## Books by Richard Slotkin

FICTION

*The Return of Henry Starr* (1988)
*The Crater* (1980)

HISTORY

*The Fatal Environment: The Myth of the Frontier in the Age of Industrialization, 1800–1890* (1985)

*So Dreadfull a Judgment: Puritan Responses to King Philip's War, 1675–1677* (with James K. Folsom; 1978)

*Regeneration Through Violence: The Mythology of the American Frontier 1600–1860* (1973)

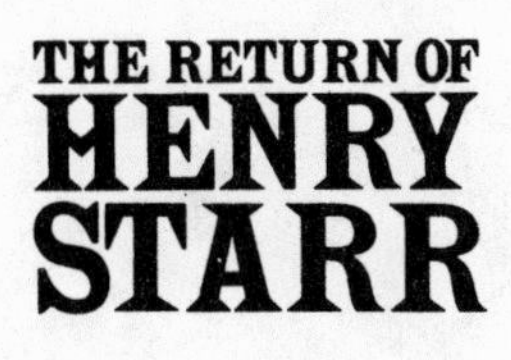
THE RETURN OF
HENRY
STARR

# THE RETURN OF HENRY STARR

RICHARD SLOTKIN

NEW YORK *ATHENEUM* 1988

The excerpt from THE DREAM SONGS by John Berryman, copyright © 1969 by John Berryman, is reprinted by permission of Farrar, Straus and Giroux, Inc.

Excerpts from *The Story of the Lost Reflection*, Verso 1985 © Paul Coates, is reprinted by permission of the publishers.

Excerpt from the manuscript "From Flickers to Todd A-O," by Edward M. Miller, is reprinted by permission of the author.

The map of Tulsa, 1921, is based on one in *Death in a Promised Land: The Tulsa Race Riot of 1921* by Scott Ellsworth, copyright © 1982 by Louisiana State University Press. It was used by permission of Louisiana State University Press.

*The Return of Henry Starr* is a work of fiction, suggested by the lives and times of certain historical personages, and by historical incidents. However, any resemblance between characters in the novel and actual persons, living or dead, is purely coincidental.



Atheneum
Macmillan Publishing Company
866 Third Avenue, New York, N.Y. 10022
Collier Macmillan Canada, Inc.

Library of Congress Cataloging-in-Publication Data
Slotkin, Richard, ———
The return of Henry Starr.
I. Title.
PS3569.L695R48 1988 813'.54 87-30722
ISBN 0-689-11811-2

10 9 8 7 6 5 4 3 2 1

Designed by Jack Meserole

PRINTED IN THE UNITED STATES OF AMERICA

For Iris

The problem of the twentieth century is the problem of the color line.

—W. E. B. DU BOIS, *The Souls of Black Folk*

Colour images lack the ghostly poignancy of black-and-white. The monochrome film spontaneously peels off interesting images from the world: it sees things we do not see, and thus insists on the existence of a phantom presence within reality, a world we cannot perceive.

The silence of beings so akin to ourselves is absurd and frightening . . .

Cinema is the dream of an afterlife from which to contemplate this one.

—PAUL COATES, *The Story of the Lost Reflection*

. . . There ought to be a law against Henry.
—Mr. Bones: there is.

—JOHN BERRYMAN, *The Dream Songs*, Number 4.

# Contents

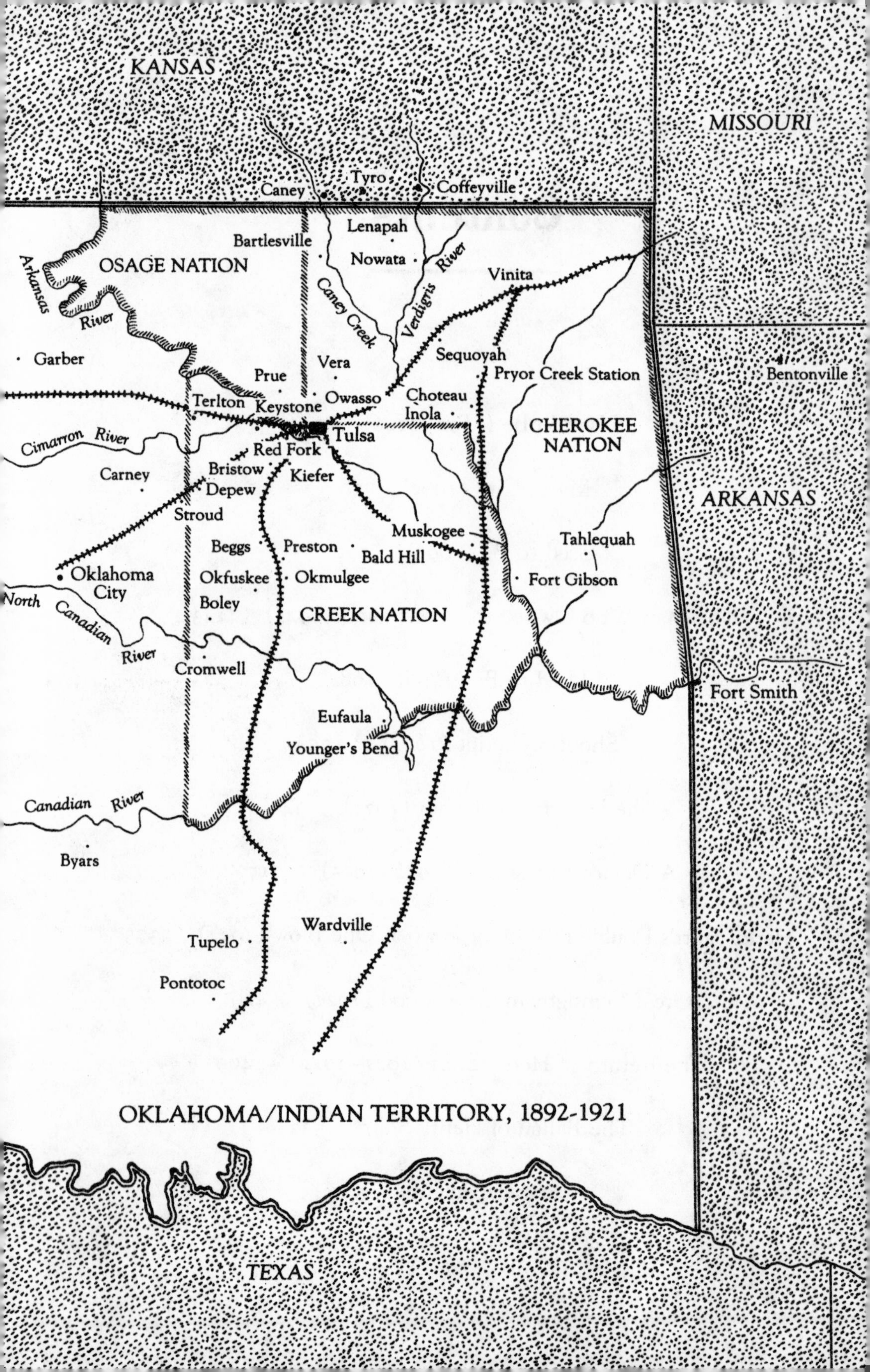


OKLAHOMA/INDIAN TERRITORY, 1892-1921

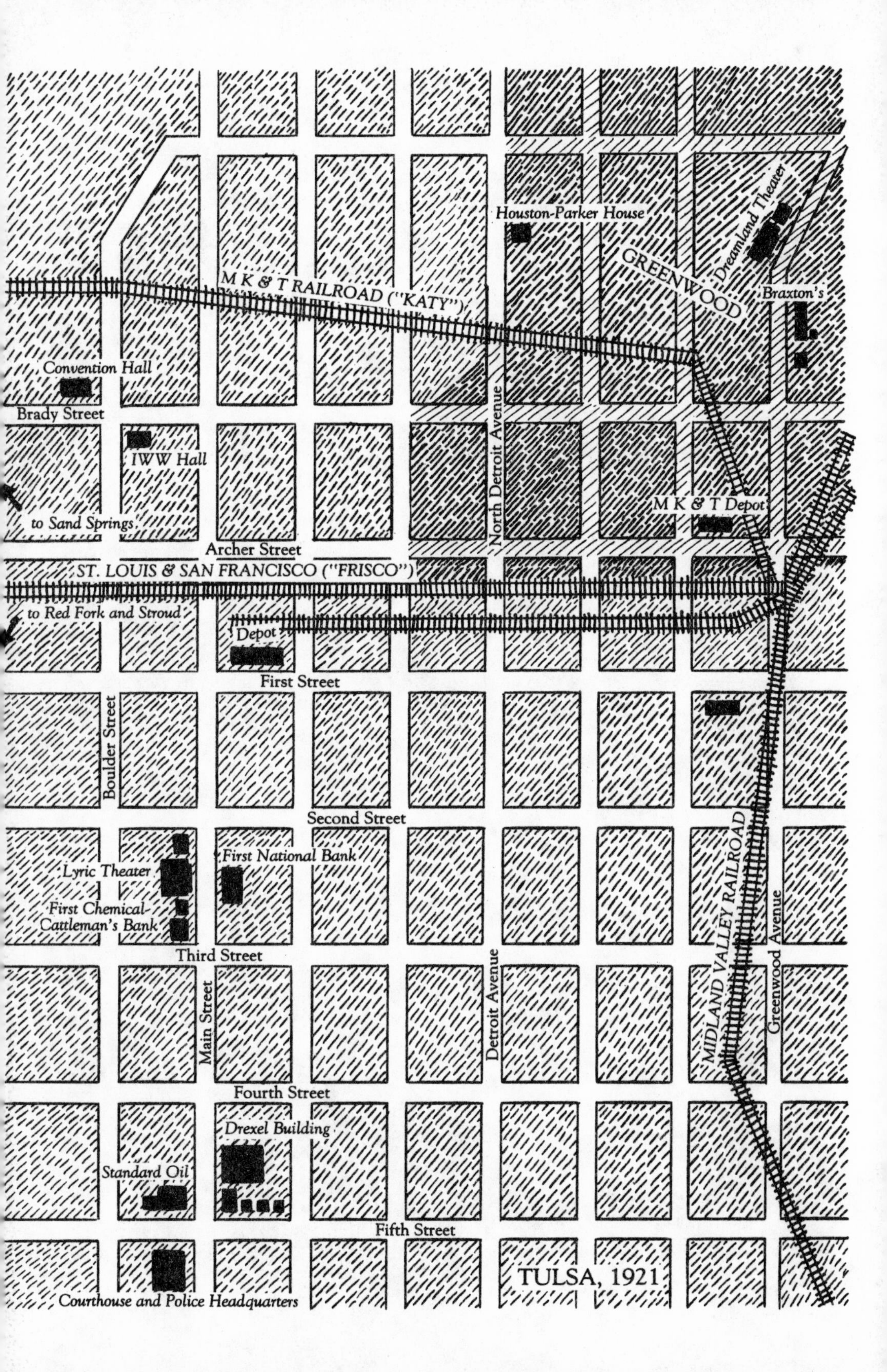

Houston-Parker House
Dreamland Theater
GREENWOOD
M K & T RAILROAD ("KATY")
Braxton's
Convention Hall
Brady Street
IWW Hall
to Sand Springs
North Detroit Avenue
M K & T Depot
Archer Street
ST. LOUIS & SAN FRANCISCO ("FRISCO")
to Red Fork and Stroud
Depot
First Street
Boulder Street
Second Street
MIDLAND VALLEY RAILROAD
First National Bank
Lyric Theater
First Chemical-
Cattleman's Bank
Third Street
Greenwood Avenue
Main Street
Detroit Avenue
Fourth Street
Drexel Building
Standard Oil
Fifth Street
TULSA, 1921
Courthouse and Police Headquarters

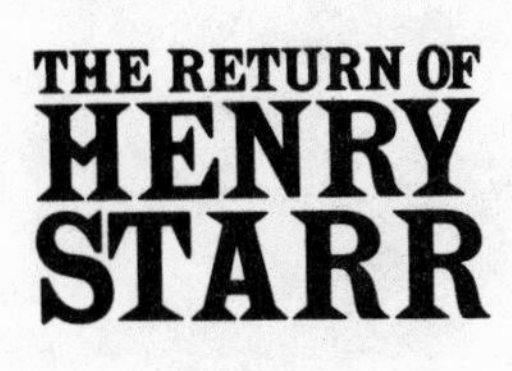
THE RETURN OF
HENRY
STARR

# Used to Be

## TSIGESU

"Let me tell you how it used to be in the old days, just as I saw it, just as it was told to me: about the outlaw Henry Starr and his partner Cherokee Bill, who rode the nightland with the wolves and heard the owl hoot, away down in the Cherokee Nation a long time ago.

"They was brave men and they kept their word, and they kept their road. Together there was nothing they could not rob, and no law man could keep them from their getaway: because Cherokee Bill was big and strong—the second biggest man for size who ever lived in the Cherokee Nation—and Henry Starr was the smartest outlaw that ever lived, so smart . . . he could charm the bark off a hickory, Henry Starr. Two times they locked him away in stone prison, and two times he come out again and found his guns, and his horse and his road and his word, that word of his with which he robbed many a train and store and stagecoach, and banks . . . *hyenh!* Twenty-eight banks he robbed, saying: 'Thumbs up and stand steady!'

"Twenty-eight banks he robbed, one for every farm that the Starr clan had owned that was taken from them by white men, in Carolina and in Tennessee, in the Southern Confederacy and the United States of America, in the Indian Nations and in the state of Oklahoma—twenty-eight farms, twenty-eight banks—and the last bank, the twenty-ninth bank, for the Nation itself that was lost or sold away, so long ago among the mountains: the bank that was too many for Henry Starr.

"He played fair, and he give like he took with a free hand; and he never killed but one man in his life and that by accident. He was outside the law but he lived by justice, Henry Starr: he knew the taste of Cherokee justice. Yes: I'm telling you. So the law could never hold him, you see?—because he lived by justice.

"Henry Starr was named to death by hanging, in the court of Isaac Parker in Fort Smith, by the word of the man that was called the Hanging Judge; and no man ever lived after Isaac Parker had named him *dead dead dead*, named his name for the greased rope and the black hood—no man but Henry Starr, who lived, and came back out of that stone prison to find his guns again, and his horse and his road and his word.

"Listen: this is how it used to be:"

## FORT SMITH PRISON *July 20, 1896*

There were two Indian prisoners (*Big Injun, Little Injun*, thought the guard) waiting in line for their stew, with slack chains dragging from the shackles at their ankles. There was a trusty, part-Creek himself, to ladle out the stew from the big battered trough. And next to him the guard, slapping his billy stick lazily into his meaty left palm, his big red face grinning a little and his soft belly bulging above his gun belt and his badge pinned over his heart. *Look at that*, he thought, *Big Injun, Little Injun*, and the idea started to work him mean. The guard's name was Eoff, but he pronounced it "Oaf."

Little Injun was in front: built small but wiry, his smooth skin smoked just a little bit—just enough Injun blood to keep color in his cheeks after three years in Fort Smith Prison—his smooth, shiny black hair full and thick on his head. Except for the old-man eyes you'd naturally get after three years he still looked like a kid, twenty/twenty-two, no more. And Big Injun behind him: Eoff had to look up at his face, six feet and better and thick muscled on his ox-heavy bones, the floorboards creaked when he leaned his heft from boot to boot. And on top of all that a big square ugly head, heavy mouth and nose, skin pockmarked like it was buckshotten, hair like a shovelful of snipped black wire ends, skin the kind of color you get when there's Injun blood in you, and maybe more than a dose of coon Eoff figured, and greaser and peckerwood and Chinaman too as far as he could tell.

The trusty plopped the first ladleful of brown stew into the little man's bowl, and Eoff touched his arm to stop him from dipping a second. Eoff waved Little Injun on, but Little Injun stood still.

"Move along, sonny," said Eoff, "this ain't no restaurant."

The little man spoke quietly. "I've got another spoon of that stew coming."

Eoff took a big swallow of breath getting ready to give Little Injun the old hee-haw, meanwhile throwing one quick look at Big Injun to see how he'd take it, and—but what Eoff saw made the air stick in his throat: because Big Injun's huge ugly face had begun twisting itself up into terrible shapes as if strong invisible hands were wringing it. Thick ridged wrinkles stacked themselves up Big Injun's forehead and then suddenly flattened, his heavy black eyebrows rose and fell with slow powerful contortions as if they were trying by main force to heave the browridge up into the thicket of stiff hair, and the muscular draw on his cheeks was making him show his corner teeth.

With his eyes stuck on this eruption Eoff couldn't look back at Little Injun, so he dropped the words out the side of his mouth. "Who in the hell are you?"

Which might have meant either one of them, but the little man took the question for his own. "I am Henry Starr," he said.

Big Injun made a noise like steam whooshing through a safety valve. "*Hhhaaaahhh! Listen* to him! That's right: he's Henry Starr! We don't want trouble now, Henry." Big Injun's neck muscles had taken a twist on his windpipe, so his words come whining to Eoff's ears, and that told Eoff that Big Injun wasn't no more threat to him than so much store cheese heaped that high. If he finished with the little one he could boot the big stupid one around all he liked.

Eoff rounded with elaborate menace on Little Injun. "Listen, breed," he said, "Henry Starr don't mean piss to me." That didn't seem to get through to the kid, but Eoff knew what would and he spat it out eagerly: "You scared to speak up yourself, breed? You got to let this nigger do your talking?"

The impassive young face of Henry Starr now softened, a look of sadness that went with the age of his eyes. The skin around his brown eyes seemed to droop. His glance flicked to the face of Big Injun, and he looked sadder still. But when Eoff followed Starr's eyes he saw that Big Injun's face had suddenly become very smooth and quiet. He waited now, and Henry Starr did the talking.

"No, he ain't a nigger," said Henry Starr. "His name is Cherokee Bill, and he's one of the Hair Twisters."

"That why he's in here?" Eoff wanted to know. "He twist up some folks' hairs? Then maybe *sculped* 'em like . . . ?"

"Ask him what his name is, Henry," said Cherokee Bill, in a slow, oddly high-pitched voice. "Ask him his clan, if he's got one."

"Can't neither one of you talk for hisself?" said Eoff.

Henry Starr shook his head sadly. "He can't talk to you no more now."

Eoff turned red as beet soup. "Pack it up and shove it along, shortshanks, you and your nigger both."

The sad expression vanished as suddenly as a shift of wind will turn a green-leaved aspen white. Henry Starr smiled, clean white teeth in a smooth brown face, a young man's smile, a nice young man. "Listen. There are no bad feelings between us. The stew is nothing to me. I don't hold that against you. I have to tell you . . . he is Cherokee Bill. His clan is the Hair Twisters. It means they get angry quick, it's too easy to insult them. And he's no nigger, he's Cherokee. Like me."

"Well," Eoff said, "if that don't make him and you both more different kinds of nigger than any niggers I ever see!"

"Please," said Henry Starr, "you should tell me your name, and your clan if you've got one . . . unless"—he paused, considering how you could say this politely—"unless it frightens you to tell?"

"My name is *Oaf!*" yelled the red-faced guard. "You got that? E-O-F-F, *Oaf!* And you better remember it, breed, because it's gonna be your misery till they string you . . ."

"You spell it Eee-*off*," said Henry Starr, surprised and pleased. "What?" said Eoff. "Eee-off," said Henry Starr, "it spells wrong or you say it wrong, one. Oaf. Eee-off. Don't you see it? Your name don't match the way it sounds." "What?" said Eoff. "Or maybe it does," said Henry Starr, "because *Eee-awph* is how a jackass sounds when he's showing off, ain't it? And *oaf* is somebody so stupid he puts his foot in it and don't know if it's his shoes or a pile of warm horseshit." Starr's hand quick as a snake's strike flipped the bowl of stew across the counter so that the blobs of meat and gluey gravy splattered the shirt over Eoff's belly and the fly of his trousers.

"It's okay, Henry," said Cherokee Bill, "we couldn't eat now anyway," but the last syllable was spat forward as three guards came ramming into him from behind—then three more from the sides, then arms and bodies swarming at them from everywhere, till finally with four hands dragging on each arm Big Injun and Little Injun were frog-marched out the door with the slack chains chinking on the boards as they were lifted and hustled along, and the door whanged shut behind them.

The Creek trusty looked at Eoff and shook his head.

"What's it to you?" snapped Eoff.

"Nothin' to me," said the trusty, "it's just that that Cherokee Bill is bound to kill you for callin' him a nigger, and pickin' on Henry Starr like you done." He put the stew ladle into the trough and ticked off the points on his fingers. "That Starr he was *tryin'* to tell you. He didn't want no bad feelin's since he's got to swing soon. It ain't good Cherokee to go down with bad feelin's left over like that. But you wouldn't listen. Then, Cherokee Bill he told you his name and his clan; and Starr got you to tell him yours."

"So?"

The trusty sighed. "If you're gonna kill a man, it's better you find out his name and his kin first. So you'll know *who* it is you gotta kill, you see? Makes it more kind of *finished* that way. Also so's you'll know who'll be comin' after you. That's just horse sense, ain't it? And anyway, it's how them Cherokee do."

Eoff snorted his contempt, but his eyes ran away from the trusty to the door that had banged shut behind Cherokee Bill.

The trusty smiled behind Eoff's averted head. "Yeah," he said, "and you could see how peaceful it come over him when you left off pickin' on Henry Starr and called him a nigger." The trusty chuckled. "You could just see it on him. Right then was when he *knowed* and didn't have to worry no more about what was gonna happen. 'Cause once you said *that*, wasn't no way to get round them bad feelin's, was there? So he just figgers he'll have to take care of it th'other way." He picked up the empty bowls. "You mark me: they won't eat none for four days, or Bill won't, anyways. And he'll try to get some tobacco to change." The trusty paused and thought that over. "Yeah, he'll need *that*. And after he gets it, you're a goner."

Now Eoff turned to the trusty and gathered the Creek's dirty shirt front in his fist and blew his meaty breath in the trusty's face as he talked. "Don't get any smarter than the mule you was fathered by. That nigger hangs in four days and his little friend in five. And if he can get at me when he's locked in his cell, with three-foot stone walls and an iron door between, then when he does it I'll be glad to shake his hand and call him Uncle."

That night in their cells Henry Starr and Cherokee Bill didn't have anything but water dipped from a bucket in a stone mug.

All of the cells of the prisoners that were named for hanging were on one corridor, and the corridor had only one door. The other end was a brick wall three feet thick. There was only one way out of that place: then if you turned to the right you were for eating or exercise or work or prayer; but if you turned to the left there wasn't anything for you but the pine-board scaffold and the gallows, the black hood and the greased rope. You could be sure of a fresh new rope, with beef grease or oil grease rubbed in to let it run smoothly through the noose knot when the floor dropped under you and you fell out into the empty air. But word said that the hood wasn't fresh, that while you waited inside it for the drop what you smelled was man grease and the breath of hanged men.

Their cells were on opposite sides of the corridor, Cherokee Bill's one stop closer to the dead back wall. If Henry Starr stood by his door leaning against the left-hand wall he could see Cherokee Bill sitting on the end of his bunk close to his own door. Henry Starr saw Cherokee Bill dip a mug of water, then look up and meet his eyes. He waved his heavy palm over the cup, and Henry Starr saw a small shiny thing fall into the water: a spent lead slug, flattened against the brick wall where the guards took their target practice, and Cherokee Bill had copped it during exercise. Cherokee Bill took a mouthful of water and held it. He closed his eyes. Then he swallowed the water in his mouth while tipping the cup so that the remaining water ran slowly out onto the floor of his cell, and without looking he caught the slug as it fell from the cup in midair, palmed and concealed it, and smiled at Henry Starr.

Henry Starr shook his head. That old conjure stuff—if ever it had worked it stopped when his Grandfather was a baby, in the old days when they still lived in the Old Place back in the mountains, where the water was. You had to be an old-time blanket head like his Grandfather Tom Starr to believe all that powwow muck-a-muck: that you could conjure yourself a gun and bullets and an open door and a horse and a clear road back to the Nations, with some water and Injun spit and a handful of tobacco.

And anyway, there was no real running water in this place, you couldn't make Anything come by fooling It, pouring water out of a cup. Plus they had no tobacco to change, not of any kind. Cherokee Bill would have to be luckier than Jack-the-Devil to work the conjure without any tobacco to make over.

But even suppose he got himself some tobacco: it was Cherokee powers he was trying to work, and there wasn't a lot more Cherokee to Cherokee Bill than the name he just took for himself and the clan he claimed—glowering down at you, daring you to deny it to his face.

*I got more than half Cherokee in my blood, and I could never make It come when I called.*

Yeah: you had to be a blanket head to believe in that stuff, or else a man like Cherokee Bill, so hopped up to be Cherokee you'd grab any piece of it you could get, whether it was any use to you or not.

He turned away into his cell. It was five feet wide and eight deep, with room for a washstand in one corner and a stool to sit on, and an iron bunk taking up most of the other wall. A small high barred window let light in the back wall: nothing to see in it but a one-by-two patch of sky, and if you chinned on the bars the roofline of Isaac Parker's courthouse across the yard. There was a calendar hung on a peg so Henry Starr could count his time, and an advertisement for revolving pistols clipped from the Sears catalog, the rest of which was set by the chamber pot for necessities. Next to the pistol ad was the front page of a dime book stuck to the wall with gum: *Jesse James's Double Daring; or, Two Banks at One Blow*, by Colonel D'Artagnan Arbuthnot. The sheet showed the marks of having been folded down small and square to be tucked in a pocket or hatband, the paper was limp and soft as a patch of cloth.

There was a shelf pegged into the stone wall, and some books lying on it: the New Testament put there long ago by the prison chaplain, marked with mildew from years in stir. Henry Starr used it to prop a slim stack of dime books—*Frank James's Vengeance Trail; or, an Eye for an Eye; The Redskin's Red Right Hand; or, Apache Justice*. Pressed for support between the New Testament and *Frank James's Vengeance Trail* was a set of frayed yellowing pages stitched together with thread, *The Cherokee Nation the New Israel Scriptural Proofs Made Plain*, crazy old "Preacher" Brown's printed-at-his-own-expense call unto the Cherokee Nation to take up the destiny for which the Lord had chosen it. After that was a pair of true-bound books, Boudinot's *History of the Cherokee Nation* from the prison library; and closing the row his own battered red-covered *Last of the Mohicans* that his mother had had slipped to him by a trusty, its pages worn blunt and tobacco brown by the wear his fingers had given it, reading and rereading its pages over and over every year since he could remember:

*"Go, children of the Lenape; the anger of the Manitto is not done. Why should Tamenund stay? The pale-faces are masters of the earth, and the time of the red-men has not yet come again. My day has been too long. In the morning I saw the sons of Unamis happy and strong; and yet, before the night has come, have I lived to see the last warrior of the wise race of the Mohicans!"*

His mother liked him reading *Mohicans*. According to her, it was reading those dime books put him on the owl-hoot trail. What a power she saw in those trashy little books—to turn a man's ghost bad! And that husband of hers, that C. N. Walker—he said it wasn't my books but my Injun blood, Tom Starr blood, outlaw blood going back three generations and halfway across the country, back to the Old Place and the Old Time, in the trees and mountains of Carolina and Tennessee we come out of: Boudinot, he tells how. Grandfather Tom Starr, he had his own way of telling it: how John Ross and Jack-the-Devil sold the Cherokee Nation to the Americans for, what was it? Three hundred nigger slaves and a piano for John Ross's daughters and a big white house for John Ross to live in and lord it over the Nation. Grandfather . . . what do you think turned me bad? You too, worrying at me about the books—only not just the dime books, and hell: maybe not them at all, they was almost like family history, wasn't they? All about Aunt Belle Starr and Cole Younger and Buck and Dingus James that you run with after the War. You figured it was Ma's books done the harm, bringin' up the white in me too much, wasn't that it?

*I have nothing to teach you, little white man. You know too much. Your head ain't empty, it's full of white, full of white papers, all little white papers with names on 'em. Papers like John Ross made to sell away from us that Old Place, the mountains where the water was, back there in the Old Time.*

Henry Starr felt empty. Maybe he was hungry and wanted something to fill his belly so he could stop thinking about being hungry—and something to fill his mind so he could stop thinking about hanging. Whiskey would do both—but never a taste of it again, not unless they sold moonshine for a nickel a glass in the Happy Hunting Ground or Heaven or Hell or wherever it was they were sending him out of Fort Smith Prison. Not unless the worms made whiskey down there among the bones.

Nothing to fill his mind but white papers with names on them.

No dime books tonight, I have enough family history in me, I don't need no more.

No *Mohicans*, which anyway I know by heart (I am Uncas, the son of Uncas!), because the last chief of the noble race of the Lenape is just as dead as I will be in five days' time—except that people coming after will read him in that book of his and learn his names while mine goes blowing down the street in throwed-out scraps of Fort Smith newspapers.

And no thank you, no more *Cherokee Nation the New Israel Scriptural Proofs Made Plain*. No comfort in having chapter and verse prove the truth of that same crank sermon Preacher Brown had been declaiming at Cherokee celebrations for the last ten years: That the Indian Nations were the Ten Lost Tribes of Israel, the Trail of Tears from Carolina to Oklahoma just the prefiguration of a greater Exodus that would carry the Nation over seas to the Holy Land . . . "For I will gather you again as a Nation, as a Nation of Nations, and neither East nor West will prevail against thee!"

The Cherokee Nation? No: no Boudinot tonight either, the women and children and old men that died of grief or sickness or no food along the Trail of Tears out of Georgia and Carolina sixty years ago ain't any deader than I will be in five days: the grief of the Indian Nations is not greater than what I've got in my own head, because I've got to die and I don't want to.

*If you were true Cherokee, said his Grandfather, you'd always be ready to pay out your blood, if that's what you owe.*

Grandfather. Well, he is right about the books tonight: a head full of white papers. All I can think about is *book* when what I need is some conjures.

From outside he heard the complex rattlebang of the trap drop on the Fort Smith gallows, where Maledon the Hangman and his crew were repairing and testing the apparatus for the big day.

Henry Starr lay down on his pallet. The darkness in the high barred window above him was blue. The darkness in his cell was gray and black. He thought about the old conjures and about his grandfather Tom Starr, who knew them all. He was the biggest Cherokee there ever was, Tom Starr, bigger even than Cherokee Bill. But he was good-looking, he was Indian blood through and through, not all kinds throwed together like Cherokee Bill. Not two kinds, like me.

*Look in the water while it's quiet, he said. His voice rumbles and makes your backbone shake. He stands overhead making a shadow that blocks the sun all over the pool so that the wind stops and the dancing lights on the water and it's still. You can't see his face for the sun blazing out of his ears and over the top of his head as if he had eaten it and it filled him to bursting. But the shadow of his finger points from the shadow of his fist that is bigger than a Colt's .45-caliber Dragoon pistol, the water: Look! You look into the water to see your soul. It is a small being, a small man. It is in your eyes. You look into the water and first it is your face you see. The round smooth brown face . . . you smile at it—*

Pah! *like a gunshot. The head of fire spits and breaks the water's face.*

*Now you know it, says the head of fire. You think if you are charming and you smile at the water, you think if you flatter the water by looking pretty in it like a white man that it will show you your soul. But water don't lie, and you can't make it lie by flattery. You have no soul. There is no soul for you to see. You have pretty white blood in you, but your soul is dead. The Seven Clans are sitting over your ghost. Your blood is poison. You have never lived.*

Henry Starr squinted at the gray darkness and tried to make the memory there. Tom Starr used to say there were conjures for remembering anything, but he'd forgotten to remember them. I need some conjures to remember my remembering conjures. He snorted at himself. The only memory conjures his Grandfather ever actually showed him were the ones for making memory go away, *words to make them forget with: black/ yellow mockingbird, you have just come to cover it up, you have dissolved it in blue smokes, in blue* ha! *in blue smokes, you've put dogshit on its trail.* Words you said to make your name go out of my head, Grandfather; for making my name not be in your head, not be in my clan's head, for making my name not be: not be *Starr*: Henry Starr, son of Hop Starr son of Tom Starr, the biggest man, the strongest man in the Cherokee Nation, *ha!* not be—

That's the worst kind of Cherokee death you wished on me, ain't it, Old Man? The death of no name, or a name no one will say because it's gone bad in the Nation.

I ain't going to let you do that, Old Man. One way, one time, I'm going to make my memory *be*. Listen! you used-to-be Grandfather of mine, you used-to-be Tom Starr, you remember who I am . . . ?

> If you want a story, children, then listen here to me,
> About Henry Starr the outlaw, and the days that used to be.
> He robbed a-many banks and railroad trains also
> Way down in the Indian Nations, a long time ago.
>
> 'Twas in the town of Tahlequah, that's
> where it all began . . .

---

## TAHLEQUAH, INDIAN TERRITORY *July 4, 1892*

They drove the string of horses right up the dusty main street of Tahlequah, with Cherokee Bill riding point and Henry Starr clucking them up from the left flank, Gus on the right and Petey riding drag, yipping them along and keeping them bunched. The horses nodded nervously and rolled crazy eyes as they shuffled up the street—the best of the bucking stock culled from the remudas of the Dodge ranch. They shied at the blue-starred, red-and-white-striped bunting that flared at them from the storefronts and awning posts of the long street, jerked up a little speed, then slowed down as they passed under the blazing banner that swept overhead from the M K & T Land Office on one side of the street to the M K & T Hotel and the Cattlemen's Bank on the other:

JULY 4 TAHLEQUAH IND TERR JULY 4

—and under that a strip of new cloth with smaller letters, WELCOME BOOMERS.

The rodeo grounds were at the other end of town, and Henry Starr kept his eyes out that way, disdaining the crowd already forming in front of the Land Office—nesters looking for a slice of the Cherokee Strip, step right up and show us the color of your money. And on the other side of the street, lining up in the hot early sun in front of the Cattlemen's Bank, old Cherokees in loose cotton shirts and battered slouch hats, soft pouchy moccasins molded to the shape of the feet, and their women with them in heavy dark dresses, faces round and dark as ripe pumpkins.

In the center of his vision Cherokee Bill dropped his left hand to his side and tapped his left thigh twice. *Lawman.* Henry Starr's side vision took in the lean shapes lounging against the pillar by the Cattlemen's Bank—gray shirt and pants, tan hat, droopy mustaches; and next to him red shirt, black hat—federal badges, not the territorial police but a couple of federal marshals out of Isaac Parker's court in Fort Smith. Henry Starr felt his fear walk prickle-foot up the inside of his chest, then out again. *Nothing to me,* he said inside his head, *nothing to me with the whiskey off my hands two nights ago, and just those good clean golden eagles in my pocket. Nobody ever prove where a dollar's been or what it's done, all I got on me is dollars.*

Cherokee Bill tugged his hat brim lower and eased his horse back so the herd's dust came up around him.

In front of the brick facade of the Cherokee capitol building a stage of raw timber had been hammered together and draped with bunting, two hundred black hats and pale bonnets below it, and at the podium a Cherokee Indian in a business suit—"How long?" he cried, flourishing his arms. "How long shall we flourish the broken scepter of our treaties, and like Canute, bid the waves of commerce subside? We cannot silence the white man's ax. We cannot check the advancing multitudes. We cannot resurrect the birch canoe. We can but join the resistless army of civilization and progress and thus save our people from destruction!"

Boudinot, that would be, and the other Indian in blue pinstripe, hair brilliant with pomade, would be William Ross, old John Ross's son, waiting his turn to answer Boudinot.

*Two big men up there, but the biggest one of all is missing, and nobody seems to know it.* Henry touched the small wrapped parcel that bulged the side pocket of his jeans, the gift he had bought the Old Man in Bartlesville. *Just 'cause you brought it don't mean he's got to come here and get it.*

Dodge was waiting by the gate of the corral out by the fairgrounds, and as Henry Starr came up with the herd, Dodge leaned in the saddle to grip the gate and swing it out. Henry pulled up next to him, Cherokee Bill and Gus and Petey swept the horses past them. With his side vision Henry Starr could see Dodge ticking off the count in his head as the horses mobbed their way into the pen, and he said, "All there, Mr. Dodge."

"Course they are, Henry," said Dodge—a man of fifty-five or so, with a big red face marbled in cheeks and nose with broken blue veins. He reached into his vest pocket and took out a roll of bills, yellow and green, and passed them over to Henry Starr. "Why don't you pay off the boys, Henry, then git back over in town for some fun." He gave a conspirator's wink. "I reckon your month's wages ain't all you and Bill got to spend. That Holcomb over at the 'Katy' Hotel pays a good dollar for his whiskey, I hear."

Henry Starr looked at him, his features stiff. "I suppose he does, Mr. Dodge. I wouldn't know myself . . ." and Dodge threw back his head and laughed.

"All right, Henry, all right: keep close, boy, that's the ticket." He leveled his eyes at Henry again. "Just remember, you got a friend in William Dodge. I admire a man knows how to do business, specially when he ain't no older yet than you are. You got more sense than most grown men amongst your people. If there was more like you, Henry, more business sense amongst your people . . ."

The others came drifting over, and Henry Starr began peeling bills off the roll under Dodge's approving gaze, the rancher's head nodding as if he were ticking off each bill. Cherokee Bill came last, and the others gave way a little, watching him carefully. He swiped his stack of bills out of Henry's hand—then held them like he'd forgotten why he'd wanted them so bad. He looked stupid, like his ghost was someplace else, not in his eyes. "You hold mine, Henry," he said like a man talking in his sleep, and slapped the stack back in Henry's hand. "You take and buy me a quart of that good whiskey over at the Katy and we'll drink her while we watch the riding."

Gus dug Petey in the ribs and said, "Whyn't you come in to the Katy and have a drink with us?"

"Yeah," said Petey, "and maybe buy *us* a round 'stead a holdin' so tight to a buck."

Cherokee Bill looked at them, his eyes solid and glazed like the eyes of a dead fish. "My clan don't like four walls when we drink."

"Oh yeah," said Petey, "I plumb forgot about that." He rolled his eyes at Gus and they swung away for town.

*His clan don't like four walls! Everybody knows they don't serve niggers in the Katy.*

The other three sat their horses quietly for a minute. Cherokee Bill hummed a little tune to himself and let his blank gaze slide from this to that. Henry Starr watched him. *He ain't even heard Gus and Petey, he must be thinkin' about the badges back there.* Dodge let his eyes flick from Henry Starr to Cherokee Bill and back, and when he saw that the big buck was going to stay quiet he said, "You going to ride today, Henry?"

"I might."

"They got a full-blood boy from over by Nowata that people says is on the horse like a bear and don't let go. Name is John Rises Early."

"I've heard of him," said Henry Starr, looking closely at Dodge. "I might ride or I might not, Mr. Dodge. But if I do you can put your money on me."

Cherokee Bill woke up. "Let's go, Henry. I'm thirsty."

Dodge raised his hand to check them. "They might not sell you a drink at the Katy . . ."

Cherokee Bill rounded on him with his blank face suddenly full of blood. "*Who? Who* ain't gonna sell me? Who do you—?" and Henry Starr pushed his horse between Cherokee Bill and Mr. Dodge, whose hand still hung frozen in the air, palm outward like the sign language for *peace*.

"Hold on now, easy there," said Dodge, sweat breaking out on his forehead. "Today's when they're distributing the Strip money. Agent don't want no whiskey going out to Indians till the distribution's over."

Henry Starr kept his smile on, like a bandanna pulled up to the eyes to hide the face behind. "Agency don't never allow nobody to sell whiskey down in the Nations, Mr. Dodge."

"You and me both know better, don't we?"

Henry Starr held his grin, but now there was a little skin-crawl of fear behind the mask along with the anger. *Why is he talking about all this now? Bill and me been running whiskey with his cattle for two years and he never puts mouth to it till today.* He tipped his head back and looked a dare into Dodge's eyes. "Holcomb'll serve me," he said, "seein' how I sold him the whiskey in the first place."

"Just take it easy, Henry, take it easy." Dodge's voice became low and confidential. "People is bound to be edgy today. The Strip money deal don't sit right with a lot of folks around here, and I don't mean only the full bloods. There's federal marshals down from Fort Smith to see that nobody makes trouble, and a troop of nigger cavalry camped a mile west of here." Dodge bit his lip at what he'd just said, but Cherokee

Bill just sat there stolidly, muttering something under his breath that Dodge couldn't hear [*Cherokee word for the color blue, for the color black*]. So Dodge picked it up again: "What I'm sayin' is, this ain't *territorial* today, this is downright *federal*. And not wanting trouble today means playing it *federal*. Savvy?"

Henry Starr felt his wolf lift and rise in him, wolf-light in his eyes straight and icy, anger then fear and now hatred, like a sharp ugly scent in his nostrils, coppery taste on his tongue. *Those egg-sucking federal sons of bitches.* "Yeah, I savvy, but if I don't take their damn Strip money I ain't any goddamn federal government Injun, am I . . . ?"

"Whoa, Henry!" said Dodge, the alarm in the rancher's eyes checking him in mid-breath. He held it: *Quiet. Smooth water in my mind.*

"I ain't looking for trouble with you, Henry. You know me better'n that. There's folks amongst your people that don't think any white man at all has got a good heart for Injun's business, or cares two bits about their interests or their rights. But I know you know me better'n that, because you been working for me five years, since you was practically a little kid, and I've always treated you white, haven't I? And you're smart, you keep your eyes and ears open. You know me and the other white cattlemen around here been tryin' to tell your leaders, we got to pull *together* against that damned railroad, that Katy Railroad and that Katy Bank and that Katy Land Office and Katy every damned thing it can put its brands on. We been talkin' ourselves blue, Henry, and you know it, just so's to keep the gov'ment selling that Strip land out from under your people. Not our land, Henry, but yours. Because who's gonna end up getting it but just that blood-suckin' railroad, and sell it off to these damned nesters that won't *last* on the land anyway, so the railroad gets the land back and sells it again . . . and then where's your ranches, Henry? and where's your Injuns too, that lives off what me and Roberts and the rest pays in leases? And where are we too, damn it! I ain't denying that! Injuns ain't the only folks gets robbed by the Great White Father in Washington, no sirree. But would any of your people listen to a white man long enough to find out we's on the same side, and fight this damn thing together? Would they? Would they play white with *me?*"

The ghost of Henry Starr's fear stood off from him now, distant and separate from his blood: but it made a little shadow around Dodge like a halo round the moon, which Henry would not look at or speak to; he wanted no more struggle today with that black shape. "Yes," he said, "I know you always played white with me." *You paid me for work I done same as anyone else done the work. You closed your eyes when me and Cherokee Bill made our deliveries, and never asked where the keg came from you found on your back porch once a month, but drunk it right the hell up and even gave the boys a glass or two if they was special good. If that makes you an Injun, then you are one damn white Injun, Mr. Dodge.* And he smiled, clean white teeth in a smooth brown face.

They left their horses at the livery stable and walked toward the town. Bill stopped before they turned onto Main Street again. "Listen, Henry, I think I'll just stay around back where it's cool. I don't like who's out front there."

"Dodge ain't gonna turn us in for selling whiskey."

"Not that." Cherokee Bill looked a little embarrassed. "Those marshals they got? Bill Tilghman, he's one of them. He's got a good strong memory, Henry, there's things about me he don't forget. But there's nothing he remembers about you, so don't worry. Just go get us some of that whiskey, and I want to go and see if I can get some of that Strip money. I got it coming, you know, Henry. Land they taken from us and our clans—we got a right to our cut."

"Why shouldn't we?" said Henry Starr, and he was ready then to take some of the Strip money when ten minutes before he had told Dodge he could go and drink with the white men in the Katy Hotel bar because he wasn't any federal Indian because he wasn't taking any damn Strip money. But why in hell shouldn't he? Money is money, there's no red or white or nigger about it, it don't get old or sick and it don't ever die, and getting it don't make you nothing but richer than you was. Then it struck him funny how he kept hauling in and paying out, and he smiled at Cherokee Bill. "How you gonna get your Strip money with Bill Tilghman dogging you?"

"*Ch*-shooo! I don't worry about that. He can't stay around there all day. Ain't he got to take a piss? Don't he need a drink? Ain't he gonna go see who-all is up there at the rodeo, when everybody's up there to see you riding against that blood from Nowata? *Ch*-shooo! Go get that whiskey." He slipped away behind the buildings, and Henry Starr turned up Main Street and headed for the Katy Hotel.

Henry Starr kept to the shade of the covered sidewalk opposite the green square of the capitol grounds. Across the square he could see that young Ross had mounted the platform to speak against Boudinot. A black crow and a white crow, but the song is the same: they say *no* to each other, but one says *yes* to sell the Nation to the ranchers, and the other says *yes* to sell it to the railroad. If Grandfather was up there he would give 'em a different word, Tom Starr's word, just one huge blank plain and perfect: No.

But Tom Starr would never be up there. Henry Starr dreamed the Old Man sitting off alone there in his cabin in the woods, he wouldn't even come to look at Cherokee people like these, coming to town to give up their justice and their names on the land for less than three hundred greenback dollars each. Henry Starr felt his Grandfather's murderous pride rising in him like anger—but maybe it was not pride in his Grandfather's standing out for justice like that, but only a feeling of reprieve that he still did not have to face the Old Man again: because he was also glad he could not see the Old Man's hard wrinkled face and those small eyes sharpened to bright points with the power of his wishing death on whatever he saw.

*I used to wonder why you didn't try to stop 'em selling the Nation, Grandfather: till I figured out you didn't have no Nation bigger than your own shadow at high noon.* He touched the small wrapped gift in his jeans pocket. *It ain't going to be enough,* he reminded himself, stilling the ghost of coming disappointment.

A long, bony white man in a preacher's black frock coat and striped pants jammed into battered boots came working his way down the sidewalk. A Sears Roebuck guitar was slung over his back, his left arm cradled a disordered heap of papers, with his right hand he was tearing out crumpled sheets from the pile and thrusting them into the hands, shirt pockets, reticules of everyone that tried to get by him, jabbering all the while in a scrappy insistent voice: "Days of wrath a-coming in the Cherokee Nation, days of wrath! The birthright sold for a mess of pottage, brother, and the Nation for thirty pieces of silver!"

Henry Starr fended off the thrust paper with his arm, but the man reached over and jammed the crumpled sheet into the pocket of his dirty white shirt. "Don't set yourself against a man called by the Lord, Henry Starr." Preacher Brown looked into Henry Starr's eyes like he might challenge him to a fistfight. "It's shame enough you ignore your own gifts and calling without hindering another man in his."

"The white man's gifts are not as the red man's," said Henry Starr in a portentous guttural, and Brown snapped his goggle-eyed head back so that he looked like an outraged turkey—but he mastered his anger and said coolly, "You are smart enough to quote cheap literature to mock a man of the Word; but it is still cheap." Brown's eyes gripped him, tight as if his fists were twisting up Henry's soiled shirtfront, but with more eagerness than anger. "You could be a power for good among the People," he pleaded, "you have the name for being a smart man. Your family's name is strong in the Nations."

Henry Starr glared back at Brown, but he took the broadside out of his pocket and uncrumpled it: DAYS OF WRATH TO COME IN THE CHEROKEE NATION. Below it in minute print and double columns were scriptural evidences that the Katy Railroad was the Whore of Babylon and the American Indians the Ten Lost Tribes of Israel, who must be converted and gathered home to Jerusalem before Christ could come again.

*White papers, his Grandfather said, they always say the same thing: that the Cherokee must get off this earth of theirs and go someplace else.*

He held the paper out to Brown. "You got the wrong boy, Preacher. You want the John Ross family. The Tom Starr family got no land left to sell."

"You will think on it," said Brown, and he jerked away from Henry Starr, leaving the crumpled tract in Henry's hand. He moved off down the sidewalk.

Henry tucked the paper back in his shirt pocket, thinking, *Seems like everybody I meet has something in mind for the grandson of old Tom Starr,* but he was feeling the dangerous pressure of all these eyes around him, recognizing his face, remembering his name. There were all those federal marshals spotted up and down the street, what if they had something they wanted to call his name about?

There were two marshals out of Parker's court who held Henry Starr in their memory, as they were in his, two of them from six years ago. *Do they want me again?* It made him shake, it leaped in his belly and made his hands itch. *This time, I promise my ghost, I'll leave them out in the bushes with dogshit in their hands if they're coming after me.*

He walked carefully up the board sidewalk on the side opposite from the Cattlemen's Bank and the hotel. The lawmen standing in front of the bank watching the line of Indians would be in the full glare of the sun; he himself was hidden in shadows made blacker by the glare. Red Shirt was there by the bank and now also a new one: *pinto vest, black hat*, and Henry Starr kept on without breaking stride along the inner edge of the sidewalk till his side vision picked up Gray Shirt, the tall one with the droopy mustache, lounging now against a pillar by the Land Office, sweeping the street with his eyes from the open covert of the shady side of the street. *I don't know him and he don't know me*, thought Henry Starr as he walked securely behind and past him—till he came opposite the far end of the Katy Hotel, walking slowly, waiting for the passage of a large wagon to cover his darting across the street and into the alleyway that led to the Katy Hotel's backroom bar.

---

The sign over the louvered doors said HOTEL DELIVERIES. Since liquor was legally forbidden in the Indian Territory, there could be no such thing as a public saloon. The "storeroom" of the Katy Hotel was large and cool behind the brick walls, ventilated by windows set well above eye level that let out the smoke of cigars and cheroots. The board floor had been smoothed and molded to its grain by years of scuffling boots. The round tables were bare now in the early morning, but at night might be covered with green baize and heaps of red, white and blue chips. The long bar was of smoked and polished oak, the brass rail gleamed along its base, and behind it rose a beveled pier glass flanked by parallel temples of fluted glasses and columns of dark whiskey bottles set like fetishes each in a scrolled-wood niche. Above the mirror was a painting of a naked white woman stretched at full length, her right hand clutching the hair of her crotch that spilled out through the small soft fingers like bunches of grapes.

Holcomb was behind the bar, absentmindedly polishing it with a cloth. There was one table of white men off to the right of the door as Henry Starr came in, Gus and Petey not among them. He caught the sharp foul smell of oil, recognized them as oil riggers from the drilling out at Roberts' Standard Ranch. Not everybody was waiting like Dodge for the federal government or the tribal council or God Almighty to save the ranches from the sooners-boomers-nesters and the Katy Railroad.

Henry Starr walked across to the bar, his boots tom-tomming the hollow boards, each tom marked with the tinny shake of his spurs. Holcomb looked up and Henry Starr saw his face purse itself unpleasantly. But Henry Starr smiled and said, "I'd like to buy back a bottle of what I sold you, Mr. Holcomb." He heard a chair leg whine as someone behind him pivoted to look.

Holcomb looked down at the polished bar, then up. "Well now, Henry. Well now. I'd like to accommodate you, and another time I would, but . . . Well, it's the Strip money, Henry. The town's under fed'ral jurisdiction till the money's been give out to your people. I can't sell no liquor to any Indians whatever today, Henry. I like to accommodate my customers, but not to where I got to spend a year in Fort Smith Prison if one of 'em gets . . ."

"That's how it is, Injin," said a scratchy bass voice from the oil riggers' table.

Very quiet, his smile like a bandanna covering his face to the eyes,

Henry Starr said, "There wasn't no trouble about your buying liquor from Indians, was there, Mr. Holcomb."

Holcomb pursed his lips again. Behind Henry Starr the voice said, "Now ain't that the Injin for you? First he'll sell you whatever he's got, whiskey or his woman or his goddamn pants, then he turns around and wants it back."

Henry Starr studied Holcomb's tight-pursed mouth and pink, faded-blue eyes. Holcomb didn't like this, any of it, he'd like Henry Starr to shut up and back off, but Henry Starr wasn't letting him drop his eyes. "You can't run no saloon in the Nations, Mr. Holcomb, because the Territorial Act says you can't, because Indians can't handle firewater and got to be protected from it. All right. But you run a saloon anyway, because the Lawmen around here are as thirsty as the next man and wouldn't take trouble to piss on the Territorial Act if they ever even heard of it, let alone read it. All right. Now you stand here in this saloon that can't rightly be a saloon, selling the whiskey you ain't supposed to have to a bunch of crackers that work for a rancher that rents his place from the Cherokee Nation; and you can't sell me any of that whiskey you ain't supposed to have, and that I sold you in the first place, in this ain't-supposed-to-be saloon you rent from the Cherokee Nation, because I'm a Cherokee Indian."

"Hey," said gravel voice, "he's a talkin' Injin."

"I said I was sorry, Henry," said Holcomb. His eyes watched Henry Starr, flicking once and again to the men behind him, and his hands dropped down below the polished level of the bar. "The town is full of federal marshals that come down from Fort Smith with the money. The whole place is under court order from Judge Parker and the council sheriffs got nothing to say. If it wasn't for that, you know I'd sell you . . ."

Holcomb's straitened face took on a look of deeper trouble, and Henry Starr heard the door swing to behind him. He raised his eyes to take in the door in the mirror and he knew immediately the shape silhouetted in the light pouring through and over the louvered doors—the round shoulders and the fat gut and the little porkpie hat—but Holcomb gave him notice too. "Howdy there, C. N." C. N. Walker—the trash who married Henry Starr's mother.

The bartender's hands were still down below the bar. Behind him Henry Starr heard Walker greeting the oil riggers, anybody already in a saloon was going to be a friend of his and likely buy him a drink. Looking past Holcomb's shoulder, Henry Starr saw the ghost of C. N. Walker cross the pier-glass mirror and come up to the bar. C. N. Walker slapped the bar with his little hat. "Holcomb, let's have a couple bottles. I'm buying for the boys." Chairs scraped behind Henry Starr and the smell of oil got sharper as the men approached the bar. "Yep, it's my lucky day today. You can put it all on my score."

Holcomb reached two brown bottles up from under the bar and slid them to Walker, then backed up to take some glasses off the stacks by the mirror, all the while keeping both eyes on the group forming around Walker and never moving far out of reach of the place behind the bar where he had stood talking to Henry Starr. "You got a long score with me already, C. N. Maybe I ought to ask you to settle up before you drink any more of my whiskey."

"Ha ha ha," laughed the fat man. "Well I guess today's gonna be lucky for you too. That office across the street won't be open fifteen minutes before the United States government be putting two hundred and sixty-five U.S. dollars and seventy cents into this hand. And another two hundred sixty-five seventy to my amiable wife. And another the same to that old used-to-be redskin father-in-law of mine, which ain't gone to hold back long from payin' what he owes yours truly. Even as mean an Injun as Tom Starr ain't gonna beg off payin' what he owes today, not with the federal laws thicker'n cooties. What d'I owe you, Holcomb?"

"Dollar a bottle," said the bartender, who once again stood in front of Henry Starr with his hands below the level of the bar.

"Dollar a bottle," said Henry Starr. Walker's palaver shut suddenly, and Henry Starr saw his round sweating face rise to look in the mirror, and each man looked there at the other man's ghost. "Dollar a bottle, Mr. Holcomb. And you bought 'em from a mean thieving redskin for . . . what was it? Two bits a soldier, wasn't it?"

"Henry," said Walker very softly, speaking to the ghost in the mirror.

"You'd better not serve any whiskey to old C. N. Walker here, Mr. Holcomb," said Henry Starr, low and slow and giving only a little breath to the words, saving the rest for something else, something more sudden. "No: I don't think you better do that."

"Why not, Henry?" Tiny movements in the white cloth shirt over Holcomb's arms told Henry Starr that the bartender had reached to touch something below the bar.

"Because old C. N. Walker here is a redskin Injun his own self, ain't you now, C. N.? With your fat white belly and your fat white hands, you just an old Cherokee Injun, ain't you?" His side vision registered the arms of the oil riggers shifting like reed stalks in an air. They all had guns at their belts, but he knew how this play would go and he ignored them, drilling Walker face to face and eye to eye. "And you left her standing out there holding your place in line till you get finished drinking my redskin whiskey and go out to collect your share of the Strip money, paid to the Cherokee Nation. But they ain't serving no Injuns in here today, C. N. You got to choose: you can drink like you was a white man or take your Strip money like an Injun, but there's no way you can do 'em both."

The drillers had their hands on their pistols, rustle of steel on leather, eyes fixed on Henry Starr so that until they heard hard iron rap twice on the wood of the bar they didn't see that Holcomb had drawn down on them with the two-barreled sawed-off riot gun from under the bar.

"Stand steady, gents," said Holcomb quietly. "Henry, you'd better leave."

Walker's face was boiled with rage and shame. "Goin' to collect your share, ain't you, Henry? Money don't stink for nobody, so don't give yourself airs in front of me!" His voice got louder as Henry turned his back, became strong when he passed through the doors in a blast of light from outside, yelling as the doors swung to again.

"Goddamn it, Holcomb," ranted one of the riggers, "they hang niggers where I come from for less'n what we had to stand for in here . . ."

The doors stopped vibrating behind Henry Starr, and Walker's good fellowship revived instantly. "Never mind, boys. I am that lucky man who is white enough for whiskey and Injun enough for a suck at Uncle Sam's sugar tit. Drink up!"

The sun blazed into the narrow alleyway as bright and condensed as an acetylene torch. Something whistled at Henry Starr from behind a stack of barrels at the back of the alley; Cherokee Bill bobbed his head out. "Hey Henry, it's me! You got the whiskey?"

"No I ain't." He was rankled that he hadn't got it after all, they had treated him in there like he was a nigger, like he was Cherokee Bill. He felt hot toward the big man, then ashamed of himself. Trying to swallow his anger twisted his speech. "No I ain't, it's federal like Dodge said it was," but Cherokee Bill just nodded at the words and never listened to the tone.

Cherokee Bill's eyes kept jerking around. "Well listen, don't mind about that now. I'll get some one way or another when I got time to think about it. Right now I'm thinkin' how I got to get on that line to get some of that Strip money I got comin' but can't for those damn marshals out there watching for me. You got to do some figurin', Henry," he complained. Henry'd been neglecting him.

The twist went out of Henry's thinking, and all sorts of notions and bits of information that had been blowing past him all morning began with a whirl to settle down in his mind. "Listen: you just put it around that I'm gonna ride against that buck from Nowata, that John Rises Early, this afternoon in the chicken pull. You get Young Charlie and that little greaser kid, what's his name?—Julio. Get 'em out there makin' talk and takin' bets. Clear most of that line out by two, three o'clock, everybody going up to watch their bet come home. Some of them marshals got to go up and see what's going on at the rodeo, see if somebody they might remember is gonna show up there. That leaves you a short line, and less law to worry about."

"I can do that," said Cherokee Bill, his face lighting up. He grinned at Henry Starr. "Hey, you think you really can beat him?" He threw back his head and laughed at the look on Henry's face. "I'm just joking you, Henry. John never rise that early in his life. Nobody *ever* rise up early enough to get ahead of Henry Starr. You bet all my money on you, Henry, never mind about that whiskey." He slapped Henry Starr's arm, looked around, and dodged off behind the buildings.

His arm tingling from the slap, Henry Starr decided he needed to do more than he'd said. How about a real blind for whatever game Cherokee Bill was going to run? He stepped to the edge of the alley: Gray Shirt was still on watch. Henry Starr pulled his hat low and dodged out into the street, as if he were trying to use the cover of a passing buckboard —which was no damn good for the purpose if he'd really meant to keep covered; if Gray Shirt was worth his pay he ought to spot one little Injun boy sneaking out the alley from the Katy Bar and acting spooky. Who did Cherokee Bill think these lawmen were? Bill Tilghman, Heck Thomas and Chris Madsen—they had a big reputation for being tough and you couldn't buy them off, and the Fort Smith papers called them "The Three Guardsmen" or "The Three Musketeers" or something like that that sounded like it was out of a book by Colonel D'Artagnan Arbuthnot, *Jesse James's Double Daring*. Well, let's see if we can't show the old Colonel a few new tricks.

Henry Starr crossed the street, hopped up on the sidewalk and walked past Gray Shirt and into the newspaper office (Tahlequah *Chieftain*) next door to the M K & T Land Office. The sign in the window told contestants to register here for the rodeo. Henry waited a bit in the entryway, felt Gray Shirt slip in the door behind him, stepped up to the desk and said, "Sign me up for the chicken pull. I am Henry Starr." The clerk raised his eyes and looked at Henry—flicked to the badge behind him—"Yes: that's who you are all right."

He wrote his name, *Henry Starr*, paid his fee, then turned and walked right past Gray Shirt and outside like a man with no reason in the world to suppose the federal badge was following him.

He was out in the street again, people passing by and every other one shying a look at him. "You're Tom Starr's grandson," said a quiet voice behind him, and Henry Starr turned to look at Gray Shirt. The man was tall—would be maybe six feet even without the high-heeled boots and tan Stetson—fair droopy mustaches threaded with gray, gray eyes looking very cool and quiet. The ivory handle and silvery steel of a Colt's revolver jutted clear of the marshal's hip, inviting his hand. He closed the door of the newspaper office behind him, as if the open street was his private office and now he had Henry Starr by himself. "You ride for Bill Dodge," he said.

Henry's wolf was alive in him again, not an angry wolf like with Dodge, but a playful wolf now, a sly wolf: "That's right, Marshal. And for Roberts on the Standard Ranch before that." No flicker of recognition; this man had nothing to do with six years ago.

"My name is Tilghman," said Gray Shirt. "I am looking for Cherokee Bill. They say you are a friend of his."

"They say true."

"Do you know where I can find him?"

"I do not."

Tilghman nodded as if he expected that answer or approved of it. "A man should keep track of his friends," he allowed. "Sometimes they get too far ahead of him and it gets hard to catch up."

"We're having a talk about friendship," said Henry Starr. "It's an interesting subject to me."

"A man should side his friends," said Tilghman thoughtfully. "A young man should start that way, and it'll keep him straight, probably. Unless his friends are crooked. Then he's got to make a choice. Hard to make a good one then, but he's got to."

"Sometimes there is no good thing to choose," said Henry Starr.

Tilghman nodded again. "Your friend, Cherokee Bill, shot and killed a partner of mine, a deputy named Jack Houston."

Henry Starr's heart jerked like a steer on a short rope. *That's what he was doing away from the ranch two weeks ago*, and he said quickly, "Nothing to do with me, Marshal." He had to look away when he said it—and his eye, flashing along the front of the bank across the street, touched a dark shape jutting up above the low shapes of the Indians waiting in line. There was no mistaking him: the biggest man for size who ever lived in the Cherokee Nation waiting on the main street of Tahlequah for his Strip money and his half-breed grandson to come to him.

He looked back at Tilghman: the marshal was easier. "I don't know where he goes when he isn't riding for Dodge."

"Yes," said Tilghman, "I know that. That's why we're standing here talking about friendship."

Henry Starr was calmer now, wolf crouched, careful. "I don't know where my friend Cherokee Bill is at. But you're just gonna have to keep on looking for him, because he shot your pal Houston. All right."

"That. And Cherokee Bill is wanted on a dozen or so other charges as well. Partner or not, friend or not, those would be enough for me to keep looking for him."

"I don't know what he does when I'm not with him. I don't ask and he don't talk much."

"Nor you." Tilghman paused. "The law has got to catch up with a man one time or another," he said. "Might be a good thing all around if it was me that brought it to him."

Henry Starr felt the breath stop in his chest, as if he stood on the edge of something and the next breath would blow him over one way or the other. His plan for decoying the marshals away from the bank was like a gun under his hand; if he went for it maybe there wouldn't ever be any going back, maybe Tilghman's gray cold eyes would drill his heart and send his ghost out crying [*black into the black*]. Maybe the marshal was right, maybe it was better to give Cherokee Bill to Bill Tilghman, at least there wouldn't be anything extra, no breaking his neck trying to escape, no hooded men with knives and ropes stepping suddenly out of the woods into the firelight.

The shape of Henry Starr's fear suddenly became the raging face of Cherokee Bill, betrayed by his friend his brother, and Henry felt a stab of guilt and then of fear and rage, a blind wordless picture of Cherokee Bill and everything that went with him somehow erased, forgotten, wiped out, swallowed in blue smoke, *ha!* in blue black smoke: no more dreams of riding that road his Grandfather and his Uncles used to ride, robbing and killing but claiming right out what they wanted and what was theirs, and to hell with the law that stole and killed the same but did it on the sneak or from the back, like it did to every one of them one way or another from Jesse James to Belle Starr, shot in the back by someone in the family, cousin brother or son that had sold out to the law. No more dreaming of that, your heart banging so hard that you can't tell if it's how bad you want to start doing it or how bone-deep afraid you are, so that waking up is like getting a pardon—no more of that. And no more of a friend to claim protection, kindness, aid, the brotherhood of a clan and a blood—but that was too much the color of a lie, that clan brotherhood, too much something Henry Starr never really believed in anyway even when he gave Cherokee Bill the words he had to have, one of the Hair Twisters, my friend Cherokee Bill.

How would it be to give Cherokee Bill to Bill Tilghman, and bury the past six years in blue smokes, in blue, in the color of blue?

His eyes jumped to the tall shape of his Grandfather looming over the line of Cherokees in front of the bank. Wouldn't it make old Tom Starr shine if that's what happened. Because it would prove that Cherokee Bill is a no-good murdering nigger who ought to be hung for calling himself Cherokee, and also that I am a worthless half blood who can't be trusted to stay sided with his own.

Henry Starr's heart speeded up, and he set his face in the mask that went with his plan—the look of a sharp kid glad enough to find a way out of a tight spot, as long as nobody could name him a traitor. "No," he said, "I don't talk much. But if you want to see what I do, why don't you come up to the rodeo and watch me ride."

Tilghman's thin lips lifted the droopy mustache in a small smile. "You think you can beat that blood from Nowata?"

Henry Starr looked him hard in the eyes, as if to bang the words in: "Yes I do. I told all my friends to come up and bet on me."

Tilghman blinked, that was all—that, and the mustache settled seriously back in place. "Well then," he said—*was he doubtful? or somehow disappointed that Henry Starr would betray his friend?*—"I might come up and try my luck."

"I'll show you something, I guess," said Henry Starr, turning away on the words—almost feeling a tug holding him there within Tilghman's concentration—and he walked past Tilghman into the street.

He was jittery now, spooked as he walked back to the line in front of the Katy Hotel. *Suppose Tilghman saw through the trick, knows I never would sell Cherokee Bill, just wanted him out of town and up at the rodeo. Don't that make me part of Cherokee Bill, who killed Tilghman's pardner? But suppose Cherokee Bill shows up at the rodeo somehow, didn't say he wouldn't, did he? Won't that make me just the very goddamned Judas I been pretending to be?*

It felt as if Tilghman back there was drawing a bead in the middle of his back; and as bad as that was, it was worse walking away from

Tilghman toward the giant shape of his Grandfather, where it stood next to his mother in the middle of the line of Indians waiting outside the bank. His Grandfather already thought he was a traitor to his blood, no surprise to find he would sell out his half-nigger friend to save himself.

*Oh yes,* he thought, *Tilghman will believe my lie, because I might almost have meant it.*

He could see the two of them standing in the glare just three places up from the bank entrance: the small, round-shouldered woman in the black bonnet and red-brown shapeless dress and the huge old man next to her glaring out over her head into the street, eyes fixed on an unmoving point far beyond the stores and offices that faced him, *probably blind too by now, so why is it that I think, that I know he has seen me, even in the shadow of this sun?* The Old Man's eyes ate up the street, and Henry Starr felt that even if he had stood still, his Grandfather's bright dead eyes could have reeled him in like a fish.

Up close Tom Starr was like an outsize statue of an old-time Indian stood up for a sign next to the bank window. Even slouching, he stood head and shoulders and chest above the woman, above the other Indians lined up in the street waiting to go into the Cattlemen's Bank—where, inside, an agent of the Indian Bureau sat behind a table heaped with papers, flanked by federal marshals, verifying each claimant's right in the color of his or her blood, the blood constituting right to a proportionate share of land in the Strip now confiscated by the federal government; and offering in payment for each duly verified claim of blood and the land attributable thereunto the sum of exactly two hundred and sixty-five United States dollars, and seventy cents: this representing the total assessed value of the Cherokee Strip divided by the number of bona fide Cherokee Indians as counted in the census of 1890.

The Cherokee in the line looked ahead toward the door of the bank, or peered in the window trying to see how far it was and what was going to happen when they arrived at that place they were waiting to be let into. But Tom Starr did not appear to be waiting in line. He was standing in the street, staring across it. The line had nothing to do with him. His eyes were full of other things.

His face was a huge wrinkled brown gourd, hard and dead: his eyes buried in stiff wrinkled folds were like a pair of agates, glittering at something maybe two/three miles off away through and out the other side of the Katy Land Office. The two people in front of him, this woman and just now this cowboy in a dirty white shirt, had nothing to do with him. These Indians, standing in line in the sun? Nothing to do with him. Anyone could stand where he liked in these days. It was a free country. It was none of his business now.

"Grandfather," said Henry Starr. The gourd sat on his Grandfather's shoulders and under his Grandfather's high-crowned black hat. His black shirt hung loosely on the huge ungainly bones of his frame. A woman's gilt locket, heart-shaped and bordered with tiny metal rosebuds, swung against his chest. People said that Tom Starr had taken it off a white woman he had raped and killed and scalped when he was riding the wolf trail with Quantrill or Stand Watie during the War, or with Buck and Dingus James and Cole Younger after. And they also said that it was a judge's wife's that he took and killed for vengeance, washing the filth of one insult or another in her blood—but kept it now for a sign (some said) of his vengeance made good and he did not care who knew it, or was it because of a strange deep feeling in him about the woman?—maybe her beauty or her goodness even while he gripped her in his hands and meant to cut the strings of her blood, her Christian forgiveness (some said it was), none of which weighed against the terrible stone of vengeance in the giant's heart (or was it she who wished to stay with him, seeing a thing beneath his cruelty that no one saw, till she died of hard living and left him to bear the small locket as her sign?) . . .

Really, it was Henry Starr's mother's locket. Inside was a gray and white picture of Hop Starr, Henry's father, Tom Starr's only son—the small shape of his ghost. The woman had thrown it away when she married C. N. Walker, and Tom Starr had picked it up out of the trash and wore it. It grided the woman high and low whenever she saw it swinging against his chest, but of course she couldn't say anything. It was his power over *her*.

But he had nothing to work against *this one*, this cowboy in the white dirty shirt: so he filled the air between himself and "Henry Starr" with silence, with forgetfulness: blue, with the color of blue.

"Henry!" chirped his mother, and she bobbed her head at him like a bird will do, puffing and rumpling herself to ward an intruder off the nest—in which there was no chick, but an old Indian big as an elephant. "Henry! Why don't you say hello to your Grandfather?"

"I did," he said but she was off: "I ain't seen C. N., Henry. We've been here since sunup, waiting on our Strip money, and C. N. gone for some lemonade and never come back."

A sound like the clack of a tongue of wood came from the gourd, and Tom Starr said without looking at Henry, "What did you come back for?"

"Why not? Why shouldn't he?" she chirped again, now pecking her head at the standing trunk of Tom Starr. "He's Cherokee, ain't he? He's got a right to his people's money."

The slab lips of the gourd split and let Henry glimpse broken yellow teeth. "Cherokee," he said. "Anybody can be a Cherokee in this time. Is that right, you 'Henry Starr'? There's men as white as a snake's belly get to claim on Cherokee blood just for one little time they stuck it into some Cherokee cunt."

The woman snapped to rigid attention. "Bad mouth! Nothing is left of you but a bad mouth! If you said this to me when C. N. Walker was here . . ."

Her words pecked and bounced off the knotted rind of the ancient gourd, whose dead eyes held level on the face of "Henry Starr," this one standing here in that name. This was between the two of them. The woman was in a different place.

"I don't care about this money," said Henry Starr.

"No Cherokee money for you?" said Tom Starr. "I guess when you can have white money you don't care about Cherokee. Then what do you want from me?"

Henry Starr reached into the side pocket of his jeans and pulled out the small wrapped parcel. "Grandfather, listen to me a minute. I brought you something from Bartlesville."

"You go to Bartlesville to buy whiskey," Tom Starr said flatly, "you and that half-a-nigger, calls himself a Hair Twister."

Henry shied at the words, let the bandanna, the cool smile, slip. "No whiskey this time. Look, I'll show you," and he started to snap the string that bound the crumpled brown paper around the object.

"You sure you didn't run whiskey?" said Tom Starr softly. "I remember when you was too stupid to know you *was* running whiskey. Sitting in your wagon, reading one of those white books you read, you didn't know you was carrying whiskey for somebody else, no, not till them deputies got ahold of you." Tom Starr opened his dead mouth in a breathless laugh. " 'Don't let 'em lynch me! I ain't done nothing!' " he mimicked in a nasal falsetto. "You say you don't want my money today. Maybe you want me to save you from the law again? Maybe you want me to eat some more shame for you, so the white men won't hang you? I had to eat shame for you once, a long time ago, *hyenh*, long time, if I said no you'd still be hanging onto their boots, *hyenh, hyenh*. I told you I would not eat any more for you. You pay your own debts now, you got no Grandfather to pay them."

Henry Starr's head snapped up, the rage still there for the last six years leaped up in his belly, he felt his wolf show in his eyes and mouth and shoulders and arms. "Eat?" he said very quietly. "I'll tell you what I want you to eat. I want you to eat C. N. Walker's meat and bread in C. N. Walker's house."

But the old gourd was solid, dead, *break your teeth biting that old gourd.* Henry Starr's wolf curled in, bit at its own flanks. "Here, Grandfather." He stripped the paper from the package and held out a pair of smoked-glass spectacles with brass wire ear hooks. "Look, it's to keep the glare of the sun out. So you can see better."

The Old Man stood silent and unmoving.

"So the glare of it won't hurt your eyes," said Henry Starr. Then his hand quick as a snake striking snatched the huge dry left hand of his Grandfather, turned it palm up and slapped the glasses into the hand. Held the hand a moment. It was made of wood.

"Can't you stand looking in my eyes, you? You want to put black over my eyes?"

"It's for you to see better," the woman said softly.

"I see good enough. I know who this one is: the little white man who stole my son's blood. Now he's come for some of my son's money too. I see him good."

Henry dropped the hand and it swung loose, dead, not even dropping the glasses but just letting the earth tug them out of the palm, spin in the air, hit the sidewalk shattering one lens, the left.

With his other hand unseen by Henry, Tom Starr had taken a pinch of tobacco from a pocket or pouch somewhere. Tom Starr houghed his breath on the fragrant tobacco shreds; made a little spit and dropped it on them. His left hand slowly took a pipe out of a beaded pouch at his belt, raised it. He stuffed the tobacco in, tamped it with his thumb, all the time looking right at "Henry Starr"—no, right through "Henry Starr," the Katy Land Office, and two/three miles of empty country beyond.

Henry picked a match out of his shirt pocket, popped it flaring on his belt buckle, looked his Grandfather eye for eye and held out the match flame like a gift. "What kind of tobacco do you think you're making, Granddad?"

"I am like Something," said Tom Starr, speaking Cherokee, "I am like a Person. You have come from under the Great Thicket."

"What memory are you erasing, Old Man?" said Henry Starr, so his Grandfather would have to remember that he once tried to teach his conjures to his grandson.

Tom Starr smiled, the smile a man might wear teasing a caged wolf with a piece of fresh meat. Henry Starr saw that the Old Man only thought Henry was afraid of the conjure.

"*In blue, ha!—in blue smokes I have wrapped you. I am like that Great Serpent, that Tuft of Feathers. I am like that Wizard who finishes what he starts.*"

Henry felt cold. The old man was working one of his damned conjures, which looked and sounded like *erasing memory* but it was working on Henry Starr like *make my enemy crazy.*

The match flame gave Henry Starr's fingertips a cruel lick and went dead.

"Forget whatever you want, Old Man. Forget who I am, forget who your son was, whatever you damn please to forget. Just be sure you don't forget who you are, or how much money you got comin', or that Cherokee son-in-law of yours C. N. Walker won't buy you no lemonade."

Tom Starr stopped muttering suddenly. "Who are you? If you're a white man, why don't you just go and be white? Why you keep hanging around us poor Cherokees, hmmm? You can read like a white man, you talk like one, you look like one, so why don't you just go away and be what you are?" His head began to shake so that his heavy lips shook and the loose skin at his throat trembled. "You think you got to have some Cherokee money for yourself, but white men don't get no Cherokee money."

"He thinks you are C. N. Walker," said his mother in a loud whisper, as if the blind old giant were deaf too.

"No, he don't," said Henry Starr, "he knows who I am."

The old man split his face in a terrible grin, mocking and self-satisfied, that showed the black jagged spikes of his ruined teeth. "Heh!" he said, a laugh that was also a puff of breath into the tobacco cupped in his palm, and melted into the rhythmic mumble of the conjure, *In blue, ha!—in blue smokes I have wrapped you. I am like that Great Serpent, that Tuft of Feathers. I am like that Wizard, who finishes what he starts.*

Henry snorted breath through his nostrils and showed a slash of grin that mocked his Grandfather's power, and inside he was ashamed for Tom Starr, working his old-time powwow muck-a-muck magic like a senile old blanket head as if it only needed his words to erase "Henry Starr" from the air and memory around them. But Tom Starr kept mumbling, and Henry Starr had to stop him. He was too much man now just to stand like a wooden dummy in front of the whole Nation on the main street of Tahlequah on the Fourth of July, and let this giant old man put shame on him like dogshit in his hands . . . and something in Henry

Starr snickered. *What if there really is Something, Something that listens when Tom Starr changes tobacco?*

## TSIGESU

"Listen now:

"Henry Starr's people were of a certain one of the Seven Clans of the Cherokee Nation a long time ago. I think I won't tell you the name of their clan—maybe I don't remember. But if your name was Starr that was all the clan that mattered. It's a big family, it counts many important men and women—judges of the clan and of the Nation, sheriffs, ministers of the Gospel, officers of the territorial and the state governments, schoolteachers (Henry Starr's mother was a schoolteacher, she was almost white), members of the legislature . . . also many men and even some women who rode the nightland with the wolves and heard the owl hoot. Even some white people have heard of Belle Starr and her daughter Little Pearl—who kept ranch at Younger's Bend near Eufaula for Cole Younger, and for Buck and Dingus James and all of those boys that rode with Quantrill in the War, and afterwards became outlaws. Belle Starr was Henry Starr's aunt, and Cole Younger and Frank and Jesse James and all of that gang, they was like Uncles to Henry Starr—not Uncles to see and to live with, not Uncles in the blood, but Uncles for children to listen to stories about, Uncles to grow up like and ride their kind of horses on their kind of road. That kind of Uncles.

"But the head of the Starr clan was old Tom Starr: he was the biggest man for size in the Cherokee Nation, and he kept his road no matter what, Tom Starr's road. He was like a Nation to himself, Tom Starr, he had no law but what he made or took for his own; and he was the only single human person with whom the Cherokee Nation and the government of the United States had to make a private treaty of peace, to keep Tom Starr from making war on them for as long as there was power in that giant body of his, the biggest man in the Cherokee Nation.

"Used to be in the Old Time, when we lived among the tall mountains and the great trees, in that Old Place that was full of the sounds of falling water and the silence of water resting in pools: back in the Old Time that was, Tom Starr met a bear in his road. They were walking down the same trail under the trees, the bear walking east and Tom Starr walking west. Now most men will give trail to a bear, but not Tom Starr. Once he had chosen a trail it was his, and he would not turn aside for anything. The bear lifted himself, and rocked his upper body left and right, and houghed out his breath that smelled of dead meat, and showed his yellow teeth. So Tom Starr, he did the same: hauled his breath up into his chest, and rolled his big body round his hips, his arms hung out like thick tree limbs, his teeth bare and shining under the trees. And the bear come with a rush, sort of toppling as he come, but Tom Starr took one sweeping step that brought him inside the bear's rush and he swept his right hand up as he come on like a man swinging a giant iron maul, and he chopped his big fist down right on top of the bear's nose with the whole swinging weight of arm and body and hips behind it, and he drove the bear's head right down to ground the way you drop a steer under a poleax, yes: I'm telling you—the skin of that bear made a good coat for one of Tom Starr's three wives, the young one. A good coat: not a cut of knife in it, not a bullet hole, the skin beaten so soft it needed hardly any chewing.

"Tom Starr: that was the Grandfather of Henry Starr. He was too much Grandfather for any man to have.

"This was his way: if the chiefs said it was wise to do one thing, he would do the other. Listen:

"In those days we first brought among us the black people whom the whites kept as slaves. We were of too many voices about this thing. There were those who said that it was not wise to take these strangers in among us to do a man's or a woman's work, because their work would mix with ours and change it; because living with us there would be a mixing of blood with us, and a changing, and whether from this blood or this work we would become other than what our Grandfathers made us. And there were others among us that said, great wealth and power came to white people from the doing of this one great thing, the holding of black people as one holds cattle or dogs. If we would be rich and strong as white people, it was a wise thing to follow them in this way of power. The quarrels and arguments whirled and spun, men of the old belief speaking their grief: first the way of the white missionaries to turn our minds, now the way of the black people to turn our bodies white. And the men of the Christian belief answering two ways: that the way of the holding of black people was not owned by the Jesus; and that it was. And between the two kinds of Jesus men and two or three kinds of old-believing men finally the Council seemed to become a boiling cloud of blue smoke, of blue in which nothing could be clearly seen: until Tom Starr stood up.

"Tom Starr stood up and lowered his big scarred head forward on his heavy shoulders like a bear menacing before he charges. 'I name John

Ross,' he said, 'and the family of John Ross, and the other families of the Nation who have gotten fat on the meat that black dogs carry to them in their mouths.'

"The family of Ross, and the wealthiest families of the Nation—although some belonged to Jesus and some still sang the songs of their Grandfathers—they all thought the way of the black people was the way of wisdom and power. And so did many who had no great property but dreamed of John Ross as of a kind of Uncle, an Uncle whose horse you will ride when you grow up down a road like his—that kind of Uncle.

"Then Tom Starr shook his head and rocked his heavy body on his hips. 'John Ross owns many niggers,' said Tom Starr, 'but he does not own me. I am not one of John Ross's niggers.' He took up each man of the council singly in his fierce eyes, and put them down again, one by one. 'My word is against it,' he said, 'and so my hand is against it too.'

"And John Ross, who was the greatest man among us in those days, turned pale and said, 'Tom Starr will do as the Council decrees.'

" 'No,' said Tom Starr, and he held John Ross in his hard angry eyes as if he would shake him. 'You've heard my word against it. You know I keep my word.'

"That was Tom Starr's way. If there was a thing the wealthy Cherokee like John Ross wanted, he was against that thing. Another man might have stood up that way with his whole clan behind him, but I'm telling you that Tom Starr had no clan: his own name, his own skin, his own blood was clan enough for him, just like his own word was all the law he would let belong to him. It made him strong—but also it was a weakness that allowed men of more cunning to abuse his strength.

"It was like Tom Starr kept meeting Jack-the-Devil out in the woods, and giving that one his names, so that all his power for his family turned against his family, and everything that made him strong made him weak. Jack-the-Devil, you know how it happens with that one—some call him just plain devil, and some call him Coyote, you can't ever learn his real name: but one day your uncle Rufus Tenkiller meets a stranger in the woods, and it seems like he brings luck so that the deer walk right up into the sights of his rifle and the fish jump into his creel spilling over the top like too much water, and all the while the stranger is talking and learning his names and the names of his family—then he kills Uncle Rufus somehow, or gets inside his skin and his name, and comes back home pretending to be the one he killed or got inside the name of and runs the same game on all the man's kin: and only after he's done and the house burnt by the neighbors because the deer and fish turn out to be stolen, and the women and young girls fucked this way and that by their brothers and fathers that might or might not also have been Jack-the-Devil—only after, when you're looking round for the bodies do you figure out it wasn't Uncle Rufus come back from the woods it was Jack-the-Devil. And if Rufus comes home next day, you can add his body to the pile because nobody will take *that* chance again.

"Listen:

"In that time the Old Devil Jackson was President of the white Americans, and he betrayed us. We who had fought by his side against our cousins the Creeks became black in his eyes when white men came to him seeking our land. Old Jackson was against us, and many other whites: too many for us to fight and win. It's an old story and you whites don't tell it to yourselves that much, maybe you don't like to hear it. Our homes were stolen, the Old Place among the trees where the mountains were and all the many different sounds of water, and its quietness; and we were driven out like the Indians out here used to drive the buffalo, crowding and stumbling to get away, with the books that the whites had given us, and the Jesus-speakers the whites had sent to us, and all of the things they had given us, all of the things we had bought from them to own them and be white, all these things—they drove us out with them as if we were black in their eyes. So.

"Do you think they could have driven out Tom Starr if he was not willing to go? He would have died in that place. Or he would have lived on there, and be alive still like an old black bear in the mountains, the whites who stole that land would never have eaten meat or made fire in that place without feeling his eyes upon them, lifting them one by one out of their place; without feeling the ghost of his arrow out of the dark striking deep between their ribs.

"How do you think they got him to go?

"This was the way: at first, John Ross was unwilling to go, and he called councils to keep the Seven Clans behind him in his stratagems, for he had many devious ways of working upon the whites, walking among them in his suit and ruffled shirt and silk tie as if he were one with them. John Ross wanted to keep his plantation worked for him by his many black people, so he worked against the move to the west and set his heart on the law of white councils in the east.

"So then what was there for Tom Starr to do but to fold his arms, and lower his heavy brows, and take his stand: 'Let the law speak with the mouth of the white man or the mouth of John Ross, and it is still nothing to me. My word is against it. And so my hand is against it too.' But that must also be against the trees and the mountains and the different waters, for leaving the Old Place and going to the west. Well . . . you see what it is like here. Tom Starr had not seen it, but how could he not know it must be wrong to leave the Place of that Old Time? But what else could Tom Starr do once Ross had spoken, but go himself to spite John Ross, and send his sons before him into the Territory.

"And then: when the whites gathered their warriors against us and locked the people in stinking forts, helpless and starving among their own shit—then Ross collapsed like a rotten dogwood stump when a bear butts it looking for honey, he surrendered to the white paper, he packed his black people, his wives and his daughters, he packed his food and his seeds and his furs and his furniture, he packed his books and his pens and his preacher and his piano, and started the Nation on its long trail to the west. Many people died on that trail, for not carrying enough food or losing their heart for the road as the air kept opening in front of them and closing behind, the new place further than dreaming, the Old Place buried behind deep clouds of blue, of black.

"But John Ross had fooled Tom Starr: though old Tom could still say, 'Nobody drove me out, I came myself.' Could still say, 'I didn't follow John Ross to the Territory; John Ross followed me.' Because when they came to this place John Ross still had his black people and his house and his books and his furniture and his piano in the parlor, and Tom Starr had only his little cabin away back in the woods.

"So there were quarrels between them, there was blood spilled. And then the War came. John Ross owned slaves like the Graycoats, so did many other great ones among the Nation. So when John Ross agreed to let the people fight for the Graycoats there was no surprise. Maybe it was his kind of fight, a fight for his kind of Cherokee people. But the other kind of Cherokee, the 'Pin Cherokee,' whose name was a mockery because they had no buttons, what business was it of theirs to fight for John Ross's niggers? So Tom Starr drew his family back into the woods, and John Ross would rather send his people to fight Bluecoats far away than into the brush after Tom Starr and his family.

"But John Ross had no heart to own the gray coat. He had heart for his lands and his daughters and his house and his piano, and he had enough money and power so he wasn't afraid his black people would run off and leave him—to go where? to dig roots for the Pins? to be staked on the prairie by horse Indians? So as soon as the Blue began to reach closer to the Nation John Ross changed his coat, and now his men went scouring into the brush to bring Cherokee out to fight for the Bluecoat. Bluecoat, Graycoat—it was all to fight for John Ross's house and land and piano.

"And so what could Tom Starr do then but send his sons and go himself to fight with Stand Watie and the Cherokee Graycoats, to ride with Graycoat Quantrill, who drank his enemies' blood at Lawrence and Centralia. So once again John Ross had circumvented and humiliated Tom Starr for all his great courage and strength, so that the man who had no slaves had to be fool enough to shed his blood for the Graycoats, and lose his lands in punishment; and the man who held black people as one holds a horse or a dog, he was the friend of the Bluecoats, his judges sat in judgment on Tom Starr—who never held slaves, whose word and hand were both against it, who always held himself a man for freedom.

"It was as if one of those night doctors had changed some tobacco on Tom Starr and put a twist on his ghost, or like he had met Jack-the-Devil in the woods and Jack-the-Devil got inside the old man's bones and come back in his shape to make his good luck bad luck, so what made him strong become the very thing that give him into the hands of his enemies, so that he never could get justice.

"Out there in the woods alone, far from his home in the mountains, far from the waters and the trees of the Old Place, out there in the black in the blue dark Tom Starr gave his mind and his ghost to studying justice. How you can think about justice all alone, with no people around you, I don't know. But he could not think when he was with people anymore. 'Here I can get no justice,' he would say, 'here there is no justice for a Cherokee man. There can't be no justice when there is white men all over the place, and Indians like John Ross who are white men too. Because in those white eyes a Cherokee is just a different kind of nigger, and there's no justice between white and nigger: there is just what do you own, what can you hold, what can you make him do. You see? I know about niggers. John Ross taught me all about niggers, he owns many of them but he does not own me, I am not one of John Ross's niggers. I am Tom Starr, my blood is Cherokee water in the Cherokee country, and I can't get justice anyway, as if the color of my blood was black.

" 'In the Old Time, back in the Old Place, in the mountains where the water was, we had us some justice then, *hyenh*. You hear me telling you? Some justice. If there was blood laid to your name, if a man had done a thing to you so you must walk on his ghost or else turn into a woman, turn into a nigger in your own eyes, I'll tell you: I stood up in front of them, the whole Council, and I told them . . . right there in their eyes, in their face: how a thing was done and what to do to make it right. And you could see how your word tasted to them, they would eat it like food, real food—you could wait while they chewed it, and it was beginning to be better already, knowing they could taste the truth of it. If they said *Peace* after that, all right, a man could swallow that if he had to. Or if it happened that blood had to come of it, mine and then his and then mine again . . . even if there was no other way but that, still you would know, everybody would know whether it was justice from the taste of it in the mouth like food, something to chew on. Law is for people that don't understand justice, don't taste it. Kill a man, you hang: that's law. Rob a store where you been cheated: prison. That's law. Law is what you teach children until they can learn the taste of justice—food for babies who can't chew meat, that's law, that's what white men live by. That's what they should live by, and let the people here live by justice, like in the Old Days, *hyenh*? When everybody knew the taste of it, like food.

" 'But these people . . . white men and law paper all over the Territory, and nobody against it. Cherokees taking law into their eyes, it turns their ghosts white. Nobody knows the taste of it anymore, what justice tastes like, you know? You know why that is? Because that John Ross with his pockets full of dollars, with his white house and his white wife, and his daughters that he makes to be like white women, and his racehorses and his niggers that he buys and sells, his niggers that work his land and make his food, his books and his preacher of the Jesus and his piano in the parlor, that John Ross sold the mountains and the trees and the water of that Old Place for money, and sold the food and the justice for money, and brought us here where nothing tastes right, the water stinks, the land stinks, little small trees, little mountains, the justice stinks, there ain't no justice—you can't taste it for the stink, but only law everywhere you look: tribal law and territorial law, federal marshals out of Fort Smith, *pah!* No justice. Here I can have no justice like it should be, sitting down to a feast with the Old Men. Now you have to make your justice like you make your whiskey, out in the woods, out in the dark. Now you make your justice with this [*he lays a Colt's .45 revolving pistol on the table*] with a gun like this.'

"Tom Starr: that was the Grandfather of Henry Starr. He was too much Grandfather for any man to have."

## TAHLEQUAH *July 4, 1892*

It was a bit cooler inside the bank, the windows were shaded, the air cooled by a fan stirring slowly round the ceiling. There were four of them together now—old Tom Starr, and his daughter-in-law, and his grandson Henry Starr, and C. N. Walker had joined them at the last minute, his face still glowing with the whiskey Henry Starr had sold but could not buy again. He gave Henry a conspiratorial wink, no hard feelings. "I figured you'd turn up for your cut," he said—the wink was more of an insult than the words, but his mother said, "Please, Henry," and put her hand on his arm: there were white men watching, they had money—and outside the Nation waiting, watching, listening.

In front of them was a large table, a white man behind it in paper-collar shirt, bow tie and blue suit, his hands folded before him on the table. Two other white men sat on either side of him, one with a stack of papers, the other with an open strongbox. Behind the table stood a deputy with a shotgun, chewing tobacco slowly, stewing in his sweat with the heat. Off to the right of the deputy in leather chairs along the wall were five white men in dark suits, white shirts, black four-in-hands, carrying briefcases.

"Your names?" said the middle white man at the table.

Tom Starr still stood as straight as he had outside. Perhaps he had not really moved his feet at all to come in here. Perhaps the room had moved in around him, respecting his power to remain in his place unmoved.

C. N. Walker stepped up to the table. "We-all are the Starr family. That's old Tom Starr, head of the family. This is Mrs. Hop Starr that was, his daughter-in-law, remarried to myself, C. N. Walker of Tulsa. And that's her and Hop Starr's boy Henry: now my stepson."

The man with the papers leaned toward the white man in the middle and muttered, "Tom Starr's a blood, sure. But is she? Because if she ain't, then . . ." and the white man in the middle raised his hand to stop the talk, nodding—he understood all that.

"Are you claiming on your husband's blood, or your son's, ma'am?"

"Me?" she chirped. "My husband's . . . my son's . . . I am Cherokee myself! I can claim for myself. Here's the names written down, the names of my parents, of their clan, written down . . ." She handed them papers, official birth certificates: her people were not Pin Indians from the backwoods, but upstanding townfolk, citizens, Christians, even one, even two generations ago, even in the mountains and hills far back at the other end of the Trail of Tears, where the water was, even then . . .

The two white men leaned together. "That makes her good any way you look at it. Him too," and he tipped his head toward C. N. Walker, who stood there beaming, as he had when the boys at Holcomb's had bought the next round of drinks and included him.

"All right," said Middle White Man, and he gestured with his left hand and the third white man opened the cashbox. "As computed by the government assessors, the value of the Cherokee lands seized in forfeit for tribal activities on behalf of the late Southern Confederacy amounts to a share of two hundred and sixty-five dollars and seventy cents for each man, woman or child now belonging to the Cherokee Nation." The third white man began counting out bills and coins, building four stacks on the table in front of him.

Now one of the white men sitting by the wall, with the dark suits and the briefcases, rose and came up to the table. "Morton," he said, nodding to the middle white man, "as you know I am here as the agent of the M K & T Land Company, which has purchased the outstanding notes of a number of businessmen and sales agents trading through the Nations. These here folks are the Starr family, Tom Starr family? From around Eufaula?"

"That is correct," said Middle White Man and sat back a little in his chair as if he had now done. C. N. Walker turned slowly and looked at the new man, never seen him before but . . . he began to flush red from the jowls up, he smelled something. The woman had her eyes on the little growing piles of money. Tom Starr stared off, his eyes piercing the back wall of the bank to find and fix on a place, empty place miles off out there in the country.

"I have a set of invoices and bills of sale which I place before you on the table," said the agent, and he did so.

"Noted," said Middle White Man, and he raised the papers perfunctorily and displayed them to his colleagues, who nodded, they saw them. It was like some sort of white man's church, slow serious words matched by measured, strange gestures, the Injuns watching the mystery.

"Mr. Starr," said the agent to old Tom, "do you recognize these notes of yours, given in your own hand?"

It was a place, a far place—many many miles distant. The strength it took to look toward that place turned the walls into thin panes of ice, the people into shadows, their sounds into gray smoke.

"He seems to be blind," said the white man on the left.

"Or . . ." The man on the right tapped his head.

"I turn to you," the agent said, still speaking and moving formally like a priest, "Mr. C. N. Walker, as being, in lieu of Mr. Thomas Starr, head of the household. I ask you to verify that these signatures are his."

Walker, boiling now, jabbed at the papers with his eyes, but they skidded away in uncontrollable panic. "How in the hell should I know, I didn't even know the old idiot could write." He slapped the limb of the dead standing stump draped in its ragged black shirt. "Hey! Who in hell knew you could write, you goddamn fool! Didn't I tell you not to . . ." Something hit Walker, some fear maybe hidden in the stump, his rage spun him off Tom Starr and onto the woman. "What'd I tell you? Didn't I tell you to keep those goddamn drummers away from him? Didn't I?"

Briefcase smiled. "I guess it is clear that the signatures have been recognized, and therefore that the purchases made and the bills due . . ."

"Wait a goddamn minute," said C. N. Walker. "The only thing I bought on this here Strip money was that piece a land Roberts was leasin' from the Nation. You can't hold us to a sale made to this pore worn-out old blanket-head, that some drummer probably got him drunk before he . . . and carryin' whiskey, by God! in the Nations too. That's agin the law, and you know it, so if you think those goddamn papers you got gonna stand up in court . . ." He looked at the papers again and that kicked him off in another direction. "A piano! Oh my sweet Jesus dead upon the cross! Look at him, for Chrissake! Look at him! What's a thing like that gonna do with a piano? What did you do, old man? What in hell did you do? Goddamnit, you just about ruined us!"

Middle White Man was rearranging the stacks, taking off bills of the largest denomination first and piling them near the stack of papers. "Wait a minute!" yelped C. N. Walker. "You can't take my money too!"

Middle White Man looked up. "If you're part of the Starr family, Mr. Walker, then you share in its debts as well as its entitlements." He reached over and began peeling bills off the fourth stack.

"Hold off," said Henry Starr.

They all turned to look at him.

"I said hold." His voice was very quiet, as if he gave only half his breath to it. The deputy with the shotgun stood there half asleep, blinked, then gathered his attention suddenly to a point. Trouble.

"Who's the fourth stack for?"

"That's your share, if you're Henry Starr, the son of Hop Starr."

Henry Starr looked at the stump of his Grandfather. The eyes in the stump were someplace else, not this place, *a place far off, many miles beyond the wall that is not really there, far . . .*

Henry Starr looked at the middle white man. "I am Henry Starr, but no kin to these. No kind of Cherokee at all." Nobody moved or spoke. "So I reckon you better just throw that money back where it come from."

"Henry!" cried C. N. Walker. "Take it, for God's sake, maybe there'll be somethin' left if you . . . Holy Jesus, boy, they'll skin us all the way back to Tennessee without you take your share of that money."

Middle White Man sat there, uncertain. The agent with the briefcase looked annoyed; if they threw the money back he was going to have to collect the bills these Injuns owed by suing against their land, and that was doubtful, expensive and time-consuming. "Take your money, son," he advised, "you got it coming."

"Not that," said Henry Starr. "I ain't got that coming."

"Money don't stink, son," said the Briefcase. "What do you care where it come from or how?"

"That's Cherokee money, boy," said C. N. Walker, "your own people's money."

Henry Starr looked at his Grandfather. "Then it still ain't my money." He looked up, all around the room. "Come over to the rodeo and watch me ride. That's how my money comes to me. If anybody wants a piece of it they only got to bet on me."

## TSIGESU

"So they come packing and piling in, hundreds of people, racked up the slanting frames of the bleachers and crowded up and onto the fence rails that ringed the big arena. On each of the half dozen telegraph poles that marched past there were people of all colors hanging from the iron step-rods the repairmen used to climb and repair the wires. Behind the crowd behind the fence folks had pulled their wagons up, and these become box seats for clumps of people packed in to see.

"Hawkers come through the crowd selling American flags and Cherokee warbonnets and firecrackers and pop and lemonade and probably some whiskey and Choctaw beer on the quiet too. And the odds takers was working the crowd, taking in all kinds of money today. There were serious gamblers who meant to win, who checked this boy's record on a bronc, and dug out of memory where in hell it was they'd seen that lop-eared roan with the Roman nose and the mean eye—different name on him but the same look, you can't fool me about a horse, didn't he near kill that Guthrie cowboy rode him over in Bartlesville? And there was some that bet by the numbers, give 'em the longest odds for their dime or dollar and they'd try it, work whatever their number magic was to make it come true, not knowing or caring who the riders or the broncs was, just watching the numbers come up on the board.

"But there was more folks who had come there to bet on their kin and their clan and their blood. Money on the white boy, that blond dude-y lookin' one, his father owns the big spread out east of here where the nigger cav'ry is—no, leases it, I expect, like everybody else around here, from them Injuns. Money on this one [*name of this, clan of that*]. Money on the full blood or the breed kid. 'That kid, why mister, I wouldn't want to just take your money, he's only a . . . well, if ya got to lose it, I'll oblige ya.' Because how can you not put your money on him who rides today in the name of your blood and your clan?

"That's how it was done in the Cherokee Nation in the old days.

"Bronc riding they had, bareback and saddle. Roping and tying, bulldogging.

"And then they come to the chicken pull.

"There was a dozen riders to start, only two of 'em white boys, the rest all different kinds of blood from all over the Nations. Around by the bleachers they had set up a table, with a couple of shotgun guards around it, and that was where the Old Man sat to judge the riding and to keep the prize. The judges brought some money with them for the prize, but then they set the box before them and opened it, and others came forward to make the prize greater still. One after another they walked up to the table, the old men dressed in whatever their best might be: broadcloth suit and derby hat, a leather case of bills and coin (he is a judge in the tribal court), 'For my clan . . .'; next spurs and a gun belt, chaps, a weathered face under a broad-brimmed hat, 'For mine'; old buckskin worn soft as velvet, 'For my clan.' And so the prize money became greater, bags of it—maybe, I don't know, five thousand dollars there in different kinds of money, gold eagles and silver dollars, Mexican pesos, probably some old Continental money, probably some old British pounds and shillings, probably some old medals like they used to give out bushels of back in the old times, when we lived under the trees, up in those mountains, and the Americans were first coming through Cherokee country to trade for furs or tobacco or land or slaves. And I'm not even mentioning all the money that was being bet outside, that personal money bet on the clan, but not officially in its name. All that money and all that glory for the winner to take under that big sun, the sky blue, the flags waving off the tops of the poles like the gas flares burning off up top of the oil rigs. That's how it was in that old time.

"You ever see one of these chicken pulls? You got to have a bunch of chickens, supposed to be white ones, the tougher the better, *hyenh*? or what's the good of it? And you dig a hole in the middle of the ground at one end of the arena, and the boys is all down at the other—leave just enough room for a good man to stop his horse after his run.

"Then they bury the first chicken, and the boys start taking their runs at it. One of the white boys from Claremore got no patience, so they let him try it first. He sets his horse one count then kicks in his heels and spurs and yips, and his horse jumps out and starts to churn it up coming all out down to where that little white chicken head is stickin' up out of the packed earth sort of peekin' and peckin' around, and the white boy leans as he comes in on it down off the right side of the horse, his arm swinging and everybody's looking in the dust to see did he snatch the head off—but those who had seen this many times before could tell from the line of his body that he never leaned over far enough to get that chicken, not if he had an arm like an elephant's nose. You can't keep your seat firm and catch the chicken, no: you got to hold with your legs, with your knees, you see? and slide off the side and hang yourself out there in the air, so far out you could lean forward and start shooting people from under your horse's chin *hyenh*! and then you snatch that chicken's head off!

"And so the next one come down, a strapping boy from over Muskogee, good people there, and rowels his pony down the track looking very good—and then, just a little bit you could see him guiding his horse, correcting him as he run, and I knew it was no good even though he come up square over the chicken and swept low enough hanging off the horse by one leg and you could hear that chicken *scraw!* as he wrung its neck out of the ground, see how the white neck wrung his arm back like a whip hand jerking against the crack, jerking him out of the saddle rolling over and over as his horse went by, over and over his arm broke under him.

"Because you see, if you're gonna snatch the head off that old tough bird buried in there up to the craw in hard-packed earth you, you got to come on, you know? You got to rowel that horse and get him a-comin', and his head got to be set just right when your heels give it to him and kick him forward, and you can't shift or change none because it's got to be all your speed, all your power rushing forward there, and you not even thinking about slowing to lean and get your grip, and never thinking about how if you don't check him after you grab the head how in hell is that crazy bronc gonna stop before he busts the both of you and that bloody goddamn chicken head right through the side of the corral? You just got to get up and come on, and go on, and come on, and get over it and pull through it, *mm! hyenh-heh*, that's how it's done!

"And that day there was some boys that could do it. There was Rogers from Oolagah, and the Ridge boy from Muskogee. But mostly there was John Rises Early, a full blood from Nowata that maybe was kin to John Ross; and there was Henry Starr, grandson of old Tom Starr.

"One after the other they come down, kicking in the spurs and letting the long whip end of the reins fly free, hanging on with their knees and sweeping down for that little white head bobbing in the white sand, one quick grab in the dust with your horse's hooves flying an inch away from your nose, a quick snatch, a hard grip, and then throw yourself up against the pull of the white bird's neck trying to wring you back into the ground, and as you come up twist the horse's head in and down to tuck him into himself, sliding on his hooves and rump to a skidding halt in front of the barrier.

"One after another till only four was left, and those four had each pulled the heads of three chickens out of the ground that way. And then, on the fourth run, the Oolagah boy—he got arm-tired maybe—stripped feathers and never made his pull but held his saddle, and got a cheer for it, and turkey gobbles from his clan. And they buried another chicken, and the Ridge boy come down smoking, and he missed it and come up with a shake of his hand scraped raw on the ground. Some yells for him, not so many from outside his clan. And that left it to Henry Starr and John Rises Early—a big boy, that Rises Early, from Nowata up on the Verdigris, good cattle country, and he was dressed as a cowboy should dress for a rodeo, with hand-tooled boots and a silver belt buckle and a red plaid shirt and a white Stetson hat. They say he was some kin to John Ross, maybe. I don't want to say, one way or the other. But maybe that was what made it seem like something important was happening, something maybe dangerous even, not to speak about: that of all that started, in the end these two were left. Maybe. I don't want to say whether it was so. But the Ross family were all there. And old Tom Starr come too, with his daughter-in-law, and his white son-in-law whose name I keep forgetting to remember. That's how they say it was. It was a thing to see, to be there in those old times."

## TAHLEQUAH *July 4, 1892*

Henry Starr was breathing heavily, standing by his horse, the two of them bathed in sweat. *Glad now I didn't have no whiskey*, he thought. The Old Men were talking over by the prize table. Nodding heads. "What's that about?" Henry Starr asked his cousin—Edward Starr, sixteen, proud to be helping Henry Starr with his horse on this great day.

Edward made a face. "Old Tom. Up in the stands there, back of the table. The whole Ross family too. Nobody wants that old trouble to start up again."

Henry Starr grinned at that old Cherokee trouble. "Got to let it run, don't they? Got to be him or me?" *Give me this,* he said to himself, *give me this for that old dead gourd-head Grandfather, with his damn full-Cherokee blood.*

One of the Old Men trotted over. "Last one. Win or lose, this one. Both pull, both split the prize."

The Nowata boy, John Rises Early, said nothing. *That's the Ross clan's mark: listen to the Old Men, especially if it gets you off of a* "Ride till one of us don't come up, wasn't that the rule?" said Henry Starr. "Wasn't that the law for this contest? Ride 'em till there ain't but one rider left up, or no more white chickens left in the Cherokee Nation."

The Old Man looked at Henry Starr. "You are the grandson of Tom Starr. Don't talk to me about the law. The law is for peace. This is for peace. One more ride: win, lose, or split."

John Rises Early swung up into his saddle. His red shirt was bright in the sun, which struck a white spark off his silver buckle. He pulled the brim of his new white Stetson low. Set himself. Looked his way to the white speck of the bird down the long hard strip of packed earth. Took his breath and gave it back. Again. Then his legs lifted and kicked and he screeched as loud as he ever had before, cracking the dryness in his throat and the horse jumped out, its hooves boiling up the torn-up sand, thundering straight as an arrow run down the arena, the boy's long body bending, plaid shirt flashing red as he swung, hat gone to hell, a sweep, a scree-*crack!* and then he was wringing the horse around to a stop in front of the barrier, trotting past it to the judges' table, holding the bloody head and neck in his hand.

"Where is my Grandfather?" Henry asked.

"Just off to this side of the judges' table. Close enough to taste the blood, I guess."

"Oh yeah?" Henry was smiling, and he felt his wolf get up and shake itself. "You want to see, Eddie? You want to see Henry Starr, of the clan of Tom Starr?" He reached to his chest, twisting the wet dirty white shirt in his hands till the buttons popped and the seams split and he stood bare-chested. "Get the saddle off him, and the bit-bridle too," he said, sitting down in the dust hauling off first one boot, then the other.

"Holy Jesus, Henry, what you gonna do?"

"Just get that damn saddle off, and run me a hackamore with your rope there. Goddamn it, move!" He had his knife out, slashing at the legging of his jeans, "Damn it" nicked his thigh, but he had them cut down to like breechclouts with long ragged blue streamers trailing to the ankles. He dabbed at the string of red blood on his bare leg with a finger, dabbed again—lifted it and touched quickly, two dots above the eyes, stripe down the nose. Tore a strip from his shirt—he felt the crinkle of paper in the pocket, *The Cherokee Nation the Lost Tribes of Israel*—tossed the shirt away, binding his hair with the torn strip of white.

Jumped onto the bare back of the horse and gripped the hackamore, white teeth flashing in his brown and bloody face above the smooth naked chest. "Hayee, Eddie Starr! Watch how it's done, cousin! Watch how it was done in the old days."

He didn't lift and rowel, no spurs on his bare heels, but his body seemed to twist and wring down on the horse and lift and spring and shoot him forward, hooves slashing forward straight out through the dust, charging fast and light and crazy and furious straight down the fairway to where the small white head of the bird poked out of the earth this way and that, smoking down, burning down, the smooth brown body sweeping down on the side of the horse, the brown arm swung like a whip, the snap of the neck too fast for a cry, and then horse man and bird all gone into the huge smoking boil-up of dust where the horse come skidding on heels and rump up to the barricade head and neck wrung away and back against the roar and rush of their speed.

Then still.

And there they were, their shapes resolving slowly out of the smoke. Horse rising to stand, rider on his bare back, naked chest and legs, blue streamers, white headband, face painted with brown-red streaks on eyes and nose. In his right hand the beak and the beady eye and red comb of the chicken, and the open neck draining blood from the bottom of his fist.

The whites began to clap and cheer, and the Cherokees were making sounds like *yu-yu-yu-yu* and here and there the wild turkey gobble of the old-time warriors remembering how it was in the old days.

Henry Starr walked his horse up to the judges' table. The head of John Rises Early's chicken lay on the table next to the prize money. The judges did not look at his face, but at his horse's face. "Both pulled the chicken," said the middle judge. "The prize is split."

"No," said Henry Starr. You could hardly hear him for the yelling and the *yu-yu-yu* and the *ooblooblooble* and the firecrackers and guns popping off. "You listen to the people there. They know who won."

"Give us the head and you can take your share of the prize money. That was the rule."

"No," said Henry Starr, "it may be the law but you know it ain't justice," and with his knees he eased his horse on to where Tom Starr sat in the grandstand.

"Grandfather," he said.

The shouting and yelling and popping of guns kept on and on, and old Tom Starr did not move, but sat there looking straight ahead. A place off there, two/three miles. Not here. A withered gourd with agate eyes, set on a black shirt stuffed full of huge old mastodon bones.

"Did you bet, Grandfather?" Henry Starr cried. "Did you bet your Cherokee Strip money?"

Tom Starr's head tilted down and up.

"How did you bet?" yelled Henry Starr, yelling to be heard over the uproar, shouting, explosions, "How did you bet?"

"On my blood."

"Your Injun blood, goddamn you! Your Injun blood or your son's blood, which?" and Henry Starr threw the bloody head of the bird into the dust right at old Tom Starr's feet. The yelling got worse, the shooting louder . . .

Somebody on a horse came roaring by in the back of Henry, bumping his horse, the crowd was boiling, everybody suddenly gone crazy, and Henry swung around, trying to get control of his horse with the rope halter.

"Hey! Hey! Goddamn it, you men, I want a posse over here!"

It was the red-shirted marshal, just behind him Gray Shirt—Bill Tilghman sitting his horse there, looking at Henry Starr, very cool and still in all that eruption, his partner yelling "I want every ablebodied . . . goddamn it, boy, get out of the way!"

"What's happened?"

"Cherokee Bill just robbed the Cattlemen's Bank. Come in while everybody's out at the rodeo, just like he was there for Strip money. Deputy recognized him and tried to arrest him and the murdering half-breed son of a bitch shot a hole in him with a forty-five, grabbed the cashbox and run."

## EUFAULA *July 6, 1892*

No moon. Starlight turned the tall grass white, cottonwoods black along the creek bed. There were yellow squares of light in the squat black block of the Starr cabin and the wind tilted the plume of chimney smoke forward across the dooryard and toward the cottonwoods. There were a couple of horses in the corral standing quiet. There would be a dog somewhere, probably tied by the front steps. Three black figures in the cottonwoods stood still. The starlight made no shine on the blued double barrel of the cut-down shotgun carried by the tall one, nor on the Winchesters of the other two.

The men waited. The stars moved.

One of the shadows touched the arm that held the double barrel, and that one shook his head, *no*. He held up three fingers, three. A pause. Then the tall one gestured, pointing to the right; caught the eye in the third shadow and gestured left. The two shapes shifted off through the cottonwoods, then out into the open still downwind of the invisible dog, moving up to take position behind a bush on the right flank, a smokehouse on the left.

Door and windows covered.

Bill Tilghman stood in the cottonwoods, the wind gave him little drifts and hums of sound from the cabin. Too faint to hear anything clearly, but there might be some arguing going on, still, after a couple of hours waiting. If he was in there, would he be jawing all this time? And where in hell would that other murdering son of a mule be waiting? There are odds that the two of them are long gone, the trail getting colder under the stars while the three of us wait here trying to figure out what in blazes they are doing in that cabin. But there's no percentage rushing things either. Like when you hunt buffalo: you got to take your stand and your sight, and wait for your bull to stand clear of the herd. Start worrying at 'em and they'll stampede and leave you empty or stamp you flat.

But once you've got your sight you must squeeze trigger. Wait the shot past and you lose it. There hadn't been but three of them showed in the windows all night: the old man, the porkpie hat and the woman. The kid would have to be stupid or scared silly to come back home to hide. If they hadn't seen that little bit of track where a horse carrying one cracked shoe on the left forefoot had stepped in soft moss they'd have given the cabin a pass, left it to one of the other deputies coming down from Fort Smith tomorrow. But he had to take what the kid had given him, which to give him credit was as near to nothing as might be. Smart mouth, maybe; but he knew how to ride a horse, and if he wasn't being just dumb lucky he could cover his trail pretty fair.

He dodged out of the cottonwoods, smooth and quiet, at a running crouch from cover to cover. The yelling in the cabin got louder as he came up to it, kept on even when the dog under the door got up and bristled and started to growl down in his chest, nobody paying it any mind at all. Then the dog bolted off the stoop heading for Tilghman's legs, and he stopped short and swung the double barrel sideways as the dog charged in on him and knocked it yowling to one side, and Tilghman didn't wait for it to land, whimpering, but ran for the door and planted himself to the left of it where—as it opened inward—he'd have a clear shot into the room with the double barrel.

He leaned into the doorframe and with the butt of the shotgun gave the door a *ramramram* and the yammering inside shut down sudden.

"I am Marshal William Tilghman," he said loud and clear into the silence. "I am out here with a posse. Windows all covered. I want Henry Starr, if he's in there: out this door, hands high, no tricks."

There was scuffling inside and then C. N. Walker's voice: "You could have him if he was here for all I care, but he ain't!" There was a low growl from somewhere inside, and Walker yapped, "Shut up! You want us to get shot on account of some stupid thing he—"

"Open the door," said Tilghman. From the tail of his eye he could see Madsen and Thomas shifting toward the two windows. "Throw it wide and stand clear," and he flattened against the wall as light rushed out onto the stoop. Madsen and Thomas were under the windows—Thomas, hatless, bobbed up to look, down, nodded and held up three fingers. Tilghman held the shotgun squarely in front of him, butt cradled between elbow and side, stepped into the light and into the room, and it was just the three of them there: the woman like a heap of laundry at one end of the bench at the back wall, the old Indian sitting still and tall behind the table, his shape enlarged by the dome-crowned black hat he still wore as if indoors/outdoors was no difference to him, his face shadowed, his outsize twisted hands flat on the table in front of him, empty—near them a tumbler of clear liquid. C. N. Walker stood in the middle of the room with his arms spread and raised out straight like the forepaws of a coyote skin stretched out with nails on a barn door. Tilghman bobbed the double barrel up and down, and when Walker still stood there he said, "Okay, take 'em down."

"You come for him, and that's all right by me!" snapped Walker, hoarse in the throat. "He's ate my bread long enough. That's right now," he yelled over at the woman on the bench, "and don't you say not another thing, you hear me, because I ain't standing for no more of it, no sir. You want to talk about blood? Look at that old man there, and listen him talk up his blood. You don't like it much but it's told, ain't it? Run true in one goddamn *pa*-poose anyway.

"Takes the bread out my mouth and the money out my goddamn pocket, by Jesus! His own family's money, that raised him like he was my own son instead of the quarter-breed pup of a dead renegade and a used-up old used-to-be big shot in the Cherokee Nation. My God, the thanks—all the thanks I've got, and he just throws that money back like it was dogshit.

"And comes back here after helling around all night and day for two days, spending that prize money he won on whores and whiskey, and slaps his gear together and takes my Winchester and who knows what else if I hadn't right that minute come in and put a stop to it. Who'd a stopped him walking off with every red cent in the house? Huh? Not this blind old excuse for an Injun, and not that one over there either, who lets on to bein' respectable, a *respectable* lady and a *school*teacher bless you, but she lets her own get run hog wild as ever you please. You hear me telling you, don't you?" he yelled at her. "That's one damn thing Tom Starr got right in his life, it was you spoiled him for—"

"He's been here and gone," snapped Tilghman. "When? How long gone?"

"Far's I know this morning. I come back in and there he is, lookin' like he slept in a pigpen and grabbing my Winchester and a bag of shells and grub and this one jawing at him some damn nonsense, and that old wooden Injun sitting there not doing a goddamn thing but sit there like he done two days running with his jug a white mule under the table gettin' his head paralyzed. And what does the little bastard do but throw down on me, with my own goddamn Winchester, and make me drop my gun belt and sit on the bench.

"He'd a liked to kill me soon as spit, but I didn't care that for him. 'You son of a bitch,' I told him and he starts puttin' that foul mouth a his on everything and everyone, his name, his blood, his kin . . . Jesus Christ, even his own mother, who was as good to him as pie. 'Blood will tell,' I told him, 'and yours is worse'n most.' "

*"Don't you talk to me about blood, you poor excuse for a Cherokee white man. You and this old used-to-be Tom Starr and your blood. I'll tell you what, C. N.—Cherokee white or nigger, it ain't in your blood, it's like some kind of clap, you know? You catch it like some folks catches the clap. This one here, she's a little bit red, little bit white, but she marries Hop Starr and gets herself a good dose of Cherokee clap, and look what come of it. But it goes both ways, don't it, 'cause she clapped old Hop Starr too, ain't that right, Grandpa: that little tang of white blood clap finished Hop Starr off pretty quick. And that left me like the walking-around clap of the two of them—red, white and whatever all in one little package. Then you come along, Mr. C. N. Walker, and clap her white again; and get yourself enough of a dose of Cherokee to get your hands on some of that Cherokee money . . ."*

"Then he turns on Tom too, sittin' there like a cigar store Injun, and he says, 'It ain't blood, Grandfather, it's just the clap. And I done took myself the cure.' "

Sound like a bear's chest rumbling came from the shadow-faced shape at the table, and Tilghman nearly lost his guard on Walker with the surprise of hearing anything at all out of that wooden presence: "Sometimes I get tired," the words came falling slowly out of the shadowed face. "Sometimes . . . I get tired."

Tilghman waited.

"I get tired of being . . . Tom Starr. I get tired of being . . . I get tired of the whole Cherokee Nation. I get tired of having to keep looking for justice in this place where it stinks too much, and you can't taste it anymore. My blood is tired and the whiskey don't help it, I'm tired of my blood. I don't like to live this way. You know, it would be easier to be John Ross, it would be easier to be white, that's what makes me tired. It's got too hard to be Tom Starr, to be Cherokee these times. Look what happened to my son. He was a good boy, he knew the ways it should be—but even he, you know, his own blood wasn't enough, so this woman . . . because she had that white in her. You do that, it breaks your strength, it makes you tired having two kinds of blood in you, two kinds of blood in your head like that. And if you got a son, you know what makes me tired? Because if you got a son it's like what comes to his blood comes back to you also: Cherokee water in Cherokee country and I got to have this white woman in my blood. And then he makes me a grandson that's no damn good at all, that don't listen, that don't know how to be Cherokee, that don't know he's supposed to be white—like his mother wants, and it's easier anyway to be white man than Cherokee so why not, *hyenh*? why [*black nighttime*] not? He can't be so good a Cherokee as his Grandfather, nobody in the Nations, nobody ever, I'm Tom Starr and my word is against it. So I told him, better he should be white, if he was so smart why wouldn't he know that? And he wouldn't listen to that either, and you know why? Because nobody gives a pile of dog turds for a man who is true Cherokee, of the blood, Cherokee water in Cherokee country, where we came from when we lived in the mountains, under the trees. He, that grandson: with your blood in him, woman's blood, white man's blood. No respect in him. No understanding of justice, *hyenh*?

"If he was Cherokee like me I'd change some tobacco and you Little Wolves would never find him. Yes, that's true. With blue, with blue smokes, with blue . . . Justice could find him, but that's all right, you always got that justice with you anyway if you got it, so that's all right.

But a white man I don't care, the law belongs to a white man so the law can have him if it wants, you must pay what you owe. If he was Cherokee . . . then only justice, only justice for him."

Bill Tilghman sighed; he was getting tired of this himself. It was too damn bad that the kid had to live in a place like this, but you have to ride the horse they give you the best way you can—the kid could sure ride a horse anyway, couldn't he? He cut the memory with an abrupt jerk of the shotgun. "What time did he go? Where was he headed?"

"About ten in the morning, I don't know or give a damn where," said C. N. Walker. "Back to Dodge's place probably, where him and that nigger half-breed hang out. I don't know and I don't give a damn." His eyes dropped to the shotgun still leveled at him as if seeing a rattlesnake for the first time, and doubt flickered in his little eyes. "You federals finally gonna take him in for runnin' whiskey into the Nation?"

*He don't even know*, thought Tilghman, *the kid never told him so that means he don't trust his own, can't say I blame him, but they don't run for long if there's no kin or clan they can claim trust from*, but he kept them covered with the shotgun anyway. "Not for whiskey," he said. He made his voice a little larger, to take in the still figure of the old giant Indian sitting at the table, and the heap of blankets on the bench. "Yesterday while the marshals and the Indian Police were mostly out tracking Cherokee Bill, Henry Starr and two other cowboys came back to Tahlequah and stuck up the Katy Land Office. They got the cashbox with about three hundred dollars, dumped a couple drawers full of land titles and blank claim forms that they thought was mortgage papers and tried to light 'em up with matches. Then they busted out of town up Main Street, heading west, shot up a couple of storefronts and plate-glass windows keeping people's heads down . . ."

"Son of a bitch," said C. N. Walker.

"Nobody killed. Clerk put out the fire in the land paper."

C. N. Walker sat down.

Light was beginning to fall through the windows, and Tilghman could see that the woman still sat crumpled in her corner, blanket over her face. C. N. Walker looked pasty-faced, hung-over, elbows on knees and his head drooped like a man thinking about a puke. "Three hundred," he said.

Old Tom Starr sat bolt upright at the table, hands lying like dead meat on the table in front of him, a glass of whiskey white and clear as water next to his right. If he had dropped his hands below the table Tilghman would have switched the shotgun and fired one barrel into the shadow, he'd been waiting for something like that all night, but there was nothing. The light picked out a woman's gold locket ringed with tiny metal rosettes dangling against the black shirtfront—the shirt like a coarse bag full of huge old stone mastodon bones, and above it now a face showing in the cold light like a great brown wrinkled gourd under a dome-crowned black hat.

"*Hyenh*"—a soft sound hidden in the chest, maybe a sound of surprise, numbed in the throat by the white whiskey. Then a single word as weird to Tilghman as if a standing stump had spoken it: "Justice," he said. Then nothing more.

Tilghman looked at the old man and saw that he had been sitting there all night paralyzed drunk at the table wearing his big black hat and a pair of smoked specs with the left lens busted out.

## CANEY, KANSAS *March 27, 1893*

From the Caney *Tribune*:

Our local branch of the First National Bank of Coffeyville has had some unexpected withdrawals made. The affair was carried off in a remarkable—indeed, a somewhat eccentric—style, evidently intended to mark the appearance of a new combination in the old trade of the

**Frontier Desperado.**

Two men, one of them perhaps of part-Indian blood and the other a mulatto, walked coolly into the bank just before the close of business at 3 P.M. yesterday. The only persons in the bank were Cashier F. S. Hollingsworth, Clerk Henry Scurry and M. McEniry, vice-president of the bank.

As they entered the mulatto proceeded toward the back room. Cashier Hollingsworth, looking up, spoke, saying, "How do you do." The robber merely nodded and replied "How d'do," and passed on as if looking for someone. Hollingsworth turned to tell him there was no one there, when something attracted his attention in the front of the bank, and when he turned back, there stood the other man right in front of him with two six-shooters pointed in his face, saying, "That's all right, hold your thumbs up and stand steady."

The gang then moved with rapidity and precision to take possession of the loose money and dump the contents of the vault in a sack, showing a perfect acquaintance with the bank's arrangements.

They then locked the three men in the back room, ran out the front way and turned down State Street toward their horses. The larger of the two men (the mulatto) carried the money, which was quite a load. The smaller man, evidently the leader, exchanged his six-guns for a Winchester with which to protect

**Their Retreat.**

Just across the street were three men passing up from Burris' Livery Stable. These were Mr. Shinn, George Carlinghouse and Harry Dunn. The little man with the Winchester called to these men to *hold up their thumbs*.

The three did not comprehend the import of his remarks, nor why he, a stranger to them, should be addressing them in this fashion, meeting them casually in the open street. So they nodded and continued walking, when he called to them in louder tones:

"Hold up your thumbs!"

Even then they paid him but little attention, thinking he was some waggish young fellow amusing himself at their expense. But when he called out to them a third time,

**"Thumbs Up and Stand Steady!"**

and raised his Winchester to his face, they realized that something was amiss. Mr. Shinn dodged in at Henderson's Hardware, in his haste putting a crack in the glass of the front door, and the other two ducked around the corner, overturning a barrel of wastepaper which the rising breeze blew into the street like confetti at a parade.

The robbers then quietly got on their horses and rode out of town the way they had come in.

Then there was such hurrying and scurrying as has not been seen this side of Gotham since the Great Chicago Fire. Men rushed hither and thither, everybody calling everybody else to do something and nobody doing anything.

For coolness, smoothness and daring this adventure has not perhaps its equal in the history of the state. It has perhaps not been equaled in this interesting line of human activity since the days of the Daltons and the Jameses.

At least twenty-five men were within calling distance of the bank, and yet not a single person knew what was going on until the robbers were on their horses and riding out of the city. Not a single shot was fired, not a drop of blood spilled. The two men were doubtless experts, and to this fact we owe the remarkable good health which all of our citizens continue to enjoy.

'Twas in the town of Tahlequah, that's where it all began,
When Henry Starr robbed the Katy Bank with his pistol in his hand.
"Thumbs up and stand steady!" were the words that he did say,
And he burned the mortgage papers when he made his getaway.

## TSIGESU

"Listen: this is how it used to be in those old times away down in the Cherokee Nation, just as I saw it, just as it was told to me: Henry Starr and Cherokee Bill became robbers, and there wasn't anything they couldn't rob: stores, stagecoaches—railroad trains they robbed whether they were standing in the station or racing sixty miles an hour flat out across the country, blow down the express car door, charge the clerks and the guards in the smoke with pistols and sawed-off shotguns, 'Thumbs up and stand steady!' And banks—*hyenh*, a certain number of banks they robbed.

"What they wanted was money. They didn't rustle cattle, or steal horses unless they were running too fast from the Little Wolves to stop and pay. If they robbed a store they left the food and goods and took the money—unless it was guns or bullets that they needed. Once they robbed a store in Honey Springs and cleaned out the till, and Cherokee Bill grabbed him a big smoked ham-leg off a hook; but Henry Starr reached into the money sack and took out a whole handful of the money never counting it, and dumped it back in the till.

"So people could understand from these things what kind of outlaws they were: that would take money but leave a man food to eat; that would rob a rich man before a poor man, and a white man before an Indian; that insulted no women of any kind or color. That give like they took with a free hand, and the man who gave food or shelter or a lie to cover their trail was as sure of his reward as the men of the gang that done the work, blowing the express car door and charging the guards in the smoke—Henry Starr, Cherokee Bill, Kid Wilson and Linc Cumplin, 'Thumbs up and stand steady!'

"When they rode through a town or across open country they went like a war party, like soldiers ready for anything—flankers out, Winchesters jutting up like war lances. The local sheriffs and town police watched them ride through, tilting up one slat of the blinds that closed their offices for the day, and wired Fort Smith for federal marshals. But there wasn't but three riding out of Fort Smith who would go against Henry Starr and Cherokee Bill—Bill Tilghman, Heck Thomas and Chris Madsen. The rest would be too busy—or here they would come piling off the train with Winchesters shotguns field glasses maps and federal warrants after the dust was three days settled behind Henry Starr and Cherokee Bill, and ride from farm to farm hazing the sodbusters for information the people would not give, and those marshals not have used in any case.

"Because how can you kill or take a gang who rides always ready, whose leader can see in the dark and around corners and break a trail or double it, who can pass through the eyes of thousands of people whose vision wraps him and his names in blue, in black, in blue smokes because they are afraid or grateful, or maybe just because they trusted Henry Starr to be the kind of outlaw who knows the taste of justice, who lives by justice though he rides the night air with the hunting owl and hears him hoot upon his kill.

"Henry Starr and Cherokee Bill: together there was nothing could stop them, because Henry Starr was the smartest outlaw that ever lived, smarter even than Jack-the-Devil, he could make you think black when you saw white. And Cherokee Bill was one of the biggest men who ever lived in the Nations, almost as big as old Tom Starr, big and ugly and strong: and his hand as fast and keen to kill as a rattlesnake is to strike.

"They had robbed seven banks by the time Henry Starr was twenty, seven banks. In Nowata and Muskogee and Tahlequah, in Bartlesville and over the line in Caney Kansas and in Arkansas, Cato and Bentonville, seven banks—Henry Starr and Cherokee Bill. And Henry Starr never shot anybody any of these seven times, not one.

"But Cherokee Bill, he was a killer. Only when he was with Henry Starr could he hold his hand from blood, because of his friendship, because he trusted Henry Starr to take him through. But by himself he killed seven men. He shot the deputy robbing the Cattlemen's Bank in Tahlequah, and Deputy Jack Houston riding through the gate of Cherokee Bill's hideout cabin, and some other deputies he dry-gulched when they come after him. His brother-in-law George Brown he shot down in his own kitchen, blowing holes in him with two different forty-five pistols because Brown's father give Cherokee Bill's sister six hogs and Cherokee Bill five, which was treating him like a nigger. And he shot a man once who was painting a sign over Schufelt's store, and looked down between his boots and there was Cherokee Bill.

"But Henry Starr never killed but one man in his life, and that was Deputy Wilson and by accident, who came on him unawares at the Dodge Ranch, and never said who he was but started shooting from the back—and Henry Starr was even sorry for that one killed, he never knowed him for a deputy, what kind of deputy would back-shoot a man like that?

"But the law don't ask itself questions about how or why a thing is done, not when one of its own has been put under. So they tracked Henry Starr and Cherokee Bill through the Territory for two years, Bill Tilghman and Heck Thomas and Chris Madsen, two years all across the Nations and into Kansas and Arkansas and Colorado, like wolves on a blood spoor, not thinking about anything else only how Henry Starr killed Deputy Wilson and he had to pay for it, and if they asked you and you covered Henry Starr's trail with blue smoke or lies they would smell it, and they'd put your name on the same white paper as Henry Starr and Cherokee Bill: and in the end they found and took Cherokee Bill wounded in his cabin, the roof on fire and two deputies already down when he stumbled out the door with his guns empty and eyes smoke-blind to kill them with his hands if he could only see to get to them. And they jumped Henry Starr in bed with a saloon lady in Colorado Springs.

"And in the end it was the one thing for both of them: Isaac Parker's courtroom in Fort Smith, the Hanging Judge in his black robes looking down—both guilty, both named for the rope. The same death for Cherokee Bill who was in his heart and his bones a killer; and for Henry Starr who killed a man by mistake, who was carefuler than any man, than any policeman or even any judge that nobody get killed by mistake when he was working, so you were safer to be robbed by Henry Starr than to be saved from Henry Starr by any of those that come hunting him.

"So you see how the law is, stupid in a way? How it don't taste like justice?

"*Tch-shaaa!* That's how it was. It didn't do no good to tell Isaac Parker killing was just Henry Starr's bad luck and he was sorry for it. It wasn't being sorry that got Henry Starr out of Fort Smith Prison, and cheated the Hangman that time.

"Listen: I'm telling you how it used to be."

# Magic City

TULSA, OKLAHOMA *April 23, 1921*

Marshal Bill Tilghman stood by the window of his office on the second floor of the Tulsa County Courthouse: a lean old man, six feet tall—gray hair, gray mustache, gray eyes, pale gray Stetson and a light gray suit-and-vest relieved by faint white pinstripes. The jacket was side-vented to clear the ivory handle of a .45 Colt's revolver, an old single-action Peacemaker, the ivory yellowed by the oils of his hand to a color like amber. The brown leather scabbard was molded to the gun's shape, the original chasing of its surface rubbed smooth in decades of use.

The marshal's face was smoothly and evenly tanned by seventy-odd years spent mostly out of doors, the skin still taut on the bones showing only sharply incised squint lines around the eyes, and the finer almost invisible network in the skin which is what well-worn leather shows, softened to the texture of cloth.

It was getting on to noon, and Captain Blaine of the state police looked up from his aviation magazine and saw Tilghman still standing there by the window as he had been all morning. *Studying it out*, thought Blaine, *studying how to track those Chicago whiskey-runners they've set him after, though how he's going to do that from two hundred feet in the air I can't tell.* Then he smiled and thought, *Aerial reconnaissance.* Above Blaine's desk was a swatch of red cloth with a black stripe running up the right side. Blaine had cut it from the wing of a Fokker he'd shared the killing of three years ago in France. There was an ashtray on his desk made of an antiaircraft shell casing, and a framed photo on the wall of twenty smiling young men wearing leather hats that fitted close to the skull.

"Bill," he said quietly, and the old man turned. "You are watching Tulsa grow," said Blaine.

The gray mustache lifted a little in response.

"I've been talking with Mayor Egan," said Blaine, insistently sociable, "and he's sold *me*. When I asked him about the chances for getting a police air patrol he said that was progressive thinking, Tulsa could use that kind of thinking these days." Blaine fell into a version of the mayor's Oklahoma drawl. "Your Paris, now, that might be a fine town . . . *is* a fine town, he'll allow. Crows over Tulsa some ways, he'd *reckon*. But Paris—Paris got nowhere to *go*, don't you see? No *sir*: for *growth*, for *improvement*, give him Tulsa every time. 'Magic City of the Southwest.' "

"It doesn't improve," said Tilghman, "it gets bigger."

*How old is he? He moves slow, but he doesn't waste anything. I'll bet he moved that way at sixteen.* "You must have seen it change plenty," said Blaine.

"Yes," said Tilghman, turning back to the window, "I've seen it change some." Through the window to the north the brown steel skeleton of the new Standard Oil skyscraper put the Osage Hills behind bars. Soon he'd need an office in Standard Oil to see the hills, and how long before he'd have to move again because they were sure to throw another one up right behind that? All over the downtown rusty frames and grates were elbowing each other to grab chunks out of the sky, the whole town just ramming itself up into the blue as fast as a thousand men could slap steel and stone together.

It was no better looking out the southwest window across the Arkansas River toward Red Fork. You could still see prairie out there, but they'd struck oil in Red Fork and there were derricks jerked up out of every quarter acre of ground firm enough to take a drill: crude iron or wood skeletons like a city of unfinished church steeples, with maybe the plume of a gusher or a flare-off of gas at the top for a cross—oil derrick steeples sticking up out of brush thickets and marshes and lined up like corn rows in the broad flats, poking up creek beds and into the city streets like some newfangled kind of ugly leafless brush running into a cornfield nobody takes much care of.

One man struck oil sign digging him a root cellar and there was his house now with the kitchen end knocked off and a derrick of naked boards stuck onto the end of it like a bull's pizzle on a she-goat. Now there were derricks of all sizes stuck up among the houses, jabbing up out of the clusters of roof peaks, matching the churches steeple for steeple, poking up out of people's backyards and front yards and chicken yards and kitchen gardens, and even a half dozen out among the stones of the cemetery like they were pumping out the ghosts of dead men and women from under the ground, two bits a gallon and rising.

The dust and heat rose out of the city below Tilghman, warped and dazzled the images that passed to him through the air. April not done and the place was baking already, God pity the farmers if it keeps up like this. The air from the southwest was solid with the reek of oil, sharp and bitter and slightly foul with sulfur.

Behind the bars of the Standard Oil skyscraper and the air twisted by the heat, Tilghman's eyes made the low line of the Osage Hills where they had camped, and the shape of the land under the houses and the derrick frames and the skyscraper frames was still there for him. Thinking:

*The Arkansas River used to be good country, back in the '70s when I first come into the Nations hunting buffalo. We made our first big strike across the river by Red Fork, brown humped backs packed thick together, must have been a couple thousand animals in that herd . . .*

## RED FORK, CREEK NATION *Summer, 1872*

. . . The wind brought their smell down to us, strong and thick *brown* kind of smell, buffalo-shit smell like a kind of rich earth and the odor of the animals too, a kind of sharp smell like . . . like nothing else I guess, and too much of *it* too, too much smelling of it out there on the prairie while you're walking toward it from behind the cover of a low ridge, the herd invisible to you and you've never done this before. Man, it was like walking up to the feet of a giant, walking up into that smell, just the ten of us, carrying those Sharps buffalo guns so big you had to stand 'em on a stick to aim and they'd kick your shoulder out of joint if you weren't careful, but damn they felt like peashooters walking up against that big brown smell.

Then we topped the rise, crouching forward through the brush to our stands, and there the valley was just black with buffalo from one rim to the other, so damn many you could never miss them just firing into the brown, and packed so close it was like one tremendous *thing* that your bullet would nick and puncture but never kill at all.

But you don't think about that, not for more than a second, and not more than once in this life. You come from downwind, and you move patiently like you are nothing for It to fear, nothing more dangerous than a bush inching down the slope root by root. You take your stand like you've learned, far enough off so the little pig eyes buried in the shaggy bulk of the head can't see you. You don't think about It, about the herd and the giant brown, but you pick your bull. Take your rest. Take your breath. Take your aim. Hold for your shot like you was just a bush standing there rooted in the sun-struck ground, even the wind don't move you. When you get your shot: *take* it. Let it pass and the animal melts back into the brown and you've spent time and breath and eyesight and patience for nothing.

*Boom!* Puff of dust under the foreshoulder and the bull drops like hay cut with a sweep of the scythe. The herd just stands there still and huge and stupid, chawing and flicking tail and dropping shit and shifting from grass to grass. And it hits you that you can do this all day, that you can kill this giant thing one piece at a time and it'll never notice at all. Seven thousand buffalo packed hump to hump; ten men and ten buffalo guns and we could kill 'em all in a couple of days if the powder and ball held out, and if we'd had a Gatling gun my God what we could have done . . . we did enough with Sharpses, but with a Gatling . . .

As it was we worked that herd for two days, slow-booming away at them one shot at a time, careful to kill with one shot, not for the sake of marksmanship nor yet for the animal, but for bullets being so dear, and not wanting a gut-shot bull to spook the herd standing so still and stupid, listening to the slow repeated booming off out past the edge of their sight till the lightning struck them too, and the valley was full from one end to the other with spoiled red meat and white bones and the smell of seven thousand dead buffalo going rotten in the sun.

Well, they called it hunting. I called it hunting. But there was no difference between me out there in the Indian Nations in a buckskin jacket and moccasins, and some poor Hunky poleaxing steers in the Chicago stockyards. Except the Hunky is a meat killer at least; we just took the hides and left the meat for the maggots. When we got done Red Fork was red right enough, piles and piles of peeled carcasses red-white in the sun, vultures sliding down and coyotes loping in. By the time the skinning was done the buffalo skulls would be crawling with white maggots, like the brains was trying to come alive and think a haunting on you.

Put that smell against the oil stink and which is worse?

*How many times did I have to do that before it turned sick inside me? Like when you've eat too much fat meat and you feel all swole up as if your innards was clogged and clotted with fat and it's rising in the back of your throat and spoiling your breath. Too much. Too damned much. Think of what we'd have done if we had a Gatling. We'd have killed everything we could see fast as thinking, we'd have killed so much even the hides would have begun to rot before we could get to the skinning. We'd have killed everything from ridge to skyline in maybe an afternoon and then bragged on it for weeks in*

*Wichita. The only good I had of it was that first time, one bull I chose from the black herd, one shot and the great black thing was just hauled right down to size, one man with one gun against one bull.*

## TULSA *April 23, 1921*

"You've run down some bad characters, I guess," said Blaine, and Tilghman came back into his faded gray eyes and looked at the young policeman. *I am getting old and dreamy*, thought Tilghman, *and I'd better take hold or it will get me killed.* Blaine had a funny look on his face, the studied flatness that an untried poker player will think is a mask, and Tilghman's attention tightened. "These Chicago hoods," Blaine asked coolly, "they're pretty different from those bad men you used to chase?"

"Back when the West was wild, you mean?" Tilghman smiled. His eyes glanced toward the framed photograph above his own desk, three men with mustaches, Stetsons, pistols, Winchesters, and a badge on each chest above the heart: Madsen, Thomas and Tilghman, the "Three Guardsmen" of Judge Isaac Parker's court who rode out of Fort Smith to bring federal law into the Indian Nations, a long time ago. When the West was wild. Blaine was a good enough kid, if he *was* a Yankee: he did his job, when he wasn't fussing to get back up in one of those aeroplanes. "There's differences," Tilghman allowed, resting one ham on his desk. "Old-time bad men used to ride *out* of things. Made 'em hard to catch but easy to track. These Chicago boys like to stay in the brown. The more herd the harder to mark your bull."

*He's feeling talkative this morning*, Blaine thought, and his professional curiosity stirred: Tilghman had been hired as a special marshal to work on the Prohibition rackets, and he was close and cagey about it all. "It's different since the war," said Blaine, baiting his hook. "This Prohibition law's changed a lot of things."

"Go on." Tilghman smiled, and Blaine blushed; the old man was not fooled a bit by his subtle probing.

"Oh, nothing," said Blaine, "but it's a whole different set up for the law to handle, saloons closed up front but open for business out back, and how many millions for the Chicago boys to keep 'em full of whiskey?"

"Not so different," said Tilghman. "Back when this was still the Indian Nations they had a law against selling firewater on the reservation. Difference is, now the whole country is reservation."

"I guess," said Blaine, not knowing how Tilghman really stood on booze. Blaine liked a drink himself, but he knew it for wrong from the word *go*. He'd seen enough in the war to convince him that booze and ugly dying went together. Tilghman never touched a drop as far as Blaine knew, but he wasn't as hard on whiskey as some who drank the bottle dry. He shifted his ground slightly: "Price says it isn't the dagoes, it's just local niggers like Bub Houston bootlegging white mule and Choctaw beer like they used to."

Tilghman's eyes narrowed and the gray mustache shifted slightly, masking the tightening of his lips. "Price," he said. "Deputy Price thinks it isn't anybody from Chicago, but just some local colored. And Chief of Police Casey thinks it is the Reds and the Wobblies and the Grangers brewing moonshine behind the union hall."

The gray eyes looked sharply at Blaine and the state policeman felt the blood rise in his face and a little bump of fear—it was like seeing the eyes of a man squinting over the machine-gun sights at you while you wheeled round each other in the empty middle of the air, because Blaine didn't like to talk about Casey; it had been made clear to him that Casey was out of bounds and he'd accepted that until just now, when something in Tilghman's look made him ashamed of having taken those orders. So he paused, and let himself resent a little what Tilghman made him feel, and then shifted his line of approach: "Price just has *nigger* on the brain. It doesn't leave enough room for Chicago."

Tilghman's look was still straight, but the muscles of his face had lapsed into a poker player's mask: he had noticed that Blaine was not talking about Casey. "Deputy Price checked in with Police Chief Casey this morning at eight A.M. Banker Wilberforce stopped by to chat with Casey and said he was going to watch his motion picture company working out by the Springs Road." Tilghman kept his eyes on Blaine as he spoke. "Deputy Price left Casey's office five minutes after Wilberforce, took the patrol car, and drove out in the direction of the Springs Road. At ten minutes past nine Bub Houston, and his son-in-law that owns the colored movie theater, drove by in a buggy headed the same way."

"Price is working on the case his way," said Blaine. "He wants Houston."

"No doubt about it," said Tilghman. "A good tracker will know when to leave the trace and figure the animal's next jump, and he'll get there ahead of him, take his stand and wait." Tilghman's eyes now frankly measured Blaine, and he asked, "You figure Price is that good a tracker?"

"No," said Blaine, and it struck him just then that Tilghman was watching Price pretty closely, and that the old man probably *was* that good a tracker. He ran his mind back over what Tilghman had told him,

Banker Wilberforce, the motion picture company . . . "Wilberforce had Miss Woodly with him!" he said, and Tilghman nodded. Blaine smiled. "I guess Price is tracker enough to follow *that* case," but he was thinking, *Why? why is he watching Price like that?*

"Maybe he is," said Tilghman, but he wasn't really interested in Price tracking after Miss Woodly. He kept moving straight ahead on some trace of his own. "The colored in this town were making moonshine and Choc beer when Red Fork was a buffalo wallow. I don't doubt they still are. Bub Houston used to be a peace officer around here, when it was still the Indian Nations; but he made moonshine himself then, and since too I wouldn't doubt. I don't doubt Deputy Price wants to put Bub Houston out of business."

The old man was after something, Blaine had no idea what. *Keep him talking.* "Some peace officer, Bub Houston, making moonshine when he wore a badge."

Tilghman's eyes shifted focus, lost their straitness of concentration, seemed to look far off through and beyond Blaine. "The way things used to be . . . Bub Houston wasn't federal or territorial, he was a tribal officer and it was Choctaw and Cherokee law he undertook to enforce. The no-whiskey law was none of his or his people's making so he left it to be taken care of by those that owned it. It was the same law we have now, and it doesn't make any more sense now than it did then—it's just got almighty bigger.

"But it don't belong to most people around here any more than it did to Bub Houston, does it? So now you've got these Chicago boys coming down here, and more bad whiskey in the state of Oklahoma than ever was in the Indian Nations."

His eyes tightened on Blaine as he spoke, more words than Blaine had had from him in the two months they had shared this office. *Why now? Why is he talking to me now?*

"Maybe it's still Bub Houston making and selling it," said Tilghman, "just doing more *of* it, but I don't see how he can. There ain't trees enough within two days' ride to hide the size still he'd have to be using. No way he can meet the demand, unless one of these oil drills struck a vein of whiskey and he's pumping it out of the ground. So no, I don't think it's just Bub Houston. And then . . . do you see Mayor Egan or Chief Casey running to some colored barrelhouse in Greenwood whenever they want a drink?"

Blaine didn't think so but he wasn't saying. Mayor Egan was out of bounds too. "Everybody gets thirsty," he said.

"Yes," said Tilghman, his pale eyes cool and blank, "people used to get thirsty even in the old days. It's a question of what a man is willing to put up with just so he can get a taste when he wants it." He was looking straight at Blaine, no threat in his eyes now, but an intensity that was palpable. "Even if you got the best kind of law there is, there's people who won't be able to live inside it. I've seen times myself . . . But it takes a certain kind of man to sell his badge for the price of a drink. Bub Houston never sold his badge. Nobody ever bought me off a trail I was set to follow. And nobody ever took a prisoner in custody away from me and tarred and feathered him or strung him up. Nobody. Not in the woods, and sure as hell not out of any six-story stone-walled downtown Tulsa City Jail. But maybe I just never got that thirsty."

Blaine hung fire and his eye flicked nervously over to Casey's door. It was none of his business, he'd been told off by his boss to leave the matter alone and it had been five years ago while he was in France dodging German bullets and flying high over the Western Front—but what kind of police chief *was* Casey if a mob could walk into his jail and take out forty Wobbly prisoners duly convicted by the court and whip, tar and feather and ride out on rails all forty of them with deputies "keeping order" in the streets where it was going on and not doing anything else about it? Not that Blaine gave a good goddamn for any Wobbly that ever . . .

Someone cleared his throat behind him and Blaine saw Tilghman's pale eyes widen the least bit as he stood up, and Blaine pivoted in his chair to see who it was.

It was a small wiry man in a dark suit bagging on his frame, white shirt made to have a collar and tie but without the collar, without the tie; the skin above the shirt a smooth light brown, Cherokee cheekbones and black hair swept smoothly back from the forehead. On second look there were lines of silver in the black, and the baggy suit and creases at the eyes made him forty-odd. The stiff clumsy cut of the clothes, the odd shyness of manner, the slumped line of shoulders and head told Blaine the man was just out of prison. The man smiled a little bit.

"Maybe you remember me, Marshal? I am Henry Starr."

"I remember you," said Tilghman, and Blaine noted a slight softening that was courtesy in the old man's manner. Then a sudden broad grin opened under the gray mustache and marked Tilghman's face with strong lines at the eyes and lips. "You are not hard to remember. I spent twenty some years looking at your picture on wanted bills. I arrested you twice, under interesting circumstances."

Henry Starr stood a little straighter and smiled back, clean white teeth in a smooth brown face—a light-up smile that made him look years younger, almost a kid. "I didn't think you'd remember me with my pants on," he said, and Tilghman laughed and gestured to Blaine.

"Henry Starr, this is Captain Blaine, state police."

"With his pants on?" said Blaine.

"The first time the marshal caught me I was in the hay with a lady in Colorado Springs. The second time I had a bullet in my ass and a lynch mob gathering outside when the marshal got there. That was in Stroud, six years ago."

"Before my time," said Blaine. In 1915 he had been in France, in pilot training with the Lafayette Escadrille. His life on the other side of that year was as distant from him as a childhood remembered only in studio photographs. He noticed that Tilghman's smile had disappeared.

"You've been paroled," he said to Starr. "You were always a good hand with parole boards."

Starr's look held to Tilghman's face, the smile gone, a tighter set to his shoulders. "I made my case to them, Marshal. As good a case as I could. No less."

"It's a better prison system now," said Tilghman. "They can fix a man up in six years like they couldn't do in a dozen in the old days."

"It's better," said Henry Starr. "Also a man learns things sometimes. Things that will let him change."

Tilghman said nothing.

"They took seven years to pardon me the first time I was in Fort Smith Prison." Henry Starr spoke deliberately, like a man arrested but not yet charged emptying his pockets out onto a table. "You know what I did to earn that pardon. You know how long they made me wait after I'd earned it."

Tilghman's tight stare at Henry Starr eased its bite just a little, but his voice was still flat: "You killed Deputy Wilson, Henry. They reprieved you for Wilson because of what you did to stop Cherokee Bill. Life for life. That was justice."

"You knew Cherokee Bill," said Henry Starr, "you know what he was like. You know how the two of us . . . You know I talked him into giving up his guns, and the guard he had hostage, knowing they would hang him dead the next morning." There was no pleading in Henry Starr's voice, but an urgency, like a man in a tight poker game laying down his cards quickly one after another on the table.

"And they give you your life for that," said Tilghman. "Pardon is for a man that's ready to go straight. That wasn't you."

"There were circumstances," said Starr and Tilghman said, "Yes, there are always circumstances," and he paused.

Starr stood in front of him, small and straight-backed, and as far as Blaine could tell the cringe was gone now, there wasn't anything in Starr's face but just a patient waiting for Tilghman to say he could go on and lay out his "circumstances," and that would mean maybe his would not just be the kind there always were. Tilghman's eyes flicked to the photograph of the Three Guardsmen on his desk, to the shape of the Standard Oil skeleton looming at the north window. "What kind of circumstances?" he asked.

Starr's voice was soft and smooth and even, a story-swapper's voice; it compelled Blaine's attention and woke his suspicions at the same time:

"I had a store in Cromwell, in the old Creek Nation: general merchandise in front, beer and sandwiches in back. I'd been out of prison a bit when I met the woman owned it: Cora Munson. We got married a year later, '04 it was. She had a small son, name was Jiminy, by her first husband. It was a good 'nough store to start with, but we made it something different—it was sort of comfortable to buy stuff there, or maybe just to stop in for a beer and a bite and a little talk between working. Kind of place I'd have liked myself when I was punching cows for the Dodge Ranch, except there wasn't no way to mix beer and groceries in the Indian Nations—just pop up front or red-eye in the back room, wasn't it? But we had that kind of good, comfortable place. People mostly didn't know me, a dozen years since Floyd Wilson and ten since Cherokee Bill. So we didn't have the kind of trade you get when some famous western desperado opens a place. No damned Wild West.

"We had a lot of oil riggers and drillers around there, would come in and sit and jaw. They was most of my business. Maybe they was Wobblies, maybe not; but that *wasn't* my business, long as they were clean and quiet and paid the score. They complained some, but they talked like men who did the work. They was regular customers.

"Then this fellow Kinsley starts coming in with them, a new man, at first just like the rest of them—laugh about stuff, gripe about this and that, low pay or it's dangerous work when you pop a gas vein and a spark can blow her off . . . Only this Kinsley, he seems to take it all more personal, like it was a particular meanness done *him* and wasn't no more than fair for him to answer up in kind. If the boys talked low pay, he talked theft and slavery. If the boys was down on their ramrod, he named him a bully and a murderer, blood in his eye and nothing to meet it with but the same. If the boys talked strike, he talked dynamite."

"An anarchist," said Blaine.

"Maybe I should have showed him the gate," said Henry Starr, with the shade of a smile passing and going on, "but it wasn't my business, was it? Not being a law officer . . ."

"Shouldn't have made any difference," said Blaine, "if you knew . . ." But he stopped, uneasy because Tilghman wasn't talking and all this was for Tilghman.

"But the difference was *him*," said Henry Starr with a little smile, "because he *was* a law officer. Which he showed me the night after the dynamite talk, coming up to me at the counter while I'm closing down, and he lays a stack of papers on the counter: a bunch of arrest warrants from Kansas and Arkansas for robberies along the Oklahoma line—stores and small banks and such. No name on the warrants. 'You are Henry Starr the bank robber,' says he. 'No,' I say, 'I am Henry Starr the storekeeper.' And he shows me his badge: 'The Eye That Never Sleeps': he's a Pinkerton."

Starr looked over at Blaine and back to Tilghman, as much as to say, *I don't know what you think about Pinkertons. Take it any way you like.*

"Go on," said Tilghman.

"He said he had me in mind for those robberies. Nobody better situated. I asked him were these robberies he wanted done for himself or was it company business, but he didn't think that was funny. No, the robberies were all taken care of, it was just a matter of sending somebody away for them. And that was me. Except that he had some other projects in hand a lot more important to him, and he'd let me off the robberies if I'd help him out."

That hit Blaine like a rude jab in the chest, waking him suddenly to the subtle twist hidden in the smooth run of Starr's voice, and his resentment almost leaped out in defense—damnit, that *was* how it had to be done to ever get anything on those Reds, and if Tilghman was too old-fashioned to know it—but he bit it short because it was already too late. "You wouldn't play along," said Tilghman, and Starr didn't answer, but just picked up the story:

"So he wrote my name on the warrants. It looked pretty certain they'd extradite me back there, and that meant the rest of my life in prison. There wasn't going to be any more Cherokee Bill for me to talk out of his gun and into a noose, not this time. In the meantime, just the naming of me as a bank robber and the store started to go under. And the woman . . . maybe it was bad enough for her that I could even just be named again that way. She wasn't cut from the same cloth as my aunt Belle, to keep ranch for a bunch of night riders. Her first husband had stood for something in that town, I guess, and the kid, her son, still had the man's name—but I was his pa now too, wasn't I, and getting myself named for robbing general stores and penny-ante banks in two states. Did I say . . . ? Cora was her name, Cora Munson, and the boy's name was Jim but was called Jiminy."

"So you run out," said Tilghman.

"I had the name," said Henry Starr, "I thought I might as well have the game."

"You should have waited on the law, Henry. You had all those people for alibis . . ."

Henry Starr shook his head. "After the Pinkerton got through the riggers wasn't any good as alibis. And the other people there . . . you don't know what it's like when you just get *named* for an outlaw with folks like that. They spooked at buying crackers and calico from my wife. How could I trust them for witnesses?" He paused for a minute, thinking. "And the truth is, I had no trust in the law and never did. Maybe I was wrong. I had reasons . . ."

"There's always reasons. If you can't get past those reasons, how can they trust you to stay straight?"

"I got a new set of reasons this time. Reasons to go straight."

"Stronger reasons than a wife and kid?"

Starr's mouth got a little grim. "For me stronger, yes."

Tilghman waited, watchful.

"I need a favor," said Starr. Tilghman said nothing. "You know the people that own that motion picture outfit? I come to ask you, would you take me over to see them? Would you help me get work with them?"

There was tension in Starr's body now, Blaine could see it even under the set of the prison suit stiff and lumpy along the line of his shoulders. "This time . . . in prison this time . . . I looked back to where I'd been, and it was different to me. It's like I'd been running around all my life after things, gold and greenbacks and my name in the papers, chasing and getting chased for years and years, and there was nothing, I just had nothing left of it at all. And the one thing I had got hold of, the thing that was really gold, I never knew to value it at all till I threw it away. I mean Cora and Jiminy and all that . . . I don't know, Bill," said Henry Starr, "you ever lose a thing like that? You ever look back down your own trail and there's nothing there of what you had, but only ghosts of what you missed or mistook or did wrong to? Knowing there wasn't one thing to be done about it anymore, because all those years and chances was gone like the buffalo and the Last of the Mohicans."

"No," said Tilghman softly, "I never left anything behind me that needed watching," and it just then hit Blaine that Starr had called the old man *Bill*.

"These motion picture people . . . I saw some of their stuff in prison, way back. I don't know . . . I've got the idea in my mind that if I could get my story told that way, if I could just lay it out like that for folks to see, it might do somebody some good. Some kid, maybe, like I was, who reads dime books and wants to be an outlaw like Jesse James or Bob Dalton. Might make it all add up to something . . . even what I missed, maybe, would mean something if I told it like that. I don't know . . . or maybe folks would just be interested to know how it was, how it used to be back then, before all this . . ."

Blaine saw Tilghman hesitating, his eyes flicking toward the north window filled with the skeleton of the Standard Oil tower—his face now drawn in, nobody in the world could tell what was working under the fine worn leather of the old man's cheeks. Did the old man really believe the line Henry Starr was handing him? It hadn't taken Blaine long to see that they were dealing with a jailhouse lawyer here—no, a jailhouse preacher ready to come up to the mourners' bench and cleanse his soul of sin. He must have had those sob sisters on the parole board dabbing at their eyes over his sad fall from grace, and none of it his fault, all he wants is the chance to tell his sad story as a warning to the rising generation . . .

"Besides," said Henry Starr, white teeth smiling out of his smooth brown face, "besides, if you take me out there, I'll tell you what it was I said to Cherokee Bill: that made him give up his gun, and let Judge Parker hang him dead."

Tilghman stood up suddenly, decisively. "All right," he said, "let's go," and with a quick stiff nod to Blaine he walked brusquely past Henry Starr toward the door, Starr following like a shabby shadow, leaving Blaine to look out the windows for answers to his questions.

Alice Farnham shrieked and clasped her folded hands to her bosom: "That is the man! That is Slick McClain!"

The man with the mustache in the black frock coat sneered and jerked his pistol from the holster and waved it at the woman and at the tall man in fringed buckskins and white Stetson who stood by her side in front of the bank. "Hands up, all of you!"

Buckskin Bill Bonham glared, Alice Farnham cringed against his manly shoulder, the half-dozen men in suits behind them shot their hands straight up in the air. Behind them an ancient Indian sat against the base of the wall, as immobile as a heap of laundry with a gourd on top.

"I'll take the strongbox and this pretty thing too!" sneered Slick McClain.

"You'll pay for this," said Buckskin Bill Bonham. "*Some* may think you a romantic Robin Hood, but I know you for a common thief!"

"Stop! Stop, damn it!" said Foley. "Just stop it, *cut*! Esterhazy, damn it! Stop cranking. Do it again, and for Chrissake will you people try to look scared? This is Slick McClain, he's a *killer*, he's stealing the strongbox with your goddamn life savings in it. And Bonham: he's stealing the woman you *love*! Jesus!" He sat down again in his canvas chair, gestured to Esterhazy behind the camera. "Again."

Alice Farnham shrieked and clasped her folded hands to her bosom: "That *is* the man! That *is* Slick McClain!"

The man with the mustache in the black frock coat sneered and jerked his pistol from—but it caught in his coat skirt and he had to flap it free and then wave it up at Buckskin Bill Bonham and Alice. "Hands up all of"

"Cut! Jesus, *cut!*" yelled Foley, jumping up to stand there with his hands on his hips glaring at them. Alice Farnham rolled her eyes up and flounced. Buckskin Bill looked sheepish; maybe he was practicing looking scared, or was it angry he was supposed to be? The extras put their hands down hesitantly, as if unsure whether Foley would shoot them down like dogs. It was breathlessly hot and half-moons of sweat showed in Buckskin Bill's armpits and small dark patches under the arms of Alice Farnham's calico frock. The old Indian was heaped like tossed tinderwood and rags against the wall of the bank. The bank was a facade with nothing behind it.

Esterhazy took his face out of the black square tunnel of the viewfinder and looked down at Foley from the horseback-high seat of the cameraman's stool. It was much more interesting out here. In the viewfinder, it was like being locked in a small black cell with nobody to talk to or look at but Buckskin Bill and Alice Farnham and Slick McClain. Solitary confinement would have been more pleasant, even more stimulating. Esterhazy could think this unsentimentally, since he had spent some time in the jail cells reserved by the Austro-Hungarian authorities for those of impetuous politics.

Slick McClain jammed the pistol back in his holster and glared at Foley, who was holding his pose of indignation, hands on hips over by the camera. "This is just stupid, Foley!" he yapped. "It's a stupid way to set the scene up. Why make me wear a damn frock coat to hold up the bank, hey? When it's a hundred and forty-eight fucking degrees out here? And what kind of sense is it robbing the strongbox out in the street, when *inside* the bank is how it's usually done, ain't it? That, or out on the road, stopping the stagecoach? Ain't it?"

"You wear the coat because the script says you're supposed to be disguised as a wealthy eastern philanthropist, until she recognizes you as Slick McClain. It isn't my script, it is Mr. Poole's script, who pays your wages and my own. But there's better reasons than that," and Foley's eyes flicked to the left. Esterhazy needed only a glance to put that together with the hands-on-hips and the high dudgeon, to know that Foley would from now on play this scene to Miss Woodly—who stood next to Esterhazy slim and cool-looking in her blue dress, her head even with his hips as he sat on the high cameraman's stool. "It's outside," said Foley, "because you've got to put the girl and the strongbox on the stagecoach you're going to steal, so that Buckskin Bill can chase you across Death Valley, then the girl jumps off onto his horse while he's racing alongside and he shoots you out of the box."

"Just like Broncho Billy Anderson in *Broncho Billy's Christmas Dinner*," said Esterhazy helpfully—the *B*'s shading into plosive *P*'s, the *k* sounds cut off sharp. He smiled at Foley his "mad Hungarian" smile to deflect all offense and nudged Miss Woodly gently with his foot. He couldn't see her face, only the top of her amber hair, but he could imagine easily the smile she would have for all of this, a small intense one like the bud of a flower, its full force held discreetly in reserve—she had a delicate mouth and cool blue eyes and many, many ways of smiling, all as fine and particular as the different wines of France.

He wished she had been with him all day, or that he had had his camera pointed the right way so that he could have shown her later: how it had been like a play or a dance, a comedy with entrances and exits in the manner of Feydeau or (better!) Mack Sennett, and if he had been filming it he would have cranked the camera with a certain nuance of *easiness* in the wrist, not quite slow, so that what she would have seen on the screen would have had just that least touch of speed, not quite excessive, that gives you the tickle in the belly, the emotion of comedy, the sense of running falling headlong hysterically out of control.

It had started in the early morning, Foley trying with desperate haste to get the scene set up before the owners could arrive to bully him with admonitions or to enslave him with suggestions—which Foley was helpless to resist or resent, being as much a refugee from Hollywood and failure as Esterhazy was a refugee from Hungary and politics. But Buckskin Bill had fussed about his makeup like a tart, and Slick McClain needed pots of black coffee to restore his sangfroid after a hard night's drinking in Greenwood, the wranglers couldn't hitch the horses to the stagecoach and the extras were late except for the ancient half-dead Indian who had spent the night squatted cross-legged on the porch of the bank.

Foley had just that moment managed by putting the highest pitch of strain into his voice, pleading and haranguing and demanding and actually pushing and hauling, to get all the things and people into place—Slick sobered, Buckskin Bill rouged and powdered, Alice Farnham petted and cajoled—when the first Intruder enters (left) and parks his white open-topped Stutz under the cottonwood tree behind the camera stand: Mr. Dexter C. Poole, editor and publisher of the Tulsa *Lamp* ("A Light Unto the Nations") and half owner of the Pan American Motion Picture Company, Incorporated of Tulsa, our esteemed landlord and proprietor (or half of them, anyway)—thirtyish, lank, thin-haired, in white linen suit and straw hat, a petulant pink mouth and the eyes of a fanatic: a comfortable, well-off, smug, well-educated fanatic. In Hungary perhaps he would have been a nobleman's younger son writing revolutionary propaganda in some cell of extreme anarchism, or perhaps (it also went with his type) a high official in the state police apparatus specializing in the treason of the intelligentsia and clergy. Here in America he was a Harvard man; the heir of money gotten originally out of cotton, then oil, then from the cotton/oil money itself; a businessman in the business of journalism exercising his moral faculties in the editorial pages of his own paper and his own movie company. Foley's bête noire, the man was naturally full of ideas which, as seigneur, he of course felt entitled to see Foley execute. Esterhazy's nights were made wretched by his having to sit in on their conferences, Poole insistently trying to pack every frame and dialogue card with editorial matter, Foley as usual thinking only of his little bag of tricks, worrying desperately that he might have to abandon the well-worn path that led from the Look to the Kiss to the Ravishment, to the Chase to the Rescue to the Clinch, which was all he knew and trusted in the world.

So with Poole looking on there was another Power to be played to, no? So if Foley said come forward Alice thought the light better for her a step backward, and Buckskin Bill had sweated off his paint, and Slick craved a hair of the dog but settled for abusing the wranglers because the horses in the scene kept upstaging him.

But with Alice *placed*, and Buckskin Bill repainted and *fixed*, and Slick McClain shaken into obedience, and Esterhazy perched behind the camera and Foley's hand raised for the start . . . enter the Second Intruder (left): Banker Edgar W. Wilberforce, the other half owner of the Pan

American Motion Picture Company, Incorporated of Tulsa, president and proprietor of the First Chemical–Cattlemen's Bank of Tulsa, in a touring car driven by himself—a big burly man but the burliness all soft, podgy, a florid white-haired sixty in a beige suit and vest with a heavy gold watch chain across the globe of his belly.

And, as usual, next to him Miss Woodly slim and straight and cool in her blue dress and a fall of amber hair—his clerk, his secretary, his bank teller, and Esterhazy in grief and despair had guesses about what else possibly, but could never discover, because there was never between Miss Woodly and Banker Wilberforce anything suggestive of the erotic or indiscreet, save for the fundamental indiscretion of her always being carried about with him, like a field flower in the lapel of his overstuffed pale suit.

She stood between Esterhazy's camera and Banker Wilberforce, who took his stand next to Poole, who left enough space between himself and Foley for the latter to wave his arms a bit but close enough to look over his shoulder—"to spit in my soup" Foley would inevitably say this evening while Esterhazy tried to get his supper down—and Foley signaled for action. But now Miss Woodly was there, standing modestly just within the shadow of Banker Wilberforce and watching the action with a brilliant intent interest, her blue eyes shifting from the actors to Foley to Esterhazy on his perch—

Which of course Buckskin Bill Bonham and Slick McClain and certainly Foley and probably Poole (and who needed even to think about Wilberforce?) took for lascivious interest in themselves, and so now there had to be a certain amount of strutting and preening, and it was obvious when you looked in the black box of the viewfinder that they were no longer playing to Esterhazy's lens but to the blue eyes and the blue dress. Even Foley, haranguing and abusing them, stood so as to give a quarter of his profile gratis to Miss Woodly—except that Poole abruptly stepped forward to upstage him. Only the old Indian slumped against the bank facade was staying in character, faithfully and with complete naturalness representing both his personal extinction and that of his race.

At which point enter the Third Intruder, Deputy Price, the brute-heavy of the piece, the boorish servant Hans or the upstart official von Blunderbronck, in a police car rolling its dust right across the first take of the day, jerking to a stop by the cottonwood, hauling up the brake with a raking scrape, and sauntering into the scene with a rolling swagger on his high-heeled boots, the pistol holstered on his hip jutting out at an arrogant angle, his face under a white Stetson long and square-jawed and abused that morning by a straight razor, his badge hung on his left shirt pocket from which the string of a tobacco sack dangled. "Howdy ma'am, Poole, Mr. Wilberforce. Foley."

Then the dance began again: Foley in the middle of the set pushing the actors into place, bluff, busy, professional, looking anxiously over his shoulder to the audience, thrown suddenly into despair because the brute bulk of Deputy Price has been hunching forward to impinge on, to eclipse, to cover the blue eyes and amber hair and blue dress. But Banker Wilberforce feels it too, the loom and pressure of the deputy's courteous, almost fawning advance, and so he too sidles, shifts away—as you do when a man with foul breath engages you in conversation, and you don't wish to be rude, but you *must* put a bit of free air between you—and of course Miss Woodly would fade back with him, drawing the great bear of a deputy after her as a magnet would draw a lump of iron.

And Poole? He had noticed the script on Foley's chair, glanced at it—seen the pencil marks where Foley had made last night's alterations, picked it up, read it, *aha!* Noticed that Foley had elided certain crucial pieces of business, certain essential lines of dialogue, which had supposedly been agreed upon between the two of them in a week of negotiations more intense perhaps than anything since Versailles, and: "Foley! You, *Foley!* What's all this . . ." And below Esterhazy Banker Wilberforce and Miss Woodly and Deputy Price had actually turned a full circle, pivoting on her slim blue shape as if she were a maypole, Deputy Price courteously, fawningly advancing, agreeing vehemently, passionately, explosively with Banker Wilberforce's politics, clothing, choice of car, preferences in weather while Wilberforce backed subtly, placatingly round the circle, keeping always an edge or angle of his shoulder between Price and the girl, yet never reaching out one of his large pale hands to claim title.

Then with all rivals present and the plot launched, arrives the First Complication, exactly on schedule: a two-horse buggy driven by two colored gentlemen, a tall old man with heavy features shaded by a black slouch hat, dressed for work in the open; and a natty younger man with smooth tan skin in three-piece cream suit and light straw derby. They too blew dust across the take in progress, pulled up under the cottonwood tree, dismounted and came forward.

And this arrival broke up the maypole dance, because when Deputy Price saw the two colored gentlemen he turned red and stood himself up tall and came at them with a rolling, pistol-jutting swagger and a harsh "What the hell is *this?*" Banker Wilberforce startled at Price's abrupt desertion, recovered, then hurried after Price as if he had missed his cue to drop the girl and start dancing round the colored gentlemen—banker and deputy just two vaudeville hoofers, one of them a little off his timing, the team of Price and Wilberforce . . . who seemed to remember Miss Woodly all of a sudden, because he turned and looked at her so that she must excuse herself from Poole's courteous inquiries (he had come up in Wilberforce's vanishing wake) and rejoined the banker.

"Esterhazy!" yelled Foley. "Will you start cranking that damn thing?" and so he missed a part of the next scene, but there was no danger that things would go smoothly today—no more than a minute and Alice Farnham's coiffure was fatally disarranged by a florid sweep of Buckskin Bill's rhetorical right arm—and when Esterhazy looked back some kind of trade had been struck: and Wilberforce the loser, by God! Red-faced, obviously uneasy, with many a backward look and second thought, Wilberforce had traded Miss Woodly to Deputy Price for undisputed possession of the two colored gentlemen, and he was taking them off to the woods to make what use of them he would. Deputy Price was squiring Miss Woodly back toward the camera, like a lustful ox following a wind-blown leaf, unaware that his own hot and heavy breath is the very thing that lifts the leaf lightly and keeps it up and out ahead of him.

She threw Price a look of her blue eyes that cut through him like a straight razor through beef suet; but just that way, the fat closed over the cut and he came on. If she weren't careful he'd pin her against the property and costume boxes—but at the last second a lithe shift of balance swept her under Price's jaw and into the clear. He paused, then came on again, stalking her across the cleared space between the property boxes and the camera. She had small shoulders and a slim, strong, graceful neck, and Esterhazy had the image of à gazelle stalked by some kind of great ugly carnivorous rhino. But when she looked up at him she didn't look the helpless gazelle at all—but a little bit fierce, a little bit amused. Playing the game, you see, taking certain chances with oneself, walking upon a certain kind of edge quite deliberately.

But now at long last, with Poole pacing restively by Foley, and Foley posed with hands on hips profiled toward Miss Woodly, and Miss Woodly sheltering against Esterhazy's stool and Deputy Price—warded back by an elbow she cocked apparently unconsciously at his ribs—Deputy Price balked and trying to twitch unobtrusively into some more advantageous position, with everything at last in place, Alice Farnham shrieked and clasped her folded hands to her bosom: "That is the man! That is Slick McClain!"

"Hands up all of you! I'm taking the strongbox and this pretty thing as well!"

"You'll pay for this, Slick McClain. *Some* may think you a romantic Robin Hood, but I know you for a common thief!"

"Oh for Christ's sake," said Foley quietly, and it took Esterhazy a moment to see what was wrong because his eyes were locked in the black box of the viewfinder and it took a second longer for the dust stirred up by the pair of horses to blow across the scene—horses ridden by yet another set of Complications making their entrance left—or upwind would be the more appropriate stage direction.

And then, to complete the ruin, the ancient Indian hunkered down on the porch stood up like Lazarus from the tomb, and with his shroud about him hobbled like a sleepwalker right across the scene, right through the space between Slick McClain and Buckskin Bill Bonham and out the left side of the frame.

"Well I'm damned," said Foley, "even a dead Indian . . ."

"They can't play the scene because it doesn't make sense," snapped Poole. "It isn't probable or accurate, and everybody knows it."

Meanwhile the old Indian was hobbling toward the two newcomers, a tall man in a gray suit and a smaller man in a dark, lumpy-looking suit. Banker Wilberforce and his two colored gentlemen emerged from the woods, their business done, and the three groups converged beneath the cottonwood.

Bill Tilghman paused and let Henry Starr step up next to him just inside the shade of the cottonwood, and gestured toward the three men coming out of the woods. "The white man's Wilberforce," said Tilghman, "he's the bankroll for this outfit. We'll talk to him first. The other partner, Poole—he's a little too . . ." He wobbled his right hand.

They both noticed the dark shape of the old Indian lurching their way, and the tableau around the camera and the false-front bank behind him.

Tilghman gave a quick glance to Starr and looked away. He knew what prisons took out of a man, the tone in the muscle, the reflexes; and what they put in, the look in the eye and in the angle of the back that's like a man who's been living in a dugout all winter: he keeps expecting the roof will smack him in the head or the air outside walls thick with his own stink will freeze him blue and dead.

Without thinking about it Tilghman had been testing out some notions about Henry Starr right from the start. He had let Starr walk ahead of him down the stairs and out into the breathless heat between the buildings of downtown Tulsa. He noticed there was a hitch in the little man's stride where he crimped his walk to favor the shotgun-torn muscle in his right ham and thigh. Got that when the butcher's boy shot him down on the main street of Stroud, Oklahoma, robbing two banks at the same time like Jesse James had done, like the Daltons had tried in Coffeyville and got rubbed out trying. The hitch and the stiff baggy suit, maybe that did it; or maybe it was the pleading note in him, in just the fact of his coming in like that to tell his tale (true or not?) and ask a favor—who never asked a thing but a sip of water lying there in the doctor's office over the butcher shop with the doctor working on his torn-up ass, and the mob outside beginning to stamp and pound and howl, and I'm alone there with my badge and a cut-down pump gun and the rest of the marshals six hours away at the other end of the telegraph wires Henry Starr had cut himself before he rode into Stroud. What is it makes him come in now to ask a favor like this one, and ask it so hard? What's in movies for him beyond the dollar and the reputation, same as anybody else?

They had stopped on the sidewalk, and Tilghman had looked at the smooth brown face, noted the droop at the corners of the eyes. "You want to drive out there? They give me a car to use when I want to. Since I got old." He colored at his own awkward courtesy.

Henry Starr smiled a little and said, "I figured to ride. I've got a kid holding my horse in the alley." And in a couple of minutes they were riding out toward the Springs Road, the horses' hooves clacking sharply on the paved streets of the downtown, north on Main to Archer, west on Archer, booming the planks of a bridge, patting softly in the dust of the road going west along the Arkansas across the open prairie. Tilghman gave Starr a look with his side vision. Prison had not dimmed his eye for a good horse: the Appaloosa mare he was riding was maybe a little old but beautifully set, showing the strength and quick feet and clever eyes of a good cow horse, and she had the perfect mix of colors, mottled gray-white in the forequarters and a white rump splashed with black spots like Indian paint. Henry Starr sat her easily, no hitch in him at all anymore, and Tilghman remembered the first time he'd seen Henry Starr ride in the rodeo at Tahlequah, smooth as running water. He was a pleasure to watch on a horse that day.

*But twenty-nine years is a long time ago.*

Now they stood under the cottonwood tree and let Banker Wilberforce come up to them, walking with vigorous stiff strides like a man walking through ankle-deep water, the two black men in his wake, the older of the two towering over the others under his big slouch hat, the younger man in the straw derby walking slowly at his side. Wilberforce's face was red with heat and strain as he greeted Tilghman, puffing, out of breath.

Tilghman's greeting was a slight inclination of the gray Stetson. "I'd like to introduce somebody to you," he said, a little shyly. "This here is Henry Starr . . ."

"Any friend of Marshal's is . . ." Wilberforce was still puffing.

"Henry Starr," said the tall black man—a deep gravelly voice. "Well, Henry Starr!"

"Howdy, Bub," said Henry Starr.

Wilberforce mastered his breath. "What brings you out here, Bill? Well never mind, I'm just glad you are . . . it's that Price I want to talk to you about, hanging around here, making a damned nuisance of himself," and he punched a thick thumb toward the group around the camera. "What's his business here anyway?" It was apparent that as far as the banker was concerned, Tilghman had come out the Springs Road just to see what Wilberforce wanted.

"Deputy Price thinks I come out here to sell you some moonshine whiskey," said Bub, and the smaller man with him scowled, looked down at his boots, said nothing.

Wilberforce spread his hands—as if *his* colored people would do that sort of thing, as if he would *countenance* it, I ask you—"Bub here, and this is his son-in-law William, are owners of the colored theater in Greenwood, the Dreamland. We have simply been arranging for them to exhibit some of our recent productions."

Bub grinned, a double line of teeth pressed tight together. "We find it more convenient to do business out here in the brush than in town. It is the heat, you see."

"You don't bootleg *whiskey*, do you, Bub?" asked Henry Starr.

Bub smiled and gave his head a little toss. "Not any more, Henry. Only dreams son Parker and I sell are the kind Mr. Wilberforce and Mr. Poole make. Not the kind comes in bottles. You got to go to Chee-*khah*-go for that. I haven't made white lightning since I used to be a law man."

"That's a long time," said Bill Tilghman.

"Yes it is," said Bub flatly. "Old times long gone."

"Why, Bub!" said the banker. "I didn't know you had been a policeman." He said it like he wasn't sure how it sat.

"No sir, Mr. Wilberforce," he answered with a toothy grin, "not a police man. I was one of those jack-leg Choctaw sheriffs they used to have round here back when it was the old Indian Nations."

"And that's why . . . ? Whiskey, I mean? You being a law man and . . . ?"

"Yes sir, Mr. Wilberforce," said Bub, "that's how it was. Things are different now. Police men don't do whiskey no more, do they, Bill?"

"Why did you ever stop being a lawman, Bub?" asked Wilberforce, but wondering as he said it how it was Bub could have gotten *started* at it.

"Well sir, Mr. Wilberforce, I didn't rightly *leave* the law. It kind of got moved out from under me, you might say. Yeah, that's what you might say," and he grinned and nodded once, sharply, looking not at Wilberforce but straight at Tilghman—who met his eyes coolly, gray for brown.

"It's law all the same, Bub," said Tilghman and Bub didn't answer—maybe his smile said that he thought he had.

Wilberforce reclaimed Tilghman's attention, clearing his throat. "It's Price I need to talk to you about, Bill." The banker rolled a nervous eye back toward the camera crew, caught the flash of a blue dress eclipsed by the deputy's swollen khaki back. "He's been making himself obnoxious. Whatever suspicions he may have of Bub here, he has no right to be rude to me, or to push himself into the middle of my arrangements."

"Unless you're trading moonshine for moving pictures," said Bub, Wilberforce not hearing him.

Tilghman considered Wilberforce a moment, then spoke blandly, quietly: "Deputy Price isn't in my department, but I will see what can be done."

"Talk to him yourself?" asked Wilberforce.

"All right." He let that sit a moment. "I wanted to introduce Henry Starr to you . . ."

"Yes yes," said Wilberforce, "any friend of the Marshal's is . . . of course . . ." He kept looking over his shoulder toward the camera, the false front of the bank.

"He's looking for work," said Tilghman.

Wilberforce's head pivoted back to Tilghman. "A bank job?"

"Oh brother," said Bub Houston, shaking his head.

Tilghman looked judicious. "No," he drawled, "he's been thinking more about working for your movie outfit."

Wilberforce looked at Henry Starr for the first time to notice him. He saw a little swarthy man with shiny hair (probably greasy), the stiff baggy suit and the shirt lacking collar and tie, the battered Stetson and the old cracked boots—he looked like someone you'd see on the Mexican streets or over in Greenwood sitting on a stoop with a bottle of rotgut in a paper bag, except that his face was clean and the suit wasn't stained or ripped . . . yet. Wilberforce looked back at Tilghman. "What does he do?"

Tilghman hung fire, it came to him right then that he didn't really know what Henry Starr had in mind, anything from acting to horse wrangling to hauling wood and water.

There was a sound like a rumbling scratchy cough made deep in the chest. The old Indian—who looked to be a hundred, wrapped from neck to heel in a greasy red blanket—had finally hobbled up to look Henry Starr in the face.

"*Hunh!*" he said. "I think you used to be Henry Starr."

Henry Starr smiled. "Still am." He looked over at Wilberforce, and the smile made him seem suddenly younger because the teeth were white and clean and the brown skin of his face so smooth, so if you forgot the baggy suit . . . "Mr. Wilberforce, I think I could be of some help to your people making movies out here. Which I understand are about the Old West—having seen several when I . . . Mr. Wilberforce, I used to be an outlaw. My aunt was Belle Starr, who rode with Jesse James and Cole Younger. Maybe you heard of her? My grandfather Tom Starr, he was pretty famous too—in the Indian Nations? In the old days?"

"Used to be," said the old Indian.

"*Apf!*" said Wilberforce. "Well I don't . . ." and he looked helplessly at Tilghman. "Are you serious?"

It wasn't the sort of question Bill Tilghman answered.

"Yes," chuckled Bub Houston. "I can testify to that. Mr. Henry Starr did rob a certain number of express cars and stagecoaches in his day. I believe he may even have touched a bank or two when he wasn't careful. When I saw you with the marshal here, I thought he was takin' you in again, Young Henry, just like in the old days." Bub gave Tilghman a look, a flash of the eye the way you might brush your coattail aside sitting down at a card table to show the handle of a revolver. "I arrested Young Henry once myself, but he was too smart for me—got away. You don't want to land in Tulsa City Jail, Young Henry. It's an easy jail for a man to get into . . . fact, it's gettin' hard keepin' folks *out* of Tulsa Jail, ain't it, Marshal? Yeah, any number of folks find it easy goin' in, but the comin' out, Henry: that's *hard*, you know, that's *hard.*"

Tilghman stood rigid and vibrant as a steel rod. "I wouldn't know, Bub. It's none of my jail."

As he looked steadily into Tilghman's face Bub's own tension seemed to still and settle. "No," he said deliberately, "I guess it is not."

"Used to be," said the old Indian, feeling Henry Starr's shoulders with his broken hands. "That's how it used to be."

"Yes," said Bub. "How it used to be. How do they name you, old-timer?"

"*Tsigesu*," said the old man. Wilberforce's eyebrows shot straight up, he couldn't tell if it was a name or a sneeze, and Henry Starr chuckled and so did Bub, and Tilghman looked the question at Henry Starr. "It means *Used-to-be*," said Henry Starr. "That's what we used to call him, old *Used-to-be*. Because of the stories he used to tell us, hey old man? Those stories about the old times . . . ?"

"*Hyenh*," said the old man. "*Hyenh*, how it used to be."

"Mr. Wilberforce," asked Henry Starr softly, "I could sure use the job. I know a lot about how they used to do things. I know a lot of stories"—and he smiled again, that surprising young smile above the old pensioner's baggy suit and unfinished collar—"though I guess if you've got this old *Used-to-be* here working for you, you got stories enough, maybe."

Wilberforce was upset and disconcerted by all of this, his attention swiveling between Tilghman, the tableau around the camera, Tilghman and Houston, Henry Starr, and he looked dubiously at the old Indian's moist toothless grin, the eyes so buried in wrinkled dead skin they might have been empty sockets. "Well I don't . . ." He looked anxiously over toward the set and his feet followed the tug of his eyes. "You'll have to come talk it over with Mr. Poole and our Mr. Foley, they're in charge of productions, I . . ." and they tagged after his broad back heading for the false-front bank, the small group around the camera, the actors sweating in the Oklahoma sun.

Esterhazy was soaked with sweat, his head beginning to buzz, he wished they'd get done wrangling or take a break for lunch, anything! He saw with relief that Wilberforce was finally headed this way, and he tried to animate the banker's bulk by projecting his own nervous energy through the aether toward him. *Come on, man, before we are dying out here*. Esterhazy had great faith in Wilberforce and the money he represented. With a belly like that, with the capital of the firm in his hands, Wilberforce *must* be the final authority, the one man who could sit on Foley and Poole (if he would) and make them shut up and get on with it.

"Look," Foley was saying, "this isn't *Birth of a Nation* we're making here, it's *Buckskin Bill's Outlaw Trail.* I've been making pictures like this one for ten years—in Hollywood!—and I know my trade. If you don't believe that, then why in *hell* did you hire me? Maybe these stunts have been done before, Jesus! *Everything* has been done before. These things keep coming back because they *work*, because they'll fetch your audience each and every time."

*And*, thought Esterhazy, *they're the only tricks you know.*

Poole drew himself up. "Maybe you're right, Foley. Maybe we can't make *Birth of a Nation* yet. We haven't got the equipment or the people or the properties or the capital for it. Maybe we haven't got the know-how either . . . *yet.* We're about good enough for these one- and two-reelers you've been making for us. But if you can't think bigger than one or two reels, then that's all you ever *will* do—and let me tell you that this company isn't getting stuck in any two-reel philosophy, not while I'm running it. You get that, Foley? Just because you started out pumping nickels in the nickelodeon doesn't mean you stay with nickels and dimes for the rest of your life."

At which point Wilberforce at last came up, throwing a sharp look at Price leaning over Miss Woodly, and the lady dipped a shoulder and moved toward him. "What's the problem here, gentlemen?" the banker wanted to know.

Poole and Foley both turned toward him and saw the others coming up behind the banker—Marshal Tilghman tall and gray, behind him a swarthy little man in a bad suit, and the two colored men back of them.

"It's about the bank robbery scene," said Miss Woodly.

"Poole wants to scrap *Buckskin Bill* and make *Birth of a Nation.*" Foley threw up his hands, at the end of his rope.

Poole answered with a death's-head grin at the director. "Mr. Foley prefers to dispense with the luxury of the *story* and give us instead a set of circus acts." The two men glared at each other.

"Mr. Foley thinks it should be done in an exciting manner," said Miss Woodly in a smooth, reasonable voice whose authority made them look at her in surprise. "Mr. Poole thinks it should be staged with more authenticity. Isn't that right?" Foley and Poole looked sheepish.

"Well now," boomed Deputy Price, bulling his way past her into the circle, "well, you folks are in luck there! Because Marshal Tilghman and me, I guess we could tell you a thing or two about bank robbers and bad men. Took our share of 'em, ain't that right?"

The others gave ground around the bull's rush, but it didn't seem to exist for Tilghman, who touched the brim of his hat to Miss Woodly and said, "Well ma'am, this is Mr. Henry Starr here. I guess he could tell you some about how they used to do things in the old days."

That was when Esterhazy and the rest of them took their first real look at the little man. Small, wiry, with that suit standing stiffly away from his frame like it was his father's suit, and *starched* in the bargain; and the unmade collar and the black hair all haggled at the ends like it had been trimmed with wire cutters, the lack of tone in the skin and eyes, the way he hung back behind Tilghman . . .

"Mr. Starr used to be a bank robber himself," said the marshal, and Esterhazy recognized the type in that instant: the jailbird. More than one time in, and ten years on the last stretch, maybe, or at any rate no less than a hard five. "He rode with Cherokee Bill and the Cook Gang," said Tilghman, but the names seemed not familiar even to the Americans present. "He had his own bunch," he added, as if hoping that would make a difference.

"Jesse James?" said Miss Woodly, and the rising note in her voice made Esterhazy look down at her. She stood quite still but the tilt of her smooth strong neck told Esterhazy what her expression must be—that intent look which seemed to draw the reins of her body into her eyes. He could see her look register in Henry Starr's eyes: brown eyes, deep-set, looking at her in a way that Esterhazy was prepared as always to resent, but despairingly, he should be used to it by now—but why did she have to draw that kind of look? Hanging on to that fat old rich man, how does she expect men to look at her? Not every man has Esterhazy's eyes!

"No, ma'am," said Henry Starr. "I was too young to ride with him. But he was kind of my uncle." His voice was very low and smooth, held back as if he did not give all his breath to it.

"Henry Starr," said Poole. "I never heard of you."

"I have," snapped Price, and he loomed forward, his big chest pushing into the space in front of the little man as he moved in on him. "The bank jobs in Stroud six years ago. The little Injun bank robber. *Hen*ery Starr! You got shot in the ass by a sixteen-year-old white boy with a shotgun, and they nearly strung you up, didn't they? Humph!" and he houghed his breath in the little man's face. "You wasn't much of a bank robber, was you, *Hen*ery?"

Deputy Price stood there with his big red face looming over his heavy chest no more than six inches from Henry Starr's face and his breath blowing into the little man's eyes and mouth and his little reddened eyes glaring down from under the brim of the white Stetson, two big meaty thumbs hooked in his belt making twin dents in the bulge of his gut.

But Henry Starr didn't step back out of the loom of his heavy chest or the sour fragrance of Price's breath, not even to lean back, not even to hold his breath, not at all: though they stood and stood there, and he should have leaned back at least, being so small, and it began to look strange and even a little bit horrible that he hadn't flinched or leaned or even held his breath but just stood there too damn close to the big mad hulk of the deputy till you wanted someone to make him stop, make him stop not doing anything at all or else something terrible was going to happen.

"Sixteen?" said the big colored man in the slouch hat. "You folks trains your back-shooters young," and Price stepped back and turned quickly away from Henry Starr as if he was eager for some reason to stop having to lean over into the air in front of that little man, glad to be free to round on the nigger and turn red in the face and get a mean squint on. "What's that, nigger? You talking to me . . . ?"

"Why doesn't he show us?" said Miss Woodly in a voice light and sharp that made them all stop again. She was looking at Henry Starr, and he was looking back, and Esterhazy couldn't see her face but the jailbird's face was very stiff and still looking except for the liquid lights in his brown eyes. From the front of the false bank the actors had wandered up, drawn to the argument like bees to nectar, Buckskin Bill and Slick McClain and Alice Farnham and all the rest. "Well, Henry Starr," Miss Woodly said quietly, "why don't you show us how it was done?"

Henry Starr felt a thing like the touch of a cool ghostly finger in the eye of his chest. *Does she know me?* he thought. *Her eyes are blue, but she's just like a deer, isn't she? The eyes wide open and ready to see everything, the small lips, and breath like sweet grass, I'll bet; and the fine head set on the long neck that way, narrow shoulders like a young girl, but she moves real strong on those long legs, even just standing there she looks set for a leap or a glide, one move and she'll be gone like someone opened a door in the air and shut it behind her. Well miss, Miss Woodly ma'am, well,* "Well yes," he said. "All right, I'll show you."

"Well, what happened then?" Blaine wanted to know, because Tilghman had paused in the telling to think about something, or maybe just to get it set in his mind, because it had all happened just too much faster than your eye could rightly follow. Henry Starr had been standing there in the stiff baggy prison suit, looking like the two-time loser that he was, and in custody of that big angry pussle-gutted pistol-jutting Deputy Price, you felt so sorry for the pore little Injun boy . . .

And suddenly the small lean body clenched and uncoiled itself, instantaneously lashing out an arm like a snake striking in a single thoughtless whipcrack so fast that you were still seeing the reaching hand snatching the gun while the gun was flashing up in the dark hand snatching it out of the deputy's hip holster, thumb-cocking it with a snap as the arm uncoiling in a straight sharp thrust pointed like a finger right between the eyes of Buckskin Bill Bonham—who choked on his own scream that the pistol shoved right back down his throat (Wilberforce cringing behind his own fat left shoulder, Poole and Foley frozen with hands halfway up to their faces, Price twisting away with his hands over the back of his head *don't kill me!*)—right between his eyes, and the voice as sharp and clear and deadly as the cocking of the pistol: "Thumbs up and stand steady!"

Only the old half-dead Indian and Tilghman and Bud Houston and the girl were still simply standing there, the girl looking like she had seen the elephant for the first time. The extras stood up stiff as boards with their hands shot straight up over their heads and their eyes racing for cover, and not a sound, not one, not another sound for miles and miles. Not one.

"Well," prompted Blaine, "I guess he got the job?"

"Yes he did," said Tilghman.

Blaine waited, and when nothing more came he said, "Well, did he tell you what he promised? What it was he said to Cherokee Bill that made him give up his guns and his hostages?"

"I didn't ask him," said Tilghman quietly.

"And naturally he wasn't volunteering information," said Blaine.

"No," said Tilghman thoughtfully. "He just wanted to show them how it was in the old days."

MOVIE MEN HIRE
FAMOUS OUTLAW

Ex–Bank Robber
Henry Starr to Make
Movies for Pan American
Motion Picture Co.

The Company Owned by a Bank!

Nephew of Belle Starr Knew the James Boys, the Youngers and the Dalton Gang

Premier Appearance in "Buckskin Bill's Outlaw Trail" at the Lyric Theater on April 30

## TULSA *April 30, 1921*

The premier at the Lyric was conceived, organized and carried off by Dexter C. Poole, editor and publisher of the Tulsa *Lamp*, whose columns bannered it for days. The main branch of the First Chemical–Cattlemen's Bank of Tulsa stood three blocks down Main Street from the Lyric, and Poole talked Wilberforce into turning the bank's facilities over to the promotion. The intervening light posts were decked with bunting that looped the Lyric to the bank in streamers of red, white and blue. The bank itself was hung with American and Oklahoma flags, and a large sign proclaiming it THE FIRST BANK OF THE MAGIC CITY. Inside the lobby there were banners welcoming the producers of *Buckskin Bill's Outlaw Trail*, and "Pioneers of Cinema in the Magic City." Directly facing the main doors a wall-high transparency imposed on the eye of the visitor the heraldry of the Tulsa *Lamp*—the paper's motto, "A Light Unto the Nations," and its trademark: "Liberty," bearing a torch whose flame had been exaggerated to equal in size the female form of Liberty, the flame bluntly marked with a heavy black cross.

A space had been cleared in front of the teller's cages, and there were Wilberforce and Poole in dark blue suits and ties shaking hands with a bloodless little man (Mayor Egan, grateful for this new occasion for civic self-assertion), next to them Foley in a director's trademark safari jacket and golfing cap, Buckskin Bill Bonham in his buckskins and white Stetson, and Alice Farnham in a froth of lacy stuff like a cloth meringue. And there was Henry Starr standing quietly among them, in a dark brown suit cut for his spare figure and a light tan Stetson above his red-tan face—diffident in his stillness, as if the others and not he were the objects of all this attention.

But in fact everyone had come to see the real old-time Jesse James/Dalton brothers badman, and (with a few exceptions) to celebrate Pan American's capture of an authentic bit of Oklahoma legendry. The exceptions stood in a bunch to one side of the photographers' arena, half a dozen men with grim mouths so engrossed in whispered talk among themselves that they could barely spare a glance for the celebrants: These were the "Pioneers of Cinema," Poole's and Wilberforce's competitors in the race to make the "Magic City of the Southwest" the new center of moviemaking in the United States, "with a better and more reliable climate than New York or southern California, and all the advantages of a geographical position central to the whole continent." It had been bad enough when Pan American raided Hollywood for a big-time director and a cameraman trained in Europe. With Henry Starr in the combination they had an authentically legendary Western star property to compare with Tom Mix, Al Jennings and William S. Hart—there would be no catching up with Pan American after this.

Photographers stepped in and out of the cleared space by the cage, popping flashpowder and begging for better poses. Each pop and flash of light printed a pair of characters on the watcher's eyes, ghosts of the images that would appear in tomorrow's *Lamp*:

**Director Foley Shaking Hands with Henry Starr, Famous Outlaw**

**Buckskin Bill Shakes Hands with Henry Starr: "No Hard Feelings"** [Buckskin Bill gives his best three-quarter profile to the camera, Henry Starr's face is half-averted.]

**Marshal Tilghman and Outlaw Henry Starr: Once Foes, Now Friends** [A reluctant, dead-fish handshake, both men turn awkwardly full-front to the camera and so are overexposed by the flash. When they try to get the marshal to draw his gun and Henry Starr to raise his hands and look captured, Tilghman stalks out.]

**Banker and Bandit** [Henry Starr shakes hands with Banker Wilberforce, while behind them looms the tall figure of Dexter C. Poole, who seems to urge these two to shake and be friends at last. Banker Wilberforce's mouth is open in a hearty laugh, but his eyes are rolled sideways watchfully toward the camera.]

Flashpowder racks popped off in a ragged volley and Poole arched an eyebrow to his own reporter to bring him into play. "Well, Henry," he said, "now that you're here, what do you think of *this* bank?"

That was a straight line you couldn't miss, so everybody hushed and in the awkward silence Wilberforce's hearty smile lost some heart while holding its grip. Starr answered softly, "It's a pretty strong bank, Mr. Poole. They build 'em a lot stronger than they used to."

"Suppose you wanted to rob it, Henry. How would you go about it?"

"Well," said Henry Starr, dragging it out a little, "I guess if I could get me one of them German Big Bertha cannons out there in front, that might do her . . ." and since that was good enough for a laugh there was laughter amid the next round of pops and flashes.

"Well well, Henry, well well," said Wilberforce, whose smile was again a genuine pleasure to look at, "that's good to hear, a Big . . . yes, that's about, that's what it would take," and he turned to the crowd. "It's a mighty *strong* bank we've got here, folks, and that's from an expert!" That got a big laugh, a prairie-thunder-and-lightning outburst punctuated by flashpowder bursts. Wilberforce enjoyed it, and then he wanted more, so he waved them quiet and added in a stage whisper, "I just hope you don't intend to try it!"

"No," said Henry Starr quietly, "not when I'm working for you," and Wilberforce's laugh was already primed and half-cocked so it went off anyhow before he thought and he was right in the middle of the noise again when something . . . what was it?—some tone or inflection of the answer gave him a sudden pang of anxiety that lingered after the crowd swept out the double glass doors of the bank and down the street toward the Lyric.

Two rows had been reserved for the Pan American Motion Picture Company and its invited guests. Gilded statuary and *faux* opera boxes overlooked the crowd in the plush-bottomed seats. The darkness came, there was fiddle and piano music from the pit, thrilling rumbles like hoofbeats or Indian drums and violins whining in romantic melancholy. The film opened shakily, shifting abruptly between spurts of bright action and the black intrusions of expository title cards, Foley in despair, Editor Poole most attentive at this point: did the audience appreciate the significance of Slick McClain's two-faced character of putative eastern philanthropist and western desperado? *Some* may think you a romantic Robin Hood, but *I* know you for a common thief. Well, they were attentive enough, no chitchat, if they watched they might learn.

Esterhazy sat slumped between Henry Starr and Miss Woodly, both of whom had what could only be called a good seat, erect and well balanced. Miss Woodly: her posture was lovely, it showed the curve of her shoulders and back and the fall of her hair past the pillar of her neck—so maybe it was a pose of *conscious* beauty? *Ach!* It also made a space of clear air around her, so there would be no small touches of shoulder or forearm with Buckskin Bill on her right or Esterhazy, Melancholy Magyar, sighing inaudibly on her left. What a one she is: the gesture that invites is the very thing that makes her untouchable. Ah well! . . . (he stole a glance to his left) and the "Famous Outlaw" sits that way because he thinks chair is a saddle? No: I would say, because he is nervous, maybe even frightened, our famous bandit, rigid with readiness—for what?

Why does he do this? Esterhazy asked himself. What is in it for him? What he is paid is nothing, he could make more clerking in store. Foley treats him like a nigger to his face, treats pictures of him worse: makes Henry Starr look like tailor's dummy. It is not even his trade. So why?

Then the screen lit and took Esterhazy's eyes and he forgot the other two for the moment. Some internal shutter allowed him to black out all the dialogue cards and every foul or useless image on the screen, so that for him the movie would consist only of the best of what he himself had put there. There were moments he waited for to savor and dissect, images embodying the resolution of complex difficulties. He waited impatiently for one long shot of the street in which the precise placing of his camera had not only allowed him absolutely and flawlessly to conceal the falseness of the buildings, but had allowed him to catch a single bolt of sunlight shot from upper left to the rear middle ground of the scene of Buckskin Bill riding into town out of the desert with the limp form of Alice—actually a bag of cotton waste that could (Esterhazy thought) pass for Alice in most circumstances—draped across his horse's withers. "Lucky shot, that," said Foley, and Esterhazy hated him for it, because he had watched the clouds all afternoon waiting for that conjunction to occur, inventing small technical difficulties to slow down the takes, cheering silently at every idiotic demand of Alice and Buckskin Bill because for once they were helping him, letting him place his camera in time and space at the moment when the sinking sun would pass into that mass of clouds and give the whole chiaroscuro to the eye of his camera. *Lucky shot*, you ass.

*Pop!* There was the face of the Famous Bandit! Absolutely wooden except for eyes that show nothing but terror, as if the big camera were some kind of cannon, Big Bertha, *Thumbs up and stand steady, Henry Starr!* He and Foley had worried extravagantly about the difficulty of working with a man crazy enough to pull a loaded pistol out of Deputy Price's holster and cock and point it between the eyes of their leading man. But Henry Starr had been sweet and docile under instruction: jail must have gotten him used to obeying arbitrary and (to him) meaningless orders. That resolved, all that remained was the simple technical matter of deciding where a one-shot of Henry Starr could be slipped into a scene of Slick McClain talking drinking playing cards passing wind or whatever it was he was doing. Then just take Henry Starr, stand him up straight, Esterhazy points the camera and *bang!* take one: Henry Starr standing at the bar. Pick him up, haul him to the next spot, stand him up, point the camera and *bang!* Henry Starr in a corral, Henry Starr in a street, Henry Starr peeking from behind a rock . . . Easy as pie: the man made no more fuss than a wooden Indian, and didn't do a hell of a lot more acting but who cares as long as his name's on the marquee and in the paper; as long as Poole and Wilberforce are happy.

Esterhazy looked over to see if the Famous Bandit was happy too.

Henry Starr's body had relaxed somewhat, his hands rested on the crown of the Stetson on his lap, and he looked intently at the screen that washed his face with cold light and flickers of darkness. His lips were moving. An ignorant man reads with his lips, but a glance at the screen showed Esterhazy only pictures (the stagecoach scene—Christ, *that* again!) . . . lip-reading pictures as if they were a book.

The lights went on catching everybody by surprise, as they always did, freezing for a second like a flash picture the hidden expressions that had crept out in the dark. Then, as those vanished, the second, slightly pale and sickly look replaced it, as if passing from movie dark into the light involved a kind of convalescence. Henry Starr's face was bathed in sweat, he looked as if he had ridden for miles. Miss Woodly?—she looked cool still, as if that air she kept clear all around her were also chilled.

But she avoided Esterhazy's eye and sought Henry Starr: "Did you like the movie?" she asked.

"Well," he said, "it wasn't exactly . . ." and she chorused ". . . *how it was done in the old days,*" and Henry Starr laughed, clean white teeth in a smooth brown face marked only now with crinkles at the eyes. *How old? How old is he?* Esterhazy tried to remember. *Robbing banks with Deadeye Dick and Buffalo Bill and he looks like young man . . . Well, maybe being behind bars all those years keeps you young—in this country, maybe so. Two years in Austrian prison I feel like old man, chill is still in my bones.*

"Did you like yourself in it?" she asked.

Henry Starr lifted a convalescent smile. "Well, I don't know, I guess. I never seen myself like that, with no colors like that. And how it looked like I was places I never been. But I was there somehow, I guess."

"Yes you were," she said, with an emphasis that made Esterhazy's heart sink. *Oh Miss Woodly*, the thought wailed in Esterhazy's head, and he called himself a fool for wondering why Henry Starr would put up with this nonsense, when he of all men should know that besides making money the most important reason for a man's wanting to blow his image up to gigantic size was to fill and make shine the eyes of a woman like Miss Woodly.

The piano drum-rumbled, the audience began applauding, and they looked up to see Editor Poole in a spotlight before the curtain, waving the applause to silence.

"Ladies and gentlemen of Tulsa," he said, smiling broadly, "you have witnessed the beginning of what we of the Pan American Motion Picture Company hope and expect will be a long and fruitful association: between the art of the motion picture and the enterprise of moral and historical education! And between ourselves and Mr. Henry Starr—a man whose past is one with the history of our state, whose life has shown that in this country of ours no man, howsoever born and raised, lacks for the opportunity to rise above his circumstances, to reform his life, and to become a profitable member of American society. Ladies and gentlemen, I give you . . . Mr. Henry Starr!"

He began applauding *at* Henry Starr and the audience took the editor's cue, turning to clap their hands and tug at him with their eyes. Esterhazy saw the outlaw's face take a wooden set as dead as in the worst close-up he had shot, and rise slowly from his seat holding his hat in his hand.

But as his head rose above the level of the seated men and women around him, Henry Starr's face suddenly lit with that bright and boyish smile, he strode to the stage and mounted it with his limp barely perceptible. He stood there next to Poole looking out over the massed faces and the clapping, clapping—then he looked at Editor Poole . . . the look holding until the editor (perhaps a little flustered?) backed off the stage, leaving Henry Starr alone.

Henry Starr held up his right hand, palm outward—and the noise stilled. He licked his lips and took a breath.

"I want to thank all you folks for coming here today. I hope you liked this here . . ." Suddenly he smiled again, as if some thought had suddenly put him at ease. "It's like a friend of mine once said on a different occasion, 'I came here to' " (the slightest hesitation) " 'to see a movie, not to make a speech.'

"So I'll keep it short. I would like particularly to say to any young people that might come and see a picture like this, that although a life of crime may seem to possess the quality of romance, may seem more exciting and lucrative than a life of honest labor, that such is not the case: and my own life is proof of what I say. The life of an outlaw is like that of a hunted beast, every man's hand against him, and no good woman's heart for him. His bread is not enjoyed with quietness, his sleep is broken by pursuit and the fear of capture, in rain or freezing cold he must live without roof or fire, his few moments of dear-bought pleasure are earned with labors more difficult and continual than those of the honest workingman or farmer. Add to this the continual rebukes of his conscience—for no matter what resolves an outlaw may take to hold his hand from vileness or violence, the life he leads will weaken and break that resolve. He will know himself guilty of crimes for which the law, perhaps, has no name; but these will dog his tracks and haunt his sleep, inflicting a punishment whose justice is harder to escape than the police and more impossible to evade than the warrants of the law.

"I make no apology for myself. As Mr. Poole has said, this country of ours offers peculiar advantages to youth. Perhaps I did not make proper use of my advantages . . . though I mean to, now.

"For I have learned an inestimable lesson, which I hope this little story of ours" (he gestured to the screen) "will help to fix upon the minds of our young people." He turned his gaze upon his two employers, Poole and Wilberforce, sitting in the first row just below him. "Remember!" he said seriously, "that Crime Does Not Pay."

Amid the thunder of hands and piano, Henry Starr stepped off the stage and worked his way up the aisle, the audience pressing out to shake his hand and touch his back. Esterhazy would just as soon have hung back, but Miss Woodly kept giving him little jolts in the back, driving him through the press toward the Famous Bandit, whose progress could be tracked by the movement of the dense knot of admirers—which did not begin to loosen until it had passed out the doors and under the marquee in the open air.

They were out in the street now, the crowd breaking up, jostled and interrupted by handshakes for Henry Starr as they worked their way toward the sidewalk. A boy, maybe twelve years old, twisted past two mustachioed gentlemen in pin-striped suits, his face burning red. "Hey mister! Are you really Henry Starr?"

Henry Starr stopped and said, "That's right."

"Oh brother!" said the kid, and twisted back through the crowd the way he had come as somewhere an outraged mother began yelling, "Billy! Billy Claybo!"

Miss Woodly was grinning like a cat at a mouse. "That's your public, Henry Starr, just trying to see you up close."

To Esterhazy's surprise, this seemed to embarrass the Famous Outlaw. His eyes flickered away from Miss Woodly and the crowd into which Billy Claybo had vanished, looking away down the street toward the railroad depot. Instead of basking in limelight, flashpowder and the blue glow of Miss Woodly's eyes, he wanted to get away from this whole scene, and obviously didn't know how. His right hand tugged the brim of his Stetson down to mask his eyes with shadow, and that suggested the next move. "Ma'am, Mr. Esterhazy . . . Evening." He stepped back and turned, walked swiftly away down the street, turning the first corner he came to.

Miss Woodly watched him all the way to the turning, and her eyes lingered on the place in the air from which he had vanished. "He watches everything so closely," she said, "he's got such good eyes."

*Ay me*, thought Esterhazy, *all through my movie she was watching his eyes*. But his resentment tangled with another feeling: that she needed protection. His tone was biting as he warned her, "Listen: he's maybe still dangerous man."

"That's all right," she said. "I think he likes us."

## TULSA *May 5, 1921*

Though he told himself he should know better, still it seemed possible to Esterhazy that the only reason she had been coming out to the set was because Banker Wilberforce brought her. But one day into the shooting for their second and third and fourth "Henry Starr" features—*Henry Starr, Scourge of the Southwest; Henry Starr, the Robin Hood of Old Oklahoma*, and *Henry Starr's Vengeance Trail*—Wilberforce began to show symptoms of boredom and distaste. It was late spring, after all, and a banker's fancy must turn to lending money against the year's harvest. His assistant would no doubt return with him to her duties behind the teller's cage of the Chemical–Cattlemen's Bank.

But the next day she was there, having driven out with Editor Poole, whose thin white-shirted form was redolent of bay rum. She carried a sheaf of papers for him on a clipboard and disappeared with him into Foley's offices for script conferences. Esterhazy believed he had scented some sort of change in the state of affairs, and he felt a degree of jealousy of Poole that Wilberforce had never evoked. But even so, for some reason it was a relief to think that she had not transferred her . . . interest? . . . to Henry Starr.

Two days later Poole was gone to wage paper wars against the League of Nations and the IWW, yet she was still coming out every day, driving her own light-sprung buggy, the leathers held expertly in her long-fingered hands. She seemed now cool and independent and capable, enshrined in the sheath of clear and impenetrable air that she seemed able to draw about herself. From being certain she had been the plaything and receptacle of Wilberforce, Poole and Foley, Esterhazy was now equally convinced that she was somehow still virginal and unutterably new. He also had wit enough to recognize that on the subject of Miss Woodly he had become slightly crazy.

Her presence distracted him, so much that he lost track of which of the three movies they were filming—which was not hard to do, since Foley made no attempt at following story lines, but just kept busily squirreling up piles of footage like nuts for a long winter. With judicious copying and splicing, he'd have enough for a dozen films even if Henry Starr dropped dead tomorrow.

She was busy here and there around the set and the offices, yet every so often, when Esterhazy thought she had disappeared for good, he would discover her standing near the set, watching while Foley put the Famous Outlaw through his paces: on the horse, off the horse, stand at the door and glare; stand by the bar and glare; enter the door of the false-front bank and glare, a pistol in each hand: *Reach for the sky, you varmints!* Point the camera like a gun and *blam!* you're dead.

In his distraction, Esterhazy took to thinking of the Famous Outlaw as one of the stage properties, a slightly more flexible cigar store Indian. It surprised him when he noticed that between takes the Famous Bandit was observing not Miss Woodly but Esterhazy himself, closely and calculatingly. Though it made him feel uncomfortably like a coquette, Esterhazy now "ignored" the Scourge of the Southwest, waiting to see what the outlaw had in his mind.

"All right!" yelped Foley, clapping his hands like a machine gun. "Let's get ready for the Starr Gang. Everybody in front of the bank, horses . . ."

They were filming the last part of a bank robbery sequence, the Starr Gang to come bursting out of the bank, mount the horses they had neatly ranged along the hitching rail in front and ride out of town shooting. Simple enough you would think, but no, they couldn't seem to get it right. One two three takes and something wrong every time. "No! No! No! Cut! Stop! Get back here and let's try it again!"

Henry Starr spoke to Foley hardly at all, but spent the long spells between takes tending his gear or his horse, or talking business with the extras on the lot—the "Starr Gang," most of them young out-of-work cowboys from ranches around Oklahoma City and the western part of the state.

"Bottom fell plumb out of beef when the Germans quit, I bet the whole spread on one more Hun offensive and lost her."

"Drought's bad. Bank int'rest's worse. This job gets done I'm thinking about Montana or California somewheres."

"I tried me some oil drillin' a while? Man, that's some stinkin' work. They had a bunch of us in there riding shotgun on these Hunkies they hauled in to bust the Wobbly strike."

"Let the Hunkies have it, they won't notice the stink."

"If they'd got them in some niggers you'd have seen some trouble."

"Hell, they *had* niggers down in there with the Wobblies and . . ."

Even to an Englishman, these men would seem to speak a foreign language:

"You always use a dally, ropin'? Got you a goodnuff cow horse it's a waste a time and cost you a thumb you ain't careful."

"You ever throw the long rope, Mr. Starr, you don't mind me askin'?"

"Never did," said Henry Starr. "You get you a goodnuff bank, buy all the beef they'll sell you, let some other fella do the ropin'."

They laughed, but the first cowboy added, "Bank got my spread, anyway. Maybe I ought to go get me that bank?"

"Why don't you just take a dally round your own neck and save yourself trouble," said another one.

Foley called for the next take, and Henry Starr said, "Save your pennies and buy you a bank. Let's get this done."

They mounted and rode in, horses jostling and upstaging one another; paused and looked foolish sitting there, the horses switching tails and dropping shit in the street, the men trying to remember that their more ghostly selves were supposed in this interval to be inside robbing the bank—which was difficult to keep in mind because the false-front bank in front of them had no insides, and they might not go to the "studio" to shoot the bank interior for days and days, by which time some of them might have quit or been fired or broken legs and gone to hospital or died and gone to heaven. Yet there they would seem to be, waiting outside while Henry Starr went in to rob the bank, then whirling their horses to escape in real time again—losing a couple of hats, and one going off the wrong way so that Foley yelled, "Cut! Stop! Cut! Goddamn it . . . let's break for lunch, I can't stand any more on an empty stomach!"

It was just as Esterhazy had concluded that Henry Starr and his gang were entirely too foreign for his comprehension that the Scourge of the Southwest ambushed him.

As he came back from the break, Esterhazy saw him up on the stool peering through the viewfinder looking for the empty set, which was covered in black because the lens cap still plugged the eye of the camera. Esterhazy stepped up and plucked it off.

"Aha!" said Esterhazy with a grin.

"Aha!" echoed Henry Starr, looking down. "So that's where they hid it."

"First lesson of photography is take off lens cap," said Esterhazy—feeling very smug and sure of himself because the outlaw had come to him at last—and as Starr started to climb down he pushed at him with two hands, *stay*, and climbed up to stand on a rung of the stool with one hand on the outlaw's shoulder to steady himself. "I show you. Look into viewfinder, so. Sharpen image turning this . . ."

"I've been watching you," Henry Starr said slowly, and Esterhazy blurted "I know!" but Starr just nodded (he had noticed him noticing) and went on, now with a small, slightly conspiratorial smile, "I been trying to put together in my mind just how it is you do all of this." His wave took in camera, set, warehouse studio and cutting room.

"Oh well," said Esterhazy, "isn't just me—Foley is directing and editing, and laboratory . . ."

Starr shook his head, having none of it. "You're the man puts it into the camera, aren't you? There used to be lots of folks around when I was conducting business, too: but you could always tell who the banker was, because he had the money; and you could always tell who I was, because I was the man with the gun."

Esterhazy grinned. "Well, maybe movies is more complicated than robbing banks."

Henry Starr nodded agreement. "That's why I come to you."

"Yes," said Esterhazy, as if Starr had done the right and proper thing, "all right—ask."

"You made it look like I *was* places I *wasn't*." He gave a sad smile. "In my old line of work, they used to call that hanging a frame on someone."

"That's cutting," Esterhazy said offhandedly—Henry Starr was so damned sure of himself, he would tell the Famous Bandit a thing or two, let him see what it was to be Esterhazy, what his skill and his knowledge were. "They take set of pictures, let's say is Slick McClain sitting in bar playing cards. This is Tuesday. Wednesday you arrive, they take few frames of you standing at bar, Slick McClain himself is off somewhere Wednesday drunk. Then cut piece of pictures of Slick"—he made a scissor snip with two fingers—"cut piece of your pictures and splice in. You see? Then another few frames Slick, snip, piece of you, snip, and splice in. When it runs audience sees first you, then Slick, then you, as if was their own eyes jumping around—Tuesday, Wednesday, all looks same, they are in barroom watching Slick play cards and you get drunk."

"You take the picture," said Henry Starr, "then you cut it up and put it together that way. All right." He nodded a grudging acceptance.

"Good," said Esterhazy, softly ironic. "I'm glad you don't mind."

Henry Starr cleared his throat and a little color came into his cheeks. "I thought they just picked up the camera and moved it around, back and forth."

"You can move camera sometimes. But is best from fixed position, with light just so, everything placed for shot."

Henry Starr smiled. "Like hunting buffalo. You take your stand downwind, with the light so it will help you pick your animal out of the brown—though I guess for buffalo it's the wind more'n the light you worry about. Take your stand. Get set. When you've got him in your sights pull the trigger and *blam*!"

"*Blam!*" said Esterhazy sarcastically. "Look, is not just like reporters popping flashpowders, pop! blam! boom! Not like shooting gun, *blam*, and something is lying dead and don't move no more. Maybe is how it looks when Foley shoots you, but not if was mine to do. Film is moving in camera, light is moving outside on people and every thing, all moving too. Only camera is still."

"What about when Bill rode out of town chasing . . . ?" asked Henry Starr, softly and shyly, looking at Esterhazy with an intensity that spoke his respect.

"Panning shot," said Esterhazy, throwing it away, a little thing. "Camera is fixed, but makes pivot, you must turn slowly to follow action, so . . ."

Henry Starr seemed satisfied: "Like a running deer then, not a buffalo stand. You got to lead your buck . . ."

"Ach," said Esterhazy, but he wasn't annoyed now, the conversation delighted him, "still shooting 'em dead, eh? But look, camera don't stop him, it follows as it can, trying to keep rider in frame till it can't no more, he slip out and gets away. Panning," he said decisively.

Henry Starr peered down the lens, then swiveled the camera carefully, panning. "It's different," he said. "You cut things off and put them in the box here, and it's different. Then you suck the colors out of it, and it becomes something else. This place looks like shit in daylight, but it ain't half bad in your movies."

*Your movies* made Esterhazy blush. "Art," he said in a tight voice. "Is nature of my art. Reality, I make better than itself." Esterhazy hesitated, but the urge to tell was finally too much, the attentiveness of the outlaw's brown eyes an appeal to the loneliest part of Esterhazy's being. "All right," he said. "There are two things for me. Could be more if I worked with someone who is not Foley; but with Foley"—he shrugged—"story gives nothing. Also acting, nothing. So what is left? To make picture, to set frame around it so light comes onto it to show what happens; and also, what is feeling you can have about it. Do you know what I mean? Tell me any picture you remember from that movie. I mean, forgetting your own face, which is all any actor ever want to see. Any *picture?*"

Henry Starr sat there a moment, gathering his thoughts. "All right," he said, "let's see how I do. The one I remember is that picture of the man riding in, the girl over his pommel, and the sky behind him looked like it had caught fire. It was the damnedest sunset I ever saw, not a color in it, but it felt like color. For a minute there I thought he and that gal was something . . . something more than you could say. They never lived up to the sunset, though."

Esterhazy nodded, pleased, blushing. "You got good eyes." Then he heard the echo of Miss Woodly's words in his own voice, and that made him blush more profoundly. To cover himself he spoke didactically: "That's first thing. But secret in movies is, it *moves*. Not just how light falls on things that are still, dead things—but things, people, moving talking running around, flowing even . . . you see? And for this . . ." He reached across Henry Starr and put his hand on the crank. "*This*. To use it you must have right feeling from your eyes into your hands. What I'm watching gets me excited, I'm cranking film faster and faster and what happens? Picture comes out moving slow, slow, slow. Just as slow as I was cranking fast."

Henry Starr shook his head.

Esterhazy waved him off. "Don't worry, all *you* have to know, it works by opposite, yes? Crank fast, what you see after comes out slow; crank slow and pace is fast, hip-hap-hoop! like that. Is very funny to see sometimes, that way. Is my talent to know how to play with speed, with time of things happening. Sometimes I let you see things just like they happen. Sometimes I crank just so, give them little speed or slow them little bit—like music, if time and people you could play like music, and this . . . it gives an *effect*, a feeling in what you see. You see?"

"I got to go over it some," said Henry Starr.

"Why?" said Esterhazy. "You want my job?"

"No," said Henry Starr. "It's just something I need to know if I'm going to do this kind of work."

Esterhazy looked at him seriously. "You could make better living robbing banks, my friend. If I told you what they pay me, maybe you'd think I was not any good at this."

"Show me," said Henry Starr seriously, "and I'll see how good you are."

Esterhazy pulled his head back: Henry Starr was so charming, and then there was that little edge, as if behind the smile a cool mind really sat in judgment of each new person, each new experience that approached the Famous Outlaw. "Better you should teach me how to rob that bank," he said, looking away.

Henry Starr grinned. "If I were to teach you, you'd know how."

"Would you teach him how it was done in the old days?" she said, and they looked down and saw Miss Woodly, and felt a touch sheepish at being so snuck-up on. Esterhazy blushed and hastily climbed down, and Henry Starr cleared his throat, and Miss Woodly said, "Hello."

"I was just showing Henry how to use camera."

"Fair trade, ma'am. I'm supposed to show him how to rob a bank."

"Show me too," she said, her chin tilted up so she could look at Henry Starr's eyes. It wasn't a question. He didn't know how to answer. She smiled, and something in the line of her body seemed to ease. "I think Mr. Wilberforce worries that you have your eye on our bank."

"Your bank?" said Henry Starr, with a little half-smile, and she blushed, and Esterhazy winced at her slip of the tongue. Henry Starr went on, gently, "No law against a banker worrying, ma'am. But I only rob banks in the pictures now, and Mr. Wilberforce pays for the pictures. I'm satisfied with that arrangement if you-all are." His eyes crinkled just the least bit. "But now, if I was to give some thought to it . . . well, I'd give it lots of thought. Take my time. Not something I'd just jump at."

"What are you doing out here?" asked Esterhazy, cutting in sharply.

She cleared her throat uneasily, but then as she started to speak her shape itself seemed to change, what she said straightened the set of her spine and sharpened the blue light of her eyes. "I suggested to Mr. Wilberforce and Mr. Poole that since their affairs would keep them away from the production here, I ought to be on hand to inform them of any difficulties Mr. Foley might have with the scripts, and to convey their . . . advice to Mr. Foley when necessary."

"Aha!" said Esterhazy, delighted, *wonderful! wonderful!* What a girl this one was to have made those three march to her tune, what a . . . And then he stopped, stunned at this revelation of what she was capable of, what *politics* she had—and what was it, I ask you, that she had for political capital with those two? What indeed! Esterhazy is romantic idiot who thinks this girl has a crown between her legs when is simply a tool, a kind of wrench perhaps for wringing *concessions* out of . . .

"Here's something to tell them," said Henry Starr, "if you don't mind," and they both looked at him because his bantering tone had suddenly changed. "Why don't me and Esterhazy go out and look at some country around here? Mr. Poole wants us to shoot some real old-time stuff. I know where it is. It's places I used to live in. What about it?"

"Yes!" said Esterhazy. He wanted to get away from all of them, all of this, Foley Wilberforce Poole, and especially Miss Woodly, yes. "We finish shooting in two–three days. I leave editing to Foley and he is just as happy I am not looking over his shoulder making him get it right. Very good idea, very practical, very economic!"

"Yes," said Miss Woodly, setting her round strong chin, "all right. But I'm coming along."

Esterhazy's heart sank; it just confirmed every worst thing he thought about her, his Miss Woodly. Evidently Starr's thoughts ran the same way because he said:

"Well, ma'am, camping out and all . . ."

"I am twenty-seven years old," she said, "I've camped out. I go my own way. People think a lot of things about a woman that goes her own way, but what they think is none of my business." She had lifted her face toward Henry Starr again, the round jaw stubborn, sticking it out on a dare, but her light eyes were focused intently.

"No ma'am," said Henry Starr, "I guess not."

*All the words sound like* "*No,*" thought Esterhazy *but they come out meaning yes, she comes with us. Everything goes by opposite. Even Famous Outlaw cannot say no to her.*

Henry Starr studied her, his eyes serious, his mouth curled the least bit. "You handle these folks pretty well," he said. "Near as well as you handle that team."

*So*, thought Esterhazy, *he has been watching her too.*

Miss Woodly blinked. Then she narrowed her eyes and said, "It's my team, bought and paid for with my own money."

Esterhazy realized with a shock that the outlaw's remark had broken her poise and made her defend herself—awkwardly, and the awkwardness made it somehow more shameful. *So he thinks of her that way too*, thought Esterhazy, and though he felt sympathy for her shame he was also spitefully satisfied.

"Time!" yelled Foley, his megaphone pointed at Esterhazy. The cameraman nudged Henry Starr to dismount from the camera stool and he mounted in the outlaw's place, turning away to concentrate on the image in his viewfinder.

But she was not letting it rest there. "We are all of us in the business of making movies." Esterhazy looked back at her and saw she was poised again and had a dangerous tilt to her head as she talked to Henry Starr. "Mr. Poole and Mr. Wilberforce don't do things just on a dare." She grinned, reminding Esterhazy of a small predatory cat. "Why do you think I am so sure they will pay for our excursion?"

Esterhazy had to eat his answer to that one, and he suspected Henry Starr did too.

"I wrote something for them," she said, "a plan for our next script." She paused for effect, the catlike smile broadening slightly. "It is to be the story of *The Life and Adventures of Henry Starr.*"

Now it was the Famous Outlaw who looked embarrassed, shamed as if at the exposure of a kind of nakedness—a look of strange intensity made him squint and his mouth draw back, then his eyes seemed to empty suddenly, leaving him looking hungry and slightly sad. Then his mouth set, and his eyes focused and narrowed. "My life?" he said with soft emphasis. "Well: what do you know about that."

She was quick enough to hear the irony and sharp enough to answer it literally. "When you were in prison the last time you wrote that autobiography for that Denver newspaper," she said, smiling in a way that was both fierce and slightly arch. "I've been looking you up." Then she let the smile slip, and her look was suddenly straight and serious. "Oh listen," she said, "let's not be clever and sneaky about this. I have an idea, and I think it could make a good movie. I'm asking the two of you if you want to work with me. It's not going to happen if you don't. I don't know how to make the pictures. I don't really know anything about you but what the papers say, Henry Starr. I want to do this right, and if either of you would rather not work with me there's no point in even starting." She stood very still and straight; whether they said yes or no she would not let the least alteration of line or shadow in her face or the set of her back show them that it hurt.

Esterhazy was about to speak, but Henry Starr was quicker on the draw: "All right," said the outlaw, "I'll work with you," and Esterhazy —flicking a jealous glance at Henry Starr—had to say, "Yes, me too, count me in."

Miss Woodly grinned, a fierce triumphant flash of teeth and eyes. Her words thanked them both but the look was for Henry Starr, who was watching her too, with a studied coolness.

Esterhazy looked at the two of them looking at each other and felt like screaming, but Foley did it for him: "All right! Let's get this show going! Places for the Starr Gang, and for Chrissake let's do it right this time!"

Esterhazy said "Ready," and Foley pushed at the air in front of him, yelling at the riders milling in front of the bank. Miss Woodly stepped up close enough to the camera so that she could have touched Esterhazy's knee. He looked in the viewfinder and framed the Starr Gang. Fourth try today, the Starr Gang has robbed the bank and rides out of town. Esterhazy centered the field on Henry Starr—it was easy to pick him up because of the strange pale horse he rode, a " 'paloosa" they called it, as weird to Esterhazy's eye as a zebra: the front three-quarters of its body a lovely marble-mottled gray-white, black mane and tail, and a brilliant white rump splashed with irregular spots like dashes of black paint. It shone like a full moon against the bay mounts of the other riders, and he saw the outlaw turn his horse and ride a little bit toward the camera, flourishing his hat to attract Esterhazy's attention.

He was grinning. "Don't stop!" he yelled. "Keep it on me and don't stop!"

"Ready to roll it, Esterhazy!" snapped Foley. "Start the camera first. *You men!* On my signal, you *go!*"

Esterhazy felt a light touch on his knee. "What does he want?" she asked, and Esterhazy answered, "He just said, 'Don't stop.' "

"Roll it, Esterhazy!"

"Keep it on him," she whispered intensely, "keep it on him the whole time and don't stop till he does," and Esterhazy had no time to think then because Foley yelled "GO!" and the Starr Gang's horses reared back and away from the railing in front of the bank, Starr's moon-rumped Appaloosa pivoting on its rear legs and the other four mimicking its motion just one tick behind as if someone had been drilling them, and then they were firing blanks in the air, at the bank, at the camera and gathering to a gallop across the false fronts of the street as the camera panned after them, Esterhazy fixed on the brilliant black-splattered rump of the horse so that the camera was on the spot when the rider behind Starr reeled in his seat and dropped a sack full of "money"—and who told him to do that? Foley was cursing *Cut dammit, cut!*—but Esterhazy kept turning the crank, a little faster now because it was all going so fast that the motion would need to be slower in the final image, as Henry Starr wheeled and came back, his crazy zebra-horse flashing brightly backwards against the rush of the dark horses, the outlaw tipping off the side of his horse toward the camera and sweeping the sack up out of the dust, reining the animal back with the same motion and splashing dust back toward the bank as he whirled the horse on a dime, the horse springing back into full gallop in two strides as Henry Starr flashed out of the viewfinder leaving banners of dust shining in the vacated air.

"Did you get all that?" she asked softly, and Esterhazy said "Yes," glancing swiftly down at her. "He told *you* what he . . . ?"

She shook her head *no*, but did not say how she had known or guessed what Henry Starr had in mind. "He just knew you could get all of it," she said.

Foley was standing off to the side, his megaphone held limply in his left hand. "I don't believe this, I don't believe my goddamn luck. The son of a bitch stands around here like a wooden Indian, messes up three takes, then that yokel drops the goddamn bag and he does this *stunt* . . . What do you want to bet if we ask him to do that on purpose he falls off the goddamn horse?"

"You won't need to ask him," said Esterhazy. He pointed to the camera: "I got all of it."

Foley glared at him, hands on hips. "I thought I told you to cut." He shifted his glare to Miss Woodly, then back to Esterhazy. "I still give the orders here."

"Yes," said Esterhazy, lamely. "Didn't hear you." He looked back into the square frame of the viewfinder, and felt her moving away toward her buggy, while Foley yelled Starr and the riders back. *I'm sorry*, he thought to himself, as if being politic were something to be ashamed of.

He watched the outlaw trot his horse back to the set, saying nothing to anyone, smiling a little to himself at a secret joke, moving easily through the air in exact harmony with the motion of the animal. What was working in that criminal intelligence, what did he mean by that little game with the horse? Not just the circus trick to impress Miss Blue Eyes: but that business before, *Don't stop!* he says, and she's in on it, the little Miss Woodly—*Keep it on him till he stops*.

They were too much for him, these Americans, the men and the women alike—well, perhaps he could figure out the girl, big men and big money, what else? But the Famous Outlaw, who was a grown man obviously capable of making his way by himself, who was neither an ambitious young lady nor a poor Hunky immigrant: what was in this business for him, that he should put himself under the thumb of men like Foley and Poole and Wilberforce?

That was the question that bothered Miss Woodly too, after the first blush of her triumph had passed like whiskey heat—a cold finger touched her in the eye of her chest and made her suddenly tense and watchful. Riding the forward drive of her conquests of Wilberforce and Poole, she had taken Henry Starr's agreement as the natural response to her own irresistible charge. But on second thought she was not so sure. There were things about Henry Starr that just didn't add up. He was old enough to be her father, but she found it almost impossible to see that age in him. He had a quality that was more like an older brother than a father, and sometimes—like today, when he had grinned at her and played that trick on Foley and Esterhazy, snatching the bag of bogus money out of the street like Tom Mix—he seemed more like a younger brother, reckless in his play, let the big ones worry about broken necks. But then under the grin and the joking there was a frightening intensity in the way he looked at everything; she had felt it that first day when he came to the set and she had dared him to show her how it was done, and he had showed her . . . brother, he *had*, and she grinned a grin that went right down to her feet when she thought of that lard-assed bull-bragging Deputy Price cringing under his arms, yelling "Don't kill me!"

But how could the man who terrorized Deputy Price, the man whose eyes fastened on you like a pair of hands gripping and lifting you by your shirtfront—how could that man let himself be patronized by Poole and Wilberforce, and accept Foley's bullying? Did he need so badly just to be in the movies? Maybe Henry Starr's weakness was vanity; to be a little famous and celebrated, he'd let himself be made to look ridiculous. Men were constructed that way, they could be absolutely shameless about it, overriding their own intelligence and dignity and common sense if they thought you could satisfy the hunger their vanity made in them. It was the idea that Henry Starr had that weakness too that had given her the courage to go forward—although in an odd way it also disappointed her that Henry Starr might be less than what he had seemed the day that he disarmed Price and showed them how it was done in the old days.

But then, just when she and probably everyone else was thinking they had figured the Famous Outlaw out and got him where they wanted him, suddenly he turns it around, shows Esterhazy that he knows how to do pictures, and shows me . . . what, exactly?

That somehow or other Henry Starr had been waiting there all the time, ready if not exactly for *her* then for someone like her, with her kind of project to offer—waiting in ambush as she came stalking so carefully (and so proud of her skill!) down his back trail.

It worried her to think that Henry Starr was really that clever; and it also excited her that he was as smart and watchful as herself—although that excitement seemed dangerous to her, it might fog her vision when she most needed to look out for herself. But maybe now she could begin to show him something too—something of the hidden powers of Miss Barbara Catherine Woodly. "HENRY STARR," she wrote at the head of a big sheet of yellow legal paper: HENRY STARR, by B. C. Woodly. Her *nom de plume*. Also her *nom de cashier*—B. C. WOODLY on the wooden plaque on her teller's cage at Wilberforce's bank—another of those coverts in which a woman had to conceal herself in order to get her work done in a world of men.

She was a good deal younger and newer to things than she meant anybody to know. She declared herself twenty-seven years old, and when she put on her business clothes and composed her face for the bank she carried it off, stepping out with the assurance of someone who had been somewhere and knew where she was going.

But she was twenty-one years old when she stood naked and alone in her skin before the mirror in her furnished room: the up-tip and tightness of her nipples exaggerating the liftiness of her small breasts, reminding her of how recently they had seemed like things that had happened to her rather than part of herself. She could still recall as a kind of glow along the surface of her skin the way she had felt as her daddy's her mommy's little girl-child, peering out of ambush at her mother in the kitchen wrapped in smokes and steams, the smell of beef and carrots and onions, bread and milk, the funk of cheese and churned butter, her mother lifting her head to look out the window and call, "Barbara! Barbara Catherine!"

—And she ducked outside, she'd rather be playing with her brothers in the ranch yard, *they* called her Bob-tail and Bobcat and that was who she really was, someone small and fierce and quick and clever, and her real place was with her brothers in the yard or the barns or swimming naked in the thickety pond hidden in a fold of prairie—her place as much as the house and kitchen were her mother's and the horse barns her father's. There her differences of size and shape and name were powers, there were people and animals only she could become, and more: her brothers needed her quick mind and tongue to make up stories for them to play—

(Although even then—it occurred to her—she had felt some subtle weakness in her position, because she always cast her brothers in the heroic roles, as if she understood that that might be one of the conditions under which they condescended to play with her.)

They did *Treasure Island* and she let them be bold muscular pirates or noble sea captains; she was clever Jim or mad secretive Ben Gunn or calculating crippled Long John, whose crutch was a disguised weapon. They did Jesse James and they were courageous Sheriff Timberlake and sagacious Allan Pinkerton, but she was Jesse, whom they could hunt to a back-shotten death but whose name they would sing as they rambled back for supper. They played *Last of the Mohicans* and she cast her brothers as the tall white captain and the sure-shooting scout: but she was Uncas the son of Uncas, the last chief of the noble race of the Mohicans bare-chested and in breechclouts, and they would swell up as she laid the plot out for them, pleased that they would be victors in the end, *never realizing that I had taken the best for myself, the roles of deeper power and knowing, the hero the martyr the hidden chief and unknown Messiah of the Red Race: that underneath the mask, the hero of the story was always me.*

When she looked over her shoulder, back toward the house from the middle of their play, she sometimes saw her mother come from the kitchen to stand in the doorway; and even if she said nothing, there was a suggestion, almost a command in her presence there, that told Barbara Catherine she wasn't unique at all, was out of place in the middle of her brothers' play: because her mother could see through her masks, and even through the hidden heroic shape that she dreamed for herself behind the mask—her mother saw that the truth of it was that Barbara Catherine Woodly was a girl, "only a girl," whose true place was the smell and smoke of the kitchen, whose work was a matter of feeding the men and boys for their exploits and play, arranging the place they would come back to—played out, tired with pleasure, the best of them spent before they put their butts to the bench and their lips to the spoon.

There was a league of her mother and aunts, sister-women, a kind of conspiracy against her play. She was a girl, she was going to be a woman, someone for whom her kind of play was wrong, "regrettable" —not sin, exactly, not the kind of thing that went with talk of hell and falling into a pit, but something for mothers and aunts to shake the head and look sad about. It was time she started acting like a girl, not a tomboy: a girl was someone more interested in finding ways to keep dirt off her body than in inventing new ways to get dirty. It was time she got ready to be a woman: a woman was someone whose body was shaped for weakness, for houses and kitchens—burdened with breasts, hips and legs badly put on so they could no longer fork a horse but had to set together for support, skirts and dresses weakly fluttering in every breeze not hardly competent to the task of covering what women were afraid to let anyone see.

Bobcat Uncas Woodly at eleven in warpaint and breechclouts was lean and smooth and swift whether covered or naked, and now when she saw or felt her mother's eyes on her it gave her play a keen bright edge like the blade of a knife, as if she sharpened herself against her mother's look and expectations. When they learned to ride half-broken ranch horses, her brothers had merely to master their own ignorance and fear and their mounts' resistance; she had to ride down all three, and then overcome or circumvent her mother's fear and the disapproval with which she infected Bobcat's father (whom she called "Mr. Woodly"). The afternoon Bobcat forked Old Addie's unbroken two-year-old and with her mother looking on in terror rode him bucking and bolting out of the corral and into the yard it felt as if girl that she was she had absorbed the whole strength of the animal through her thighs and crotch and hips and would be mounted now forever, transformed like a girl in a Greek myth into a female centaur, and never go like a woman on foot or in a buckboard again—her mother was watching from the door as the colt tore through the corner of the kitchen garden and kicked the laundry bucket till it rang like a gong and there would be hell to pay, but Barbara Catherine Cowboy would pay it gladly . . .

Only (now that she remembered it) there hadn't been more than a little clucking—that and a look in her mother's eyes that was like fear or physical pain, and her mother's long fingers had made red marks clutching her own forearms as if she had thought that grip could be magically transferred to Barbara Catherine on her crazy mustang. But all she said was "I never knew you could ride a horse like that." If it had been her father saying that (her father was angry about being disobeyed and "having the stock ruined"), if it had been her father she'd have said that that was praise: but what was it coming from a soft, breast-burdened woman who had to ride buckboards to church, whose play was feeding men and boys and cleaning up after their games?

She had never asked. She had been afraid that the answer would still be that she had to give up games and boys and horses and heroics, give up her horseback strength and pride and she couldn't bear . . .

And then, suddenly, what she wanted stopped mattering to everyone but herself. The shape in the doorway got inside her—the sister-women were right, it had been inside her all along—and now it began to come up in her, her form swelling out painfully into breasts and inward till she bled inside and felt crazy with weakness. It was like her changing body breathed some kind of poison all around that made her father avoid her and brought the sister-women like flies to meat. It made her brothers suddenly serious and rude and cut the strings of their play like a knife, it killed in their eyes the excited joy they had had taking her words and playing them out; putting in its place a sniggering private thing that they had together and she was the butt of. They began spoiling the games with their *looking* at her, and with *looking* and laughing they stripped away all her disguises and names (Uncas the son of Uncas!) to make her see herself all new and naked and silly looking, her smooth bare chest broken by tender points, her newly erupted brush flaring against the milkiness of her smooth belly and thighs like the brilliant target flag of a whitetail against its smooth dark fur, the cleft of her sex and buttocks seeming to deepen and darken like a split to expose in her a secret and unsuspected core of vulnerability.

She closed in on herself, curling around that core of what she thought was weakness, as if the inward curve of her sex was a command to *be hidden* and her brothers' jaunty outward jut the sign of their rule over everything visible.

But with the shame there was also the gift of a kind of power, which at first she despised, mourning the lost world she had once made of words and peopled with brothers—a power that registered in the changing eyes of boys and grown men too when they watched her pass, their eyes filling with smoke and a hapless thickening in the groin, turning helplessly like mares when a stallion's scent comes by.

She chose her time for *that* the same way she picked the time for leaping Old Addie's wild colt and buck-jumping him out of the corral and through the kitchen garden, letting her edge come up to the keenness she needed for cutting loose, and when she knew it was something she could do: did it. She picked one of her oldest brother's friends, a big nice awkward blockhead of a boy named Curly Joe—who in the whole crowd that loitered after school, cock-proud and coolly disdainful of the girls whose secret places they were really greedy-mad to get into, was the only one who would just go flat-out red in the face and hopelessly pokey in the crotch of his jeans whenever she walked by. He was two years older in the heat of that June when she turned seventeen, but she had to choose *him*, and lead him to the hayloft in her father's horse barn, and tell him yes and show him where and how with her own hands, and she was right about him because he wasn't proud or cocky (only awkward-blunt, too quick and so a little hurtful), and afterwards grateful and embarrassed for *himself*.

Then there was only the terror of two weeks to get through till she was sure she did not have any stupid little Curly Joe baby growing in her belly—only that and then she could say that her girlhood was done with, and the ranch and the brothers and Mr. Woodly her father, and her mother standing in the doorway: silenced now, no use calling because Barbara Catherine was gone.

She had enough book learning to be about anything short of a schoolteacher that a woman was allowed to be—clerk, secretary, bank teller —and brains enough to make her good at whatever work she put her mind to. But cleverness wasn't all, and certainly wasn't enough (she knew that much) to get ahead with. Her power was in her body, which she held like a fine, high-strung animal that belonged to her, at first jealously, under the eyes of the men who employed her . . .

But the more jealously she held herself, the more their eyes tugged hungrily at her or shifted between hunger and a dangerous rising anger, so that she didn't know whether the man was someone she could handle or someone to be afraid of.

There was something rising inside her body too, something like hunger and like angry pride, something weak but with it something that had the feel of the strength she had taken from the wild colt held in the controlling grip of her knees, and she wanted to let that strength out, to let it play and feel itself, knowing it was a dangerous kind of strength, to herself and others. But she had to test it, had to learn how to put its powers to use in the world.

She made mistakes, the first one a reckless *yes* thrown back in the grinning teeth of the Assistant Manager of the Coffeyville Bank after she'd worked there a week; there was obviously no other way to make him stop leering and preening and bullying her and why shouldn't she, she had seen the elephant, she had learned how to take care of herself taking her own pleasure too. He'd come over with whiskey in his breath, the front of his trousers loaded with a lump of iron that was so magnetized to her crotch it didn't hardly let him say hello let alone give her a chance to take breath, but kept slamming him up against her till he had hammered her back to her bed, spread her legs and stripped her underpants like a man tearing off corn husks, nailed himself into her and pounded as hard and fast as he could till he beat them both flat—and the next day it was sniggers and hee-haws with the other men in the bank, the rest of them preening and pointing toward her as if she now bore some kind of target between her legs.

*Don't give yourself away for nothing, or they will make you pay for it.*

So she would be more careful of herself the next time, not letting the proud animal in her body show itself except in small ways—placating ways, since they would not let her simply ignore the demand that rose in them when they looked at her, it made them furious when she refused to notice. But part payment was not enough, was worse than none at all: "You lead a man on, Barbara," said the manager of the Sapulpa Bank and Trust, "and then you don't pay off. It's cheap, really cheap of you. If a man promised something like you do, he'd pay off." She had pride and a sense of honor; if this was a horse-trading world, all right: she wasn't asking special treatment, she'd play fair—but only when it was too late and he had finished himself wetly off inside her did he tell her he was married and pulled back quickly and efficiently, buttoning himself into his pants, moving toward the door at the same time: and the next day there was a note on her desk, and the next teller smirked and said "Promoted?" but it was notice that she had been fired.

*They talk fair play, but the game they play is cat and mouse, it ends when they've had their fill. When that's done you can forget fair play, hell you can even forget thanks for the feed. All right. I won't make that mistake again.*

It was a cruel lesson, there was a mocking sneer in it: the odor of her hidden sex that gave her whatever power she had in a world of men was the very thing that opened her so dangerously when they came confidently blundering at her, eyes blind with the smoke of their own desire. She had to learn to use that blindness as a concealment, a space in which to keep herself, in which to grow.

She would find more space in a bigger city: Tulsa, and the big Chemical–Cattlemen's Bank on Main Street. Bank President Wilberforce was a soft cushion stuffed with money, his wife looked like a maiden aunt. He would walk about his bank like a pasha in a harem, winking at his "girls," parting his jacket to display the splendid gold length of his watch chain—but if a girl winked back, he popped his eyes wide and bustled away in fastidious agitation, brushing at himself as if the wink were a slick of dust.

If she had just wanted safety she could perhaps have found it there, adopting the protective coloration of ink-stained hands and dowdy dresses and pallid indoor cheeks. But the proud animal inside her wouldn't be quiet: there were things she wanted for herself, not just money but a name for who and what she was, a name she could sit up on like it was a good horse, a name that showed her strength and her powers—but what were her powers, other than what she could do to men by looking back at them a certain way?

She remembered: she had never felt more powerful and more herself than when she spun those stories of hers like webs in which she and her brothers played and played.

And Banker Wilberforce was not only a banker—he was the half owner of the Pan American Motion Picture Company.

She would be careful and disciplined now: not putting herself boldly forward, only dressing herself in colors, letting her hair shine and fall freely—shaking it sometimes so that you could no more fail to notice her than you could miss a branch of peach blossom on a heap of firewood. Wilberforce's bulky form gravitated toward her, then shied away when her look answered his. She picked her time and one day when he turned to flee he nearly bumped into her; she had jumped into the middle of his retreat and he couldn't brush her dust off his clothes without brushing her . . . and then the flattery of her attentive closeness warmed his belly and face, he beamed at her—a little nervously still, but this was none of his fault, if the young lady wanted to put herself forward he was not morally responsible—and she read in his face that he would not take responsibility for any of it, not even to name his own desire, when it came to *that* she would have to name it for him.

It took only two or three trips to the lot for her to decide that being an actress was not the form of her desire. Alice Farnham was immersed every working moment in the glare of men's eyes, hungry, demanding, sullen with repressed anger. But to be the hand behind those scenes, the weaver of stories that all these men and women would play out, and finally print on the blank screens of a thousand theaters "Photoplay by B. C. Woodly"—that smart young woman, that rider of wild horses, that proud fierce female animal—that was the shape of her desire.

She wove her tales on yellow pages in her room at night, gave them to Wilberforce to read by day, and at first he beamed at her, patting her shoulder as if he were a visiting dignitary and she a schoolgirl whose composition had won first prize. But the stories sank into Wilberforce's attention like raisins into suet pudding. He was ready enough to praise her efforts but to take them on his own initiative and put them before the company was beyond him.

His colleague Mr. Poole though—he was another sort entirely. Whenever Wilberforce brought her to their offices or to the lot he would watch her, not just with the angry smoky lust of Director Foley (although that was also in his look), but with a sharper more insistent focus, his eyes at once careless and intent—the way an angry man, idling for a minute, will look at a twig while his fingers peel and strip its bark down to the slick naked layer, running his thumbnails in to split out the pith; the twig isn't the thing he's really interested in, but there it is in his hand.

Poole would not wait for her to name his desire; and if he waited to hear her desire it would only be to ascertain the exact terms under which he would lay his claim to her. She knew what came after that, the rage and punishment if she said no, the contemptuous humiliation and dismissal after she had said yes. Either way she might be cracked in splintering halves like the stripped twig and chucked on the tinder pile. But if she didn't risk herself with Poole she might be stopped, with the suety bulk of the banker between her and the world she belonged in, the world she could remake to the shape of her will and imagination.

And then Henry Starr had come along and showed her how it was done in the old days, and it was bright-blinding like the flash of magnesium powder that the newspaper cameramen used in the bank, printing pictures with light and shadow reversed on the inside of her eyelids—the idea came to her that quickly and she jumped at it, threw herself on it with the same sense of danger and power that put her up on Old Addie's black colt . . .

Well: not quite the same. Because she was no little girl in her home ranch yard now, keening her edge against her mother's softness, but a woman who was on her own hands, a woman who knew things like the need to keep hidden while you played your game and worked your powers in a world of men. But what her mother might have said to her about all of this—the men she had let put the nail to her, and Wilberforce, and Poole whom she never *exactly* promised to—that was something she would never hear. She imagined it would be something a good deal worse than what her mother might have thought (but didn't actually say) about little girls riding wild mustangs. The grief this time would be real tears and her face twisted in a knot, it was worse than "regrettable"—what do you call it, what do you feel when someone blood of your blood and name of your name disappears into some deep black pit?—and how would her mother grip herself this time, so hard as to leave the marks of her fingers in her flesh, if she meant to send her daughter the power to hold on . . . to hold on to what, exactly? But the figure in the doorway was gone, finally and utterly evaded, her rebukes and her silent call from the doorway irretrievable.

## TULSA *May 2, 1921*

She had brought the project to Poole: because he was smart enough for cleverness to work with him, because he wanted more than just money out of the movie company, as he wanted more out of herself than one night pounding his nail between her legs. He needed a project that would allow him to push Wilberforce and Foley aside, and mark the company as his own. That was what she could give him.

They had sat in his office at the Tulsa *Lamp* with his desk between them and the editorial staff roaring and teeming on the other side of the glass door, but she heard none of it and the desk wasn't much of a barrier between them. She was on her own with him, under his eye, and he was watchful—every statement between them was in code, and they both knew it. It made her nervous. He seemed amused.

She had laid out her idea for a movie about the life of Henry Starr, sweetening it to his taste: an historical film, of the kind she knew he wished to make, something with the seriousness and scale of *Birth of a Nation*.

Had she seen that movie? he wondered. There was more to it than scale and historical detail, a vision of *historical forces* at work, the proving out of certain moral and social values . . . Did she understand what he meant?

Oh yes, she did. She looked down shyly. "I read your editorials. I've heard you talk to Foley often enough . . ." Foley: they needed to talk about Foley: she shared Poole's belief that Foley didn't understand the potential of motion pictures for portraying historical forces and values. If his role could somehow be limited?

But then who would direct?

Esterhazy.

"Hmmm. Foley will insist on playing some role. I'm not sure I wish to drive him into leaving us. Esterhazy: a foreigner, and untried. Perhaps we can keep Foley at work on other projects, but he will have to have an editorial role, reviewing the finished work. Of course, I'll work closely with him at that stage," Poole said, "so the original vision is not compromised for merely technical reasons."

He smiled. She smiled back. They understood each other. But he kept looking at her anyway, until she blushed.

"And then there is yourself," said Poole. "I am risking a good deal, placing so much trust in you."

"I do appreciate . . ." she said, holding her eyes steadily on his.

"Yes," he said, "I'm perfectly certain that you do."

Closing Poole's office door behind her she felt light as a locust husk, drained, her dress was wet in the armpits and down the back and she smelled herself—a little rank and salty, the smell of her clothes after a day with the cows on her father's farm. Then suddenly the closed door became the sign of recovered safety, and the lightness became a sense of powerful lift. She had won herself as good an arrangement as she had hoped for, because it freed her to work with Esterhazy and Henry Starr, freed her to make the script with them, talking over Henry Starr and his life, playing it out on horseback and on foot. Daydreaming, she saw Esterhazy and Henry Starr glowing with the pleasure of the dreams in which she wrapped them.

Then she wondered what her two colleagues would think of her work on their behalf. She would have liked to tell them . . . but that would run against her first and only wisdom, which was that for someone like herself to do anything, she would have to keep her powers hidden.

## TULSA *May 6, 1921*

From the covert of the teller's cages she watched Henry Starr and Esterhazy arrive together. They were to sign the contracts today. The uniformed bank guard bowed them in, and the long leisurely strokes of the Negro janitor's broom seemed to smooth a shining path for them across the marble floor to the low railing that segregated Wilberforce's reception area from the main lobby.

A few feet away was a man in farm boots, overalls and a worn khaki army shirt, talking with a man behind a desk, ARMBRUSTER: VICE-PRESIDENT, LOANS—a smooth-faced man with a clean shirt and a sharp-looking bow tie. They were talking crop loans, talking wheat. "Trade's down. Price's down," said Armbruster with a shrug.

Miss Woodly opened the barrier and walked softly toward her colleagues, who were too busy to notice.

"You read the contracts?" Henry Starr asked Esterhazy.

He shrugged. "Is usual thing. We work, they keep pictures and money."

Henry Starr looked closely at Esterhazy. "I don't know how to rate the money on a job like this."

"Is all right," said Esterhazy, "for first time, is even not bad. We shoot what we want, they don't like it, they bury it."

"They put money into it, they won't bury it," said Henry Starr, and Esterhazy said no, unless it was more junk than usual, "and if I shoot it," he said, "won't be junk."

"Nor will it be if I write it," said Miss Woodly and she could see she had ambushed them again—men were easy to catch at things, judging by her brothers and these two. She smiled. Her light hair was gathered into itself to make a businesslike bun, and the sleeves of her white blouse were bunched above the elbows by black garters.

Henry Starr's surprise became a smile. "Well," he said, "it's a good thing you're with us."

Her smile stayed set, but she felt herself drain out from behind it. Was Henry Starr making fun of her, or was he trying to shift the weight of responsibility for what happened next onto her shoulders? She couldn't read him, and that upset her—almost as much as the thought of seeing Poole again, whom she could read too entirely well.

The conversation between Armbruster and the farmer suddenly got hotter, a fortunate distraction.

"Goddamnit," said the farmer, his screwed-down voice sounding loud in the bankerly hush, "I got my wife and kids to millwork bringing in cash, I got my vet's bonus on the way and you just sit there and—"

"Shuh-shuh," said Mr. Armbruster, "let's not . . ."

"Mr. Starr?" said the receptionist. "Mr. Esterhazy? Miss Woodly?" Wilberforce's office door opened behind her.

Wilberforce rose from behind his desk like the moon coming over a rise, there was Poole lounging a little in a leather armchair and Foley scowling in the corner.

There was a hubbub from the bank behind them, and when they turned to look they saw that the farmer was standing arguing loudly with Mr. Armbruster—the uniformed guard had come over, and the Negro janitor paused in his sweeping to lean on his broom and watch, and somehow despite the farmer's loud yammering the clearest words were Armbruster saying very calmly that there was no use, none at all, in making this kind of fuss, but if he wanted to make it a *police* matter that was just fine with . . .

The farmer shrugged the guard's hands off, took three steps toward the door, then turned and violently kicked the Negro janitor's broom—grabbed the broom and shoved it into the Negro's chest, knocking him to the floor. "Keep this nigger out of my sight!" yelled the man, jabbing his finger at Armbruster so they were goddamn sure they took his meaning. "You just keep him out of my sight!"

The receptionist shut the door.

The contracts were on Wilberforce's big desk, long sheets of paper with Gothic-lettered "Whereas"s at the head, and numbered paragraphs, down to the signature blanks for the parties of the first part and the parties of the second.

Mr. Wilberforce cleared his throat and began. He allowed that the whole procedure was somewhat extraordinary, but since his colleague Mr. Poole had agreed with Miss Woodly that there should be special arrangements . . .

He looked around, beaming indulgently, and Miss Woodly smiled back at him; if she didn't show him she understood how very generous he was being, he might start fussing.

Wilberforce settled in his chair. They would find everything as Mr. Poole and Miss Woodly had agreed. The production to be in the hands of Miss Woodly and Mr. Esterhazy, in association with Mr. Starr, subject to the general advice of Mr. Poole and budgetary constraints agreed on by the contracting parties. Script to be provided by Miss Woodly, after consultation with Messrs. Esterhazy and Starr as to (a) the technical feasibility of filming each scene and (b) the historical veracity of the depiction. The company to retain all rights to distribution and/or sale of the finished product, and was to exercise through its designee, Mr. Foley here, the right to make such editorial amendments as appeared prudent and conducive to the financial success of the venture. Messrs. Esterhazy and Starr and Miss Woodly would receive in consideration salaries as previously agreed, plus a royalty on the film's net receipts. Was this satisfactory? Mr. Esterhazy? Mr. Starr?

She felt a spark of resentment that Wilberforce had taken her agreement for granted, but she knew that was unreasonable—after all, she had been the one to propose it so . . . then she realized with a pang that Wilberforce had as much as put her in the same party with Poole and himself, that made the contracts and left Esterhazy and Henry Starr only the right to say yes or no.

Esterhazy seemed to think the deal was all right—she was relieved.

Henry Starr held himself erect and watchful, like he was sitting a horse and scanning for sign on the horizon, on Poole's face—then he shifted suddenly to look at her as if he was going to ask a question, but he said nothing.

For an instant she wondered what he would do if she shook her head *no*—but why should she, when this was exactly what she had worked to achieve? She shot a look at Poole, whose long face was blank and bland.

She looked back at Henry Starr and nodded her head.

He smiled at her, reached the pen off Wilberforce's desk and signed his name with a flourish. "There you are," he said with a smile, "party of the second part, for as long as the grass shall grow and the waters flow."

Miss Woodly found herself once again drenched in sweat.

"Well," said Poole, "now that's done we can get to work. I know you mean to start looking over locations as soon as you can." They rose to go, sidling toward the door as if they were afraid to show their backs to the banker, the editor and the sullen director. Poole had a satisfied smirk on his face; as they reached the door he said, "Oh by the way Miss Woodly," and she stilled like a bird at a twig snap. "You haven't thought of a title since our"—there was the least hesitation—"*conversation*, have you?"

She hadn't, as he well knew, and she frowned when she realized that the point of his asking was simply to display to all present that she had had a private and very special conversation with him—that perhaps Mr. Poole could have such private talks with her whenever he wished. She saw that Wilberforce had taken the point in his fashion, which was to pretend nothing existed but the papers he rearranged on his desk. Henry Starr she did not dare look at.

Poole warmed to the subject. "Well, I've given it some thought and come up with one we might use: *Henry Starr: A Debtor to the Law.*" He shifted his smile to Henry Starr. "I was remembering that fine speech you made at the opening, about paying one's debt to society, and it seemed to sum it all up quite nicely—*Henry Starr: A Debtor to the Law*"

Miss Woodly's lips tucked downward in a frown—it was supposed to be her movie.

"Just think it over," said Poole, "I don't insist: I only advise." He shifted his eyes to Henry Starr. "I'm afraid I must also offer some advice to our principal performer. My newspaper's informants in our colored community tell me that you put in an appearance at the opening of our films at the Dreamland Theater in Greenwood. We have now a considerable investment in you, Mr. Starr, and in the success of this film. What private associations you may have are your own affair, but your public reputation directly affects the value of our investment. Given the state of the public mind, and the conditions of your parole from prison, I would . . . *advise* discretion."

Henry Starr stood quite still.

That was all.

Poole blinked and his face flushed red.

Henry Starr just stood there in perfect stillness, and the quiet went on a shade too long, began to take on some of the terrible implications that had been there on the movie lot when Henry Starr had stood in the too close wind of Price's breath, stood there till Price had to break away—as Poole himself had to do, abruptly turning to chatter something businesslike at Wilberforce, who was still sullenly shuffling the contracts.

Miss Woodly felt the blood spark into the points of her cheeks—she saw Henry Starr's compact stillness as proof that he was impervious to any thought or look or word of Poole's, and as they left the office she felt that it strengthened her position to have him on her side—and he *was* on her side, wasn't he? Because before he had signed the contract he had looked to her . . .

Why to her? If he was that cool and strong and compact in himself, why did he look to her before he signed?

She didn't know the answer, and she took that as a warning to keep her eyes open; Henry Starr was altogether a trickier case than he looked. The surface was all simplicity of speech and action—the hand flashing out to snap the gun up out of the deputy's holster, the body leaning off the side of the galloping horse to snatch the money bag out of the dust right in front of the camera—but behind that there was something uncanny, as if his body were a thicket in which the real Henry Starr was hid out, watching you from ambush, casing you like a bank.

*I can't read him at all. Why would a man who could ride like an Apache, shoot like Buffalo Bill, play a crowd like Billy Sunday and generally take care of himself like Henry Starr want to put himself in the hands of men like Poole and Wilberforce and Foley?*

Or, for that matter, in the hands of someone like herself, a young woman strange to him, with no name or record of her own for him to know and trust?

# Used to Be

## FORT SMITH PRISON *July 21, 1896*

*What do you want to call this day? Second day of Cherokee Bill's conjure to get him a gun or a knife or something to kill that big Eoff/oaf guard with, and while he's at it why not the key to the prison and a clear road back to the Nations. Or you can call it three-days-left till they hang Cherokee Bill; or four-days-left till they hang me. Pouring water out of a mug to make it run, a flat lead slug not a bullet and no tobacco to change, even if that old-time powwow muck-a-muck worked, which you know damn well it don't, it don't work for god-sure certain if you do it wrong.*

They brought Cherokee Bill and Henry Starr food in their cells. A guard and kitchen trusty came by, left the plate of cereal and the mug of coffee that was breakfast; and at noon the plate of bread and beans with salt pork that was lunch. He put his hand to the bread, spoon to the beans, put the food up to his face. It was just too damned ignorant for Henry Starr to sit there not eating for the sake of a conjure that couldn't work even if you believed in conjures, which he did not. But his stomach turned on him. No matter what his head told him, his belly seemed to want a piece of Cherokee Bill's conjure more than it wanted food. *Maybe Grandfather was right about two bloods in one body.*

Suppertime: he heard Eoff's voice even before the corridor door whanged open. The big guard pushed that loud bellow of his along in front of him the way a man would pole-prod a bad-looking piece of swamp. The sour salty smell of the stew came with him. He came up to Henry Starr's barred door with a rolling shoulder swagger and as the Creek trusty shoved the tin-covered bowl of stew through the door slot Eoff slapped a folded sheet of paper on top of it. "You are one lucky nigger-loving Injun," he said, his bark banging an echo off the stone wall. "Just you take a look at that and thank God they're gonna string you up legal." Eoff's red face split in a hectic grin, as if his big square teeth had suddenly swole on him so his mouth couldn't hold them. His little blue eyes ran right-left-right in his head. "Got one for your nigger too," he said loudly, then jerked himself away as if it took muscular effort to uproot him from Henry Starr and start him toward Cherokee Bill.

*If you don't like the work, why do it?* Henry Starr said in his head. But the saying was to put off the looking. Down the corridor he heard Eoff's yammer at Cherokee Bill but didn't listen enough to hear the words.

Well, he must look at it, knowing already what it had to be. He unfolded it and let his breath escape. Well, it was that thing. You've seen more than you want to count and something about them was always the same, like the pictures of Jesus cut up and staked out they show at the Catholic missions, the same pink guts in the same ripped-open chest. But still each one was different enough so you knew each picture meant a different man dead in a different place, with his own kind of screams maybe, or his own silence in the face of what it was they were doing to him.

It was a handbill on coarse paper such as the Klan would send to advertise a lynching. The date and place below the picture never belonged to what the picture showed, which had to be of a lynching done before and somewhere else; so the picture told you not just how some man had once been made to die, but like a prophet dream it told you what was going to happen to someone else on the night they named, someone maybe reading the handbill himself like Henry Starr was doing now, seeing:

The pinioned body twisting against those ropes used to be a man, but it wasn't anymore because there was the ragged blot of black where the legs forked like a hairy cunt in a whore picture which was where they had cut it all out of him. The smooth torso arched with the pain as if it was a bow strung with twisted rawhide, the cords of the throat stood plain, the head was flung back so hard that half of it was missing as if they'd chopped off his face and brain above the jaw—all of it frozen fiercely dead-stopped right there in black and white.

If you looked at it hard it might seem to waver, but that was you that wavered; it never did, it was always there. There was a can of coal oil by its bare right foot; the foot was flat-soled, pale to the body as if the foot had been stepped into pale dust or flour. The white faces and bodies crowded up all around behind it and bulged in from the margins, as if the bulk of the crowd was outside the handbill frame shoving itself into it with a huge pressure: as if the body opened and blotted out in the fork of its legs was something they needed to feed their eyes deeply on, like their eyes had to have it, had to eat up every last bit of the thing that they had made to be. And one man with a round face and a small mustache looked straight out of the handbill and into your eyes and pointed down at the thing, his face tight and swollen with something bulging behind it, popping the eyes a little and spreading the lips, a small smile and proud and terrified and reckless, glorified that the eye of the man reading the handbill was on him. That made Henry Starr think of a man standing there, taking the picture of this, and he saw the crowd bulging in from outside the frame, too big to all fit in, must be a whole damned county back there, trying to fill your eyes with themselves too, so you'd see them there, making the thing that they had made in the night there.

The more Henry Starr looked at it the more it still kept happening, the cut body and the chopped face and the crowd bulging in and the man pushing his swollen face and its little just-et smile at the man looking into the camera to take the picture, at the man looking now at the picture. All of it was always there every time he looked, never different, like a remembered thing that will not become just a dream but keeps coming out and being there. This picture was all these people had ever been and all they could be: the nigger they'd caught and cut, and listened to him screaming while some of them did the work on him, knives and razors and hard hands and their eyes eating it up; and throwing on the coal oil to burn him, and looking while they was doing it and making this thing out of him and making a picture of themselves that would make it keep happening forever just the same way.

He heard distantly the loud blat of Eoff's laugh. He heard, loud enough to fill his ears, the silence of Cherokee Bill that was his answer. *How will he kill that bastard? I don't know yet, but Cherokee Bill seems to know, and that fat-gut peckerwood oaf-bastard, he seems to know too. That's why he can't let it alone. Got to play with it to show how scared of it he ain't. And he'll poke and poke at it till it just reaches right out and bites the feet from under him. What the hell kind of conjure is it that that kind of fear makes, that it makes you make your worst vision be?*

He looked in the eyes of the handbill man again. *I know your eyes,* he thought. *You are afraid of a thing so much that it ain't enough to just kill it, you got to cut it, you got to cut its balls and its pecker off, you got to make it bleed, you got to make it beg, you got to cut mouths into every part of it so it begs its blood and its guts and its slimes for you, you got to stuff yourself up on its begging so that you ain't never going to be hungry for anything again. "Look: look how I made him beg me like I was God like I was Jesus Christ Almighty, look how I make him start and make him stop, look how I make him a woman, look how I made him an animal, look how I make him into meat and garbage, look look look.*''

Henry Starr still looked at the handbill: the man with the swollen face wouldn't stop tipping his small smile and pointing at the thing he had made, which Henry Starr no more could stop looking at than the others bulging in from outside the white box that framed the picture. He hated having to do it, it put him right in there next to Mr. Handbill Man, who he'd like to grab by the throat and ram a knife into his gut and rip it up to the throat so that all that ugly stuff inside the man could just come sliding and pouring out like a load of entrails slololloping out of a hooked hog—like it wasn't enough to just kill the man but he had to . . .

He had to get out of there, out of that picture. He looked at the blank wall of his cell. *Grandfather*, he thought in spite of himself.

The big heavy head framed in its lead-colored braids resolves itself on the wall of the cell. He's got the tinted glasses that Henry Starr gave him the day of the rodeo in Tahlequah, the left lens busted out—but instead of the eye in its wrinkled lips there's a hole. There's nothing.

''*Do you want me to die for you? A man might cut the cords of his blood for his own, but you are none of mine. You said what you wanted me to eat: aren't you satisfied that I ate it? I ate shame for you once; not again.*''

## BARTLESVILLE, CHEROKEE NATION *Summer, 1886*

. . . Henry Starr was riding for Roberts on the Standard Ranch. He owned boots and shirt and pants and a good broad-brimmed hat all paid for with his own money earned from Roberts, with a saddle just about worked out to put on the horses they gave him to ride. He had the name of being a good man on a horse. He had all of that and more: the name of Tom Starr's grandson, and the ghostly shapes of all those others swelling out around him—Tom and Hop Starr, Aunt Belle and Little Pearl, Cole Younger, Buck and Dingus James, all that tribe that was as famous in the Territory as presidents and judges and chiefs of the Nation.

This time he had an easy job, and one that showed him a trusted man even at thirteen, taking the buckboard all the way to Bartlesville to pick up packages and bring them back. He had time, a whole day with nothing to do but let the horses find their way through sweetgrass and sunshine to Bartlesville; spend the night on Roberts' account in a clean rooming house, with drummers and ranch foremen and cattle buyers; load up and back the same way in the morning. When he got back he'd be a couple of dollars closer to owning that saddle. On the strength of that he had plumped for a bag of lickrish in Bartlesville to keep his mouth sweet on the road, and a couple of those dime books his mother never wanted him looking at: gaudy forbidden peepholes to the dark side of family history. *Frank James's Vengeance Trial: or, The Doom of the Regulators*—that was Buck James circumventing half a dozen posses to settle with the vigilantes that strung up his youngest brother during the War. *Belle Starr's Wedding; or, The Outlaw Queen's Triumph*—that was Aunt Belle, about ten years younger and any number of times better looking than the real thing. And the best of 'em, *Jesse James's Double Daring; or, Two Banks at One Blow*, by Colonel D'Artagnan Arbuthnot, *damn!* a name almost as good as the book itself. He could read it, looking at the pictures while the horses ambled along the familiar road.

Or there was his "redskin" book to read, or even just to let his mind run on—he knew it inside out and back to front, didn't need but to have it tucked away handy among his gear for its words and pictures to be there for him: the battered copy of James Fenimore Cooper's *Last of the Mohicans*, the original covers torn off long ago and replaced with red cloth stiffened with sizing, the pages blunted and battered and edge-cracked by fifty-odd years of getting shoved into and out of pockets and saddlebags, bought long ago by somebody's grandfather—Ma's must have been, her folks was all for schooling, reading good literature, but it might have been some Starr kin too, one of the uncles who was a judge leaving it as a present for the kids to read. But whoever's it was originally now it was Henry Starr's, because he'd spotted it on the bookshelf stacked with the Sears catalogs, Bible, and the other heavy dark-covered schoolbooks and battered journals and ledgers, hauled a stool over, climbed up—the red cover drawing him—and slipped it out and into his room, opening it to discover its name in secret. Nobody ever asked about it or came to look for it. So it was his, like original finding on a gold claim, almost like it was his making.

He'd just let his eyes touch the cover a little, and let his memory shine up and voice those things that were like a small private bank of dreams. Dark, brave and voluptuous Cora Munro shaking out her heavy black hair, her blood so hot with secret things you wished for someone to pierce her center and find her out. And Hawkeye so cool and deadly, true to his friends, "I am a man without a cross," a free man perfect with his weapons, dealing justice that ran as straight and swift as a bullet from the rifle of a true man. And there was Uncas, who was born to be a king, son of Chingachgook, who was the great father such a king should have: Uncas, whose black eyes could pierce the heart of Cora and strike fear into the evil Magua, Uncas the last of his race standing before the ancient prophet of the Lenape, Old Tamenund: "I am Uncas, the son of Uncas, last chief of the unmixed race of the Mohicans, grandfather of the Lenape!" And Tamenund looked, wondering if the years were running backward and the youth of the Red Man come again . . .

When he raised his eyes Henry Starr saw two men trotting toward him, and he slowed the team to say howdy. They never returned greeting but came up on either side of the wagon and suddenly something in the set of their bodies and their brisk unbroken movement made the blood bump hard in Henry's chest, but by then they were on him right and left jerking rein to a sudden stop. Light flashed from badges over their hearts and on the barrels of pistols swung out from under their coats.

"Thumbs up and stand steady!" snapped the left one, his face a shadow under his hat. Henry stopped the team, dropped the reins, his hands slowly climbing his shoulders as he stared at the man.

He felt the grip on his shirt collar, then something jerked him back, his ribs jabbed and scraped by the side of the wagon as he went over and the ground beat the breath out of him. "I'm gonna blow this little bastard's brains out his mouth," said the horseback shadow above him.

"Take it easy," said the other. Henry Starr stared at the dust and pebbles in front of his nose and heard the other deputy fumbling with the packages in the wagon. He heard a pounding of metal on wood, a crack, a liquid gurgle and the raw smell of whiskey came to him.

Hours later in the jail he was still telling the marshals that he never knew it was whiskey, and it wasn't his whiskey but Mr. Roberts', who was a white man and . . .

"Don't think we stupid, boy. Injuns just love they firewater, don't they? Never saw one could get enough of it. And you just a smart little Injun boy turning a dollar running this corn likker to the bucks down the Nations. Now ain't that it? Ain't you that smart little Injun?"

The other one sat apart, behind a desk, and Henry had to swivel his head to see him. "Oh yeah, he's Henry Starr, ain't he? Kin to that old bastard Tom Starr and that murderin' bitch of a Belle, and probably every other renegade red nigger in the Nations."

Henry Starr licked his lips. "I never done a thing against the law. It ain't my whiskey."

"I bet you want us to let you go," said the first marshal.

Henry was sick with fear and hatred and all he wanted to say was *yes*, but something in the marshal's tone told him that that would be a mistake, that it would somehow set him out there naked for the butt of some terrible joke. So he ate the words and the desire to be set free and it tasted like shit.

"He don't want us to let him go," said the second marshal, smiling. "Maybe he *is* a smart Injun. Maybe he knows what's gonna happen if we let him go, and all those white folks out there waitin' on us to make an arrest of these damned murderin' renegades—too many killin's lately. Was a white woman raped by some buck over the Arkansas line."

The first marshal said, "Well that explains the hangin' talk."

"Myself I'd ruther hang than be cut."

"One they catch is the only one ain't got to decide which. Maybe get 'em both, one after t'other."

*He knew it was a trick but what if it wasn't?*

The second marshal stood up. "I think the kid's an honest Injun." He grinned. "I say we just let him go." He stepped over, his key clicked in the lock of the manacles on Henry Starr's hands. "Go on, kid, git out of here."

Henry Starr didn't move. The nerves of his spine jerked at his hips and thighs but he held himself still; they were joking, maybe not joking.

The first marshal punched him hard in the back with a blunt fist and he felt the blood rush to the spot. "Come on you red nigger, get your ass out of here." The marshal hauled him out of the stool by the shirt, he was hustled off his feet and thrown toward the door that the other kicked open. The shadowy hallway was at his back and he was looking at the man's boots, and his hands froze on the doorjamb as he half-sat in the doorway. The boots kicked at his fingers, numbed them, then stepped hard on the wrist. "I thought you said you wanted to get out of here. Didn't you say that? And now we can't get you to leave nohow, can we?" The other man grabbed his foot and jerked him flat while his partner slammed the door. "Stay if you want, but I want to hear how you been running whiskey down to the Nations, and who . . ."

*And all I could think of was how glad I was they had slammed the door . . .*

## FORT SMITH PRISON *July 21, 1896*

The afternoon swelled in the high barred window, one-by-two-foot square of yellow light. The light sickened and grayed, the air got old, the window light was blue. Maybe it was the "second day" that was ending, second day of Cherokee Bill's conjure. Maybe it was the fourth day ending, fourth till Henry Starr gets hung up in the air in the eyes of the whole people, his pecker limp and his feet kicking and the cords of his breath cut off in the center and the bright spots in the middle of his eyes squeezed out like a man might pinch the pits out of a couple of fat grapes.

*Tom Starr's ghost looks at him from the high barred window full of blue light. His right eye is covered by the smoked glass, his left blank black in the empty frame: "I had to come beg and buy you away from those men. You would be hanging to their boots even now if I hadn't. Begging them to let you stay in jail."*

"I thought they meant lynching. I hadn't done anything."

*The glazed eye and naked socket begin to fade. "And you think that doing nothing being guilty of nothing gives you some kind of power so that nothing should touch you, no ropes be slung for you no knives sharpened. If you had done something maybe you would not have tried to cheat your death, to make me pay it off for you, to bribe it with heaps of white paper. What is it to you how you die or pay your debt to the law? If you were Cherokee you'd know your justice and it would make you strong for your death. But you had done nothing. I was ashamed to save you; but more ashamed that when I saved you you were not guilty . . ."*

## COURTHOUSE, FORT SMITH, ARKANSAS *August 10, 1893*

". . . not guilty," said Henry Starr's lawyer, and Judge Parker patted his white spade beard and said, "I have seen about every twist that a smart lawyer can put upon the truth, I might as well hear yours . . ."

. . . in the Circuit Court of the United States of America for the Western District of Arkansas, August Term 1893, *United States* v. *Henry Starr*, on the Charge of Murder, the Honorable Isaac Parker presiding: the Grand Jurors upon their oath present:

"That Henry Starr on the 13th day of December A.D., 1892, at the Cherokee Nation, in the Indian Country, within the Western District of Arkansas aforesaid, with force of arms, in and upon the body of one Floyd Wilson, a white man and not an Indian, then and there being, feloniously, willfully and of his malice aforethought, did make an assault; and that the said Henry Starr with a certain gun then and there charged with gunpowder and one leaden bullet, which said gun he the said Henry Starr in his hands then and there had held, then and there feloniously, willfully, and of his malice aforethought, did discharge and shoot off, to, against and upon the said Floyd Wilson and that the said Henry Starr with the leaden bullet aforesaid, out of the gun aforesaid, then and there, by force of the gunpowder aforesaid, by the said Henry Starr shot off and discharged as aforesaid, then and there feloniously, willfully, and of his malice aforethought, did strike, penetrate and wound him the aforesaid Floyd Wilson in and upon the left side of the breast of him the said Floyd Wilson then and there, with the leaden bullet aforesaid, so as aforesaid discharged and shot out of the gun aforesaid by the said Henry Starr in and upon the left side of the breast of him the said Floyd Wilson one mortal wound of the depth of four inches and of the breadth of half an inch; . . ."

> Now Henry Starr was running with the posse on his track,
> When Deputy Floyd Wilson approached him from the
> back.
> A rifle shot he fired, the bullet it went wide.
> Henry Starr he . . .

## DODGE RANCH, INDIAN TERRITORY
*December 13, 1892*

Five days dodging through brush and tall timber, switching horses, doubling back on the trail, using water and rock to wipe the memory of his passage from the earth, Henry Starr had left the posse far behind, hands full of dogshit and eyes full of cold trail, like he had just wound out this ribbon of sweet candy for them, and they come following, following, just so eager and hungry and happy, and then quick as a magician will vanish a bunch of feathers the trail broke off under their noses and the bunch of them stood around it bellyaching and looking pitiful. He was still laughing when he pushed his horse through the gate and across the hard-packed flat of Dodge's front yard, just time to swap horses again and pay off Dodge for his long friendly silence, laughing so hard thinking about Dodge afraid to take their money and too afraid of Cherokee Bill *not* to that he never noticed:

*The wrong horse hitched to the rail in front.*

And all of a sudden right then it was too late, by the time he wheeled the tired horse around and started him shuffling back toward the gate, stepping gingerly on sore hocks, the door was slamming open and boots drumming Dodge's plank porch and someone yelling, cursing, cursing Henry Starr and adding a rifle shot that spat up the ground in front of his horse's forefeet, and another as Henry Starr ducked down—it sang by with a tug at the back of his sheepskin coat.

Henry Starr reined the horse around following the movement of his body as he bent under the shot, the ducking movement becoming a roll-off down the off side of the horse. He dropped to the ground, down to a half-crouch and he saw between the foot-stuttering legs of the animal the man running toward him twisted sideways, jerking at the lever of his carbine as he came on trying to clear a jammed shell, the goddamned back-shooting son of a bitch.

Henry Starr stepped away from the horse and pulled his pistol from the shoulder holster as the man finally threw the rifle away in disgust and jerked at the gun at his hip, jerked it out and his face came up with it but it was too late, Henry Starr was already pointing the finger and cursing him for a back-shooting son of a bitch and pulling the trigger just as he saw it was Wilson it was the law that stupid back-shooting bastard, and the .45 slug popped dust out of the left center of Wilson's chest and knocked him stumbling back the way he had come flat on his ass in the dirt.

Henry Starr was there right behind the bullet, quick as thinking, quick as if he was trying to run the bullet down and bring it back, and there was Wilson gasping like a catfish in the air. "You stupid bastard. You stupid back-shooting bastard," *he come on me sudden and from behind and never showed he was law, and I killed him, I killed the law*, and the price of it was right there in Henry Starr like a rising sickness in his belly. He saw Wilson's face turning blue, turning black as he choked on the air he couldn't suck no more, and it was Henry Starr's own death that was dying right there turning black in the face, the cords of his breath cut and the cords of his blood, dead as a dead nigger strung up in the middle of a dark night and the glare of a million straining white eyes, and Henry Starr gripped his gun hard as he could and pointed it at the blue-black face and killed it blowing off a corner of the forehead, and Wilson's black face was still there till he pumped the center of the face full of bullets till there was no face there at all, and stood there with the gun pointing at the thing he'd made thinking, *Black black, no-name no-clan, this is the death of Henry Starr.*

"I know that I am dying," the deputy did say,
"And for my bloody murder the law will make you
pay:

For robbing banks and property is laid unto your score,
You owe a life for my life, a debtor to the law."

## FORT SMITH COURTHOUSE *August 10, 1893*

". . . of which said mortal wound, he the said Floyd Wilson then and there instantly died. And so the Jurors aforesaid, upon their oath aforesaid, do say that the said Henry Starr him the said Floyd Wilson by the manner and by the means aforesaid, feloniously, willfully, and of his malice aforethought did kill and murder, contrary to the form of the Statute in such cases made and provided, and against the peace and dignity of the United States of America."

Charge signed in proper form and delivered.

Testimony.

Argument.

Verdict: Guilty, as charged.

Judge Parker looked down at the prisoner in the dock. His face had grown thicker over the years, his eyes were as still as glass beads, his lips were pursed and in his hands he held the text of the sermon he would preach upon Henry Starr as he passed sentence, but to clear the path for that he had to ask, "Before you are sentenced have you anything to say why the sentence of the law should not now be passed?"

The prisoner made no reply.

"Oh yes I robbed the Katy Bank with my pistol in my hand,
And for the laws and property I do not give a damn.
The white man robbed the Indian, the banker robs the white,
And so I rob the banker to set the balance right."

## FORT SMITH PRISON *July 21, 1896*

The blue darkness in Henry Starr's high barred window turned black. His eyes filled with darkness as with pools of oil. He heard the dip of Cherokee Bill's mug, the slosh of the water in the pail, the bubbling hiss that meant it was poured quickly onto the floor, he believed without seeing that even in the darkness the lead slug flashed in the air as it fell from the lip of the mug and Cherokee Bill caught it. Still working his conjure, working and working it, the end of the second day.

He's more Cherokee than I am, even if he is mostly nigger.

Henry Starr stepped to the barred door and looked toward Cherokee Bill's cell, but Bill was back away from the door: no sight, no sound. *I* know what is in his mind, as if I was thinking it myself. Because I have heard it before: first he'll feel that crazy-mad he gets when you put the name on him, when you put the look on him, thinking: *you call a Hair Twister a nigger and your body must be dead, your ghost is under my feet, I'll cut the strings of your blood you no-clan no-name . . .*

And when he can't do any of that he goes cold and silent inside and out.

And then inside his head he starts cursing the handbill and yelling at the nigger, *so what? Hey? So what? He probably had it coming to him, yeah, you had it coming to you, you probably called it on yourself, you stupid nigger, you black no-name no-clan son of a bitch, I don't get killed like that, see? I'm one of the Hair Twisters, I do the killing, see? You want to see? I'm walking I'm spitting I'm pissing on your ghost right now, you see?*

That's when he does those things he does, his father-in-law gives his brother-in-law six hogs and Cherokee Bill five and that's *treating me like a nigger*, so he has to walk into his sister's house at suppertime with two.45s and yell the brother-in-law's name and clan and start firing one two three four five from each pistol, each shot kicking the brother-in-law back, opening his chest up and his skull, biting a chunk of cheek, of shoulder, finally smashing ribs on the way through and out the floorboards of the house, the sister and kids gone screaming away or maybe he'd have reloaded and used the next two cylinders on them.

Only now he ain't got his guns, all he's got is a busted lead slug and a cup of water and a head full of old-time powwow muck-a-muck conjures, and he's working them as fast and hard as ever he worked the triggers of those two .45s shooting his brother-in-law full of holes.

It was worse sitting there in his cell filling his own silence with Cherokee Bill's thoughts, worse than listening to Cherokee Bill's voice. "Bill?" called Henry Starr.

There was a deepening in the quiet. Then: "You know what I hate about it, Henry?"

"I know."

"It ain't the getting killed I mind. It's the nigger of it that I hate."

Henry Starr strained to make Cherokee Bill's huge bulk rise from the bed and come to the door, but he could only feel the ghost of Cherokee

Bill in pain, twisting this way and that, walking on Eoff's ghost and then feeling the ghost of the rope around his neck and Eoff and all the rest of the hanging crowd climbing over his ghost as he fell down black into a blackening hole in the air. "Think quiet, Bill. Think about still water."

"I only wish I had some tobacco, Henry. That's all I need. If I had some tobacco I could . . . I'd be able to . . . I could climb over."

It was useless, hopeless. *Tobacco.* Henry Starr closed himself, he didn't want to hear any more from Cherokee Bill or Cherokee Bill's ghost, because there was no tobacco and no power even if they had some to climb over this. He couldn't even get rid of the damned handbill; if he crumpled it in his hands the picture just made itself again behind his eyes, it was all still happening the same way. It ain't the dying it's the nigger of it I hate, the being held like that like they could just take you and make you any damn kind of animal or woman or meat or thing and your arms no better than water against it, not even good to keep you out of their eyes, watching you, making you like that in the way they look. I wish I could climb out of that damned picture, out of those damned eyes of theirs but there ain't no way: that's just how things are. There's white and nigger, those that does and those that gets done to, those that cuts and those that bleeds—there's those that gets to watch it done, sitting there safe like it was done just to make them laugh; and then there's those looks at the picture and falls out of their eyes and down into it like it was a deep black hole and that white man's ugly face smiling at the bottom, look what I made you, look what I can do to you.

If I could climb over, if I could climb out of that black hole I'd do it any way I could. I'd climb over you too if it would do any good, my brother Cherokee Bill, because you got that nigger-death already wrapped around you, already there tight to you as your skin. You say you ain't black, but you are: I been lying for you, my brother, but I know what's true. You know that nigger you hate, that name, that black, it's just the name it's just the color of your fear, the color of your no-name no-clan death, the color of your memory frozen forever in black without no face and the swole-head white man pointing and smiling at how he's made you. But truth to tell, my brother, I rather be that handbill white man than you. And I'd rather be the man that took the picture than him, because the handbill man he's got his head so full of you, don't he? that someday your ghost is gonna look in his eyes and make him leak cold black misery out of every place he cut a mouth in you. So yes, I'd rather be the man taking the picture than the man done it, the one to make them all freeze like that: to be a man could look at that picture, frozen, like you look in a window, in a book: I opened it, I can close the book and walk away.

But every time I look and no matter where, my brother, I see your face and it tells me I'm going to die the nigger death you hate.

The silence between the stones made the sound of his Grandfather's dead breath.

Henry Starr rose and went back to stand by his door.

It's as if Cherokee Bill has been waiting for him to look. Their eyes meet. Cherokee Bill hasn't opened the lid of his stew. He dips his mug full of water, the slug falls out of his level palm into the mug. He holds the swallow in his mouth. He sits. He lets the water dribble out of the mug as he swallows the water in his mouth, and his left hand sweeps the lead slug out of the air as it falls.

Still just an imitation of running water. Still no tobacco for him to work.

## FORT SMITH PRISON *July 22, 1896*

In the late afternoon they let the prisoners out of their cells and marched them all into the large mess hall. Up on the platform where the preacher preached on Sunday they had hung a great white sheet. From the sheet to the back of the room they had cleared a path. At the back end of the path there was a machine set up on a large oak table, a contraption of black metal and bright spools and gears of brass and steel that flashed light sharp as shards of mirror, a piggy snout of brass and thick bulging glass, two projecting arms going up and down holding wide flat metal wheels on which a shiny tape was wound. A white man in a checked suit was fussing around the contraption, polishing bits of metal and glass with a cloth, blowing his breath into the snout and wiping it.

Henry Starr watched the man, paying little attention to what the warden was saying standing there with the sheet framing him. Very grateful. Kindly agreed. Tulsa Motion Picture Company. Modern science. Wisdom of the ages in a form the humblest citizen. A salutary and object lesson in crime and punishment.

The lights went out, the dark closed in. The machine began to click and rattle like stones clipping each other in a spinning pool. A white bubbling sort of shape burst out of the sheet and in its horrible pallor

Henry Starr saw the two wheels turning slowly feeding the shiny ribbon into the spools and grinders of the machine and taking it out again smooth and whole as water over rocks.

Then strong white light flashed behind him, he snapped back to confront light which was now bubbling out of the sheet. The white sheet was swollen with nauseous white light, there were shadows in it that bubbled and moved. Then suddenly the bubble contracted, its edges hardened like the sliding edge of an egg broken into hot grease. The bubble squared. Gray and white patterns broke out all over like a patchwork quilt, white and black triangles in a snowstorm of black and white flowerdots. The quilt . . . *split!* a black hole in the center started and bulged and Henry Starr heard Cherokee Bill next to him suck his breath in tight as the black became the face of a train hurtling out of broken space right down their throats, and even as the thing came at him Henry Starr's eyes composed the frame around it, the station platform, tracks, the million flowerdots that were people, people moving and waving, only a certain number of people waiting for a train: but all in silence, gray, without color.

The train stopped. The two of them had held their seats and never moved, though he could hear Cherokee Bill breathing short and quick next to him. They looked at the people in the blob of light, the silent shapes mocking human speech, the shapes of being leached of their colors.

The world of the ones who were like people and a train split down the middle and a giant white head with slitty eyes and a spade beard boomed out of it, big enough to take the whole space of a train, huge bearded giant creature from the nightland of the train. It had a white beard. It showed its teeth. Henry Starr must have blinked because with no sign of movement at all the face dropped back, there was a body, there were two faces, two bodies, it had become two.

There were two men standing under a gateway with writing above it: UFFALO BILL'S WILD WE

"Henry," came the awed whisper from Cherokee Bill, "look, Henry, if that ain't Buck!"

There was no mistaking it. That was Jesse James's brother Frank standing there in a three-piece suit next to the shape-changer with the beard, whom Henry Starr recognized as Buffalo Bill, same face as the playbills and photographs as you could see once the image stopped jumping and swelling and shifting shape on you making you feel sick and crazy in your stomach. Buffalo Bill and old Buck James in a frock coat and a vest and no gun belt.

The nightland ate them, suddenly: black. Then there were letters: **Frank James the notorious Desperado, in Buffalo Bill's Wild West!**

White light blazed at them, Buck James with a drawn six-gun among the passengers in a railway car, is that Jesse behind him *Jesse fourteen years dead back-shot by Robert Ford?* A black-coated giant blotted out coach, passengers, the Jameses, a huge six-gun looking into Henry Starr's eyes with its one empty black socket, the blackness erupting with the ghosts of smoke and fire, silent all of it and without color as the ghosts of huge black bullets blew through Henry Starr's eyes and ghost and mind, black and silent.

Buck James and Buffalo Bill stood there under the sign.

The nightland ate them, blackness.

**The Reformed Outlaw: "Crime does not pay."**

The slumped figure of an old Indian appeared, moving his gray hands in the graceful movements of the sign talk. The shape of Buffalo Bill's ghost answered.

Then black: **Jack Red Cloud—the former foe, present friend, the Red Man!**

Black shapes swarming huge, vague, legged, a black body with many legs swarmed in the bubbling whiteness, there was a snap and the screen went pure white . . .

They heard the man in the checked suit cursing.

The lights swept the room with brightness that hurt their eyes. In the harsh glare Cherokee Bill's face looked like it was made of wax, stiff and dead. "I didn't know Buck was dead," said Cherokee Bill. "I knew he turned evidence, but I never heard he was dead." He held up manacled hands, shaking with rage and fear. "His ghost trying to shoot me and my hands tied like a . . ."

The guards ordered them to rise. They began shuffling into lines, getting ready to return to their cells.

Henry Starr felt dizzy, nauseated, as on waking out of a nightmare, but now it was settling. "It ain't ghosts, Bill. Buck ain't dead. It's just pictures. Photographs, and they make 'em move on you somehow."

Cherokee Bill's face looked clotted and swollen, as if his head was pumping up like a hot sore. "If that son of a bitch thought he could send his ghost to kill me, let him kiss my ass! My magic is strong, Henry, ghost bullets and all, and I never even blinked but looked that big son of a bitch in the eyes, and if I get me some tobacco I'll walk on his ghost too, by God I . . ." But the line of prisoners was already safely beyond the Tulsa Motion Picture Company man, shuffling out the mess hall door. "That little dude white man with his box, it's like to wish a man dead making his ghost be that way, Henry! I'll cut the strings of his breath, Henry, I'll cut his blood, I'll walk on his ghost . . ."

But Henry Starr felt quiet inside now, full of still water. That night in his cell, waiting for the trusty to bring the pails of dinner, he took out the handbill again. Frozen and flat: everything as it had been, dead-fixed forever, the crowd pushing its way in around that no-name no-clan no-cock no-face no-man lying black/dead there and the white man pushing his face at your eyes and pointing proud and reckless and swole to busting with the mess of terror he'd just fed off—flat and complacent and quiet as if this in the picture was all it come down to.

It wasn't so damn much of a picture after all, was it? Flat and dead. A piece of paper you could fold blank or rip up or wipe your ass on and bury it in the dark. But that other one, now, that other one: it moved, didn't it? Like the picture could almost reach out and shoot you down, suck you in and spit you out. Like someone took a picture and then reached down that long tunnel into it and stirred it up with his fingers like a kid stirring quiet water to see the fish jump. That's a power, that kind of making a picture. If this handbill was that kind you'd have to see it being done, and it would be worse, almost as bad as having to be there.

Only if they kept it going, kept the pictures making, you'd see what come after too, what kept happening: the crowd sliding out of the picture, breaking up like ice in March and dropping off home alone with the terror of what they'd done. And the white man pointing there, Mr. Handbill Man: him too—keep the picture coming and he can't hold that look up over his face like a bandit's mask, it's going to freeze first, stiffen up on him; it's gonna crack some, and begin to slip, little bulges and lumps of the underneath popping out like boils, like spots of blackness when he begins knowing how the big fear he just cut and burned and made to scream, how it's still there, only it's educated now, it knows his name, it knows the things that will scare his ghost black and blow it out like a match . . . *Hyenh,* keep it coming, keep it coming on and let him feel it too.

And let him feel it too, that's what, that's what I'd do if I could. If I had the power to make that picture I'd climb right over this handbill I'd climb down inside the picture and make it go. I'd put the no-face back on the black man with his head chopped, and I'd show how he looks into the white man's ghost with his no-face and turns him black, yeah we'd walk all over that white man's ghost, and I'd clear those crackers out too . . . no, I'd flip the picture around on 'em, so it wasn't them showing off to me how big they been, how they took a man and made . . . so it was me showing *them*, goddamn it, showing them looking at the thing they killed and it's becoming aliver than them, coming after them, coming to look in their eyes and tell them that their ghost is black.

He smiled in the dark, eyes shut, seeing a picture of himself behind the machine that ate people and made pictures, black/white ghosts on the sheet—what kind of machine could that be? Some kind of crossbreed of that pig-snouty thing with the spindle wheels today and one of those black-box things the photographers use. Like some kind of a gun, he figured, you got to point it, don't you? Like some kind of a gun, and Henry Starr behind it, not just coming after the greenbacks and gold and silver this time, not even after the mortgage papers, land warrants and notes-of-hand this time, but after the ghosts of all those sons of bitches out there: Henry Starr and his gun that shoots pictures, ghosts, memories, visions, his gun pointing straight between your goddamn blue eyes, "Thumbs up and stand steady!"

He felt quiet inside.

Eoff and the Creek trusty came stamping and yapping down the corridor and Henry Starr heard the sound of them plumping the bowl of stew down on the wooden shelf by the slot in his iron-barred door. He heard Eoff's voice go blatting off down the corridor saying something at Cherokee Bill—it did not touch Henry Starr at all. The door banged behind Eoff and it was as quiet again outside his head as it was in.

Thinking about that vision gun was like thinking about smooth running water, it made a clicking sound like water swirling smooth stones around. Like to get my eyes my hands on that gun—hell, on any kind of a gun.

He rolled off his bunk and stepped to the door, looking down toward Cherokee Bill's cell. On the shelf by Cherokee Bill's door the bowl of stew stood untouched. Cherokee Bill stood near the door. As soon as he saw Henry Starr he dipped his mug in the water pail. He passed his hand slowly over the cup and dropped a thing from his level palm into the water. He held the palm higher than before so that Henry Starr could see clearly what he dropped.

It was not any flattened lead slug but a shiny, steel-jacketed .45-caliber bullet.

---

That night in his dreams Henry Starr's ghost killed the ghost of Deputy Wilson again. But this time it was different. From behind his head he heard the voice cry *Henry Starr!* and he felt the bullet tug his sleeve and it was silent. He dismounted slowly, rolling off the horse as slow and easy as rolling out of a bunk, floating to the ground and between the horse's dancing legs saw Deputy Wilson stepping forward slowly, very calmly and slowly. Henry Starr pointed his pistol at Wilson's chest. *You should never have come on me back-shooting*, he said, *you were in the wrong.*

*Yes*, said Wilson. Out on the porch behind him stood a giant shadow with a tall black hat that might have been Dodge but it wasn't, because it wasn't ever really Dodge's ranch, it rightfully belonged to an old giant Indian man with a pair of smoked spectacles, the left lens busted out.

*You can't treat me like I was John Ross's nigger*, said Henry Starr, *that ain't no justice*. He stopped.

*I'm sorry*, said Wilson. *Me too*, said Henry Starr and he pointed and shot Deputy Wilson in the

*Bang!*

in the chest

*Bang!*

Henry Starr was awake. The light was gray. He smelled the gunsmoke acrid-sharp, and heard the rattle of metal on the stone floor. Something heavy dragging. The ringing of keys in a lock.

## FORT SMITH PRISON *July 23, 1896*

"Henry Starr! Goddamn it, Henry!" It was Cherokee Bill yelling from down the corridor and the smell of gunpowder was sharper than the jailhouse funk but there was something sharper than gun smoke, with an edge on it like copper and a little whiff of rot, and that was blood.

By this time Henry Starr was off his pallet and on the floor, worming toward the barred door. From up toward the closed end of the corridor he could hear wood breaking and people yelling from out of the other cells and Cherokee Bill telling them all to shut the hell up. Down to the left the corridor door slammed open and Cherokee Bill fired out of the dead end and everybody fired back, the bullets whee-ranging off bricks, metal and smashed-all-to-hell furniture. Henry Starr lay there trying to push his face and belly out through the floor of his cell not having any better luck than before.

The racket stopped abruptly leaving absolute quiet. "You there, Henry?" boomed Cherokee Bill.

There was a sudden ear-splitting blast from the doorway, one of the guards with a sawed-off shotgun, the buckshot rooted up what sounded like wood and rang off the bricks and the bars, and the prisoners began yelling all together.

"*Oobloobloobl*e," yelled Cherokee Bill, like a crazy wild turkey the size of an elephant. "*Ooobloobloobl*e."

The shotgun went off again with a roar-whang-boom! but through the rattle of the buckshot Henry Starr could hear the bark of a .45, somebody yipped from the doorway and heavy metal rang on the stone floor. Cherokee Bill gobbled a long loud looney gobble. *Shot the gun out of that bastard's hands.* Then there was a sound like snuffling from Cherokee Bill's end, a sound like ripping, somebody groaned.

"You hear me out there?" yelled Cherokee Bill. "I got that son of a bitch Eoff, and I got that smart little trusty, only his brains is blowed out. So you clear out. I'm comin' out of here."

"Come on then," said a voice from the door, "you just come right on."

"*Ooobloobloobl*e," yelled Cherokee Bill and blasted six shots into the doorway smashing the glass window across the corridor and singing off the stones. They must have figured he was pumped out, because there was a scuffle sound at the door as if they were going to rush him—but Bill was running it on them, must have got Eoff's pistol and shells. He blew three quick hard shots back at them and they never made it to Henry Starr's cell but had to scramble back out the door yelling for someone to cover, the shotgun booming again over their heads, blowing the load into the ceiling to keep from hitting the guards. Cherokee Bill gobbled two or three times, real high-pitched. Then he got quiet and you could hear the ripping sound, it was real ugly to hear.

"Come on out, Henry! Here's Eoff's keys!" There was a whizz and a clank, and the brass ring of keys skidded on the stone floor in front of the bars of Henry Starr's cell. *Bawhang!* went the shotgun, and there were pistols barking from the door also trying to pick Bill off as he threw the keys. But nobody was going to try rushing Cherokee Bill behind a shotgun blast, not with thirty-five feet of corridor to run and barred iron doors to either side, and that damned half-breed giggling and gobbling like some monstrous goddamn turkey behind whatever cover he'd thrown together down there in the dead end.

"Lock yaself out, Henry," he called. "I'll cover you."

Someone yelled from the door in a cracked voice, "You make a move out that door, Starr, and I'll blow your ass to hell."

Henry Starr lay still with his body flat to the floor, and he felt the stone hard under him, and stone all around. This is the day that Henry Starr beats Jack-the-Devil, he thought, the day of my luck. Make my vision be, *poof!* and no tobacco needed. "I ain't going with you this trip, Bill. But I'll get out of the way and let you play your hand."

"Henry?" said the complaining voice. "That ain't you, is it, Henry?"

"I'm getting the keys," he called, very loud and slow, "but I ain't doing nothing crazy. I just want out of the shooting gallery. Just want me a nice quiet peaceful hanging, like my grandpappy always said I had coming." There was a snort of laughter from the doorway side, and that gave him nerve to snake his arm out for the keys, and he heard a soft voice say, "No, let him, it'll work better if . . ." And he knew just what they were thinking, he could see between their ears and behind their eyes today: if he swung the door open and ran for Bill's end of the corridor they could blast him and follow behind the shield of his body, maybe get Cherokee Bill if he exposed himself to shoot past his friend. If he walked out their way they could use him for cover and rush Cherokee Bill behind it. And if he snake crawled Bill's way they'd have that shotgun pointed right between his legs and just purely blow his asshole out between his eyes, so what did they have to lose?

"I'm opening the door," said Henry Starr, rattling keys in the lock. "Just keep it all hokeydokey." The door swung and creaked open. "I'm gonna go out on my belly, boys. I'm comin' straight for the door. One of you peckerwoods shoots me, gonna make Judge Parker mean enough to spit." He snaked out into the corridor and seemed to feel a cold blue wind blowing down toward Cherokee Bill. "He likes his hangings, the Judge does," crawling on the gritty stone flags, light ahead, shattered window, "don't like 'em spoilt, main attraction get all shot to pieces." A quick glance to the back: pile of broken furniture, pallets, bunks, no sight of Cherokee Bill, but the ripping noise started again and somebody groaned, pretty *damn* ugly sound. "Ain't no joke hanging a man when it takes a roll of baling wire just to hold all the different parts together." Up ahead was the open door and the corridor going left and right. Henry Starr snaked toward it, got his shoulders through the frame. Someone grabbed him under the armpits and hauled him to the right behind the shelter of the wall.

He got up, batting the grit from his baggy prison suit. There were eight guards, with Marsden, the chief, at their head holding the shotgun, a bloody cloth wrapping his hand where Cherokee Bill had winged him.

"How in hell did that nigger get a forty-five?" Marsden yelled.

"I don't know," said Henry Starr. *Neither of us would admit to believing he conjured it, would we?* "I don't know," he said again quietly. "Would you like for me to go back there and get it away from him?"

"Ha ha," said Marsden, with a stagy sneer. Then he looked at Henry Starr a second time, and there was a sudden quiet in the corridor inside which you could hear that ugly ripping sound from where Cherokee Bill and Eoff were lying in the stone dead end.

The quiet held on too long. "Dammit," said one of the other guards, "what in hell is that nigger doing to Eoff? Sound like he's *cuttin'* on him down there . . ."

Henry Starr held his face very still and peaceful. Thinking about water helped him do it: smooth water in a pool, you can see the smooth speckled stones at the bottom. "No telling what he'll do if his blood is up." He paused to let them think about Cherokee Bill's blood, nigger and redskin and peckerwood and Mex, like he was every kind of half-breed a man could be—and he thought to himself, *wouldn't it have been enough to say he was a Hair Twister, and it's easy to get him angry, ain't that what you would have said if you was really . . .*

But he didn't have time to think, he had to play the cards as fast as the dealer turned them up. Just thinking about Cherokee Bill with his blood up made Marsden's eyes run back and forth like weasels in a pit, and Henry Starr said helpfully, "You boys could probably rush him."

There was no answer to that.

Marsden's shoulders slumped and he leaned back against the wall. "What's your proposition?" He held his right palm outward, a gesture of denial before Henry Starr even spoke. "There's no way I can let you out of here, Henry. And I can't speak for the judge."

But Henry Starr could see what was moving around under Marsden's hair, and he had to calm his own face to keep the smile down, quietness like a bandanna drawn to the eyes. "Well," he said sort of thinking about it, "you could go over now and ask the Judge if . . ." and he saw Marsden's words flitting across his face before they touched his mouth and drew his breath. "Nnnno," said Marsden thoughtfully, "no, it won't do. I can't take the time with that renegade cuttin' on Eoff like that," and his eyes flicked to Henry Starr's and then flicked down. *Lying*: because old Judge Parker would never cut a deal just to save one of these fat-ass no-good guards one of whom had probably sold Cherokee Bill that pistol himself for a gold watch or just a set of smokes. "But I'll talk to him, Henry," said Marsden. "You've got my word I'll talk to him and do my best to get you off."

Henry Starr turned it over in his mind. Judge Parker would probably as soon pass wind in meeting as give Henry Starr a pass on the gallows. But Parker had a hatred for Cherokee Bill that ran deep as his spine. At the trial he'd as much as threatened to shoot the jury and hang the district attorney if they failed to find Cherokee Bill guilty, and when Bill's lawyer had raised too many formal objections he'd told him to write out his will before he raised another. Anyone who stopped Cherokee Bill from cheating the Hangman had a claim on that hate, strong and true as a mother's love, you could count on it. And Henry Starr hadn't killed but one deputy, and that in circumstances. Maybe Judge Parker had lived close enough to the Nations to recognize that a life could pay for a life—Eoff's (if he was still alive) or Marsden's or one of these other guards here, for the life of Deputy Floyd Wilson *who I swear I never meant to kill but he come on me so sudden from the back and I—*

"All right," said Henry Starr. "You give me a bucket of fresh water, a pouch of tobacco and some matches and forty-five minutes, and I'll get you Cherokee Bill."

What would he say? He would be giving Cherokee Bill to the Hangman. The wrong words would put his spirit on the black road of the giant's ghostly vengeance. There was something in Cherokee Bill, some dark thing, some power, or how had he made the conjure work? Wilson's ghost was bad enough. Cherokee Bill's would be too much weight for him to carry. *You see, Old Man, I remember what you taught me . . .*

They brought him the water, slapped the pouch of tobacco and matches into his left hand, Marsden tapped his watch. "Forty-five minutes."

"Bill! It's me, Henry Starr! I'm comin' down to you. There's no tricks, I swear it. I'm comin' down to talk."

"Come ahead."

He stepped into the corridor, a cold circle in the small of his back as if the eye of a ghost were sighting a pistol barrel on his spine.

# The Man Who Owned the Dreamland

NORTH DETROIT AVENUE, TULSA *May 6, 1921*

Bub Houston lived in a two-story white clapboard house on North Detroit Avenue, which he shared with his daughter and son-in-law. The houses on North Detroit were new and built to roughly the same plan, each with its patch of front lawn and evergreen foundation plantings and nearer the street a pair of spindly saplings that promised velvet shade to the coming generation: two rows of houses so alike it was as if a mile-long mirror ran right down the center line of the street. The only difference between the two sides was that every house to the west of the line was owned by whites, every house to the east by colored.

From his second-story sitting porch Bub Houston could watch Henry Starr riding that line all the way up from the intersection with Archer. Bub showed himself early, rising to his feet as soon as Henry entered the street, and the outlaw smiled at the old man's courtesy and his choice of a stand. It was just the spot Bub Houston would pick, gave him height and a 180° line of sight and when he was on watch there—riding the same tipped-back bentwood chair he had ridden for twenty years on the front porch of the Boley Sheriff's Office—there was nobody could cross that line he couldn't have seen and stopped dead, if he wanted.

Behind Bub Houston's house to the east stretched the roofs of Greenwood, where the colored lived, shingled peaked roofs giving way to square brick mesas and ragged tar tops. There were two colored high schools in Greenwood (Dunbar and Booker T. Washington), a colored public library, several colored restaurants, one big colored barrelhouse (Braxton's) and a dozen blind pigs, two colored newspapers, colored churches, colored groceries, colored shoe stores, colored barbers, colored hardware dealers, colored gun shops, colored farm implement and feed stores, colored pharmacists and colored doctors and colored dentists. One of the most imposing of the brick mesas belonged to the Dreamland Theater, which Bub owned in silent partnership with his son-in-law, William Parker. It was the larger of two colored movie palaces, located right in the heart of Deep Greenwood, Greenwood Avenue north of Archer.

The matinee performance at the Dreamland this week, by special arrangement with the Pan American Motion Picture Company, had been a double bill of *Buckskin Bill's Outlaw Trail*—retitled *Buckskin Bill Against the Starr Gang* for showing at the Dreamland—and *Henry Starr, Scourge of the Southwest,* which had been so rushed into release that there had been no time to provide a colored title for it. Since there was only one print of each film, William Parker provided a courier who picked up the reels of the second film while the first was showing at the Lyric; then after the colored showing, rewound and shuttled the film back to the Lyric just as the first was finishing; picked up the first film, which showed second at the Dreamland and was returned and exchanged again for the late afternoon and evening performances. It was an elaborate procedure, arranged at some cost, but worth it because it gave the Dreamland access to the first run of Pan American's films, while it reassured Poole and Wilberforce that they were avoiding even the appearance of allowing white people and colored to drink out of the same bottle.

The operation required exquisite timing—as Henry Starr had told Bub (when the two of them sat over a beer in Braxton's), it was almost as complicated as trying to rob two banks at once, and Bub threw back his head and laughed, and invited Henry Starr to come and get his hand shook at the opening and dinner some night later in the week.

"Howdy Bub," called Henry Starr, dismounting, and the old man nodded down from the porch, "Henry," and from inside they could hear the yipping of Houston's grandson. "He's here! Hey Ma! Hey! He's really here . . . !"

Bub Houston smiled. "He been to the Dreamland every afternoon this week looking at Henry Starr. Sooner have dinner with the Scourge of the Southwest than Teddy Roosevelt or even Mr. Jack Johnson."

Henry Starr winced a little, "I've got an alibi on that *Scourge of the Southwest* job, Bub," and Bub said, "I've heard your alibis before. You can save this one for the indictment," at which point William Parker opened the screen door—dressed in a cream-colored linen suit, smiling with cool politeness—and ushered him into the front parlor.

Henry Starr heard Bub Houston clumping down from upstairs. In front of him a man and a woman rose from a tufted loveseat and an easy chair, and a little boy about six years old half-leaped toward Henry Starr and was jerked back by his mother's strong hand at the scruff of his shirt. The woman was tall and athletic looking, a match in height for William Parker, her skin a creamy light brown, with broad shoulders, long arms, and graceful long-fingered hands, her size and the sharp look in her eyes and confident smile marking her as Bub Houston's daughter. The man next to her was heavily muscled, maybe taller than Bub Houston and as dark, with smooth tender-looking skin and a very high round forehead, but something about him made you mistake his size at first—a way of holding his body that suggested a folding of himself inward, and something about his eyes.

"Henry Starr," said Bub Houston. "This is my daughter, Harriet Parker, and you've met my son-in-law, William." He indicated the big man. "This here's our good friend Dick Rowland—he's the man hauls those pictures of yours back and forth," and the man gave his hand to Henry Starr, more like a quick reluctant touch than a shake, and now up close Henry Starr could see what was strange about his eyes: they had that look you see in a baby's eyes, not blind exactly because they get all the light there is, but it doesn't connect inside yet, it just passes on through and shines back out again pure and bright and blank.

Bub looked around as if forgetful. "Now let's see who else . . ."

"Grandpa!" yelped the little boy.

"Oh yes," said Houston, "and this here is Shaker." The old man's face seemed to fill up like a balloon, his smile getting broader and broader as he looked at the boy.

"How do," said Shaker as Henry Starr stepped forward and took his hand.

"That's a good name, Shaker," said Henry Starr. "How'd you come by it?"

It was a story he got to tell lots but he liked it so too much that it always came out tumbling. "My baptize name is William Chaka Tubman Houston Parker, Junior, because my daddy is William Senior, and Chaka the name of a black man used to be King of the Nation back over Africa. He was a black man, but Zulus are like Injuns only colored . . ." but at that he popped his eyes open and zigged them nervously from his father to his grandfather to Henry Starr and around again, because Grandpa says Zulus is *sort* of Injuns but Daddy get mad when he do, and maybe being named like that was maybe rude to Henry Starr for not being colored but an Injun, and and . . .

But it was all right because Henry Starr nodded, and looked seriously at Shaker's father and Bub Houston, and said, "That's a strong thing for a boy, to carry a chief's name like that." He looked down at Shaker. "Your folks must think you're a man who can be counted on."

Shaker was pleased so suddenly and fiercely that you could see it just freeze him for a second so he fairly buzzed until he could find a direction to let it out. "Right! so I got to help Clary with the . . ." and he raced his words out of the room, beating them to the kitchen.

Dinner was served by Clary, "a little-bit-Cherokee colored woman," who worked for the Parkers: chicken soup with okra and hot peppers, a roasted loin of pork with chili barbecue, sweet potato pie and greens, and ice cream for dessert: cold beer for the menfolk and cold tea with mint in it for the women and Shaker. Most of the conversation was Shaker asking Henry Starr, and his grown-ups telling him to let Mr. Starr eat some of his food; to which Shaker could answer truthfully that he *was* eating his food, because Shaker already knew an awful lot about Henry Starr from his grandpa's stories and he saw every movie Henry Starr had made three times this last week, and what he didn't know he could guess or make up (not noticing the difference), so all Henry Starr had to do was give him openers and Shaker would fetch the rest of the tale by himself.

"So did you really know Jesse James and Belle Starr and all them . . . ?"

"Yup. I was just a kid, you know, but my grandpa'd take me to Aunt Belle's ranch, and one time Frank and Jesse was there. Now I was too young to remember, but they tell me Jesse picked me up and . . ."

"Rode you round on his horse! And showed you how to shoot a gun and . . ."

They talked about the train robbery at Pryor Creek, and all the bank robberies from Tahlequah to Caney to Bentonville, and Prue and Owasso and Keystone right on down to the two-at-a-time robbery at Stroud "and I bet you were just about the greatest outlaw that . . . weren't you, Mr. Starr? I mean when you rode into town like that, *k-pow* with your gang and everything *k-pow! k-pow!* and just come *wham!* into that bank and tell 'em who you was and they just fold up like they backbones busted and . . ." which was exactly the way it had happened in *Henry Starr, Scourge of the Southwest* to Shaker's certain knowledge no fewer than three times that week.

Henry Starr put his silver down and looked round the table. Dick Rowland was eating slowly and with concentration, his eyes making no contact with anyone or anything outside the field of his plate. Mr. and

Mrs. Parker were looking at each other in a silence of increasing sharpness, *somebody* got to take a hand with that boy, but they each liked to give him his head and would rather the other one checked him. Having finished giving William her *look*, Harriet Parker recovered her softness spooning another serving of the sweet potato pie onto Dick Rowland's plate, as sure in the movement as if he had asked some of her, which of course he hadn't. William Parker was dividing his purse-mouthed disapproval between his son and the bad man who had aroused his son's criminal enthusiasm. And Bub kept shoveling his food down, looking up every once in a while to watch the boy going on, then back to his food grinning as if that look gave him a bigger appetite.

"I was a pretty good bank robber, Shaker—good as a bank robber *is*. But good as I was, son, I got caught. Got sent to prison for it." This made William Parker set a little easier.

"Well," said Shaker with a dismissive shake of the head, "but they snuck up on you, didn't they? It ain't like they could have got you fair. Even that white crack . . . even that Bucksican Bill, he never would go up against *you*, but only that Yankee you was with, that Slick McClain."

"Can't fool the boy 'bout what he seen with his own eyes, Henry," said Bub with an evil grin.

Henry Starr puckered his eyes in discomfort. "Bub," he said, "I've got an alibi for that one."

Bub laughed. "Heard your alibis before, Henry."

"Well now that's true," said Henry Starr softly, with a little grin. "Now I'd 'most forgotten that . . ." and he let the gap in his words draw their attention to him. "Now Shaker, you're right about one thing: it took a mighty good man to put the law to me fair and square. There wasn't but two men ever did in my whole outlaw career. And of them two there was only one that ever done it face to face, and not when I was wounded or took by surprise. Now I bet you ain't even been told who that man was." Henry let Shaker race memories around his story-riddled head, and while the boy's eyes were blanked with inward concentration Henry Starr glanced at Bub Houston, who frowned, then shook his head, resigned to letting Henry go on.

"Bucksican Bill?" said Shaker. "Marshal Tilghman?"

Henry pointed solemnly at Bub. "Your grandpa. Only man ever met me face to face, stopped my play and took me in."

"Grandpa? Really? But you never told me . . ." He wasn't sure he liked this new information, it just confirmed his grieving anger at how they always hid "big stuff" from him, letting him think he knew so much and then laughing at him because he didn't know *nothing*. "Well if it happened, then how come they didn't put it in the picture?"

"You'd be surprised what don't get into those pictures," said Henry Starr, with a look at Bub. "Here's how it was:

"It was in '93, me and Cherokee Bill and two other boys was on the run from a bank up near the Kansas line, half a dozen posses out to get us . . ."

". . . dead or alive and better off dead," Shaker finished with dreamy satisfaction, and Henry Starr nodded.

"We'd about run our horses to death, out of food, and to tell the honest truth we hadn't got much money out of that bank, and already spent *that* just to keep ourselves running. Then we come to this little town, looked so quiet and peaceful. They didn't even have a regular bank, but just a general store with a post office and a little bank sign next to the yard goods and millinery. So we figured, bold as we was, we'd just ride in and clean it out as quick and easy as you'd eat some of this sweet potato pie."

Bub shook his head and hid his glance in his plate.

"That was Boley, wasn't it?" said William Parker, and when Henry Starr nodded Parker gave him a small bitter smile and said, "I guess there were some other things you calculated on"—and Henry Starr felt the blood stiffen his cheeks a little, because if Parker was wrong on the detail he was right on the principle, *although it wasn't until they had actually shoved through the double doors of the general store with guns drawn, "Thumbs up and stand steady," that they saw the dozen or so faces—*

"From the outside," said Henry Starr, "it looked like any other little town. So like I say, we walked in the front door drawing our guns as we come. And there were all these people in there, men, women, and kids, and this one big old fella behind the counter, and I say, 'Thumbs up and stand steady!' like I always done, and all these folks turn around, and *bless* me if they wasn't all—"

(Henry hesitated just long enough to let William Parker jump to *niggers* as the next word out, it was funny how sometimes two people can practically hear what's going on under each other's hair but damned if he'd let Parker know how close he'd come.)

"—all pointing some kind of weapon at us, forty-fives and Winchesters," said Henry Starr, "the women pulling little bitty derringers out of their purses, and I swear one little bitty baby bust his bottle on the counter and shakes the claw end of the glass at me . . ."

(But he couldn't stop the flash of memory: *flash of surprise and sudden fear when every last one of the faces was black and Cherokee Bill looked around at the whole arsenal and grinned and said, "Jesus Christ, Henry, a whole town full of niggers, this is gonna be easy . . .")*

". . . and your grandpa over here, he's leaning on a sawed-off shotgun over the counter.

"You see, that was Bub Houston's town, and he had all his people *ready* for whatever trouble might come.

"Well. And we just stood there like that for what seemed like an hour or more. Because if anybody had moved that place would have blown up like flipping a lit match down a gas well. And your grandpa looks around as calm and happy as a preacher giving the benediction, and he says, 'It looks like we got us a *situation* here . . .' "

Shaker was torn now, looking from his father's displeasure to his grandpa to Henry Starr and around again. "Well why didn't you shoot . . . or he . . ."

"Well now," said Henry Starr, "some men might not have seen a way out of that situation but shooting. There would have been some fine people shot who didn't deserve it. Maybe also a couple who *did*. But your grandpa, he kept his folks steady; and my gang—well, my orders always was, 'No gunplay unless there's no choice,' and they minded me. So I looked your grandpa in the eye and said, 'Bub, it looks like you got me fair and square,' and stepped up to the counter and put my gun down . . ." Bub was shaking his head and remembering what Henry Starr was leaving out:

*"You ought to talk nicer when you come vis'ting folks where they live," Bub Houston said quietly, and they stood there through thirty hard slow pounding knocks of the heart everybody with the drop on everybody else, everybody frozen except for Cherokee Bill—"the big colored man" as Bub called him in his head then, not letting his concentration loose yet to hunt his memory for the names he was sure to recognize, but watching with critical judgment the crazy rage gathering and swelling in Cherokee Bill's eyes. It was like watching a rattler's head tight with poison lifting up out of his coils, "Niggers," he kept saying, "niggers niggers niggers a whole damn town full of niggers" and Bub felt his own finger begin to tighten on the triggers of the shotgun to beat the big man's finger on the .45—and then he saw Henry Starr shifting his weight toward the big colored man, and he recognized the look in the bandit's eyes: they were in the same place the same way, almost like kin against this moment, and Bub willed everybody in the room to hold as tight and cool as himself when Henry Starr whipped his pistol across the back of the big man's head, dropping him like a grain sack off a platform . . .*

"But if you give my grandpa your gun, how did you get away?"

"Now Shaker, you don't figure any man could have got away from your grandpa, if he had a mind to hold him, do you?" Shaker didn't but stubbornly refused to say, because then he'd have to give up believing that if Henry Starr was minded to escape, there wasn't a jail in the world could keep him. "Lucky for me he didn't have that much of a mind to hold me . . ." said Henry Starr, but William Parker stirred impatiently so he finished, ". . . maybe that's a story for another night."

All the food and talk seemed finally to slow Shaker down; he yawned, his mother hugged him round the shoulders and he would let her do it if she wanted to that much. "Time for bed, little man." "All right," he said, "if Dick can come sing to me . . ."

Dick Rowland had been silent, his hooded eyes seeming not only to cut him off from the people around him, but almost to make him invisible, so that Henry Starr was half surprised to be reminded he had been there. All during supper, the only recognition of his reality and presence had been Harriet Parker reaching over unasked to spoon sweet potato pie onto his plate. But when Shaker spoke he came up into his face the way sunlight will rise in the bland face of a pond when the wind ruffles it. He picked up a steel-strung guitar that had been leaning against the wall. Shaker ran past him up the stairs, and Dick said, "Good night Miz' Parker, Will, Bub. Mr. Starr," as if he too were being put to bed, leaving the grown-ups to talk.

They heard the sound of Dick Rowland chording softly upstairs. Then his fingers started to ruffle and jab and slide on the strings, a hard blues softened and sweetened for a little child to hear, but underneath it an insistent walking heart-beat rhythm, bass notes dark, the middle ranges supple and rubbery, and once in a while a high string sang like a train whistle or a steel thread on black velvet.

"Listen," Harriet Parker said softly. "Shaker love this, he just love this part . . ." She sang a little, whispery, her eyes half-closed, enjoying how her little boy loved this part. ". . . John Henry said to his Shaker,/ Now Shaker, why don't you sing . . . ?" her voice faintly echoed by Dick Rowland's bass now doubled by Shaker's high-nasal "Throwin' fifty pound / from my hips on down, / Won't you listen to the col' steel ring Lordlord . . ." She put her lips together, satisfied, smiled and came back into her eyes. "He always think that the Shaker is him. Ever since Dick first teach him that song." The corners of her mouth drew down, and her eyes darkened. "He's a man got a calling for children, but he still . . . Every time he come back I think, this time he get quiet, this time he be ready."

"Well, Harriet," said William Parker quietly, "I guess the bad time ain't over him yet."

"Or the right woman come," she affirmed. Bub and William Parker flashed quick looks at each other, Bub (seated where his daughter could not see) lifting his eyebrows as if she astonished him. She said, "Sometime he seem like he used to be before the war. The other day they had this *row* outside, some of the white boys from over the street ganging up on Shaker in front of the yard . . ."

"Tell me *what?*" snapped Bub, and William Parker said, "Never told *me* . . ." but she said, "Just some boy-fuss that amount to *nothing*, and will you *hush* up and let me tell you why? I'm coming out the front door and Dick come driving up with the wagon"—she leveled a finger at her father—"which I guess you got him working on, making deliveries, you bad old man—and he jump off and step up behind the boys and drop his shadow *down* on them. They turn 'round, and he says real quiet, 'What's the trouble?' Don't nobody answer, because they been pointing and calling Shaker names, and they scared. And he says, 'I can tell you boys ain't doin' no *serious* kind of scufflin' here. Because five against one ain't fair fightin', it's just meanness. Man who fights five against one, he'd be mean enough to suck eggs.' And one of the white boys says, hidey-like, 'Less'n the one was bigger,' and Dick look all the way down at him and says, 'Big man who'd whup a little one, he'd suck eggs too.'

"I say to him after, 'Dick, how come you treat those boys so gentle?' and he says—that don't put ten words together in a week, unless he's pickin' under them—he says, 'Meanness just gets more meanness. That's why their daddies is so mean. But you catch it in a boy, maybe you can sweeten it out of him.' The boys been okay with Shaker after. You'd have whupped them," she told Bub, "and they'd have laid for *him*."

Maybe it was that he had just told that story leaving out all the part about Cherokee Bill—sometimes not saying the name could draw a ghost as easy as speaking it—but now there was something about Dick Rowland that reminded Henry Starr of his old partner. They both had the kind of size that was a menace in itself, the huge heaviness of body and those eyes that didn't connect, and that awful crazy peacefulness that was like a mask, and if what was behind it slipped out into the eyes and hands it could just blow a room full of people all to scraps, the air all gun smoke and blood smell, sister nephews nieces screaming out the door and George Brown shot dead in his own kitchen because one less hog was treating Cherokee Bill like a nigger.

Except that with Dick Rowland all the ugly hard edges had been smoothed and softened somehow, so that you could trust Dick Rowland to take care of a little boy, even if it wasn't his own. That's more than you could say for Cherokee Bill and hell: it was more than you could say for Henry Starr, *riding home to Cora from the movie in Okfuskee,* The Great Train Robbery, *and Jiminy smaller even than Shaker was, bouncing on the wagon seat next to him pumping ghost bullets into the brush shadows, "Pow! K-pow! When I'm big like you I'm gonna rob trains just like . . ."*

"That's a mighty fine little boy you have," Henry Starr said to Mrs. Parker.

"That Shaker," she said, as if the wonder had happened to her instead of being made by her.

"William Chaka Tubman Houston Parker," Bub chanted, "a lot of name for a little boy, but he can carry it. You liked that 'Chaka' idea, didn't you, Henry?" Bub looked a little sly and shifted his glance to Parker. "See now, I told you that way of naming a boy was more Injun than colored."

His daughter rolled her eyes theatrically and began shooing invisible flies off the tablecloth. "Well we're going through *that* again . . ."

Parker leaned back in his chair, waved a hand. "Go on, Bub. Lay it all out." The edge of old arguments was showing, but he wasn't going to let anybody get cut.

Bub's face angled toward Henry, away from Parker, his speech loaded: "Son Parker here is a disciple of Chief Charles Albert Sam. You heard of Chief Sam? The great *osageefoo*, wants to ship all us colored back to Africa."

Henry Starr shrugged. "Okay by us Injuns, long as you take your paleface friends with you."

"Ruins the point of it," said Bub, "which is to get where there ain't any palefaces. Out there 'mongst the bush niggers, us *colored* Negroes be the Great White Father."

Parker looked at his wife, it helped him ride hard feeling down. "You can lay all the bad words on it you want to, Dad, and it doesn't change the reality . . ."

"Of which there ain't none, and never going to be! How many of you got on that boat Mr. Sam had down in Galveston to ship you all over to Liberia?"

"But I'll tell you what does get to me, Dad," Parker continued, "it's that you got to *beat* on it so hard, when if there was ever a man should understand it's you. What was Boley, if not the very same thing? When you went for a sheriff, were you playing the white man? Or trying to make a place for the black man to be *for* and *by* himself?

"But you couldn't make it work here, could you, Bub? Big as you *is*, you wasn't *that* big. Now *ain't* that what gets you? Everybody in that little old town packing guns, ready and waiting twenty-four hours a day every day for somebody to ride in from outside and rob 'em or shoot 'em or lynch 'em or burn 'em out. And maybe you spot them coming, three, four, fifty times. But you can't stop 'em coming and coming at you, because they want you off of this earth, and if you stand long enough they'll do you like they done Dick Rowland's daddy. Now you tell *me* if that ain't the true history of Boley, Oklahoma."

Bub's face set stubbornly. "What you aimin' at but *let* the white man drive you right off the face of the United States of America, like he always meant to do? I got no blood in Africa. I got no land there and nobody of mine ever did. What's mine is here. Even every bit of a thing that ever was taken *from* me, it's still here. As long as I got a foot here, I ain't *give* up any of it. I can still draw that line and say brother, you better not cross it."

Parker leaned across the table. "You been drawing that line all your life, and every time you do it gets closer and closer. Right now that line is about as big as your shadow around your feet at noontime. Next stop is your skin, Bub. I'm telling *you.*"

"Son Parker," said Bub softly, "what you gonna have to declare for in Africa but your own skin? That and your forty-five, because nobody *out* there but some bush niggers got an idea Africa belong to them, and not some high yellow dickity American Negroes carpetbagging into the territory. Man, talk to my Henry Starr over here, ask him how Injuns take to palefaces in the territory . . ."

Parker's lips curled as if he tasted something bitter. "If I have to choose between going to Africa and live like what you say is a white man, or stay here and live like a nigger . . ."

"Live like a *nigger*?" said Bub. "You tell me Dr. Jackson in the next house be livin' like a *nigger* next door to me? Dr. Jackson? Who been a surgeon, cuttin' on white folks and colored both, up there at that Mayo Brothers Clinic up north? Livin' like a—?"

"Right *here*? Yes I do, I *do* say it! Because when it comes to riding a streetcar or getting his hair cut or sending his children to a school, they call him that *nigger* Jackson from North Detroit, if he was surgeon to Jesus Christ himself, goddamn *Mayo* Brothers . . . So what's a self-*respecting*—"

"Ho, self-res*pect*ing!" snapped Bub.

"—colored gentleman to do? You tell me what's left to do, old man, according to your lights."

"You're a college man," said Bub, "you figure it out."

---

Henry Starr and Bub Houston sat on the upstairs porch, cigar ends glowing softly in the dark. "Son Parker's a good enough man, he's good to my Harriet. But his *notions* . . . 'the solidarity of the colored race,' Africa, *Zulus* . . . He got what I call that 'high yellow fever.' People raised in this country live and die black or white. And if you're black they say git back; and if you're white, you're all right. That Cherokee Bill of yours, he had it too, they so close, so close to being white . . ."

"Cherokee Bill wanted to be Cherokee," said Henry Starr, but Bub waved that away:

". . . or whatever it is that ain't *black*, that's what I'm saying to you. And it make them angry-crazy—so close to the line they can feel it run up their middle, so close they can look across it and smell the cooking, all the pretty things they could have if . . . you know what I'm talking about here, Young Henry?"

"Yes." *Only you left my color out of your story, Bub, you got to add a line: if you're black get back, if you're red, good as dead.*

Bub pulled on the cigar so that its light lit his face and made two sharp red points in his eyes. "It take different folks different ways. Son Parker's got a lot of *head*, it take him cold and make him think about putting himself where he don't have to see or smell or think about anybody else being white anymore, even if he got to put himself and all those he supposed to take care of out in the middle of the jungle . . . You hear me talkin'?"

"I hear you, Bub."

"But your friend, Cherokee Bill: it took him murderous, make him mad enough to kill out everything he could see between morning and sunset. But it's the *nigger* he want to kill so bad, and who in hell did he think he was himself? Now you tell *me*: standing there in my bank-store, going on about *a town full of niggers a town full of niggers*, and him standing there just as much colored as . . . and then after that he says to *me* . . ."

*In Boley jailhouse: Henry Starr sitting on a stool talking to Bub through the bars. "I'd like to talk us loose if I can, Bub." Two of the gang rolled up asleep in their blankets, Cherokee Bill heaped against the wall staring ahead with those dead-fish eyes as he had since waking up after Henry Starr had cold-cocked him. And Bub said, "Go ahead and try, you already underestimated this place and me one time today," and then the voice came rumbling out of the dead heap of old clothes and giant's bones at the back of the cell, "Brother . . ."*

". . . he says to me, 'Brother, don't you let 'em hang me.' *Brother!*"

"You didn't let 'em," said Henry Starr. "We was worth a thousand dollars apiece dead or alive, and that posse wasn't half a day back of us."

"A peckerwood posse like that?" said Bub. "I'd never see ten cents on the dollar."

"Money is money," said Henry Starr, grinning down Bub's guff till the old man rared back and said, "Listen, I told you I knew how to lay down that line," and Henry said quietly, "I'm just real glad you decided to put us on your side of it."

Bub ate smoke, then shook his head. " 'Brother nigger, *don't* you let 'em hang me!' Huh! I suppose I can't blame you all for being crazy like that, because you ain't had my advantages."

Henry Starr said, "I guess we can't all be lucky enough to be born black in the state of Mississippi."

Bub gave him his look. "It ain't luck, Henry, and it don't just come to you in your blood—you got to learn it. My daddy was born black as me, and in the same place, but he could never draw the line. He was like a man got no walls to put between him and the weather, you know what I'm saying? I see him busting his back like a mule on that same plantation where he been a slave to the white man, and him a free man and the world in front of him, but he won't go off and take it. Because of his children, the five of us—because we was like a ball and chain on him. He get up and go, who put food in our mouths? And how he take us with him when he got to go not knowing where till he gets there, and maybe he never does. So he broke himself on that white man's cotton land like he was somebody's mule, and every bale of cotton that old man made laid on my shoulders. Bury my body, Lord, anywhere in this world but under cotton. The day come when I got to live or die, and I drew that line right before his own eyes, him on one side and me on the other. You hear what I'm telling you?"

"I hear you, Bub."

Bub drank the smoke of his cigar, and let it flow out his nostrils and down his chin. The smoke roughened and blurred the edges of his voice. "Yeah, you hear me all right. We come from the same place some way, Henry. We seen some of the same times. Sometime it feel like where you come from run deeper than what your blood is. Only one of Son Parker's age I can talk to more than five minutes is Dick Rowland, and that's 'cause he don't hardly say nothing."

"This Chief Sam idea," said Henry Starr. "Reminds me of old Preacher Brown, that said the Cherokee Nation was the Ten Lost Tribes and prophesied us out of Indian Territory and back to the Promised Land."

"Times come around serious," Bub murmured, "if my folks got to start thinking like that."

"Looks like it's your turn to play Injun, Bub," said Henry, thinking, *They had mine playing nigger long enough.* "Brown got a little smarter after I talked to him one time. We did a little business together . . . but he still wanted to ship all us Injuns back home to Jerusalem, and never knowed where in the world Jerusalem was—probably reckoned it was just south of Pittsburgh, because he didn't know where Pittsburgh was either." He made the cigar end glow. "At least your son-in-law seems to know where Africa is. He serious about going there?"

"Serious as a man can be who been to college and owns a movie house."

"Movies can get pretty serious," said Henry Starr. He was thinking about signing those contracts in Wilberforce's office; and about Miss Woodly, who when she wasn't startling at him like a skitty doe was glaring at him like a bobcat at a rabbit—just what kind of game was *she* playing?

Bub chuckled. "I forgot who you was, old 'Scourge-of-the-Southwest.' "

"I told you I had an alibi. They put the whole thing together without my knowing . . ."

"That ain't the best alibi you ever had, seeing how I *saw* you myself, scourging the Southwest in there all week."

"What they done was take little pieces of pictures from the other film I done and kind of cobble 'em together to make it look like I was runnin' around makin' a goddamn fool of myself with those . . . those —and robbing grocery stores and chicken coops." His voice was shaking a little, in the dark he felt again the little electric lick of the fear he had taken from the movie, seeing his ghost do things he had never done and appear in places he had never been—as if Foley had stolen his ghost and put his pale hands all over it and conjured it into performing shameful things in the face of the Nation, and if he could figure out a way to drop that son of a bitch down a trapdoor in the dark by God he was going to do it.

"Well, Young Henry," said Bub, "even the best of it ain't a lot better than a lie."

"I got something working there, Bub." He wanted Bub to believe him.

Bub looked skeptical. "You call that work, Young Henry? Man, I call that *play*-foolin', no better than my little grandson makin' believe his finger is a forty-five and the broom is a horse named Zulu." He sucked fire into the cigar, enough to redden his face and light red sparks in his eyes. "Now you want you some *work*, I could find you something serious."

Henry Starr grinned. "I been wondering when you'd get to it, Bub."

Bub shook his head. "Watchin' you carry on up there in those pictures make a man wonder can you still draw the line between what's serious and what ain't? When you operated round my county you was that good at walking the edge—and then I always wondered: if you was that smart, how come you let them push you over after you had got yourself pardoned and in the clear? and smart as you was about your business, why did you ever make that fool play in Stroud?"

"Maybe I just wanted to get my name in the papers."

Bub shook his head. "Then you fooled me. I thought when it come to business you knew how to draw the line."

Henry Starr said nothing. Bub had to answer the question for himself.

Bub sighed. "I'm easing around to asking you to do a job of work with me. I know you got parole to think of, and here I been telling you to draw yourself a *line*, so I got no bad feeling if you say no."

"What's the job?"

"I had a pretty good whiskey business here for a few years: dealing with buyers for the white speaks, and colored direct. Protection paid to the Tulsa police, nice and regular. Then these Chicago boys come in, and first one of my trade gets shot, then another burned out, another run off. I got to get out the business, or find me some new trade, and new trade means white. My protection man, my police, wants to put me together with this white man MacKinnon from up north, owns the big speak where the mayor and all of them big shots get their liquor. Meet me at your still, he says, but that's a fool's play. All right, he says, then bring your still man along and let my trader talk with him about what's wanted." Bub paused. "I want somebody behind me with a good pair of eyes. Case they figure to take out the competition all at once instead of one at a time. Still man no good with a gun. Dick Rowland be with me, but I'd like to have someone good as Henry Starr used to be."

"I show my face, Bub, and your protection will have all he needs to send me back to McAlester."

"I can fix it so he don't see you."

"Word gets around. Once he's got my name, all he has to do is lay for me. You know it ain't possible to keep every single condition of that parole and . . ."

"Well, in the first place he ain't going to be doing anything very legal himself . . ." Bub smiled wolfishly. "Anyway, if he do find out, you can't be in no more trouble than you already are. My protection is that lard-ass Deputy Price—the one you buffaloed at the movie that day?—and he be laying for *you* already. Yeah: you see what kind of trouble play-foolin' can bring to a man?"

*Yes*, Henry Starr was thinking, *only the police trouble ain't the worst of it. It's the ghost trouble: that's what worries me*. While they were talking Miss Woodly was lying in the dark dreaming pictures of Henry Starr, spinning them onto reels of smooth shiny snake skin, and Foley was sitting in the dark cutting and moving the little gray pictures of Henry Starr, till they raced like fast water through the darkness, pictures of his ghost doing things he'd never done in places he'd never been, ghost trouble, *I'd rather ride shotgun for Bub Houston where the worst that can happen is I get my head blowed off*.

And it was Bub Houston asking him, who never asked anything even of his own, let alone someone as far outside as Henry Starr; and didn't Henry Starr owe Bub Houston, not just on his own account but also on Cherokee Bill's?

Because it wasn't Bub Houston who had drawn the line and put Cherokee Bill on the wrong side of it, when the men with the greased ropes got their hands on them.

## NORTH OF TULSA *May 6, 1921*

The moonlight between the pine trees lit everything blue—the buckboard and team driven by Bub Houston, Henry Starr sitting his black-and-white horse alongside Bub, Dick Rowland mounted on the opposite side. The man next to Bub leaned across to shake Henry Starr's hand as Bub introduced him: "This here is T. J. Hanks. Cooks mash for me, and he's better at it than any of us ever be at anything."

"Give you white lightning," said T. J., "pure as mountain air and bite like a lion. Or mellow brown juice like there was honey in the mash. Or anything in between."

"Henry ain't the buyer, T. J."

T. J. grinned. "Just practicing."

"Dick will put you where I want you," said Bub. "Price will figure I got *somebody* watching my back, but I want him to think hard about who and where. It'll tire him out, thinking. You'll be able to hear what goes on." Bub looked intently at Henry Starr. "Listen all you can. You always was smart, Henry; I need someone can figure white folks better than I can."

"My record on white folks ain't much to brag about either," said Henry Starr, annoyed that Bub put him down white. But this was business; he dropped the feeling and said, "I'll listen, Bub."

Dick Rowland didn't say a word, moved into the trees like he expected Henry Starr to follow but didn't care if he did or not. Henry didn't like having to depend on someone who looked and acted like a dummy or a crazy man, especially one the size of a standing grizzly bear, but Bub Houston trusted Dick Rowland and that had to mean something. Rowland certainly moved like a hunter, sure and silent in the woods, and the stand he picked in the brush gave them sight on the whole of the small blue-lit clearing, and put them in deep shadow where no moon could light an eye or a gunbarrel.

Rowland pointed Henry to a position behind a tree trunk and took his stand about ten feet to the right. He licked his lips in obvious reluctance about speaking—but this was business, and even in the dark you could see Dick Rowland set himself to it. "Bub will bring the wagon in there," he said, pointing to where the road came through the brush to the clearing, "and he'll stop her *there*, by that broke-down pump." The spot was twenty-five yards away; they would have a clean shot at Price, and Henry Starr could hear them if they talked loud, which Price probably would.

"What do you hunt?" asked Henry Starr.

"Deer sometimes. Ducks." Either Rowland was sharp enough to see where the question came from, or too crazy to care. He spoke in a kind of no-breath voice that carried less on quiet air than a whisper hissing urgently between your teeth. He looked over at Henry Starr. "Mostly I don't shoot. I just put myself where I could if I wanted to."

"Like this," said Henry Starr, thinking, *what was it Bub had said about why he needed more guns behind him than Dick Rowland?* and at the same time he was listening intently for the approach of wagons.

Dick looked back into the clearing. "If Price does anything ugly I will shoot him."

"All right," said Henry Starr. In the dark it seemed Rowland could hear what was working in Henry Starr's head, and it made his hair prickle and rise. Sometimes a dummy or a crazy man could do that, but the more this one says the less dummy or crazy he sounds.

They heard the wagon and then Bub Houston drove his rig in from the left of the clearing. The roar of an engine and the banging of metal slammed over road ruts announced Deputy Price—then his open-topped Dodge sedan jumped into the clearing all at once in a glare of electricity that stopped Henry Starr's eyes with light-blind and lit Bub Houston stark and clear, and dead if they meant that because their ambush had been turned back on them. Henry Starr looked quickly over to Rowland and saw the big black man leveling his gun, crazy-dummy or not maybe he had been smart enough not to be surprised by the headlamps, *smarter than Henry Starr anyway*, and Henry leveled his own piece into the glare, aiming between and above the headlamps. If anyone started shooting he'd fire six rounds there and hope he was lucky enough to take out the driver.

Someone switched off the lights, and he heard Price's bellow of greeting through the green fog the headlights left in his eyes.

The green faded, blue-white moonlight glowed up. There was a man with Price who was shaking hands with T. J. Hanks, but Price had his hands in his hip pockets to show he hadn't shook hands with anybody. The other man must be MacKinnon, which was good news. It wasn't likely that Price would try to bushwhack anybody with his money bag standing there.

MacKinnon said something and they heard T. J. Hanks's penetrating voice answering, "Yes sir, any kind whiskey yo' *clientele* prefer." Henry Starr imagined Hanks smiling as he popped the French word into his minstrel-show singsong, and he mouthed the next words along with him: "Give you white lightning pure as mountain air and bite like a lion. Or mellow brown juice like there was honey in the mash. Or anything in between."

Hanks and MacKinnon adjourned to Bub's wagon to try samples, leaving Houston and Price facing each other. Henry Starr swung his rifle to cover MacKinnon, wondering could he rely on Rowland to keep his sights on Price. He looked over: the line of the black man's shadow held firmly on its target; his unblinking steadiness was a rebuke to Henry's uneasy shifts of vision.

Houston and Price just stood there facing each other, saying nothing.

Then MacKinnon and Hanks returned to them, MacKinnon nodding, the rising tone of his voice marking a question. "Oh yeah," bellowed Price, "sure you can. I've known both these boys a coon's age, and you can sure trust 'em." Starr heard an intake of breath from Rowland, but Bub Houston made no move, said nothing, and the words passed off harmless. MacKinnon shook hands again, Price didn't, the two white men walked to their car and Henry Starr hissed to catch Dick's attention and shifted off catlike through the brush, moving his stand to get out of the lights for an angled shot into the Dodge. But there was still no trouble as Price cranked it, and turned it jouncing back the way he had come.

Bub and T. J. still stood by the wagon as Henry Starr and Dick Rowland came out of the brush.

"Well?" said Bub.

"I don't like it," said Rowland, and T. J. put in, "You don't like whiskey or money neither."

"Tell me how you heard it, Young Henry," said Bub.

Henry Starr felt reluctant to answer, he was sore inside: those damn car lights had caught him out, maybe he wasn't up to business anymore. Maybe it was time to get old and take a set by the fireplace.

But on the other hand, how smart did you have to be to see that something about Price's deal was wrong? "You've swapped knives once or twice before," said Henry Starr. "So when you lose some of your outlets he brings you some business, because he's the kind of man got a good heart that way. You can tell that's so by the way he talks to you."

Houston just grinned back. "If I don't draw the line at his talking, Henry, maybe I got my reasons."

"Your reasons!" Dick Rowland spoke suddenly and sharply, taking them so much by surprise that their hands strayed toward their weapons: "Old Man, unless you *told* him your reasons, Price ain't bright enough to figure them out. If he talks that way to you, dumb as he is, he's got to believe he don't have to treat you white no more, not even in private and damn him ever doing it in public!"

Nobody took that tone with Bub Houston, Henry Starr would have said, but Dick Rowland did, and it wasn't just that you had to make allowances for a dummy or a crazy man (especially when he was that size), because Bub was looking seriously at the big young man, he was explaining himself. "I know the man, Dick. If Price think I won't stop him using his bad mouth on me like that, he ain't gonna be worried enough about me. He think this just old times, him yelling nigger in the street and swapping knives with us in the brush. It's just that old game we been playin' down South forever. So sometimes maybe he bust a still, but that just keep his badge shiny while he bring us the trade."

"He don't just bust 'em behind the badge," said Rowland. "He does it under a sheet too."

Bub's voice rose, justifying himself: "Well, that's part of the old game too. Who gonna think Captain *Kukluck* dealin' whiskey with niggers? . . .

"And anyway what's the difference," said Bub looking off into the black pines, "that's what I think: what's the difference between any of 'em, in sheets or out, if there was somebody lynched they was all in on it, either hauling on the rope or selling them the knife or writing it up for the papers or reading it out to the chil'ren like it was Uncle Billy's Whizbang. If you do business with one you can do it with anyone."

Henry Starr stood outside the talk wondering if *anyone* included him.

But Rowland bored in on Bub: "If you can't draw the line any finer than that, maybe it's time you got out of business."

To Henry Starr's surprise, Bub Houston seemed almost apologetic now. "Maybe you got it right, Dick. Maybe this the last time we deal. He cookin' somethin', or somebody behind him. But I got to find out what's behind him and how bad it is if I'm gonna keep goin'."

"You're going partners with a man that wants to bust you, and that's just the start," said Rowland.

"He don't know where my still is so he can't bust it. Long as I'm in business he got to deal with me one way or another, because I can price him down."

"He could try killing you instead," said Henry Starr.

And that made Bub Houston smile. "Well, he could . . . it's been tried before, Young Henry. It's been tried before."

"There's no man so big he can't be killed," said Dick. "Even up on that porch you can't cover the whole circle."

But the threat just made Bub show his teeth. "That's what I got friends and kinfolk for, brother: to watch my back . . ."

"And who be watching their back, Bub?"

"Damn it," said Bub, "I do what I got to to take care of my own. You either in with me or . . ."

"With you," said Dick quietly, but he gave only half his breath to the words and you could feel what he held back swelling in his throat like steam pressure, "like you been counting on from the start. Your family watches your back, and you got me to watch theirs, just like always"—Rowland's heavy head swung toward Henry Starr—"though Brother Henry here, he ain't so sure I can be trusted to kill for you if I have to," and Henry Starr saw Rowland's teeth flash briefly in the blue light. "With you, Bub," said Rowland with his head close to Bub's, almost too close, his voice whispering now, his throat screwed down like a pressure valve, "even if you go partners with Price and it tastes like you given me shit to eat."

Then Rowland broke away, moving smoothly for all his size, up on his horse and out of the clearing at a sharp trot, never looking back.

To Henry Starr it felt as if the darkness around them lightened a little when Rowland disappeared. There was too much jammed into every word and gesture between Rowland and Bub Houston, rage and grief and something stronger and worse than both, more than could get out of a man's head at once, more than he ever ought to have to say, you'd live happier longer not knowing what it was. It reminded Henry Starr of himself lying face to face with Cherokee Bill behind the barricade of smashed furniture in Fort Smith Prison, watching Cherokee Bill's ghost raging and pleading in his little black eyes like a man in a cell, like a giant shrunk down small shaking and shaking the bars of his cell while his brother Henry Starr talked him to death.

T. J. Hanks sighed and shook his head. "In with you any way at all, brother, but I hope what's in it is worth the chances."

"You ever know me to be stupid about business?" Bub glared at T. J. When the still man looked away he glared at Henry Starr.

"No," said Henry Starr, "you always knew what you were doing."

"Mr. Starr is a man of judgment." T. J.'s speech was mock courtly. "A reader of human character: he got doubts whether Dick Rowland can pull trigger on a white man."

Bub was too serious to smile, but he shook his head. "Henry, Henry: my my my. You walk the edge and don't even know it. You got to get away from those play-foolin' pictures, 'fore you lose your judgment entirely."

"When you let me in on the joke, Bub, I'll know what you're talking about," said Henry Starr.

Bub squinted at T. J. "That mouth of yours get you in serious trouble some day." He spat, and looked uncomfortable. "Well," he said reluctantly, "if you're in with us, you got a right to know. I just hope you still got some judgment, Henry, 'cause if you look at me and Price from where Dick Rowland stand you might forget to remember that I am still Bub Houston, and I know what I am doing. And I can see it from Dick's side too—I ain't blind, and I know how smart a man he still is anyway . . .

"But T. J., you remember what a smart boy he was." ("That's right," said T. J.) "His daddy was postman in Greenwood, they had money put by, and Dick their only son, and they fixed it for him to go up north to school, somewhere in Ohio. He left smart and come back smarter. That boy could hunt and fish like an Injun, run like a horse, he played baseball in college, you hear me telling you?"

"I hear you," said Henry Starr.

"He'd come back summers from that college, looking better and smarter every time. Girls and women they'd just rare up when he walk into a room, look at him like he was good enough to eat. You know, even my Harriet . . . well, but all the girls was sweet on Dick Rowland then."

Henry Starr saw a still image of Harriet Parker spooning sweet-potato pie onto Rowland's plate without him asking, and her eyes gone half-lidded listening to Dick Rowland singing to her little boy upstairs in his bed.

"When he run with the boys," said Bub, "they followed after; when he talked with the men, they listened. Him and his daddy liked to go at it furious, but like it was playing too: the old-fashion colored gentleman on one side, and his smart newfangle Yankee-college Negro son on the other, the old man talking 'bout how you got to learn to live with the white man against you, learn how to fend off and hang on, and the son talking a new day for the Negro in the twentieth century. But when talk was done Mr. Rowland would swell up proud at how his son held his ground, and Dick knew it, and it made him shine.

"Only time they come to serious differences was the war. Mr. Rowland was a clay-dirt Socialist, like I used to be, and we was all of us against Mr. Wilson getting into that war. We was for not going when they called us up for the draft, even got some of ourselves shot or jailed not doing it. But Dick, he signed himself up with the colored infantry, because if it was a new day for the Negro, the people have to prove themself alongside white folks, like he say, 'doin' the work of the world.' Prove themself! Like it ain't been done before, and done no good . . . Like I say, the arguing got serious.

"But even so when Dick come home with sergeant's stripes and polished brass and leather all over, and the khaki cut to the cut of his build—honey, he was a sight to see. Never mind politics: while Dick was home that last time his daddy preached a new day for the colored man, and there it was in the front pew—you hear me telling you? With *college* up inside his head, and a soldier in his body, a sergeant. *That* kind of day for the colored man."

"Tell it, Bub," whispered T. J.

"Uh *huh.* So Dick went back to the colored infantry and his new day, and Mr. Rowland went back to preaching hanging on, hanging back and hanging together. By and by the elections come around, and Mr. Rowland working Tulsa, where it was meaner than blue weather and no place to hide. He was a good talkin' man, he made folks stir and not just colored. Well . . . what was gonna happen out of that, you tell *me*? Hm? *Hm!?* Now *ain't* that so? Well you're goddamn right that's what happened—a couple hundred of them one night with sheets on and pointy hats, and guns and knives and a rope out by the Katy trestle on Spring Creek, and what could one man have done against a hundred?"

T. J. said, "That's true."

"Dick was in New York, shipping over to France, and his momma said, 'Don't tell him till he's across the water, I don't want him coming back here now.' And there was some said, Amen to that: let's not have no more trouble. Amen to that: keep the boy safe out the way of them that killed his father, because who knows what he might say or they might do? And some said, Amen to that: let the boy learn him how to kill white folks over there in France, and when he come home . . . You understand what I'm sayin'?"

"I hear you, Bub."

"So they was over in France, in the line. Son Parker was with Dick, they was buddies—an Oklahoma-Arkansas colored outfit with cracker officers, understand? There they was when Dick Rowland heard what they done to his daddy.

"He freeze up sudden, and askin' Son Parker, over and over again, 'They shame him first? They shame him? They shame him first?' Son Parker say nothing, what he gonna say? And Dick can't leave it, 'Did they shame him? Did he try to fight 'em off? Did he try gettin' away? Didn't any of those niggers stand up for him? Didn't he know what was going to happen, but he just stand there till they cut him down?'

"Then he grip my son Parker by the arms and push his face up close and say, 'Somebody gonna *die* for this.' Parker look at the size of that boy, and feel the power of his hate in his hands, and Parker say he knew it was lots of people could die starting just about anywhere and no end in sight.

"Next day they went over the top, three hours of artillery coming both ways beforehand, but Parker says he wasn't scared of that as much as he was sitting there nose to nose with Dick Rowland, hate blowing out of his face like snow in a blue north wind, blind and cold.

"Then the cracker officer blow his whistle and they go up and over, dodging forward through the wires and mud and shell holes and shells, losing men all the time, pushing through the smoke and the machine-gun bullets and the shells chunking up the mud and slop, but all Parker can see is the cracker officer running forward and Dick Rowland right behind like he was chasing him, his bayonet on the end of that long Springfield rifle like one of them Zulu spears.

"And then a shell come close and knock Parker in a hole, and when he come up all he can see is Dick's helmet going behind this churned-up hump of ground. So he starts after him, because Dick was his buddy. He's crazy, my son Parker, but he's a good man . . . you hear me telling you?"

"I hear you."

"He jump into the German trench, and he's alone. Bullets going by overhead, shells roaring through like the Katy Flyer overhead, but he's alone in the trench: except for the cracker officer lying there looking up at him with a red hole between his blue eyes. Parker say the eyes was crossed like the man trying to look at the hole in the middle of his own head, he look real *stupid* dead like that. There was Huns too, three of them, Parker could see he had shot the first one trying to stand up and knocked him backwards over the machine gun, and the second in the back turning to run, and the third he'd pinned to the trench wall with his bayonet, and gone off around the corner of the trench.

"Wasn't hard following Dick Rowland's trail. Somewhere along the way he busted the Springfield and switched it for the pistol of the officer he busted it on, beating the helmet off his head and bust the head too. Then he switched the pistol for one of those trench shotguns. The last dozen or so must have heard him coming and been running away from him, shot in the back as they was, or from up close in front like they had tried surrendering and Dick never paid no mind, but most of them shot down as they run for the bunker—which Dick come to, and chucked one of their own grenades in on 'em just as Parker caught up, and see Dick disappearing down into the smoke, and he stood outside and listened to that trench gun woofing under the ground like some big mean son of a bitch dog was down that hole . . ."

"That's how it was," said T. J.

"And when Dick Rowland come out of that hole he was empty. Like there wasn't nobody left at home in back of his eyes." Bub shook his head. "Man, it make you think about death and judgment every time he walk into a room. But my son Parker, and my Harriet—you know, they was true to him, just like it was still Dick Rowland inside there, that nobody could see. I told my daughter she's crazy, hangin' onto something wasn't no more Dick Rowland that used to be than a picture on the wall, and her a married woman and a child comin'—what's she mean tending that big crazy man with no more sense inside him than a baby, but big enough to break you in his hands like a stick? I used to think she still . . ." Bub shook that off. "But they done it, her and son Parker, I got to say they did all right . . ."

"Yes Lord," said T. J.

"And so he's come back, little by little. You see yourself, he's gettin' smart again, he'll talk like he used to. And he can be so gentle. But that quiet he get sometime . . ." Bub leaned forward intently, his nostrils flaring like he was on a scent: "That kind of quiet that make you afraid, like that partner of yours used to get—that Cherokee Bill."

"Yes," said Henry Starr, and he remembered the terrible quiet of Cherokee Bill in his cell waiting to hang, holding the lynching handbill Eoff had given him and thinking how he needed to kill somebody now, conjure himself a gun and kill somebody, *it ain't the dying, Henry, it's the nigger of it that I hate.*

"Only there's difference between them too, and it ain't just that Dick been to college and Cherokee Bill was just a crazy-dummy."

The difference, thought Henry Starr, was you could trust Dick Rowland to take care of a little boy, and watch out for a family that wasn't his own making, and to stick by his friend even if he had to eat shame and swallow his rage for the friend's sake—and that was more than you could say for Henry Starr, never mind Cherokee Bill.

"No," said Bub, "the difference is that your Cherokee Bill, he never really done what was in his head . . . hell, how could he, not knowing was it niggers or crackers or redskins he needed to kill, not knowing where the shame was coming on him? Not knowing just how and where to draw his own line. But Dick Rowland, he saw it clear that one time, and the Lord give him leave to *do* what was in his heart. And he done it, brother. He done all of it, right down to the very bottom. And they never killed him for it either, but he come back out of it alive, knowing what it was he wanted in his heart—knowing what was in him to do."

Henry Starr was silent, Dick Rowland and Cherokee Bill kept changing places in the dark behind his eyes. *I wonder which is worse,* he thought, *to know or not to know what the thing is you really want, and what power is in you to make it be.*

# Used to Be

TSIGESU

"That's how it was in the old time: that's how it used to be. Henry Starr spoke to Cherokee Bill, and that giant killer of men gave himself up to the Hanging Judge, knowing there was nothing for him then but the greased rope and the black hood. Henry Starr—what a power he had! If he changed tobacco, if he worked tobacco then, if he used certain words—what words they must have been, *hyenh*? Don't you wish that you had those words?

"But nobody knows them, nobody ever knew them but Cherokee Bill, and Cherokee Bill did not know them long. They were in his mind the next day, Friday, when he stood on the gallows, with Maledon the Hangman holding the black hood in his long white hands, his beard like a bib on his chest; and Eoff next to him standing by the lever waiting to pull it with his one good arm. Cherokee Bill looked around at the crowd of people standing there in the sun to see him drop through the hole and into the blackness of the air, and he remembered those words, and he smiled:

" 'Sure is a lot of people come to see me die.'

"And Maledon the Hangman fixed the rope on his neck with his long white hands, and Cherokee Bill grinned again.

" 'Any last words?' said Maledon, the black hood held in his hand with its mouth breathing on Cherokee Bill.

"Cherokee Bill made his face stone, but he was still smiling inside his face, as if he was satisfied.

" 'I come here to die,' he said, 'not to make a speech.'

"And they hooded his head, dropped him through the hole, broke his neck and let him swing.

"Six months later the Hanging Judge Isaac Parker died of a stroke. But maybe he was satisfied too.

"And Henry Starr, he must have been satisfied: because the Hanging Judge let him keep his life . . .

"And get out of Fort Smith Prison seven years later in 1903 with a pardon from President Theodore Roosevelt himself, and got married, and a store in Cromwell in the Creek Nation, and went straight that time—straight for as long as his blood or his luck or the law would let him. Because he went bad again, you know: yes. They say, maybe, that the ghost of Tom Starr and Hop Starr and Belle Starr, and the ghosts of the Daltons and of Cole Younger and Buck and Dingus James, and the ghost of Cherokee Bill come after him and whispered him they was so lonely, the trail they made was empty and nobody riding it like it was in the old days, nothing but law and cheating on the law, sneaking around—not like it used to be. Maybe that's why he started robbing banks again, only banks this time, not any trains or stores, only banks: just like in the old days, slide into town loose and cagey, into the bank slick and greasy, 'Thumbs up and stand steady!' open the cashbox, burn the mortgage papers, and then out into the street firing at windows streetlights signs clouds to just hoo-raw and buffalo that town so that every head with a hat on is squinching down for cover and every gun hand froze.

"Twelve banks he done that way, twelve banks: and with the seven that made nineteen. Marshals after them, and sheriffs and police, even the state militia—a regiment on horses with carbines sabers and pistols and a Gatling gun that could fire two–three thousand bullets like you were cranking a hurdy-gurdy, and I'm telling you that they never saw him, never smelled the ghost of his trail, he just put dogshit in their hands, he just disappeared in blue *ha!* blue smoke.

"Till something got to working on Henry Starr. Who knows what it was? Maybe some old doctor working tobacco was climbing over Henry Starr. Maybe it was those ghosts of Tom Starr and Belle Starr and Cherokee Bill and Buck and Dingus James come back and told him: *Henry, you rob those banks too careful. You rob banks like a banker banks 'em. Rob 'em hard, why don't you?—like your family done in Lawrence and Glendale and Liberty and Northfield and Coffeyville. Rob 'em two-at-a-time, nobody but Buck and Dingus ever robbed two banks in one swoop. The Daltons got shot to pieces when they tried it in Coffeyville, remember?—the same year you won the prize and robbed the Land Office in Tahlequah. Remember how it used to be in those old times? Let's see now what Henry Starr is made of.*

"So they hit the two banks on opposite sides of Main Street in Stroud,

Oklahoma, and everything was running along like smooth water until some little squirt with a shotgun bigger than he was pops out of a butcher shop and shoots Henry Starr's ass full of buckshot and down in the street there in Stroud, Oklahoma, the whole town mobbing up and sending round for some rope while Henry Starr is bleeding on the counter of the butcher shop, Bill Tilghman standing by the door with his riot gun . . . and that was twenty-one banks before Bill Tilghman got Henry Starr again, and kept the mob off of him, and sent him back to prison in 1915.

"But you know, he got out again. He was so smart . . . he could charm the bark off a hickory. Henry Starr in his life robbed twenty-eight banks, one for each of the farms the Starr clan had taken from them in Carolina and in the Indian Nations. But the twenty-ninth bank . . . that was the number that was too many for him.

"Some people say: because it wasn't his bank, it wasn't justice for him to rob past twenty-eight. Some people say: the last bank was the most justice of any bank he robbed, because it was not for any of the Starr clan's own farms, but for the land lost in the Old Time, when the Cherokee Nation was among the mountains and the waters that lie under the tall trees back in the Old Place. But I've told you already what I think: that it was too many for him. Those things were lost so long ago that the power-that-is no longer remembers them, and you can claim no justice on the names of that Place because they are out of remembering now. I don't know any words to bring them back or make those old stories be.

"But me . . . I still wish I had those words that Henry Starr gave to Cherokee Bill, to make that giant killer of men give up his ghost to be caught in a black hood and strangled with a rope by the Hanging Judge in Fort Smith Prison, away down in the Cherokee Nation, a long time ago."

## FORT SMITH PRISON *July 23, 1896*

They sat quietly behind the barricade of wrecked furniture. Henry Starr rolled two cigarettes, lit them, and passed one to Cherokee Bill. The giant took the smoke like a thirsty man drinking water, and breathed it out again in a great cloud. "It almost worked real good, Henry. I had the running water and the bullet. If I could have changed some tobacco it'd have worked me all the way outside. As it is I got Eoff here," and he leaned over and gave the guard's body a proprietary slap. Eoff was bound and gagged with strips torn from sheets and blankets—that was the ugly ripping sound that the guards had thought was Cherokee Bill a-cuttin' on old Eoff. Cherokee Bill had built his body into the barricade, tucked among the splintered chair legs and busted tables and bed frames, it was interesting that none of the bullets fired down this way had killed Eoff yet but there was still time. The red-faced guard had a big purple bruise on the side of his face where Cherokee Bill had pistol-whipped him, and a bullet through his left shoulder meat, but he was still breathing, his eyes were swole out and his face mooning up and turning blue-black as if his fear was a head of steam building behind the gag.

Cherokee Bill's fear was working too, hiding under the pocked ugly mask of his face, lifting itself to peek out his eyes like a small black man hanging onto the bars of his window.

Henry Starr shook his head. "It's no use talking about it, Bill. Even if that old-time powwow stuff did work, which I ain't saying it does, you know you never done it right. Pouring water out of a cup ain't no more running water than piss is. You changed a slug for a bullet in the middle of the charm. And you never had no tobacco to begin with."

"No," said Cherokee Bill, "I traded all my tobacco to that damned trusty for the forty-five and bullets. That tricky little Creek bastard. He knew I'd need that tobacco if . . ." His face split with a grin that showed his big square yellow teeth. "I give him all my tobacco, and a roll of greenbacks I had stashed, and a treasure map, *hyenh*, to all that gold you and me buried out there in the Nations, gold and silver and jools, *hyenh*. So he give me the gun and took all the tobacco and figures it'll never work for me without tobacco so he's safe, that smart little fucker. Then when he come round with Eoff today I blowed his brains out the side of his head right after I took Eoff down, and him so smart." The two stiff feet in their cheap boots protruded from the barricade, the wrecked head and outflung arm were on the other side—Henry Starr had walked toward the dead trusty down the long corridor to Cherokee Bill.

"It was a good play, Bill," said Henry Starr, "it could have worked, maybe, if you'd had some luck."

The giant looked down and blushed a little. "Thanks, Henry." He looked up. "I got 'em stood off pretty good anyway."

"It don't matter now, Bill," said Henry Starr. "If you don't give it up they'll just bring on that Gatling gun they've got over at the armory and just naturally shoot this whole damn place to little pieces and you with it. You've heard how that thing goes on, just cranking out the slugs like . . ."

"Not while I got Eoff here," said Cherokee Bill uncertainly.

It was awake now, the ghost of Cherokee Bill's fear: like a smell off his body, like a little black man walking back and forth in the cells of his eyes. And Henry Starr looked at it and spoke to it again, knowing it for what and who it was: "You think Judge Parker's gonna let you walk away just because this stupid peckerwood let you catch him?"

Cherokee Bill shook his head. "They'll shoot hell out of both of us."

"And hang whatever's left: like blanket heads drying jerky."

"I'll charge 'em . . ."

"And get the legs shot out from under you," and Henry Starr could see Cherokee Bill's ghost turning round and round and round inside him, black as a shadow, sucking the skin of the face inward. "Just blast away till you can't crawl and then come down and get you."

Cherokee Bill was very quiet. His muddy face had a thick, numb, dead look. "What should I do, Henry? I got a horror of hanging." His eyes dilated as if to draw Henry Starr's ghost inside with his own and make it twist with him in the locked cell. "It's a nigger's death, Henry. It ain't no way for a Hair Twister to die."

Henry Starr felt that his smooth brown face was quiet and still as water, he listened as if he could hear the giant's ghost whispering to itself, and he didn't smile but he felt his own charm like a glow from his face as he spoke to the black ghost of Cherokee Bill's fear, thinking, *You out-traded that Creek trusty, Bill, swapping him your tobacco and greenbacks and a phony treasure map for the .45 I got to outswap you, my brother, for the .45 that means I am maybe going to live past Saturday, and all I got to trade you for it is your own death.*

"You got to go out the right way, Bill. Nothing left but that one thing. You've got to say your say, and put your word on 'em. You've got to let your people know you went out like a man, not twisting like a snake with a broken back on a dirty jailhouse floor."

Cherokee Bill thought about it, his eyebrows straining up and down as the thoughts wrung them. "I meant to thank you, Henry, for telling this dumb peckerwood that I was one of the Hair Twisters. I hope that clan don't find out and hold it against you."

"No," said Henry Starr, "it ain't to thank me. You got the claim of blood on them."

"But I thank you," said Cherokee Bill softly, his face still and quiet again. "They'd name me a nigger if I claimed them as kin and you know it. But all these peckerwoods, all these . . . they heard you, Henry. When they talk about how I tricked 'em, how I got this here gun, they'll tell what you said about me too." He looked down at the gun. "I got to go the right way. They got no right to treat me, to hang me like a nigger, Henry. I'm Cherokee and a little bit Mex, but mostly I'm as white as anybody. They ain't gonna string me up and cut on me like I was a—"

"They won't unless you let 'em." Henry Starr snapped it out. *Hold it for truth*, he told himself, *hold it for truth which it maybe is.*

"I'll go down shooting first."

"Listen, Bill: that hanging and cutting stuff, that ain't how it is when it's done according to the law. That's if it comes down in hot blood, like if they take you running, or they had to do something dirty like blow off Eoff's own head, one of their own, to get at you. Or if it was a woman . . . It just cuts 'em loose for meanness, then. But it don't have to be that way, not when it's according to law. It's got respect. It's as fast as a bullet. It's quiet. There ain't any cutting before or after, no pushing or hauling 'less you push or haul. They march you up and it's quiet. Quiet for you as for any white man, for the whitest man that ever was, whether a chief or a judge or anything: the same for you. Quiet so if you got words to say you can say 'em, and they can be heard. Quiet as a picture. And folks watching in the quiet, hundreds probably, white and Cherokee, to take in what you're going to say and to watch how you take your dying. And showing respect too, for the law and for him that's got to hang, same as if it was a judge of the Nation.

"There'll be hundreds of people there when the word gets out about how you tricked 'em, and got your gun and your hostage, and how you bluffed all of 'em to a standstill. They'll remember it for a hundred years. I'll tell them myself, Bill, I'll"—and suddenly he saw it as if it were real—"I'll tell it into those light pictures, just like Buck James. I'll have it written out in the light, with your face and everything . . ."

"My face without colors, my ghost," said Cherokee Bill, "like a picture. But how will they remember what I say?"

"And the shadow of your words too, made out of the same stuff. I swear."

Cherokee Bill sighed and looked sadly at Eoff's purple swollen face. He turned the .45 butt first and handed it to Henry Starr. A wistful look came over his huge ugly face and his hand lingered on the barrel. "Maybe we could just say we was surrendering, and when they come down for us . . ." Then he smiled. "No good, hey Henry?" And took a second .45 from under the heap of torn blankets on which he had been sitting.

---

And it wasn't until the next morning that Henry Starr asked himself why Cherokee Bill should have believed his promise when according to the sentence Henry Starr himself was supposed to hang in one more day; had spoken right from the start as if he never expected Henry Starr was going to hang at all, but was going to be there to hear from some angry Hair Twisters, and to tell the people about the dying of Cherokee Bill.

But then Cherokee Bill had always said, there wasn't anybody ever got up early enough to climb over Henry Starr.

# Shooting Script

## TULSA TO STROUD *May 7, 1921*

Miss Woodly had them up early for the Frisco line's morning train to Stroud fifty miles southwest of Tulsa. She laid out an itinerary, beginning with the scene of his last and most spectacular robbery in Stroud, where they'd rent three riding horses and a spring wagon, charged to the Pan American Motion Picture Company, and strike out across country to look at some other sites of Henry Starr bank robberies.

They needed the wagon because Esterhazy insisted on taking his equipment: a still camera that required a tripod and a portable viewfinder of his own design that would let him frame a scene as if through the eye of his movie camera. A set of glass filters in a range of colors and darknesses allowed him to transform the scene into monochromes of various intensities, to analyze any scene into pure contrasts of black and white. With the image cleaned of extraneous color the scene became a field into which Esterhazy could infuse the special qualities of softness, allure, intensity, grief, *angst*—whatever emotion it was that, when the occasion arose, he would decide to capture or project within the camera's frame.

Henry Starr had some special equipment as well, which surprised them: a wooden crate marked AGRICULTURAL EQUIPMENT, about which he would only say, "It's farming country, ain't it?"

They rode in the regular coach in a set of facing seats, the two men looking forward and Miss Woodly watching the blue-green plains of alfalfa ambling backward as the train carried her toward Stroud. The window made flickers of white light in her pale eyes, glossed the smooth texture of her skin and showed corn-silk down on her cheeks. It felt too close at first, sitting like that looking at each other. Esterhazy was excited by this chance of looking his fill at her, but something in the situation depressed and frustrated him—the way Miss Woodly and Henry Starr, like magnets put wrong side together, kept touching eyes and looking away. Esterhazy grunted irritably and tugged a broad-brimmed straw hat lower over his eyes, pretended to go to sleep.

She kept looking at Henry Starr, then over at Esterhazy, and her eyes suddenly took a set on Henry Starr like a bobcat looking at a hare. "You're not going to tell me anything, are you? Not unless I ask."

Esterhazy sat up and took notice.

Henry Starr's color darkened a little. "What-all do you need to know?"

She laughed, a little fiercely. "As far as I can tell right now," she said, "I might need to know everything: why you did all those things that you did, or that they say you did: why did you start robbing banks, and why did you go back to robbing after you'd gotten clear and been pardoned?"

*And why are you so interested in making movies?* Esterhazy thought silently. *The money or the vanity, which?*

"I'm not sure I can show you why," he said quietly. "I only figured to show you *where*."

"*Where*—all right," said Esterhazy, "but *how* is all camera cares about."

"Yes," she said, and the line of her body changed, she gathered and concentrated herself, sitting erect in her seat. "I'd like to know how it was done. How about . . . trains? When you robbed a train, like Jesse James—how did you do it?"

"Well," he said uneasily, "I never pleaded to train robbing. Fact is I never liked trains. Banks are better."

"Why?" said Miss Woodly, and Esterhazy held up his finger pedantically: "No," he said, "*how*? How would you rob train? This one, for instance."

Henry Starr tilted toward the aisle and looked quickly forward and back: just themselves and an old man with a head bald and pale as an egg and a farm wife in a sunbonnet with her little daughter, their fingers strung together playing cat's-cradle. "Not worth the trouble," he said. "Midday coach and freight to Oklahoma City, no express car, coaches full of farmers that spent all their cash money in the big city."

Esterhazy would have none of it. "I attach express car at next station. I fill empty seats with wealthy merchants in best clothes, with wives and watches and jewelry and fat wallets."

The train slowed and the weathered Gothic facade of a station filled the windows: DEPEW, OK. POP. 625. Esterhazy started to speak, but Henry Starr held up a hand for silence and watched the station.

The train jerked and pulled out, and when the windows emptied he relaxed and said, "All right now. You pick a station out in the country.

You look it over: how many men at Depew station, how many guns, when does the train get there?"

He looked quizzically at Miss Woodly, and she grinned back. "Stationmaster with a blue hat, clerk in the ticket office and three men on the platform. Twelve forty-five, and I don't know how many guns."

"Good!" said Henry Starr, surprised at how quick she'd picked up his play and joined it; he almost laughed. "But we've been by here three-four times already in the last couple weeks. So we know there's never more than three men on duty at the station after dark, which is when you want to do it. Rifle and a six-gun in a drawer in the office, maybe the stationmaster packs a gun in his pocket, anybody robs the Depew ticket office must be so stupid or hard up it won't pay to draw down on him for the six bits in ticket receipts and eighteen Sears catalogs in the mailbag.

"On the train itself you figure maybe one in four of the men passengers are carrying guns, rules say they got to be unloaded, and they are anyway somewhere unhandy. Engineer and fireman too busy even if they're armed. Conductor might be a problem, or the brakeman, so you ride the train a couple times to see who they are, and where they put themselves when the train pulls into Depew at nine fifty P.M. on a Thursday night. Where it gets serious is where the real money is, in the express car. The idea would be to take the station before the train comes in, jump the engineer and fireman while they're trying to coal and water. You need three men riding on the train, making small talk with the brakeman and the conductor . . ."

*Kid Wilson always liked that part, liked trains and wanted to work on one, he'd talk the brakeman's head off and ask could he turn the brake wheel or pester the conductor to let him punch tickets and generally have a high old time, and them trying to ignore him back to his seat (pesky young punk) finally turning their back and there's the Kid's .45 making a dent in their spine as the train slows toward the lights of the station.*

"Yes?" said Miss Woodly. "Then what?"

"I'd want . . . say three men for the station, maybe two more in the brush. One man to buy a ticket, 'Here's your change,' and when the agent looks up there's a forty-five leveled on him through the cage. Second man asks the stationmaster the time, he takes out his watch, looks up and the man says 'Thumbs up.' Walks him back into the station, takes and puts on his hat with the brass button."

"Got you!" said Miss Woodly. "The boy at the telegraph."

"Right you are, ma'am. Boy sees Linc . . . sees the man at the ticket window, the agent's in his way and maybe the boy don't like the agent much or maybe he's just not thinking two jumps ahead, so he dives for his key and *tappity-tappity-taps* away till maybe I kick the door in and say 'Stop that now, sonny,' and the kid does, all red in the face because he got the message off and stood by his duty and showed his quality. And to tell the truth I'm of two minds, whether to let him go on thinking that or to tell him. But I figure it's better he should know: next man who robs this train may not appreciate a boy with sand in his craw. 'Son,' I might say, 'you done brave, but foolish. We cut the wire before we come in here, and if we hadn't I'd have had to pop you with this,' and I let him look at the Colt, cocked and ready, pointing at his middle. 'You showed sand. Next time show sense,' and he says 'Yessir,' like I was his uncle or something."

"Yes," she said with a pleased grin, "I can see you doing that."

"What did you do next?" Esterhazy asked, but Henry Starr stared out the window for a few seconds. *To his eyes it was black out there, and in the blackness Cherokee Bill was standing out in the brush, his ugly buckshotten face shadowed by the brim of his high-domed black hat, chuckling a little bit while he waits to go for the baggage car, he makes a small* ooblooble *in his throat.*

"Axes," he said, "for the express-car door, and someone who can convince the agent he'd better open the safe . . ."

"Or . . . ?" she said, and Esterhazy snicked his index finger across his throat, and suddenly her eyes jumped wide open and she looked quickly up and down the car—there was the woman in the sunbonnet and her little girl playing cat's-cradle, the old man with the bald head, in the next second the woman would open her eyes and shriek, the bald head crack like an eggshell, brains blood-slimy like a fetal chick—and she looked back at Henry Starr, asking.

Well, what could he say that wasn't just a damn lie, when the truth was too hard and ugly for him to say? That wherever he went Cherokee Bill was with him, his partner and his brother, mad and ugly and ready to blow holes in this one or that one, kin, kind or total stranger at a look or a word or the red flick of a thought—because Henry Starr needed Cherokee Bill, because without Cherokee Bill's crazy magic Henry Starr had no strength, no power to make the world put its thumbs up and stand steady.

Esterhazy's impatience rescued him: "All right, so you come into train, everybody wearing masks, pull out pistols and—"

"No masks," said Henry Starr. They looked skeptical. "Well look," he said, "after a while there wasn't much point keeping your face hid.

You get a reputation, and people can spot you by the mix of people you got with you, or by the way you handle yourself."

" 'Thumbs up and stand steady,' " said Miss Woodly, "you've got a style or a trademark . . ."

"Yes, like that." He thought for a moment. "Say you've got the reputation for taking banks with a bandanna over your face. Every green kid with a gun who robs anything upwards of poor boxes and country stores uses a bandanna, but getting your train or bank knocked over is big doin's—you lose all that cash, insurance goes up if you can even get it, newspaper's in an uproar, sheriff's up for reelection: you don't want folks thinking any squirt kid with a popgun can take your train or bank down, do you? So it's got to be Henry Starr and Cherokee Bill, or the James Boys or the Dalton Gang that done it. Your score gets heavy enough without all the extras. If you were seen face to face robbing a train in Texarkana on October 25, then that can't have been you that hit the bank in Colorado Springs twenty-four hours later."

"If they catch you for one, why worry about other?" Esterhazy asked, and Henry Starr popped the answer right back: "Because maybe somebody got shot robbing that bank. And nobody got killed at the one I was doing."

She was looking at him sharply: "How could you know nobody would fight back? How could you have been so sure?"

"You have a certain reputation," he said. "People know it's Henry Starr they're looking at, so they know every hole is covered, it's smile and take your medicine and nobody gets killed or even roughed up, because that's how Henry Starr does business."

*You sound like a banker,* said Henry Starr's ghost inside his head, and he lifted a lip at himself, *you make it sound as easy as keeping store.* "All right," he said, as if conceding something, "you've also got someone behind you, maybe, who's got the reputation—maybe he's earned it, maybe not, but the express agent only has to believe it could happen to him and he'll open that safe."

He looked at Miss Woodly: her eyes, slightly dreamy and unfocused, held on his face and his mouth, her small lips parted, and if she had understood what he was trying to say about Cherokee Bill she sure didn't show it. She looked like Jiminy listening to a bedtime story, eyes full of fog and lids slipping down, or Shaker sleepy–full of having dinner with the Scourge of the Southwest—and he suddenly felt bad for her for looking at him that way, he felt an impulse to warn her. "Listen," he said sharply, "there's some folks that it makes 'em happy to know they been robbed by somebody famous, and famous for being good at it."

"Yes," she said, coming to herself again. "If you put it that way it's just like that little boy who wanted to touch you in the lobby after the movie—"

She made Henry Starr blink, echoing his thoughts like that, as if she could hear what whispered under his hair.

"—only it's better than going to see *The Scourge of the Southwest,* because it's all real," she said.

He hesitated. It wasn't going like he had figured, her questions kept spoiling his balance, shifting him toward places he didn't want to go, things for which he never figured to have to answer to *her*. Some things she saw too damn much of too damn fast; but others, she didn't even know enough about to ask the right questions. What would she think if she saw his partner, his brother Cherokee Bill, this little Miss Woodly here with her milky skin and clear eyes and the corn-silk down shining over her cheeks, looking so young that if her lips was milk wet it wouldn't surprise you—*and there's things you can't tell a child, not without putting a twist in their ghost, if I ain't learned that much out of my life then* . . . No: if he said it flat out she'd give him one look like she had to puke, drop him and his movie and run like hell, or else make up some pretty story like a kid would do, that would suit her notions and have nothing to do with him. But it made no sense for him to lie to her either, because that was like conjuring against your own ghost, she'd make the movie and then there would be Something walking around inside his name that had nothing to do with Henry Starr.

His words hung fire. He didn't know what story to tell or how to tell it. For a moment he wished he was riding shotgun on a load of Bub Houston's moonshine, at least there you could say who and what you were, bullets were easier to dodge than Something when it gets its holts on your name.

He made a gesture, like a man throwing something away, giving up. "Yes," he said, "it was real."

"Very neat!" said Esterhazy. "Like taking candy from baby. Good rehearsals, perfect timing, right costumes, actors you choose well for part. You are better director than Foley, and not with blanks in gun, yes?"

Henry Starr found himself disliking the compliment, and it gave Miss Woodly's face a toothache twist. Did she think he was some dime novel bullyboy snitching gimcracks from little pigtail girls? "I told you I never did like doing trains," he said apologetically. "Too many different kinds of people on trains. Rob a bank and all the bankers get down on you, but there's lots of folks is down on bankers. But trains . . . you got all kinds mixed together, maybe you take some poor widow's last dollar that was to see her buried proper, or some little girl's birthday presents. Banks are better."

"Why better?" asked Esterhazy, but Miss Woodly said, "Wait, let him finish robbing this train first. The widow's mite and the poor man's savings . . ."

"Look," he said, "it wasn't like that, we tried not to do that, we . . . I'd tell the boys, leave the women alone, and don't take a thing from any man who works with his hands. I'd come right into the passenger car and say it again so everybody could hear it, 'You remember my instructions about the ladies, men. And Henry Starr don't take money from any man poorer than himself,' and they'd say 'Right boss,' and 'Sure enough,' just like they was told."

"How'd they know who was who?" she pressed him. "In their Sunday-go-to-meeting how could you tell . . . ?"

"A man's hands'll show it," he snapped back and she answered, "You checked each man's hands?" and he didn't answer but raised his own hands slowly to his shoulders, palms forward, as you would do when a bunch of train robbers had the drop on you.

"Aha! So that's how you manage 'robbing from the rich,' " said Miss Woodly with a laugh. " 'Some may think you a romantic Robin Hood . . .' "

He smiled at her, a peculiar smile: "But I know you for a common thief."

"Well," she said, "not common." She was smiling at him delightedly, her eyes foggy with pleasure, and it hit him suddenly that what he had told her was as good or bad as a damn lie because of what he had left out.

He could almost see Bub Houston laughing, shaking his head, *The best of it ain't much better than a lie.*

"Robin Hood," he said. He was disgusted with himself for telling her this in a way that only made her see him more and more like a dime book hero, and all the time thinking that that was the genuine dyed-in-the-wool truth of him. He wondered, *Do I have to tell you all of it, can't you see for yourself, Miss Woodly?—how it was doing it that first time at Pryor Creek station and only after the train was stopped and boarded and the axes ramming at the express car door realizing that I'd got to be in two places at once, it was like I was being split in half, I had to leave the express car to Cherokee Bill so I could keep my eye on the boys in the passenger car because suppose some poor wife was foolish enough about her tin wedding ring or necklace of paste pearls to snatch it back from an armed truant schoolboy who learned about gunplay from dime books—because that was the place where it could all go wrong, not just the money lost but some hideous explosion of pistols and shotguns leaving dirt farmers women and children dead in the cars, and that would raise up the world against me, not just the paid marshals out of Fort Smith but anger out of the countryside to help them, no more trust no more silence to cover the track of Henry Starr in blue smoke. But that meant leaving Cherokee Bill out in the express car with only Charlie Taylor or Linc watching him, and suppose the express man looks at him queer . . . ?*

But that still wasn't enough of the truth. *Listen, Miss Woodly*, his ghost whispered, *this is how it used to be: when I started there was Cherokee Bill so they would know that we could kill. But after Floyd Wilson we didn't need Cherokee Bill, because we had me.*

He thought for a moment. "Look," he said, "a man on the run needs some friends somewheres. I was telling those people what kind of man, what kind of outlaw I was. I was telling 'em how far they could trust me—to rob 'em complete, but careful—no unnecessary gunplay. To not go after somebody's last dollar in the world that's between his kids and starvation"—he looked at her intently—"because that's what's no good about trains, you're always coming up against folks that can't afford to lose it, that's got all of it in a little sack in their pocket. Because there's things you'll risk your blood for. Not for a hundred thousand in a bank vault: bank president maybe stands there with his hands in the air and thinks about the insurance, or about all his property and cash that ain't in that vault, which is mostly other people's money, and he thinks and thinks till it's too late. But the dirt farmer heading back from Tulsa to Stroud thinks about his kids' next meal, and how he's busted his back sharecropping ten or twenty years and nothing to show for it except a long line of debt at the plantation store and if he don't get clear he might as well be a nigger; and maybe the little bit he's saved moves him one inch of the miles he's got to go to get clear, but that's his blood in the inch, and mister if you want a piece of it you'd better get ready to do some dying for it. You kill a man like that and you can't live with it, because it don't taste like justice—not to you and sure as hell not to the people who you got to get food or shelter or information from.

"If you live outside the law, people will treat you like you wasn't anything but a rabid wolf or a wild renegade out for blood—unless you can make 'em see you ain't *their* enemy, that you see the world and walk in it like they do, just like you were human too. So you got to do things to show 'em, to teach 'em what you are and that they can trust you, or else your name is just black and they'd as soon rub you out as get rich. So you got to see the way different people take their money differently, you got to understand some rules, you got to let them know you got some sense of justice—that there's things you won't do for money or even to save your own skin. If that makes me Robin Hood—

"Listen: I'll tell you how it was:

"There was a time we was on the run, after we robbed a bank over the Arkansas line in Bentonville, and the bank was okay but it gone bad after . . ."

*Rode in it was quiet as Sunday, just a little shirttail kid playing mumble-peg under the Confederate statue in the square, and us like farmers come to town for seed money except maybe for Cherokee Bill scowling under his big hat, then chuckling, his belt stuck with three different .45s and a Winchester in one hand. Shirttail kid took one look and run to the hardware store, and when we come out of the bank there was six rifles poking out of the store popping away at us all the way down the sidewalk to our horses—and I asked the banker, ducking behind his back, was he holding paper on those people? because they sure did not seem to care a whole hell of a lot if they killed him killing us—but they missed the banker and hit Linc Cumplin four-five times, and he come crabbing along the boards on one arm, glass was shattering behind us, Cherokee Bill spanging wild shots off the Confederate soldier's ass.*

". . . three of the boys wounded, one pretty badly. There's a posse back of us, it's been two days and time enough for the marshals from Fort Smith to organize things on the Indian Territory side.

"There was six of us when we rode up to the cabin, and even without Bentonville added to the list there was probably ten thousand in reward money for information leading to our capture" *and for Cherokee Bill and me, 'Dead or Alive'* "and if you never did more than hear our names mentioned at the general store you'd have to be bone stupid not see who six men, three of 'em gunshot, just had to be, riding horses that was nothing but raw bones slicked over with sweat. And it wasn't much of a cabin either, more of a lean-to cut into a hillside, with a scrappy-looking yard of corn in front, a pen with three chickens in it that *we* was just about poor enough to steal but a Digger Injun would have passed. And a woman in it who looked worse'n the chickens.

"You've got to see that she knew who we had to be, sixty miles from anywhere you'd be in the Nations if you had any choice. Which I guess she didn't either. She might have been afraid of us, should have been." *Any minute now Cherokee Bill would rouse himself from the torpor he'd fallen into since the shooting stopped, he'd know it was safer to leave her dead than have her laying words on our back trail, just look at this place, she's got nothing, you could buy her for a nickel.* "I told her just who we were: the Starr Gang. That we robbed banks. And we'd pay her for whatever we took."

"That made her feel safe and cozy?" said Miss Woodly.

"Well," Henry Starr allowed, "I told her I would pay her when I could as easy have pulled a gun and said 'Gimme.' Or shot her down and helped myself."

"There is other things to be afraid . . ." Esterhazy started to say, then stopped abruptly, embarrassed by Miss Woodly's presence.

Henry Starr gave him a toothachy look and said a little grimly, "If she didn't know our reputations, or didn't believe them, she might have been afraid of that. I guess just seeing what we looked like, she wouldn't have needed to think hard to find something to be scared of." *Linc bent double off his horse like he was going to puke, and the side of the horse smeared with his blood.* —*No,* he thought, *you did not think about spreading her out and doing her, we were bloodied and thinking blood, if you thought about anything it was Cherokee Bill shooting holes in her with his .45 like he'd have done to his own mother if he thought she might point the finger at him.* "But she stood in the door looking at us, and she says, 'I don't mind robbing banks. I had me a place before a bank got it.' 'Which bank would that have been, ma'am,' I ask her, and she answers, 'The Condon Bank of Coffeyville, Kansas.' I looked at her, and she looked like an old woman at first, but if you looked close she wasn't that at all, but like a young woman with an old woman mask on her face. But that was her face. There was a cradle by the front door out in the weather but I see no child there. 'Ma'am,' I told her, 'that is the very place we have come from.' We was dismounting while I talked, getting the hurt men down and inside . . . 'How much did they get your place for?' I asked her and she said it was for a three-hundred-dollars loan.

"When we rode out next morning I gave her three hundred dollars out of the small bills in our poke. 'You don't need to pay me,' she said, 'what you done to that Coffeyville bank was justice.' But I gave her the money and said, 'If it was justice, ma'am, then that's your piece of it.' "

"Coffeyville?" said Miss Woodly. "I thought you said you had come from robbing Bentonville?"

"That's right, Miss Woodly," he said quietly, "Bentonville."

"But why . . .?"

"Because it was a lot simpler that way. Because it told everybody who heard about it what kind of men we were. Because money doesn't have any names that belong to it, so I could use it whatever way suited me. But you tell me was it justice I give the woman, or was I just blowing blue smoke in her eyes, to cover my trail?"

"Is business investment!" said Esterhazy. "Only, in style of Robin Hood. Like Mr. Rockefeller's little charities, he steals oil company and for charity gives beggarman one dime. Ha! I like it! Is system, very neat, very elegant—like our little photoplays with cast, with story, with script . . ."

Henry Starr didn't like that, it put a twist on what he said that made it all seem too neat, as if robbing banks were as easy as keeping accounts in them. "It's not that simple," he said. "There's always something you can't keep control of, something that gets away from you. Something you bring with you, or that takes you by surprise—or something you call down on yourself somehow. Something: there's always something like that."

"You don't like that way of looking at it," she said, her eyes brilliant, "because you weren't any dime book Robin Hood, what you did was real, all of it—who you took from and what you took for, and how you did it—the bullets were real, and so was the prison, and that poor woman from Bentonville . . ."

"Coffeyville," he said softly, and Esterhazy gave him a wink, damn him—they had him in a spot, these two, between Esterhazy who wouldn't see anything at all in what he said but just trickery from start to finish, and all for the money; and Miss Woodly, who saw too damn much and too damn little, made him out a Robin Hood one minute and a dime book bullyboy the next—so that to answer her he had to figure out whether he was gold certificates or greenback shinplasters, *Last of the Mohicans* or *Jesse James's Double Daring* by Colonel D'Artagnan Arbuthnot.

Henry Starr looked even more uneasy at that thought: because he had just remembered that his perfect plan for robbing a train, with everything timed to the tick and even that speech about Henry Starr don't rob women or men that works with their hands—all of it had been taken word for word from the pages of *Jesse James's Raid; or, the Scourge of the Union Pacific* by Colonel D'Artagnan Arbuthnot.

"Stroud!" called the conductor, "passengers for Stroud!" and he was glad of the distraction.

So was Esterhazy: "At last!" he said. "We arrive at scene of crime."

The small passenger depot in Stroud wore sun-battered Gothic ornaments along its roofline. Malodorous stockyards stretched southwestward along the tracks and an ugly brick jailhouse flanked the station to the north. The townward side of the depot looked at the rear of a row of one-story cotton warehouses, built of rough round country stones mortared sloppily together and plastered over with cement that the weather had cracked and windowed. Wooded hills lifted a little to the southwest, but otherwise the country round about was flat as a billiard table. North, a rusty water tower rose on spindly stilts into a cobalt sky.

They walked a block up to Main Street. Esterhazy could take the whole town in in two looks, left and right, but he'd be damned if he knew how to frame a photograph that would show the place. Its architecture was senseless, the buildings mixed as if one had taken two unrelated decks of cards, shuffled them together and dealt them just as they fell. The most imposing structure at this end of town was the telephone office, a two-story building of incompetently whitewashed brick whose roofline made a crude W shape, in the central apex of which "1903" was inscribed in raised stone letters. It looked like it had been cut out of a photograph of some suburb of Chicago and pasted into a collage with the cotton warehouses, Wild West saloons, brick and gimcrack storefronts that alternated for seven blocks out to the three-story redbrick bulk of the "Opera House"—after which there was just a slice of empty road rising up an imperceptible slope to the blank cobalt sky beyond it.

They stood in front of a two-story building whose plate-glass windows in fluted cast-iron frames seemed entirely too fancy for the establishment—which a sign proclaimed to be STROUD PAWN.

Then Esterhazy noticed the stone plaque over the door that said FIRST NATIONAL BANK and the street seemed to swirl and suddenly sharpen as the world did when he focused his lens. There ahead of them, across the street and on the corner a block away toward the Opera House, was the second bank, the Stroud State—yellow bricks and a red tile roof, and large arched plate-glass windows.

"*This* is place? That famous place of two banks at once?" Esterhazy was annoyed, he was being cheated again.

"It's come down some since I was here last."

"Tell us about it," said Miss Woodly, "tell us how it happened." The place puzzled and repelled her too, but maybe if he helped them to see how it was . . .

"The idea," said Henry Starr, "was to take the two banks at the same time."

When he hesitated Esterhazy prompted him, "Yes, good plan, you get twice as much money for same hours."

"Yes," said Henry Starr, "I guess that was the idea. Twice the money. It's more than twice as hard to do it, though. Because of the timing—you've got to make sure everything happens at the same time, so you need people with you who you can trust to follow a plan and keep to a timetable. It's a different kind of trust from just knowing a man will stick by you when it gets rough. You've got to be able to trust them out of your sight, too—" *Cherokee Bill would have sided me to the death, hell: that's what he did do, isn't it? But I could never have sent him into the second bank alone.* "It's a different kind of trust."

"I thought you said banks were better because they were simple," said Miss Woodly.

He looked at her with a sudden caution that she liked, because with him it was a mark of respect. "They are," he said, "unless you want to make things complicated."

"And that's what you wanted."

"Yes."

"I thought so," she said. "But I don't suppose you're able to tell us why," and she smiled at him, happy as a bobcat grinning at a cornered grouse.

*Complicated or simple? I could never have done a job like Stroud if Cherokee Bill wasn't dead. But if he wasn't dead, maybe I wouldn't have had to do it at all.*

Esterhazy was peering through the dusty glass of the pawnshop. They could never shoot inside, it was too dark and the only remnant of the building's banking days was the long counter, now heaped with all sorts of junk taken in pawn that looked as if it had been sitting there for years. "When you rob this place," he told Henry Starr, "it stays robbed."

"Huh!" said Henry Starr, startled, taking the joke seriously. He looked around the dilapidated Main Street with a sadness that seemed like a kind of remorse.

A voice behind them made all three startle and turn: "Pawnshop's closed, probably permanent." A young man in a white apron had come out of the grocery store—Brogan's—two doors back from the pawnshop. "Mr. Pike asked me to keep an eye on it till he can sell the place."

Henry Starr recovered quickly, and his eyes took on a snaky look. "Mr. Curry," said Henry Starr, "I believe you do not remember me. But I remember you very well." When Esterhazy glanced at him, the outlaw was grinning that white-toothed smile of his, a young smile that sorted as oddly on a face with his history as the telephone company building did with Stroud's board-front saloons and dry-goods stores. Something in the outlaw's manner seemed to have caught Miss Woodly too: she was focused on Starr now with sharp attentiveness.

The young man let his jaw swing just a little. He thrust out a large roughened hand, gritty in the ridges of nails and skin, then broke into a grin as Henry Starr took the hand and shook it. "Well I . . . Well I," he said and you could see he was grateful that Henry Starr had been willing to shake his hand.

"Miss Woodly," said Henry Starr with a slightly evil look, "Mr. Esterhazy, this here is Mr. Paul Curry. He and I go back a ways."

"Old associate?" said Esterhazy dubiously. He knew that criminals started young, but this boy would have been about sixteen at the time of the Stroud robbery.

"Well, not exactly," said Henry Starr as Curry blushed furiously. "Mr. Curry did his Christian duty one night, sitting up with me when I was feeling poorly."

"Well I," said Curry, "well now," grinning at Henry Starr's funning these city folks but not sure if he was invited to join. "It was the least I could do considering."

"Considering I was feeling so poorly 'cause you'd shot me down with that hog-killing gun of yours." Henry Starr shook his head, the world was a damn funny place. "Shot down by a boy with a hog-killing gun. A man of my years and experience. Teach a man that crime don't pay."

"You . . . ?" said Esterhazy, his eyes running around the street, trying to see how and where it might have happened, and he saw Miss Woodly suddenly go white and still like a heron freezing at a twig snap.

"That's what you tried to tell us," she said in a queer voice. "Something always happens, either you bring it with you, or it comes on you by surprise, or you call it on yourself."

"That's right," he said, as if she had pleased him seriously. "I finished my bank the same time my boys got done with this one here, right on schedule. We come out bringing tellers and cashiers as hostages, and started easing back toward the horses. Everybody else was tucked away behind doors or windows, except for two men popped out across the street there not knowing, and we scared 'em back . . ."

"Yeah," said Paul Curry. "I heard the first and seen the second—you practically picked Al Carlock's pocket watch out of the fob with that one . . ."

"And that was when you shot me with the hog killer," said Henry Starr softly.

"Oh God," said Miss Woodly quietly, her eyes opening just a little, because all of a sudden it was real to her—the talk about trains and plans and methods and reputations and weapons was talkytalk, but here was the man or boy who had shot Henry Starr down with a hog-killing gun while the outlaw was menacing his hostages and firing at citizens, and maybe if it had gone differently some of the hostages killed too and

Paul Curry dead at the age of sixteen which was her little brother's age when she left home, and Henry Starr running from a sentence for murder—*no, from another sentence for murder* . . .

Curry looked shamefaced again, a gust of anxiety pulled his face tight, what was Henry Starr doing back in Stroud?—but he'd faced it out before and he'd do it as many times as it took. "Back-shot you, Mr. Starr."

Henry Starr's smile was a little bit soft now. "Don't give it a thought, son. You was the only one with sand enough to try and stop us, and you done it after seeing we could shoot. And you stuck with me afterwards."

"Ah!" said Curry with something that wrung him worse than embarrassment. "Well I, well maybe I . . ."

"You stuck till Marshal Tilghman got there," said Henry Starr.

"What if he hadn't?" said Curry quickly, and Starr shook his head and said gently, "You can't figure on things that never happened. The way it come out, you stuck for as long as it took," remembering:

*The crowd downstairs muttering, starting to yell at itself, the doctor kept wiping his hands with the bloody towel and looking at the frosted glass door wondering if there was any point in the gesture of locking it, and Henry Starr looked at the boy and knew he wouldn't stick much longer, that he wouldn't be able to stop them or even stay and look but would have to run for some hole he could pull in after him—but he couldn't blame the kid, hell: if he could feel anything but a great big ice-cold blank below his belly he'd run for it too, any way at all to climb over this.*

The outlaw's gentleness didn't seem to soothe the boy. "What brings you back here, Mr. Starr?" asked Curry, as if the answer were something fearful he was determined nonetheless to face.

"I'm working for a company makes moving pictures," said Henry Starr. "These are my partners. We have an idea folks might like to see a movie about a real old-time western badman."

Paul Curry beamed his gratitude and relief at Henry Starr and his city folks. "Hey," he said, "why don't you come in and have some of this lemonade we got. I put some mint in it. It cuts the heat real good . . ." and they followed him into the store. The lemonade was in a big stone jug with a bung-tap in it, beaded with sweat, and Curry drew three glasses.

"This is a nice store," said Miss Woodly, looking at the shelves of boxed and canned goods, smelling the slightly rotten smell of the barreled vegetables.

"It ain't mine," Curry said. "Mr. Brogan bought my daddy out the year before Mr. Starr here . . . I just work for Mr. Brogan."

"Killing hogs?" asked Esterhazy, who was then taken aback by the flare of sudden rage in the young man's eyes.

"Whatever I have to," he snapped. "I just do whatever I have to." His eyes blinked and his fists clenched unclenched, he grabbed back out of his breath what he wasn't supposed to feel let alone say. The color of the feeling showed in his cheeks.

"What happened to all that reward money?" Henry Starr asked softly.

Curry shot a confused look at Henry Starr, angry and appealing at the same time, as if he wanted very badly to ask Henry Starr for something he couldn't hardly name, and was already resentful of having his petition frustrated. Then he shrugged his shoulders as if giving all of it up, wish and resentment both. "Well, shoot, you know . . . Once it come to paying out, there was a lot of people had a claim on a piece of the reward: the bank cashier, the sheriff who wasn't even in town, Doc Vincent. I never saw but four thousand, and that went right back to the bank to pay off my daddy's notes. Only thing I got out of it for myself was Brogan raising my pay a buck a week, and keeping me on regardless." His mouth twisted, and he gestured toward a glass display case next to the counter. "Mr. Brogan doesn't much care what I do or how well. He figures my name is enough to bring in the local trade."

Inside the glass case, the focus fuzzed with dust, Esterhazy saw a pair of newspaper front pages with a black-framed photo set between them. The photo was of a much younger Paul Curry, with a cut-barreled Winchester rifle across his lap—the rifle itself, its steel lock stained with rust, lay along the top edges of the newspapers, the *Democrat*: ROBBERY OF TWO BANKS BY HENRY STARR AND HIS BANDITS and the *Messenger*: HENRY STARR CAPTURED ROBBING TWO BANKS IN STROUD.

"People remember," said Henry Starr, but Curry snorted, "Remember! They remember it any damn way they please, till they think they know more about it than me! But what do you expect? You robbing them banks was the last thing ever happened in Stroud, Oklahoma. It's like when that was done, there wasn't nothing else for us. Oil went bust, cotton and beef went bust, one of the banks went bust. Opera house went bust—she's the Stroud Trading Company now. Took out the seats and they use her for a warehouse. Hell, you know: I think the picture that was playing here that time you come through, that was the last one they ever showed at the opera house. You can still see some raggedy signs hanging onto the wall out front. Pass the damn thing every day. *The Squaw Man.* Other towns get *Ben Hur* and what-all, and all we got is this half of a poster about a picture probably died its own self after it come here."

Then something else seemed to strike him, and he looked hopefully at Esterhazy (who looked like a gent). "Well but hey," he said, "you're *in* the picture business, ain't you. Maybe you'll open her up again."

Esterhazy nodded noncommittally, but Henry Starr was determinedly straight: "Theaters isn't our game, exactly. We're going to make the pictures."

"Here in Stroud," said Curry pleadingly, "you could do it here in Stroud. Hell, nothing much has changed since you was here, except the bank becoming a pawnshop."

"You could be in it with me, if you want to," said Henry Starr (ignoring Esterhazy, who, out of Curry's line of sight, was shaking his head *No! No!*).

"You'd want me in it with you," said Curry quietly, seeming more solid on his feet than he had since he first surprised them in front of the pawnshop. "Well I guess then that it is all all right," he said softly, passing a judgment on himself. He looked up at Henry Starr and laid his right hand on the glass display case, as if swearing an oath. "Whenever you say, Mr. Starr, I'll be ready."

"Why did you say no when Henry Starr asked the boy if he wanted to be in the picture?" Miss Woodly asked Esterhazy, when—waiting for Henry Starr in the hotel restaurant that night—they had a moment alone. "Poole would like the idea of shooting the scene where it actually happened, with the original participants."

"Poole! Look, Miss Woodly: nothing has ever happened here. Nothing could happen, not anything you could make a picture of. This . . . it isn't even a place. I don't know what it is. And even if we use scene, that Curry is impossible. Too old to play sixteen-year-old, he moves already like old man who pushes broom thirty years. Plus I don't like some bit player walks on and shoots my hero, especially shoots him in *back*, especially in this Stroud, Oklahoma, which I am never coming back to. Trust me: nobody would ever believe anything really happened here."

## STROUD TO FORT GIBSON *May 8–9, 1921*

She agreed with Esterhazy that there was something wrong with the whole scene in Stroud—with the whole day. Nothing had seemed to match anything else: beginning with that weird moment in the passenger car when she had looked at the woman with the bonnet and the child and the old man, and at Henry Starr sitting quietly talking about the old days, his words conjuring robbery and murder, blood in the aisles, the child screaming, the woman fending off hands pulling at her, opening her purse and taking everything, the old man with his head broken. She had had the same sense with Paul Curry, that nothing in him or in the town was equal to what had happened there in 1915, when Henry Starr came to Stroud and robbed two banks in one day. *Banks are simple, unless you want to make them complicated.*

And then she saw part of what was peculiar about it: that the boy who had been part of it all had somehow slipped out of the frame of action, and was now like one of those kids in the audience at the Lyric Theater, his name and experience counting for nothing even to himself: he was just proud to be noticed by somebody as famous as Henry Starr. It was like he had told her on the train: some people feel important just knowing they'd been robbed by an outlaw as famous for being *good* at it as Henry Starr.

Henry Starr—that's what it was to have power in your name, she thought: so that whatever people were or had done or been to you, in the end all they or anyone else had to remember was a single fading image, like a photograph of someone you know standing next to a famous person, standing next to Henry Starr. That was all that was left to show that they had been in that place with you.

But if that was true, if all Paul Curry had left was that memory, then there wasn't all that much difference between Paul Curry—who had really been there, who was really a part of Henry Starr's story—and herself, who had come on the scene too late even to be a spectator. All that either of them had of that moment with Henry Starr was a picture in the mind—that brought her level with Curry already—and someday she'd even go past Paul Curry, because before she was through she would have caught up to Henry Starr and got him to talk all of his moments to pictures inside her head; because when she had done her work those images would have been changed from fading still dream-pictures to actual moving pictures on a silvered screen.

When they left Stroud in the early morning, Miss Woodly driving the rented wagon and the two men riding as her flankers, she was alert and eager for whatever Henry Starr would show her next, scanning the landscape intently for the ghost marks of his passing.

But there was nothing to see. He took them eastward, across billiard-table flats on which the sun lay like a layer of burning cement. The heat and dust painted her skin with grit, the sun pressed her small inside her crackling skin. From an airplane, she thought, they would look like three bugs crawling across a pane of glass. Even in Stroud there had been those wooded hills rising southwest of town, here there was nothing. She thought of Henry Starr, a young outlaw hunted across that space like a bug hunted across a pane of glass.

The plain was broken at intervals by seams of brush, which marked the places where streams furrowed the plane of the flats—relief for the eyes as well as the throat. When they left the open road they escaped the oppressive weight of the sunlight, but the trails became more difficult. Henry Starr made them dodge into hollows thick with brush on stony and rutted bypaths—at the end of each of which they would find a small hamlet by a railroad siding, buildings covered with scabby paint and a cur scratching his ass in the crossroads, and there would be a post office and a pawnshop that "used to be a bank," and Henry Starr said he had robbed it in the old days. They would sit in the crossroads, looking, not knowing what to say or do, Esterhazy rolling his eyes or muttering in an ambiguous but clearly sarcastic tone.

She was getting tired and disgusted herself. Angry at Henry Starr for . . . for what? If this was all there was, it wasn't his fault. But it wasn't enough, no more than Stroud and Paul Curry were enough to add up to Henry Starr quitting bank robbing for the movies. It wasn't enough for her, and she kept thinking that she had missed something in all that he had said—but damn him, why didn't he just say it, instead of holding it back? If there even was an *it*: maybe he was just an old jailbird, maybe there was nothing special for him to tell. Thinking that made her angrier than ever, at him and at herself: because, damn it, she needed for there to be something special.

He insisted that they camp on a small hilltop and led them up a stony trail, over which the wagon banged and rolled protestingly. The strain of getting the wagon up brought Miss Woodly out of her seat, gee-ing and haw-ing, clucking the team up, slapping their rumps with the reins and once even producing a handful of small stones from a pocket of her skirt to sting them over a deep rut in which the wheels threatened to rock back and forth all day.

"You can handle a team," said Henry Starr when they reached the top, but she shot him a look from under the straw hat that opened his eyes again, *'scuse me*. Her face was flushed with the heat.

Making camp was quick work, Henry Starr and Esterhazy buckling to it with fierce concentration, centering all attention on the lifting and placing of gear, the choosing of spots for campfire and bedrolls, because there were a whole lot of questions that neither man wanted to be the first one to raise and so with all their talk they had never discussed them. But Miss Woodly, moving briskly, saying nothing, answered the unasked questions point by point:

While they were unpacking their bedrolls she put hers by the fireplace. Esterhazy approached leaning against his burden and she stood up and faced him squarely, and he swerved to dump his gear in the shadow of a standing boulder several yards away. Henry Starr took this in, then followed suit with an easy carelessness that got a smile from under the straw hat.

She answered the next question by asking Henry Starr where the spring was—certain there would be one and he would know where—and walked off to it through the bushes. So that was what they would do about *that*. But they worked in silence; it was as if she'd walked off with their voices. When she came back her hair was wet, she'd changed her blouse and was carrying a freshly filled waterbag.

So that was that. All they had to do was let her alone and she'd make matters plain enough for them. It was suddenly restful there in the heavy air.

"You *can* handle a team," said Henry Starr again, and this time she smiled and said, "Yes I can."

Henry Starr still looked melancholy, so she spared him her questions and turned to Esterhazy: how did he get started making pictures? He spun it out for them, a little modesty about his war experiences (just an interruption of his real business), left out his politics entirely; but gave them the comic rendition of his arrival in California and his meeting Foley (gliding over the shameful way he had let himself be taken advantage of, just off the boat with no equipment and not even a good set of forged documents. Foley had bought him the way they used to pick up coolies on the San Francisco docks).

They turned into their sleeping sacks early. Miss Woodly lay awake for a while, listening to the fire whisper itself asleep, listening for the sounds of the two men settling into their blankets and the deep indrawn sound of their breath in sleep. She felt her apartness from them as a kind of loneliness, but it felt good to her. She felt safe with them tonight: without saying anything they had recognized and accepted the line she had made between them—and their silence about it was as important to her safety as the fact of their recognition. Because she knew what could happen if they began to put into words the thought of her sex, even if they thought *she'll say no* they would start to wonder *but does she mean yes?* Her fear was not just that they might be too strong for her:

having both of them together was a kind of guarantee against that; she knew Esterhazy well enough to know that where she was concerned Henry Starr might be a rival but never a partner. But she knew that once the question was asked the wish would be there, and it would breathe a kind of poison fog around her, in which they would see neither herself nor the work they were doing together, but only the split of her sex like a target they had painted between her legs.

She knew all about what went on in that kind of fog, knew it the way Henry Starr knew his trains and banks and his queer terrain.

Yes: and it was more complicated terrain than anything Henry Starr had showed her so far—plains as flat and dry and barren of interest as concrete slabs, and creek hollows full of brush and broken-down hamlets and dead banks and sidings with grass sprouting between the rusted rails. It made her wonder if "Henry Starr" wasn't just entirely some character she had made up out of her own head—what he showed her of his real life had none of the color or fire or horseback-dashing power she had imagined as his.

He had gotten smaller for her today—that was part of what made her feel safe lying here just across the fire from his dreaming body—but she found herself regretting the loss of that smoky, dark, threatening shape she had sensed in him when they rode into Stroud on the train, and she had looked around the passenger coach and seen his ghost stepping in through the doorway, six-guns in his hands and a crowd of crazy laughing boys behind him, armed to the teeth and ready for anything.

Well, he hadn't seemed ready for anything that had happened since that conversation with Paul Curry. Even the terrain seemed to surprise and disappoint him: as the day had worn on he had become almost shamefaced about it, as if he knew he was letting his partners down, sensing Esterhazy's annoyance and her own deepening disappointment.

But as she thought about the hamlets they'd visited, she realized that it wasn't Esterhazy's disappointment or hers that registered with him: it was his own. Nothing was as he remembered it, nothing was there of what he wanted to show them. In Preston and Beggs the banks had become pawnshops, just like in Stroud, as if that were a stage in the evolution of banks: maybe when a bank got sick or failed it became a pawnshop, still lending on security but on a lower plane, like—she remembered Henry Starr riding hunched over in the saddle, tiny movements of his head the only sign of his continuous and now purely ornamental vigilance—like an old-time outlaw, she thought, who's come down to making movies about old-time outlaws.

She retraced their journey in her mind, trying to re-create the shape of what she had seen—trying to see it not as Esterhazy did, through the intently focused lens of the cameraman; but as Henry Starr, as an outlaw would see it, reading the shapes of things to learn how to rob banks profitably and safely, and make a perfect getaway.

It came to her suddenly that there was a difference between Henry Starr's country and the rest of Oklahoma. The places Henry Starr robbed were always tucked into a creek hollow or a fold in the plains cut by running water. There was always a railroad running in and out; it came to her that banks lived by railroads the way people lived by creeks. And always, tumbling down from the hills into the creek valleys and even in among the houses of the town, there were trees and brush. They could ride for hours and not see more than two or three willows or cottonwoods starving by a slough, past weathered board houses where the yards had been fenced with twisted deadfall limbs stuck upright into the ground, as if the fence had withered in the terrible heat, and then the ground would begin to lift just that little bit so the team had to lean into the traces. Then it would lift higher and roll like a wave, a line of trees at the top, and on the other side a stream-cut furred thick with trees and brush right down to the silver lick of the water, and down in there somewhere was a little town and a bank in it for Henry Starr to rob.

Behind her closed eyelids she could see the country with his eyes now, and though he was still out there ahead of her she had the feeling she was getting closer to overtaking him with every tick of her blood. Henry Starr country was not out on the blank open flats, but in the hideaway valleys with their tangles of brush and the railroad track twisting down into them through the gullies like a taproot out of Tulsa or the Frisco trunk line. The lines of the terrain that his ghost ran were like the lines of her own body, she felt him ride the lifts and smooth planes to find the places that answered his need, which were the secret places of the landscape, the hidden tucks and folds furred with brush . . .

She opened her eyes, awake, alert and alarmed. Am I getting closer to him, or is it Henry Starr who is sneaking up on me?

She lifted in her blankets and looked at his muffled shape across the low gleam of the fire. She reminded herself to remember: Henry Starr was a good deal trickier than he looked.

But she was confident now that she had begun to master the trick of seeing things through his eyes, and on their third night out she was ready to show him a glimpse of her mastery. It would be an answer, of a kind, to that display of power he had given her the first day they met, when he had answered a simple question by disarming Deputy Price and pretending to be ready to blow out the brains of Buckskin Bill Bonham.

They were dining at the National Hotel in Fort Gibson and Esterhazy's patience had run out. His head had that backward tilt that he used to glare imperiously down from the high cameraman's stool on all those who did not understand how movies were made. He was trying to keep the razor edge out of his voice, and it made him sententious: "My friends," he said, "perhaps already we have seen all we need to see? To make this picture . . . *ach*, I think we have seen as many little hamlets with crossroads and feed store as I can stand."

Henry Starr seemed apologetic, but there was urgency in his tone: he didn't want them to stop just yet. "Things changed a lot more than I figured. Somehow I never figured how different they could get to be. Maybe we just picked some wrong places to start. But there's places out there that are still the same, or close enough anyway so you can see right through 'em to what used to be. If you give it a little time . . ."

Esterhazy was suddenly decisive: "Listen to me—my friend. Is your life in this film—I understand this. But film is not same thing as your life. Even if we could find this place you remember, where old days are still going on, maybe it don't look like right place when we put it in camera. And that is all that will matter at end: what camera can make of it."

Esterhazy looked to Miss Woodly for support, but all he had was her attention. So it was on him to speak for realism in this affair. The Famous Outlaw was lost in his scrapbook of memories, and his producer and screenwriter was a virgin where movies were concerned (whatever else she might be!) and probably her judgment was totally fogged with sentimentality about her Oklahoma Robin Hood. They needed the shock of seeing the world through the camera's eye, rigorously framed and reduced to the merciless simplicities of black and white. "Shall I tell you truth about what we have seen? As camera sees it? You say that no place we have seen can show how it used to be. Well, I have seen one such place, which I could make to show how western bank robbery happens that you would believe. Is not Preston or Stroud, is none of places you *did* rob. Because in none of those places can camera see *anything*. Little houses like cheap bungalows and stores all different kinds, like it was national dumping ground for bad architecture—brick wood stucco Spanish Yankee Texas—all too close together. No place to put camera where it can command all angles! And all around these bushes and trees, as bad as smoke or fog—two jumps and horses are completely invisible.

And pursuit? How can I give feeling of pursuit through that jungle? Horses bump through branches ten feet, I pick up camera and twist it through jungle twenty feet, put down, shoot two seconds of film and then pick it up and move it again, all I'm getting, I *swear* you, is leaves in front of camera."

"Which place was it you thought you could make to look real?" asked Henry Starr.

"Do you remember place on main road—Bald Hill? Brick general store, Baptist Church, half dozen wooden buildings alongside big wide road, big wide fields all around it. Six, seven places I can put my camera, and from every one I command street, which is open like stage, open to light. Anything you do robbing bank, any piece of business small or big, I shoot it eight different ways and pick best shot for movie. Town is little small, but okay—better I fix it up with couple extra false fronts here or there, than we have to shoot so they don't notice somebody has slapped stucco all over log cabin to make it look like is *palazzo* next to Bald Hill Feed and Grain Emporium. And that store—beautiful brick, big windows, wooden pillars framing door—you just paint out Feed and Grain and paint in First National Bank: it already looks more like bank than any banks you showed us, which were (excuse me) most convincing pawnshops." Esterhazy's eyes were dreamy, he was seeing it all: "Yes: and lovely flat fields all around, chase car could follow you for miles and miles, wonderful long-running passage, it would seem to go and go endless, picture of life that becomes *eternal* pursuit . . ."

She could see Esterhazy's picture and what it would show, he was right about the way to make a picture of the sense of an outlaw's life, racing away in desperate escape from your crimes across an empty plain perfectly alone and perfectly visible to an eye that never sleeps and never ceases searching for your trace across the glass. But Henry Starr couldn't see it, though he was trying to—and she guessed, maybe, what he was seeing. "Esterhazy is looking at these things like a movie cameraman," she said. "You're still seeing them like an outlaw. The things that make a place good for him are the kinds of things that make it impossible for a bank robbery." She looked intently at him, she wanted him to see and understand just how close to his own way of seeing she had been able to get. "The street's too open, and there's a dozen different places from which they can take a bead on the bank door. There's no woods for you to duck inside of, they don't even have to track you—they can see where you're going till the sun goes down." She paused for emphasis. "There's no railroad there," she finished, "and so there couldn't have been any bank."

Henry Starr's attention was so close it made her nervous, until it broke in a slow smile. "Well, if Esterhazy and me see things too different, maybe you can split the difference for us." He seemed easier, in command again. "Listen," he said to Esterhazy, "I don't ask a man to do what can't be done, and I sure don't put my judgment ahead of a man that knows his own trade. If there's no way you can make a picture of . . . of things the way they seemed to me, all right, I'll take your word and give it up. But you got to give it a chance." He grinned, clean white teeth in a smooth brown face. "You got to come see the country like an outlaw would see it."

And she thought that yes, that was it: that was what they had come out here to do.

## TAHLEQUAH *May 10, 1921*

Henry Starr led them out of Fort Gibson, across the bridge of the Grand River and eastward toward Tahlequah, Miss Woodly driving the wagon, Henry Starr riding point, Esterhazy shifting restlessly from flank to drag. Country roads, rutted by wagon wheels, led between small woodlots and fields of wheat already beginning to burn brown in the strong sun. Cicadas and june bugs razzed them, and the heat was heavy, a burden on shoulders and lungs. When Henry Starr turned in the saddle he saw her sitting slim and limber in the wagon box, rocking easily as the wagon took the ruts, her face shadowed by a big faded straw hat.

Esterhazy pulled up next to the wagon to complain to Miss Woodly. "We must do all things like old days, of course. And ways of Cherokee are perhaps not like those of paleface, but they must have had better idea of how to get from *here* to *there*."

She measured Esterhazy with a look from the cool shade of her hat. "Outlaws don't go in straight lines," she said.

"We're not outlaws," snapped Esterhazy, annoyed at her seriousness, "we make movies."

Henry Starr waved them off toward a line of low hills about two miles from the road, and they followed a winding track even rougher than the roads they had taken. Tall weeds rose between the wheel ruts and tickled the belly of the wagon.

Once off the open roads and into the woods, the feel of things changed sharply. The Cherokee country was nothing like the plains between Stroud and Fort Gibson. It was all of it Henry Starr country, broken by mounds and bluffs and hills, their peaks worn down to nubs, their sides roughened with blackjack oak and cut with ravines where creeks hid among swamp maple and creeper. The sky was gone along with the shapes of the worn-down mountains. The unfalling dead limbs of the blackjacks stiff-armed them onto a narrow trail, like a corridor between walls of barbed and twisted bars, hard as black iron. Virginia creeper hung in tangled beardy masses of heavy green hair. Thick woody vines looped and slung themselves from branch to branch like the petrified intestines of some fossil monstrosity.

The narrow trail forced them to go in single file, and she was grateful for the sight of Henry Starr riding ahead of her and the sense of Esterhazy riding behind.

They came to a creek and the sky looked in on them again. She let the horses drink, and Henry Starr sidled his horse alongside the wagon box.

"My Grandfather hated this country," he said. "It was like a prison to him."

"I can understand that," she said.

"Yes?" he said vaguely, looking off elsewhere—at some place miles off, invisible behind the bars of the blackjack thicket. "He would always talk about how it was back in the Old Place, back in Georgia, Carolina and Tennessee, where we come from. How there was real mountains there, and real trees—not like here, where the mountains got beaten down, and the trees just eat 'em up, these little dusty shite-poke trees. Where he come from the trees was giants, shooting straight up from the floor of the forest that was like the floor of a theater or a church. And big as they was, the mountains was bigger. They was hard rock, sharp as the head of a spear, climbing up and up and up, till you left the air of the world and come to a place where the air was smoke, was blue smoke, like when you dream or when your mind becomes dark or . . . and still they pushed up higher, till you was above the trees and above the smoke—because the tops of those mountains was bare, he would tell me, 'Like heads shaved to let in wisdom' or like the skulls of scalped men—and if you was strong enough to climb that high, you could see the whole world and everything in it below you—the heads of the other mountains and the blue sky, and the blue smoke hanging there in its place, and the big trees in their place, and underneath them people hunting, people farming . . ."

"Why did he leave it?" she asked, and Henry Starr blinked, as if a branch had snapped in his eyes.

"That's a fair question," he said. He looked around to see if the answer might be lying out in the open. His eyes lit on the line of the creek and he said, "He was the biggest man for size and strength who ever lived in the Cherokee Nation, and he had a name for holding by his own idea of what was right. And if you come against him with your own idea, he'd draw a line in front of you and dare you to cross it while he had his eye on you. It didn't matter if you was stranger or blood kin, if you was the President of the United States or John Ross Chief of the Cherokee Nation, he'd draw that line."

Henry Starr looked at Miss Woodly, and she saw that his eyes had softened their grip on things. His voice became smooth and rhythmic like the rocking feel in your hips when your horse drops into an easy gallop, and she felt herself lift away from the hard wagon seat and into the dreamy speed of his words:

"I guess what happened is, a day come when he drew his line, and the one on the other side didn't back off, because this time it was nobody but himself, who was the biggest man in the Cherokee Nation, and never give the trail or the ground or the right to anything, bear man or ghost, that ever walked in the world.

"I used to wonder, when I was a kid, what was it gave him the power to draw that kind of line that nobody was brave enough to cross. He used to talk hate around that John Ross, about his big house and his white lady wife and his piano in the parlor, like what there was between them come down to a little mixed blood and the money it took Ross to live like that. Maybe that's how it started, and maybe that's what Tom Starr thought himself by the time I come along. But lately I begun to think there was more to it than that. Back there in Georgia, Carolina, and Tennessee, when the whites started trying to push the Cherokees out, Ross wanted to hold them off and stay; and old Tom sided with the ones that signed the treaty that give the land away and moved on out here. He said it was because the only reason Ross wanted to stay was to hold onto his lands and his slaves, and live like a white man, but that ain't no reason for Tom Starr to leave. Maybe old Tom was afraid that if he lived up close to white people, he wouldn't be strong enough to draw the line, their ways and their blood and their money would just plain eat him up.

"Because he saw coming what Ross was too much the white Injun to see, that the Americans meant to clean out every last Cherokee between the dot of their shadow at noon and the edge of the sky, whether it took scaring or killing made no difference to them, and no law on any piece of white paper would make them stop. And when the two of them met again out in the Indian Nations, Tom Starr looked into John Ross's eyes and saw a man whose ghost had been defeated by what the Nation had suffered following him—herded into stockade pens where bad food and shitwater and the stinking spots killed them like sheep until their Chief John Ross erased the line he had drawn and said, 'Yes yes, all right, okay, yes, I give it all up, I will go where I am sent.'

"I think that when old John Ross looked in Tom Starr's eyes he saw his own shame, because Tom Starr drew the line between them saying that the man who stays and suffers with those who are helpless and weak is a fool, who cannot draw a line: and in the end he saves no one and nothing, and loses even his honor as a man, that honor which tells a man to draw a line that no one may cross, that tells a man to find his guns, and his horse and his road and his word, and turn his back on home and ride away.

"But I think old Tom was more afraid of John Ross than John Ross was afraid of him. I think that every time old Tom looked at John Ross he saw that same kind of no-name no-clan blue/black death that Cherokee Bill saw when he thought about dying strung up like a nigger—death that don't just rub you out but buries you in shame deep and thick as a bumper crop of Mississippi Delta cotton."

*Death? Strung up like a . . . ?* Miss Woodly's dreaming mind dropped out of the smoky air of Henry Starr's voice and hit the wagon box with a distinct bump. She looked across the line of the creek into the dry-branch jungle of the Cherokee Nation and she was suddenly repelled by it, she was afraid of it, afraid to cross the line and see what was inside it—afraid of names like John Ross and Tom Starr and Cherokee Bill, whose meaning she knew from her reading, but whose shapes now seemed larger and darker, knotted in bony barbs and twists like the blackjack thickets across the creek.

She shook her head and looked at him. He was sitting his horse, cool and uncanny and almost bonelessly relaxed in the saddle while his horse lapped creek water.

The blood snapped into her cheeks; he had sucked her into letting her guard down, got her dreaming and then frightened her with his damn ghost stories, and *then* sat there watching her be afraid. She felt spied upon, she flashed angry at him, and under the anger she was still a little afraid—enough so that for a moment she wondered if she really wanted to know the truth about Henry Starr, or if it was better for her to stick to the "Henry Starr" she had invented on the sheets of yellow legal paper in her room.

Then suddenly it was not Henry Starr she was annoyed with, but herself for her own confusion, and she cast it off by slapping the reins on the horse team and taking the wagon across the stony ford. Henry Starr followed, splashing the creek water as high as the stirrups.

They arrived on the edge of Tahlequah just before three o'clock, discovering it suddenly and by surprise as Henry Starr took them over the top of a low hill that had concealed them till the last minute. The sun flared blindingly at their backs, and their shadows pointed stubby fingers toward the town, whose buildings rose from among trees, marking the straight line of Main Street and the cross lines of the intersecting streets—which ran straight for a block or two before the hills bent and twisted them to the shape of creeks and cow paths.

They came into town past the big open flat of the rodeo grounds, fenced with broken boards and worn plank grandstands turning their backs to the road. There was nobody on the road, the grandstands were empty and so were the bull pens and the horse corral, Fourth of July 1892 was long long gone. Henry Starr paused, sat in his saddle looking over the grounds as the wagon creaked up behind him. There were rags of paper blowing around the field.

"Is this it?" Esterhazy asked. "Have we finally come someplace?"

*I can't see it anymore*, he thought, *not even the ghosts in the bleachers: old Tom Starr and John Ross's family, the judges behind the table, the flags, the horsemen,* "It ain't like I . . ." They were waiting, watching him, the audience he had brought here to tell, to show them . . . what, exactly? How it was done in the old days? "I won a prize at the rodeo here once, Fourth of July, 1892. The same week I robbed my first bank, here in Tahlequah. Or something like a bank, anyway—the Katy Railroad's Land Office. They bought and sold land, lent money same as a bank . . ." He looked at her and she looked back, waiting, and behind her Esterhazy said "Aha!" and began unpacking the Kodak, tripod and viewfinder from the wagon. "But first I won a prize for riding." She was waiting and watching intently, almost demandingly, and he felt that electric hum up the center of his belly, and suddenly he felt it was too difficult even to begin telling her how it was exactly, what-all it had been and still was to him, and he felt like he had only a blunt clenched fist for a tongue in his mouth. "*Injun*-style riding I done." He pushed the words out and left them there, *hell, let her figure it out.*

"Bareback?" she asked, looking away out over the rodeo grounds.

"Near bare-*assed*," he snapped, then he felt bad seeing her stung face. "Excuse me," he added. "It was a kind of riding where you come in at a hard gallop and lean off and . . . pick something, snatch something up off the ground," *a small white red-combed head, feels like you're jerking a root out of the ground, smell of fresh raw blood and your hand sticky with it . . .*

*Clickup!* went Esterhazy's Kodak. "Like you did with money bag in bank scene?" He spoke without looking at Henry Starr, making adjustments in his camera.

"Sort of," said Henry Starr, tight in his throat, looking out at the rodeo grounds. A brown dog nosed at a blowing newspaper, then moved on. "It was dead even between me and another Indian boy from a different . . . different part of the country. Both of us dressed like cowboys at the start, riding saddled horses. Dead even. Judges told us we'd have one more run, only one no matter what—win, lose or split the prize. So he made his last run, he pulled . . . he made the pickup. Then I . . . I changed, I took off my shirt and boots and the saddle and ran the last one in breechclouts and bareback, and the people there, the Indians there they said that I had won it. The judges said no, it was a tie because we'd both picked it up; but the people up there in the stands knew I'd won it, because I rode it like it used to be in the old days. They said it wasn't justice, splitting the prize; it was politics, because that other boy, his family was very big in the Nation. They say that I robbed the Katy Land Office next day to get even."

"Was it true?" she asked.

"It could have been."

"Was the prize that important to you?"

He looked at her looking at him, as if he could make a distance behind his eyes and conceal himself in it. He wanted her to know the truth without his having to tell her. How was it possible to make her know what it was to have Tom Starr sitting there in the stands with his black hat and his smoked specs with the left lens busted out, and the John Ross family in their Sunday-go-to-meeting behind the judges' stand, and the old Cherokees coming up to the prize table with their wallets and bags of coin, *For my clan.* Suppose she didn't understand it after he told her? Suppose she said she understood it and he couldn't believe her? But if she could see:

*The sweated coarse hair of the horse between his bare thighs, iron smell of new blood, the tightness of the cut on his thigh and the drying blood on his face, the air full of gunshots and turkey gobbles, his right hand sticky with the blood draining out of the torn-off chicken head, the Old Man sitting among the crowd like an elephant in a herd of buffalo, the smell of blood, "Who did you bet on, Old Man?"*

*"On my blood."*

*"Which blood, Old Man? Which blood, your Injun blood or your son's blood, which?"*

"I didn't take half the prize, because I wanted justice." He kept looking at her and felt himself, felt something in his head swelling, filling the distance in his head and bringing him into his own eyes again. "Maybe I wanted even a little bit more than justice," he said, and lifted the reins to tell his horse to walk on into town.

"Wait! Wait a minute!" yelped Esterhazy, hastily fumbling the Kodak and the tripod back into the wagon.

The main street of Tahlequah still had the same shape, the same series of buildings marching through its heart side by side, built of boards on which the paint was sun-cracked and laddered, or brick washed with sun-faded logos. COCA-COLA, SOZODONT, CHEW RED MAN TOBACCO. The street had been paved but the paving had cracked and the underneath dust was coming up through the cracks and sifting over the pavement. Main Street was nearly empty of people under the dusty trees, half of the stores opposite the brick tower of the Cherokee capitol were closed, even the upper-story windows blocked with boards like eye patches. On the left side of the street the Cattlemen's Bank was now the Chemical–Cattlemen's Bank; and the M K & T "Katy" Hotel was the Tahlequah Commercial. On the other, the Land Office and the Tahlequah *Chieftain* were still in business.

"This is it?" Esterhazy wanted to know. "Does it look like when you robbed first bank?" He stepped into the back of the wagon, grabbed the tripod and his viewfinder and began setting up in the street.

No danger of being run down by traffic, the street was empty out to either end of town. Three horses drooped by the hitching rail at the hotel, and a loafer snoozed by the wall with a spot of sun in his lap and his face in his hat. *The Last of the Cherokees*, thought Henry Starr, *the white man's dream come true*. "The buildings are the same, older. But there were people . . ."

"In street?" said Esterhazy. "When you robbed . . . ?"

"No. Before. The day before I robbed it. The rodeo."

Esterhazy was set up, and he swung the viewfinder around, framing things, *the street no good unless you covered it with dirt to hide lousy paving, but buildings looked right, little paint maybe, horses look good at rail, change loafer into real Indian wrapped in blanket snoozing on steps of saloon, only where used to be the saloon . . . ?*

She watched Henry Starr and saw the uneasy set of his body on the horse, the shoulders wrung out of line as if he were turning away from something, the eyes shifting restlessly away from her, up and down the street as if he were . . . the way he had looked up and down the aisle of the train planning the robbery, only now he was afraid, licked his lips as if they were dry. She wanted to help him. "Can you tell us how it was?"

He straightened, nodded as if conceding something. "It was a big day, the Fourth of July. Not just because of the holiday . . . not much in that day for us to celebrate. But because of the money. The government had confiscated a whole lot of the Nation because we was the wrong side in the war."

"The Civil War?" she asked running the tally of years backwards in her mind, and he answered, "That one too.

"But they didn't just take the land, they said they'd treat us white. So they wrote all that land into some paper—it's easy done. Then they write the paper into money, it don't matter what numbers, ten cents or five cents on the dollar, it's your paper and you can write anything you want. Then they put all the names of the Cherokees on paper—full blood, half blood or just married Cherokee don't make no difference, you can write any names you please, it's your goddamn paper, isn't it? Then they put the two papers together and cut it up: two hundred and sixty-five dollars and seventy cents a head. So there was a lot of money come into Tahlequah that day, that Fourth of July, over there in the Cattlemen's Bank, and the people lined up in the street waiting for their piece of it."

They waited for him to continue. Esterhazy fussed with the viewfinder, changing filters. "Which one was it you first robbed? Bank over there?"

"No," said Henry Starr, "the Land Office on this side. There was money here too, lots of nesters coming in to buy up that Cherokee land as fast as the government took it away." He leaned over to peer into the dirty window. Behind the foggy glass a white-shirted shape moved, the ghost of a plump white man who had taken Tom Starr's Strip money, who had made Tom Starr eat the shame of having had and not being able to hold on to it, like the shame of eating C. N. Walker's bread and C. N. Walker's words, *Look at him, for Chrissake, what's a thing like that gonna do with a piano?* "Some of them never even got their money out into the street so the stores and the rodeo touts could get it. They had debts, and the bankers was right there, all of 'em come to town that day to collect everything all at once."

"Did you plan it out," she said, "carefully like you did the others?"

"No. I just walked in and did it."

"Why?" She waited. *Why?* she thought. *Please say why, I need to know why.* "How did it . . . ?" she started but he hadn't waited for the question, he kept on telling it, glancing across the street to where no more Cherokees were waiting in line for their Strip money, then looking into the gray dirty screen of the window of the Katy Land Office.

"Because it's what my Grandfather would have done, what he would have expected me to do if . . . if he had expected me to do anything at all." He wanted to look at her but couldn't, and spoke instead toward the small blurred ghost she made next to his on the gray screen of the window. "He was Tom Starr, the biggest man for size in the Cherokee Nation. He fought Andrew Jackson and John Ross both; he fought the Civil War with Stand Watie and he rode with Jesse James. He was the only single human individual ever to force the Cherokee Nation and the United States of America both to make a treaty of peace with him, personally. His brother was Sam Starr, who married the woman they called Belle Starr, who the dime books called the 'Outlaw Queen,' and she had a child named Pearl by Cole Younger of the James Gang, and Pearl hid out the Dalton Gang on her ranch at Younger's Bend while they was planning the double bank robbery at Coffeyville. His son was Hop Starr, who was my father, and he was with Jesse and Frank James and the Youngers the day they robbed two banks in the same town at the same time, and nobody ever got away with doing that again." His mouth made a grim line and he added, "Not *clean* away." Now he looked at her directly again, and he saw that unfocused look in her eyes as if he had gotten too big somehow for her to see all of him up that close, and he regretted having made that look come there even while he felt himself glowing with it. "That's who Tom Starr was," he said. "That's why I robbed the Katy Land Office."

Her eyes sharpened suddenly, surprising him with their concentration and clarity. "Because Tom Starr was your grandfather?"

"Yes: and because they took his land first, and then the money they were supposed to give him for the land, and then . . ." He waved his hand vaguely at the empty street.

"So maybe," she said, "maybe you wanted a little justice here too."

"Ha!" he said, "maybe. Or maybe more than justice again, I don't know. But I'll tell you what I got. I got to rob the Katy Land Office and ride out of here shooting out every light and window on Main Street. I got three hundred dollars out of the strongbox, split three ways for the boys that rode with me makes it a hundred apiece, and it cost me every cent of that to get away and hide out at Aunt Belle's ranch. But let's say three hundred. Put that next to what they took from us the day before, for debt and for . . ." *Starr clan or Cherokee blood, it ain't my money I ain't got* that *coming.* "They got two hundred and sixty-five dollars and seventy cents each for me, my mother, her no-account husband and Tom Starr. Hell, I'd have done better to take my cut of the Strip . . . Well, like I said, a hundred dollars minus expenses was what I got, so you tell *me* what kind of justice I took out of Tahlequah."

"You can't value justice with money," she said.

"Money don't die," said Henry Starr, "it don't smell, and it don't get old; it don't get droughted or weeviled out, and it ain't guilty because you can't ever prove what a dollar done."

"Justice dies?" she said. "It gets old? It . . . ?"

"It's hard to count it. It's hard to know when you got it or if, and so how can you hold on to it?"

"So that's why you went back to robbing banks, after you'd got your pardon and were free and clear with the law? Because you could make more money at *it* than you could keeping a store?"

Henry Starr said nothing, because the air had stiffened in his throat. *He stood in the darkened store, the air dense with the odor of cloth and herbs, grain and smoked meat, and Cora stood opposite, the orange light of the lantern on her face, her body framed by the shelves of unsold canned and boxed goods. Her grief scratched lines at the corners of her eyes and mouth, but something strong inside her smoothed her face again. "So you let him," she said, "you let him drive you back to it. You couldn't hold on just a little . . ."*

*"Maybe he didn't have to drive me to it. Maybe I'm just not cut for a storekeeper."*

*"Nor a husband. Nor a father."*

*"I have the name, Cora. I might as well have the game."*

"Where's all that money then," said Miss Woodly, "that doesn't die or smell or get old, all the money from all those banks you robbed?"

"Injuns: they can get, Miss Woodly, but they can't hold. My Grandfather couldn't as big a man as he was, and neither could I." Her blue eyes were serious and straight, and he felt a cruel urge to mock her seriousness, her taking him so seriously—to turn her eyes aside. "It is enough," he said in a rumbling guttural. "The anger of the Manitto is not done. The pale faces are masters of the earth, and the time of the red men has not yet come again."

Instead of bridling at his mockery, she grinned and answered solemnly, "In the morning I saw the sons of Unamis happy and strong; and yet before the night has come have I lived to see the last warrior of the wise race of the Mohicans."

"Ha!" he said. And then he couldn't say anything.

"What is all this?" said Esterhazy with his head inside the viewfinder.

"James Fenimore Cooper," she said, smiling and smiling at Henry Starr, "*The Last of the Mohicans*."

Henry Starr cleared his throat, "I didn't think girls read Hawkeye kind of books." *My book* he thought, *my redskin book, she knows my book.*

"You didn't think girls knew how to drive a team either, did you, Henry Starr?" she said, shaking her head.

"Ah!" said Esterhazy, standing up and looking at them. "*Cooper!* The American Karl May!" They looked at him blankly. "Karl May?" he said. "Old Shatterhand? With Indian companion, Winnetou?"

"No," she said, "I never heard of any of them. But Hawkeye, Chingachgook . . ."

"And Uncas," said Henry Starr, "the last chief of the noble race of the Mohicans."

"I would play with my brothers," she said happily. "I had two brothers. One was Hawkeye the Long Rifle, and one was Chingachgook, his faithful Indian companion. Guess who I was, and *don't* say the treacherous Magua or I will . . . . I will *scalp* you."

He shook his head, grinning. "If I judge you by your hair, then you are the fair Alice—sweet but with a tendency to wilt in the sun."

"Ha!" she said.

He looked seriously at her, cleared his throat and said, "Maybe Cora, set aside the coloring . . ." He seemed embarrassed again, but she just said, "Ha! Better, but still not close enough," and she smiled and smiled at him till Esterhazy was nearly frantic, understanding not the least bit of what was happening except that he was not meant to understand it.

"Uncas," he said, softly and strangely and she nodded happily, and he went on, "you were Uncas, the son of Uncas."

"Yes," she said, "for as long as my brothers would let me be. And that was longer than they wanted to. You see, I was the only one who knew the book, and knew how the game should be played. Without me they had no story, they didn't know what to do next, how to play . . ." Suddenly she looked bleak. "Till it finally came to the point where even that wasn't enough to keep me in the game."

Henry Starr looked at her and shook his head. She kept being a surprise to him. Just when you had written her down for one thing, she showed another: she came on like a woman who had seen the elephant and knew what the world was and how to handle herself in it, who knew what she needed and where to get it and don't need no help thank *you.* And then again she'd look young enough to make you want to warn her to take care, skittish and run-away in the eyes as an unbreached doe. But just when you decided she needed careful handling she'd show enough catamount in the eyes and teeth to make your hair rise and your back hunt a corner.

Then suddenly he felt real easy inside, because he saw what she was thinking as clearly as if he was behind those blue eyes of hers, and he knew just what to say: "Let's go take a look inside the bank." He glanced at Esterhazy. "Why don't you watch things out here. See how we look going in . . . and coming out."

He grinned a little wolfishly as they dismounted, took Miss Woodly's arm, and Esterhazy watched them cross the street, and vanish into the bank.

The front of the bank was bland and boring, a square window in a square block of a building, thrown into shadow as the sun lifted over the roofline. Esterhazy stood now in the heavy glare of the afternoon sun, sweating. The wait became prolonged, empty like the street. What were they doing in there? Opening an account? Making a withdrawal? He bent to frame the bank entrance in his viewfinder, but the sun slicing in over the building seemed to spit sharply in his eye so that he blinked and flinched, *we'll never be able to shoot them leaving bank this time of day*—then Esterhazy snapped to sudden nervous attention as if his thought had been repeated to him with a new and frightening emphasis. *Never shoot them coming out of bank with sun in my eyes . . . ?*

The bland face of the bank stared emptily at him, like the numbed face of a drunkard who may instantly wake and begin spewing obscenities at you. The horses were restless, and Esterhazy kept taking his head out of the black cell of the viewfinder to glance nervously up and down the street.

"What *were* you doing in there all that time?" he asked them. It was evening, the sun painted the clearing a deepening yellow and the campfire flickered invisible tongues among the heaped sticks in the firepit.

She looked happily at Henry Starr sitting cross-legged opposite her, then up at Esterhazy—the same silly smile she had worn since coming out of the damned bank and telling him "Wait" when he'd asked the question the first time. "Let me tell you how it was"—she could barely contain laughing and her skin glowed. "We went into the bank. There was a guard to our right asleep in a chair tipped back against the wall. Two clerks in the teller's cages and the bank president sitting in his office with the door ajar. The vault door open a little bit. It was exactly two fifty P.M." She laughed, rocking back a little bit on her haunches. "Mr. William Smithers here was thinking about buying some cattle, wanted to arrange for his bank in Denver to transfer funds . . . That's how you'd do it, isn't it?" she said. "That's how you'd play it if you wanted to do that bank?"

"You liked it," said Henry Starr blandly. "I told you banks were better."

"You're right," she said, "banks are better. I did like it." Esterhazy grumbled at his stew, and his jealousy tickled her as much as playing bank robber with Henry Starr had done. She felt warm and close to the men across the fire, as if she were playing Hawkeye and Uncas with her brothers.

"The strange part," she said, "was sitting there like a pair of ordinary citizens, talking bank drafts and insurance rates, all the time knowing you don't mean any of it, that it's all a joke on that little old banker. I kept thinking he would see right through us, but he never did, as if we were wearing masks . . ."

"Yes," he said, "that's how you start. Later it can get complicated . . ."

*He is feeling pretty smug, isn't he?*—having showed off for her, having let her play his game. It made her flash a little bit—did he think he could let or not let her play, when this was her game too?—but she tried to damp her fire down, keep her face soft so that Henry Starr would not be on his guard. "I kept thinking of you talking to Wilberforce the day your movie opened. He was like a mouse, and you were a cat talking shop but thinking *dinner*." She grinned, and looked (to Henry Starr) just like that cat. "I kept wondering what you had in mind for . . . *our* bank."

"Well," said Henry Starr, "now that *would* be complicated . . ." and she said, "Simple—I thought you said banks were simple."

Henry Starr looked at her face, sharp-eyed and with that bobcat grin, glowing with the firelight and the fun of playing outlaw, you could see she was up on herself the way a good rider was up on a good but unbroke horse, and he said inside himself, *Well, if she ain't ready now she never will be*, and he tipped her the corner of a smile. "All right," he said. "If you're ready for the next lesson."

He rose and walked over to the wagon, took an iron pry bar from the boot, hopped into the wagon box and began popping slats off the top of his crate of "Agricultural Equipment." Esterhazy and Miss Woodly came over to watch.

Inside the crate, set into a framework of notched crosspieces cushioned with rags, were three Winchester repeating rifles, of an old model newly refurbished and blued dark so that the iron ate the light; four .45-caliber Colt's pistols, three of them single-action Peacemakers and one an old hog-leg Dragoon model; and a pump shotgun with a radically cut down barrel. Packed under these were leather scabbards for the rifles, shotgun and pistols, and boxes of ammunition, steel and brass and copper cartridges, red-and-white-topped shotgun shells.

"What is all this?" Esterhazy wanted to know. He looked a little frightened. "We are really going to rob bank?"

"Not today," said Henry Starr. "I just want to show you the tools of my trade, like you showed me yours."

Esterhazy took one of the Winchesters, Henry showed him how to load and lever it—Miss Woodly seemed to know by herself, or maybe her eyes were quick and her hands cunning enough to pick it up by watching. They set up a row of stones along the top of a flat table rock on the far side of their clearing, and Henry Starr stood at the other side and shot two of them into powder. Esterhazy stepped up next to him. "We had bolt rifles in war, more heavy than these."

"She's light but she'll bite," said Henry Starr. "Squeeze careful and be ready for the shoulder punch." The POW-*pwee!* of Esterhazy's ricochet punctuated the sentence. He levered the next shell up waveringly. Took his rest, adjusted his aim, and blew a second rock to powder.

Miss Woodly walked off to one side and took her rest with the barrel of the Winchester on the wagon box. Her first shot powdered the rock next to Esterhazy's, then she lowered the rifle and braced it against her hip to lever it. Took her rest. Aimed. And popped another rock off the ledge.

"Winchester's too long in the barrel for me," she said, "I have to rest it on something."

"Nice shooting any way you do it," said Henry Starr. So she had been around guns and knew how to handle herself with them. He felt easier, as if that settled some questions he had about her, although he couldn't exactly say how.

She stacked the rifle against the wagon, then said suddenly—impulsively, with a force that was puzzling—"My brothers taught me how," and she seemed embarrassed and proud at the same time.

"Same fellas taught you to drive a team?" said Henry Starr, teasing her—but softly, remembering how she had shied and bridled at the remark before, as if in spite of the way she handled a rifle he *did* have to be careful of her. But this time she just narrowed her eyes at him the least bit and said, "The same," and the line of her chin dared him to say more.

He decided to change the subject. "Rifles for distance work," he said, "keeps the sheriff from getting too tight to your tail. But bank robbing gets done close, so you want these," and he handed them the Peacemaker Colts by the barrel, leaving the old-model Dragoon in its notched rack.

They stood closer to the rocks this time. Miss Woodly had wrapped handle and trigger in one long hand and cradled the weight of the barrel softly with the other. The blue-barreled Colts were a lot heavier than they looked. Henry Starr buckled on an old worn gun belt and holstered the Colt by his right hip. He stood square to the line of rocks, then reached easily for the gun, sliding it smoothly up pointing and cocking in one movement and firing three shorts sharp barking shots, and three rocks popped into the air.

Esterhazy profiled toward the target like a duelist, his right arm squared at the elbow, the pistol pointed straight up; then he slowly lowered it, squinting a little as he extended his arm, trying to sight it like a rifle. He squeezed the trigger, but the pull jiggled the barrel off line so the first shot went right, and the recoil made the second high. He stood, smelling the bitter smoke, staring at the row of rocks. Then squared his stance determinedly, lowered the gun so that it centered in him and his body gave backing to his arm. Two shots, both steadier, the second scoring the rock face and singing into the woods—both misses.

Miss Woodly stepped up, stood square, the heavy revolver on the end of her willowy arm as weird as a prosthetic hand on the victim of an industrial accident. The pistol wavered when she pointed it, but then she reached up and steadied her right wrist with her left hand. It took two thumbs to cock the pistol. She tried to squeeze the trigger, but the action was hard as a rock; she squinted with the strain, the barrel making tight loops almost imperceptibly in the air, k-*pow!* The recoil threw hands and arms up and back. She took the body of the pistol in her left hand and shook her right. Esterhazy watched her, flushed with heat and effort; perhaps he wished in rivalry that she should fail too, but his mind repressed the thought.

Henry Starr watched her silently.

She took the gun in her right hand, refusing to look at him, cocked it with two thumbs pointing it forward and down, then raised it in a swift pointing gesture firing as the movement flowed, k-*pow!*—and a rock flew into fragments as the kick of the pistol threw her arm straight up so that she almost dropped it.

"Ach . . ." Esterhazy tried to stop himself, but it was too much, too much, all these looks and private games and jokes, and himself reduced to the role of some useless and impotent male duenna, and he had to tell her, "Just lucky shot." And was instantly ashamed of himself.

Henry Starr lifted an eyebrow at Esterhazy and said, "Sometimes it's better to be lucky than good." He gave Miss Woodly a nodding bow: "You shoot real nice . . ."

"You mean for a girl?" she said. "Maybe I'm just talented. Or maybe I had good training," and she grinned. The bones of her hand, wrist, forearm and shoulder and the tips of her breasts still rang with the shock of the recoil, her nostrils prickled with the sharp tang of gunpowder smoke, and it all felt so good to her, the three of them standing around taking turns and showing off—

—and suddenly she felt like laughing: she remembered playing like this with her brothers when they were young, peeled down to the strange difference of their skin by the pond, her brothers displaying the sweet complicated bunches of their sex, matching dick against dick as they pissed for distance, and she the impartial witness and judge, not envious or excluded at all but woven simply and completely into the game as if every difference between them were just another part of their kinship.

Now here she was a woman alone in the woods with two armed men, one of them a foreigner and the other a convicted felon, the two of them swapping eyes the way boys in a schoolyard would trade insults and double-dare-dast-you's, it was about the guns and it was about her too, and she knew she was walking a line, but she wasn't scared at all. She could handle a horse, a team, a gun—and a man too, or two men if it came to that.

She didn't know the name of the game they were playing but she loved it, it was better than Robin Hood or Jesse James or even Uncas and Hawkeye, and she was so good at it, that was what made her love it: she was the best at it. If Henry Starr was the famous chief of the Starr Gang, then she was something subtler and larger than that—she was the hidden chief of the Woodly Gang, that vast combination of which Henry Starr and his merry men were only a part or aspect, masked even among her fellows, moving secretly and swiftly to fulfill her inscrutable purpose.

And it was in her hands now, to bring Esterhazy out of his sulks, and put Henry Starr back in his place. "I suppose you gave some demonstration of your skill to keep your victims cooperative."

She could see from the way Henry Starr looked watchful that he had already learned to recognize when she was going to start working him over again, but she knew he could never anticipate just what she would do.

"No," he said, "you wouldn't want to make noise. One of us would be carrying the shotgun."

"A cannon like that . . ." said Esterhazy. The blunt-nosed weapon was leaned against a rock; its large empty eye and distorted proportions made it seem peculiarly murderous.

"Not just the weapon," said Henry Starr, "it's your eyes and the way you hold yourself. You don't need to shoot the buttons off some bank guard's shirt. In the bank you're so close it don't hardly matter how you aim as long as you can cock. Why it works is that the man looks at you and he knows you think you could shoot his buttons off if you had to. And that you would."

"How did they know you could?" asked Esterhazy. "Or would?"

"You get a name for things, and it sticks to you. People made up stories about us, and sometimes we helped 'em along, and some of 'em anyway was lies, but I never called a one of them. Because we lived by that kind of stories as much as by being smart or fast or well armed. They'd say, 'Henry Starr will not be taken alive,' or 'Cherokee Bill'd as soon kill a man as . . .' Or they'd say how I wore a steel plate under my shirt so nothing could kill me but a head shot. They said I was a dead shot with shotgun, rifle or Colt forty-five; that I had once shot a jackass rabbit dead in full jump at a hundred and fifty yards while riding my horse at the gallop; that before I rode into Bentonville I raced my horse under the telegraph wires and clipped all three with pistol shots as I charged into town."

"Is any of that true?" she asked.

"You've seen me shoot some."

"Not telegraph wires at a gallop. Not jackass rabbits at a hundred and fifty yards from the back of a bucking bronco. Buffalo Bill I have seen do that, but not you."

"Well," he said, and he looked a little smug, which graveled her, "maybe I could and maybe I couldn't. But the point was the people believed I *could* and that I *would*, and ain't that all you need? When you're afraid of a man he ain't just a man to you, it don't seem like he can be as much afraid of taking a bullet or eating the dirt as you are, as far as you're concerned he might as well be wearing that steel plate . . ."

"Suppose they called the bluff," she started to say, but suddenly the truth jumped out at her: "It wasn't a bluff," she said, her voice coming small as if there were a hand clenching her breath, "you weren't bluffing at all when you . . ." and he said, "All right, no, I wasn't—but what did it matter as long as they thought . . ."

But she wouldn't let him duck away from the fact that had nailed her attention. "You went in there ready to kill, and if somebody, some bank teller, some bank teller like *me* . . ."

*A teller like you, Miss Woodly?* he thought. *There never was a teller like you, for I do believe you would have called the bluff. But then I . . .*

*But no I would never have done that, because I was smart and careful to keep the killing chances out of it, so that you were safer to be robbed by Henry Starr than to be rescued from Henry Starr by some clumsy rube of a bank guard or a posse man hot for reward money closing his eyes and blazing away from the back like old Floyd Wilson—*

*You remember old Floyd Wilson, don't you, Henry?*

*Listen:* said Henry Starr's ghost. *Tell her what you want to, but don't you lie to me. You know there is a moment, always, sitting the horses out in the brush before you go in, with the shape of the street and the bank clear and simple as a picture in your mind, and you tug your hat tight and check over your weapons, all of you together, making a chorus of click-snaps and the chirr of spinning oiled cylinders like a field full of iron crickets, and you take the sound and let it into your head so that it makes a kind of blind inside you, outside of which the shapes of people don't signify no more than if they was wooden statues or nightmares or meat on the hoof.*

She was looking at him now with a fierce intensity—it was the look Jiminy used to give him when Henry Starr was going to tell him something he didn't want to hear even if it was good for him, and maybe that was the way he looked when Cora told him Daddy-Henry was gone some time last night without saying even good-bye, and never coming back . . .

*But I can't say any of that to you, Miss Woodly, no more than I could say it to Jiminy, to my little boy who wasn't really my . . .*

"Listen," he said, "I understood how it all worked, Miss Woodly, and nobody ever made any mistakes or got killed inside any bank I ever robbed."

"What about outside?" she said, she had an eye for loopholes that was as good as her line on a rifle target. Esterhazy looked at her in surprise: her voice was sharp, her eyes narrowed in that razor look she used to slice up Deputy Price. "You make it all sound so *simple*," she said. "Everything goes like clockwork," she said, "like one of Foley's Westerns, right? The plans are perfect, the equipment just what's needed, force calculated to frighten so far but no further, the men carefully trained and absolutely obedient. The clerks do not call you because they are scared and it is not their money. The bankers do not call you because they are scared, and because it *is* their money and they want to live to enjoy it. The law fears to pursue because they can't be paid enough to risk their lives against such terrible men; but the people befriend and protect you because they know you are a robber with a heart of gold, rob from the rich and give to the poor . . . It *is* neat," said Miss Woodly. "Perfect in fact. I can see why you kept going back to it. In fact, I can't see why you ever stopped. You make it sound less risky than keeping a store. So tell me, Henry Starr: what went wrong? Why are you working for a bank instead of robbing it? Why did you ever have to stop? Did you get tired of hauling off the cash? Run out of banks?"

To Esterhazy's sly delight it seemed that someone had finally asked a question that the Famous Outlaw could not answer.

She kept looking hard at him, she had the drop on Henry Starr and did not mean to give it up. "I'm asking, Henry Starr: because if I'm going to do a movie of your life and get it right I need to know."

"Excellent!" Esterhazy snapped. "We are not here to rob banks or shoot targets but to make script for movie. Miss Woodly, dear colleague: is any of this useful to your work?"

She grinned like a bobcat at a trapped squirrel, predatory and playful. "Yes it is . . . all of it. Do you want to hear?" Esterhazy nodded, instantly pleased to be on his own strong ground; Henry Starr looked discomfited, the shotgun an awkward implement in his hands. "Well," she said, "the details need to be worked out, but I know what the *shape* of the story will be." She looked at Henry Starr, her eyes snapping. "And if you tell me even *once* that this 'ain't the way it used to be' so help me I will kill you."

"Go ahead," he said.

"All right then." She took a breath. "You're a boy, a young man—Henry Starr is a young man, an Indian, he's proud of that, but . . . but he has a sense of the injustices his people . . . of how they have been driven down in the world. Then the whites . . . the railroad" *(Henry Starr stood stiff and stony-faced, pleased? insulted? stricken? what . . . ?)* "wants to take his land so . . ."

"Wait!" commanded Esterhazy. "This is literature. Movies is *picture*. Tell me what it is I can see."

"All right," she said. "How about this: as if we were on a hilltop, turning and looking, there's a wide open grass prairie sweeping by us, dotted with . . . with cattle, with buffalo . . . buffalo! A grove of trees, a cornfield and a cabin. He's sitting and reading . . ."

"Lying down and reading," said Esterhazy, "in the shade of the trees . . ."

". . . among the corn rows," said Miss Woodly. "Reading a book, what book? A dime novel about Jesse James!"

Henry Starr said, "*Jesse James's Double Daring*. By Colonel D'Artagnan Arbuthnot," but his voice had an edge.

She gave him a savage look of glee, *Welcome to the party*. "All right: but how about Fenimore Cooper's *Last of the Mohicans*, because Henry Starr is *that* kind of boy. Reading and dreaming: 'A boy's dream of the lost grandeur of his ancient race.' How about that?"

"Literary," said Esterhazy, "but with pictures it might work. Go on."

"Some white men come—banker-looking types, with some toughs to provide the threat, they try to bully Henry Starr's mother into selling the land . . ."

"My Grandfather Tom Starr," said Henry Starr. "If they'd been crazy enough to try *that* he'd have killed them."

She was ready for that objection, ready for days in which she had dreamed his life over, knowing that the boy, the mother, the grandfather and squaw-man stepfather were too many for her movie to contain. "No grandfather," she said.

Esterhazy came to her rescue, as if on cue. "Of course not grandfather! Henry Starr is hero of this epic, yes? Hero protects his mother is more *hero* than protecting grandpa. So: family is *mother*." The outlaw looked bull-headed, but on this ground Esterhazy was not afraid of him. "Listen, my friend. In movie you live in eyes, you have to abide by law of eyes. Eye has no patience, eye don't think about it, ask question—it looks, bang! what's there it sees, then it wants to see next thing, and next and next. If movie stops and starts and goes back and reconsiders, eyes won't listen long enough. Picture has to be instantly, instantly and total, instantly and complete. To make movie, you can't tell history of Cherokee Indians and United States of America. You can't even tell whole life of Henry Starr. It takes you twenty-five years to live from Tahlequah robbery to Stroud robbery and we have for this maybe less than hour, and only to show *pictures*, understand? So that's why only mother, no grandpa."

"But that isn't how it . . ." Henry Starr started to say, then jerked up short and looked at Miss Woodly in surprise. She grinned happily, she had got ahead of him on that one all right, heard the words while they were still behind his eyes and told him they had no power tonight. That rankled; he reached back for a word that had some force to it and found the one Bub Houston had laid on him: "Even if you make a man out better than he was, Miss Woodly, it's still pretty close to a lie."

"Ha!" she cried. "It's all right for you to ride around pretending to be the Robin Hood of Old Oklahoma for the purpose of robbing banks: but if I tell a story . . . in which *you*, for God's sake, are the *hero* . . . ! you call *that* a lie," and in the very next breath she was going to ask him *who did he think he . . . ?*

When suddenly she remembered that the answer was that he thought he was Henry Starr. And he *was* Henry Starr: standing there just across the fire glaring down at her, with his wounded leg and gray threads in the black hair and the hard prominent bones of his head, crinkled skin at the edges of his dark hooded eyes, compact and dangerous and full of his age and his uncanny history and his secrets all as hard set as the bones underneath his well-used muscles. She felt suddenly and sharply her distance from him in age and sex and knowledge. She knew suddenly and with absolute clarity that she and Esterhazy had been perfect idiots, inventing a story that probably had no more to do with Henry Starr than Henry Starr did with Robin Hood—it made her despair about her work, and herself.

"Listen—" Esterhazy came to her rescue. "Of course you come out looking better in movie—like in story, like in dream, everything is better, everything make more sense. In life you make all kinds mistakes, you get it wrong. So this time you get it right, hey? You make it happen like it should be."

Henry Starr was silent, but she could practically hear the buzz of their words through his brain.

Then he seemed to let go of something, so that his muscles slumped on the rack of his bones. "They wouldn't need to bully her into selling," he said softly. "It would have been enough that she was in debt and the railroad held the paper. All they have to do is show her the paper." *Even Tom Starr had been defeated by that*, he thought.

Miss Woodly's anger and confusion blew away like dust off a doorsill, and she had to take a rein on the sudden charge of energy that filled the muscles of her arms and legs and made the breath expand in her chest. She did not guess what his reason had been, but she recognized that Henry Starr had accepted—however tentatively, implicitly—her right to make her fable of his life, and she took the legend now in both hands and began to spin it out.

"Well. I wasn't sure where to go from there . . . there was a lot to cover even before you told me about the rodeo—your first robbery, your gang getting together, the early success and the failure at Bentonville and the killing of Wilson, arrest and prison, pardon and release, your new life with . . . and then the second time around leading up to the famous double robbery at Stroud, prison again and . . ."

"Law of the eye!" Esterhazy commanded. "Why do you send him to prison twice?"

"I didn't send him, the law did . . ."

"Yes, that's true history, 'how it used to be.' Is dead and gone. Can't get it back." He looked defiantly at Miss Woodly. "Story don't need Bentonville *and* Stroud and all other robberies. Which one you want to see? Only which is most full, most spectacle, that makes most difference. Story don't need two times prison: only one that makes difference to him so when he comes out . . ."

"But it didn't," she said, thinking hard about her densely written pages, "it didn't make a difference the first time he got out, because he went right back to it."

"But you can't use if it don't make difference," said Esterhazy seriously and quietly. "Not like life. Movie has to keep adding up to something, and life don't. Movie must come to *point*, not life. If next scene don't make difference, then eye stop looking and you are dead."

Thinking so hard, her eyes flitting from object to object, she heard "dead" and saw: the fire: the gun: Henry Starr—and with a shock realized they had lost their sense of his presence, as if he were a ghost, withdrawn and silent. She focused on him, trying to wake him up: "Well, why did you have to try and rob two banks at the same time? When you'd already been to prison once, and got free and made a new life . . . ?"

Henry Starr's stillness became a weight.

Esterhazy stepped in to keep them moving forward. "Maybe reason don't matter so much. Why does Mr. Poole want to make *Birth of Nation*? Maybe just because is biggest thing of its kind. Is all anyone wants, especially people who come to see this movie—something so big, like that: such spectacle . . . !"

She could see it: "So we have to make it all seem to come together at once: the biggest robbery, the most important time in prison—the decision to do Stroud rather than to go straight, to . . ."

"To stay with my wife," he whispered. "Her name was Cora. The boy's name was Jiminy. We had a store . . . she owned a store . . ."

She waited for him to say the rest, poised in electric tension, her mind bubbling with disconnected words and wordless thoughts, the rippling of the firelight on his face seeming to her overheated imagination like evidence of the visions surging and falling behind the skin of his face. But he did not speak.

She had been so intent tracking the ghost of Henry Starr from bank to bank across the Nations that she had somehow forgotten the woman, but suddenly now she was there, like the touch of a cold hand on your back when you thought yourself alone in some warm place—there, but Miss Woodly still couldn't see her, she was just a looming black shape, the wife his wife, the woman he married, was married to, the child the store the house, what was she to him really? Why had he married, why did he leave her, what did he do to her, did she drive him out, did he run away, why did he leave her to rob two banks in one day of complete disaster at Stroud, why? The question became bigger and deeper and darker as she thought it, an undertow in which the shape of her script danced like a chip, worthless, utterly without importance beside the reality of his . . . .

And just as she thought she was letting it go she saw with absolute clarity how the woman, the robbery, the reasons and the climax would all come together:

"The lady in the cabin!" she said, and they didn't get it. "The woman with the child . . . the one you took shelter with after Coffeyville."

"Bentonville," said Henry Starr.

"That's right," she cried, triumphantly, "and which one it was made no difference to you, or to what you told her. It was a bank robbed her, and you'd robbed a bank, and you gave her some of the money and told her it was 'a little piece of justice.' "

"It was a lie when I told it, Miss Woodly. It was to give me that kind of reputation . . ."

"Which you would live or die by . . ."

"But still not true."

"But true enough!" she cried. "True enough to live and die by! And wasn't it justice for the lady to get that money? And what difference *which* bank it was, isn't the idea of it the same?"

"I didn't rob the bank for the lady's justice."

"But you robbed it for *somebody's* justice, didn't you? That was part of why you did it, the best part, wasn't it? And you knew that, you did!—that was why you wanted that kind of name, that kind of legend, instead of a blind killer reputation like Billy the Kid or Cherokee Bill or . . ."

"So: they come riding up to house . . ." prompted Esterhazy, leaning forward eagerly.

". . . riding up to the cabin," she said, "and the woman comes to the door—like Henry's mother at the beginning, the same image!" She felt herself glow as Esterhazy bobbed his head and pursed his lips, so pleased with her grasp of the image. "She's frightened—the men are rough, bloody . . . Especially Cherokee Bill, he's . . . he's huge, he can barely contain his . . . his fury, and you're the only one who can hold him back, but you . . ."

"I'd just killed Floyd Wilson," said Henry Starr, his face unreadable in the shadows, but her heart leaped because she recognized that he was playing the game with them, Henry Starr rewriting the life of Henry Starr.

"Yes," said Esterhazy. "So audience is not sure of what you are capable."

"And you see the woman and the child," said Miss Woodly, "you see them . . . she's poor, the clothes ragged, but she has fine features, a kind of light in her face, and she stands . . . she's afraid, but she holds herself well, pride in spite of the rags, the hair blowing, her sad face—the way she holds the child to her breast you . . ."

Henry Starr's shadow shape made a sound, a grating breath. It scraped on her nerves, raw and painful; had her words hurt him too? She would revise them, she wanted to make it good for him: "She's the reason you go to Stroud," said Miss Woodly, softly, "the reason you have to rob two banks at once: because you keep seeing her, the woman and the child and the cabin, and you want to win her some justice, you want . . ."

She could see it herself in the blackness, clearly and suddenly, and it seemed so absolutely and terribly true that she felt an inward whirl of horror, as if her playful fibbing had turned up a secret truth as awful as a corpse found by children playing a game of death. She knew with absolute certainty that there was such a woman, child and cabin, these were ghosts full of power in Henry Starr, the woman's shape swelled and flowed and shifted like boiling smoke or fog or the poisoned water of a swamp, she had so many shapes: his mother, his wife, his lady-in-the-cabin—

And herself.

"I did it for her . . . for the woman, and for her justice," said Henry Starr as if he were teaching himself a lesson. "And what you said, that's just the picture of the reason I did it, which was for somebody's justice."

"For lady," said Esterhazy. "All they can see of that is lady. Something that makes difference in story, so when he is in prison, yes? and Cherokee Bill makes his break, and Henry Starr stops him . . .

Scene: As they are marching Henry Starr and Cherokee Bill to the scaffold, Cherokee Bill suddenly breaks free, seizes a gun from one of the guards—the crowd falls back as the outlaw savagely menaces all around with the weapon, thrusting it against the head of the guard who kneels at his feet:

Title: **"Spare me! My wife and children . . ."**

Cherokee Bill motions for Starr to pick up a fallen rifle.

We see Starr's face in close-up, and across his features the image of the woman and child passes like the shape of a ghost . . .

Starr strikes the gun from Cherokee Bill's hand, the guards rise up and seize both of them roughly.

Starr's face is calm and pale, with a light on it like that which illuminated the woman in the cabin.

In shadow silhouette, we see Cherokee Bill hanged.

Title: **The Law takes its Course . . .**

Bill Tilghman appears at the door of Starr's cell. He holds out a paper:

Title: **. . . but there is such a thing as justice.**

Starr looks at Tilghman; at the guard whose life he saved.

Title: **"I have pursued you for ten years, Henry Starr. You have courage, and you always played square. In your heart, you are a good man."**

We see Henry Starr riding his horse slowly over a hill. He pauses and looks down—dreamily, as at the beginning. We see that he is looking into a valley, in which sits a poor small lonely cabin, with a curl of fire at the chimney.

Fade out as Starr rides down the hill toward the cabin . . .

"I know none of it happened that way, exactly, I know," she said. "I've read your story, I've been listening to what you've said. But it can't just be laid out like a history or a novel. It has to be a picture leading to a picture leading to a picture. I have to condense all that, all the meanings of everything, all the things that happened, into a few pictures. But I . . . I'm trying to be true to what you . . . You *did* mean to get some justice for your family when you started, they had suffered and been pushed . . . and they won't *see* it, won't see the truth of that unless there is an image they understand, the mother, the child who tries to . . . and you *did* care about the woman you told us about and you must have . . ." and she stopped her running tongue, frightened suddenly at the line she had almost crossed, finishing in her own mind: *You must have cared about the woman you married and the little boy, even though (and*

*I don't know why) you left them behind you when you started on the road to Stroud.* "If you think I got you all wrong, if it doesn't make sense . . ." She spoke softly, pleadingly: because if he did not give his life to her, then she would be weaving with smoke and it would all blow away with a breath.

"It almost makes too much sense," he said, "this Henry Starr you're talking about, he moves so straight from one thing to another, he seems so clear about what he . . . You make me too much better than I was, Miss Woodly."

Her eyes lit with the hunting-cat fire again, and she pounced on the idea he had given her: "But it's always better, it's always too perfect. There's never anything *but* heroes in stories, so anyone who gets remembered in a story has got to seem to be that way. And you, you know that, you lived and would have died by that yourself, even when you were racing around in that used-to-be real life you always talk about: you kept telling stories, playing out stories of yourself, so people would remember you a certain way. The movie is a story too, it isn't against your life, it's part of it, it . . . it's . . ."

". . . all that gets remembered," he finished, and she answered, "Yes."

"All right," he said. "I understand you can't show exactly how it used to be, truth for truth. All right. I couldn't tell it that true either, so I don't blame you. But it's got to be *right*, even if it can't be true. This time it's got to be right. All I was ever trying to do those other times was get it to come out right and . . . but you've got to know"—and his eyes leveled on her and she felt their weight—"it ain't just pictures of things. It was . . . the things was real, used to be real. So these pictures, they got to show so you know there is something real behind 'em, or it's just" (*and he muttered words she didn't understand, Cherokee word for blackness, for black sorcery*) "it's just plain shit, you understand?"

"Then show me more," she said, focusing intently on his half-shadowed face, "as much as you show me of what's real I'll put into the story. Only we'll have to make it smaller to fit in these pictures . . ."

*Could it work?* he wondered, and he looked at the pictures her words left in his mind: *Suppose he gave her all of it—Tom Starr, Hop Starr, Aunt Belle and the whole Starr clan, and Jesse James, and the Cherokee Nation; his mother, and his redskin book, and Colonel D'Artagnan Arbuthnot; and Cherokee Bill, and justice, and all his dark reasons and conjurings and dreamings and the ghost workings—let her have all of them, let her make them over again like you change tobacco,* hyenh? *like blue tobacco, like red.*

The names and their ghosts made one shadow, like smoke swelling to a vague hugeness, wordless, speechless; it was as if Miss Woodly breathed that smoke in through her nostrils, drank it with her small parted lips, with her blue open eyes—and the smoke seemed to give her size and weight, as if her light body was the seed of a gigantic shadow shaped like a woman, a woman whose eyes were bright with eagerness, and bright with drinking the names of Henry Starr.

But behind Henry Starr's back, breathing as cold and dark as the fire was warm and bright in front, there was another shadow shape, huge and strong and male and full of a rage and a hatred large enough to kill out everything between his shadow at noon and the horizon, the shape of Tom Starr, the shape of Cherokee Bill: *I don't know what she can do, but she hasn't give me a picture yet that can stand equal to that.*

He looked at her. Why did his goddamn name and story matter so much to her, so much that she seemed sometimes full of a witch's magic with them, a woman full of lightning and the smoke of changed tobacco in which things themselves are remade—and then like now, looking at him like a child, like a child of his own, hungry for a thing from him, a word she needs to be able to live.

There was nothing he could say about it, nothing that made sense except that that wasn't how it used to be. Which she had said she would kill him if he said, but judging by the sad eager look of her waiting on my answer, probably meaning she'd feel like killing herself.

Now why in hell should she feel like that? What did she want from him? His body answered with a flash of blood upward from his loins through his belly, but he rode it down like you ride a half-broke horse and refused absolutely to name it. It buzzed wordlessly in his brain and nerves, making him feel edgy and a little drunk. So what if she had her own reasons for making him the hero of this story, everybody always had their own reasons for everything they did, and he was dead sure she meant to show him good, to do right by him. That was a kind of truth, even if the details come out a little bit wrong. So what if she had all these moods and shapes that he couldn't keep track of; girl, witch woman, bobcat or deer, if shape changing was her gift, maybe she could make a shape for him. All he had to do was take the chance and put his ghost in her hands.

"All right," he said, "I'll show you."

"Good," groaned Esterhazy, "wonderful . . . but not tonight, eh? No more tonight."

---

It was late, they felt the accumulated weariness of the long day, the energy of talk was spent although the impulse and need to continue, to finish the unfinished, hung in the air. They went off one at a time into the brush, then returned to the fire—which Miss Woodly strengthened, sitting cross-legged before it, while Henry Starr cleaned the guns and set them with a soft knock back into their racks in the crate; at last rapping the nails of the crate home again with a hammer. Esterhazy came back to sit across the fire from Miss Woodly. But he had nothing to say to her, and the dark shape of Henry Starr moving restlessly like a cat outside the firelight oppressed and annoyed him. Were they just waiting for him to go to sleep so they could finish whatever it was they had started here? Esterhazy suddenly felt disgusted with himself, stood abruptly and said, "Good night, Miss Woodly," walked into the darkness, rolled himself in his sleeping sack. He could still see her sitting by the fire, hear Henry Starr bustling around by the wagon. *How do you know,* he thought, *that I am not lying here watching you?* He smiled, and sleep came up around him like fumes.

She drifted sleepily too, feeling the warm tongues of the fire on her face and breasts; the echo of the pistol's blast and recoil made a dimmed buzz in the muscles of her arms and chest. She was contented as a cat, neat and balanced and edgeless. It had been difficult today, there were passages of feeling she had been through that had surprised and frightened her, but she felt all right now, and that everything was going so well. Maybe it was dangerous to relax and let herself feel so comfortable, let the tight cords in the groove of her hips and thighs slacken to the fire warmth—because it wasn't finished yet, he'd have to tell her more if she was going to know what she needed to learn, and he had to be goaded and teased and poked and winked at or he would just close up again, silent and self-contained.

It was funny that that was what drew her, that sense that he could close over himself and be all right, compact and secure—because she wouldn't be happy unless she could pick that compactness apart: no, not pick apart, but open it up, unfold it and lift out what was inside.

He was solitary and self-sufficient, but Henry Starr needed her more than her brothers ever had, even at the beginning of their games when they still relied on her to bring them stories out of the books she read: because Henry Starr had a story, but no voice to tell it with. Oh, he talked smoothly enough, but it never got said with him, did it? It was always held back or turned aside somehow. She was the only one who could tell it all for him, and when she did, even if it was his story to start with it would be hers too. She had worked, thought, dreamed it so intently that already she couldn't be sure that what she saw in him was not just the reflection of her own yearning: to be strong and sure and compact, to ride everything the way Henry Starr rode that horse of his, that ghost-gray Appaloosa with the moon-bright rump whose body read and followed the shifts of your mind in the grip and guiding of your knees and thighs.

His image was so sharp in her mind that it seemed almost to be an aspect of herself, another being's ghost projected among her bones and the strings of her nerves and blood, a stranger's ghost, but somehow also it felt like it was kin or kind with her, like a baby might feel—something woven out of yourself but also come into you from outside, out of that odd lovely pushing opening up of you by the strange lovely prong of a male body, which she knew and enjoyed except for the fear that would clench her even in the top of her pleasure when she thought of that strange thing starting itself over again inside her.

Henry Starr. I love to watch the way you move, I envy the way you seem like a veteran of your body, at home in its easy motion, settled among your muscles and the hang of your bones like a cat in a corner.

She remembered her own body feeling like the way Henry Starr moved, when she was a child. She had loved the feeling, and it made her warm toward her outlaw that he could recall that sense to her. But she had to watch the illusion: it was a snare, if you weren't careful. It had betrayed her before. One day she was quick and limber among her brothers, the next it seemed that her strength had become a useless unwanted kind of burden or embarrassment to herself and everyone else—and her quickness of eye and thought and invention useless as well, something to be mocked and evaded. One day she had felt her own power rising in the pulse of blood in her own belly and sex, the deliciousness when she touched herself as if her fingers were wet sliding tongues, in the way men's eyes and bodies changed at the touch of her eyes or her scent: and the next she was just one more dick-nailed cunt, used up and spraddled out on a rented bed.

But watching Henry Starr's black edgeless shape gliding back and forth among the random licks of firelight, that other self woke up and stirred inside her skin, it was still there, as slick and lithe, as smoothly muscular and perfectly articulated as an otter, an otter that could sing like a bird and tell stories like a crystal set. When she looked at Henry Starr he seemed like an otter too, silky slippery and wild and strange to most people as a wild animal, just like her. He was her brother otter, they were two of a slippery muscular kind, she would open his throat and teach his breath to talk and sing and the gush of his stories would fill her until her muscles rested as easily on his bones as if they were her own . . .

That image seemed to leap at her out of the fire, and an electric shock of fear bow-strung the muscles in her thighs—as if she had felt the lick of a blunt smooth tongue in the deep socket of her hips. She hunched forward, gathered herself protectively around an invisible center. *Don't let the game play you.*

He moved around in the darkness, fussing with the guns and equipment and horses, and still he could see her face reflecting a small gem of firelight from the flames. He was having second thoughts.

How had she got him to say *yes* so quickly? She has got me to spread myself out for her like a map, and she don't let on about herself—who she is, where she come from, those brothers that taught her things, what's between her and that fat banker or that peckerwood Deputy Price or that egg-sucking weasel of a Poole. Hell, she don't even give away her front name, unless it just happens to be *Miss*.

She's got an angle on asking questions that covers the ground, and the eye to take advantage of it. What makes her think I got to answer? What makes *me* think I got to answer?

She acts like she has been around and has seen the elephant, and she can handle a horse and a rifle pretty fair, and she says she is twenty-seven years old, which makes her not just a woman grown but she has had some practice, has had some getting used to it. And then I say something and she shows the color in her face and looks like she'd like to take a little bite out of me, I can see she'd like to think just about as well of me as I'd let her, if I'd let her; questions sharp but the answers she wants is just the ones a man would want her to have *some may think you a romantic Robin Hood . . .*—and it don't add up, you look at those little fine lips and maybe you should take off five or six years, and it makes you want to, makes you think you ought to be a little careful with her . . . careful *for* her, because she does take her chances don't she?

Miss Woodly. Miss B. C. Woodly. She has read my same old red-cover *Last of the Mohicans*, and both of us grew up being Uncas the son of Uncas. But when I make a picture in my head of her reading that book, she's ten years old and built like a birch-tree sapling, I bet she ain't decided yet whether she's girl or boy, lying in a field reading about the noble race of the Mohicans. And depending on what's her real age I am either thirty years old, just pardoned out of prison for tricking my best friend into a hangman's noose; or I am thirty-seven, I have one more year left of living in Cromwell Oklahoma with Cora Munson and her baby Jiminy, one more year of thinking how if I can just get them to belong to me I will finally be home free—one more year till I throw them both away and go back to robbing banks, and every word I had spoke or thing I had done for them out of love turned into black trickery, false sign to hide my true name and my trail.

False sign: I have laid a lot of that in my time. Used to be I had to stay covered to keep from dying, but what good does it do me to leave false sign now, as the name the people will have to remember me by? She keeps asking and I got to keep deciding whether to come out in the clear or keep blinding the trail—plead to her like she was to judge me guilty or not, or just look at her soft and talk pictures into her eyes until she can't see me for blue smoke and sweet music, and then I . . . and then we . . . ?

*Damn.* He couldn't think about Miss Woodly for five minutes straight without his eyes filling up with blue smoke and his body taking the bit like a runaway horse, and in his business that way of drifting off could get a man killed.

Or no: in the business he used to be in, smoky dreams could get you killed. In this movie business blue smoke was the name of the game—except that Henry Starr needed for this movie to be the making of his own name, *Henry Starr*: and for people to believe in it, believe it was true as if they saw it happening with their own eyes, and if he was right about movies then somehow in spite of all the blue smoke that's what they *would* see.

Only first he had to tell the truth to Miss Woodly so she could make his words into pictures of the things they really was.

He'd showed her his guns, told her he knew how to use them, and she already knew he'd killed Floyd Wilson "by accident" because she had "looked him up"; but that still wasn't enough of the truth to escape being a little bit a lie. He'd never actually said with his own breath "I killed Floyd Wilson, I'd have killed anyone who" nor said what was inside the name of Cherokee Bill, who had gone under the black hood so Henry Starr could climb over everybody and return to find his road again, and his horse and his guns and his word: that word of his, which he gave and took away again, promising he would work with her and tell her the truth and then—

He stepped suddenly out of dense blackness into the firelight, and she startled. "The only reason I quit," he said, as if an hour had not passed since the last words they had spoken, *Why did you quit, did you run out of banks or get tired of hauling off the money?* "—the only reason was, I got caught."

She was alert again in a second. "Ha!" she said. "But when you got out of prison you went right back and picked up where you left off. Getting caught never stopped you, it just . . ."

"I didn't go right back," he said, looking at her closely, a little bit in pain. "But all right. I'll tell you how . . . There's things," he said staring into the fire, "things you can't keep control of, that get out of hand . . ."

*He looked in the fire and thought of Cherokee Bill shooting his brother-in-law full of holes with two different .45 pistols because he had got one more hog as a present from his father-in-law which was treating him like a nigger; of Cherokee Bill gobbling softly in his throat waiting for the signal to ride into Caney Kansas or Bentonville Arkansaw or to stop the Katy Flyer at Pryor Creek Station or for the prison guards to rush his barricade in the dead end of the stone corridor in Fort Smith Prison, and nobody wants to know what's happening behind those small weird eyes of his; Cherokee Bill so strong and crazy that even Fort Smith Prison couldn't hold him but he'd conjure so hard and furious that Something would finally have to give him a gun, and kill a trusty and stand off the whole garrison except for Henry Starr his friend his brother coming to talk him out from behind his barricade and his guns and into Judge Parker's black hood and greased noose.* Beyond the firelight a huge shape of darkness seemed to shift its heft uneasily on its boots, and the earth creaked like boards. "There's things that get away from you" said Henry Starr.

"All right," she said softly, but emphatically, as if his admission had settled something. "So you wanted, you had to do those things knowing all the time, *all* the time what could happen, having people with you who . . . what did you say? Who had the reputation that they might, that they would just plain . . ."

"Cherokee Bill," said Henry Starr, as if confessing something. "You could see it in his eyes, anyone could, just looking at him: most of the time there was no more in them than what there is in the eye of a dead catfish, like the world wasn't there at all; and sometimes like a little black man locked in a cell, shaking the bars and cursing at you, and the bars just about to break to pieces in his hands. But he was my friend, he wasn't that way to me." *Henry Starr! Nobody ever rise up early enough to climb over Henry Starr.* "He was my friend. He'd have give his life for me if it come to that," *which he did, didn't he? Gave or had it fooled away from him by the friend he would have give it for.*

He couldn't talk to her about Cherokee Bill, not yet: couldn't put the words into the night that would make that shadow solidify, because he hadn't kept his promise, not in twenty-five years he hadn't, and he wasn't certain yet that he could keep it this time, and if he couldn't he must never look into the eyes of Cherokee Bill's ghost to see that small terrible shape in them shaking the walls of his cell.

"All right," he said, looking hard into the fire until it blanked his eyes with brightness and the black of the night itself was covered, and no shape in the blackness could be seen. "All right, maybe I can tell it to you so you can see why I could never quit it, never, no matter what I had to . . ." *It's just that I can't look at you, can't bear to see you while I'm doing it because what if you don't understand, or if you do understand and then can't?*

"He was the biggest man in the Cherokee Nation," he said, "and I think he hated me right down to the bottom of my blood. When I looked at his face it was like, like I had to *eat* that, eat that [*Cherokee word: for black, for a thing which is black in your eyes*]. And I wanted, one time to show him who in hell I was—what did he think, that he was the only man under the sun could look at a man and make him eat shame and eat fear, make the man know that you held his life in your hands and you're just thinking about what you want to do with it . . . ?"

*She was lost, all of a sudden, was it Cherokee Bill he was telling her about? But it sounded like his grandfather again.*

"So I stepped out of the street and into the Katy Land Office, it's almost the end of the day and the whole street is in shadow, the raggedy bits of all that Fourth of July welcome-boomers trash blowing up the street with the old newspapers and rodeo programs and firecracker scraps, the shank end of everything and time to close up shop—and I come stepping through the door of the Katy Land Office. The white man behind the desk looks up, and he is Mr. White Man in the Middle"—*Who? she thought, who was he?* but he went rushing on too fast, sweeping her question down the street with the scraps of paper—"who had sat behind that desk and give it to Tom Starr—give Tom Starr his own shame to chew on, standing there taking it like he was a goddamn dead tree stump blind and deaf, gone all rotten inside and out—give it and took it back again. Mr. White Man in the Middle: he had a round pale face with a bow tie under it and a white shirtfront, and a smile put on like a paper collar till he sees who it is come in the door. And the smile closes up like the stores on Main Street, because this ain't a boomer come in to buy some Injun land, this here is some little Injun kid come in here for some tomfool reason or other when I'm a busy man. So he says: 'What can I do for you, sonny?' the way you'd say *scram.*"

*So it is Tom Starr then,* she thought, *Tom Starr and not Cherokee Bill—or somehow both of them together?*

"What does he see, I wonder what . . . I just stand there for the time of one breath—like a boy walking a fence rail stopping to hold his balance between this side and that. It's all still inside my head, all still behind my eyes where nobody can see it yet: who I am, who Henry Starr is, who he's going to be in just one more tick of the heart, one more breath: Tom Starr's grandson. A cowboy who rides for the Dodge Ranch. A good man on a horse. A whiskey runner. The breed kid who won the prize riding against that Nowata buck, pulled off the chicken's head riding bareback and buck-naked" *and he lost her again. Chicken's head? Buck naked? When all she could see of the rodeo was Henry Starr in Foley's false-front cowtown swinging off the side of his horse to snatch a bag of stage money out of the dirt.* "The goddamnedest thing you ever . . . And already I was *inside* just what I was going to be for real in one pulse of the blood from now, Henry Starr the Outlaw, the bank robber Henry Starr . . ."

*Who looked in the face of the Katy Land Office manager and smiled, clean white teeth in a smooth young brown face as the right hand loosely dangling by his hip snapped up and swept the big Colt out of the scabbard thumb-cocking it in one unbroken move as the barrel came up to point like a big black empty eye socket right between Mr. White Man in the Middle's two blue eyes . . .*

" 'Thumbs up and stand steady!' "

He had risen to his feet and stood there pointing into the darkness across the firelight, the light washing up his chest and turning his face into a reddish mask with blank pools of black at the eyes, which might as well have been stopped with black hoods for all they could see, blinded by the wash of the firelight. "And all the time Linc Cumplin and Kid Wilson are cracking the cashbox and filling the sacks with greenbacks and paper and silver—and we never even knew what kind of paper to take but just jammed everything in we could lay hands on, half of it useless blanks or IOUs we threw out that night—and heaping up big armfuls of land papers that we thought was mortgages and busting the coal-oil lamp on 'em . . . all that time I am eating the light of the white man's eyes, I am having a meal on his fear. It tastes good to me. It tastes as good as Tom Starr's shame tasted to Mr. Briefcase and Mr. White Man in the Middle when they sat there holding Tom Starr's Cherokee blood money in their hand, and give it to Tom Starr and took it away from Tom Starr just as they pleased.

"And when I was *full* I yelled 'Let's go!' and we come out that door like bulls out of the chute, we come yelling, we come blazing, we were on the horse like a bear, two jumps and the street was boiling up clods and dust clouds under the horse hooves, and we blew out every streetlight and plate-glass window from the Land Office to the bank to the Katy Hotel to the Schufeldt store, the citizens jumping out of the light out of the air down any hole behind any wall they could find to put between their soft bodies and the hard iron of Henry Starr, of Henry Starr and his gang, of the outlaw Henry Starr who just robbed the Katy Land Office and got clean away, with the town of Tahlequah hoo-rawed to hell and the posse miles behind on a cold cold trail.

"That was when I, when I climbed over, climbed over that fence, climbed over Tom Starr and the marshals that had me in the Bartlesville jail, and climbed over William Dodge and C. N. Walker and John Ross and Jack-the-Devil . . ."

He heard her take her breath back in a small gasp, she was suddenly afraid of what she was seeing, aware all at once of how distant and uncanny his life was from hers and now that he was telling all of this it was as if she saw his body strange and naked, and she wasn't sure she could, wasn't sure she was ready to . . .

The small breath sound made him remember her. A little distance came back to him, a little watchfulness—not enough to stop the flowing outward of ghosts, which Henry Starr felt crowding at his eyes and spilling from his breath, but enough so that now he listened to himself, deciding which ghosts she could hear and which ghosts he would see himself but not name for her.

"The posses coming after, they was part of how good it was, like all those people sitting racked up the bleachers and fence rails and telegraph poles at the rodeo. Sometimes we could feel them back in the air behind us like ghosts, but we crossed their paths with black, with blue smoke, I'm telling you we just put dogshit in their hands and broke the trail off short right under their noses and they never come close. Two, three times we'd be sitting up on a hill over our back trail and watch them come up to the break, smoking down the trail, reading it close, getting their peckers high, getting that itch all up and down inside and out like hound dogs on a coon scent, and then jerk up short what-the-hell because it just vanished, the ghost of Henry Starr printed clear in the earth just went plumb blank. I couldn't see their eyes but I could dream them, and it was almost as good to eat as the fear in the eyes of Mr. White Man, almost as good as watching him eat the same shit he fed to Tom Starr —to disappear out of somebody's eyes when you want to, it was almost as good as putting the fear of you in those eyes there, because that was my power.

"And finally I come back to Aunt Belle's ranch. In the old days, when I was a kid I'd go there—Buck and Dingus was there sometimes, and I remember seeing Cole Younger, I must have been less'n two because he and his brothers got shot to pieces in Northfield, Minnesota, in '76 and Cole was in prison twenty-five years. And Aunt Belle would always say to me, 'Well, *Cousin* Henry . . .' and it was a question, same old question it always was: you got big *enough* yet? You *done* anything yet? Anything at all to show you can come in here like the son of Hop Starr, like Tom Starr's grandson?

"Aunt Belle was dead three years when I come at last. They buried her in the front yard, right in front of the main house, in a little square fort of flat stones with a monument like a finger pointing up, which was just her way of pointing the final posse in the wrong direction.

"Her daughter Pearl kept the ranch now along with her son Ed Reed, a sneaky back-shooting son of a bitch that probably was the one murdered Belle. Ed is standing, blocking the gate as I come up, like maybe I ain't big enough yet, now he is the one to say, 'Well, Cousin *Henry*.'

"I throw the leather saddlebags down on the ground and he hears the clink of the eagles inside, and he says, 'Well well,' and grins me a grin like a cheap whore. 'Welcome to the family, Young Henry Starr.'

"It seems like people kept coming into the ranch all night, every bushwhacker in the Nations, and they had all heard about the big doin's in Tahlequah: how Cherokee Bill robbed the bank one day and Henry Starr took the Land Office the next . . ." *Cherokee Bill: who rode in himself that evening his face already numb with drinking white whiskey and teeth marks cut into the back of his hand, and what happened to the man who held his horse when he robbed the Cattlemen's Bank and rode out with him after Cherokee Bill never told and nobody asked; but he had heard all about me and the Land Office and he started laughing as soon as he saw me, and all he did was laugh and laugh and call me 'Henry Starr! Henry Starr!' till he passed out with a bottle of Ed Reed's whiskey on his chest.*

"Return of the Prodigal," said Henry Starr, "that's what it was. Except Ed Reed took pret' near the whole hundred to pay for the fatted calf, smiling and patting at me till he had it all . . . Hell, I didn't mind. It was like coming home, you know? Coming home and your own folks see you, think you're *famous*, you know? . . ."

(Yes, but it wasn't Belle Starr's ranch that Miss Woodly saw, where her mother had stood in the doorway calling Barbara! Barbara Catherine! The yard was blank, brothers hiding, Addie's black colt run off and gone.)

"He taps me on the shoulder, shushes his lips and says, 'Come on,' like it's something special for me, 'there's folks at the bunkhouse you ought to meet.' I cross the ranch yard with him, my head buzzing with whiskey, towards the low log bunkhouse, light slipping out through the chinks and from inside the sound of men talking low and throwing gear together. He raps the door, opens it, and I come in out of the open dark into the smoky insides of the bunkhouse, oil lamp stinking on a table, and there they were: sudden, sharp in the yellow light like pictures printed on a black page:

"Fat, mean-looking Grat, too tall for the low roof.

"Young Bob, looking smart and sharp and go-to-hell.

"Emmett, young and serious, chewing his bottom lip.

"Bill, looking like a preacher or a country politician dressed up for a cowboy, which I guess is what he was.

"The Daltons. It was the Dalton Gang.

" 'Boys,' says Ed, 'I want you to meet my Cousin Henry.'

"Grat *umphs* and Emmett looks up, angry, 'This place is about as private as Buffalo Bill's Wild West. Why don't you sell tickets, Ed?'

" 'Cut us in for ten percent,' says Bill, laughing.

" 'Never mind them,' says Bob, smiles at me and sticks out a hand. 'My daddy knowed your daddy, way back when.'

" 'We don't need nobody else,' says Grat.

" 'I ain't lookin',' I say, but I am looking, looking: the Dalton Gang, Grat and Bob and Emmett and Bill—and Bill Doolin probably off somewhere keeping an eye on some bank or riding back and forth on a railroad train—packing up their gear in Belle Starr's bunkhouse to ride off that same night to wherever or whatever it was, you'd be reading it in tomorrow's papers and for years in the dime books.

" 'Henry just come from Tahlequah,' says Reed. 'He took the prize at chicken pulling' ('Do tell,' says Grat) 'robbed the Katy Land Office of three hundred in gold and greenbacks, burnt a bunch o' land papers, hoo-rawed Tahlequah to a good night, and dodged Bill Tilghman off his trail.'

"And they straighten up, all but Grat, who turns red and goes on stuffing underwear and ammunition and oily cleaning rags into his saddlebags like he was filling a hole. 'Well sir!' says Bob, he smiles at me and puts down a neat-folded shirt, and comes across and gives me his hand, lean, cold and hard. 'Seems like the start of another fine career in the Starr family. Glad to make your acquaintance, Henry Starr.'

" 'Likewise,' says Emmett, but with sad eyes, looking from me to Bob and back. 'You sure,' he says to me, 'plumb sure you dodged Bill Tilghman before you come here?'

" 'I dodged him all right,' " *but it jumped up at me, saying it. Did I? Did I dodge him? Or was that lean gray man sitting on my back trail laughing at me, watching me watch the other posses getting thrown off, coming on and coming on slowly, his time is his own and he uses it all and he'll be waiting for me out ahead there somewhere: his gray eyes, they saw my ghost back there in Tahlequah, maybe he can smell me even now?* " 'I lost him good,' I say.

" 'We run his back trail when he come in,' says Ed Reed suddenly very businesslike: 'Nothing—he done it right.'

"Then the Daltons were packed and ready, and we shifted out of the stinking oil lamplight into the darkness, there were stars enough to see by. Grat pushes by and bulls through the blue air towards the horse corral not looking back. 'Keep doing right,' says Bob Dalton, 'and you'll *do* all right,' and he grins at me, but Emmett jumps in with 'and some day you'll be as rich as we are,' and Bob answers, 'You ain't as much fun as you used to be, Emmett.' And he looks at me: 'You be careful now, Henry Starr. Bill Tilghman don't shake easy, if at all. Appreciate it if while he's dogging you, you keep away from *my* back trail. Go anywhere you like, as long as it ain't Coffeyville, Kansas.'

" 'Shut up,' says Emmett, 'you talk too damn much.'

" 'Sure you ain't lookin' for a job, Henry Starr?' says Bob, still grinning. 'I could use another brother. This'n's about wore out.'

" 'Let the boy be,' says Bill Dalton, a deep resonant voice like a preacher's. 'This here's going to be just family—no offense to Young Henry here—just between the Dalton brothers and Jesse James,' and he winks.

" 'You *do* talk too much,' says Ed.

" 'You watch us, Ed,' says Bill Dalton, 'you see if we don't call Buck and Dingus and maybe raise 'em one.'

" 'Take care and do it right,' Bob Dalton says to me, 'and next job if you want you can ride with us like your daddy rode along with Jesse James. Just you remember: banks is the only thing, that's where the money is. You steal a horse or a cow and it bust a leg and die on you. Steal somebody's land and if *he* don't drygulch you then you'll just get droughted or weeviled out, and some bank'll get it for your debt. But money don't die: it don't get sick, it don't get old, and it don't never die . . .'

" 'It don't talk so damned much neither,' says Emmett pushing past to mount up, but Bob just laughs and says, 'That's what you think.' Then he was up too, and they pushed out of the corral, big hunks of shadow in the starlight, and they was gone down the road to Coffeyville, Kansas.

"My head was full of whiskey and full of names, dizzy with whiskey and names, Daltons and Jameses and Youngers, and Starrs—Tom and

Hop and Belle and Henry, Young Henry Starr that robbed the Katy Land Office and then hooked up with— What's all that shooting? It's the Daltons, the Dalton Gang and Henry Starr, they just robbed the Cattlemen's the Katy the Exchange the Wells Fargo the First National . . . *Henry Starr's Double Daring. Henry Starr's Vengeance Trail. Henry Starr the Outlaw* by Colonel by General by Field Marshal D'Artagnan Arbuthnot . . .

"Names and whiskey and names, and me stumbling around in the dark, looking for . . ."

He saw the rest of it, but he felt Miss Woodly again, felt her eyes and something told him to keep it dark, this part of it dark, and he wondered what she could hear behind his words and how much of all this she wanted to understand.

She saw him close his eyes but she didn't know why, and she said, "Henry."

He looked at her straight and she thought that he was still drunk on whiskey and names and talking and a finger of fear ran up from her belly to the tips of her breasts because she didn't know what he would do next in the dark. Esterhazy was locked in sleep, Henry Starr looking down at her, and her legs gathered under her so that she rose to meet the look and stand up against it. But he just kept standing there looking and silent, and she could guess easily enough that the rush of words was still going on behind his eyes . . .

*Drunk on whiskey and on names, and I went fumbling around in the dark looking for my saddle and sleeping blanket, whiskey and names and the faces of Mr. White Man and Tom Starr and Bill Tilghman and Bob Dalton all of them rising up in my belly and chest and lifting my head off over my shoulders for a stilty-walking look around, and that's when I saw her come out of the main house and close the door behind her. She come down the steps and stood by the square stone box Belle Starr was buried under, her body rotted away to hair and nails and bones and a pair of rusted pistols. Her pale dress was shining a little, but her face was shadowed and her black hair melted into the darkness.*

*"Hey!" I said, and she stopped. Because my word made her do that. "Thumbs up and stand steady!" I said, and she turned and put her hands on her hips, and the starlight was blue on her cheekbones and chin but her eyes was blots of shadow, and she said, "Thumbs up your ass whoever you are."*

*"I am Henry Starr," I said, and come towards her.*

*Her face was Aunt Belle's with twenty years washed off it, she was a ghost till she said, "I'm your Cousin Pearl."*

*"I didn't see you before," I said.*

*"I been busy, Henry Starr."*

*I stood in front of her, my heart jerking in my chest like a bull calf on a short tether, looking into the shadow pools of her eyes and mouth, wanting to see inside them, to push my eyes inside them and see, but it was too dark, and she laughed, "Well I guess you got everything else a boy could want but that, didn't you, Henry Starr."*

*She pulled her dress up over her head and stood up to me, the starlight turned her white-blue and black, two black eyes in her breasts and a wedge of black at the bottom of her belly ate the light that glistened and shadowed the long heavy muscles of her horseback-riding legs. "How do you like it, Henry Starr?" she said, and stepped up close so I could smell her smell sharp salty sweat and tobacco smoke and something under it dark and sweet like a, like a kind of fruit or, "Or don't you know how you like it yet, Henry Starr? It ain't like robbing a bank," and I felt her hand slip my gun belt and belt and flip flip the buttons down the front of my pants, and she took my lips into her hot mouth and bit them open, and her tongue went into my head hot and slick as the worm in a bottle of mescal, and she pulled me right over onto her as she lowered to the ground and leaned back, and took my thing in her hand like she was grabbing a Colt by the barrel—only the barrel was kind of popsy-shaky—and she pushed it all at once into the smooth hairy socket between her legs: and I was mounted but she did the riding, gripped me and roweled me in with her legs and heels. "Like that, Henry? Like that, Henry? Like that henry henry henry Henry Henry Henry Starr?" till I busted apart inside her name and blood and ghost and all.*

*And lay there breathing her smell, flat out empty, smooth as still water.*

*Then a step! Twig crack! and I rolled over sudden, tried to—but tangled, stuck in her goddamn it, pants around my ankles, gun belt off in the dark, and out of the nighttime it was Tilghman's goddamn Winchester snicking when he cocked it, and me on the ground snarled in a woman ass-naked and backside to the bullet . . .*

*"Hh! . . . 'scuse me."*

*Cherokee Bill. It was Cherokee Bill, "and goddamn you sneakin' around in the dark like that you," and Pearl Starr under me laughing fit to bust. "Thumbs up! Thumbs up, Henry Starr, and stand steady!" I started laughing too, laughing till my head was as high on laugh as it had been on names and faces and white whiskey, rolling over and over buck-ass naked on the grassy ground of Belle Starr's ranch yard with Belle Starr's Pearl, sweet smelly just-been-fucked by me over me under me over me Pearl . . .*

"That's why," he said, eyes blanked again but not with looking in the firelight, so she couldn't be sure if it was herself he saw and spoke to and she had to hold and hold onto his blank eyes until she knew.

"That's why I started and why I always come back to it. It was my night, you see? Nothing else ever made me feel as good as that; nothing else ever made me feel my . . . my powers, not even riding in the rodeo and taking the prize Injun style, nothing—like I could climb over everything, like I was a horse run and run till he was completely stretched out and used up, except you couldn't ever use him up because this was a horse with no bottom *to* him, no bottom at all . . . Because I, because I loved all of it, you see? Even the Cherokee Bill parts of it I loved . . ."

"Henry—" said Miss Woodly, and he came back into his eyes, and let her go, and suddenly she felt empty and cut off in the dark. "Why," she said, "Why did you stop?"

"Because I got caught at it, ma'am," he said, looking at her from farther away than he had ever been—

*And only after he'd said it realizing that he had misunderstood the question this time, that it wasn't bank robbing she was asking why about but the interrupted spill of his ghost, and that she had been ready there, waiting for him, that he could have stepped into the sheath of firelight around her, as close to her as the flickering on her skin and yellow glints out of her shadowed eyes.*

*And that this was where he had meant to bring her from the first.*

"Why did you stop?"

He looked at the fire with surprise, as if it had just become another thing entirely.

"I never did," he said. "It took something else to stop me. I got to ask myself what was it, did someone put a twist in my ghost, hey? Somebody climb over my ghost, somebody change tobacco on me, or was it something I done?" *The face of Tom Starr, one empty eye socket: a dead man's laugh, breathless. The face of Cherokee Bill: You'll think of something, Henry, you give your word to think of something. The face of a woman and a child . . .* "Yeah: that I done myself—so maybe what happened to me was justice, some goddamn old-time Cherokee justice."

She saw his face change—or it might have been some shift of the firelight—but it seemed to her that his eyes, nostrils and mouth resolved themselves into a glare of complete and wolfish ferocity.

"Well then maybe that ain't enough for me," he said. "Maybe a piece of justice, maybe that kind of Cherokee justice ain't enough for me, and my name made to be, to be right in the Nation. Maybe like you said I wanted more than justice, something bigger. Maybe I want my name to be so much, to be so right that it don't matter that there ain't no Starr clan anymore, ain't no Nation anymore to remember it. So . . . so big that my name be remembered when even the name of the Nation blows away like . . ."

"I'll make it right," she said, wavering a little on her legs, "I promise, I'll give you, I'll make a story that will do you justice"—and it flashed into her head that she was saying just what Paul Curry had said, that whenever and however and for whatever Henry Starr called her she had now sworn she would be ready. But she couldn't hold back, she had to promise him that she would make her movie absolutely as true to him as she was able to, because he had given her what he had promised, given her almost too much more of what she had asked for than she could hold in her hands at once, so much too much that she was a little drunk on his secrets, the details all smeared and blurred and no clear sight of him but only the sense that she had seen him fully open and naked for once and then he had closed on himself and disappeared, and somewhere inside was the vital secret of him that she needed, that she had wished for and he had given her, if only she could recall all of it, and the only thing she could be sure of was that it was real, he had showed himself, it had happened . . . The dull soreness in the cusp of her shoulder the next day reminded her, they had shot rocks into powder, they had talked, she had been there with him and it had been like that. Only the details were blurred, so many details.

Including a most trivial one that bothered her later: that she never knew how he disposed of the case of AGRICULTURAL EQUIPMENT. It was not among the boxes offloaded from the train at Tulsa when they returned on Wednesday night.

# The Lady in the Cabin

## TULSA *May 12–18, 1921*

The work began smoothly and efficiently under Esterhazy's management. Miss Woodly had completed an outline of the script, and on that basis Esterhazy established a filming schedule, determined to begin shooting exteriors and action sequences even while Miss Woodly was still writing some of the major scenes.

Most of the cast was ready to hand in the "Buckskin Bill" company. They had Alice Farnham for the lady in the cabin and Slick McClain for the crafty railroad agent/banker, the cowboys for the Starr Gang. Buckskin Bill was hopeless for the Tilghman role, but when Esterhazy suggested he play Judge Parker, Henry Starr laughed out loud and said yes, by God, it would serve the old bastard right—and don't worry about casting Bill Tilghman, he had a notion about that, and it seemed to make him happy.

Miss Woodly found a Mexican kid of about sixteen to play Henry Starr as a boy. They agreed that though Henry Starr's mother was still living somewhere near Tulsa, they could never use her in the movie—she would be far too old to be the mother young Henry tried to win the rodeo prize for in 1892. Miss Woodly and Esterhazy felt a kind of delicacy about even discussing the problem with Henry Starr, and they were grateful that he was too uneasy himself to raise the subject.

The only thing they disagreed on was the casting of Cherokee Bill. They ran through every one of their cowboy extras, darkening their faces with walnut juice when Henry Starr complained that they didn't look the right color. But he didn't like the full blood she found in Tulsa, who was a clerk in Shoemann's Hardware and distantly kin to the Starrs. Cherokee Bill's place in the cast and script was like a gap tooth, she couldn't talk or eat without her tongue worrying the empty space. "I just can't see Cherokee Bill in this feller," he would say over and over again.

"But any one of these men could play the part, it isn't all that large or difficult. He's just got to look *mean*, just be around you, like a kind of shadow of all the things Henry Starr could have been but wasn't . . ."

He answered with the expression of a man talking around the pain of a toothache: "I got to see him clearer, Miss Woodly, I got to, before it's gonna make sense to me what happens between us."

He saw her swallow her own anxiety and doubt so she could give him what he was asking for: "All right, we can wait for you to make up your mind. We can work around it," and Esterhazy nodded, they'd discussed this and it was simple enough—if you knew Cherokee Bill was going to be the lurking shadow of evil in the life of *Henry Starr: A Debtor to the Law*, you could shoot everything around him—settings, reactions, the works—and fill him in later.

What Miss Woodly found most troublesome was having to abandon her step-by-step progress through Henry Starr's life and adapt her writing to Esterhazy's shooting schedule. Esterhazy had marked for her the sequence in which he would shoot specific scenes—it was all out of order with the chronology of the movie, marching instead to the discipline of logistics, the necessity of using first the characters and properties most immediately at hand.

Her imagination balked. She had based herself on the solid structure of his biography as he had given it to the newspapers, a simple and inevitable movement from his boyhood as a persecuted child of the Vanishing Americans, to his first impulsive crimes, to his emergence as a legendary robber of banks and trains. Now she had to commit herself to a series of deep plunges into moments arbitrarily chosen out of the flow. It required of her a more dreamlike and intense imagining, but it gave her a sudden thrill of power and achievement when she realized that it had become possible for her to recreate his life that way. She recognized with pleasure that the story of Henry Starr was not just an idea, a set of words, but it had become an environment, complete and complex, a space behind her closed eyelids in which she could move with absolute freedom, discovering new things each time as if she were exploring a woods, yet finding in each specific scene she touched (no matter how or when) signs of its kinship to things she already knew, its connection to the imagined whole.

So she worked days at the bank and gave her nights to imagining Henry Starr in his age and his youth and his manhood, riding his zebra-spotted Appaloosa down long roads out of spoiled and blazing towns into the black pit of prisons and out again into the air, the sunlight, the road to the cabin and the woman and child to whom he had given a piece of justice.

Weekends she would come out to the set to watch the shooting, and these were the best times for her—the only moments in which she could see (and so believe in) the process that was transforming her evanescent and wordful dreams into hard facts. These were the moments in which she most felt herself to be part of that tribe she called the Woodly Gang, whose horses would carry her out of the teller's cage and beyond the reach of the banker, the editor and the lawman to a place of pure freedom, her home and hideout, her hole-in-the-wall with the world below, where the bandit queen removes her mask and shows her true face to the members of her gang.

Esterhazy's judgments held more instruction than terror for her. It was showing her script to Henry Starr that gave her night sweats and heart-thudding anxiety, because his judgment was not a thing of words: but the fact of himself, standing in front of her in his hard, compact, well-worn shape—and if the eyes in that shape met her images with ice or sarcasm or ridicule then (she was afraid) he would kill inside her that dark, swift, flexible, laughing, dreamy, dangerous boy of hers.

Her first test with him came when the three of them met in the warehouse-studio to try out her courtroom scene: Isaac Parker sentencing Henry Starr to death by hanging in Fort Smith. She had been up all night worrying, dreaming Henry Starr's responses, and all of them were the worst she could imagine, but when she handed him the script her nervous vulnerability changed in a flash to prickliness, and she thrust the pages at him, ". . . and if you tell me that this 'ain't the way it used-to-be,' Henry Starr, I'll . . ."

"Kill me," he finished for her. "Yes, I know."

And she had had to sit there, her nerves grating on each other, her dress sticking to her with sweat whose sharp smell somehow appalled her, while he read and read and read, sometimes moving his lips like a yokel in a classroom, until she was ready to kill him for *not* saying something even if it was that this wasn't at all the way it used to be.

When he finished he folded the papers and looked down at them in his hands—she noticed their thickness of muscle and bone so odd because he had such a light-looking body, and a tiny constellation of star-shaped scars at the base of the right thumb that she recognized as old gunpowder burns—and she heard him say "Yes" very quietly. His face when he raised it had a look so unexpected that it shocked her, the skin smoothed and blank against the pull of some strong feeling that showed only in the eyes—which showed something both intense and soft—and was there a little fear in it, or something like that? She wasn't sure, but it was a look that made her feel her own size and weight, as if she had suddenly grown older, taller, denser. She had been feeling very much like a little girl in school showing her composition to her elders.

"Well? What do you think?" asked Esterhazy.

He answered Esterhazy but looked still at Miss Woodly: "It's good enough, I just hope it isn't too good for *me*."

"So," said Esterhazy, "we try it and see."

Esterhazy stood for Judge Parker, nodding his head sagely while Miss Woodly set the scene: the witnesses sworn in, faces of the jurymen, the crowd—"Try to see them in your mind. What are they like, the faces of crowd? Friendly? Hostile?"

*The Hanging Judge in his tall pulpit, the Fort Smith jury looking at the Injun desperadoes from across the river in the Nations like you was the nigger in the woodpile, the Wild Man from Borneo, like you was shit.* "Not friendly."

"But they're going to change their minds when you stand up there and tell them . ."

*Miss Woodly, they will not smile until they hear Judge Parker name me dead dead dead.* But he set himself to try the trick. " 'Injustice I suffered,' " Henry Starr read as if he were quoting an editorial, " 'and I answered it with . . .' "

Esterhazy clapped his hands, "No! no! You don't look like convincing anybody. You look *apologizing*."

He looked at them, feeling cornered. They didn't believe him, and he didn't believe him either. He was not in the Judge Parker's courtroom that he remembered sometimes too well, where he had not said anything like these words. *Where he had not said anything.* He was in a warehouse with Esterhazy and Miss Woodly, speaking words from a page.

"They drove you into a corner," said Miss Woodly, softly and intensely, "the railroad men and the bankers and Cherokee Bill and the others: put you where you had no chance for justice, no choice but to strike back for your own. You *had* to! And after they back you into that corner, they're going to hang you for defending . . ."

" 'Injustice I *suffered* . . .' " No: he waved Esterhazy quiet, he knew it himself—sounded like a Cherokee politician getting ready to "flourish the failing scepter of our broken treaties." It had to be what he would say, what "Henry Starr" would say, the sort of boy who had dreamed the lost grandeurs of his fallen race, and ran afoul of an unjust law trying to keep the white man's paper from eating up his mother's home.

He closed his eyes and felt again as he had in prison, as if the darkness in his mind were a powerful blue acid smoke in which all hard real shapes dissolved, became anything, became nothing, no-name/no-clan/no-history Henry Starr, he felt a little tic of anger as if her words had stolen his ghost and made it *Something Else* [*Cherokee word for black, for blue-blackness*] . . .

Miss Woodly was watching him, her blue eyes focused on his face with the sharp hot precise intensity of acetylene—and suddenly he saw himself as if it was with her eyes, he knew the shape he made in her eyes (shape of a man in a blue-white space shining, shining as if his body was full of sunlight) he knew the place he held inside her dreaming ghost, he knew exactly what "Henry Starr" would have had to say, and he saw her sudden delighted smile coming so close on his that he knew the same ghost was making it up out of each of them:

His body standing in the ghost of the Fort Smith prisoner's dock fell into a relaxed pose—not a slouch: the lounge of a quiet predator. His hands fell unconsciously into parallel rigid lines suggesting manacles, but his head was reared back and he gave Judge Parker a defiant grin that was at once grim and debonair.

"Don't try to stare me down, old Nero! I've looked many a better man in the eye. And save your wind for your next victim. I killed one man who could have killed me, while you and your kind have slain unjustly your thousands and tens of thousands! I may be outside the law, but I know the taste of justice!"

"That's not in script," complained Esterhazy.

Miss Woodly was glowing like a coal as she folded her papers decisively. "But that's the real Henry Starr all right."

"You liked it?"

She felt as if her smile would keep growing until it split her in two. He was in it, he had come so far inside her story that he could make things up for himself that were just what she would have invented for him. She felt no jealousy for her word against his, they were two minds spinning one single story.

And Henry Starr thought: *She liked it. Well.* Standing there in front of her all dressed up as "Henry Starr, a Debtor to the Law" he felt for the first time really sure of himself, as much at home in his movie clothes and his play of youth as he was in his own Cherokee-dark skin and the wounded muscles that wrapped his bones.

For Henry Starr the days were tense and vivid with expectation and impatience. Miss Woodly was usually hidden away with the secret shape of *Henry Starr: A Debtor to the Law*, emerging suddenly from time to time as Esterhazy invoked her. But what she showed him of that secret was never enough, always something partial and out of sequence. His days were false-front buildings, the surface action palpably real but mindless, happening without motive or consequences, like a body without a ghost of its own inside it doing things over and over for no reason at all, ride into town rob the bank ride out of town ride into town rob the bank ride out ride in rob ride out ride . . .

Shooting those scenes was almost as bad as what he had done with Foley. Esterhazy was more careful about changes of costume; you knew there would be consistency of appearance when in the final cut Henry Starr would seem to move from an interior close-up to the horses to the bank front, the street and the road. The cameraman worked ingeniously, making the same poor sets work in a multitude of ways, choosing different angles and times of day for shooting, altering camera positions so that some of the robberies would show the Starr Gang sweeping the screen from right to left, and others the Starr Gang thundering straight into the cameras out of the gunsight V of buildings, or out and up a rising slope toward a sky in which distant thunderheads exploded with the aura of a hidden sun.

But it was hard to keep believing in the camera. It stood there glaring with its glass eye, as cold and penetrating and unaffected as Bill Tilghman staring at a trail or the face of a liar. When he put on his "Henry Starr" costume and played himself for that camera his sense of himself and of the solidity of his story began to shift and lose its edge like a cloud of blue smoke. The story was a crazy and broken thing—begun in the middle with robberies robberies robberies each and every one exactly the same to the man riding the horse although he knew that Esterhazy's lying camera would fool those who saw it into believing the eight ratty facades were the streets of fourteen different towns in three states.

But when Miss Woodly was on the set it worked for him again, he could imagine himself as he looked in her clear blue eyes and then the stupid cycle of ride-rob-and-run began to have an aura, a coloring of warmth and intensity that was the ghost of their journey to the night by the campfire, a sense of shared understandings that she was bringing into the daylight. She was the one who could make these crazy pieces be the story that he had to tell.

It worried him how much he counted on her. Sometimes he would see her through the window of the bank talking to fat Wilberforce; and once he saw her with a file of papers coming out of the Drexel Building where Poole and the Tulsa *Lamp* offices were. It gave him a little whiff of fear; just what were they doing together, with all of those papers he had signed hidden away in steel vaults?

Then he thought, What did it matter who she talked to? Hell, it was business, and she had to take care of that side of it for all of them, since neither he nor Esterhazy was any good at it.

And she was good at it—good at lots of things, and that was the best reason he knew to trust anybody. What she was best of all at was making up his story, and that was what he needed most. Bill Tilghman or Bub Houston might think it was all lies and play-fooling, but how could a lie make such a true difference in the look and feel of the world? No, she was using powers all right, she was working powers, but brother: *true* powers.

He waited for her appearances impatiently, thirsty for the images of himself that she would bring, fragments of the shape of a Henry Starr whose ghost would walk with power in the lights of the world, gray and swift and true beyond the dirty facts of the case, clear and deathless and invulnerable. It was like the huge shadow shape of a man in his mind, that shape—unfilled and unfinished, and each scene she brought him was like a gift that took him a touch closer to filling and finishing it. But it was more than a gift: she came herself to teach him how to play the scenes she had written, as if she was teaching him how to be "Henry Starr," how to fill the shape of his own name—how to make that name mean not just the dead loss son grandson brother husband father bank robber he used to be, but something else, "Henry Starr" the way he should have been.

When she was watching him he felt himself becoming the hero of the movie. The routine and absurd ride rob and run began to echo and resonate, it didn't matter that he was playing scenes that were like hallucinated memories, half-false and out of the sequence of time. He felt meanings and connections radiating from himself like webs from a spider, connecting his every least action to the huge heroic shape they were forming here.

For days, that first week, he walked around with the sense of being accompanied everywhere by her silent invisible observation and understanding.

He began wearing his costumes as street clothes, playing unwritten scenes in his head while the traffic of downtown Tulsa swept by in front of him, wagons and automobiles and trucks in the road and people continually walking by—the unconscious audience for his triumphant exit from "Bank robbery scene number 24, take 5." And he could imagine their observation and applause, seeing the eyes turn to him on the street, recognizing Henry Starr by his face, or by his costume, or just recognizing the presence of a costume. It made him feel like a giant ghost spread out on a screen with an audience of eyes stretching far out into the boundless darkness of a great theater.

We see Henry Starr in the street, watching the closed door of the Land Office.
Title: **When a man cannot find justice inside the law . . .**
Interior of the Land Office: The Railroad Land Agent, Morgan, and the Clerk are laughing over their papers, a bottle of whiskey. Suddenly the door bursts open, and three masked men with pistols stand there. The two white men start to reach for their guns, but the leader of the outlaws gestures sharply with his pistol:
Title: **"Thumbs up and stand steady!"**

And this was just the start of it, the tobacco and the water and the wizard all in place but the sun still up and the first words dreamed but not yet spoken: *Listen! You who come from under the Thicket: I am Henry Starr of the family of Starr, of the clan of . . .*

His ghost was restless, hungry, eager for the taste of that justice Miss Woodly had said she would do him, working there in her dark and dreamful room at night: sometimes he rode by her rooming house and looked at her window making a yellow eye in the blue darkness.

In the late afternoons, when heat and dust made shooting impossible, he took long rides around Tulsa, looking at those banks again, banks he had robbed years ago in Keystone and Terlton, Owasso and Vera, Kiefer and Kellyville, dusty windows in dusty streets, sun-cracked macadam and unrepaired gas lamps like gallows in rows all down the streets of the bigger towns. He said he was looking for someplace they might go to shoot it like it used to be, but he knew he'd never find anyplace that convinced Esterhazy—and hadn't he learned himself by going back to Stroud and Tahlequah that all that used-to-be was blown away like dust off a doorsill? Gone so far he had as well make it up new as try to remember it like it used to be?

Well, these places he went to now had changed too, although it was only ten years or less since he'd been there: and then not as the wild kid bandit he had been when he rode with Cherokee Bill, but as a man who had seen the elephant, a man who knew more about how and why and when you rob banks than any man in the Nation: *with Cherokee Bill dead, and his life with Cora dead, and all of that now like a dream while he lay in that small bed in his mother's house in Tulsa, dreaming a map of the whole of central Oklahoma, and drawing circles in circles on it, every circle larger than the next, every circle marking a new stage in Henry Starr's Secret War on the Bank—and when the last circle was swung the secret would open up, and Henry Starr's name would be written in letters of gold and gun smoke and blood all across the heart of the Indian Nations.*

Used to be. Nations that used to be.

Well, he enjoyed taking his pleasure these hot afternoons, letting his ghost loose on these banks to dream robberies of them again. He would case the bank the way he always used to when he was planning a robbery. He took a casual stand on the street in the early morning, a man checking the gear on his horse hitched to the rail across the street. He'd fool around to watch their opening-up routine, feeling a peculiar sense of warmth and safety, as if his character as movie man was a kind of magic bandanna that not only concealed his face but conferred an actual and complete innocence that covered him as deep as his ghost. When he had savored that enough he would go in and make businesslike inquiries, just as he had when planning a robbery: except that nowadays his method was to go in and identify himself to the banker as a representative of Pan American Motion Pictures of Tulsa, out scouting up locations for some of their movies—historical pictures about Old Oklahoma, that was their line. Would the banker like to have them rob his bank for him (strictly on film of course)?—and they would have a chuckle about that. Then he'd pace off the distances from door to counter, observe the fall of light through the big plate-glass window, and look for a stand for Esterhazy's camera with the same kind of care he had used to position his inside men before making his move through the street doors, "Thumbs up and stand steady!"

It felt real funny, at first, having the banker for an audience while you laid out the robbery of his bank, and looking real gratified about it all, too: gonna be in the movies, Mr. Banker-man, lots of free advertising. It was a sign of how well the powers he was playing with could work in the world, a sign that the movies were going to climb him over the world and the Cherokee Nations at last. It was, he thought, like it must be learning to be a sorcerer and to make that Power *come*, knowing that when you get a few more words inside you you will be able to remake your own ghost and to put yourself over like Jack-the-Devil on everyone that walks and everything there is.

## OWASSO *May 19, 1921*

And then, in Owasso—the day before they would start shooting the "cabin" interiors back in Tulsa—the world gave him a sign of his power, as clear as if a bear had stood up out of a thicket and tipped him a wink.

He was outside fussing with his saddle leathers and peering over his horse's back at the First National Bank (on January 5, 1915 he had gone in there armed and alone and come out with $1500) when he saw the tall man in the bad suit coming up the street. It was the kind of suit a drummer would wear, or that a cowboy who had come into some money would think was "real respectable"—kind of a sour yellow-tan, with a grid of large black boxes laid on it—and the man had that mincing kind of walk a cowboy will have when he switches to store shoes, his toes scrinched up front and the flat heels throwing a weird pitch into the rolling gait that Texas boots would have carried as a swagger. On top of it all was a too-little derby hat, under which Starr recognized the heavy red features of Deputy Price shining with sweat.

Price disappeared into the bank. Henry Starr waited, as patiently as he would have if he had been studying the opening-hours trade, spotting regulars and occasionals, and did the guard hold open the door for the merchants coming in to fetch a bag of change for the registers.

About ten minutes later Price came out the door, looking left and right as edgy as if he had just done a robbery in there and like a greenhorn thought he could sneak his way out of town unnoticed. Price walked quickly, legs stiff with nervousness and his gait still hobbled by his store shoes, back the way he had come. He turned the corner into an alley, there was the sound of an engine bellowing, and a minute later Price came smoking out of there behind the wheel of the open-topped Dodge, spun left and headed out of town on a road that would take him to the bottom of the Verdigris River if he stayed on it—but he wouldn't, he'd take the first right after the feed store and swing behind town to pick up the Tulsa road on the south side. It was a pitiful performance all around: the suit was about as good cover as wearing a Klan sheet at a colored camp meeting, the getaway was laughable—a shirttail kid could have seen through that miserable attempt at misdirection. He should have left town due north, where the road ran straight for the Kansas line, if he wanted to keep anyone off his back trail to Tulsa. Price was not only an amateur, he was stupid enough to have learned nothing from years of tracking robbers—but then, why should he bother with all that incompetent slinking and misdirection when he obviously had not robbed the bank, there was no hue and cry, and nobody was staring down his back trail except Henry Starr?

Henry Starr walked across to the bank and opened the door. It was the same layout he remembered from six and a half years ago, only a little worn-down, the buff walls a shade paler, the base of the counters more scuffed. Behind the teller's cage a man in a suit (the bank president) was explaining something to a clerk in shirtsleeves and a green eyeshade. Henry Starr was supposed to talk to the president, show his card, Pan American Motion Picture Company.

Instead he waited, allowing the president to finish instructing the clerk, raise his head to see and dismiss the road-dusty rancher standing by the door, and retire into his sanctum. Then Henry Starr stepped up to the cage: "Morning," he said, "name's Claiborne. Just bought a ranch over between here and Caney-creek? Been lookin' for a bank to put my accounts in. Got to have cash in the cattle business these days—can't deal on a handshake no more. But I guess you know all about that . . ."

The clerk did, and flushed with pleasure to see that the rancher recognized a man expert in fiscal matters. How could he help Mr. Claiborne?

"Well now, I mean: is this here a good *strong* bank?" (The clerk looked nervous, times were chancy and the assets weren't what they ought to be, too many bad loans out, but Mr. Claiborne relieved him with his next question.) "What I mean is, you get robbed much?"

"No sir. Not since seven years ago. We've taken extra precautions since then, and nobody even tried since." The clerk noted Mr. Claiborne's smile of satisfaction and believed he had won the account. "All the biggest merchants in this part of the county deposit with us!"

"Well that's good, real good to hear . . . in fact, wasn't that Mr. Dolphus from the feed store over in Turley I just saw in here?"

"In here? Oh no, no: that was Mr. MacKinnon. I don't know where his business is at, but I believe it's down around Tulsa somewhere. Yes," said the clerk, warming to his subject, and pushing a little hard on the truth, "yes, he could bank at the biggest places in Tulsa, but he comes out here to us, every Monday morning and Thursday afternoon regular as can be. Puts as much as fifteen or twenty-five hundred in at one time."

Mr. Claiborne looked skeptical. "Well now, I do a cash business. I'd want to be able to draw a substantial amount in cash as my affairs required. Country banks just don't have the reserves . . ."

"Mr. MacKinnon just withdrew five hundred in cash, without any notice whatever. I'm sure you would find our reserves sufficient for a still larger amount."

Mr. Claiborne nodded over that, it was good to hear that, but he was a careful man, he'd have to talk with Mr. Dolphus—would probably be back . . .

Once a week, thought Henry Starr, probably in that same drummer costume that wouldn't fool even that fool of a clerk for very long. And the wrong name on the account: the name of MacKinnon, Bub's new customer and the owner of the biggest white speakeasy in Tulsa. It looked like Bub Houston's protection was carrying the bag for Bub's competition. Dick Rowland had smelled it at that meeting. Henry Starr owed it to the two of them to tell them so. They had done a job together, even if he wasn't quite kin or clan.

And then an idea hit Henry Starr that made him smile, the kind of trick you can't make up for yourself but Something comes out from under the Thicket and gives it to you if you have that kind of powers, that kind of luck.

He could swap Price to Bill Tilghman, the marshal would nail Price and MacKinnon and take care of Bub's competition. And owing Henry Starr a favor, maybe Bill Tilghman would give Henry Starr a hand with his little problem of casting the role of the marshal in *Henry Starr: A Debtor to the Law.*

## TULSA *May 19, 1921*

The windows framing Tilghman's desk were open to let in whatever breeze the furnace air of downtown Tulsa might generate. What little there was brought the sharp-edged reek of petroleum and the braying of noontime traffic. Blaine's uniform shirt was stained at the armpits, sleeves rolled to the elbows; Tilghman in his gray vest and white shirt managed to look cool and sweatless. Henry Starr was comfortable in a blue shirt elaborately embroidered with tomahawks and six-guns, a belt with a silver and turquoise buckle, riding pants of soft blue twill and a new pair of boots with Texas heels and "enough carving and inlay to decorate a whorehouse piano, as the fella promised when I ordered them. Nice of you gentlemen to notice."

Blaine was red in the face with heat and annoyance. "Movie business pays well for honest work" came out with more sneer than he meant to display.

Henry Starr grinned at Tilghman. "Well, it's legal work, anyway.

Whether it's *honest* or not remains to be seen. Either of you been to see any of my pictures?"

Tilghman nodded, friendly enough, but his eyes were watchful. "It's all right, I guess, if you don't take it serious. If you had carried on back then the way you been doing in those pictures, police work in the Nations would have been a lot easier. You been telling those poor movie folks that *that's* the way it used to be?"

"I know what you mean," said Henry Starr, "which is what I wanted to talk to you about." He leaned forward eagerly. "You did me a favor, getting me in with those people, and I'd like to return it. I . . ."

Blaine looked quizzically at Tilghman, who shook his head. "It's sort of funny, you coming in like this, Henry," said the marshal. "I just this morning sent to ask you to stop by."

Starr's posture and expression did not change, but they seemed to gather and set, and Blaine could see how alert he had become. "Well that's all right," he said, "seeing I owe you for getting me the job, chance to return a favor." He looked from Blaine to Tilghman. "Shoot."

"You know Bub Houston," said Blaine.

"We go a ways back," said Henry Starr.

"Bub Houston makes moonshine and peddles it in Greenwood to the colored speakeasies." Blaine rapped out his words. "We hear rumors he's spreading his trade over to the white side of town."

"Tulsa was always a cheap-talking town," said Henry Starr. "Mr. Houston's in the movie business, same as me."

Tilghman spoke softly. "I don't care about Bub Houston, Henry. One way or another, he won't be doing business for much longer. We have T. J. Hanks in a cell downstairs, waiting on five hundred dollars' bail. Arrested delivering a wagonload of white mule to a warehouse off Third Street."

"We'll find out who he works for, and who he was selling it to," said Blaine.

"I am glad to see the police are doing their duty," said Henry Starr. "How come you didn't just wait around in the warehouse to see who come by to pick up the goods?"

"Deputy Price made the arrest."

Henry Starr grinned mirthlessly. "Well, congratulations in the newspapers to Deputy Price."

Tilghman's eyes never let go, he bored straight ahead. "Either the law will stop Bub, or the competition will. In the last year every colored whiskey runner and barrelhouse owner has either been bushwhacked, arrested or run out of town. Sometimes it's the Klan does it. Sometimes it's the Chicago boys from this side of Archer. Sometimes it's even the police. Bub Houston is a small-time, hill-country whiskey man, with maybe one friend on the police force who gets a keg of snake poison every Fourth of July to keep Bub where the law won't notice him. These Chicago boys, they got the kind of money you don't find outside of banks. Bribing hired help don't interest them: they just buy whatever kind of law they want: mayor, judge, chief of . . ."

"Wait a minute . . .," said Blaine, thinking how can you tell this to an ex-convict who is probably working for a bootlegger himself, when they had no proof of any of it yet and maybe if they were lucky it was not true, or not as true as they thought, or they couldn't prove it . . . because if it was true and they could prove it they'd have to watch their backs against their fellow officers as hard as they watched the gangsters out in front.

But Tilghman ignored Blaine. "Maybe you can help me track 'em, Henry. Maybe you can tell me where to pick up the trail."

*How much does he already know?* Henry Starr wondered, thinking about his night's work riding shotgun when Bub met with Price and MacKinnon to arrange for the shipment of whiskey which Price was supposed to run protection for, but instead had arrested Hanks. If Tilghman said he didn't want Bub, you could trust it; and not arresting me for breaking parole by associating was probably proof of that. But Blaine was different, and he had made no promise that Henry Starr could hear. He could give them Price's visit to the bank in Owasso in his tinhorn plaid suit, but he'd have to tell them about the account in MacKinnon's name, and why he had been curious enough to pump the teller about it—and that would lead right back to Bub Houston's meeting with Price and MacKinnon. He had to hold that back till Tilghman or Blaine gave him a reason to get interested, and that meant he had to trick Bill Tilghman into thinking this was the first Henry Starr knew of any of it; and he had to be careful what he promised to do about it, because you didn't break your word to Bill Tilghman.

"I owe you a favor, Bill. I can keep my eyes and ears open. Any names you want me to listen particularly hard for?"

"Price," said Tilghman.

". . . and MacKinnon, who runs the best speak in Tulsa," added Blaine. "And his boss: a Mr. Scarpione, of Chicago, Illinois."

"I'll keep them in mind," said Henry Starr. There was a moment's silence, in which Blaine had the sense of the two men weighing their exchange like horse traders between sales or poker players while the dealer shuffles.

Tilghman sighed, as if conceding something. "What was it you wanted to see me about?" he asked, the faintest stress on *wanted.*

Starr smiled and appeared to relax a bit. "A couple of the people out there in the company want to put together a picture that'll show how it *really* was, back in the old days. She calls it . . ." Henry Starr colored a little as Tilghman's eyebrows rose. "Miss Woodly, from the bank—she's the one writing it all out—it's called *A Debtor to the Law.*" He paused, looking earnestly at Tilghman. "I figured you might like that title, Bill. For a picture about an outlaw."

"It says something," Tilghman acknowledged, "supposing you mean to live up to it. Why does it matter what I think of it?"

Starr grinned and leaned back in his chair. "Because we want you to come in on it. No fancy acting, just like it was: you tracking me down and taking me in."

Tilghman looked embarrassed and shocked. "The hell," he muttered. "Henry, you do take liberties . . ."

"But only as few as may be. I got their promise, Bill. They'll tell it straight, only for a little bit of shortening-up and smoothing-out to keep her running, and to bring out the . . . the inside parts, Bill—what the whole thing adds up to. *A Debtor to the Law* and why the debt had to be paid, and how he . . . how I done it."

Tilghman shook his head. "It sounds like more smart talk, Henry. That was always your weakness—though I guess you take it for strength. Talk your way around parole boards, newspapers, judges, talk your way around the law—talk so much you get to talking your way around yourself, believing your own alibis, maybe start believing you never done what you know goddamn well you did. You know what was the best talking I ever heard you do?" Tilghman waited, his eyes cool and steady. When Henry Starr stayed silent he nodded as if approving and said, "Yes: it was what you said to Parker that first time he sentenced you to hang."

*"Has the prisoner anything to say before sentence is pronounced?"*

*And the prisoner said nothing then, nothing while Isaac Parker named him dead dead dead, by the Hangman's noose and the black hood dead—but inside maybe there was this ghost, see? This small black this small blue ghost of who Henry Starr would become after the twenty-eight years he would live in spite of Parker's sentence, saved from death by the dying of Cherokee Bill, and that ghost would say, was maybe already saying, "Don't try to stare me down, old Nero! . . ."*

*Maybe: maybe that ghost had been real then, I think it should have been real.* "Give me a chance, Bill. At least come by and take a look."

Tilghman sighed. "All right," he said. "That's as much as you promised us, isn't it? To look things over? I'll come and look. When I can take the time from serious business."

Out in the street again, Henry Starr felt like he used to after trying to talk with old Tom Starr: like no matter how old he might be or what he might have done, he'd never be anything but a no-account kid to the Old Man. Well, what kind of quality had he showed, swaggering up to Bill Tilghman, expecting to climb over him on the strength of one dumb-lucky break? It was just more dumb luck that he still held Price as a hole card, if the talk hadn't started off someplace else he'd have swapped Price before he had looked hard enough to know what the deputy was really worth—and got just what in return? Bill Tilghman in greasepaint playing cowboys and Indians in *A Debtor to the Law*?

Close-up of Marshal Tilghman:
Title: **A true peace officer, he enforced the law with an even hand, and could recognize virtues even in an opponent.**

Talking all that silly shit—Bill Tilghman? No, talking like that is for men like Henry Starr, that got things they have to talk themselves around. Bill Tilghman, he doesn't have to talk himself around anything. Those ice-needle eyes look right through you and your hat and that wall and two–three miles of country out the other side, and when he says nothing he still says all there is.

Just for a second as he stood there he was aware of the ghostly look of Tilghman's eyes, watching him now right through the wall of the courthouse just as they had that day in the courtroom itself back in Fort Smith twenty-seven years ago, and he knew the old marshal would see *A Debtor to the Law* as a lie pure and simple, Henry Starr strutting and bragging like a silly cockawhoop in front of that Hunky cameraman and especially that Miss Whatisit Woodly, whose front name nobody in Tulsa seemed to know. She had made him make a fool of himself, just purely conjured the natural jackass up in him to where its ears could be seen and its heehaw heard. Damn how a woman like that gets inside a man and . . .

*And gives his ghost a twist.*

He stood outside the bank and through the window caught the bright flash of her hair behind the teller's cage. *She's got my name on a paper and the paper in the bank, and that's all they needed to climb over Tom Starr and walk all over that giant old ghost of his.* There was only one way to settle things between them and one time to do it and that was right now . . . and he was already through the door of the bank, as quick as reflex behind the flash of the idea, faster than his own thought—moving deliberately but still without stop or pause the way you'd carefully depress the coil of a steel trap spring to set it, pressing low against the strain but always in the one direction—

She raised her head and he saw her eyes go wide and track him as he crossed the room sidling toward her window by an angle that let him absorb everything in the bank through eyes, ears, hair and even the skin at the base of his skull, where the guards were, and the bank officers, the vault door is open, it's the close of business, the sun is going down and the flare of it is at my back—everything as and where it should be, the timing perfect for—

"Yes?" she said in a strangly voice. "What do you want?"

"I," he said, "I," *what do I want?* He had come in to the bank to set something straight, to balance . . . What was it he had wanted to say to her? He had never put it in words, and for a second here out of pure reflex he had almost told Miss Woodly to—

He blinked and saw her with sudden clarity, she was as scared as if she had *heard* him thinking, *Thumbs up and stand steady*—the pressure of her small lips showed how she held her poise against the force inside that made her eyes run away and back to his face and away again.

It was as if he could see himself through her eyes, as strange as if you were looking in a mirror and suddenly found yourself looking out: she had seen his style when they played bank robbers in Tahlequah, and with all the rehearsals and scenes since she must have it by heart. So when he came in just now it must have seemed like all those jokes she made about *how would you rob my bank?* had come home to her like a wish spoken careless and Something hears it.

Well, he didn't want her to see him like that, he was sorry, he hadn't *meant* to scare her—but just what was it he *had* meant to do? If there was a wolf inside him now it was a mighty puzzled wolf, easing its hackles down, showing a little bit of a grin maybe—but you know what a wolf's *grin* looks like, even a wolf that's just having fun?

Then he noticed her nameplate; B. C. WOODLY incised in a prism of wood. "I just came by to ask you what that 'B. C.' stands for."

She huffed a breath at him as if he were a candle she was trying to blow out, and fear became anger in her face. "It stands for my name, Henry Starr."

"Which is what, Miss Woodly?"

"Which is mine to know, and mine to tell." She was getting angrier, he was bullying her, trying to get his hands on what was none of his damn business.

He let the spring unwind. The game had gone far enough, he was too old for games and this one was getting complicated. He would say what he had come to say, or part of it, now that he remembered what it was: "It don't seem fair," he said, "you knowing my name, and me not knowing yours."

For some reason that seemed to sweep the tension and anger out of her face swiftly and cleanly. She was smiling—no, she was grinning, standing back a step from the brass bars easy and confident and poised like a bobcat setting up on a branch and look what's just stepped under my tree. "You want to play fair?" she said. "You made a name for yourself, Henry Starr, and you're stuck with it. Maybe when I've had a chance to make mine, I'll let you see what it is." Her eyes were lit up, and she smiled her bobcat smile, jaunty, sharp and delicate.

"All right," he said seriously, even a little grimly, "that's a deal." He paused, as if he couldn't decide where or how to move next. Then he touched the brim of his hat and smiled—holding the smile till you could see it take his mouth, cheeks and eyes, becoming real and full of himself. "All right," he said, "but in the meantime I reckon I'll just call you Bobcat."

*Bobcat? Bobcat?* Her blood bolted against the cage of her ribs, seized with fear at this awful naked discovery; how did he know *that*, the name her brothers had given her when she was their little sister, playing . . . how much did he know about her?—but he couldn't know, he could only guess, oh but that was an uncanny good guess . . . And he was enjoying her discomfort, *damn* him!—like he was tasting some rare fine whiskey, so absolutely goddamn sure of himself giving me a name like that—she felt herself arch and bristle up, just *like* a bobcat, damn it! She flared back at him again, "What are you *doing* here?"

Unfortunately for Henry Starr that was still a good question. He held his smile, but it lost heart, became a mask for his uneasiness. "Just having a little rehearsal for that big bank robbery scene," he said lamely.

She wryed her mouth to something between a smile and a frown, let the man have his fun. "The one in the movie, I hope."

"That's our game, isn't it?"

"It *better* be." She turned her annoyance and worry into a joke. "For a minute there it looked like you were figuring out how to rob my bank."

"No," he said seriously, "you couldn't just walk in and take this bank. It would have to be an inside job."

She felt the blood run up the core of her chest and into her face, and she despised herself for showing it. *Damn him damn him damn him again, was he standing there thinking* he *was the cat and* she *was some damned canary, fear-frozen in her cage and as good as meat in his claws?*

His smile faded in her blue glare. "But not while I'm working for you," he said quietly.

"Some of us do actually work," she said, "while others just ride around . . ."

"Locating," he corrected her, "I been locating for those bank robbery scenes."

". . . playing at cowboys," she finished, reached under the counter and handed him a large manila envelope. "While you've been having fun, I've been working."

"What's in here?" he asked.

She narrowed her eyes and said, "You are."

She liked what the words did to his assurance, and she added: "While you were playing cowboy, I went out and found you a mother."

He read the script in his room, it was just three pages copied out in Miss Woodly's spidery script, but every time he read them they seemed to swell and extend, like ripple circles when you drop a stone in a pool. *I found you a mother.* Not that mother you saw the last time in the house in Tulsa, wrinkled like a raisin and bones brittle like charcoal wood, chewing and chewing her old trouble over again: *your daddy dead and C. N. took my money and drank it up and old Tom rotten with whiskey putting his foul tongue on me, I was a schoolteacher, Henry, my family wasn't no trashy Pin Indians, why couldn't you have took after them why couldn't you have been good*: but a new mother, a dream mother, the mother made out of Miss Woodly's dreams and words younger than my mother ever was, young enough for her little boy to stand by her and stand up for her . . . a cabin in the Indian Nations, in "the Red Man's Promised Land," *and we see a young boy reading a book near the cabin . . .*

He lit a space in his mind with white light, and put the cabin in it. All right. And then his mother . . .

*You was such a good such a smart such a handsome boy, Henry, you could have been a doctor or a lawyer or a judge of the Nation if it wasn't for those dime books, Henry, if it wasn't for you running with that murdering crazy nigger, Henry, the pitch that defileth . . .*

When was the last time I saw her? I remember I was still in prison, I can picture her there . . .

*She is waiting on the other side of the barred door when they walk him down the stone corridor, the echo of the steel shackles ringing back off the walls, he remembers Cherokee Bill walking down the corridor to where they would string him up, smiling that terrible smile of his . . .*

. . . but I don't remember which time, was it the time after Cherokee Bill or the second time, when they put me away after Paul Curry shot me in the back at Stroud? or was it when I was hiding out after I left Cora and Jiminy, and I lay up in that pantryroom of hers that had no windows, and there was no difference between that and prison except the prison had windows, and she could only come visiting days . . . *and it don't seem like there's enough difference between the different times to make you notice:*

## FORT SMITH PRISON *1896–1903*

*. . . like when you've been deep-fever sick for too long, or hurt yourself bad and been lying up with the pain for too long time, the pain crawls up all through you and into your head and pulls your eyes shut from the inside and locks you up inside your head. After a while you can't tell is the pain down there in your body or is your body all inside your head, washed and heaving with waves of black heat and sickness, your thinking hurts and your hurt does all your thinking, inside/outside don't make no difference. I'd lie on the bunk watching the damp form and shrivel on the gritty wall, one day and another day: I'd walk down the corridors to food or exercise, one day and another day. But it all come down to no difference: maybe I walked down one stone corridor with echoes banging off the metal doors on the insides of my ears, months and months and months. Maybe I laid there on my bunk walking down stone corridors months and months inside my head.*

*The only difference was when she come visiting, but the difference didn't take. Seldom as she come it was always the same thing, like it was one visit at the end of the one walk down the stone corridor that went on month after month, one dream at the end of the corridor I visited month after month lying on the bunk with my eyes closed tight to keep myself walking inside my head, because walking was better than lying there . . .*

Ma on one side of the cage and himself on the other. "When they goin' to let you out, Henry? I talked to that lawyer like you said, but he don't say. After what you done for them, Henry, after you helped them kill that murdering nigger half-breed, they got to let you out—ain't you bein' good, Henry? You got to try and be good so they will let you out. You just do what they tell you and don't make no more trouble, Henry, please don't, because I can't stand no more trouble. Grandpa just gets worse and worse." (*Grandpa's real sick, he's dying, Henry, he's dying slow, I wish he'd die sometimes Henry it's more than I can stand to watch him.*) "Henry: Grandpa's dead."

*Sometimes her eyes are awash in red as if she wept blood, sometimes her cheekbone is stained yellow where a bruise is going stale.*

"You were always a good boy, Henry, so smart, people liked you, they thought you was smart and good-looking, and why couldn't you have stayed that way, Henry? Why couldn't you be good as I know you was, and me with no husband because your father just up and died, and Grandpa . . . and C. N. going on and on at me like he done, why couldn't you, why? Why couldn't you have had just that much consideration, Henry? Why couldn't you be good, and they'd let you out of here sooner, and you could come and help me Henry, because C. N. just drinks everything up because ain't none of them Starrs give a hoot if their own kin has to beg bread on the streets, because C. N. run out, Henry, and how can I stand it in that cabin alone, me and the dogs and it's hard, Henry, I'm scared to go outside, Henry, I just sit inside and sometimes I think I see old Tom glaring at me from the bench with his old dead eyes and C. N. sneering at him for his Injun blood he was so proud of, and C. N. no better about being white, and both of them trash that left me alone with nothing, and you . . ."

*So that I, so that you would start to wonder, after a while, whether it was you visiting her instead of the other way round, you coming seldom to see her in her prison that got smaller and darker and more solitary every time, and she'd look a haunting at you too for coming so seldom, sitting there small and shrinking into herself on her side of the cage asking for the kind of food the kind of words the kind of strength that you couldn't pass through the bars, the guards would confiscate it, eat it themselves. And you'd walk away back down the corridor to the dark place inside your head and for just that minute you'd think it was you that was free, walking away out of her prison ashamed but cut loose from the darkness.*

*And that was a dream too: and her visits convinced you that both sides of the bars was the same dream, and both still prison, locked behind closed eyelids inside the darkness of your skull, warm and black and sick and safe as death.*

Until that weird moment when his pardon came through; he was washing his face for the last time in the basin in his cell, and he looked in the cloudy tin mirror nailed to the wall and saw that he had grown old and faded in the long dark years of his cell—realized that for the seven years since his reprieve he had not once looked at the image of his own real face, but lived only with the ghost of his youth in the nightland of his head, so that when he came out of prison and finally looked in mirrors again—the shaving mirror in his mother's house, the eyes of old friends showing their age in crows' claw marks at the edges—his age had taken him by an ambush every bit as complete and naked as the one in which Tilghman had caught him.

*So when they finally let you out it is like someone slams open the shutters of the months-closed sickroom and the sunshine bangs off the back wall, and in the blare and rush of the sunlight the inside is just blanked-out empty: no words no thoughts no dreams no body, just that white light coming in.*

*And I stood outside in that white glare feeling like a ghost, like a hand of corn shucks with the ear out of it, the light and the wind blowing through me.*

## TULSA *May 19, 1921*

No: cut that. No light on that cabin that cell. No camera, no voices.

*Henry Starr and his mother, take two.*

The white light, the cabin in it, the woman standing in the cabin: in his mind he kept trying to get close to her, hungry, pushing, trying to find a way to get close enough to her so that he could give his breath to Miss Woodly's words and be that child she had made up for him.

*Not like Tom Starr saw her, that white-blood bitch that stole my son's ghost. But my mother, you know, how she should have been . . .*

A white man with a mustache, in a business suit, holding a sheaf of papers, pulls up in a buggy, accompanied by three rough-looking men. The boy rises from his book, eyes narrowing suddenly. Close-up of the stranger:

Title: **Morgan the Railroad Land Agent: he enjoyed exacting the "price of progress" from those who could least afford to pay it.**

Morgan and his men approach the cabin door in which stands a woman, Henry Starr's mother, who watches the men with growing fear, then stiffens to hold her ground. Morgan speaks sneeringly, then thrusts the papers at her: she recoils—

then the boy Henry Starr pushes Morgan back and stands protectively between the men and his mother, snatches the papers from Morgan's hand and throws them down. He speaks calmly but with unmistakable defiance: his mother restrains him, but he shakes her off. Morgan is taken aback, retreats a step.

Henry Starr snatches a gun from his belt and orders them off his land.

Morgan sneeringly answers:

Title: **"If you don't pay your debt in two days, it will not *be* your land!"**

Interior of the cabin: Henry Starr comforts his distraught mother. She is in despair. Henry Starr gets an idea—it is as if a light begins to glow inside his face.

Cut to: Banner—JULY 4 TAHLEQUAH RODEO; to street scene; to rodeo arena, man riding a bucking horse; to sign, FIRST PRIZE $1000.

Title: **July 4: a festival of American independence and fair play—a young boy's best hope.**

*That kind of mother.*

When you get out of bed and wash, and dress yourself to be "Henry Starr, a Debtor to the Law," it will be that mother you are going to meet. She will be there: she will have a breath in her—*whose breath?* You will become another thing with her, you will become this mother's son.

That other mother, that used to be—that other mother and her son: will not come back. Will be forgotten, be covered in blue, in blue smokes, in the color of blue.

## TULSA *May 20, 1921*

He came in through the side door of the big warehouse where the studio was and they were all there before him, faces turning from the white-lit space of the "cabin" that opened in the blackness. The heels of his boots thumped the wooden floor, spurs chinking like single shakes of a tambourine.

The bigwigs were over by Esterhazy's camera. There was Wilberforce like a tethered balloon, and Poole looking like a man who sucked lemons and *liked* 'em, Foley doing a slow silent alcoholic burn, and Miss Woodly with the script in her slim strong hands.

"Well, good morning," she said, running her eyes over his costume—the blue embroidered fringed shirt, the fancy belt and tight pants stuffed into those carved and inlaid Texas boots—"You came ready for business today."

"Yes, ma'am." He smiled. "I think I've had enough rehearsals."

She gave him a scratchy look, as if she'd be damned if she'd get the joke, but Henry Starr was looking past her toward the white-light space in which his mother's cabin was waiting for him.

"Well," said Esterhazy, lifting his head out of the viewfinder, "such pleasant surprise."

Henry Starr glowered at him; was the little Hunky being sarcastic about his coming late? It was half an hour before the usual . . .

A small olive-skinned woman stepped onto the stage: there was her little boy with her.

Only it wasn't her kid, it was that little Mexican pup Miss Woodly had brought back with her, wasn't it? Standing there with this supposed-to-be mother of mine in the light of my cabin and the eye of my camera.

*Damn fool,* he named himself, *goddamn fool.* He wished a black hole into the center of his head, one that would suck down his damn fool's face and his brain like a block of wood, and make his face and name not be. But the hole wouldn't suck, he had to stand there in his fancy shirt and whorehouse boots while they grinned behind their hands at him. She had really put it to him, hadn't she? Got him hankering and hankering so hard he couldn't remember what day it was or what was the job of work in front of him, couldn't hardly remember where some chicken-scratch marks on a page left off and a forty-seven-year-old two-time loser half-breed thief named Henry Starr began.

Miss Woodly was smiling, and he damned her for it even while he asked himself how he could blame her not guessing that the smartest outlaw who ever lived was going to forget everything they had said about this scene and come to work limping in his fancy cowboy suit, expecting to play himself at age sixteen with a mother who was not more than thirty herself, small like Henry Starr's mother but standing there with her arm around the boy's shoulder so easy, friendly, more like Cora in the store with Jiminy than Mrs. Hop Starr and me.

Miss Woodly just stood there looking like she had just unwrapped him a Christmas present. "Couldn't stay away, could you?" she chortled, gave him a grin like a slap on the back. "Me too!"

He couldn't say anything to her. He stepped back out of the light, and as he did so Poole sidled up to Miss Woodly, smiled and dipped his head, and Henry Starr saw his lips move, spilling words sideways toward her. But she seemed scarcely to hear Poole, her eyes kept their hold on the scene unfolding in the cabin, her lips moving to mouth the words as little Henry Starr spoke and his mother answered him.

It was her show out there in the light. Henry Starr could see it by how she watched it, her small lips moving silently over the words, head nodding a little, all of her energy focused in her eyes that reached out and into the scene, and roved over it, like tender hands on a beloved face. It was her dream there, her makings, hers—a little boy whom she made be Henry Starr and the mother she made for him, they needed all the ghost she could give them.

*All right then, if it's yours, why don't you just enjoy it and leave me out of it?* It wasn't himself out there, not himself young—or if that was young Henry Starr, then his young self was a stranger to him, as separate and alien as this Mexican pup Miss Woodly found, I never knowed his name and I'm damned if I'll learn it.

He felt a hand on his shoulder, and he turned around gladly: and there was Dick Rowland.

"Bub sent me," he said, and Henry Starr turned his back on the white-light cabin and guided Rowland toward the rear wall of the warehouse. It was dark, but the glow from the cabin reached far enough to show Rowland's face had a numb, set look to it. He didn't wait for Henry Starr to ask him what Bub wanted: "You been to the police building yesterday, talking to Tilghman."

"I heard about T.J." said Henry Starr and Rowland stepped on the heels of his speech. "Heard what?"

"Heard he got arrested at the pick-up spot, and Price done the arresting."

Rowland waited. Then he said, "Then you *ain't* heard: T.J. got bailed out last night."

Henry Starr shrugged. "I figured Bub would take care of it."

"That's what you figured," said Rowland, dead flat.

It was not a good day to fool around with Henry Starr. "Well, what about it?" he said. "Did Bub expect me to bail him out?"

"No," said Rowland softly. "Bub figured to do that himself. He takes care of his people."

Henry Starr waited.

Dick Rowland smiled a bad smile, a smile that was sick to death of itself: "Time he got the money together and got over there, somebody already paid the bail. Duty officer forgot to do a receipt. Been no sign or scent of T. J. Hanks since. Not anywhere."

Henry Starr swallowed his breath waiting for the rest of it, because none of this was right at all, cash paid and no receipt and all of it done in the middle of the night.

"By coincidence," said Rowland, "the arresting officer himself was on duty, and logged the prisoner out."

"Deputy Price," said Henry Starr.

"But even so it don't make sense," said Rowland. "Even Price isn't dumb enough to lose the receipt and pocket the bail, because T. J. Hanks is *gone*, and if there isn't $500 cash in the till next morning then . . ."

"You said it was $500," said Henry Starr, and Rowland nodded. "Then it's bad," said Henry Starr: "Price got himself $500 cash out of a bank yesterday—I spotted him doing it." Rowland's eyes narrowed and Henry Starr said, "Think whatever you damn well please, it was just dumb luck me seeing him." But anger wasn't enough to give Rowland, not after what had happened just because Henry Starr wasn't smart enough to see all the way through Deputy Price. "He keeps a bank account in MacKinnon's name, puts a big wad of cash in every month. I saw him making a withdrawal and figured he was just taking his cut. I better tell Bub."

"No," said Rowland, his face pursing up as if with a physical pain. "Bub is gonna be too busy for talk. Busy looking for T. J." He knotted his face as if clenching something in a fist, then it got away from him. "Oh goddamnit, if Price bailed him out and then . . ."

There was a burst of noise from the fake cabin, Esterhazy yelling "Cut!" and that seemed to bring Rowland out of his feeling. His mouth slid sideways and he told Henry Starr, "Sorry to bother you, *boss*, when you so busy yo'*self*," and Henry Starr said "Tell Bub" as Rowland swung the door open and shut behind him.

*Tell Bub what? That I was too dumb or too busy playing cowboy to think through what Price banking MacKinnon's money in Owasso could mean? That I'll go riding with him till he finds where Price and MacKinnon got T. J. Hanks and blow the door down and go in with him, shotguns and .45s and whatever else it takes . . .*

The white light of the fake cabin was brilliant in the darkness of the warehouse, a magnet that drew him back. Young Henry Starr who was him and was nothing to him stood out there in the light and tried to take care of that supposed-to-be used-to-be Henry Starr's mother. Like she should have been.

*Someone has put a twist in my ghost so hard I can't tell my ass from the front of my head.*

He looked around to see where Miss Woodly was and missed her on his first sweep. Then: there she was, standing just under the judge's podium. Talking with Editor Poole—or no, looking downward, nodding her head—yes, no, maybe—while Editor Poole looked at her intently and talked and talked. He felt a little chill run over him; the joke was you were supposed to feel that when somebody was talking about you, or somebody just stepped on your grave. Only this chill come from thinking that Poole and Miss Woodly were not talking about him.

Henry Starr stood in the dark, watching the young woman who had made all this, and for the first time he felt the depth of his distance from her, felt the levels of her strangeness. Who in the Nations was she? He didn't even know her right name, and he'd give his ghost and his name practically into her hand. And here she had give his name to this Mexican kid he never saw in his life, that she conjured up out of no place, like she could do anything at all with him or anyone, take their ghost into the cool of her blue eyes, into the blue, the black inside and make them over any way at all, any way it come to her in her power to do.

He looked away from Miss Woodly, but there was nothing else to see but the fake cabin, and a woman in it who to hear Miss Woodly go on about it was Henry Starr's mother just exactly as she should have been, and a kid in there with her who was supposed to be what grew up to be a used-to-be badman named Henry Starr. But Henry Starr was no such rare bird: this is him over here, the old man with the busted ass and the gray in his hair, the one all dressed up like he was a kid gonna play cowboys, looking at the back of a young woman like she was sweet candy he'd never get to taste—an old man like that and all he wants is girls and candy and playing cowboy.

It was like looking in that mirror in the white glare after they broke up the long overnight of prison, and seeing his young face old.

The torn muscle in his ass ached. He was glad neither Bill Tilghman nor Bub Houston had seen him like this.

He peeled his eyes off the picture of the mother and kid, and his nose off the glass between him and Miss Sweet Candy, and stalked outside into the glare of the white sunlight. The door closed behind him.

He spent the rest of the day trying to get a line on Price, but the deputy had apparently disappeared after signing out as duty officer at the jail last night. His bungalow on the Broken Arrow Road was silent, the bed not slept in. MacKinnon's speakeasy was closed during the day: the boy sweeping out in the alley hadn't seen Price either.

It was getting dark when Henry Starr gave it up and went to see Bub Houston. But Dick Rowland stopped him before he reached the door: a low whistle out of the covert of a bush. "He isn't inside. Left me to watch. He's gone looking."

Henry Starr stepped into the shadow of the bush next to Rowland. Through the screen of leaves he could see the yellow squares of the windows in Houston's house. "I came to tell Bub: I can help him put the nail in Price. I know where he banks his graft, and under whose name. Bub gives the go-ahead and I'll hand Price to Bill Tilghman trussed up with an apple in his teeth."

Dick Rowland shook his head, "It's gone too far already. Too far for T. J." The look he gave Henry Starr had pain in it. "Looks like the deputy got ahead of Bub Houston this time. He never meant anything from the start but putting Bub out of business. Set it up to find out who was our still man, jail him. Then Price bails him and they got him in their hand." He noted the intensity with which Henry Starr was looking at him and said, "How do I know *Price* bailed him? I been watching, Mr. Starr. And listening. Friend of mine sweeps up at the Drexel Building"—his voice dropped into mock-dialect—"you knows de Drexel, dat's where yo' boss got his office?"

Poole: the editorial offices of the Tulsa *Lamp* were in the Drexel Building, Tulsa's tallest skyscraper.

Dick Rowland's smile faded. "It was in the morning edition, how the colored criminal classes emancipated one of their own in the middle of the night when nobody see them unless they smiled. The paper put it on one of the colored cops supposed to be on duty."

"Price was on duty," said Henry Starr, and Dick Rowland overrode him: "Yeah, Price: and Bub wants to know how come the Tulsa *Lamp* can break that story at eight A.M. when the man bailed out at one in the morning? So I go and talk to my friend, and he says oh yes, that fat-gut redneck deputy been in to see Mr. Poole just the evening before, they come out smilin' and shakin' hands like they children was getting married, and Poole don't go home—stays in his office, keeps the pressmen on, and about one thirty by the clock he comes down with a new story for page one and that editorial on 'Colored Criminal Classes and Civic Corruption.' "

"Price laid it out for him before it ever . . ."

"You listen good, Mr. Starr," said Dick Rowland. Then his look shifted, the eyes tightened so that the sadness had an edge of anger to it: "You know what's possible, don't you."

"Yes, I do."

"Then *say* it," said Rowland savagely.

"They take him out and beat him up bad, scare him like they did the others who worked for Bub or took Bub's trade. Or they kill him. Either way, Bub's got nobody to make whiskey for him, so he loses his trade." But those were the small possibilities, too small when you looked at the risk Price had taken handling the release himself: he wouldn't do that just on the *chance* it would hurt Bub's trade bad enough. "Or they make him tell them where the still is hid and they go bust it."

"And how they gonna do that, Mr. Starr, when T. J. Hanks is such a *tough* little man, and one of Bub Houston's own?"

No words: the image of a handbill, and on it the gone-gray ghost of a body split and spread and stretched on a rack of wood for burning, that used to be the body of a man but wasn't no more.

"That's right," said Rowland, as if he could read the thoughts behind Henry Starr's eyes. "If he's in town, or if he just got run off, Bub will find out tonight. If it's the other thing . . . Bub has five stills located in a circle around the city. We'll start at the east and work around by south to north. Week from now we'll be in that thicket back of the marsh where the Caney comes into the Verdigris."

"I know it," said Henry Starr. "We used to hide out there sometimes when we were working the northern part of the Nations."

"I'll go with him when he goes up there."

"If you want me . . . ?" said Henry Starr, as if he wasn't sure what Bub expected of him, and in any case how could he swing it? They were filming him tomorrow . . .

Rowland shook his head. "Don't need you up there. But if you could watch the Parkers' backs at night, at least till William gets home from the Dreamland."

"Of course," he said. Then something odd in Rowland's tone struck him, and he asked, "Did Bub tell you to ask me?"

Rowland studied a moment: "No. I'm asking for him."

That stopped Henry Starr flat. You had to be kin at least, and maybe more than that before Bub Houston let you have his say-so.

Rowland saw his question and shook his head. "You know Bub. He holds what's his own, doesn't let anybody touch it but himself." He gauged Henry Starr for a moment. "The watching is my idea," he said, "it's not something I take his orders about. I got my own reasons for watching."

"Those must be *some* reasons," said Henry Starr.

Henry Starr and Dick Rowland looked at the bright windows like eyes in the dark bulk of Bub Houston's house. They heard softened thuds and thumps, maybe doors being closed and drawers sliding, the rhythm of a voice questioning, a lighter voice answering. Henry Starr could imagine the tall woman and the little boy, the look-talk they would make between themselves that was like the hum of a big engine under the little rattles and jingles of their words, *the baby balancing on his butt like a boy on a fence rail, Cora behind the brass register in the yellow window light, a picture sharp and still and perfect in his memory, in one more second she will raise her eyes and see Henry Starr, and it will begin, it will begin to come together and come together until the day when he would take it in his hands and tear it in pieces.*

"Listen!" said Rowland sharply, and Henry Starr snapped alert out of the fog into which he had fallen, dreaming himself in through the walls of the house. "Listen," said Rowland, "there isn't anything like that at all, not a thing. I don't hardly say, don't do a thing about her except keep watch so those bastards can't get to her and her boy."

"It's the same way you hunt ducks and deer," said Henry Starr, watching the black man carefully, "close enough so you could if you want to, but you just don't want to."

"You remembered that?" said Rowland. "Well: I guess you do listen good." He held his breath, hesitating. Then he let it out. "You got to understand about Harriet and Will Parker and me. I guess Bub told you some, far as he knew to tell? How they killed my daddy, and how I paid 'em back?" Rowland showed his teeth. "Man, I tell you, it was like I got religion, God give me grace to see what I did wrong and what I had to do to make it right. I used to spend so much time studying things out, but it was just words I studied on, and I should have been studying war, you know? I should have been studying war. Maybe if I had then he . . . he wouldn't have had to die like that all alone, you see? When I saw that, it was like I had to get back to him somehow, get back to him but he was all mobbed-around with white, white faces, white men, and I had to . . . to tear my way through them to get back to him, you see? So he wouldn't have to face that all alone.

"That's why I went through those Germans like I did, and that cracker officer: he came in behind me and he said, 'Give me a hand up, boy,' and I shoved the bayonet right into his guts and when he screamed I shot out the middle of his eyes like you'd blow out a candle.

"Then I went after the rest of them.

"And when I come up out of the hole, it was like I was just full up the throat with dead white . . . like maggots in a week-dead body. Like I had died, so long before I had forgotten how and when. Couldn't talk, talk about it, couldn't talk a long time after—afraid everybody would see that white crap stuffed up to the top of my throat. And the fact was I didn't have anything else in me to say: dead man opens his mouth what comes out is flies—yeah, if I had said a thing in those days it would have sounded like the buzz a cloud of flies makes coming off a dead man.

"I used to wonder, how could you have killed all them white folks and still wind up dead yourself? I thought, if you got that much power of killing, should be nothing—*nothing* ever come over you again . . . But I never could kill my way through 'em back to my daddy, that was just a damn dream, make me crazy."

Rowland had become a black shape enclosed in the larger blackness of the bushes, talking about killing and the power of killing, how much you can do when your power is as big as the rage and terror inside you, *and I wonder what Cherokee Bill would have done if he'd had Dick Rowland's reasons and advantages, Cherokee Bill with a war to run around in, with hand grenades and Gatlings and tommyguns to do his talking with, laughing laughing and that ooblooble turkey gobble, once he starts killing they'd never stop him, not this time, this time nobody would trick him into a noose . . .*

"But it didn't work that way for me. My daddy was still dead, and those Germans and that officer: and me too. And nobody even knows it, but slaps you on the back or gives you a medal like you were still people.

"But you know, it still wasn't like being alive. It wasn't like having a body, you know?—walking around among people, bumping into them, touching them. It was like a ghost was sitting in a house looking out some windows—anybody's windows, maybe it ain't even his house, you know?

"So I sit inside there looking out, and I see that all those other people wished they could have done what I did, it was like themselves they pinned the medal on or slapped the back of, themselves like they thought they should have been. Because these people been . . . they been stepped on, they been eating shit so long, so maybe they wished they could do something like I did to save themselves and everybody else all the way back to . . . to Africa, Mississippi, wherever it was it started for them. Even Will, who saw what it did to me . . . sometimes I'd catch him looking at me like I had something he wished he could own, like he wished he could have done what I did, crazy as I was and useless to myself or anyone else.

"And all I wished was that I *couldn't* have done it. Because if I was strong enough to do that, then why didn't I stop 'em killing my daddy, why didn't I get out and stop 'em killing anybody else again ever? So I said nothing, did nothing, because if I could do any of it then I'd have to do all of it again. It's like I said, it can stop here if you're willing, and I'll never say a word or do a thing in my life, but if they give me reason like that again . . . and it's got to happen, you know, they'll never let it be." His voice twisted down low in his throat. "And I wonder am I gonna have to go out and keep doing it again, and again and . . .

"And what's the point? If all of it just leaves you dead your own self, like a no-name ghost in a house ain't even his, and every time you talk those shiny green flies come out? You know what I'm saying?"

*A small black shape imprisoned in his eyes, Cherokee Bill's eyes, like a man in a cell screaming to get out: I saw it and I said I would help and make him quiet, but it would cost him his dying.*

"Yes," said Henry Starr.

Dick Rowland took a breath and let it out. "They took me in, the Parkers—after I got out of the hospital; Bub gave me a job. Bub and Will, they understood about half of it—though like I said, even they looked at me like they wished they had my chances, even if it put them all alone in that room. But Harriet: she took one look at me and she knew. She looked at me, and then I knew I had got myself dead, because she was just grieving me . . . you know? Just grieving me. And I watched her out of that wasn't-mine window and said thank you for it.

"Well, it was good even one person knew, you see? Knew you were alone dead inside that house? It was like company.

"I would watch how she was with Will—wasn't even jealous, I . . . no I wasn't, because it wasn't me watching, who she used to be sweet on before the war, called her Harriet the Lariat, always out trying to rope herself a boy . . . Wasn't me. That man, he had had certain kinds of possibilities, you see, and I didn't have any, I'd used them all up all at once. Not jealous at all, because it was watching them that helped me get back as far as I've come. I'd watch how they'd be with me, taking hurt from the way I was, and then they would take that hurt and turn it into kindness to each other. So when they look at each other it's like you saw something through a window no outside person should see. But it was all right for *me* to do it, because I wasn't hardly any kind of person anymore, just like a painted picture on your wall and you think you see the eyes turn and follow you when you go by. No more than that."

"Maybe a little bit more," said Henry Starr. "You get down off the wall enough to keep watch on 'em, you turn up when Shaker gets in trouble. You sit at the table like you belonged in the house, and you feel like you're kin enough to ask me to do Bub Houston a favor. Watching will come to doing, if you keep at it."

Rowland looked hard at the house, as if he were looking for permission to speak. "All right," he said, "I guess I am ready to kill somebody if I have to, on their account or T. J.'s. I guess I have to do that much, even if it puts me back on that road again."

"Yes," said Henry Starr, "I know: it's no good staying still, but whichever way you go you're afraid you'll wind up in the same hole you just before climbed out of." He looked at the house, shuttered in darkness. It was like the old days, with Cherokee Bill, standing outside some cabin in the night, listening to the family sounds, wondering could you take the risk to let yourselves be seen and maybe known for the sake of a little bit of food, the comfort of a roof and company that wasn't electric with fear and vigilance. The house was silent and black, the woman and child asleep and neither by dream nor by thought were they aware that Dick Rowland and Henry Starr were on watch over them, any more than people in a painting knew you were looking in on them. He knew why Dick had to keep it that way. But didn't Dick want them for his own, want to be inside the picture with them, or with people like them?

"Man," said Henry Starr, "you aren't that old that you've used up *all* your chances. You aren't just some picture of a face on somebody's wall. You can't let yourself just be that. My face been a picture on the wall in every post office, sheriff's office, bank and police station in four states, and when they get you like that, brother they have you nailed. You have to get down out of it, go make yourself a new picture . . ."

Rowland smiled. "I forgot you're the moving picture man."

"Yes," said Henry Starr, with a twist in his mouth, "I am the man whose picture learned to move."

## CROMWELL, OKLAHOMA *June, 1903*

MUNSON'S STORE GEN'L MDSE.

Help Wanted
Inquire Within.

The light on the storefront was white and dry, but the brick walls lined with shelves of store goods kept the heat out and the cool inside. The air was a rich texture of smells, cloth and dried herbs and leather and cheese and tobacco and gunpowder. There was a young woman behind the marble counter by the high embossed-brass cash register: her boy, one year old, sat next to it, dabbing at it with his right hand and waving his left as counterbalance, his eyes holding hard to his mother's face as if sitting on his butt on the counter was like walking a fence rail and he needed hands and eyes both to keep him from tipping off. She was calculating something in the register, but she never lost track of the boy. One long-fingered hand rested lightly on him here and then there, she made a little song out of her counting for him, and every now and then broke her concentration on the register to give him a lick of her dark eyes with a smile, and the baby would stiffen his body and point a rubbery finger at her face. The light, mellowed to a soft orange by the window blind, molded the strong shape of her cheekbones and chin. She was broad in the shoulder, full-breasted and deep-waisted, and she seemed very tall somehow, standing there with her baby behind the counter.

They made a picture at that moment, sharp and still, printed in his memory: the boy whose name he didn't know yet, the woman he didn't know either but guessed was Mrs. Munson, who seemed taller than she was—when he stepped to the counter her eyes were on a level with his own—but she had a quality that made her larger somehow, what was it? An impression she gave of filling up completely the space and light she stood in, of being so dense and deep within herself that her shape was just a suggestion of her size.

She looked up and so did the baby: and there he was.

*There who was?*

*A dry stand of corn shucks burnt white and light as ash by the white light blast of the sun after almost ten years in black fever-dream prison, an empty old wreck walking around in Henry Starr's name—Tahlequah to Muskogee to Tulsa to Oklahoma City, there's people will give him a job or a drink for the sake of the name, it reminded them of this old-time bandit who robbed a stagecoach a train a store a bank right near by. But no, can't be the same one, look ain't right nor the years, and hell: he don't even seem to know where he is, don't recognize nothing—thickets cleared off for farms and the farms cleared off for oil, oil derricks popping up everywhere like brush in a fallow field: Roberts' Standard ranch where he used to ride now a rolling derrick-forest from the home ranch across the corrals and feedlots and out onto the range, he remembers when it was just a few ugly-talking riggers poking at the ground and getting slammed in Holcomb's saloon under the Katy Hotel; derricks pimpling up around the station where they stopped the train at Pryor Creek, derricks all around Bartlesville like the Indian Nations had come together for a giant powwow and built them a village of half-assed wooden tepees, gas flares waving and stinking in the air like war banners at the topmost knot of the lodgepoles.*

*This old thing? He can't be* that Henry Starr, *who rode the nightland with the wolves and heard the owl hoot, who kept his guns and his horse and his road and his word, away down in the Indian Nations a long time ago—so long there ain't a taste of it left, the Nations gone and the owls and the wolves, and the guns, and the road, and the word (that word of his with which he robbed many a bank,* hyenh!*—a certain number of banks), gone*—not that *Henry Starr . . .*

Who stood there in Munson's Store seeing woman and child as sharp and uncanny as a picture that was somehow looking back at him, and suddenly his ghost jumped back into his eyes and his name leaped to his tongue as swift as ever he had drawn Colt from scabbard as a kid in Tahlequah, looking into the eyes across the counter knowing that in one more tick of the heart he would have become Something Else, something he had never been except in dreams:

"Ma'am? My name is Henry Starr."

"Yes," she said, and he knew that "Henry Starr" was nothing to her, not legend or reputation, not even a recollected name, but a name like any other, blank and new and as free of ghosts as a newborn baby.

"I can read, I can cipher. I've worked ranches, and know that trade real well." His name was a blank to her, he could lie to her but he wouldn't, Henry Starr played fair. "I've been in prison. For robbery. And murder. I was guilty. I was pardoned by President Roosevelt for stopping a prison break seven years ago."

She looked at him strangely. Was that look embarrassment, fear, surprise? He didn't know her looks, he would have to learn them; was he looking too closely at her face and did that seem too familiar or cheeky or . . . ?

The child turned and gripped the front of her blouse to pull himself toward her, and she was suddenly businesslike. "I own this store, Mr. Starr. Mr. Munson . . . my husband died about a year ago. Hired help I can find, but I need someone with experience to be responsible for the place when I can't be around. Someone who can be . . ."

"Trusted? If you give me the job, ma'am, you can trust me. I haven't robbed a bank in ten years. I don't want to go back where I've been." She looked at him intently, her concentration parodied by the small face next to hers, and Henry Starr felt himself smiling, the smile rising up to fill his face, because he knew she would decide to trust him as surely as if he could read the ghost behind her eyes.

"Well . . . yes," she said, as if answering a question she had asked herself, "I guess I can trust you. If you hadn't told me about yourself, I'd never have known." Her answer seemed to satisfy her, and her face opened to him, smiling a welcome: "My name is Cora, Mr. Starr—Cora Munson."

*Cora Munson*, he thought, and he felt the touch of Something, of some kind of power in the center of his body, because the name of this woman—and it was his luck that he met her, wandering lost in the world—her name was close as never-mind to the name of that dark, brave, raven-haired Cora Munro of his old red-cover Indian book, his *Last of the Mohicans*. And her look was the same too, strong and deep, with a kind of power in her way of standing so you'd think of her as a lady no matter if she *was* standing behind a counter, and rich with womanly secrets that asked you to find them out—and the first thing he'd ever asked of her, which was to trust him, she had answered *yes*.

Henry Starr did not know what It was, what power he felt; but he felt it rise in his body like light in the morning, felt it break out in a smile of his own that answered the welcome she gave him—a clear sweet smile, clean white teeth in his smooth brown face, that melted prison years away and made him look (to her eyes) like a little boy whose wish had been granted against a world of expectation.

## CROMWELL *1903–1905*

He seemed so different from Stephen Munson—Stephen whose mind and body had so grown into hers that she found herself thinking his thoughts alongside her own, and confused the smell of his body in hers with the odors of her own skin and sex. She could list for herself even now—fourteen months after his death—all of his qualities one by one, his customary gestures and words and what was behind them, the touch that meant he wanted her and the one that said he was thinking of something else, the flash of the eyes when he had finished with a wholesaler that meant he had made the deal on his own terms, had won something for himself and for her. She remembered the look of his eyes when the sickness had sucked the marrow out of his bones and the strength from his muscles, as if the life in his eyes was falling backwards down a deep well, out of the light and the touch of her eyes, the well was his own dying body and not even the baby growing inside her body that was as much Stephen as herself had power to call him back, *Stephen* . . .

Whereas Henry Starr was all a clean blank slate to her, when she looked at him moving about, his hands and his eyes on everything, she saw just his clean health and good will and power, it had no taste of the terror, pain and loss, the hurtful emptiness that came back to her when she thought of Stephen. There was just the man himself, standing there in stiff, ill-fitting clothes like an ear of corn in dried, half-stripped husks, as he was.

As he could be: charming to the customers behind the counter, clean white teeth gleaming in his smooth brown face, polite but with a little dash of something in it. Folks got a laugh with their change, the women went off with a pleased blush, the men with a story to pass on to the man at the livery or a pal at the saloon. If a rancher came in Henry Starr could talk to the point about the quality of gear and the manner of its use: when it came to running cattle he had preferences and good reasons for them.

And more: she could leave him with Jiminy. He could handle business and the boy at the same time, and what other man had she ever seen that could be trusted that way? To not get his eyes and head lost in the cash register or palaver with a man buying harness while the boy fell off the counter, or got himself avalanched to death under a tipped sack of unmilled grain, or his small hand caught in the grinding gears of a cast-iron coffee mill. He seemed to be able to hold the boy in his attention, talking to him while he talked with the trade; if Jiminy put the harness strap in his mouth, he was testing its quality: "Always value your advice there, little partner, but how's about we let Mr. Simmons get a feel of this bridle." She stepped out of the storeroom in the quiet hour that always came just after noon, and saw the two of them sitting on the floor in front of the counter with a few heaps of assorted-size washers in different size stacks arranged in front of them. In perfect silence they would shift washers from one pile to another. It was no game she had ever seen, it was not clear which of the two of them had taught the other, but they seemed to be very good at it.

Some people seemed to have known about Henry Starr's past. They'd wink at her as if there were stories they could tell if they chose. But the truth was that she didn't take them all that seriously: people were always making too much of things, making up stories to give their small lives and memories importance. She knew he was good in the store, he was good with her little boy. She knew she liked him. She knew he liked her. She liked feeling his eyes follow her when she walked across the store.

She liked to listen to him talking softly to Jiminy, telling him stories, or singing him songs in a high, slightly nasal voice unlike his soft speech. "Come along boys and listen to my tale, Gonna tell you 'bout my troubles on the old Chisholm Trail, Come a ti-ti whoop! yippee-ay, yippee-ay . . ." Or more slowly, sadly: "If you want a story children, then listen here to me . . ."

One evening she suddenly realized that he knew she was listening, studying him, riddling his riddles—and she noticed now a subtle reaching out in his soft storyteller's voice that meant to draw her into the circle of light in which he sat, face to face with Jiminy—two years old now—and told him about the Indian Nations and the days that used to be. Seeing him with Jiminy, she felt a sudden rush of emptiness—she had been so busy taking care of the store and the baby since Stephen died that she had had no time, no strength to look up and see him not there. She was suddenly utterly overwhelmed with grief for his being gone, worse than when she had buried him and her mind was filled with accounts and bills of lading and funeral expenses piled deeper than the earth on the coffin—Jiminy's loss and her own now climbing over her in waves, every day of that emptiness washing over her again, the baby looking for his father and there was nothing, for him there never had been anything not even a ghost to hold in memory, nothing.

Except Henry Starr: who was no kin to either of them, but he had a fathering voice with the baby, there was a fathering music in his voice when they talked that the baby recognized—and so did she: the music of his voice filled her head, she could hear it simply by thinking about him, as she could stand in the empty store at night and conjure the shape of him moving quietly, taking stock of the cans, barrels and boxes, careful and sure now of everything around him as if it belonged to him, as if it were his own makings.

Yet he wasn't Jiminy's father, he wasn't Stephen Munson who had built this store with her and left it to her, and she had kept it and made it grow. Henry Starr's comfortable movement among the shelves and counters spoke of how he had molded himself to the place she had built and kept. With Jiminy he was more a kind of uncle than a father, and sometimes he almost seemed like an older brother, another child in the house. When she took Jiminy that night and kissed and tucked him into his bed, it seemed to her that there was a kinship between the small soft shape of her son and the soft voice of the darkened man now sweeping up back in the store: something in him that might be as small and vulnerable as the child, a thing to be carefully wrapped in wool blankets masked with muslin sheets.

She stepped into the store, and he was standing just out of the wash of light that fell from the single kerosene lamp. "I've never really asked you to tell me anything about yourself," she heard herself saying, but it didn't matter really: her strong body carried her, driven by the sudden plunge of blood into her nipples and the core of her hips, so that she reached out to take him with both arms, wishing to have him as deeply inside her as it was possible for him to go, wrapped in her skin and cradled in her bones.

Mr. and Mrs. Henry Starr took a brief honeymoon in the timbered hills of the Cherokee Nation, on the border with Arkansas (where he had ridden with the boys after Bentonville, dropping blood and pieces of gear, horses, money by the stack and the handful to buy their safety from the posses coming on behind), and then came back to Jiminy Munson (who missed them both) and to Munson's General Store.

"Which we should change to 'Starr's General Store' just as soon as we can get Mr. Hurley to paint us a new sign." She pushed herself to be bright about it, but it sickened her a little, even now, even two and a half years later, as if Stephen Munson's ghost were somehow bound up in the gilded wooden letters above the door of his store, as if by erasing his name she wished to make him die again.

Henry Starr looked at her with that look of softness she saw in him when he looked at Jiminy: "Well, there's no hurry. We have time to change things, if we want."

She read his kindness then, and that he was sharp and attentive enough to read her trouble.

She learned, in time, to read *his* trouble, a trace of grief or fear or anger veiled by that same softness of tone. He was still reluctant, a year later, to change the name from "Munson's" to "Starr's."

"Because somehow it ain't mine. I never built it up, like he did. I never made it from nothing . . ."

"Why do you always say that same thing? You've changed it, you've put in . . . do I have to show you matching him dollar for dollar? I could do that, I would if I thought it made any sense. Or if you feel that way, then make it 'Starr and Munson' or 'Munson and Starr.' "

*Because if you can't accept your name on the store because it wasn't yours from zero to right now, what about me, Henry Starr? What about me and what about the boy, who was another man's wife and another man's son long before we ever knew there was any such person as Henry Starr?*

"Well, I guess I can't get used to it, to being 'Henry Starr the Storekeeper.' " He would smile. " 'Henry Starr' still seems like the name of a bank robber . . ."

And if Jiminy was there he would butt in, "Used-to-be bank robber," then Cora could let it pass with a laugh one more time: "It sure better *be* used-to-be. I'd like it better if you could get used to being a storekeeper. Henry Starr the storekeeper sounds just fine to me."

"Bang!" the boy would yell. "Henry Starr the outlaw bang!" and they'd dodge around the bales and bins and display cases, firing pistol fingers at each other, sometimes (she'd swear) as if they were two of an age. Maybe that came of his not being the boy's father, but only a stranger met . . . but that thought had pain in it, and she shied away from it, thinking it was just her own pain, afraid it would make an estrangement between her and Henry Starr—only slowly realizing that what she felt was a reflection of Henry Starr's own pain, which he hid well under songs and games and stories and jokes, but which she surprised in him sometimes—looking up after she'd been feeding or bathing the boy, to see Henry Starr watching her with the despairing intensity of a hungry child staring at a rich meal sealed behind a wall of glass.

## CROMWELL *1905–1909*

Sometimes in the store in the dark he would stop and listen to the wind sweeping eastward over the flats and think about where he'd come from and what he had been and what he had become: Henry Starr the Storekeeper, you know—the half of Mr. and Mrs. Henry Starr that wears the trousers and the Texas boots, *that* Henry Starr.

The smartest outlaw who ever lived. It took him just that one look at the woman and baby and he knew as clear as if he had been told that this was what he had to take and make his own, and if he did he could leave his old name and life behind, buried like Tom Starr and Cherokee Bill in blue smokes and black night.

She was not the kind of woman he knew how to read for himself, but when she looked at the child she was open as a book, you could read her right clear through to the bottom and not miss anything. So he had put himself with Jiminy, as if he hoped that some time or other if he followed him close enough he could come in her door on Jiminy's heels, evading the guard she set around herself—a woman alone, raising a child, running a store, hiring a man. It hadn't been just Jiminy he was singing or talking to, softening and sweetening his stories for, it was Cora—listening for her step, his side vision stretched to hunt the edge of her shadow as she passed, stopped a minute to listen. He wanted her to know him a little, enough so that she would want him.

But just a little: he didn't think it was safe for either of them to know more than part of him, his kind of life being just about completely against her nature—and hell: every woman's nature with the possible exception of Aunt Belle and Cousin Pearl. And to Jiminy he'd tell only what was fit for a kid, because there's stories that make you hate the one that told 'em every time you remember, *ain't that true, Grandfather?*

So he won Cora and Jiminy with conjuring up that soft sweet Henry Starr who sang old songs and told stories to beat Robin Hood, who knew how to ride and throw a rope and sell gear to farmers and probably glass beads to Injuns, an easy, friendly, gentle man who would never curse his Grandfather's blood and name his own mother a whore, or rob banks, trains, stores and stagecoaches like his aunt Belle Starr or his "Uncles" Jesse James and Cole Younger, or ride with Cherokee Bill and kill Floyd Wilson blowing black holes through his body with a .45 Colt revolver —or save his own neck by swapping his best friend out of the guns and the hostage he had conjured with all his gigantic and desperate strength to save himself from a nigger's death.

But without all of that, who was he?

Henry Starr: as it was the name didn't carry any more weight than wind under the door, there was nothing to it—he himself had lost its meanings and its history in blue smoke, and if names or faces came back to him from there he drove them down, he blew them out.

So he wasn't half of Mr. and Mrs. H. Starr, maybe he was less. Maybe he was more Mr. Mrs.-Munson than she was Mrs. Henry Starr. Because it was Cora's store she had put together with Munson, Jiminy was her baby that she had made with that long-gone shadow of a Munson, she carried her names like a roll call of victories, each one adding something of power to who she was, Cora Darrow Munson Starr, a name only one breath away from matching the hero-woman of his old red-cover redskin book. And what was it Henry Starr had ever made that was equal to any part of that?

He felt more level with Jiminy than he did with Cora, she was the one with size and power, the one who knew who she was: where the two of *them*, "the boys," still had their names to make, though in Henry Starr's case the word was "remake." Yet their difference on that score was less than what made them kin. There was that long tricky game he had played with the boy that was his way to win Cora; in a way they were like partners who went back a ways. And then there was the fact that the boy wasn't tied to him by blood: that helped him feel that he was safe for Jiminy to talk to. Stories you hear about a stranger, they don't take hold of you like stories of your blood, they don't come back to haunt you and whisper you into doing things like your people did, riding a certain kind of horse down a certain kind of road. So he'd tell him about outlaws that lived by justice, robbed from those that could afford to lose and gave to those that had lost, no more harm than if he read him Robin Hood out of a book. If there was teaching, it was like him teaching the boy to sit a horse and throw a rope, things any grown man would teach a boy come under his care, say they were working a job together or something like that . . .

Only after a while it got to be like blood with Jiminy too, because he was so soft and little, if you touched him on his cheek as lightly as you could the skin still showed the quick-fading mark of your finger. Until he learned to grip he held on to everything with his eyes, looking so hard you could practically feel him watch you, and you realized how he was always taking things in, gobbling them up—and then one day you'd see him swagger barefoot across the store like he had on Texas boots and spurs, or you'd see him squint a Henry Starr squint or rope a bucket with an offhand Henry Starr throw, and it was like looking into a mirror and seeing yourself again, suddenly and completely new and clean and fresh, but still it was *you*—because never mind whose blood and bones he had, all the looks and the moves on this little kid come from the same body that won the prize at Tahlequah, and robbed the Katy Bank, and killed Floyd Wilson, and sold Cherokee Bill, and lay in fever ten years in prison till his ghost was almost dead and his name an empty husk.

"The smartest outlaw who ever lived," so smart he was the only man alive who could outsmart himself: he had started playing with Jiminy to get at Cora; but the game had turned, it looked like getting Cora was just a way of tricking himself into being Jiminy's daddy.

Which brought him back by a different way to the same spot with Jiminy he had already got to with Cora. He couldn't tell Cora who he was because next to who she was Henry Starr added up to zero or less; if he tried to write "Henry Starr" by "Cora Munson" on that store sign the letters wouldn't take, they'd slide off and blow away. But knowing what he could be to Jiminy meant he couldn't tell him too much either, *because the boy's ghost could take a twist from those stories as easy as his hands take the curl and toss of the way Henry Starr throws a rope.*

So it's safer to forget those old stories, and the name that went with them: that Henry Starr that used to be, who rode the nightland with the wolves, and his partner Cherokee Bill. Safer to be Mr. Mrs.-Munson. If you've got to look at those pictures in the memory, act like they was photographs in someone else's album.

They were playing a new movie, *The Great Train Robbery,* over in the opera house in Okfuskee. Jiminy was crazy to see it, and Henry Starr had to ask himself if in spite of all his cleverness in concealing the tough parts Jiminy hadn't somehow caught the badman disease from his Daddy Henry. But Cora didn't seem to mind; and when he thought about it, the Great Train Robbery was none of his doings. Henry Starr and his boy could sit in the dark like anybody else, and watch the pictures about those funny old-time and faraway outlaws that was nothing to Mr. Mrs.-Cora-Munson and his or her little boy, not a memory, not even a name, just a set of flickers on a silvery screen.

Sitting in the darkened theater on the plain wood bench next to the boy gave him a strange, almost painful sense of the boy's littleness—and then he remembered with a shock that the last time he had sat this way had been in Fort Smith Prison, the huge heavy shape of Cherokee Bill next to him drawing breath slow and heavy as if his muscular neck was already stiffened against the rope that would break it two days later.

The wall flashed at them, like the light of a gunshot too far off for sound, and said:

THE GREAT
TRAIN ROBBERY

and suddenly it was like Henry Starr's ghost was sucked out his eyes and swooped off flying like a woodchip up and over and down and through a rapid: they were inside a telegraph office, two men shoved in from the left jerked like puppets on a string, guns in their gray hands forcing the clerk to the floor, tying him with brittle broken movements while a train spread itself through the squares of windowframe one at a time behind them.

They were outside in the loom of the water tower, ghosts with guns swarming up into the locomotive cab.

They were inside the mail car, trees ran swiftly backward in square frames on the wall, a heap of angular shadows avalanched out of the left-hand blackness and shaped a man with a gun that blew smoke at the clerk who breathed it and fell as if dead.

They were outside riding high above the coal tender, two men fighting, one of them thrown off like a sack of grain.

They were inside the cab of the locomotive, ground slid down left and right, a man with a gun was gibbering silence.

The locomotive became the passenger car. People swarmed out. The bandits pointed guns at them and they began to disgorge little bags and sacks. Then blink-fast a passenger popped right up in Henry Starr's eyes, his face torn open by a silent scream.

Vanished. A man stood there pointing a smoking gun at Henry Starr.

The engine materialized among trees, bandits climbed down it.

The trees sprouted horses, the bandits mounted them. The horses pretended to trot and canter while the gray trees ran away from them —then they accelerated and sped into the black.

But then Henry Starr was back inside the telegraph office. A girl untied the clerk, both of them jerking as if electric shocks bit at their spines. Too panicked to use the telegraph, *which so far as Henry Starr could tell the bandits hadn't cut, unless maybe it happened outside where we can't see, even boys this bad couldn't have forgot to . . .*

*Outside where we can't see*, it was there all of a sudden: that even though you couldn't see it there was supposed to be a world outside the black frame in which things happened and then came into the light and ran on out of it again, and they must still be happening when the eye of the screen blinked and opened someplace else. So now Henry Starr stopped jumping from scene to scene to scene like a man opening a series of separate black boxes; it all began to run together smoothly in Henry Starr's mind, what he could see and what he couldn't, what was there and what wasn't, what used to be and what was still going on all equally happening for him: so when they jumped him back to what must have happened in the local saloon while the train was being robbed it didn't faze him, and when they jumped him from the posse to the bandits and back again, and back *again*, he always knew where he had come from and where he was, through change after change right down to the dead end—

When the king bandit stood framed in black like a doorway and looked at Henry Starr. He pointed his gun at Henry Starr and fired smoke burst after smoke burst at Henry Starr's ghost. And Henry Starr felt the ghost of the bullets nudge him silently in the eye of his belly, and he knew he was sitting next to Jiminy Munson but the bench they was on was a long long bench, it ran all the way back to Fort Smith Prison and there was Cherokee Bill sitting next to him in the dark with the shadow of Frank James blowing black holes in him with the silent bullets of a ghost .45.

They rode the buggy back as the day darkened and cooled around them, field stubble catching the sinking light like bright saw teeth. He had figured Jiminy for sleeping his way home in the rear of the buggy, but he had figured wrong. The wild energy of the flickering screen was in the boy's eyes, fighting with the sleepy dark that tried to claim him from his waking dream.

"Pow!" said Jiminy, pumping impalpable bullets into Henry Starr. "Pow! Bang! When I'm big like you, I'm gonna rob trains like . . . Pow!"

Henry Starr smiled tentatively. Cora wouldn't like that much. "Well, maybe not just exactly *that* way."

"Pow! Why not?"

"Well, it ain't exactly nice to rob trains . . ."

"Pow!" said Jiminy, blowing that one away.

". . . and second, any outlaw with brains would tell you banks are better than trains . . ."

"Whoo-*oo*!" Jiminy train-whistled that answer down, "Whoo-oo-*hoo*!"

". . . and third," said Henry Starr, "that isn't the right way to do it."

That made the boy rein up and listen.

"No outlaw that knew his trade would have done it like that. If you're going to rob the train out in the country, why get the telegraph operator involved like that? Especially since he's sitting right in the middle of a town with enough folks in it to fill a good-sized saloon, just hollering distance from the depot by the look. No, if you want to do it in the country, you do it way off out there; and if you do it at the depot, you pick some nowhere depot that hasn't got no saloon full of possemen right handy. And why'd they let them folks off the train, when they was probably sitting down inside all peaceful, and nobody could run away and get killed? And all that killing, when if you do your job right you shouldn't have to fight the fireman for the right to draw down on the engineer, and the mail car clerk could be buffaloed and . . ."

"Right!" said the boy. "But that's how I *would* do it, and nobody would get killed, pow! pow! unless they was supposed to."

And right then he thought maybe now he could tell Jiminy the whole story about himself, there would never be a better time: the story already forming in Jiminy's own head, a dream that his own Daddy Henry could make real for him. Then there would be someone in Henry Starr's new world, his new clan, who would remember Henry Starr that used to be, and his partner Cherokee Bill, that rode the nightland with the wolves and heard the owl hoot, away down in the Cherokee Nation a long time ago—someone who would just *know* him that way and . . . and admire, and love that old used-to-be Henry Starr that was still alive inside Henry Starr the Storekeeper, inside Mr. Mrs.-Munson, *that rode the nightland with the wolves and heard the owl hoot* . . .

With Cherokee Bill. A long time ago.

What a puny thing it was, if you thought about it, telling stories to a kid so he wouldn't know better than to think you were like a hero out of a dime book or *The Great Train Robbery*—when what you should have been doing . . .

Yes: that was it. If you know so damn much about it, if you're so smart, then why ain't you out robbing those banks, instead of lying to little children about it? And if you got to talk, why can't you do it as good as those pictures do, talk so good that hearing is like seeing, and seeing is believing it is true. It wasn't the bad technique the train robbers used that racked his bones and made his blood hurt. It was that the pictures should have been his own making, that was what he had promised, what he owed Cherokee Bill, the debt he had never paid. *You owe a life for my life, a debtor to the law.* If the ghosts on the screen came out wrong, twisted and false, lying ghosts instead of true ones, and put a twist on him and on his son Jiminy, whose fault was it but his own?

He opened the door, and Jiminy went run-thumping through the darkened store to the door that led upstairs to where they lived, and Henry Starr turned and locked the door behind him—afraid of robbers?—and stood in the dark among the dry sweet fragrance of his goods.

I promised Cherokee Bill that I would bring his ghost back, to make his memory be in those pictures—pouring out of the vision gun in a flow of light. I'm a conjure man, like my grandfather, see? Give me your blood and I'll conjure your ghost back from the other side of the nightland, I'll make your memory be. (*Listen! Now you are walking on the White Pathway clothed in Red Tobacco. Now you have just come through the Nightland, they have just now come here carrying your ghost . . .*)

But I'm not any kind of conjure man, my brother. Didn't you know that? I have no box to grind out light and make the ghosts flow in it. They used to tell us stories about how Rabbit tricked the Wolf out of his skin, you remember? and how Jack-the-Devil conned our Grandfathers out of everything they owned, and sent them down the Trail of Tears to live in a desert at the other side of the darkness—remember? Well, I was that Rabbit, brother—Jack-the-Devil had nothing on me. *They'll remember for a hundred years, Bill. I'll tell them myself, I'll tell it into those light pictures, I'll have it written out in words, with your face and . . .*

"*My face without colors, my ghost . . .*"

*And the shadow of your words too, made out of the same stuff, I swear it.*

So I traded him out of his blood and his life, and kept my own—and made no ghost picture for him, but only made this store: and hell, didn't even make *it*, but only stepped into it, the store founded, the woman already wifed and childed, no *Henry Starr* about it at all. Like some old Cherokee nightwalker, a ghost coming out of the deep hole of the dead and stepping into somebody else's life and taking it for his own: that's the evilest kind of conjure there is, two names lost, two names gone black—the ghost's name buried in the wrong body, the body's name gone wailing off in black to where he can't *be* or breathe . . .

The crossroads shone blue in the moonlight, running northwest to Stroud and northeast to the Cherokee Nation.

But there's no going back to that Henry Starr that used to be: because his name went black a long time ago, and every time you start down the road to look for him it just takes you right back to Fort Smith Prison and Cherokee Bill, two more days till he hangs and still no running water, still no tobacco—only a handbill with a picture that names you for a nigger's death.

Being Mr. Mrs.-Munson is a better conjure against that than running water and tobacco and a .45 slug.

He closed the door behind him and locked it.

## CROMWELL *1909–1912*

For months after they returned from the movie, Jiminy played nothing but the Great Train Robbery, sometimes changing so quickly from the King Bandit to the telegrapher to the spunky girl to the posse to the King Bandit that unless you had seen the movie you'd think the boy was pitching a fit: but if you'd seen it you'd remember, you'd know without him saying a thing just who and where in the movie he was.

It wasn't a game that Henry Starr enjoyed. He had never liked trains, the greatest train robbery ever was worse than the worst bank. But that kind of wisdom was less than useless as far as Jiminy was concerned. If the boy listened to it, it would spoil the game for him—and what could Henry Starr offer the child in exchange, a lesson in how to rob a bank? But if Jiminy couldn't use that, then there was no place in his game for Daddy Henry.

If there's no place or thing or person that's enough of your making so you can feel right giving your name to it; if you can't keep your promises or your wife's store; if you can't make movies or magic—you make what you can.

Henry Starr took an empty storeroom and made it over into a little restaurant—nothing fancy, just a place where folks could have a beer and a sandwich, and sit around talking. It was part of Munson's Store, connected to it by a pair of louvered doors, but it had its own outside entrance too: RESTAURANT EATS said the sign. Cora had been pleased by the idea; they had talked it over, she had some ideas that he heard out, smiling to show that he was listening. But he kept his notions to himself mostly—telling himself that he wanted to see her be surprised by how clever or nice his plans were working out. And she *was* pleased too, at the way he carpentered the counter and shelves, arranged the tables to use the small space to best advantage, set out cheery red-checked tablecloths like ones he had seen in a big hotel in Denver. She glowed and smiled and exclaimed at each revelation so much that he didn't notice till much later how she had stopped making suggestions early on—and how, without their ever talking it over, it came to be that Henry Starr stopped working the counter in the main store except when business got heavy, and Cora never came into the restaurant except to look in and say she would have to go out for a while or she was closing the store and going upstairs.

The restaurant was favored by the local oil riggers, being convenient to the union hall, and Henry Starr was pleased to hear them talk about meeting over at "Starr's place" even though he had not felt ready to write his own name on the sign. Sitting around and talking with the boys, hearing some bull talk again, felt good to "Henry Starr the Storekeeper," especially after one of the riggers—a little Cherokee named Frank Little—put name and reputation together and came up with "Henry Starr . . . hey!—who used to ride with Cherokee Bill, back when I was a kid. Henry Starr—well, I'll be damned. My mammy used to scare me to sleep with you and Cherokee Bill. My grandpa always claimed you saved his little place, burning up some mortgage papers before the banker'd filed 'em."

"Well," said Henry Starr, glowing, "I'm glad to hear that old trick actually did somebody some good, all the times we pulled it."

"Come meet the fellas I work with," said Little. "Boys, do you know who this is you been buying pop and crackers from? Henry Starr, the last of the old-time outlaws . . ."

"Henry Starr, the last of the old-time storekeepers," said Henry Starr with a laugh, shaking hands all around. He didn't feel like the last of anything, though: he had a little bit of that sit-up take-notice feeling he had had seventeen years ago, after Tahlequah, hearing the boys at Aunt Belle's ranch call him "Henry Starr" as if that were now a name to put with all the others in Belle Starr's gallery.

Talking to Frank Little was easier than talking to Cora or even to Jiminy. He didn't have to worry about hurting Little's opinion of him by reminding him of his criminal past. And Frank Little wasn't a kid: he came from the same place, same blood almost as Henry Starr, and even though he was younger he had a kind of knowledge of things that made him seem older and more experienced—as if living in prison didn't add up to living a man's life, and while Henry Starr's body had got grayer and older his ghost had somehow been frozen at the level of the wild boy he had been when he went in; while Frank Little, starting later, had passed Henry Starr in learning things that matter sometime around 1901, and in every way that counted was at least five years older. He knew business and politics, not just the old cattle ranch and tribal council stuff Henry Starr grew up with, but business like oil and banking, politics like England and France and China. He knew it by his work, which had taken him all over the country, politicking for the Socialists and organizing for the Western Federation of Miners and the Wobblies. And he knew it by reading books, lots of books, his room at the hotel was full of all kinds of books, history, economics, politics. Well, what had Henry Starr ever learned from his work but how to stop a train, rob a bank, or buffalo a posse? What had he ever read but Boudinot's *Cherokee Nation* and *Last of the Mohicans* and every dime book ever written about the Jameses and the Daltons by Colonel D'Artagnan Arbuthnot? So if Little treated him like he was worth some respect, that meant something.

Their being from the same place had more to it than being born in the Cherokee Nation: because as Henry Starr could plainly see, Frank Little was putting a gang together in Henry Starr's lunchroom, and doing it just about the way Henry Starr himself might have done in the old days. All the signs were there: the watchfulness beneath the easygoing manner, the way he'd come in and sit down with one or two men regularly for a week or so, and then drop one of them—and the one he didn't drop wouldn't show up just any time, but would *always* be there on Saturday night, end of the working week, when Little would buy the beers and deal a hand or two of cards, and swap yarns and talk *serious*. The card games went from two-handed blackjack to four- and five- and eight-handed poker, and then they'd have needed two tables except that the talk finally got serious enough to take the place of cards.

And just like when you were putting a gang together, you had to get some things straight right up front. Sometimes you had to lay the law down so that it stuck. There was always somebody thought they could do the job better than you did, and like as not what they had in mind was more firepower, laying so heavy a menace down all around you that sooner or later it would come to killing, because you can't keep scaring folks to death and not expect to have someone sometime stand up and defend himself. But nobody ever killed anybody during any robbery Henry Starr had ever put together, and after listening three nights you knew nobody would do any killing in any strike Frank Little had the making of. Not without Frank's say-so. Not that there weren't a couple of wild boys who thought with their pistols, and one old buzzard named Kinsley who should have known better, and sometimes looked shrewd enough so you figured that under the guff he *did* know better—maybe that was why he passed Little's inspection.

Henry Starr wondered how he would have stacked up against someone like Frank Little, if they had been in the same line of work at the same time. Maybe their respect for each other would have started to taste sour. But as it happened, as good and smart a man as Little was, he was still pleased down to the bottom to know Henry Starr, who had been a story his father had told him in the old days, a song he'd sung how Henry Starr robbed the Katy Bank and burnt the mortgage papers, shot Floyd Wilson and told the dying deputy:

> "Oh yes I robbed the Katy Bank with my pistol in my hand,
> And for the laws and property I do not give a damn.
> White man robbed the Indian, banker robs the white,
> And so I rob the banker to set the balance right."

Which wouldn't have been Henry Starr's answer, and he told Little so. "I didn't rob banks for the Cherokee Nation, nor yet to even things up for those boomers and sooners and nesters that come swarming in to cut themselves a piece of Cherokee land."

"You burned those mortgage papers," he said.

"For all the good it ever did anyone except your grandpa. But I kept the money for myself. If the poor got anything out of it it was for something they had to give me in return—and if it was shelter or food or horses when I was on the run, you can bet they took top dollar for it."

"You burned the mortgages; and you wouldn't rob anyone who had calluses on his hands."

"That was strategy, Frank, that wasn't politics. I was in it to make money for myself. Like I am right here in my store."

Frank laughed. "Henry Starr the storekeeper! You was always a capitalist at heart. Is that what you want me to believe? That you started out to make money like a banker or a storekeeper, and that all those people told all those stories about you because they admire bankers and storekeepers so? But how'd you know the strategy that would keep the people on your side? And why take *them* when you'd been smarter connecting up with some crooked sheriff or railroad or rancher or oil man, who'd pay you for cutting loose on the competition, fence your goods and change your bills, pay your bail and fee your lawyer?"

Henry Starr had no answer. "I never gave it much thought, it was the only way I knew to go about it. And it wasn't very smart at that: because they turned on us finally, like they did the Jameses and Daltons before: as I should have figured they would, once I killed Floyd Wilson."

Little shook his head. "It wasn't the killing. If people minded killing, they wouldn't elect all these generals as governors and presidents and such. The problem was money. For a man that robbed as many banks as you did, you were a child when it come to understanding the powers of money. For changing things around money will beat tobacco every time. When you started you were just a Cherokee kid among your own folks. What you did was what everybody would have done himself, if he'd had the horns for it. Everything they owned had been eat up by the greenback dollar, and you were the man that went up against the dollar and took it down. You couldn't stay inside the law, and they didn't mind that because they knew how the law can be . . . can be stupid, can be wrong, how it ain't always justice but sometimes just a weapon that a big man can use against a little one. But you was beyond that, you was against that kind of law: and so they made a little dream about you, they dreamed that you stood for justice, beyond and outside the law, and stronger and freer than any of them lived inside the law.

"And then, when you started to get good at it, when you could just take down bank after train after bank, why, you started to look different—not like you was out for justice, but like any other man good at getting his hands on a dollar, like a man eat up by dollars. When that happened, nobody really gave a damn if it was you or the banks went down. Like you just went roaring out of town and disappeared in a cloud of dollars."

"I don't see what else I could have done," said Henry Starr. "Robin Hood is a character in a book. Robbing from the rich makes sense, and you give *some* to the poor; but being an outlaw is expensive, you've got to pay cash for friendship, or even for just a little silence and loss of memory. When we was in the Cherokee Nation folks covered for us, because we was Cherokee or passed for it. But the Cherokee Nation wasn't big enough, we had to go outside . . ."

Little smiled, like he knew something. "You needed a bigger nation than Cherokee . . ."

"Nation as big as I needed be too big to *use*. You can't ride all over three states and expect to have kin and home folks everywhere."

"Marshals don't need kin or homefolks to help them get the job done when they're tracking you. Sheriffs that never even knew their daddies will hunt right along side them. Dirt farmers that are one crop away from losing their land to the bank will turn you in for robbing that same bank. Because the banks pay the sheriff's salary, and the banks put a reward on you. It don't need blood or kinship to hold them together like that, all it takes is money. The power of blood ain't nothing against it. Look: here you got all these people, rednecks and Negroes and Hunkies and Chinamen and eleven different kinds of Indians, and every one of 'em is under the thumb of some bank or land company or oil drilling outfit. But do they ever get together against the one thing that's got them all by the short hairs? No: the rednecks mob up against the niggers and the niggers mob the Chinamen and everybody tries to cut themselves another piece of Indian territory. And even with Indians, don't tribe do down tribe, and even clan against clan?

"And meantime what do the banks do? The little ones club themselves up and become big ones, and the big ones keep marrying each other and getting bigger, till they even start eating up the land companies and the oil outfits: until what you have is One Big Bank on one side, and on the other a bunch of people without enough jack to buy beans, and no better idea than to do dirt to people no richer than they are just because they're different blood.

"There's more power in money than in blood. The power of money don't stop for state lines and it don't owe you or your family no favors. It don't let go of a thing once it's got hold of it; it don't get tired or sick or die of natural causes, and there ain't no one man who can kill it . . ." Little paused, and grinned like a wolf at Henry Starr, his eyes were hot and his face burning:

"But if all the folks that ever lost blood or sweat or land to the power of money—if they was one tribe, then you could do it. If they was all in One Big Union, and ready to stand up to the power of money, they'd know a man that robs banks is more kin than the man that owns them. They'd know if what you was doing was just a different kind of greed, or if it was their own kind of justice. Like the song says, 'White man robbed the Indian, banker robs the white . . ."

" '. . . and I just rob the bankers to set the balance right,' " Henry Starr finished the verse for him, his mouth wryed with embarrassment and irony.

"Well yes, now that you mention it," said Little. "Only what I got in mind stands next to robbing a bank the way a scrimmage stands next to a war."

"Last war any of our color fought ended at Wounded Knee."

"One battle ain't a war. After the army goes, you shift to guerillas. Didn't your family do that during the Civil War, and after? And ain't that what you and Cherokee Bill was doing . . . whether or not you knew it? Maybe if you'd had an idea what you were about, you could have made more of being for justice than you did—more than just a mask for ripping around the territory." Little smiled: "Maybe you could have done something 'to set the balance right.' "

There was a shape there, under Little's picture of his history, the shape of a thing, of a man he could have been, could be still if circumstances were . . . But there was no point thinking of that. Henry Starr the Storekeeper had no use for that kind of shape. It was enough to sit here like a good old man, listen to a younger man tell you back the story of your own life so it made some kind of sense, like a kid's story with a lesson tacked to the end of it. That's what it was to be famous, to have a name that would take hold among people—that people would come up to you, needing to tell you again the story of your own life, like it was part of theirs. Even if they got it wrong, that was still something.

So when Little asked if Henry Starr had a place where they could hold a private meeting he thought of his Aunt Belle's old ranch in Eufaula, Younger's Bend. Her house was still standing, and at night the stone on her tomb glowed blue in the moonlight, her obelisk chipped to a stump by souvenir hunters, and underneath it Belle Starr's body rotted to down to bones teeth and hair and a pair of rusted revolvers. The bunkhouse still stood, where young Henry Starr had met the Dalton Gang, and Bob Dalton—wise old outlaw that he was, at all of twenty-two when the citizens of Coffeyville shot him into the ground with eighteen pistol shots and twelve rifle and a couple of barrels from a shotgun—Bob Dalton told him *'You go for the money, Young Henry. Because money don't get sick and it don't get old, and it don't never die.'*

Frank Little said almost the same thing about money as Bob Dalton, the difference being that all Bob wanted was to get as much of it all at once as he could; and Frank Little wanted . . . what did he want? Sometimes it sounded like he thought he could kill whatever thing it was that was behind those heaps of paper dollars. Sometimes it sounded like he just aimed for the biggest bank job of all universal time, something to make two banks in one day look like child's play—the One Big Union Gang would ride in and rob every bank everywhere all at once, and everybody in the world who wasn't a banker would share in the take, equal shares for them that held the guns and blew the vault, or held the horses, or blinded the trail or gave food or even just sang the praise and told the tale of the outlaws who did the work.

Like Henry Starr was supposed to have done in the old days, give like they took with a free hand, they knew the taste of justice . . .

He offered the ranch to Little with a small breath of fear chilling the eye of his chest, what if Little didn't want any part of it? "It's hid plenty of outlaws before this," he told him half-defiantly, "I guess it will do for the Little Gang."

Little laughed. "I figured on something with a bigger sound to it."

"How about that?" said Henry Starr, and he pointed to the rack of dime novels, *Jesse James and the League of the Outlaws* by Colonel D'Artagnan Arbuthnot.

"No," said Little: "that gives away too much, as if the law was what you were supposed to be inside of. Call it the 'League of the Dispossessed' if you like the sound—but one day, brother, it will be called the One Big Union."

"Oh hell," said Henry Starr, "I thought you meant some honest work, like robbing banks. If it's *politics* . . ."

And under the kidding that was like a mask, Henry Starr was thinking seriously that he would not tell Cora about offering Little the place, or that he was going to the meeting or why, masking his plans with a story about looking over some cows which was what he would have done if he had been riding out to case a bank.

Not that she would have objected or questioned him: in fact Cora never asked him about his old life, maybe she didn't really want to know, and anyway he figured it was better for her that she didn't. How would she feel climbing into that bed with a half-breed outlaw? The same bed in which she and her lawful wed husband come together making little Jiminy, the same in which the boy came twisting out of her belly into the light and his own breathing.

Not Cora no: he couldn't see Cora in bed with badman. It was better to come to her cleaned up like he was new. But it was also too naked-feeling sometimes like that, coming to her without that old outlaw name of his, like putting himself too much, too far, too naked into her hands. No matter how deep or hard she held him in the cradle of her body, no matter how warm the breath in his ear that filled the night with the sound of his name like a cover of blue smoke, he could never answer her, the breath that held her name inside his chest stuck in his throat: because it wasn't equal between them, his name on her breath had no more to it than a baby's name new-given; while she come to him named already by someone else, for someone else, and the name went with the baby's body and ghost she had woven out of the strings of her own blood which was the most thing she had done, or anybody could ever do, and what did he have to measure with that but a certain number of banks he robbed and years he had served, and a too-late Presidential pardon for having given his best friend over to the Hangman? Henry Starr's Place was just a little corner of hers, the name of it not even painted up for showing but just whispered . . . Well he needed that, his little place apart from her. What went on there was his own business, he didn't even want to owe her words for it.

Not telling her that he was going to Frank Little's meeting at Belle Starr's Ranch was that kind of secret, that kind of place: something he wanted to keep apart from her, hidden among the things he had never said about Tom Starr and Cherokee Bill, and how it was he came to get out of hanging for murder in Fort Smith Prison.

It had been a slow day—Little away on another of his trips, not many people coming in. Yet he had stayed by the counter late as if stubbornness would conjure the company he was hungry for. Stayed there even when Cora came to say she was going upstairs, not asking him to come in so many words but . . .

Why was he obliged to guess at what she wanted? Let her ask him and he'd come—maybe. If it suited him. He waited in the restaurant while the light behind the window in the door turned blue.

Someone rapped on the glass of the door, "A word with you, Mr. Starr." It was Kinsley, the old bird who talked up dynamiting when he should have known better.

Henry Starr unlocked the door and stepped outside, closing it behind him, thinking it was probably some message from Frank Little. In the moonlight Kinsley's pale face was a corpse-blue, marred by the slash of his mustache. The color and the lift of Kinsley's smile—smug, like a cardsharp with aces buried—woke Henry Starr's ghost to the old scent of danger; without thinking he turned the key and locked the store safe away.

They stood under the small roof that covered the entrance to the store, Henry Starr with the key in his hand.

"We have some business to discuss," said Kinsley, with an insulting tilt to his head that said he didn't think Henry Starr had any choice in the matter. Henry Starr's silence didn't change his attitude: it made him grin a nasty kind of grin. "You run a hangout for criminals, Mr. Starr."

"Most of my customers are decent. I don't wonder but one of them might be the kind you'd be ashamed to know in company."

"One of them's a Red agitator, an anarchist . . ."

"Nothing illegal about that," said Henry Starr. "I was afraid you were going to tell me one of the boys was a Pinkerton."

"That's just it," said Kinsley, "I *am* a Pinkerton." He reached into a pocket and took out a leather folder which concealed his badge: the Pinkerton name and rayed-eyeball trademark, "The Eye That Never Sleeps."

"I believe you," said Henry Starr.

"But you don't like it." The detective grinned. "I don't suppose it will change your mind if I point out that what these men have in mind is a criminal conspiracy? That a couple of them are no better than Communists, and that Little fellow admits to being a member of an anarchistic labor organization? Or that you, as a property owner, Mr. Starr, are the legitimate object of their hostility?"

"A little property don't change a man that much."

"Don't it?" said Kinsley. "Well, maybe not. Maybe some kinds of people just ain't got a natural taste for property—their own, that is. Let me put it another way: you are Henry Starr the bank robber, are you not?"

"I am Henry Starr the storekeeper."

"I have a warrant here which says different." The white paper was blue in the moonlight: it was a warrant from the State of Arkansas, charging one Henry Starr, aided and abetted by certain others, with armed robbery of the People's Bank of Bentonville, Arkansas, on June 14, 1893. *Certain others: Cherokee Bill and Kid Wilson and Linc Cumplin, shot through five times, bleeding, crabbing his way up the street to where I hope to God the horses are still* . . .

"This is old hat," said Henry Starr. "They won't extradite me. I been pardoned and good behavior since 1903."

"I have here a stack of warrants which say different."

He looked at the papers in the blue light of the moon. The names were left blank. "That ain't my name."

"It's your name, all right," said Kinsley. "You just can't see it, because I haven't written it in yet. Nor do I have to."

"If?"

"If you'll testify in court about these anarchists here plotting to blow up the oil train next Tuesday."

"The only dynamite talk I've ever heard around here came from you, Kinsley."

Kinsley paused. Then: "No, I guess testifying in court wouldn't be your way. But I got something that is. How about seeing to it that Frank Little goes where the sun don't shine? Something quiet, like an accident. Not a hard way to earn a stack of bills like this," and he ruffled the warrants. "You've done as much for a lot less."

"You must think a little property makes a man a whole lot meaner than none at all."

Kinsley smiled. "The offer is only good till next Tuesday. You do Little before that and I save the cost of an oil train. You don't, my investment goes elsewhere and I lay these on you sure as death. Why don't you be a little smart, Mr. Starr. You've got yourself a nice situation here—a family, property. Isn't that worth more to you than whatever kind of prejudice you've got against law men?"

"Pinkerton ain't *law* . . ."

Kinsley shrugged. "You got some ideas about law, now ain't that interesting? They said you was a jailhouse lawyer. But what's there to talk about? The law is just a tool, like any other thing you use to get a job done. It's as good or as bad as the people that uses it. Decent, upstanding, substantial citizens with a stake in the community—hell, who else is the law supposed to be for?"

"All this that you're doing, talking up dynamite, spying, that's *law*?"

"Who's to say it isn't, and anyway, what's the difference? You should understand, if anybody should, that there's times you can't stay inside the law and get the job done. Little is my job, friend; and you are too. So why don't you spare me your speeches. You've had to dump friends before, haven't you? When it was a matter of your life or theirs? Ain't that so?"

Starr said nothing, his face hooded in black shadow.

"You watch out for Number One, same as the next man, Henry Starr. Why not get smart, and join the decent folks? Hell, you're married into the club already! So why not sign up? It's a stronger outfit than that One Big Union Little wants you to enlist in. It's just us or them now, all the old-time outlaw gangs is dead or behind bars. So where you gonna run to if you run out of here?"

Kinsley had disappeared, but Henry Starr was still standing outside in the blue air. The million bright eyes of the night sky watched him. He unlocked the door again and stepped into the warm black dark of the store, dense with the smell of goods. He locked the door behind him. A bar of blue light shone through the window into the empty space behind the register where Cora had stood that first day when he came into Munson's Store, and saw her and the boy together there, weaving their little close net of touches and licks of the eye. And himself peering in at them like a lone ghost out in the blue cold, looking in a window at the warm light, the glow, the food, the people.

Well, I come inside, and you can see where my hands touched everywhere, the lunchroom planned and built and filled every day, men at the table playing cards, beer and sandwiches, Little and the boys making up that One Big Union . . . and the goods too, bought and talked over with the folks buying them, good talk, straight talk and no damn conning or conjuring, because I know that gear and what it's worth and how to use it.

And Cora too, all the time and all the ways we've been together, it's like she's running water and wore herself a groove in my chest—inside there she's thinking about me I know, thinking about what's been with us and what's going to be, till it must feel like she's got "Henry Starr" written all over the inside of her eyelids, hums in her ear in the pillow, lies in her belly like water in a pool.

And what about my little Jiminy . . . because ain't he *mine* too when that's my games he plays, that's me he's playing at being with all that banging and k-powing and dodging around? That's my loop he makes when he throws a rope, he watched and watched, taking my movements in through the eyes till finally they spun out into the arms and fingers and he roped that calf with a Henry Starr throw and a Henry Starr loop. And I could put him on a horse, too, teach him guns—horses and guns, I know those inside and out and he will too—and how to pick your road, and ride it, and keep it . . .

*Like you kept your road, you outlaw-storekeeper, you friend-liar you . . .*

Give that Pinkerton son of a bitch Frank Little, and you get to keep the store. And the woman and the boy. That's your road now, that's what you've got to keep.

*You've got to keep . . . ? Who the hell are you?*

Henry Starr the Storekeeper. Mr. Mrs.-Cora-Munson.

Warm darkness, the smell of leather and herbs and cloth. A cash register full of money. Henry Starr the outlaw and his partner Cherokee Bill, they'd clean the register and run for the state line. Henry Starr and Cherokee Bill. Take Cora's and Jiminy's money, and run for it, and be what you used to be and always was.

Then everything of you there was with them, your name and your shape and your memory, will get a twist in it like a sorcerer can make, like a hog with the face of a man or a stick of dead wood with eyes in it, and your name be black for Cora and Jiminy, be no-name, no name that ever was . . .

So then stay and be just what they made you in prison: a fine upstanding rehabilitated former felon, a jailhouse trusty who will do whatever they ask so the law will just leave off kicking him. Hell, you know how to wear that name, ain't you the man who sold out Cherokee Bill your dark brother, so why not do the same for Frank Little who ain't half as much to you as that murdering crazy half-breed nigger son of a bitch, that's what you'd do if you *was* Henry Starr the Storekeeper.

That's what you'll have to be if you want to stay.

Or you could hook up with Little, and slide around the state holding meetings and writing pamphlets and hiding from the law, and hope they put that One Big Union together before the Eye That Never Sleeps finds you and bullies some other poor bastard into saving his ass or his store by putting a bullet in your back.

*Grandfather?* There was nothing in the night but blue blackness.

How would he have ridden this horse, that old Grandfather? How would Henry Starr have ridden, and down which road, that Henry Starr that used to be, who rode the nightland with the wolves and heard the owl hoot? Who was the best rider, the surest shot, and the smartest outlaw that ever . . .

It was like that day when he had just stepped into the front door of the Katy Land Office, scraps of the Fourth of July blowing up and down the empty street at his back, and there was Mr. White Man in the Middle looking up at him and seeing just some fresh-faced Indian kid, and in just an instant from now he was going to be Henry Starr, Henry Starr the outlaw who pulled the chicken at Tahlequah rodeo and robbed the Katy Bank with his pistol in his hand, and rode out of town blowing out every street light and store window on Main Street—into the blue distance of his perfect getaway . . .

*Henry Starr's ghost fogged the ghost of his horse through blue air, the blue-white road unwinding beneath the silent hooves like a treadmill, and far away ahead of him a giant and a young man—maybe they were Bub Houston and Dick Rowland but there were others they could have been—shrank slowly down into themselves like melting snowmen, till nothing was left but a small flat paper picture, and Henry Starr leaned off the side of his galloping horse to whip the paper up off the ground like he was snatching the head off a chicken:*

*and it was a handbill, it had a picture that made him scream and the dream blew out like a candle.*

## TULSA *May 21–23, 1921*

His bed was under him, the rented room was full of blue air, for a second he almost believed he was back in prison. Every night, for three nights after Dick Rowland left, Henry Starr had had the same dream. When every time you fall asleep you wake up in the same dream, the dream is like a place, like a room in which you live, there isn't enough difference between it and the room you fall awake into when the dream stops, which is also always the same.

Then he saw his clothes draped over the chair, the blue shirt with its fringes and embroidery, the rodeo-champion-size buckle on the jeans, the hand-tooled boots as gorgeous as reserved boxes in an opera house. Put the clothes on, and you remember that outside this room there is another room lit with white light, into which you will throw your body and your ghost: the fake room in which you are making a perfect picture of your life. That's the place you have to go for: that blue road the giant and the young man are riding, that hand-bill road isn't for you any more.

*Lady in the Cabin Scene, take one: Places!* . . .

Every night, for three nights after Dick Rowland left, Henry Starr had stood watch in the bushes outside Bub Houston's house. He would get there just after dark, and stay till just after midnight when William Parker would return from the Dreamland Theater. Watching the lights come on and go off, he would stare at the blind-blanked yellow squares and try to imagine the life inside—Clary cooking supper, Shaker charging around yelling, jabbering away through the meal, Harriet Parker moving around and about him, bending over him, smiling at him like it was good as eating just to look at Shaker, humming little bits of music for him, talking to him like it was a kind of singing.

It made him feel like Dick Rowland, a cold man, gone chilly inside with seeing and doing too many of the wrong kinds of things, he can see Harriet Parker and Shaker and he knows somehow what it's all about, but he can't step into that picture, it's just like a picture of a place somebody dreamed, you can't understand the words worse than if it was French, hell you can't even get your ears to hearing them, hearing them is as impossible as hearing what the shadows are saying in a movie, they talk and talk and talk and as far as you can know all that comes out is silence.

*Lady in the Cabin Scene, take one: Ready! . . .*

Every day, for three days after Dick Rowland left, Henry Starr dressed himself and painted his face, and tried to put himself back into that story lit with white light, where he met the Lady in the Cabin, and stood between the mother and child and Cherokee Bill and the Stroud State and First National Banks, and his bad life became something else.

But it didn't happen. The lady was Alice Farnham who put her face on with a brush and cracked like a cheap plate if the camera looked at her wrong. The baby was a knot of rags wrapped in an Indian blanket which Alice held as tenderly as so much dirty linen. A week into shooting they still had nobody who could be Cherokee Bill, they blocked him in with this or that cowboy out of the "Starr Gang."

Outside the sun was one big white dead-silent roar on the rooftop, must be a hundred and ten, and as white and hot as it is out there that's how black it is inside. "Where the hell am I supposed to be?"

They were still under the lights in the warehouse in the same cabin interior they had built for Young Henry and his mother—the backdrop of a chink-log wall with a window in it looking out on painted trees, the two other walls slanting open toward the darkness from which the camera stared like a spider swaying on jointed limbs, a cluster of cold glass eyes and a web of wires. There were shadowy figures hidden in the fog of light-blind made by Esterhazy's brilliant lamps.

"The cabin scene," Miss Woodly said with deliberate patience, "the gang has ridden up, you've seen the woman with the child in the door. You *look* at her. She *looks* at you. There's that . . . that understanding between you. Cherokee Bill moves toward her: you check him with your arm. She invites you . . ."

*Where was she, invisible out there in the light-blind, what was she thinking, what would she make him do next?*

It used to be he had felt easy about things only when she was there to watch, he had trusted her power to make her word good and make this movie do him justice, him and all those ghosts that were counting on him. But it wasn't any good now having Miss Woodly to watch, in fact it started him feeling tender and awkward in his own skin when he felt her eyes going over him, as bad as having Bill Tilghman's gray cold eyes freezing a dead spot at the base of your spine.

He held in his hands the pages on which she wrote him down a young Henry Starr with a body unwounded and a memory that never was a prison cell, young and strong and moving in straight clean lines.

But he wasn't *that* Henry Starr any more than he was the Mexican kid she'd stuck in with his "mother" that day.

He got up, costume in place, beginning to sweat under his pancake mask. What did she see when she looked at him? He felt like a nigger painted up for white in some ass-backward coon show. *I can't leave this movie thing alone, and yet it don't satisfy me at all like it used to, but I can't seem to let go of it. Or maybe I got that the wrong way around and it's it that won't let go of me: because it don't seem to change for me, but I keep having to make myself over to suit it.*

*You can use a lie or a story to make your name or cover it, but how many of them can you lay on yourself before the lies take over and your ghost disappears?*

"Is my face all right?"—Alice, with a querulous whine, the prop girl kept putting the rag baby in her lap and she kept dropping it to tease more curl into her eyelashes.

Henry Starr stood in the "doorway" of the "cabin" and watched her drop the baby. "What's supposed to be happening here exactly?" he said.

"Henry," Miss Woodly said, "we've been talking about this for—"

"Most important moment in script," Esterhazy cut in, with a silencing glance at her. "It is woman here—this woman with child, poor woman, bank takes her farm, husband is killed from it—this woman that makes difference to outlaw Henry Starr. Is like mother from first scene, she lose cabin, boy robs bank and goes to jail. He becomes hard man, but underneath he remembers, yes? And then this woman here, like his own mother used to be, what he feel for her will make him change as *man*, make him stop Cherokee Bill, win himself pardon. All from what he feel for this woman—starting now!"

"Lady in the Cabin," said the clapper boy, "take one."

"Action!"

Henry Starr saw Alice pinch the rag baby into a becoming settle in the crook of her plump arm. She let Henry Starr see her teeth and blinked at him.

*Listen:* he thought, *I am Something: you call this a human being but it is wood.*

Alice backed away from the door, simpering a little and dabbing her fingers aimlessly at the rag baby's head. Henry Starr stepped stiffly in after a hesitation that made you think he had forgotten something . . .

*You call it a hog but it has a human being's face.*

"Cut!" yelled Esterhazy. "Alice! Stop flicking flies off baby's nose. *Hold* baby softly, it's maybe asleep and you don't want wake it up."

One of the cowboys whispered behind Henry Starr as he stood in the door: "Tell her to hold it like it was a dick, she'll know right off."

"Henry Starr!" said Esterhazy. "We must see some emotion you're beginning to have, yes? Maybe you look at woman and child, you think of own mother, yes?"

"Whoops," said the cowboy behind him, and Henry Starr knew he should feel like killing somebody over this, but he was goddamned if he could tell where the insult came from or who put it on him. Maybe he put it on with the clothes and paint, made himself the kind of man whose mother is that kind of joke.

"Henry?" said Esterhazy. "This time you will let us see what outlaw feels, yes?"

"Feels? Feels what?"

"My God, what fuss! Feels love, whole mysterious passion, yes? Put in all literature you want, doesn't your Fenimore Cooper teach you this? This time literature is all right. Love, little cabin and farm, mother and baby . . . like *she* already told you, yes?"

*She*: Miss Woodly: he needed little pert Miss Woodly to tell him what it was he supposed to feel stepping into a picture of his own life. She was supposed to suck in all the breath his ghost had given her, the way Esterhazy's camera sucked up all the light of his shadow, all the words and pictures of his memory that popped and flashed behind his eyes like images seen by gun flashes in a black room, all in their hands to make it run together smoothly from spool to spool so his life would unwind itself in a pure and gigantic and wonderful flow of lights so perfect that everyone in the Nations would know what the life of Henry Starr was.

But he had lost something, whatever it was that every time she looked at him had made him feel that his life began to swell and glow and run along like a gigantic fable right out of that old Cherokee used-to-be. They had chopped his life up like you chop a snake, a piece here and a piece there, the head by the rattles and the asshole between the ears, every piece out of its right place in line—and like there was pieces of different snakes mixed into it, by God, so you couldn't tell which hunk was what, or if it was *snake* you was looking at and not a chunk of pussycat tail stripped fur-naked. It was like old Tom Starr's conjure for making his enemies crazy, you make over some tobacco, spit on it, you get your old gums working over that old Cherokee talk like an old dog on a rawhide knot: *Listen! you who came from under the Big Thicket! The name of this, the clan of that: You call this a human being but it is wood: you call that a hog, but it has a human being's face. It was a white thing: it is black! I have taken your day and made it night. I have changed your name, I have made your ghost into Another Thing. Now you are not what you were: now I make spaces in your life: now you are living in this time—in that time—in this one. Ekh! you are stopped. Stopped and started again. In the middle of the morning: look. In the middle of the forest: Look. You have become Another Thing. You were a young man: I have made you old.*

He felt relieved that he couldn't see Miss Woodly through the light-blind, as if that made him invisible to her, so she would not see whatever it was he had become.

And then he suddenly despised that feeling, he was getting like an old blanket-head where she was concerned, afraid to be looking her way as if all that old-time powwow muck-a-muck was gospel true, and there was a sorceress out of the Cherokee Nightland hiding out under that shiny honey-color hair.

"Lady in the Cabin, take two!"

"Positions? Ready?"

He should throw the script to the floor and stalk off out through the door into the sunlight, get on his horse and fog on out of there, he wasn't ever rightly himself but mounted and alone and pointing for the horizon; join up with Bub and Dick, find T. J., and then take care of Price and after that head for the open country, a long empty road with a bank to rob at the end of it, and a hard ride out and another bank after that, and another . . .

*Till they shoot your sorry ass full of holes, and if they don't blow you in half they hang you up like a butchered hog in McAlester Leavenworth Fort Smith Prison.*

But then riding out of here back into "real life" made a scene as crazy and useless as this one that they kept him doing and doing and doing over, walking into the same make-believe cabin over and over again with this stupid bitch of an Alice I'm supposed to be so in love with I sell my best friend to the Hangman for her, when she'd spread out and twitch it for a lot less than . . .

He let his eyes go blurry and tried to let his ghost fill the lighted square with its imagining. Forget that you are in a box of light inside a box of darkness inside a warehouse inside a flat square of Oklahoma under the flare of the white sun: the cabin, the woman and child, same as yesterday, like it was your own mother in her own cabin.

Like it was my mother:

*Why couldn't you have stayed smart, Henry, you was so smart and good-looking till you got to running with that murdering crazy nigger of yours . . .*

Henry Starr stepped into the cabin like a fox into a guarded chicken yard, and Alice flounced backwards with a curtsy-flourish of the rag baby and a fawning smile for this handsome stranger . . .

*That's her meet-the-white-man face, that's the face she used so C. N. Walker would marry her and make her that little bit whiter than she was married to Hop Starr son of Tom Starr, she'd have thought I was even prettier if that pork-pie sneak-thieving peckerwood had been my . . .*

Alice backed away from the door clutching the rag baby, cradling the infant in her arms that was nothing to him or to her either but an old nest of head rags and torn-up breechclouts left over from *Geronimo the Apache Fiend. Your own mother! To put such names on your own blood! Somebody sure put a twist in you, Henry, you got that mean Tom Starr streak in you . . .*

"Cut!" said Esterhazy more softly, there was a hum of whispering from the darkness.

"Listen," called Esterhazy out of the glare of the spotlight-spider eyes, "it needs to have *different* feeling, yes? You come to her like she will blow up in your face. Let it be so she is more frightened than you, yes? Behind you this Cherokee Bill, big man, brute, face like thunder, this little woman, so small, with small baby, she—"

"What Cherokee Bill?" said Henry Starr stubbornly. "We still haven't got a Cherokee Bill to—"

"Be fair," said Esterhazy wearily. "Be fair and say why we do not have Cherokee Bill with us today."

Henry Starr froze: as if the strings of his blood had been cut.

"Henry?" said Miss Woodly, with a strange tight twist in her voice. "Maybe there's no such person here—but having someone to be Cherokee Bill isn't the important thing. It's the presence of something . . . something Cherokee Bill stands for . . ."

"Yes!" said Esterhazy. "Huge, dark, dangerous, terrible, capable of everything, *everything*! . . ."

Their noise, their arguments broke the spell that froze him, if they jabbed at him he could jab back: "Just what is it I'm supposed to be stopping Cherokee Bill from doing?"

"Use your imagination."

"It seems I got to keep using *yours*," he snapped. "So you tell me what Cherokee Bill wants with the lady."

"Brother," whispered the cowboy behind him, "what does every fork-tail devil in camp want with the lady."

"Capable of everything," said Henry Starr dimly, "that's what he is to you? That's how you want him to be?"

"Please, Henry," said Miss Woodly in a clear voice, "if you don't want our version of him, think of him any way you like . . ."

*Listen to him chuckle, little turkey gobbles bubbling in his breath as he waits, and the way his eyes run here and there like a little black man in a black cell, crazy with rage and terror, so crazy it makes him laugh, laugh so hard that the walls, the bars begin to shake and melt and no stone prison will hold him, nothing keep that black turkey-gobble laughter from blowing black holes in any man, woman or child his eyes lay hold of . . .*

"Even in *your* version," she went on, "the woman was frightened, frightened of something about you—all of you—that's all we need, just the thing she saw that frightened her, and if you could put that into playing this scene then . . . then it will be okay. But you've got to show us what you're thinking, show us by how you act with her . . ."

Alice tilted her head and smiled now that the talk had come back to where it belonged, and she dipped a flouncy curtsy to acknowledge it.

"He hates this," said Miss Woodly in a small, stricken voice, but Esterhazy was in no mood for sentimentality: "He's grown man, let's get on with job if you please."

*You've just got to show us, got to, got to show us, got to show me.* Miss Woodly: who the hell was she that she could ask him—just like that—to conjure Cherokee Bill's ghost back here. Was she just ignorant, or was she too damned smart for him? She'd got him to trusting her, leaning on her, living in her blue eyes like the blue was milk, and when she'd got him floating there all light and peaceful, she says why doesn't he just conjure her back that good old Cherokee Bill, that funny old cuss who never did nobody no harm.

What other shapes of pain or horror did she have in mind for him? And why did he stay here waiting on her next breath? He could leave any time, she'd never know where. Stone prison hadn't been able to hold him, nor his mother's cabin nor Cora and Jiminy's store, nor Pinkertons nor marshals nor sheriffs, and once he had his horse and his guns and his road nobody, not even Bill Tilghman, could hope to track him unless Henry Starr practically called for him—you talked your way, thought your way, tricked your way out of every trap, when it got too thick you would just fog on out of there, close the door and find the road and cover your back trail in blue smoke, in blue.

And then one day Miss Woodly pops up in front of your eyes, and you look at her, you look in her blue eyes and it's like looking in that pool with old Tom Starr conjuring it, and you see your own soul like a little man in the water of those eyes, and everything you got away from and closed the door on and buried in blue smoke, in black—everything is still there, watching you like ghosts looking in through a window.

Miss Woodly, Miss Woodly. Who was she when she wasn't with them on the set? Who was she when she thought he couldn't see her?

He thought of her standing there with Poole the day Dick Rowland had come to the set. She could be anything at all to any of those men, that fat-assed Wilberforce and that weasel Poole, and even Price, even Foley, even Esterhazy, for all he knew. When he couldn't see her, was she lying in bed in the dark by herself somewhere, her ghost back-trailing Henry Starr's in the blackness behind those blue-white eyes of hers, *color of blue in blackness*, tracing his shape and his name for herself? Or was she? Did she? He made himself think of Wilberforce mashing her small breasts between his fingers, or Poole standing there looking at her naked between the legs, and it made his bones feel like they were grinding together, hell *no*: it was worse than that. It felt like it was done to him, and so it would be if she was their little trick on him, because he depended on her to keep the movie together for Esterhazy and himself, and if she couldn't keep it, or if she belonged to one of them . . . And she's got my name and my story and my ghost right there in her hands, makes them over any way she wants.

Damn these lights you couldn't see through. Damn her blinds and her room and her cage at the bank and her secrets and her smiles and her games, *How would you rob my bank?* Why in *hell* shouldn't he go look at, talk to her or hold up her bank or . . . anything he wanted with that little blond piece of business anytime he wanted to, like Foley, Wilberforce, Poole, Esterhazy, Deputy Price and every proddy bull in northeastern Oklahoma could and *did* as far as he could see.

No: as he could not see.

"Action! *Lady in the Cabin scene, take three.*"

Henry Starr stood in the doorway. The cowboy who still wasn't Cherokee Bill shifted restlessly, sucking his teeth. Alice Farnham gave the ruched cloth of her breast to the rag baby and tilted her head, a Madonna but with lovely, lovely bottle curls instead of that plain-looking mantle.

Miss Woodly's shape in the light-blind was like the moon ghost you see by guess between the horns of the sickle.

He had to bring Cherokee Bill back for her, make that ghost be there so he could save the woman from *a crazy murdering nigger half-breed, who put his trust in his brother Henry Starr, that nobody ever would get up early enough to climb over Henry Starr, that if he did what Henry Starr said it would all come right for him, as if Henry Starr was not only the smartest outlaw but the greatest conjurer that ever was.*

But why the hell should he, why should he do that to Cherokee Bill's ghost for her when the Lady in the Cabin wasn't anything to him, a damn fake painted up like a whore or a clown, and if he conjured Cherokee Bill here it wasn't the Lady he'd care about protecting, he didn't owe her what he owed his friend his brother his partner, whose ghost he had traded into the worst death it could imagine to save the life of that used-to-be outlaw Henry Starr.

Alice backed away from the door, holding the baby as gently as if it were Foley's dick, flouncing backwards toward the table, one shoulder dropped coquettishly, her pointy pink tongue darting between her lips to wet them.

He stepped in, he felt himself go wolf in the eyes and teeth, felt his hair prickle and rise and his fingers and the palms of his hands itched . . .

*You dumb bitch, you fake, they think that when Cherokee Bill, that when I see you all I want is to have you do my dick, but when you smile that smile he would blow you full of black holes till there was nothing left and I'd tear you up like a cheap handbill and throw the pieces in the trash.*

. . . stepped in after her so quickly that she lost her flounce, tried to get backward faster, stumbled, hit the table with her hip, jerked away from it backwards and away, she dropped the baby and . . .

"Cut!" Esterhazy sat for a moment, invisible in the darkness. Miss Woodly next to him, in the darkness. Watching. *How do you like now your romantic Robin Hood?* "Maybe is problem with my English. We got Cherokee Bill in scene, but in wrong place. In script you are supposed to push him outside, not bring in with you."

*Your Pathways are Black: that was not wood, it was a human being! Your hands are full of dogshit, you have blue dogshit in your eyes, the tree you killed was your mother, that is her flesh on the ground, the ax is wet in your—.*

"He hates this," she whispered, "he hates all of it."

Esterhazy had no patience for this, time was passing. "Listen," he said, "is not right, but maybe we get closer. So now we have feeling what Cherokee Bill brings with him: good. This is good. Now go back to lady, beautiful lady and baby, bank has starved them and driven into desert, such fine lady, so lovely, so refined—and you feel: what terrible thing for lady like this one to . . ."

Alice's dresser held up a mirror, and Alice experimented with her shawl as a wimple, a soulful tilt to her head—but then no one would see her hair.

"If I love her so goddamn much," said Henry Starr, "why don't I just flat ask her to marry me?"

Esterhazy clucked with annoyance, the Famous Bandit was getting like all actors, as vain and fussy in his way as the ineffable Alice: "Because is just starting now," said Esterhazy with hair-triggered patience, "little ghost of possibility. Feeling starts small, maybe you see woman and kid, that you-look, she-looks business happened and first thing you know you want take care of them; then you will go out and win something back for them; and then . . . then you change yourself to something else for them, but not till I tell you. Alice! you know what is required, yes? One look at this romantic Robin Hood . . ."

"Wasn't there ever a lady like that, Henry Starr?" Miss Woodly cried suddenly, sharply. "Can't you remember feeling that way about anyone . . .?"

He stood there, sweat cracking and lifting his painted white skin. He said nothing, but walked backwards till he stood in the door.

*Cora was standing in nearly the same place she had stood that first day when he came in out of the white light and found her there with the boy still a baby balancing on the counter, leaning on the strong look of his mother's eyes—only now he knew her name, and she stood in front of the counter so that he could see the whole shape of her body, the boy was a big boy and asleep alone in his bed, it was deep nighttime, and they had come to the end of everything: he had brought them to the end of everything. "You let him do it to us," she said, "you let him drive you out," and even then he only gave Cora part of the truth: "Maybe I didn't need driving. I have the name, Cora. I might as well have the game."*

"Once again," said Esterhazy softly. "Places: Lady in Cabin, take four . . ."

. . . Three days of that after Dick Rowland and Bub Houston had gone to find out what they had done to T. J. Hanks. Three nights at the bottom of which he would bolt awake in the darkness of his boardinghouse room sweating and tense, his muscles and nerves crawling around under his skin with a jittery life of their own as if his body was a sack of crazy worms.

It was like being in prison again, a box inside a box inside a box, your ghost caught inside your closed-in mind trapped in a body caged in an iron cell inside a stone prison inside a world whose bones were the iron grids of white men's law: nothing real in there anymore, only the locked-in unchanging smell and smoky ghost of yourself, a self without hardness or shape of its own, a head full of blue smoke, the color of blue alive with shapes he could almost remember; if he let himself remember them they would drown him in blue smoke, his name forgotten and his clan, the blue would suddenly become walls of black stone three feet thick and if he didn't wake up he'd be right back there and no pardon this time, no Cherokee Bill to give his life to Henry Starr to trade them both out of a nigger's death because he trusted Henry Starr to take him through, *because nobody ever rise up early enough to climb over . . .*

. . . "Mr. Starr?" said the landlady's boy. "Five o'clock, Mr. Starr." *Nobody ever . . .*

## TULSA *May 24, 1921*

He opened his eyes. His blankets and sheets were wormed and twisted like snakes he'd been fighting and killing all night. The morning in his room was the formless gray you get before sunrise. The night behind him was a blank of blue smoke, no names at all in it or else too many to name at once, but he was aware that one of the names belonged to Miss Woodly, he had been dreaming long questioning conversations with her, as close and intense as a fight with knives in a cellar.

How had she known the words that would cut him? How had she been able to see so deep? She's got her eye on me, he thought, she knows my name and she can read what's in my ghost before I can name it myself. She can stop me and start me again, send me back to where I been or put me any place at all she decides to dream up. *Lady in the Cabin take seven.*

Why had he ever told her that damn woman in the cabin story? Probably just showing off his natural smartness, a little lecture on "How to Become an Outlaw," maybe laying out a little scent for the pussy like an old tomcat. He was a clever one, that Henry Starr, the smartest outlaw that ever lived, so smart he could even outsmart himself. But there's Something that don't like a man setting himself up for smart that way: so It lays back waiting, working on a man's hunger to be lucky, luckier than he deserves, and to believe in his luck, to believe all the fish jumping into his pail and the deer killing themselves on his porch really come of his own good medicine: the parole board takes your word and sets you free, you charm Bill Tilghman into getting you this job and before you could even start thinking about the next move up pops this beautiful young Miss Woodly who looks at you like you was a mixture of Geronimo, Robin Hood and Jesus Christ and says she wants to make a movie of your life, she's got the papers written and the money laid out and the bosses and bankers greased—and her smile opens to you without any of that twisting that comes when you think of the strangeness of bloods, a smile like a sweet young woman who smiles and opens the leaves of her blouse for you—and just when you're patting yourself on the back for what a smart and lucky old tomcat you are, the pussy turns into a wildcat, you got just time enough to know that Jack-the-Devil has been walking on your ghost before she claws your insides out.

He remembered the look of her watching him in the firelight that night above Tahlequah, as his story spilled out between them, a look almost hungry, like she was licking and tasting up that ghost of his as it come out of him. Now she knew his names and the names of his clan back to Grandfather Tom Starr, she had them all on that white paper and he didn't even know her front names: "Miss Woodly": what did *that* mean? Was it her father's name or a first husband's or an alias she hid behind or the name you conjured her by in the black-night time? What was her *own* name, the one hiding under "Miss" like a face behind a bandanna?

Yeah, she had his name and his number and all he had were her two front initials and a promise that if he did like she said—painted his face white and acted like a piece of wood named Alice was his own true love and he'd do just about anything for loving her so much—then she would turn him into Something Else, something he was really going to like, yes, something really good, you bet . . . though what that was or how she was going to do it he couldn't see at all, and if he was right about her he *wouldn't* see it until he woke up one morning and found that the white paint had stuck to his face and his body had turned to wood and his tongue just made a sound like slapping two slats together.

Which would make him just exactly the same kind of damn fool Tom Starr had been—who traded off the Cherokee Strip paper and the money it stood for to buy himself a piano in the parlor like John Ross bought for his daughters, that he and none of his knew how to use; and wakes up the next morning to find that the paper had somehow fetched his land and cabin and all and give it to the white man with the briefcase, and the biggest man in the Cherokee Nation is just a toothless old used-to-be, everyone who knew his name is dead and gone, and nothing to do but sit outside the saloon smelling sick with whiskey-sweet telling stories to the upturned hat between his legs, *a black hat, the crown is deep like a hole going down, a hole full of black full of blue smoke . . .*

*No: no, not again.*

He opened his eyes, it was like kicking open a door and Something that may kill you is on the other side but you kick it anyway because fear and waiting are worse. He rolled out of bed, feeling about in the gray dark for his clothes and boots. He dressed hurriedly. Each thing he put on—the shirt, the jeans, the boots he pulled on feeling the tug of hurt healed muscle in his hip and thigh—marked and established himself more surely in the gray false-dawn that began to lighten the air.

Even his breath became visible as he led his horse out of the livery barn, swung into the saddle, the insides of his thighs grateful for the solid feel of the mare's dashed and spotted barrel like they had been starving for something solid to grip. Man and horse rode out along the Springs Road to the movie lot.

Esterhazy was going to shoot some more exteriors today, trying to clear the poisoned air that had got so thick on the Lady in the Cabin set you could hardly breathe, let alone make speeches or take pictures. It was like hearing your parole board say yes—suddenly you could bear to look at the world again.

The lot was empty, a light ground-fog fuzzing the outlines of things in the unborn daylight. The mottled gray black and white hide of the horse would have seemed like part of the fog, if he had not felt her deep chest giving and taking breath between his legs as they waited in the middle of that street of false fronts.

*The Lady in the Cabin, take one, take two . . . take fifteen thousand before it's done, if it* ever *gets* done, *another day and still no word from Bub, still nobody to play Cherokee Bill, no tobacco, no running water, this here conjure is just as dead as the other one was—just that one thing missing that you need to make it work, so you get the gun and the guard hostage, but you can't get out the door—and then they send in your best friend to sweet-talk you into a black hood . . .*

Trust her is what she says, and I'll write your name in the ghost-lights of the movies as long as grass grows and water flows—*a bargain about as good as your average of Injun treaties, as I should know, having done better swapping lives with Cherokee Bill than that Dutchman did who traded some poor blanket head a poke of glass beads for New York City, swapped him out of his life and then left his name to be black in the Nations when I promised to make it good*—so how could Henry Starr say it wasn't justice that Miss Woodly and the rest had done, justice that they had got his name to be party-of-the-second-part on a white paper in Mr. Poole's briefcase or Mr. Wilberforce's bank vault . . .

That was the worst of it: having to admit that yes, it was your name on the paper, and that what come to you was just the same thing that you had done to those that trusted your word and your name—so that even you had to admit that the thing they made you into and the dogshit they stuffed in your mouth tasted like justice.

But then, thinking like that, he remembered how it had felt when she had watched him and he knew that she was making that shining movie of him inside her, could feel a kind of electric hum from her as if a ghost-projector were actually whirring inside her with a sound like pebbles clicking together in a whirlpool, and he thought: Oh hell, if she's conjuring on me I wish she'd conjure me back to feeling like it was when we started.

*And if that don't prove she's climbed over me, then what does?*

I got to break out of here, he thought, I got to break out again to where the horses are real, and the road runs farther than your eyes, and the guns shoot real bullets, before I drown in ghosts and blue smoke.

The horse's breath and his own dissolved invisibly into the blue ground fog. He couldn't stay here waiting for them all to arrive any more than he could have gone back to his room and gone to sleep. An almost involuntary twitch of the knee turned his horse and set them to moving down the street and out the other side of the set.

The path went along the bank of the Arkansas, still shallow and brush-spotted despite the spring runoff that gave it a voice. The mist was heavier here. It enclosed him and cut him off, trapping him in his thoughts; the only real things were the slow shifts of muscle in the horse's back that pressed against the inside of his left thigh, the inside of his right. He turned her to the right, up a road that twisted over low hills, leaving the river behind. The mist thinned as he left the valley and the sun rose to burn it clear.

As they came up into the sunlight the world suddenly resolved itself into blackjack oak trees, dusty road opening ahead, things became solid with clear good edges like the black splash-spots on the mare's silver-white rump. A man can go round and round, but a horse is always going somewhere; if she got nowhere she wants to go, she's got sense enough to stay still. If her rider points her wrong, it's not her fault: it's never the horse that's lost.

The horse had carried him to the outskirts of a town. He recognized the weathered sign:

PRUE OKLA
Pop. 1000

Almost seven years ago he had come out of Prue on this road, heading for the ford of the Arkansas, riding as hard as he could with Shays's horse panting hard behind him, $1400 formerly owned by the Prue State Bank in their saddlebags and a posse no doubt rising in the dust they sprayed behind them. *That was bank robbery number eight, and it finished my second swing around the big circle I had drawn around the heart of Oklahoma from Tulsa south to Tishomingo: the circle I had dreamed and thought out for days and nights in my mother's house in Tulsa, knowing that this time I couldn't just go back to robbing banks, I had to make it add up to something else, something that would balance everything that went before, Tom Starr and Cherokee Bill and Jiminy, and Cora standing there alone in the blackened store. "If you had given me a chance, Henry, maybe we could have . . ."*

The main street of Prue was just as he remembered it. Everything was the same as when he had robbed it in 1914, except that it was earlier in the day, the streets empty as if all the people were in their graves, and no one riding with Henry Starr because Shays *was* in his grave, his name unremembered except as "John Doe" on an undelivered warrant.

*But back then everything was* there, *and I was the one who made it all come together: like living through a story you had dreamed in your head, a vision that you run through as smooth as water running downhill, coming down as swift and sure in the grooves of time as a train down the tracks from here to the end of the Nations, a vision with edges and hard sides and true bullets and fast horses—and with justice in it too,* Miss *Woodly:* hyenh!—heh, *that's how it was, like a story full of the taste of justice.*

The Prue State Bank was still in business. Henry Starr dismounted and walked toward the windowed door. His ghost appeared in the hazy screen of the glass, the white and black head of the Appaloosa gleaming behind him like the skeleton head of a ghost horse.

*Like a story with the taste of justice: why ain't that as good as a movie? Why does that time keep blowing away like blue smoke, like black? Why is it that I got to I got to I got to keep trying to get your movie right, to not only tell you more truth than I ever told anybody let alone a woman in my life, but to become your "Debtor to the Law," to paint my face white and make myself something else when and how you say: to sell my friend my brother Cherokee Bill to a nigger's death for the sake of that Alice Farnham who is no more a woman than a cigar store Indian is an Indian, just because Miss Woodly calls her the Lady in the Cabin . . . when that ain't nobody at all but a dream you dreamed up for me, Miss Woodly Miss Woodly—*

Well no: not Miss Woodly all by herself, but Miss Woodly with a little advice from Henry Starr himself, a little almost true story he told about Henry Starr that used to be:

*And even that was more than you ever done for Cora and she was your own and only wedded wife, and Jiminy's mother who was as near a son as Henry Starr will ever have in this life. She asked you why, why you were leaving and the words you gave her wasn't good enough to make a decent lie: "I had the name, I thought I might as well have the game"—as if all the time and touching and breath between us didn't amount to anything more than a joke you flip away like a cigarette butt when you've had your smoke and she had no right to know what was in your name even if she give herself to share it with you, no right to see any more of Henry Starr than the two eyes showing above the bandanna.*

*Which is just about as much as I showed you, Miss Woodly.*

So whatever conjure Miss Woodly was working on him now he was the one who had started it, telling stories with a twist in them, stories with parts switched around or left out. If she wore her initials like a mask over who she was, the fact was that he hadn't given her more than half the truth either, he'd left out half the names. He had no more found a name for Cherokee Bill that night above Tahlequah than he would let her pick a player for Cherokee Bill in the movie yesterday.

So if the conjure was going bad now, whose fault was it, Miss Woodly's or his? If all you got to conjure with is half the truth, or truth with a twist on it, then the conjure can't come good, it's got to come twisted like when a wolf gets up and walks or a baby starts to howl at the moon and grow hair all over, it's got to come half-and-half like a rotten stump with a soul in it or a hog with a man's face.

*And one morning you wake up and look in the mirror, and the man is you.*

But the shape that Henry Starr saw in the fogged glass of the bank window looked clean and straight and young, his clothes seemed to shine like they was new-made, "Prue State Bank" scrawled like a halo around the white Stetson. The ghost in the glass drew him, swelled toward him like the image of the Scourge of Oklahoma striding toward the audience out of the depth of the movie screen, till it filled the screen edge-full and blanked it out. And it was his ghost, he had recognized it because it wore the sort of clothes—white shirt, Stetson, jeans—and carried the kind of pistol—an old Dragoon model Colt .45—that young Henry Starr had worn to rob the Katy Land Office in Tahlequah with his pistol in his hand: but the clothes and the gun had been made magically new, newer in fact than they had ever really been, polished and new-made and they were shining as they had never done in the dusty aftermath of that Fourth of July in 1892, *in the town of Tahlequah that's where it all began, when . . .*

Right through screen ghost door and all Henry Starr stepped inside the bank. The bank president, bending over a stack of papers on the clerk's desk, looked up: a plump white face above a white shirtfront and a black four-in-hand. And for just the count of a single heartbeat he stood there, no-name at all to this banker but in just one more beat he would be Henry Starr the outlaw, who robbed the Katy Bank with his pistol in his hand . . .

. . . which dropped to the Colt at his hip, lifting pointing and thumb-cocking it in a single unbroken motion as he flashed a grin of white teeth in his smooth brown face:

"Thumbs up," he said. "*Thumbs up and stand steady!*"

# A Debtor to the Law

## PREACHER BROWN

> " 'Oh yes I robbed the Katy Bank, my pistol in my hand,
> And for your laws and property I do not give a damn.' "

[Stuttering guitar licks, the singer is eighty years old, his fingers are knobbed and wry at the joints: then the rough old voice]

> " '. . . White man robs the Indian,
> banker robs the white:
> And so I rob the bankers to set the balance right.' "

[He picks a steady rhythm without melody, it goes on as if the singer is thinking things over, then:]

> "Now I do not hold with rob'bry, and murder is a sin,
> But between the banks and weevils, a farmer cannot win:
> And if we don't git justice soon, then things may go too far,
> Like they did in the Indian Nations . . .
> In the days of Henry Starr."

[The last chord is a little ragged. Sound of a chair scraping, somebody bumps a mike and it booms.]

[Federal Writers' Project, Tape # 1213,
" 'Preacher' Brown," recorded by Jefferson Lomax,
Broken Arrow, Oklahoma, April 13, 1934.]

LOMAX: That's one I hadn't heard. The tune is old but . . .

BROWN: Yes, it's an old tune they put those words to back in '93 or '4, after he shot Floyd Wilson.

LOMAX: This is the first I've heard of Henry Starr, and I don't think we have anything else about him. Not to compare with Jesse James or Billy the Kid. I don't suppose he had any connection with the James Gang?

BROWN: [Pause: the machine hums.] Well, Jesse James was kind of an uncle of his, and Belle Starr was his Aunt. But Henry come too late for Jesse James. That always graveled him. He wouldn't have liked you saying he don't level with Jesse James.

LOMAX: Did you know him?

BROWN: [Pauses longer than first time—the machine hums. Then he chuckles.] Well yes, I guess I knew Henry Starr. You and that machine . . . no, let it run, let it take me down. I guess the statute has run out on me knowing Henry Starr.

Henry Starr: maybe if he'd a been born sooner you wouldn't have had to ask me about him, maybe he would have been as famous as Jesse James. But then, if he'd a come later you'd maybe just think of him as one of these here Public Enemy Number Ones, like Johnny Dillinger or Pretty Boy Floyd—so I guess I got to abide the judgment of the Lord, and say that he must have had the time the Lord intended for him.

But if it wasn't against Providence I'd wish he *was* remembered like Jesse James, because to me he was a smarter man than Jesse, and a better one. Though he made his mistakes, yes—some beauties. But take him every way, I'd say he was better than Jesse James: I'd say he was everything Jesse was supposed to have been, and should have been, but never was.

Let's see: I guess now it is twenty some years ago. It was hard times in the Nations. This Depression now, more folks in more places is poorer because of it, but it don't cut as deep as those hard times did—maybe because so many is in it now, people don't feel they was named special for bad treatment; or maybe because they figure they can get together with other folks, get themselves some gov'ment. But back then it was mean hard times, meanness again' you asking meanness back, and you didn't know where or how to get rid of it or again' who, white men down on niggers, Injuns workin' tribal rules against whites, niggers clubbing up against the other colors to keep 'em off. That's why I joined that One Big Union . . .

LOMAX: The Wobblies? IWW?

BROWN: That's the one. One Big Union, only way back then a man could get in his licks and still feel like a Christian. I used to do some preaching for them, some singing. One time we had a meeting over by Eufaula, and that's where I met him.

LOMAX: I didn't know Henry Starr was a Wobbly.

BROWN: Well he didn't exactly join up with the One Big Union. He was a man had his own ideas, and they wasn't anyway *wobbly* . . .

"I was surprised to see him at that meeting in Eufaula. I knew him from before, you see, when I used to preach in the Nations—yes, I used to have a call to preach to the Indian Nations, that they was the Ten Lost Tribes and the Chosen of God, and must be gathered to Jesus and returned to the Holy Land if we was ever to come to the End of Days.

"I don't mind you smiling at it, I can smile at it myself now. Henry Starr, he used to mock and scoff, back in '92, and I rebuked him for it, told him he was mocking no one but his self, his self and his Nation and his calling. He was a smart young kid, smart enough to have become about anything at all in the Indian Nations, a judge or a preacher or a schoolmaster or a writer, but he was wild, angry wild, angry at more things than he could give a name to, and no calling or vision to set himself on—and where there is no vision the people perish. So he ended up doing harm mostly to himself, robbing trains and banks—killed a man and wound up in prison, sentenced to die. But he had a change of heart in prison, put his old bad companions away from him—stopped one of 'em killing a guard in a prison break and won himself pardon from hanging. Come out, and he was a new man. He went straight, worked hard, all of that smartness he was born with finally come to use: had a nice little business I heard, and a wife and son of his own.

"So I was surprised he come to that meeting. For one thing him being a store keeper, with property of his own. And for another, taking the risk of being caught with us, when being in that One Big Union was the next thing to being a bank robber in those days, and him out on parole.

"But Frank Little had fetched him: Little could fetch *anybody*. That's why those sons of bitches lynched him in Butte Montana back in 1917—vigilantes, Klansmen, and Federal officers that President Wilson, that boiled-shirt son of a bitch, set in amongst them to make sure they finished the job. Frank Little run that meeting, and he fetched them each and all.

"And it wasn't like he was preaching to his neighbors and all of 'em baptized. He had every different kind of human being there was in the State of Oklahoma, oil field roughnecks and timber beasts, cowboys and ranchers from out north and west, and three or four Hunky coal miners from just over the Kansas line. He had nigger sharecroppers and red neck tenants, white nesters who had cut themselves a share of the Cherokee Strip and full-blood wheat and cattle farmers from the Cherokee Nation, even a couple of Chinamen from the Katy section gang. And he didn't stop at mixing in the women too, a few farm wives and some mill girls from Oklahoma City. And the white tenants wanted to know 'what in hell the niggers was doing in the organization, when their people just been tossed off the Consolidated Cotton plantation because they brung in niggers . . .'

" 'One of which you peckerwoods lynched . . .'

" '. . . and here's the Chinamen,' yells one of the Hunkies, 'who will put you all out of . . .'

" 'And can we get these women out of here? Who in hell thought of bringing white women in here with niggers and Chinamen?'

And then Frank Little stood up and he says, real quiet, like a man just talking to a man, "Brothers and sisters." And something about how still he was standing there in the middle of all of that yelling and threatening and waving guns around made you want to stop the noise so you could hear what he was saying, so you could find out how it was he could stand so calm and still.

"So they come quiet, and Little looked from one to another, taking each face up in his eyes and holding it for a second, the way a man picks up a baby—his grip softened down to the measure of the difference of his own strength and size. Then he started low and slow and easy, but as Little spoke he begun to creep up on them, to pick up speed and pace till he was level with them, and then started to pull ahead, climbing over them and drawing them on after.

"Well I have been a preacher, and preached the Lost Tribes and destruction on the Cities of the Plain. I could preach you a *Revelation* would raise your hair like a Comanche war party, and a Whore of Babylon that would make the eyes start in your head. But my strongest pull was always the Accursed Thing—thirty years I been preaching down the Accursed Thing, and I slew my thousands and tens of thousands crying to Jesus to put it off! put it off from them . . . But never did I hear anyone do the Accursed Thing like Frank Little done it, so calm and soft and clear like it was the voice of a little child, till you could see it there, the Thing in its actual form: the Thing out there in the dark where you can't see it but only feel the ghost of its breath, the Thing that makes you want to crawl in the dirt for shame and fear, the Thing that whatever the difference was between nigger redneck Injun or Chinaman it was their Enemy, it made them all the same and brought them here in anguish of body and spirit to hear someone preach the Word.

" 'What's the name of that Thing?,' he says. 'You know what Thing I'm talking about: the Thing that stole the Injun's land by trickery and strength, and give it to white farmers, and then stole it back again from the farmers and give it to the banks and the oil companies. The Thing that gives a man twenty cents for a day's cotton picking and charges him forty cents for the food he ate while picking it. You know what I'm talking about—what do you call the name of that Thing? That lends you money for seed and storage, and the interest eats up every dollar that the market would pay? That's the Thing I mean, and you can't tell me its name, but you know it's there, because every time it moves something changes on you, you wake up one morning and your property been turned into a piece of white paper, and the name on the paper ain't yours.

" 'Now what is that Thing?

" 'It's hard to pin down, because it's got different names in different parts of the Nations. In the oil fields it might be Cherokee Oil & Gas, in cotton country Consolidated Land, in the mines it's Continental Coal; or it might be the Chemical-Cattlemen's Bank or the First National . . . But if you look under it all there's one thing behind those different names. Some people say its name is Standard Oil and some say the Rockefeller Bank; but its name is Legion. You can just as well name it the One Big Corporation—because that is what it means to be.

" 'A corporation ain't a man or like a man, though men make it. It's made out of paper, it's a ghost made out of paper. And its power is that it changes, it makes things over into paper—tobacco cotton oil land, men's labor, men. It takes justice and turns it into law, which is just the power of the Thing put into heaps of white paper, a pile of papers that turns out to say that after you've paid out all you have, in the eyes of the law you're still a debtor to the thing that robbed you.

" 'Lynch some pore nigger looking for work, don't change a line that's on the paper. Rob a country store or a bank—you might as well work roots at it. It don't work no better but it's easier on the nerves.

" 'But suppose we could see ourselves like the Corporation does, look under the surface and see that farmers miners oil roughnecks sharecroppers is just different words for the same thing; niggers and crackers and Cherokees and Chinamen, just different colors of the same thing—which is them that ain't got, that has to pay money and eat dirt begging for a chance to earn bread to eat, and never enough; that takes their blood and their children's blood and the hours and minutes of the days God give 'em to live with, and trades 'em for a few cents, a few sorry pecks of bad flour—

" 'And then get them together into One Big Union, and say unto them that grind the faces of the poor that not a wheel shall turn, nor spinner spin nor seed get planted, until the hungry are fed, and the poor and sick provided for, and the workman receives the fruits of his hands and the hire of which he has proven worthy. The world is out of balance if a pile of paper can weigh down the scale against real food and goods and things and the work of the real people that produce them. And if it took One Big Corporation to set the balance wrong, why it's going to need One Big Union to set it right.'

"That was what Frank Little told 'em.

"It was like we had been children crying boogerman in the dark, and pappy come in and turned up the lamp to show one small definite rat in the corner, and the broom of justice in his hand to finish it off. Well my soul was refreshed and my trouble lifted off, and I was feeling full of the Lord.

"So feeling full of the spirit that way, I went over to Henry Starr to see if Little had turned his mocking to weeping, but he smiles at me and says, 'You have changed your calling, preacher. Or maybe those Lost Tribes got themselves lost again.'

"That was always his way—to joke about things everyone took serious, whether it was law or gospel or gov'ment. But I took it wrong in him, took him to be the same careless boy yet that he always was, only swelled up now with how he had beat the law and got out of jail and come prosperous. No, I told him sharp, I hadn't give up on the Gospel or the Indian Nations or my call to preach. 'The call don't change,' I said, 'it just catches up with you from a different side each time it comes.'

Because Scripture don't mislead a man, not if he's got ears to hear and keeps 'em open for the Lord's good news. When I listened to Frank Little it was like the Lord struck me between the eyes, like you got to whack a stubborn jackass mule to get his attention: that I'd got it wrong about the Lost Tribes and the Land of Israel, that it wasn't the Cherokee that was lost tribes, but everybody else:, because the Promised Land was nowhere but right here in the United States of America, the land of milk and honey from which God's children were exiled and to which the Lord was to lead 'em again in the fullness of time, and wash their sins in the blood of the . . .

"Well think about it yourself a minute: didn't those old Cherokees tell how they was drove out of that Place of theirs, that was like the Garden of Eden, full of trees and fountains? And when you consider how the Trail of Tears ain't nothing but the Book of Exodus come alive again in our own time, the word of god made manifest . . . why brother it knocked me deader'n Saul on the road to Damascus, that the Lord had sent the Indian Nations here before us to prepare a habitation in the wilderness for all his children that would come after, each with his own experience of the Lord's mercy towards him, gathering and gathering and gathering in: and not just gathering back to that old time small time

Promised Land of Canaan over the water, but a Land big enough to stand up to the Name and the Promise—because the Lord's words come again but don't ever just repeat themselves, but get bigger and wider and stronger every time they come around, starting small with Adam and Eve and bigger with Abram's family, bigger yet with Jacob, and growing to a people with Moses, and a Nation with David and Solomon, and a Church with the Disciples, and an Empire and then all the Old World, and then a whole New World . . . 'a Nation I will make of you, a Nation of Nations and One Big Union, and neither east nor west will prevail against you.'

"Henry Starr just shakes his head and says, 'Well once a preacher,' like you'd say 'once a *fool* . . .' and I come right back with 'And once a *thief* . . .'—and right there I might have known that it wasn't grace I had but self-righteous pride, returning anger for mockery instead of forgiveness.

"But he—he just laughed, and though I took it for mockery it seems to me now that that was just his way of returning forgiveness for my anger. And it never occurred to me at all that there was gospel in what passed between us. Looking at him with scales in my eyes I figured him for a prosperous man vain of his worldly success, he'd got himself a vine and fig tree and shed his old self like a serpent will shed his skin.

"And yet for all of that, he is a serpent still. And inside himself Henry Starr was still who he always was, which was never as small a thing as a storekeeper, but a thing so big that it was better in the Lord's eyes for him to seek it out than for him to become what he might have been, a judge or a law-giver or a teacher among the people of God's Chosen Nation. He had a call and a calling of his own, that the Lord give him to labor in, and he was in anguish of spirit to find and get hold of it.

"His call was from the Lord to be an outlaw.

"Yes sir, that's what I'm trying to tell you. He had a calling from God to rob banks. Just like Jonah had the call to preach the wrath of God unto Nineveh that great city—and no more than Jonah could he get away from it, not even if he hid himself in the belly of the beast. He could no more hide his gift under a storekeeper's bushel than Jesus could have stayed a carpenter and whittled sticks.

"And I imagine that he had to go alone like Jesus in the wilderness, and into the prison houses of the powerful to listen and find that call in himself, and answer the Devil's questions, and see the visions; before he could come out, and choose his chosen men, and go about his work. I wonder what sights he was showed, and what questions he was asked, and how he found his answers without the Book to guide him, and him on the run all the time . . .

[Strums a chord: sings quaveringly,]

". . . They called out twenty posses, and the Fed'ral Marshals come,
With rifles ropes and pis-tols!—and a great old Gatlin' gun—
They called out the militia!
They called the Ku Klux Klan.
They chased him for a thousand miles . . ."

. . . into the blue distance of his perfect getaway—

## TULSA *Winter 1911–1912*

. . . the most perfect getaway there ever was or could be: because his mother's house in Tulsa, where he hid himself from the Eye That Never Sleeps, was like a tomb into which he had crawled to hide, pulling his name in after him, that name that was like spoor the hunters could follow to run him down. A tomb or a prison, it amounted to the same thing. Every time he took off down the road to make his name or save his life, he wound up back in some place like this.

His mother said, "It all come from hanging around with that murdering nigger half-breed friend of yours, that Cherokee Bill. There is pitch that defileth, and he's the one, Henry, you got to promise me you won't hang around with him no more . . ."

Henry Starr tried to smile, but it was a mask to keep his terror hidden: "All right, Ma. If he'll leave me alone, I won't ask him to follow me."

It was like talking to a ghost, talking to her, she talked about ghosts like they were right there. Her eyes breathed ice when they touched him. It was worse than before, when she came visiting him in Fort Smith Prison. She had been locked up for a dozen years in her own head in this house, listening to herself mumble over and over her old troubles, Tom Starr alive and Tom Starr dead looking his hate at her from his bench in the corner, C. N. Walker taking her land and money and pissing it away, Henry Starr gone bad, it never stopped happening to her: it was like she was frozen in a picture of things as they were that time in Tahlequah in 1892, all of it still there around her in 1912 when she looked at him. It made him feel like he was a ghost himself, a dead man haunting the same cheap bungalow twenty years after he had died.

Alone in the darkness of his mother's house, Henry Starr gave his mind to studying ghosts. The pantry room was like a cell. He lay in his bed and made the ghosts and shadows come up and speak to him. They never said anything different, that was the way of ghosts: as if a ghost was just a question you couldn't answer made over into a body, the shadow of a body, those words that never changed was all there ever was to them, and till you answered them right they'd keep right on asking:

Tom Starr's question, *Why does a white man like you think he can walk around in my name?*

Cherokee Bill's question, *My name, my ghost, my words written in pictures in the light, tell me when you gonna do that, Henry, like you promised me?*

Or Kinsley's question: *You've had to dump a friend before this to save Number One, why don't you get smart and join up with the decent folks?*

Or Deputy Floyd Wilson's, only Floyd Wilson's wasn't a question, just a fact in the shape of a dead man.

And Cora's question: *Why?* and any reason at all would have been better than what I gave her, which wasn't even answer enough to make a good lie—but a joke, as if I wasn't only running out on her and Jiminy and everything we . . . but sticking my tongue out at her for ever believing—

I need to get me some new answers, or some different ghosts with some new questions.

If I had told Cora I done it for the money—it could happen to anyone, man loses his home and family running too hard after a dollar, it happens to lots of people it ain't no special shame. You do something for money, people can understand, they can respect that.

Maybe I ought to study on money. "*You go for the money, Young Henry. Because money don't get sick and it don't get old, and it don't never die.*" Yes, when it comes to money, I been advised by experts, men like Bob Dalton that made it their study all the years of their lives, which I got to admit wasn't many. Not many at all: maybe the money they took ain't dead, but the Jameses and the Youngers and the Daltons are, and all the cash they took didn't buy them any piece of that don't-get-sick -old or -die magic that was in the money; but the money itself worked like a magnet drawing bullets, especially from the back—so in the end the road ran one way for Jesse James and the Daltons and Henry Starr, one generation after another. Maybe you started out to get yourself some justice, get some of your own back from them that robbed or hurt or put you down, and every man woman or child smart enough to know the difference between law and justice—every human person that ever lost blood or sweat or pride to that difference—why you was them, you was their boy, and they'd lie to the law for you and tell stories and sing songs about you to their kids, till you had a big name in the Nation.

But it never lasted long that way, you could never make it last. Little had it right: getting the money out of the banks, that was what the game always come down to, that and making your name big in the Nations so that folks would give way to you and the law think twice and the tough hands and the smart hands want to join with *you* and nobody else. So even if you started out thinking it was about justice, it kept coming down to getting better and better at getting more and more money out of the banks: so you'd rob 'em fast and then slow, slip up on some and hooraw others, rob some plain and some fancy, some like a cavalry raid and some like a pickpocket; you'd do banks and switch to trains; if you did trains in stations then you'd do 'em in open country, trains moving and standing still; and small banks, country banks, city banks, banks that was bullion depositories and banks that held paper—and when you'd done all of those things once and one at a time, why then you could better it doing 'em two at a time, because you made twice the money twice as fast—and also because to double the deeds that way, why it doubled the power of your name and your fame, *Jesse James's Double Daring; or, Two Banks at One Blow . . .*

And so whatever it was you started out doing it for, in the end it was the banks and the Pinkertons and the federals that you played to, and when they posted your rewards up higher than the Cook or the Doolin gangs, when they posted you up toward the money they would have paid for the Daltons or the Youngers or Jesse James, that was your applause and your praise, that told you where you stood with the people and the Nations. Because somehow you didn't stand anymore for what you used to, for their justice. All you stood for was money and being famous, and your face disappeared in a cloud of famous names and the names was just a cloud of dollars, and the same people that would tell their kids about Henry Starr or Jesse James robbing the rich and giving to the poor, they'd spot you in the street and name your name just to get their own names up there with yours in the paper, just like Robert Ford back-shooting Jesse, and the citizens of Coffeyville shooting the Daltons to pieces, and somebody told them where to find Henry Starr with his pants down.

But how could you blame folks that couldn't see more of you than five thousand dollars dead or alive, when that was what you saw yourself every time you looked in the mirror, a man who robbed more banks and was worth more money dead or alive than Jesse James?

Only Tom Starr—he never done it for the money, but for the justice pure and simple.

Yes, and died a poor old crazy blanket-head Injun, hating his own kin and blood, hating everything he come across from here out to the edge of the horizon.

So Tom Starr's was a sucker's game too. His game was standing against the law, and that was his name, he wouldn't have no law but justice and no justice but Tom Starr's justice. He couldn't share it with nobody, it was just his: and finally he just eat that justice up, and if people couldn't live with that, if they wouldn't say Tom Starr when they meant justice, then let them die, let them and their land and their children be eaten up by cattlemen railroads bankers or whatever, it was nothing to him, it wasn't Tom Starr's business: Tom Starr's business was to stand against John Ross and the government of the Cherokee Nation, whatever that government might be. And when that happened he become a joke, John Ross could fool him, everyone could fool him and him powerless, locked up alone in the dark inside his blind old head with no family, tribe or nation to remember his name and help him make justice.

If an outlaw don't become part of something bigger than just his own gang, pretty soon there won't be nobody he can rely on but himself. That's what happened to Tom Starr and to Cherokee Bill, to Jesse James, to the Daltons—brother mistrusting brother, after a while. It ain't enough to stand up to something or to stand against it, it ain't enough even to be the same blood. You got to stand for something, and people got to be able to tell what that is and recognize it every time they look at you: so that what they see in you and your gang ain't just a stack of silver dollars and headlines in the paper, but their own justice.

He was still lying in the bed, his eyes still full of the blue darkness of his mother's pantryroom, but it seemed that the blue was getting clearer, it was not blue smoke anymore. He felt the weight of his own body lying on the bed, and little curls of power lifting in his muscles, like tiny animals taking a scent underground and beginning to think about getting out into the sunlight to hunt it down. If all the folks that ever lost blood or sweat or land to the Thing was on one side, and on the other there was just this great big heap of white paper . . .

Well, but then what? Just what is it we got to *do* to set the balance right? Because that ain't just trash, that heap of paper money that makes up the Corporation, there's power in it, the paper got its own guns and people to use 'em, it's got the power to get inside you and turn you around, it can change the names on things. If it didn't have that power behind it, how could it have stood so many years, weighing down the balance against all those different kinds of people, and the stuff they made or grew?

*For a man spent as much time in banks as you have, Henry Starr, you sure got simple notions about the power of the dollar.*

If you hunt bear, you got to think like a bear. Down there under the many names and faces was always the one thing, Jack-the-Devil or Andrew-the-Jackson or John-the-Rockefeller, what was the difference? Tom Starr thought the name was John Ross, and Ross thought it was Tom Starr, Dodge thought it was the Katy Railroad and the Katy thought it was Dodge. And John Ross and Tom Starr and Jesse James and William Dodge died, but the Name and the money never did, because the Name was the money and money don't die: it don't get sick and it don't get old, and it just goes on and on, coming and coming after what it wants like a blind root under the ground hunting water. And all the different things that stood against it—Indians coloreds crackers and Chinamen, the Cherokee mountain and water land, ranches cotton fields corn patches coal mines timber ranges—their names got eat up down into the one name, The Chemical–Consolidental Cattlemen's Oilroad Cottonbank Company—or call it Standard Oil, or the One Big Corporation. And why? *Because* they was all different names, and right out in the open: and Jack-the-Devil found 'em out, and set 'em to fighting each other, thinking each other was Jack-the-Devil, so he used their own strengths and names against them, and when they was worn down he ate 'em up.

Because they couldn't see that underneath it all, their justice was one thing. Cherokees only got a taste for Cherokee justice, and peckerwoods for peckerwood justice, and colored colored justice, and probably Chinamen Hebrews Hunkies and even women and children got their own Chinese Hebrew Hunky female or kid's kind of justice, and they don't know or care how another man's justice tastes to him—how maybe it tastes just the same as their own.

But suppose there was an outlaw that was like the Corporation, that you couldn't say was it one Name or a million names, that hit you here and hit you there, different every time, no way to get a fix on him, starting out secret and small so you couldn't even be sure it was one man: except that whatever he hit, when you looked at it, you found it was always the one thing—it was always the bank the store the payroll office that was Corporation in that place, you see?—that was Standard Oil or Consolidated Cotton or the Rockefeller Bank in that place. And anybody who saw that outlaw as the man standing up for *his* justice, if he looked closer at it maybe he'd see that it really *was* justice and not just a badman out after money, riding out in a cloud of dollars: he'd see that whatever the outlaw done, it was done against the Name, the Corporation.

And it wouldn't be just Cherokees looking at a Cherokee badman either, but every different kind of man that was locked in the cell of his own mind, fighting and afraid of every other man in a cell, seeing that however different the country was—oil or cattle or cotton or timber—the outlaw always found the Corporation and pointed his pistol at it and *named* it and punished it. Then there would be two powers, the One Big Corporation on one side and the Outlaw on the other—and back of the Outlaw all of those different kinds of people coming together in his name, just like they was that One Big Union Little talked about.

Slowly, invisibly, the Outlaw's Name would begin to come out of all the different faces and aliases and methods he was using—but not as his real name: no. Because if they got that, if they figured out that the outlaw wasn't the Outlaw who stood over against the Corporation, but was just some little half-breed desperado named Henry Starr, then I'd lose the power, lose parts of my Nation, and my Name would get smaller, and they'd run me down like they done before. Henry Starr could be the Outlaw as long as nobody discovered the Outlaw's name was only Henry Starr.

The trick was to make yourself a name that was so much bigger and wider and stronger than yourself that what you was yourself couldn't cut it down or hold it back, but it would lift and fly off from you like your ghost had turned into an eagle, and left you yourself just one of the other creatures on the earth, your spine hair rises and you scrunch and pray when the shadow covers you and passes by, but a piece of your ghost flies off with it, they can hunt you into your hole and kill you, but the eagle hides in the sun and lives forever.

## CENTRAL OKLAHOMA *1912–1913*

Like an eagle: he set himself to look down like an eagle, his eye taking in everything that moved between horizon and horizon. Except that all an eagle can see is what's on the surface, and now he was also seeing like a corporation, scouting the insides of things before he looked at the outsides, his ghost ranging over the whole map of Oklahoma which he held in his head while his eyes sliced through stacks and stacks of newspapers, looking for trouble: barn burnings and bank robberies, mob busting up a foreclosure auction, union men or scabs bushwhacked or riot-gunned, lynchings, lootings of company stores—not just any trouble, but the kind that when it happens you know that there is a place where the difference between law and justice is cutting deep enough to draw blood.

He made his first circle around the center of Oklahoma finding his men and the places where he could work, moving quick and putting lots of distance between stops—Tulsa to Okmulgee, Okmulgee to Okfuskee, to Tupelo in Coal County and Shawnee, to Pawnee County in the cattle country and Bartlesville in the Osage Nation, then back to Tulsa. In every chosen town he made up a different gang for a different target (and yet underneath it the target was the same). For every gang a different mask on the leader's face, a different set of moves and reasons, keeping his true name secret, hiding even the fact that there was only one man behind it all, only one name for the hunters to sniff out—drawing circles of secrecy around himself like the circles of water around the hole a stone makes when you throw it into a pond, the edges hard and separate and moving farther from the center with every pulse.

## CENTRAL OKLAHOMA *1913–1914*

It was hard times all over Oklahoma, the Tulsa *Lamp* had to admit it, "although contemplated in the stern light of economic and moral law it is, perhaps, a blessing in disguise: an occasion for purging the body politic of excess and luxury, and reaffirming the basis of social happiness in hard work, frugality, and discipline."

In cities like Tulsa young men out of work hung out around saloons, burgled houses and stores for money to live on. Out in the country men on the tramp, out of work or driven off the land, stole fruit out of orchards, butchered a rustled cow for food, or jumped strangers on the road, beat them and took their pocket money. Everywhere you looked there were amateur bank robberies, wild boys with rusty old six-guns getting shot down by guards, or coming in themselves overarmed and scared and hair-triggered, shooting too soon and too much so that half the time they had to run before the cash was delivered. Farmers along the Frisco and the Katy railroad rights of way now and again fired shots at the trains as they roared through, because the screw of rising freight rates was busting a lot of small farmers. In late May a gang of six men, three in dirty overalls, robbed the Oklahoma City Express one night between Tulsa and Bristow.

It was hard times in Okmulgee. Cherokee Oil and Gas was drilling and fighting the Cherokees to hold their lease and the farmers for their mineral rights and their own workmen over wages. On the night of May 31 a gang of five men in drillers' jackets and masks stuck up the C O & G office on payday, by unfortunate coincidence arriving within five minutes of the pay chest itself.

"What the weevil begins the cotton factor finishes," said the *Appeal to Reason*. "Grain and beef prices fall, interest rates rise and the farmer becomes a sharecropper or a tenant, till the tractor arrives and makes the tenant a vagrant. The farmer without a plow, the workman without tools, both without bread for the children who depend upon them—who can blame him if in his pain and anger he turns to crime, becomes a human beast, a traitor to his own people who for the promise of a dollar will sell his vote and make himself a slave; or rob another man striking for his life and the dignity of his work; or take up a pick-handle and bludgeon that man to death at the behest of capital?"

In Coal County they had busted a miners' strike, augmenting the mine guards and strikebreakers with "deputies" hired from other parts of the state: displaced croppers, cowboys or tenants with a strong arm, a grudge, and a need for ready money. There was shooting at the pit heads, the deputies shot up a strikers' picnic, some tunnels were blown up and the militia called in to clean things up, and just when things seemed to be getting back to normal the biggest company store in the county (Continental Coal) was cleaned out by a particularly daring bunch that had hung on somehow in the timbered hills.

Hard times all over Oklahoma, "the farmer and the laborer choking for breath in the anaconda coils of capital," said the *Appeal to Reason*.

> Wife and babies just can't eat
> With twenty cents cotton and forty cents meat.

In the cotton country of Okfuskee County, where the Consolidated Cotton Company was trying to move Negro croppers off the land to bring poor whites in, there had been shootings; cross-burnings; a robbery at a crossroads store in Okfuskee by three Negro youths, evidently unused to crime, in which a white customer (who arrived innocently on the scene) took the robbers by surprise and was shot in the ensuing panic. This was followed by a raid on Consolidated's central plantation store by bandits whose hoods and gloves made it impossible to declare whether they were disaffected Negroes or whites. And still further: a few nights later a meeting of the Klan was infiltrated by a set of hooded figures, who (as the meeting was disbanding) isolated the Grand Dragon and his Kleagle and robbed them at gunpoint. The robbers were presumably white—but rumor once again had it that under the hoods there were at least two Negroes (identified by their voices) and perhaps more.

The Tulsa *Lamp* was deeply troubled. "Perhaps not all of our citizens will prove capable of learning the lesson of the times. We hear from various parts of the state of violent outbreaks—the vandalization of factories, gins and warehouses, the formation of criminal mobs to keep honest workingmen from their toil, robbery arson and murder. These criminal excrescences should be treated with the stern surgery of the law, and where society's peril will not 'suffer the law's delay,' by the spontaneous assertion of public manhood."

Public anger at these Negro outrages resulted in the burning of a colored school and church, and the murder (by hanging and burning) of one of the alleged perpetrators of the Okfuskee store robbery in which the bystander had been shot—the tenuous character of the evidence against the boy (who was fourteen) being outweighed by the value his execution had as an example.

Oh yes I robbed the Katy Bank with my pistol in my
hand.
And for the laws and property . . . I do not give a damn:
The white man robbed the Indian,
The banker robs the white,
And so I rob the bankers—to set the balance right.

It was hard times in Oklahoma, and hard times meant gunplay and barroom brawls, family murders and arguments settled with knives and pistols, strikes and lockouts and picket-line violence, lynch mobs and riotous assemblies. Add a lot of politics to that like you had in 1912 (and '13, and '14), with Socialists running for office all over the state, and the Democrats trying to kick the niggers out of the voting booths, and the Republicans running against the Democrats, the Socialists and the One Big Union, and what you had made the old Indian Nations look like Quaker Meeting. In the central part of the state the Wobblies and Socialists had their best union organizers and even a renegade preacher, agitating against the new poll tax. Don't pay it, you ain't a voter; pay it, and what will you use to get your seed or pay the money you owe at the plantation store or the bank?

"There is God's law which is justice in one scale," said the preacher, "and man's law in the other, which is the power of guns and money.

Render unto Caesar, saith the Lord, the things that are Caesar's—but justice don't belong to Caesar, nor the bread of the sweat of your own brow don't belong to Caesar, and woe unto that Nation where the scale of justice is outweighed by guns and money . . ."

Worried officials put the poll tax collection in the Keystone State Bank, and on September 8 two men came in early in the morning and cleaned out the vault. Within a matter of days some fifteen hundred tenants and sharecroppers had come in to pay their poll tax in cash.

"This war of man against his fellow man," said the *Appeal to Reason*, "will never cease until the People itself, like the infant Hercules, rises in united and universal wrath to strangle the serpent."

The Tulsa *Lamp* rose to confront the evil of the times: "But even if the malefactors themselves are exterminated, these criminal and revolutionary outbreaks will be renewed until those that cried them up and egged them on have been chastised. That same soft-mindedness, which fifty years ago endowed the Negro race with a franchise it still abuses, persists among us to this day. We behold its workings in the wholesale addition to our citizenry of large infusions of foreign blood and alien ideas, and the fatuous indulgence with which these elements are received and accorded the privilege of citizenship and dignity of participation in the exercise of political power. In the wrong hands, the ballot is as dangerous to civilization as a bullet in an outlaw's gun."

(Sung softly, like after the heavy work has been done you're turning it over and over in your mind:)

> Now I do not hold with robbery, and murder is a sin,
> But between the banks and the weevils a farmer cannot
>   win,
> And if we don't get justice soon, then things may go
>   too far,
> Like they did in the Indian Nations . . ."

## STROUD *March 7, 1915*

They were holding the big Four-County Cooperative Fair in Stroud. It was the biggest one in that part of the state, originally run by the old Farmers' Alliance, where they'd rally and speechify how they was going to circumvent the currency and put a bunch of shit-kicking sodbusters like themselves in charge of the government and the banks. The organizations that sponsored it was different now, but the name of the trouble was the same.

Henry Starr had a funny feeling, itchy and comfortable at the same time. He was taking chances showing himself, playing with the possibility that someone here could put his face with his name and his name to the robberies that had the central counties stirring like a beehive when a wasp moves in. But he needed to try his powers, just like he had needed to run that chicken pull bareback Indian style, and rob the Katy Bank the day after. He needed to play hide and seek with his name and his safety. He needed to feel that his name could never be hid so deep in blue smoke that nobody would even know he was there.

The fair grounds were out on one end of Main Street; just like Tahlequah in '92 you rode out there under banners saying welcome and showing the colors. They had a livery stable if you wanted it, but he just hitched his horse—a bay mare, the color of his incognito—among others at the long rail and walked easily down the long midway that ran from one end of the fairgrounds to the other. Stalls and booths for livestock to be looked at and judged ran off to right and left, and there were tent-covered tables where the women sold vegetables and fruits, fresh and preserved, pickles put up in jars, fresh-made bread and pies—for eating and judging—counters for pop and coffee and lemonade, and if you knew how to ask for it beer and corn whiskey clear as water and so pure that if you lit it up in your hand it would burn off in a flash and leave no more than a baby's-lick of corn sweet in your palm.

He liked the taste of his power. He could pass through the crowd like one of them, so safe he was almost invisible. Not like the rodeo day back in Tahlequah, riding in feeling like his horse was a fence rail he was balanced on in the face of the whole Cherokee Nation, every pair of eyes down the long street with some knowledge of him like ropes looping out to tanglefoot a skitty colt, *Tom Starr's grandson Cherokee Bill's partner whiskey runner good rider half-breed* so that everything he did was like on a stage or scaffold right out in public, the robbery of the Katy Land Office no more private than the chicken pull was, the ghosts of the Nation's eyes all over him. This was better, this not being a name for all these people that he was nothing to.

Yet he should have been somebody to them.

The papers were full of the work of Henry Starr, but there was nobody in all of the Nations who could put Henry Starr's name to it. *Can't any of these people read? Don't anybody remember my name?* It was as if there was no Henry Starr anymore, but instead a huge blank shape, was it one shape or thousands? The papers shot names at the shape like a greenhorn jumped by Indians in a thicket, blazing away at shadows, bushes, birdsong and fly buzz till the air was full of blue smokes and their guns were empty: names of known professionals and political organizations and just plain insult-words like trash and red and nigger, and the warrants out with no name written on 'em.

Here he was at the Four-County Cooperative Fair, the biggest one in this part of the state: cowboys and oil riggers down from Payne County, white and black croppers from Lincoln and Okfuskee, dirt farmers from Creek—and in every one of those places he had his people, and he had helped them draw the line and hold the balance—burnt-out union halls and farmers' cooperatives built back up with money given out of our take, a mean straw boss or manager scared out of the county, money in a poke for the widows and orphans of men gunned down or lynched for taking a stand. It made him itch, little electric flashes ran along his skin when he thought how close these people should be to knowing who he was, it made the muscles in his thighs ache and jump.

But none of the people there could rightly name the one who helped them any more than the bankers or the sheriffs or the possemen could; and if they had, nobody but Henry Starr could have told them that the different names they knew was the same man in each of their different places. Because the different gangs didn't mix any more than their people did at this so-called cooperative fair. The colored croppers and the white kept by themselves when they wasn't matching teams for the sled pull or hogs for the blue ribbon. Their wives sat over tables of pies and jar preserves and piles of handmade quilts, but never swapped talk of the craft—and the colors of their quilts shared nothing at all, pale blues and pinks with million-dotted flowers on one side, black green and yellow flowers on a blood-red background on the other. The Italian construction hands from the oil fields wore funny little hats and embroidered vests, and danced to accordions; the cowboys danced squares or rode bucking horses or practiced rope tricks.

In seven seasons from the winter of 1912–13 to the winter of 1914 Henry Starr had gone round the circle seven times, firstly preparing and secondly hitting the company stores and offices; thirdly taking the banks southward from Tulsa in Keystone, Kiefer, Wardville; fourthly the coal-country banks in Tupelo, Pontotoc, Byars; fifthly the westward banks in Prue, Carney and Preston; sixthly the banks northwestward: Owasso, Terlton; and seventhly, a long swing all the way west to Garber and back home to Vera. Seven circles, some like wide roping loops and some like little pigging ties, but together they were like the concentric rings of a target around the heart of Oklahoma, homing in on the heart of things, on the banks which were the home and center of money and power, the place where they wrote down the death of justice—so maybe if there was anyone out there to read what was happening they'd begin to see that it wasn't just renegades breaking out here and there and everywhere, but there was someone behind it even if you couldn't name him or even know was it a single him or a bunch. Henry Starr wanted them to start to feel that much, just that whoever or whatever It was out there in the night, wolf or nightwalker or outlaw, It was a thing with notions, It was aiming at something—nameless as It was, It knew their names and where to find them.

Nameless as It was . . .

*I've got every sheriff, deputy, cop, town and federal marshal in the state chasing the ghost of that Outlaw, who has no name, who has as many shapes and voices and costumes and masks as there are different kinds of trouble in the Indian Nations—a regular coyote, a regular Jack-the-Devil. Grandfather, you old wizard: I am a better conjure man than you. Maybe too good, hey? Because if there's nobody can put your name with what you done, then it's almost like you never really done it in the world, but only dreamed it among the blue smokes of your mind.*

"Henry Starr."

The naming took him from behind like a gun in the ribs, and he felt that flash of pure nakedness and vulnerability that he remembered from his childhood arrest on the Bartlesville road, the flash of the badges, the deputies' boots, *don't let 'em hang don't let 'em cut me don't*, but he made a smile like a mask that hid the downward pull of terror behind his face, thinking: *If you ain't careful what you wish for you're liable to get it*. "Well," he said, turning slowly with his hands away from the pistol on his right hip, "at least *somebody* here knows my name," and looked up at the grim black face of Bub Houston.

"Words with you, Henry, that's all. Just a few, and all of 'em mine. What you been up to in God's world I don't know or care, but if you think a sparrow fall in Okfuskee County and I don't know it then you're a fool. If you still walking after busting that store, it's because I ain't sheriff no more. That Consolidated Company and these white crackers here got out a law, ain't no more niggers to vote or hold office in this state. So if you do them, it's nothing to me; and if you want to take a Klan meeting down, that's no trouble. But you keep practicing on this, the law gone use what you do to come in here and start taking names and jailing and hanging my folks, like they done that poor boy for those kids that robbed the store and shot that man comin' in—and if it hadn't been somebody else's killing they was thinkin' about, Henry—if I believed it was on your account they hung that poor boy, then I wouldn't be talkin' to you, Henry, while you eatin' pie at the Four-County Fair. I'd be huntin' you, Henry, and because I'm lookin' at you now you know damn well I could find you."

Henry Starr felt his cheeks blush and stiffen: "What I been doing ain't for harming those people, Bub. I been helping 'em any way I—"

"These people ain't no more to you than wind under the door, Henry Starr. What can you give 'em that would make a difference? You don't have no home in these folks, you ain't kin and you ain't kind. You ain't ever chopped cotton, and you never wore the chain or had the Ku-kluck come looking for you, and them that has"—his voice took on a mocking minstrel-show lilt—"they just po' niggers lookin' up fum de cotton-feels, Lawsey ef it ain't dat bad bad man, dat Henery Starr." Bub's face clenched: "And when you done, it's them that gets left behind to deal with the company, and the man in the store aiming to get even, and the sheriff and the night riders, and no lawmen of their own kind anymore to stand between—"

"I never wanted anyone to take a rap for what was my doing, Bub. I'll fix it."

"There's law here right now taking names, Henry. If I didn't think you'd set it right I'd have give him yours already."

"Who . . . ?"

"Tilghman," said Bub, turned on his heel, and walked away.

Henry Starr held his breath, held his ghost tight, turning slowly around the compass, not hasty or anxious, a man looking round for his wife, maybe, or his kid gone off for likrish and lost in the crowd—turned past the red quilts of the black croppers, the Italians around an oil drum in which something spicy was being fried, past the farmers' pyramids of gourds and jarred vegetables, then eased toward the corral . . . but there he was, the gray Stetson riding Tilghman's high head out of a crowd of cowboys. If Bub hadn't given him the name he'd never have had the edge he needed to spot him first but they would have met by chance, eyes locking suddenly in recognition ghost-to-ghost; they had guns riding their hips *and is Henry Starr the man who will draw his gun against Bill Tilghman?—faster than thought or you will not see the blood pop out like a sudden flower in the* V *of Tilghman's gray vest, but it will be Henry Starr who is dead dead dead with one leaden bullet chopping a hole in the middle of his breath . . .*

Henry Starr eased back into the crowd, keeping an eye out for Tilghman's tall shape and gray hat, walking an edge between seeing and losing him—needing to see him to be able to keep his distance, fearing when

Tilghman disappeared that his next apparition would be as a voice from behind his back: "*I believe that you are Henry Starr . . .*," walking toward the horse corral again with that feeling of having rifle sights trained at the base of his spine.

"Watch it, Jack." A rough black voice; he'd walked into the middle of a crowd of black sharecroppers, and suddenly he knew his masks were stripped, he was not part of this crowd but a stranger in it, his paler skin showing him up like a deer on the skyline. If they had been the boys from his gang, they would know him and . . . but that wasn't in the plan, was it? *Nobody knows my name*; it was a wish, a prayer, a conjure.

"Excuse me." He ducked his head and touched his hat, left them muttering about white trash, moved back toward the midway of the fair, trying to stay in a crowd.

But the crowd wasn't a thicket he could keep hidden in. Everywhere Tilghman went in that crowd he planted Henry Starr's name, and there was another set of eyes sprung up ready and able to look for him. It was an edge too sharp to walk on. He looked at his horse tied up outside the corral, if Tilghman had spotted it someone would be watching—the farmer in the red galluses? the Italian sitting smoking on the seat of his rig? The crowd was full of eyes now, it was as bad as it had ever been riding into Tahlequah like a man ridden up Main Street on a fence rail. Everybody knows Tom Starr's grandson Hop Starr's son Belle Starr's nephew Cherokee Bill's partner brother friend who sold him to the Hangman in Fort Smith Prison, his name like a tin can tied to a dog's tail to make him run himself to death, *Henry Starr Henry Starr Henry Starr Henry Starr . . .*

Henry Starr kept walking past the corral, past knots of men jawing by the fence. Twenty yards ahead the midway ran into the Main Street of Stroud; he was walking away from the fair and its million-eyed patch quilt of black and white faces. The buildings of Stroud came up around him, his eyes took in the big brick shape of the First National Bank, and a block past that the Stroud State Bank, and beyond them the marquee of the Stroud Opera House, *The Birth of a Nation.*

It would be dark inside the theater, and dark was safe. He bought a ticket from a girl in marcelled hair who looked at his money but not his face.

Inside he sat in a wooden seat, on the aisle—an exit door framed in fancy painted-on curtains ten steps away. There were people all around him, but their attention was forward to where the curtain was swaying apart, their eyes on the blank window of the screen that was revealed. As the blackness shut around him he felt safe again, his ghost cased carefully and tightly in his own flesh, the blackness like a vast cloud to hide him from searching eyes, the silence like a warm blanket pulled up around him in which he could huddle, in which he could no longer hear the rattle of his own name tailing him.

Then the pictures started coming on, and they took hold of him by the ghost, reaching in through the holes of his eyes like always: only this time it was different, stronger and stranger. It was a picture about some rich folks, southern mostly, running themselves into the Civil War proud and pigheaded as they was, and if he thought about it they was nothing to him and less than nothing—never friends (except for Quantrill and Jesse James and old Stand Watie), and even as enemies they was nothing much to do with the Indian Nations and that old Cherokee trouble that was all the Civil War Henry Starr knew or needed. But these pictures didn't just flash and declare themselves, they grabbed and they run, they stole your ghost and took it with them, moving slick and smooth and seamless and pretty as a running horse from moment to moment to moment, months and years flashing by in a few seconds with no more break or trouble to the mind than if it had been a pretty woman walking across a room, moving you fast and slow through time, putting you close in so that the Little Colonel waving his sword charged his regiment between your eyes, and so far above that you saw with the cold distance of a vulture that the regiments and the flags was all going to be meat in the end, every face and name lost in the flow and the mass and the numbers and dates and names of battles. Sometimes you was showed things that was the inside of the people turned out, as if you could see behind their eyes and between their ears—the fluttering bird in the hand was the fear that came with love, a soldier's still photograph in a frame was the young man's death.

Plunged into the flow of gray and white he was deeper and farther and safer in himself than before, he had found a darkness within a darkness, a world of liquid light-ghosts where there was no Bub Houston to stand and draw a line in the dust of the fairgrounds and tell him never to cross it; a place where the cold eyes of Bill Tilghman had no being.

Some of the stuff was damned funny. They had white men blacked up to play the bad niggers, putting the crackers and the gentry down together, and at first it was like Henry Starr's own outlaw game of the last year played out on the screen, men changing their color on the outside so they could get themselves some justice. He almost laughed out loud when the pictures showed him "Lincoln's Plan," which was to put all the niggers on a boat and ship 'em back to Africa, like Preacher Brown and his Cherokee Jerusalem. So why shouldn't he enjoy the joke, if he'd paid the price of the ticket and they were none of his folks? Damn that Bub Houston and his "folks" anyway, if they wouldn't say he had a place among them after all he'd done.

Only it gradually become clear that these blacked-up jokers was not meaning justice at all, stealing food and clothing from the poor and helpless. It almost made him mad at the picture, but what was it to him, when you come down to it? He had no use for crackers or the gentry, and according to Bub Houston had no stake or interest in niggers either, so what was it to him if these blacked-up white men give the niggers a bad name for thievery—and rape: there was one crazy bad half-breed named Gus looking fucks at the women—no, it was that crazy look like Cherokee Bill had, you couldn't tell was he looking fucks at them or shooting black holes in their bodies with his eyes. Gus was so much like Cherokee Bill it was almost like the giant's ghost made over into Something, into a joke about Cherokee Bill, who said he was just about white inside his own black skin and looked murder at anyone who noticed how all he really was was a nigger who almost looked Cherokee.

Henry Starr leaned back and let the movie roll; he was having a good time, like all of those blue-black ghosts that come hunting him was finally laughed to death. It was like whoever made this movie made Henry Starr's dreams come true: he could watch people doing each other dirt and none of it belonged to him, not the poor suffering crackers and gentry, not the good/bad angry pitiful niggers, not that dummy-crazy Cherokee Bill of a Gus—none of them belonged to him, so what was it to him what shit they made each other eat. It wasn't any of his shit; they was different kinds, the movie people and himself, the kind that gets done to against the kind that gets things done.

If he was like anybody in the picture it was the Little Colonel, the banty-cock Reb with the mustache—a man come down in the world, busted but not broke, his name still good and he's got enough pride to be angry, his word is still his own to give and one day you know he's gonna get that gun of his again, he ain't gonna stand for *this* very long: his goods spoiled or taken, blue-belly law all over the place working every way they knew to put their hands on the little man's ghost, to make the ugliness of his poverty and his losing the war sink into his ghost and turn him into a . . .

Nigger.

Turn him into a nigger.

Which was ugly and poor and couldn't ever take hold and had no show for justice . . .

Like Cherokee Bill.

Like Cherokee Bill, who could be the brother of this skulking half-breed nigger Gus in the pictures, looking out at the little white girl from behind a tree with rape and murder in his eyes. A white man, painted like a nigger—ain't that what Cherokee Bill thought he was himself? A white man or a Cherokee man that got the name and the face of nigger laid on him like a spell, and he can't get shut of it, and he tears at the name at the mask at the skin of his face like he was ripping at the bars of his cell and when he gets out he's got to start killing till he finds the one who . . .

Henry Starr felt his ghost split in two, and he ran for rape and murder with Gus, and he mounted his horse robed in white to ride the nigger down and draw the line and cut the nigger off before he . . .

Before he became the nigger who pleaded bug-eyed in the red smoke-light at the spiked hoods that rose around him like ghosts . . .

And became the Colonel who drew his sword and plunged it through the pulsing red screen at Henry Starr's attentive ghost imprisoned shoulder-to-shoulder among dark shapes in the dark . . .

And as the images flashed changing the Colonel stabbing to Gus jerking to the Colonel stabbing down with his sword to Gus cut and bleeding the Colonel screaming Gus dying as black blood bubbled like vomit from between his lips—

It was like the handbill in the prison had come alive, like a horror conjured out of scraps of hair and blood and paper and rope to walk a man's ghost down and eat it, so that Henry Starr couldn't tell where he began and the picture left off, or who or where in the picture he was, nigger or half-breed or white man colonel, a horseback killer riding to a rescue where the niggers was whites and the whites niggers, where the very thing you wanted to do good for was the very thing you had to murder shamed and screaming.

*He was your partner and almost your brother, and he'd have sided you right up to dying for you: and that's what you made him do, isn't it? . . .*

The Klan was riding to rescue all of the poor good white people of the world and save them from being turned into niggers, when somebody stood up in the movie house and said, "That's a goddamn lie," and walked out unseen in the darkness. Nobody knew who it was, but he was the only man in Stroud, Oklahoma, who didn't agree with President Wilson that *Birth of a Nation* was history written with lightning . . .

## TULSA *March 8–20, 1915*

. . . Whereas Henry Starr's name was written on trash—crumpled newspapers blowing down the street in the raw wind, old cheap handbills turning yellow on the walls of banks, post offices and country stores.

Henry Starr lay in the blue-black darkness of his mother's pantryroom, and gave his ghost to studying the name of Henry Starr.

He was safe, not even Bill Tilghman would think to find him hiding out in his own mother's house, smart as *he* was—that is, if it was "Henry Starr" Tilghman was hunting. But why should he be? Tilghman was looking for the Outlaw, the biggest Outlaw that ever rode out of the Indian Nations, that was so smart he could double a trail or break it and make you think black when you saw white, that give like he took with a free hand and knew the taste of justice. Whereas there wasn't any more to the name of Henry Starr than being smart, but it was a small mean kind of smartness, without any generosity to it, without the taste of justice, the kind of smartness that kept quiet when other people got lynched for his crimes, the kind that told him the best way to sell his partner to the Hangman, to get himself a pardon he was even too stupid or careless to keep on living inside of.

If I could have kept my word to him and made his name over in those movie pictures like I said I would, then maybe he'd lift that shadow of his off my name, maybe they'd say that whatever else he was, Henry Starr was true to his word and his friend, that he played fair and give back something for what he took. But I can't, I never even thought I could, but Somebody Else out there sure as hell can, and look what they done, look at the twist they put on things *[words to make you crazy]*, so that black is white, the poor ones is the greedy rich and the rich ones is the outlaws, you think it is a hog you are gutting but it was your mother, you know? It was your own mother and you are looking down at her and the knife is dripping in your hand.

I have no answer for that. Unless you think those scrap papers blowing up the street is what they mean by moving pictures.

I am greater than my Grandfather, and yet his curse come home, because for all anyone knows of my doings "Henry Starr" might as well be no name in the Nation, no name but traitor for giving up Cherokee

Bill. Everything good I done belongs to that no-name Outlaw, that nightwalking ghostly son of a bitch that I conjured up myself, and if I was to die tomorrow he'd just keep on, they'd keep laying holdups to him, every wild kid and cheap crook in the Nations could lay claim to it and nobody say different.

"Where are you going, Henry boy?"

*If there's nobody to remember and to read your name with what you done, then it's almost like you never really done it in the world, but only dreamed it among the blue smokes of your mind.*

"I'm going out to see if anybody remembers my name."

CROMWELL OK
Pop. 800

There were more houses and stores than he remembered; the town had grown up some. He stood masked by the shade of an awning and looked across at the store: "Munson & Todd."

In the yard a young boy with Jiminy's hair, but taller, and dressed like a cowboy, was tossing his lariat at a gatepost for practice. He looked spruce, like someone had taught him to take care of his gear. And taught him to throw a good loop.

*It was like looking at a picture of the boy in an album, small and flat and far away, and though you may have took the picture yourself and remember the taking the moment ain't in it no more, no more than life is—you can't touch through it no more, all you can do is watch like a tramp outside a window.*

Nobody in town seemed to remember his face, or connected it with the two-year-old poster on the wall of the post office naming him for the Tyro, Kansas, robbery. He wondered if Cora had posted him too. What was the difference if she had? If she did it meant he was no more to her than any thief in the world with $7500 on his head. And if she didn't, then Henry Starr had left no mark or memory there at all.

*You got no home in these people either. You ain't kin or kind.*

"Munson & Todd Genl Mdse."

What a damn pitiful waste it was, and no way to make it good, because if there ever had been a way to make that sign read "Munson & Starr" it was long gone.

*Well: maybe there never was any such chance. Nothing here ever really belonged to me—it was given, but I wouldn't take it up. The truth of it is that Henry Starr never give anything at all, and so never understood the gift —Henry Starr was a bank robber, his gift was to take things. That was his power. That was his road. That was his word.*

Maybe he had no kin or kind, no clan or Nation that was there just to keep his name for him. But he had powers of his own, and he knew how to work them, and he had something in mind to do that would write "Henry Starr" for a sign to the Seven Clans, and the whole by-God State of Oklahoma.

## PREACHER BROWN:

"Yes, there ain't no other way to say it: Henry Starr had a calling from God to rob banks. The marks was there: it come to him natural as breathing, like a gift; and he was good at it, the Lord prospered him in it according to His wisdom; and made it an instrument of good: because there's God's law which is justice, and man's law which is might, and Henry Starr had an itch, had a hunger for justice that wouldn't let him keep store under his vine and his fig tree.

"And when you looked in his eyes, you knew it was *your* call he was carrying too, and you recognized that the word he brought you was the one you would have spoken for yourself if you could have.

"Well, that's how it was for me, anyway: when he come to me I was broke in spirit, my calling come to nothing, our work broke up and the workmen killed or driven off, cruelty done to innocent children like the times of Herod, and me helpless to do anything, my words like ashes on my tongue, the Word itself become my sorrowful bread. And he looked down off that pale gray zebra-spotted horse he rode, more like some kind of spook than a horse—and he smiled, and told me: *There's more'n one way to preach folks a sermon*; and he give me a .45 pistol and a Winchester rifle and a map of the Chemical-Cattlemen's Bank of Keystone Oklahoma . . .

"A calling from the Lord to be an outlaw. Did it lead him down to Death in the end? Well: you tell me brother, what calling is it that *don't*? I used to hear folks say that the path of unrighteousness is a downward slope, and Henry Starr rolled down it like a ball of snow, gathering sin and crime as he come till the weight of it spun him faster and harder and faster and harder till he just had to go smashing all apart in one last explosion of sin and error—like he done at Stroud.

"But I say no. If getting thrown in jail and killed was proof of unrighteousness, then Daniel and Joseph wasn't prophets, and Pilate had the goods on Jesus Christ. I still say there was as much of the Lord in his going to Stroud as there is in anything, the signs was there for them that had eyes to read.

## STROUD *March 25, 1915*

"He called me to him first of all the bunch—his picked men, seven of them like it might be for the Seven Clans of the Cherokee or the seals upon the Book of Judgment—and of the Seven he called first for the Preacher to come with him and spy out the land.

"It's flat around Stroud, except for a big rise out to the Tulsa side, and low wooded hills where the creek cuts through to the south. We come in over the Tulsa hill, woods behind us where we were camped, and ahead of us half a mile the buildings strung out along both sides of the road: the Charles Hotel first, then the big red-brick opera house with a little shrunk-down steeple at the top to mock the Lord's house—as we come past they was changing over signs out front, *Birth of a Nation* was going to be held for a longer run by popular demand, folks was gonna have to wait to see Dustin Farnum in *The Squaw Man.*

"He sat on that spook-gray horse of his and looked at the sign like it made him angry. 'It's the biggest goddamn lie ever made,' he said.

" 'Held over by popular demand,' I said.

" 'So was the Golden Calf,' he says, and starts moving up the street again.

"Well: that made me look back, but he says, 'Looking for signs and portents?'—the anger switching to a laugh like it always done with him.

"On the right as we passed was the Stroud Bank—yellow brick with tall round-arched windows set into a frame of brownstone pillars. The front door was set in the corner and a man coming out that door could be covered from three quarters of the compass. A man in teller's armbands came up the street and turned in the door, his face red, the bulge of a flask on his right ham.

"The other bank, the First National, was up the street a block away on the left, also on the corner, but with two doors—one looking out on Main Street, the other fronting on Fifth. We hitched our horses across from it, by the Galloway store. Pasted to the front door was two signs: one of 'em an advertisement for a book, had this huge hooded skeleton with a scythe looking down on a picture of the globe and human bodies all tangled, and four men on galloping horses with smoke coming out of their nostrils—*The Scarlet Plague* was what the book was called; the ad said it was 'Jack London's greatest and most thrilling novel.' In little letters under the scythe they wanted to know, *'If War, Famine and Pestilence Destroyed the World, could you rebuild the Civilization in which you live?'*

"Henry Starr read it carefully. 'The real question is, if you could, would you want to?'

"That was when I noticed the sign next to it: it was a fresh handbill, WANTED FOR BANK ROBBERY HENRY STARR, with an old picture of him in the center and $10,000 underneath, as if that was his name. His face give away nothing as he saw me noticing it. 'They raised it twenty-five hundred dollars in the last week,' I told him, as if he didn't know.

"He just shrugged. It didn't make no difference to him that they had raised the price on him, despite how careful he had been these last months to keep his name and face and trademarks out of what he was doing. It should have, because the new price meant that somebody was smelling him out, and they had his face, his name hung out on the front doors of every store bank and probably ice cream parlor in the very next town he was going to hit, and that should have made a difference. But it didn't. 'Let's go in,' he said, 'I want to buy me a copy of that book.'

"So that is just what he did: went in and bought that book, and to devil me he would have to stand there jawing with the storekeeper, and give out that his name was 'Howard—Mr. Thomas Howard from St. Joseph, Missouri,' and winked at me: because the storekeeper just took his money, counted his change and give him his book, when I would have thought that every man woman and shirttail brat in the United States of America knew that 'Mr. Thomas Howard' was the name Jesse James had on when that dirty coward Robert Ford shot him dead from the back for the sake of the reward.

"Yes, and he enjoyed the joke so much that nothing would do but he must go into the Stroud State Bank to talk about opening an account, and give them 'Thomas Howard' too, and winked at me again till even I could hardly keep my countenance, only the two of us there who knew the joke.

"Yet he wasn't no wild boy like Billy the Kid, and he wasn't no cruel and greedy hypocrite like Jesse James: he was Henry Starr, and he had a taste for justice. If you asked him why he done something, why he give up his store and his goods to ride against man's law, he would joke you away: 'I had the name,' he'd say, 'I thought I might as well have the game.' He wasn't any preacher, you see, he wasn't made to bring men and women to the gospel—that wasn't his gift. Words couldn't say what he was: he was a vision, a picture of justice that you couldn't say in words, and one part of it was wrath but the other half was a way of making all the words of the mighty into a joke—yes: along with the wrath, the other half of his gift was for laughter.

"Signs and portents and taking chances for the sake of a joke—that was never the kind of thing that troubled his mind. All that worried him was the placement of the two banks, and the problem of timing the robberies to come off together; and what to do about the telephone and telegraph lines. Modern conveniences: they had a Telephone Company in Stroud, the stick-out building on Main Street, yellow brick two stories high, with a roofline notched like a 'W' against the solid blue sky, and the wires running out of it onto the poles and rising and swooping out southwest to Oklahoma City and Northeast to Tulsa. 'That's worse than the telegraph,' said Henry Starr. 'Once the wires is cut we got to be *fast*, because every gossip-mongering biddy in town will know right off that the wires is down. Don't the Bible say anything against idle chatter?'

" 'There ain't as much piety as there used to be,' I told him, for he would have his joke.

" 'Less piety, but a sight more money,' he said, as if that was all he thought about it.

"Yet he was a thoughtful man, and he studied on that book, *The Scarlet Plague*. It had a red cover, just like that other book of his he took around with him everwheres—now what do you think *it* was? Frank Little had him a red cover book that was full of political economics by Karl Marx, and he'd study on that, and I thought he give Henry Starr a copy, but no: it was just an old ripsnorter, *The Last of the Mohicans* by James Fenimore Cooper. He read that book and *The Scarlet Plague* like they was scripture.

" 'If you're in a frame of mind to think on the End of Days,' I told him, 'there's better reading than that.'

" 'If war, famine and pestilence destroyed the world,' he said, 'you wouldn't just make it over again, would you? You'd make it something else.'

" 'War, famine and pestilence,' I said, 'and greed—*A measure of wheat for a penny, and three measures of barley for a penny, and see thou hurt not the oil and the wine*.'

" 'A penny a measure,' he said, 'is that all them poor dirt farmers are getting these days?'

" 'At least that book of yours got part of it right,' I said. 'They had four horsemen on that picture, and four horsemen is what's promised—

each horse a different color, a white and a red and a black, and Death on a pale horse it don't say what color . . .' *but maybe*, I thought, *maybe it ain't colors, maybe it's white with black spots.*

"He closed the book sharp and looked at me the same. 'Then the picture's better,' he said, 'for there ain't any horses in the book.'

"And then again he smiled: 'Well,' he said, 'if it's four horses, then the bad sign ain't for us. We're seven men, and fourteen horses mostly bays. This time the different colors is on the men.'

" 'Then maybe the sign ain't for us,' I said to let him have his way —because it come to me that warning or not, the sign made no difference to me either. A man gets a call and he's got to heed it. There's nothing in the Book says he's got to make money by it, or live to a ripe age."

## TULSA *July 4, 1914–March 27, 1915*

Bill Tilghman sat in the federal marshal's office in Tulsa, the dry white light burning over his shoulder while he read the papers.

The papers talked about a crime wave in Oklahoma, and remembered the bad old days of Isaac Parker's court and the Indian Nations; but they knew what days it was, and though it looked like different gangs everywhere, down below they believed they saw the shape of a single enemy: ". . . red barbarian anarchistical race-amalgamating communist socialism, which our too-liberal institutions have allowed to flourish as a bosom serpent," as the Tulsa *Lamp* had it.

Which was about as useful to an old-time lawman as no damn idea at all. These hired-on marshals or sheriffs, bought and paid for by Consolidated Cotton or Standard Oil or Amalgamated Livestock Growers or the Katy Railroad or the Chemical–Cattlemen's Bank, they could use that kind of information: knowing it was the red barbarian anarchist race-mixing communist socialists, they could just mob up a gang of special deputies or Regulators that would wade in with rifles pistols ropes and kerosene and shoot hang burn the lot of 'em. But an old-time federal lawman like Bill Tilghman, aiming to bring law down on the guilty, not caring anything about red anarchist race-mixing communists but keeping his eye sharp for the professional full-time cradle-to-coffin outlaw—for him that kind of trail was worse than no trail at all. Like tracking a deer through a buffalo wallow.

But that was the kind of thing an old deer hunter buffalo hunter man hunter like Tilghman got paid to do.

The stack of newspapers, crime reports and warrants on his desk were the wallow: but if you looked close you could see there were some tracks in there that weren't just the herd milling around, nor yet red barbarian race-mixing communists, but sign as clear and personal as a signature—the signature of someone who knew his business.

From the welter of obviously amateur crimes, and crimes committed by known criminals, Tilghman culled out a third set where you couldn't be sure was it one or the other, picking the cases as much by a kind of hound-dog sense as by any kind of logic. They came from all over the center of the state, they bore all the marks of local troubles, the gangs varied in size from as few as three to as many as eight, varied too as to the color and apparent civilian occupations of the criminals. Yet they had some peculiarities.

In Okmulgee, for example: the C O&G payroll job. The robbers had cased it perfectly, knew exactly when and how to hit the office, knew when the payroll was delivered and where to find the file in which the company's blacklist of union workers was kept (they burned it). It looked like an "inside job," involving disaffected oil drillers. On the other hand, the smoothness of execution suggested the hand of a professional—the typical oil-field roughneck running more to strong-arm than finesse.

The robbers spoke little, communicating their wishes by means of significant gestures with their weapons—two were armed with six-shot revolvers, one with a pump shotgun sawed short, the fourth with a rifle. Indeed the manager could recall only one full exchange of words: when the gang entered the manager had asked, "What do you want?" and the leader of the band had replied, "Mr. Rockefeller sent us to collect his share of the take."

The Katy Flyer was robbed by men wearing overalls and a strong smell of cow shit, which argued for a bunch of angry farmers. But they had taken the train with a smoothness that reminded you of the James Gang. Three masked men cleaned out the passenger car, courteously refusing to take anything from ladies present, or from men in working clothes—one frugal farmer, in threadbare clothes but with nearly $900 in his pockets from a livestock sale in Vinita, saved his entire fund in this way. But they cleaned out the express car; and as they turned to leave the leader reached out and cut from the conductor's belt the leather wallet in which ticket receipts were kept. "I paid full price for my ticket," he said, "but I think I'm entitled to the same rebate you give Mr. Rockefeller." And he removed from the wallet cash amounting to 20 percent of the price of a through ticket from Vinita to Tulsa—20 percent being the amount of the rebate Mr. Rockefeller is said to have obtained from those railroads who wished to have the business that only Standard Oil could give them.

The company store robbery in Coal County: there had been a "massacre" at a strikers' picnic, when special deputies attempting to make an arrest had opened up on a crowd of miners, women and children; pistols, shotguns and Winchesters blazed away for fifteen minutes, hitting more than two dozen people running in panic for the woods and even some who had thrown themselves down on the ground, maiming a dozen permanently and killing eight, including a woman and an infant at the breast (the shotgun blowing infant, breast and blankets into a single bloody mash). Some of the miners had gone off into the hills, coming down to bushwhack the guards and deputies and steal what they needed to keep going. Robbing the big company store looked like part of that: half a dozen men, armed with a mix of revolvers, shotguns and rifles, entered the place late on a Friday, with the till full and about a dozen deputies lined up to get their pay and nobody on lookout. The bandits cleared at least $18,000 from the till and safe, enough ammunition to equip a battalion of cavalry, all of the deputies' own money, badges, weapons, boots—and pants, which they required the deputies to strip off.

As his men were preparing to leave, the leader of the gang (who wore a mask and spoke with a Hunky accent that sounded fake, like a Mex imitating a Hunky) stepped over to the counter and began testing the balances on which the storekeeper weighed the meat and vegetables he sold to the miners. To no one's surprise he discovered the scales were crooked, the bottom of the weighing pan thickened with three plates of lead. "This company never give honest weight on anything," said one man (apparently a miner); to which the leader replied, "Well then we must set the balance right." He took a large hammer and some nails from a shelf and nailed the unleaded pan to the counter. Then he took something wrapped in rags, laid it in the nailed-down pan, and said: "Tell Mr. Rockefeller that we got something here weighs more than all the coal oil and gold he's got."

On examination the rags proved to be the torn and bloodstained fragments of a cotton infant's blanket.

What was peculiar about it to Tilghman was that line about Rockefeller—that and the fact that they left the blanket instead of gunning down any of the deputies, at least three of whom had been involved in the "massacre."

The plantation store and KKK meeting in Okfuskee—that looked out of place in the series too, because nobody in any of the other robberies had been colored. But there was the same careful preparation, control and timing, the same mix of weapons displayed. And this: as they backed out the front door of the Consolidated Cotton Company, the bandit leader noticed a blind Negro with a beggar's tin plate seated in the shade of the porch. He reached into the swag sack, pulled out a roll of bills (perhaps a hundred dollars in all) and dropped it in the plate, and next to it a folded note which had obviously been prepared beforehand—a circumstance that incidentally made the blind Negro himself suspect for a time, and a candidate for lynching by a mob of those white croppers whom the company had brought in to displace the Negroes, until someone in the crowd suggested that they had probably used the blind old Negro for a lookout, at which point the lynching and the indictment were laughed to death. (The company reclaimed the hundred dollars.) The note had read: "I O U 10 cts., John D. Rockefeller"—a reference to one of Rockefeller's favorite modes of charity.

Surprisingly, the president of Consolidated Cotton himself had risen to the joke, defending Mr. Rockefeller's record as a progressive businessman and philanthropist—and the newspapers, following up the story, uncovered the fact (hitherto carefully concealed) that Consolidated Cotton was indirectly owned by Standard Oil, which was acquiring rights to drill for oil in the cotton fields. The matter would be unraveling for years in the courts and tribal councils.

So: whatever the different elements might be of each robbery and each gang, Tilghman believed he could see a single characteristic set of tracks in the paper wallow—one very smart, very good professional robber behind it all. Yet the pattern didn't match that of any of the professionals currently on the loose, whose signatures Tilghman could read in the dark—Jack Spencer, Henry Starr, Bill Coughlan, Kid Wilson, "Doc" Marquard. They were men with reputations, and proud of them. But this one: in every place he was different—never the same voice, face, clothes, color or motive twice, no territory or type of folks that was special to him.

And that, of course, was his signature. Tilghman had no human name to put to the Outlaw—as he called him in his own mind, as if he were the only one, or the only one that mattered. But that there was one man behind all of those robberies, with real tracks that could be followed till they came home to him, Tilghman did not doubt. If you plotted the robberies out on a map and marked the map for time, you could trace this Outlaw's ride like a big flattened circle through east-central Oklahoma, from just north of Tulsa to Tishomingo in the south, no farther east than Catoosa and no farther west than Oklahoma City.

Just enough time between jobs for a man who had set things up in advance to move from one place to another—a dozen robberies in all between July 1913 and August 1914, collecting once a month like he was on salary.

In all that time, he had never once hit a bank: all the bank cases on Tilghman's books were either amateurs or known professionals. But then starting in September 1914 there was a series of odd little bank robberies, beginning in Keystone and Kiefer, Tupelo, Wardville, and Pontotoc down south, then northward toward Tulsa, hitting Byars, Glencoe and Prue in December. Then two little loops south and then west out of Tulsa, hitting Beggs and Owasso, Terlton, Garber and Vera. If you weren't looking for it you wouldn't see it—no Rockefeller jokes, and it wasn't the same gangs of four and five but always two men working alone, slick and quick and professional. Nothing obviously political, except maybe for the first one at Keystone—though there wasn't a bank in the state that hadn't foreclosed on farmers or taken over a sharecropped plantation or bankrolled a company with union trouble. No, the only signature to it the first time you looked was just that same trick of never doing it the same way twice—that, and the fact that all these slick, no-name robberies followed roughly the same flattened arc south and east from the outskirts of Tulsa to the coal country, and then back to the north and west, hitting banks at two-week intervals regular as clockwork—again like a man going round a regular collection route, with plans made and a partner ready to go in every different part of the state.

Six times now by Tilghman's count he had made the big looping circle of central Oklahoma, and Tilghman was dead sure he would try for seven, though he could not say why. Outlaws like this one never knew when to stop, when to bank their winnings and leave the game. He guessed that if they were the kind to bank winnings, they wouldn't have become outlaws in the first place. A man like that will ignore the odds and the numbers to ride a lucky streak to the end, never recognizing it was done until the luck turned over and dumped him flat. Seven was a lucky number, the Outlaw had come out on top six times, he was sure to try for seven.

The only question was where would he go. The first six times around he had swung a series of elongated loops that always seemed to come back here to Tulsa. Maybe that was home to him, out of which he rode wide into the world and to which he returned for rest and praise, kids and grown men that should know better admiring the local badman in the barroom or pool hall. Maybe he had some protection here. Outside of the city the only quarter of the compass he hadn't struck was east and northeast, which was the old Cherokee Nation. Maybe that was where he'd go next . . .

Except that he'd already had the chance to do that, and he hadn't taken it. Six times around the circle from southeast to north, and never once had he touched the Cherokee Nation. Maybe he figured somehow he owed the Cherokee Nation for good that was done him there, or for bad that he done back before he begun these circles. Or maybe he had protection there, maybe he was Cherokee himself and so he kept clear of robbing his own.

Newspapers and police reports weren't enough. If Tilghman was going to put a name to the Outlaw, he needed to taste the dust in his trail and smell the air for his scent. So Tilghman now began to ride the loop in the Outlaw's trace, talking again to witnesses and victims of the original robberies and the more recent bank jobs—bored witnesses, who had answered the same questions days or weeks or months ago for local police county sheriff state cops federal marshals reporters friends relatives, and so dealt snappishly, offhandedly with the old marshal sitting patiently, looking steadily at them with eyes so cold and gray—so cold that suddenly they felt a sharp chill off them and they'd reach down to come up with something new, something they'd held back or forgotten for the others, because it seemed trivial or a foolish thing to have noticed—but they told him, just to have something between Tilghman's eyes and themselves, even if it was just noise:

"The leader, he walked like a cowboy, he might have been an Injun, he moved and talked young but his hands looked old. When he come in, before he pulled his gun he muttered something under his breath, and I said 'What?'—and then he said, and pulled his six-gun, he said, 'This is a robbery! Don't move and you won't get . . .' "

*What was it he muttered before he pulled the gun?*

"Something that sounded like 'Something's up' or 'Don't gum it up . . .' "

*Thumbs up.*

"That's right! That was it: 'Thumbs up!' was what he said, maybe just like you'd say something for good luck, or . . ."

*Thumbs up,* thought Tilghman, *what he said was 'Thumbs up and stand steady.'*

---

Well, who else could it be?—that would leave the Cherokee Nation alone because it was his people, and because he had done the Nation in the old days with Cherokee Bill; that could organize things so completely and well, keep the gunplay low but twist a joke into your ribs that was sharp as a knife blade; that would hide and dodge and duck away but give you just the whiff of his scent, the flash of his face like a tip of his hat before he disappeared in the smoke and dust . . .

So now Tilghman had the name, and he went back to the loops on the map: he might start the next cycle spinning those loops of his backwards from north to south, but he'd been six times around and never done that. Tilghman reckoned he would start to the south again—not as far south as Coal County, because he'd been swinging his last loops tighter, no more than a morning on the train or a day's hard ride out of Tulsa. Knowing that much, if you looked next for the towns with the fattest banks, a railroad line, and woodsy country to run away and hide in after, you could expect Henry Starr in any of half a dozen possible places between Stroud at one end of the range, and Okmulgee at the other.

The town of Bristow sat on the Frisco line just up the tracks between Tulsa and Stroud, with a telegraph link over to Okmulgee and a good straight road that way.

So Bill Tilghman took the train to Bristow, got himself rooms in the Frisco Hotel and arranged with the livery for a good horse to be kept saddled and ready for him every day. After breakfast he'd cross the street and sit in the telegraph office reading the papers and listening to the mechanical cricket clicking and chirping away. He was done figuring. He was just waiting like a buffalo hunter hidden in a blind made of nothing but distance and downwind.

On the afternoon of March 27, 1915, at 1:25 in the afternoon the steel cricket died. The clerk tapped away, trying to revive it, but it was no good. The line was down somewhere southwest of Bristow.

Tilghman got up and folded his paper. He asked the telegraph boy to wire Tulsa for some marshals to take the next train to Stroud. Then he crossed the street to the livery, mounted the horse that stood saddled and ready with a Winchester in the scabbard and rations and ammunition in the saddlebags, and rode out of town down the railroad line heading southwest for Depew, Stroud and however many towns southward he might have to search to find the man who was, by this time, stepping through the door of his chosen bank with his pistol in his hand saying, "Thumbs up, boys, and stand steady!"

## STROUD *March 27, 1915*

From the Stroud *Democrat*, April 2, 1915:

> They came in a covered wagon from the jungles of the Osage Nation Country, north of Tulsa, and camped in the woods two miles east of town. They gave themselves out as hunters, and came frequently to our city to purchase supplies and ammunition.

The rest of the bunch came in by ones and twos: the best of the men he had chosen so carefully in each different part of the state. All they had in common was the secret he trusted them with, which was his true name. For the rest of it, Brown was a preacher, while Romero (who had retired to Oklahoma for his health after four years with Pancho Villa) was a Catholic; Estes was a peckerwood ex-tenant and one time or another in his life most likely made one in a lynch mob, while Nat Shields was a black cropper with a warrant on him for shooting the sheriff who served his family their dispossess. Bergman (the ex-Wobbly oil rigger who had dynamited three wells and a storage tank after they busted the strike in Red Fork) was some kind of Hunky or maybe a Jew. Jack Shays was an old cowboy who had scraped enough off his wages to buy a small ranch, and he had it in for Jewbankers (it was one word to him) because of losing his place for debt —burnt it to the ground the day after the auction: house barns corrals feed . . . and livestock too. When he remembered the horses screaming he liked to get hard drunk, but when he was sober he was a cool hand.

All they had in common was their grievance, their secret and their quality—and that they trusted Henry Starr enough so that when he said *Come on*, here they were: watching each other uneasily, waiting on Henry Starr to speak the word.

They were to go masked, but he was going in with his face open. Let them go after the money, that wasn't what Henry Starr wanted in Stroud. What he wanted was to let the whole state of Oklahoma know it wasn't any Oklahoma crime wave or red race-mixing anarchist revolution they had been looking at, but just the deeds of an outlaw named Henry Starr, who come from the Cherokee Nation but understood all the different kinds of justice there was and showed people how a man could ride out after it. And when he finished in Stroud he'd have a name that would be good in the Nations for as long as people had heart to remember, not for the things he hadn't done like dying with Cherokee Bill, but for being the Outlaw who hoodwinked Robin Hood and out-Jesse'd the James brothers, who won where the Daltons lost, who knew the taste of justice and lived by it, and run the law ragged all over the Nations.

He couldn't wait anymore for the people out there to read "Henry Starr" behind the mask of the great Outlaw in which he had covered himself. Things were getting out of hand. That poor kid and old man in Bub Houston's country taking blame because nobody could put "Henry Starr" to the robberies there were just signs of what would come if he didn't take ahold of things again.

It was hard enough trying to live up to Tom Starr and Jesse James. Now it was himself he had to climb over, or something he had made out of himself, which had got away and outgrown him, and become like some kind of know-all see-all be-all bare-hand-bear-killing giant—so big and heavy that its weight made you cramp yourself all humble, so strong that it could eat your ghost and shit your name on the ground.

Yet there was something in the situation that made him want to laugh, it was damn funny a man going out to climb over his own ghost. "Henry Starr—he was the smartest outlaw who ever lived, so smart that the only one who could ever really climb over him was Henry Starr himself."

After the noon meal on the twenty-seventh, they were ready to go.

Preacher Brown, riding his old white gelding, pulled out two hours ahead of Henry Starr and Estes and Shays, who stayed behind to break up the camp. They would meet by the stockyards in Stroud, coming in from opposite directions, at 2:30 P.M. Romero, Bergman and Nat Shields rode with Brown, Shields leading the string of spare horses. Shields would wait with the horses in the blackjack thickets southeast of town—he didn't like it, but Henry Starr had to keep his word to Bub Houston that nothing he did would point the law toward the colored people of Okfuskee and Lincoln counties. When they had dodged any close pursuers off their track in the tangles of deadfall and branch bars they would switch to fresh mounts, split up seven different ways, and meet again at Henry Starr's place in Tulsa for the cut.

Shays and Estes worked with silent intensity burying the remnants of the fire, loading the gear back into the wagon even though they'd never use it again. "Bob," said Henry Starr quietly, and held out his pocket watch. Estes dusted his hands, and with his eyes buried in the air before him walked blindly to his reddish-brown bay horse, mounted and trotted stiffly out of the clearing.

After an interval of five minutes Henry Starr and Shays followed him. When they stopped at the foot of the two telegraph poles and climbed to the crosspiece they could see Estes breasting the top of the hill between them and Stroud. Six miles off invisible to the southwestward but as clear and certain as anything in Henry Starr's sight or thought, Brown and his men were doing the same to the lines from Stroud down to Oklahoma City. *And maybe somewhere out there Bill Tilghman is waiting too, smelling my ghost even if he ain't put the name to it yet, but after today I better look sharp for gray eyes.* He smiled howdy to Bill Tilghman through the sky northeastward to Tulsa.

The cut telegraph and telephone wires fell to the roadside, they clambered down, Henry Starr bent and began rapidly wrapping the fallen wire into a loop. "Go on," he said to Shays, who mounted his black horse and took off at a jerky trot, hitching in his saddle as if he had caught the jitter spark from the cut wire. Henry Starr tossed the roll of wire into the brush. He mounted and set his horse in Shays's track at an easy walk, letting the ex-cowboy disappear over the hill toward Stroud.

Henry Starr kept his interval, three minutes behind Shays, so he was the last of the three to pass up the main street of Stroud, the Appaloosa nodding her spooky black-and-white head and jingling her bridle as if on parade, his eyes checking one last time to see where sheriff and deputies, businessmen and customers, locals and visitors were standing or sitting, playing pool or sipping whiskey or licking ice-cream cones in Balcomb's or buying groceries from Baum or Brogan or Galloway—fixing every thing and person in Stroud in his mind so that he was dead-sure certain, because it was all on him and that was how he wanted it, because until he had said his word he and his men were simply hunters in town to buy supplies, and Stroud was a nowhere village calling itself a city and nobody listening, and nothing had happened there and probably nothing ever would.

Paul Curry looked out the front door of Brogan's store, northward past the hanging sign of the First National Bank, up the street toward the Opera House. Except for a farmer on a bay horse jogging past him heading for the stockyards the street was empty. He wondered was that the man who had ordered the hogs, but from the look of him he didn't have cash enough to buy a slab of bacon let alone four big hogs killed, hung and butchered out. Curry leaned the hog-killing rifle against the doorpost—a big-bore Winchester with a cut-down barrel. It was a clumsy-looking gun, a dirt farmer's gun, a butcher boy's gun, and he hated it. Bad enough his father had lost the store to Brogan, bad enough working as boy where he should have been coming into the property, but Brogan had to have him killing hogs like a butcher—stand just far enough off so the head snot and blood don't spray on you and blow their piggy brains out. There was men out in the woods hunting deer, with rifles long and lean and clean-looking. This gun was more a kind of club, beat a critter's brains out with it instead of piercing its heart with one clean long shot across a big empty distance full of morning light.

He envied Matt Taylor, who couldn't run the football on the same field with Paul Curry when they played at the high school, but who had a beauty of a Remington and let Paul Curry try it one night, shining rats' eyes on the big garbage dump east of town and popping their heads off with single shots. Paul had tried the same thing with the hog gun in daylight, but you had to come in too close for shooting anything as little as a rat. He'd tried barking squirrels out of a cottonwood tree near the stockyards, chipping bark aplenty but never hitting fine enough to knock the critter off his branch.

It was the slack of the day. He could look forward to sweeping out till Mr. Titus delivered the hogs; then the rest of the day shooting 'em, skinning and dropping the guts out, and hanging the carcasses up to drip and stink. He'd be dripping and stinking himself. He'd have flies in his eyes and nose and hair. *Buck that pigskin through the line, Curry*, said the coach. Now I know where the pigskin come from.

Mr. Penniman hitched his wagon in front of the Stroud Opera House, right in front of the big sign that showed how *The Birth of a Nation* was still playing there, and he said, "See now, I told you it would still be here" to the little girl sitting next to him on the buckboard seat.

"We'll see it now," she told him.

"No," he said (he had said this before and before and before), "they won't be starting till five. We have to see Mr. Shaffer first about Mother's pictures, then we—"

"I don't want to see Mother's pictures," she said, "I want to see the ones that move."

Mother is dead, he thought, Mother is dead and neither she nor her pictures will ever move again, but he said, "Later, we'll come see how they move later." A man rode up the street as he lifted his daughter down, just a cowboy trotting his black horse to get through town as quick as possible, horse's shoes making a rapid clackclackclackclack on the pavement, heartbeat quick, heading nowhere. When Mr. Penniman had been a cowboy he had never just drifted, but was always pointing directly toward the ranch he would someday buy, always heading somewhere. He had got this far, that the bank had notes on his ranch and his wife was dead and all he was going to have of her was pictures and a little rattle-head kid that every time he saw her smile it made his wife come alive and die for him all over again. *Enjoy the ride, cowboy,* he thought after the passing rider, *it will beat whatever you find at the end of it.*

Westward four blocks on Main Street, Mr. Patrick, the teller at the Stroud State Bank, and Dr. Vincent bumped into each other in the doorway of Burton's drugstore. Dr. Vincent's offices occupied the second story above the Stroud Bank's competitor, the First National, which sat on the corner just two doors down. They each said "Excuse me" at the same time. Maybe that and bumping into each other accounted for the embarrassment each saw in the other, as if they had committed an imprudent intimacy instead of just bumping into each other.

Patrick walked stiff-legged away, and stopped in front of Brogan's grocery, between Burton's and the First National Bank. He watched a man on horseback coming at a nervous jerky trot and decided to cross after he had passed. From the deeps of the store he heard the whisk whisk of a broom, and Brogan calling to his boy Paul Curry from the pens in back, *The hogs is here . . . the hogs is here*. He paused and popped a mint into his mouth and coughed experimentally. The mint was a lozenge for his throat, always bad in the blowing dust and pollen of spring, and also a mask for the whiskey-sweet smell of his breath after a quick sniff at Carlock's saloon. When the man had passed (a stranger on a black horse, looked like a cowboy), he crossed without going to the corner of 5th and Main, avoiding the line of sight from the doors and windows of the First National Bank looking out on Main Street. The bank clerks in this little town were all out to better themselves at each other's expense, and there were two who had already applied for Patrick's own job at the Stroud State Bank. His job had sides to it that made a quick trip to Carlock's worth the risks, but it was his, as good as anything he was likely to get, and he wasn't about to let it be tattletaled away.

As he walked up the street toward the Stroud State Bank at the corner of Main and 4th streets, he saw Mr. Penniman and his little girl standing in front of Shaffer's Photographic Studio and touched his hat, but Penniman was too absorbed in the child to notice another adult. "Please," he was saying, "it really isn't too much to expect, now is it, Emmy?" as if the kid was a henpecking old wife instead of a six-year-old spoiled brat. The little girl flounced and put out her lip. Big man like that making a fool of himself over a kid, thought Patrick contemptuously, and his hand rose unconsciously to finger the diamond stickpin that held his tie to his shirt—a gift from his mother, it had been her father's, given to him on his promotion. It would take more than mints to fool her, he thought grimly.

Up the street came another lone rider, and Patrick recognized him by the Appaloosa he was riding as one of the hunters camping out at the Bradford place—"Mr. Howard," he called, tipping his hat as the man rode by, loose in the saddle and not a care in the world likely—face all brown from living out of doors, that was the life, and Mr. Howard had property too, had been into the bank inquiring about arrangements for a transfer of funds—some men had it all, thought Patrick, as he opened the glassed door of the bank and nodded to the tellers behind the brass bars of their cages.

Two blocks away Dr. Vincent left Burton's drugstore with a wrapped parcel of arsenic powder. The arsenic was medicinal, but he felt a little ashamed of his taste for tipping a little bit into his glass of whiskey before bedtime, so he held it close to his side, concealing it from the lone rider who came jogging easily up the street: part Indian by his physiognomy, Vincent guessed—his horse was an odd one, like a white horse that had been dipped headfirst in oil-mottled water, then weirdly splotched and dashed with black paint on the rump. The rider turned the corner of 4th Street, likely headed for the stockyards. Probably a delivery of cattle on the 2:55 from Tulsa.

Henry Starr passed the yellow brick and brownstone-arched windows of the Stroud State on the right and then the store-front First National on the left, and as he came up to the brick facade and W-notched roofline of the telephone company building he saw the line crews—two of them—clucking their teams out of the alleyway, heading out of town in opposite directions. Henry Starr smiled, something must be wrong with the wires. The rapid clickclick of his horse's shoes on the pavement was suddenly deadened as he turned off Main Street onto packed dirt.

He rounded the corner to the stockyards and there they were, the five of them with their horses drop-reined alongside of the cattle pens. He dismounted and looked them over—Preacher Brown working his cud, the others showing fish-eye or bull-snort depending on how they liked to face their fear, but all of them ready to go. And no reason in God's world to stop them.

"Twenty-five minutes till three," he said. "Let's go."

He led the way up the railroad tracks, back toward town. Up ahead the tracks vanished in a long V at the heart of which was a puff of steam and the swelling node of black that was the 2:55 freight from Tulsa. The trainmen stood on the depot platform. Sheriff McCarron stepped up from his office in the jail to join them—he liked to make sure no bad characters jumped off a boxcar in Stroud, Oklahoma. He stood, hands on hips, swaying on the heels of his Texas boots as Henry Starr, Estes and Romero turned up 6th Street and headed for the Stroud State, their movement mirrored one block behind by Preacher Brown, with Shays and Bergman, who turned up 5th for the First National.

Main Street was nearly empty under the bright sun that etched geometric shadows into the macadam. To the right the sunlight spotted the penny-ante marquee of the opera house, *The Birth of a Nation*. To the left Preacher Brown with Shays and Bergman came stalking around the corner, paused in the dead spot where the corner pillar blocked street views from inside the First National, pulled masks up over their faces, drew pistols and a sawed-off shotgun from under their dusters and disappeared into the bank. Henry Starr tapped Romero on the shoulder, and the man halted, taking post across from the Stroud State Bank where he could watch the whole intersection, especially the street up from the depot and the corner-set front door of the bank. Then Henry Starr stepped into the street, empty out to the horizon at one end and to the rising line of wood-roughened hills at the other, crossed swiftly to the bank and went up three steps to the door.

Pinned inside the glass was a picture of himself.

WANTED FOR ROBBERY
HENRY STARR $15,000 REWARD.

It was a fair likeness as such things went. They had made him look like a cross between Geronimo and a Mexican faro dealer. He looked himself in the eyes as he pushed open the door of the bank.

---

Mr. Patrick was seated at his desk talking to Pike Eason, doing Mr. Charles's dirty work for him. Mr. Charles got to give charity bundles at Christmastime and preach the lesson in Bible class, and Patrick got to turn people down for loans and foreclose his neighbors' property. Mr. Charles liked to hide behind things. His daddy had given him the Charles Bank, and he had let the Stroud State people buy him out and hire him as chief cashier, only so he could say it wasn't himself squeezing the eagle's nuts so tight. "I'm sorry, Pike," said Patrick, "it ain't my say-so."

"I'm good for the money next month," said Pike—*s*'s whistling through a gap tooth. "Picked up a job drilling on the new rig out by Spooner's."

"They say the Wobblies aim to close it down . . ."

"No, Pat, no," said Eason, "I . . . there's boys needs the work bad enough they ain't gonna stop for no Wobblies. *I* ain't likely gonna stop for no Wobblies, am I, Pat?" (His eyes were narrowed.) "Not with you boys holding paper on me . . ."

"I'm sorry," said Patrick, "but it ain't my bank."

"I'm glad to hear you talk that way," said someone, and Patrick raised his eyes to see Mr. Howard standing behind Eason. "Hold to that and you and I should have no trouble."

Mr. Howard was holding a large-caliber revolver in his hand and pointing it at Mr. Patrick's nose.

Henry Starr met the clerk's eyes and winked; it was very important that things appear to be quiet, clear and controlled, and there was a kind of luck in having the farmer sitting between them not knowing what was happening—it was as if Henry Starr and Patrick were playing a kind of joke on Mr. Eason, standing behind him making faces or holding up cow horns where Eason couldn't see. He saw Patrick's fear and doubt; it was running through his head should he duck or fight or yell or run or grab for the gun in his desk? What was expected of him? What was a man supposed to do?—and Henry Starr aimed to make it easy for him, gesturing with the gun sort of friendly as he said, "Thumbs up, and stand steady."

Patrick did not seem as grateful for the suggestion as he should have been, he hesitated—

And at that lunatic moment a sound broke out behind Henry Starr like the rattle of some impossibly huge iron snake . . .

---

From the Stroud *Democrat*:

. . . or a boy raking a stick along a picket fence, and when Mr. Charles turned to look out through the bars of the teller's window he found himself looking down the twin barrels of a shotgun in the hands of the second robber—who, unlike his colleague, had muffled his face in a bandanna.

Meanwhile Mr. Eason had the presence of mind not to turn around, but had perforce to guess at what was transpiring behind his back by reading the expressions of horror and resolution that alternated on the bank teller's face. Mr. Patrick sat rooted to his chair, like a bird fascinated by the sinister eyes of a serpent, looking at the unmasked face of the outlaw, unable to move. The robber gestured with his pistol, as if to end the clerk's perplexity, and instructed him to open the safe or be shot down like a dog where he sat . . .

Patrick gave in and stood up slowly, raising his hands with his thumbs turned up.

Estes, meanwhile, had lined up Mr. Charles and the two tellers against the wall near the vault, and Henry Starr sent Eason to join them. With his bandanna muffling his face, Estes tried to throw all the menace he could into his eyes. But this didn't seem intimidating enough, so he kept making gestures with the shotgun, and felt better when he saw his hostages in comic unison haul in their bellies and try to turn away from him—yet once wasn't enough, he had to keep doing it over and over to be sure it was still working.

Henry Starr walked behind Patrick toward the safe which sat behind the teller's cages. The clerk's eyes lit on a pair of canvas sacks sitting on a shelf, and in his most businesslike manner he took the first one up and turned to give it to the robber—it was heavy, but contained only dimes.

Henry Starr looked at the clerk as if he were seriously disappointed in the lad. Then he reached forward suddenly with his left hand, and plucked his mother's diamond stickpin out of Patrick's tie. "I'll swap you my dimes for this thing," said the robber. "Now open the safe." At this point Patrick noticed that the .45 in the outlaw's hand was indeed on full cock, and somehow the plucking out of the diamond stickpin had made him feel as if a large hole had been made in his starched shirtfront and an icy bolt of air had touched the eye of his naked belly. He put the bag of dimes down on the counter. "The safe," said Henry Starr again, and Patrick turned . . . but at this point the open vault door caught his eye; he felt suddenly that all of this was a kind of dream or play in which a certain part had been prescribed for him though he could not have said by whom. He was beginning to feel put upon; they were trying to rob Mr. Charles's bank and so far he was the only one who had been robbed (his mother's precious stickpin!), and if ever he had, he now certainly owed nothing to Mr. Charles or the corporation that owned the Stroud State Bank. But this bandit had come down on him and done him hurt, and anyway if he was a man he was supposed to put off these robbers, so he headed for the vault—stopped when a hand of almost metallic hardness clamped itself painfully on his shoulder and the robber said again, "The safe," and he remembered that "Mr. Howard" had discussed with him the bank's procedures for keeping cash deposits protected, and he had told him that they used their modern safe rather than the old vault, which held only bank files and loan records.

Patrick now stood in front of the safe, his shoulder still tingled, he could not get over how in the midst of his sense of being in a dream—which made his guts feel air-light and his vision smoky—there had been the hard cold iron of that hand on him; he had never felt anything so hard in his life, like a set of steel-spring–driven iron teeth.

"Patrick!" moaned Mr. Charles, and for the life of him the clerk could not tell if he was pleading with Patrick to somehow save the bank's assets or to hurry up and give the bandits what they wanted. It didn't matter: Patrick had his orders. "I can't open the safe," he said stubbornly, thinking resentfully, *let Charles do the dirty work for once, it's his goddamn bank not mine, why should I have to stand for this, why should I have to lose my . . .*

From the Stroud *Democrat*:

"You *can* open it," said the bandit, "and if you don't I will blow your G——— d——— brains out." For the first time in the ordeal the iron nerve of Mr. Patrick wavered. The vicious Cherokee blood in the veins of the outlaw surged again through his brain, and he leveled his gun a second time at the head of the cashier.

But just at this critical juncture . . .

There was a jingle from the bells above the door and Starr moved swiftly, stepping toward the back wall and turning so that with a flick of his gun hand he could cover the door and still hold the drop on Patrick—but there was nothing, nobody there to be seen at all, and for one loud tick of the heart everyone in the bank felt the terrible eruption of absolute blank uncertainty into what had been (they now remembered almost fondly) the very safe and orderly procedure of the robbery so far.

"Hi!" said a small girl's voice, and when Starr and Patrick looked down over the counter Patrick recognized the little Penniman girl, pert and pouty in her white go-to-town dress; the little spoiled brat had given her old man the slip at the photographer's up the block . . .

The door swung open again, a man, and Patrick was afraid it would be Penniman, but the man was tugging a bandanna up over his lower face—it was another robber, whose spread hands and shrugged shoulders made him look sheepish despite the Winchester he held in one hand. "I couldn't do nothing," he complained, in Mexican-accented English, "she . . . I mean, what I was suppose to . . ."

"Well," said Henry Starr . . .

—from the Stroud *Democrat*:

"Well," sneered the bandit, "this sure spoils our play."

—from the Stroud *Messenger*:

"Oh hell, she's balling up the game. All right, kid, stick around for the big show."

—from the Tulsa *Lamp*:

"Well G——— d——— me," said the murderous half-breed, "if this don't spoil our fun."

—from the Tulsa *Democrat*:

"G——— d——— it all," he cursed wildly, "now our little game is spoiled."

—from the *Appeal to Reason*:

"Well, little girl," said the outlaw, "if you will just be quiet you may see something instructive."

"Well," said Henry Starr with a laugh, "if you hang around cattle, you got to expect some shit on your boots." He thought for a second, then motioned the man at the door to come all the way in and cover Patrick. Romero had followed orders, watching the street to keep intruders away, and also being damn sure not to pop any peaceful citizens unnecessarily, and it was funny thinking of Romero trying to bend his mind around the problem of a little pinafore girl traipsing into the bank in the middle of the robbery. On the other hand, now the problem was his, and maybe it was Romero's turn to have himself a laugh.

"If this clerk here doesn't start opening that safe," he told Romero, "kill him and get the boss man to do it."

He picked up the bag of dimes and stepped out around the counter. The little girl watched him complacently. She knew the bag was for her. It always was. The man put his gun away, bent and picked her up and set her on a low stool by the door. "There," he said, and he smiled—she knew a lot about smiles, and she liked the one he gave her. Then she felt the heavy bag plop into her lap with a chinkling sound like tiny bells.

From the Stroud *Democrat*:

For possibly the first time in the life of this seemingly heartless robber, he turned his lustful eyes from the glitter of gold to present himself in service to a human being. He put the bag of pennies in her lap saying, "Play with these; I will buy you an ice cream when I come back."

From the Stroud *Messenger*:

. . . saying, "Here kiddie, go buy yourself some ice cream."

From the Tulsa *Lamp*:

. . . saying, "Take this and shut up, or I will make you sorry."

From the Tulsa *Democrat*:

. . . saying, "Why don't you run off and go see the picture show?"

From the *Appeal to Reason*:

. . . saying, "If you sit quiet you will be perfectly safe. We mean no harm to anyone but this bank. Later you may take this money and go buy yourself some ice cream."

"There is an ice cream store across the street," said the man. "Would you like some ice cream?"

Of course she wouldn't say because she wasn't supposed to take things from strangers, but she wanted, so she said, "Well but I can't cross the street by myself," and suddenly she could tell from the man's smile that he knew what she wished, and he would, and she felt her belly and face and ears go all tingly and she thought, *Fudge-y, I'll have some fudge-y.* "You just sit there like a good little girl," he said, "and I'll take you across when I'm done here."

Patrick had the safe open and was filling the sack with currency. "Watch that he doesn't stuff it with small bills," said Henry Starr, crossing rapidly to where Estes held the others against the wall. He grabbed Mr. Charles by the lapels and rapped him sharply against the wall. "Go into the vault," he said, "get out your unregistered mortgage files."

From the Stroud *Democrat*:

"I want what's in here too," said the bandit, "we mean to make a clean sweep of you." He compelled Mr. Charles to open the vault drawers, but finding only small bills and bank records (as the banker had told him he would) the bandit became enraged, stuffed papers and currency at once into the stove where they were consumed.

From the Tulsa *Lamp*:

. . . nearly foamed at the lips in his anger, and hurled the papers into the black maw of the coal stove, where the fire consumed them.

From the *Appeal to Reason*:

"Well," said the bandit looking at the great heap of papers, in which were recorded the struggles and sufferings of the region's oppressed sons of toil, "I see that you are in the robber business yourself."

Henry Starr stepped into the vault on the banker's heels and saw him go straight to a particular drawer—correctly labeled. He used the pistol to motion him toward the coal stove in the corner of the lobby, and when the banker had stuffed the papers in Henry Starr pulled a small flask from his jacket pocket, poured a sharp-smelling liquid on the papers and ignited them with a match that made them explode instantaneously in a roar that flashed tongues at the bandit and leaped up the wide-open flue.

"Damn!" said Pike Eason. "Well I be God *damn!*" He was wondering if his own note had just gone up in smoke.

Patrick was rising from the front of the safe with the sack of currency in his hands, and Starr pointed at him and at Banker Charles, and Estes and Romero began backing toward the door, Estes covering the others with the shotgun, Romero pushing Charles ahead of him into the street, Henry Starr gripping Patrick by the scruff of his vest and gesturing ahead with his pistol. As they passed the door the little girl looked at him wonderingly and he said, "Come along, little lady, and I'll see you get across the street all right." And over his shoulder he added, "The rest of you will find it healthier to stay indoors a while."

The sun was painfully clear and bright in the street, as if the sky were glass. Keeping Patrick and Charles outside of them, they moved swiftly up the sidewalk toward 5th Street, where the First National Bank sat diagonally across the intersection. Patrick noticed that Starr was not using the little Penniman girl as a shield, but kept her inside of the group till they got to the corner. Then they crossed the street, Patrick and Charles on the outside flanks and Starr and the child in the middle, Patrick feeling in the open space as exposed as a bug on a billiard table waiting for a giant ball to roll him under—but there was silence, no one on the street, and they could hear the noise from the depot two blocks away where the 2:55 freight from Tulsa to Oklahoma City huffed and clanked.

When they reached the opposite corner, Henry Starr bent and tapped the little girl on her fanny and pointed her back down the street toward Balcomb's Ice Cream Parlor. "There you go," he said. "You go get yourself some ice cream."

Her shoes rattled up the sidewalk, her bag of dimes chinkling.

The bandit looked after her. This gave Patrick reason to hope. "Listen," he said, "that stickpin you took—it ain't worth much, and my mother give it to me. My mother, she would be—"

"I have heard that mother story before," said the outlaw.

Starr took him again by the scruff of the vest and moved him across 5th Street to the First National Bank and just as their feet touched the curb Patrick saw three more figures come out of the bank and his heart roared in his ears fearing some terrible interruption so that he was actually relieved to see the men wore masks and that they were still safe inside the robbers' careful procedure. Relief made him feel drunk; he almost laughed. "I swear to you, it ain't di'mond. It's only glass. I'll swap you my gold watch for it."

They were in front of Brogan's grocery now, and Starr paused and turned Patrick so he could look in his face. "I didn't know you had a gold watch," he said, grinning like a cat.

"No," said Patrick blushing hotly, "I mean I ain't got it with—" and God knows what other idiocies he might have said, but just at that moment Al Carlock stepped out of the Galloway Store across the street with a paper parcel in his arms, and Henry Starr shifted his pistol and it barked and Carlock's derby hat flew backward through Galloway's door and Carlock dropped the package and fell backwards in after it and Patrick would have sworn that Starr put three shots into the paper parcel shattering the bottles inside before it hit the sidewalk.

Mr. Taylor stuck his head out the door of his bakery; the outlaw pointed his gun like a finger and popped the straw hat off Taylor's head too. Patrick had the giddy sense that they would now just stand in the street and watch him shoot hats off anybody who showed himself, and just as he thought that, the outlaw shoved him violently forward stumbling and he saw that he was going to be shot down like a dog because the bandit leader had finally gone crazy, throwing himself with an insane and convulsive leap right on his face into the gutter, the careful process of the robbery falling apart all around and over Patrick's head as he crouched on all fours like a cur with bang-banging guns all around and over him, people yelling, the elongated spike-headed shadows of the killers moving with comically exaggerated violence where the sun printed them on the pavement, and his memory imposed on all of that the single tone of a rifle shot booming out of the depths of Brogan's store behind him—Mr. Howard, the robber, was lying on his face, shot, a saddle of blood riding his hips.

Paul Curry had been holding the rifle in his hands and looking at the hogs jamming their snouts between the boards of their tight pen. He had felt like shooting something, but shooting hogs was like blowing up a big bladder of crap. So he just held the heavy, blunt-nosed rifle in his hands, and listened for Brogan moving around behind him in the store.

He had heard a sound like a firecracker going off in the street, or a car backfiring. Then three more. It was like someone was calling him. He had turned on his heels and clumped forward through the darkened store on his pig-sloppy boots, Brogan peeking up from behind the counter, just the top of his bald head and his little piggy eyes. There were a bunch of men standing in front of the open door and one of them was shooting a pistol and Paul Curry had run toward him with his sawed-off rifle in his hands.

Which he threw up to his shoulder, sighted at the back of the shooting man, pulled the trigger and knocked two of the son of a bitches over with one shot easy as barking squirrels off a tree limb.

He found himself outside, as if his body had flown in the wake of his bullet, and he crouched to lay a hand on the man he had shot, felt the rough cloth of his trousers—Mr. Patrick from the bank was crouched on all fours next to the dead man. *The dead man.* "They robbed the bank!" cried Patrick. "Don't let them get away!"

Curry looked up and saw Banker Charles leaning against the front of Brogan's nursing a split lip, and the shape of a man vanishing around the corner. It jumped out at Paul Curry: the truth was that he could have been shot down in the street if that running man had stopped and waited for him, shot down while he crouched next to the body of the man he had killed, and that made him mad so he yelled "Hey!" and ran to the corner to catch the man.

There were five men on milling horses alongside the stockyard corral.

Fear bit Paul Curry in the belly so hard that he screamed, "You could have killed me!" and threw the hog gun up and fired into the mill of riders and levered and fired again. One of the robbers toppled ass over head over heels off the rump of his bay horse, which shook him and bolted after the others, who were galloping across the tracks just ahead of the engine of the 3:05 freight to Oklahoma City.

Curry ran to the man he had shot, who lay—dead—just off the tracks where the train was sliding by like a curtain of steel, cutting off pursuit as neat as if they'd planned it that way, the engineer in the cab looking down and back and wishing he could stay, waving. Three men came cautiously out from behind the corral fence, and Curry said to them, "Bring this one along," the robber lay flat on his back with his shirt-front half blue and half blood, dead as a stone. He started to run back to the first man to make sure he was still dead, still lying like a slaughtered hog in front of Brogan's store, praying that no one had stolen him.

Henry Starr flew through the air. There was a smooth stone wall in front of him, and the huge soaring fling of his flying slammed him helplessly into it flat along his whole length from forehead nose mouth to belly balls kneecaps toes, flat: slam: so hard that he stuck to the wall like a smashed insect, hanging there with the zero of empty space below him.

*I have been shot,* he told himself. *I have been cut in half like a bug.* He knew it was not a wall but the paved street, and so the wall tilted straining and failing to become a street again. When it tried that Henry Starr felt his lungs and heart suck down toward the black hole that was where his belly and hips should be and it scared him so sick that he said to himself, *All right, let it be a wall.*

Somebody picked his head up by the back hair and looked at his face and said he's alive.

*I feel like I am standing with the lower half of me in a hole. There is nothing in the hole, not even coldness: and the nothing is me. Is half of me. Is the hole.*

"Who is it?"

"He calls himself Mr. Thomas Howard," he heard Patrick say, "but that ain't his name I bet . . ."

"Howard?" said the boy. "Mr. Thomas Howard? Don't you know who used to call himself . . ."

"Henry Starr," said Henry Starr, turning his cheek to the street to look at their boots. "I am Henry Starr." *I sure as hell am not Jesse James.*

They started to bicker and palaver, but the street became a wall again, and then a ceiling and everything below his belly was the hole, they had cut him into two halves and lost one of them.

"Take him up to Doc's," said the kid. "I shot him, didn't I? And I'm saying, take him up to Doc's."

He felt himself lifted under the arms. Were his legs dragging? Were his legs there to drag? The angle at which he hung suggested they were hauling him by legs as well as arms, but that was just guesswork; a man likes to be sure about things like that.

"Easy with him, easy!" yelled the kid; these yokels would mess it all up if he let them, then all he'd have would be another dead one, like the one at the stockyards. Somehow the dead one didn't count.

Henry Starr lay on his face on a leather chaise. The air smelt of carbolic and sweet-stinky pungent chemicals. They were fooling with his lower parts. Two men stood and watched. The kid crouched down in front of him to look in his face: sixteen, meaty cheeks and a little jut jaw, small eyes, he kept licking his lips.

*If they shoot you in half you are as good as dead. Everything below my belly is zero, is in the hole, is the hole. Maybe soon the hole will be my shoulders, my eyes, my mouth zero, my ears, my hair*—"I am Henry Starr," he said.

"I shot you," said the kid halfway between brag and apology.

Henry Starr remembered sending the little girl to get some ice cream. Everything had just been running along as slick and smooth as water down a hill, and then this back-shooting little bugger comes along and cuts me in half.

But the half that's left has to act like Henry Starr.

Henry Starr smiled, and worked his right hand out—the angle was too awkward for a shake, but he gave the kid's hand a grip. "Nice shooting, boy. You bagged yourself a badman. I'm worth $15,000 by the latest quotations."

His own face—WANTED ROBBERY HENRY STARR REWARD—filled his eyes, then folded back on itself like a cheap handbill.

"Ha!" said the kid, and he looked around, shaking his outlaw's hand. "Ha!" Well, he had showed 'em this time, hadn't he?

Everybody came up the stairs to Vincent's one at a time to see his outlaw, and what an outlaw it was, too: Henry Starr, who was nearly as famous as Jesse James, and just cool as could be, cool and like a gentleman—telling Mr. Carlock he owed him for a new hat, and Mr. Taylor too, giving Patrick back his stickpin and asking if he was still willing to swap for his gold watch—so that those that had an insult or a nasty word to say come off looking poorly themselves, looking mean—and every word, every gesture was like adding a coin to the reward heap for Paul Curry, his outlaw, the man he had shot.

"Back-shot," said Mr. Brogan out of the side of his mouth, adding, "Not that that makes a difference."

The afternoon wore on and wore on. Doc's office smelled of blood and medicine. The smells always made Paul feel sick and giddy—but he didn't want to leave, he had to keep close to Henry Starr, as if to keep his claim on him, as if if they were to come for him while Curry was away his name would be wiped out of record and memory, and no one know who it was that had shot the bandit Henry Starr.

Back-shot.

Not that that makes any damn bit of difference.

Did it make a difference? Paul Curry pictured hogs standing packed side to side in a pen, like big bladders of crap, and nothing to stop your blowing them open but saying *No sir* to Mr. Brogan, and he never had done that yet.

The light got stale. The doctor, sitting in his leather chair, was pretending to read a red-covered book, but every few minutes he would put it down, come over and look at the wounded man's dressing, lift and press his bare feet to see if any sensation had returned. It hadn't.

Also the sheriff somehow hadn't come back. Nobody was coming upstairs to see Paul Curry's Wild West show, his famous bandit—yet there was still a crowd in the street.

"What book are you reading, Doc?" asked the outlaw.

"Jack London," he said crisply, "*Scarlet Plague*," as if that were the title of a technical monograph on disease.

"I've read it," said the outlaw. "It's pretty tough. 'If War, Famine and Pestilence destroyed the world,' " he quoted, " 'could you rebuild the civilization in which you live?' "

The doctor didn't answer. There was a bad noise rising up outside, darkening the windows.

"Or if you could," said Henry Starr, "are you sure you would want to?"

It got suddenly very cold.

"The sheriff isn't coming back," said Dr. Vincent wanly, rubbing and rubbing his hands with a towel.

The sound from below was a mindless boiling hubbub, a rising falling muttering yowl that was like a pack of wolves had got so sick for meat they could almost talk for hunger.

Henry Starr looked into Paul Curry's eyes. Paul Curry had lived in Oklahoma long enough to know what that kind of sound meant. He cradled his cut-down rifle as if it was a hurt thing. Henry Starr knew the feeling. He smiled at Curry and lifted his eyebrows a little, like a shrug of the shoulders to say, well: a man can do only so much . . .

*Just like Cherokee Bill,* thought Henry Starr, *it ain't the dying, it's the nigger of it that I hate. It don't even matter that they cut me in half, because the half that's still alive is still Henry Starr and I don't want to die like a nigger like Cherokee Bill: who at least could say that he took that death for my sake, knowing it would get me off so that I could make his name good in the Nations, like I give him my word I would do.*

*". . . You owe a life for my life, a debtor to the law." Yes: maybe what I hate most is that I got to say that if it comes to me that way it ain't no more than justice. That I got to admit it tastes like justice.*

Henry Starr rested his head on his hands, his bandaged ass in the air. "Doc," he said, "I don't give a damn about dying, but I got a prejudice against hanging. If you got some poison handy, I'd be obliged to you."

The doctor looked shocked and then ashamed, how did this outlaw shot down and dragged in off the street know about his little habit . . . ?

Someone was ram-ram-ramming on the downstairs door, rattling it on its hinges. The boy stood up, his cut-down gun in his hands.

*An old drunk doctor and a boy with a hog gun who is gonna disappear when that mob gets the door down, that's all the crowd I get. I reckon if Cherokee Bill got cheated one way, he come out ahead of me another. There was hundreds there to hear and remember, if they could, Cherokee Bill saying how he come there to die and not to make a speech. But I am Henry Starr,* he thought, *and if this is the way it's given to me . . .*

Listen: this is how Henry Starr dies.

He smiled at the boy. "I got to tell you, getting shot with a pig gun . . . it hurts my pride, boy. But you showed your quality, and that's good shooting you done, with a cut-off gun like that." He held out his hand again for Paul Curry to shake.

The boy seemed to take some kind of electric charge from the outlaw's handshake and praise, it stood him up a little straighter. *Maybe he will stick,* thought Henry Starr, *but I still think he wants to bolt and I don't blame him, that's what I would do in his place: or no, that is just what I did,* and Paul Curry looked at the man he'd cut down and said, "Thank you sir, Mr. Starr, thanks."

In the sudden zero stillness that rose up the stairwell from the street he thought, *Well, if they did hang Henry Starr, it would only be half of him.* He smiled coolly at the doctor.

"Did anybody find out if that little girl got her ice cream?"

The stillness in the street hung and hung, drifting up the stairs like smoke to fill the doctor's office. There was a meaning in it; if Henry Starr kept silent now he would guess it.

# Henry Starr's Double Daring; or, Two at One Blow

COFFEYVILLE, KANSAS *May 25–26, 1921*

It was still. Black night, black. No fire, fire will draw hunters like blood spoor, like your ghost's breath will draw nightwalkers once a wizard has set them on you.

He stood in a thicket overlooking the Coffeyville Road, one hand muffling the horse's muzzle, listening looking smelling so hard for the pursuit it was like he had thrown his ghost out down along his back trail as far as he could remember and sent it racing as far in front of him as he could stand to think.

He shut his eyes, closing black against the black of the thicket and the night: eyes were a weakness now, in the black your fear could conjure blue shapes in them unless you had the power to black your mind blank too—no sound or memory, no word—

He stood in the black, listening:

There was nothing behind him, absolute zero sound or scent all the way back to the time and place in which he saw the image of a man stepping into a bank: stepping in through the door of the Prue State Bank, banker and clerk looking up as pure-terror shocked as if he were a sudden ghost, as if Henry Starr the Scourge of the Southwest had stepped down out of the ice-cold silver light of the movie screen into the warm dark to blow their bodies full of black holes with ghost bullets from the breathless silent pistol in his hand.

And for just that single terrible tick of the heart he was the same way himself, *not knowing if it was real yet, if anything had even started to begin to be, not knowing if he was child again or man, ghost without name or power in the world, or Henry Starr, Henry Starr the outlaw with his pistol in my hand, and for the laws and property I do not give a damn*—his ghost and body still so wrapped around with blue smoke he wasn't dead sure if this wasn't just one more of Miss Woodly's ride in rob the bank ride out scenes—

Because lately every robbery he did was a double, a double worse than Stroud or even Coffeyville, the banks' insides in one place outsides in another so that to rob them once you had to be the same man in two different places, and then they kept changing those places on you too so that sometimes the bank you robbed was just a bank and sometimes it was a crazy puzzle made of bits and pieces of other places, Henry Starr's mother's Alice Farnham's Cora Munson's cabin in the Cherokee Nation . . .

*Where it all began, when Henry Starr robbed the Katy the Caney the Nowata the Pryor Creek the Bentonville the Tyro the Keystone the Kiefer . . .*

And if that was true then any second now Miss Woodly would yell *cut* and Henry Starr the outlaw and *the Katy the Keystone the Stroud* the Prue State Bank and everything would be drop-dead cut *like the strings of his Grandfather's blood the strings of talking wire that they cut from the pole as they rode into Stroud, Oklahoma, to rob two banks and beat the ghosts of Tom Starr Belle Starr Bob Dalton Jesse James Cherokee Bill and Henry Starr that used to be*—

—stepped through the glass door of the First State Bank of Prue, which smelled today of thick dust and old pine wood and varnish and the dry yellow smell of paper brittling and dying in big heaps. It was dead quiet, the street behind him blank empty. The gun was already in his hand, his hand moving like a snake quicker than his own thought, pointing and thumb-cocking in a single motion the words already darting out of his lips as if his tongue were hairtriggered firing at the least flick of his thought: "Thumbs up and stand steady," and the banker's and the clerk's hands climbed into the air as if his words and thoughts were inside their muscles, inside their eyes, that was his power, more real than any damn conjure than any damn movie, because the Colt in his hand was heavy but it had lift and balance too, a dense lightness full of power, he knew that whatever words his mouth spoke his pistol would make good because it was not blue smoke but blued steel—real as the money they took out of the vault and drawers and dumped onto the counter, heaps of silver coin and stacked greenbacks, Bob Dalton sure as hell was right about the money, it's the real thing it don't ever get sick or die or blow away like blue smoke—

*Then where is all that money, she wanted to know: her eyes needling him out of the black shadows thrown by the firelight: where is all that money that don't get sick or old or die like a man, the money that's stronger than justice because you can hold it in your hand or—*

—or sweep it off the counter, coins paper notes into your saddle bag, and here it is, right here, the money is right here *and that's more than that damned movie of yours ever was* and the bag swings heavy with money on his left arm as he backs out the door and turns in one light swift movement swinging the bag over the pommel and mounting into the saddle, his voice as piercing as a bird cry as he slashes his reins left and right, his horse gathers under him and churns and springs straight ahead—

*I tell you I tell you he come smoking, he come blazing, he come boiling out of that town, and behind him the long back trail disappeared in the smoke of burning debt paper, in the smoke of dust, in blue smoke, in blue so that you will never find him never catch him never, with blue, with the color of blue . . .*

—west out of Prue as if heading up the Arkansas for Osage, then north through the brush cross-lots to Wild Horse and east and north, running like a coyote runs, blinding the trail and running again by instinct as natural as breathing or eating, resting no place but touching and moving out moving over moving away—across Bird River at night, camped out above Skiatook, dodging and ducking in his old worn trace—Talala, Watova, Nowata, Lenapah, up the valley of the Verdigris running for safety over the Kansas line—

And far up ahead in the V notch of the road a small white dot, jiggling in the hard light and heat-twisted air, maybe a mirage?—not a mirage, because he was coming up on it, closer and closer, smoking down toward it till its edges hardened and he knew it was men on horses, half a dozen men, half a dozen riding north on the road from Belle Starr's ranch to Coffeyville, and he had started far back, thirty years back since they had called him *Young Henry* and welcomed him to the family and told him *you keep your eye on the money Henry that's the ticket 'cause money don't ever get old or sick and it don't ever die*—thirty years' head start but he could almost see Bob Dalton's face turning to check his back trail to see how Henry Starr was gaining on him, Young Henry Old Henry Henry Starr the outlaw, the smartest outlaw who ever, and maybe he would just go whooping right on past Bob Dalton and straight on to Coffeyville and glory.

And not any damn movie-screen glory either, Miss Woodly, not the kind you win with a gun full of blanks, but the real thing, the kind you win with real bullets the kind that gets you *gets you killed, or half killed and the rest dropped down a hole into stone prison.*

Yes, but they can't hold you in those prisons, Miss Woodly, because if you got that real kind of glory, then the law can't hold you, only justice can hold you, so you slide out between the bars between the stones like quicksilver, one way or another way—the law can't hold you because your name is bigger than the law, Miss Woodly, like a picture that prints itself in the lights of people's minds so the glory don't ever fade out of it, but when you see it it all comes back to you just like it really was, the glory as real as the bullets, the justice as real as the law, the bank robbery then as real as the money is now, and all of *it* just as real as the crowd was and the packed sand of the arena the little white chicken head poking up out of the earth at the rodeo in Tahlequah, as real as that, as real as I dreamed it would be lying in my boardinghouse room prison cell mother's pantry-room Munson's Store Fort Smith Prison the rolling wagon coming home from Bartlesville the cornfield outside my mother's cabin where I lay with the sun on my back reading red-covered *Last of the Mohicans* because I was that kind of boy until the railroad agent . . .

*No: the cornfield and the railroad agent—that never happened at all that was Miss Woodly's idea she made it up:*

And the gun he had held in his hand: the old .45-caliber Colt Dragoon: blue iron heavy in the hand but inside there was nothing but the movie blanks he had loaded it with to rob his next bank in *Henry Starr: A Debtor to the Law*, photoplay by B. C. Woodly, and if banker or clerk had had a gun ready to hand . . .

A thrill of pure terror went through the middle of his spine like an ice needle, as if Miss Woodly's blue eyes had suddenly zeroed on the soft secret core of his body—just when he thought he had run out of her eyes and her thinking here she was again, her and that nightwalking "Henry Starr" she had made up, not just eating up his tracks like Bill Tilghman would, but eating up bits of Henry Starr's memory and life too, so that he couldn't see clearly anymore where the made-up parts left off and his life began.

Then the horse moved restlessly under his hand and he knew that he had run his ghost back around the circle and into the thicket above the Coffeyville Road once again: listening for the pursuit. Not a sound at all between Coffeyville and Tahlequah as far as he could tell. *They chased him for a thousand miles and never caught . . .*

But they had caught him, hadn't they—every time he thought he was riding that horse and climbing over the world and riding right up into the notch of the V where the road goes into the sky: that was when it come to take him from behind, the punch of the hog killer in the spine, or Bill Tilghman's tap on the shoulder while you're rolled up inside that store-bought sweetie's honeyhole as snug as a .45 Colt in a scabbard, or the taptap of Tilghman's horse riding carefully up your back trail, taking his time because he owns some naked clue Henry Starr has dropped or forgotten in his haste and fear and now old Ice Eyes will follow it home to him, and come ahead of him into Coffeyville to sit in hiding, waiting for Henry Starr to finish one last run down that same old road he had run so many times before—out of Tahlequah out of Bentonville out of Keystone out of Preston out of Owasso out of Stroud—as if all that running twisting dodging was just the wriggles of a bug with a needle through his spine pinned to a paper, and Bill Tilghman's knowing white eyes was the needle, and he saves your life or the half of it that is all you have left—

And puts you back in the same prison he put you in before, Bartlesville Jail Fort Smith Prison McAlester Ma's windowless Tulsa pantryroom Stroud City Jail where they cut you in half and the blue, the black comes up like rising smoke like rising water over your face and your breath and your name till it covers you and there's nothing, no-clan no-name, this is the death of Henry Starr, and nothing to keep it away but the life of your brother Cherokee Bill: since that's the only coin they'll take—and it's not even to buy you free to find your horse again, and your road, but just to let you live in a box to breathe your name at the blue, at the black—but even so you will pay the price whatever it is, and pay it and . . .

So when you get out of those prisons they say it is because you are Henry Starr, the luckiest the smartest outlaw who ever lived, and nobody ever got up early enough to climb over Henry Starr. But the truth is they made you sell they made you bite off and leave behind a piece of who you was, a piece of your name and your ghost so every time you come out you're weaker, you're *less*—your name is smaller, and your word—that word with which he robbed a-many banks and—that word of his . . . *that he had given to Cherokee Bill, to write his death and his memory in ghost-lights so it would live forever in the Nations.*

The road and the story always ended the same: with Henry Starr dropped down a blue stone hole and Cherokee Bill sold to the Hangman to buy Henry Starr's life. Not even Miss Woodly could think of a way to get Henry Starr out of blue smoke stone prison without finding him a murdering nigger half-breed named Cherokee Bill, whose body Henry Starr could give to the Hangman and the picture-man, whose name and ghost Henry Starr would leave to die and be remembered by a nigger's death.

Miss Woodly: with her blue eyes and those small fine lips like a child will have, but a look in her eyes sometimes like a bobcat on a cornered rabbit, and her breath as sweet as . . .

You were supposed to make it over in that sweet breath of yours, Miss Woodly, you were supposed to change it and make it like your breath would be if it was singing: so that instead of everything twisted around biting on itself like a mad dog *ride rob and run over and over till they catch me and drown my breath in blue smoke* it would all flow out clean and smooth like water running, all the different circles run together and run out smooth like film on the spool, running toward a place where it all comes together and comes to an end, and when you turn and look back there's your whole long road like a silver path running straight and true from back then to here and now, and it all makes sense and it comes to good, Ma and Grandfather and Floyd Wilson and Cherokee Bill and Young Henry Starr who won the prize and robbed the bank at Tahlequah, Henry Starr the traitor and the rescuer and the Robin Hood of Old Oklahoma, Henry Starr the Last Chief and Redeemer of the Noble Red Race of the Ten Lost Mohican Tribes of the One Big Union of the United States of America, finally and forever coming together and coming out right . . .

The horse jerked his head, trying to shake off Henry Starr's hand so he could snuff the morning.

The black darkness was turning black-blue, was blue: was opening into gray.

A bird spoke behind him.

The road was still empty. Henry Starr swung himself up into the saddle, lifting his stiffened leg tenderly over the cantle. "Tsik," he said, and the horse stepped out of the thicket and moved at a touch of the reins north toward Coffeyville.

Let it all go. Dreams and conjures and prisons go together. You are outside, the sun will be up in five minutes and that's a mock-bird calling out of the thicket behind you. When you cross the line you will be safe from Oklahoma law, and when you get to Coffeyville it will be noon and you will have lunch. You will pay for it with money taken out of your saddlebags, which are heavy on the mare's spotted rump because they are topping full of genuine silver dollars and gold and silver and greenback certificates backed by the full faith and credit of the United States government, you can't ask for anything solider than that. So you remember, it wasn't dreaming got you here.

No, the horse was real, and the money, and the bank robbery had been real enough, although the fact was he had never planned it beforehand nor prepared himself but took what was given and made up the rest as he went along, dressed up like a movie cowboy and never even bothered to check the loads in his gun—and maybe if you looked at it cold it was a fool thing to do, but it had worked like a charm, worked like if you had the power, if you were a real bank robber you maybe didn't even need real bullets . . .

But no: that was one trick you didn't want to have to try a second time. Not even on purpose, let alone by surprise. Stick with what you can see, with real horses on a real road, and real guns with real bullets in them, to use when you want to rob real money from real banks.

Only, don't go down that road thinking that when it ends Henry Starr will have become something else—Something: a name greater than the Daltons or Jesse James or Tom Starr or Robin Hood or Jesus Christ, a name that don't get small or sick or old, a name that don't die, but whenever people see the difference between law and justice rich and poor strong and weak they see my face, and they whisper *Henry Starr.*

Because memory ain't like money, is it? It gets old and it gets sick, and when them that carries it dies then it is dead, dead like the buffalo and the Last of the Mohicans and Tom Starr and the Cherokee Nation, dead like Bob and Grat Dalton who said "Welcome to the family, Henry Starr," and told me that the money don't ever die so stick to that, and then rode off themselves down the road to rob two banks and have it out once and for all with the ghost of the name of Jesse James in the streets of Coffeyville—and the citizens woke up and tore them apart with pistols rifles shotguns, blowing pieces of meat and bone off them like butchering hogs in a back alley while the ghost of Jesse James laughed at them and rode on, *Jesse James Jesse James.*

Jesse James: the Daltons never caught him, and I'll never catch them; and if I did it wouldn't make no difference. What would I say if I come up with them on this road—turn back, boys, you can't beat Jesse James today or ever, this road ends one way and the only thing to do is turn around and go back to where it all began . . . and do what? Start over again? But you can't, I found that out too: the roads in this part of the country run one way.

They were ahead of him, waiting there in ambush when he came riding into Coffeyville before noon. Nearly thirty years since the Daltons: the main street was paved and gas-lit, but there were the two banks still, the First National and the Condon. The Condon was a big, two-story ornate turreted building, gilded lettering over a big plate-glass front, and carefully inset in the glass was a framed pane with a large bullet hole in it; and inside the window a framed photograph of the dead bodies of Bob and Grat Dalton, Dick Broadwell and Bill Powers, laid out under a wall with their stiffened limbs sprawling, lids drooping over dead-blank eyes, mouths sagging, bullet holes like inkblots up and down their fronts.

One road, one ending: the ghosts of the Dalton Gang were real small and gray, shrunk down and held for thirty years in a little black-frame prison, with no power to keep the eyes of anybody at all away from the nakedness of their deaths. Give them a couple of days and they'd put Henry Starr's name to the Prue bank job, put his name and his price and a small gray image of his ghost on a handbill and tack it up in bank windows just like this one, and that would be the start of the conjure that would put him back in a stone box for good, blood ghost brains sore ass and all.

Next to the Condon the marquee of a movie theater overhung the sidewalk, with bunting stirring in the afternoon breeze:

BUCKSKIN BILL VS. THE STARR GANG.

Under it a red-lettered strip of paper said:

Next Week: THE BIRTH OF A NATION!

Across the street near the First National another, smaller theater with a billboard front:

HENRY STARR, SCOURGE OF THE
SOUTHWEST.

Like looking in a mirror and you know it is your face, but it can't be your face because you are young and the face is old because you are old and the face is . . .

*"Look in the water," he boomed out of the shadow, the sun flaring out of his head, "Look in the water and you will see your ghost . . ."*

---

Henry Starr sat his horse in the middle of the main street of Coffeyville, Kansas, with his saddlebags full of cash from a bank he'd just robbed and looked up at his name in giant letters staring down from the marquees of two different theaters playing two of his movies at the same time in Coffeyville, Kansas.

He took some coins belonging to the Prue State Bank out of his saddlebags, bought a ticket, and went in right in the middle of the picture, forgetting to notice which of the two movies he had chosen.

There he was, his face and his name written *Henry Starr* on the wall in black and silver lights, an icy silver with the piercing intensity of acetylene. He had become huge, his face *Henry Starr* filled all the world that eyes could see—but then again he was small, small with distance. His ghost in silver light could bring you as close as breathing or put you as far away as the edge of sight, could carry you along or let you drop—could carry *him* along, Henry Starr! Because this *Henry Starr* had power enough to lift and carry the little body that made the ghost, carry him high and far, carry him like an eagle climbing up out and over everything in the world, Tom Starr Cherokee Bill Floyd Wilson Bill Tilghman the square black cell of Fort Smith Prison . . .

Blackness shut down like a door, then light erased it, he heard the whirr of the reel winder: but the silver light still moved in ghostly repetition behind his eyelids. All they had to do was rewind the film and they would be ready to show the movie again.

He rose and walked outside, a dozen people with him, jabbering, laughing, a kid said, *Wasn't that great?* The sunlight was yellow and blinding, full of dust—the light of the screen had been better, like cool water, very clear. Inside people would soon be watching that silver flow like running water, drinking it again with their eyes. And when they had done looking at it . . .

*Then*, he thought with a smile, *there was another movie across the street that they could go see.*

And if he went back to Tulsa to work with Miss Woodly, then there would be another one after that, till wherever he went he would find his silver-light ghost running through cabins banks and countryside, into jails and into shut-down blackness—and out again to blaze silver and black down a silver trail, his ghost and his name sliding out of the black night like quicksilver between the stones or light between the bars, to run and run and run again . . .

Henry Starr stood in the streets of Coffeyville where the Daltons had been shot full of holes by the citizens of Coffeyville and the ghost of Jesse James, with his pockets full of the Prue State Bank's cash and his eyes full of movies. Nobody knew who he was, except maybe Henry Starr himself, and maybe the ghosts of Grat and Bob Dalton staring out of their picture-frame prison. But he was Henry Starr, the smartest outlaw who ever lived, who had finally climbed over the ghost of *Jesse James's Double Daring*: Henry Starr, who had hit the two-at-a-time in Coffeyville and got away with it.

He didn't have to choose between the ghost world of the movies and the dusty world of banks and prisons. He had the kind of money that worked on both sides of the line, what he stole in one world he could spend in the other. He could step from the screen into the world with his pistol in his hand and rob real banks of real money with a gun full of make-believe movie bullets. And when he had done he could vanish into the screen, vanish not in a cloud of dollars but into a cloud of ghosts, the spirits of power and memory, Jesse James who robbed two banks in one day and Tom Starr who gave no trail to a bear, and back further, to the powers that slew the monsters and made the Nation in its ancient home back there among the mountains, where the water was.

And if Tom Starr, or Floyd Wilson, or Cherokee Bill came haunting after him in this life, asking him about blood, about all the blood Henry Starr spoiled or spilled or betrayed, he would vanish through the screen and dissolve himself in silver lights, he would weave them an answer in silver and black that would change the blood to small black shapes; if they came after him questioning they would be dissolved into his answer: an answer of silver light, smooth as running water, in which everything would be made right.

He mounted his horse again and set its head southward back to Oklahoma. He could see now as clearly as he could see Coffeyville, Kansas, the road that would carry him past Bill Tilghman's eyes and Miss Woodly's stories and Esterhazy's cameras to the place where he would keep his word to Cherokee Bill, and send that huge black shape finally to sleep.

## VERDIGRIS RIVER *May 27, 1921*

As he came through the trees he heard the snick of a rifle cocking and froze.

"Come ahead, Henry Starr," said Dick Rowland's voice.

He eased his horse forward into the clearing. Bars of early sunlight cut through the trees. Bub Houston stood up from behind the charred foundation stones of a burnt-out shed. Behind him there was a tumble of blackened pots and kettles, a smashed boiler, lengths of stovepipe. Under the sharp smell of burnt wood you could still sense the whiskey-sweet. But there was another smell too, the sweet-sick of burnt human meat, and the ugly yellow rot-stink of a body going bad. The flies told him where that was coming from: it was under a yellow canvas tarpaulin under a large alder, and a scar of charring ran up the face of the tree trunk.

Somewhere in the bushes Dick Rowland had a bead on his back, Dick Rowland who had killed white men like the old-time horse Indians used to kill buffalo, driving them panicking into a pit and slaughtering them like hogs in a pen. He was here to make a trade with Dick Rowland and Bub Houston, and right now he knew what it must have been like for those white men who first come trading into the Nations in the old days, one look at the setup and the goods in your pack don't shine no more, you wonder just what you could possibly get in trade that was worth what could happen to you here.

A *nigger's death. It seems that whenever I come to trade, that is always part of the bargain.*

"Yes," said Dick Rowland, stepping out of the bushes behind Henry Starr. "You can see how they did it. Let T. J. out of prison, so the Ku-kluck get him. And then they cut on him, don't they? Cut on him till he tells where Bub's stills are hid. Then they go around and bust them up, and when they get here and bust the last one they hang what's left of T. J. to the tree by the neck, and light up a barrel of mash under him while he's twisting. That Ku-kluck, they're real *churchy* folks, they just *despise* a man that drinks."

"Burnt out the still house," said Bub, "but they didn't bust all of it. Somebody took off the gauges and the copper worm-pipe. You know why they did that, Young Henry?"

They would trade words first. "Because one of 'em owns a still," said Henry Starr, "and he knows how much those things cost."

Bub nodded. "So you tell me, Henry," he said slowly, dead tired, "who do you know that has a hand in the Ku-kluck, and a hand in the whiskey business both? Who knew T. J. was my still man, and how to get his hands on him?"

"Price."

Bub's eyes were red-socketed, under the weariness that was as heavy on him as the stench was on all of them he was fierce. "You're gonna help me, ain't you, Henry. You're gonna help me and Dick *do* that son of a bitch."

It wasn't a question, he wasn't asking or even demanding help, he was expecting it, like you can expect things of your own blood-kin—because only your kin would take the kind of debt Bub Houston owed to T. J. Hanks as their own, as a debt on their blood; and go after vengeance knowing all the time that if they killed Deputy Price there would be no getting away with it any more than there had been for Henry Starr after he killed Floyd Wilson: because they'd all come after the ones who did it, even the lawmen that knew Price for a thief and a murderer, even Bill Tilghman, the good lawmen tracking and the bad ones bullying the families and the dirt farmers and the hideaway ranchers till it was a choice between giving the outlaws up for the reward or getting hurt yourself, and they wouldn't run long or far till someone dropped their name or pointed a finger . . . and you don't ask that of kin, because you don't have to, all you have to do is say the name of the thing and they're supposed to know—and Henry Starr heard it, and he knew.

But between that knowing and his ghost was his own debt, that he had never named to anybody, but he had to name it now; and when he did it would be like he was trading with Bub Houston, debt against debt. Henry Starr felt a little touch of cold in the eye of his chest for what he had in mind, because kin don't *trade* with each other. But he couldn't see another way. What he needed was not the kind of thing you could expect another man, a man like Bub Houston, to understand the way Henry Starr understood about Deputy Price.

He saw Bub's heat cool suddenly, and the black man stood a little stiffer, watching. The single tick of hesitation was already between them, as if Henry Starr had spoken it.

"I'm with you, Bub. But . . ."

"But," said Bub.

"But there's something I got to ask . . . something I need to do first, because I . . ."

Bub said, "I'm listening, Young Henry."

"I need Dick Rowland." He shifted his glance to catch the younger man, who stepped over to stand next to Bub. "I need you for my movie. I need you to play Cherokee Bill in my movie."

Bub started cursing under his breath before Henry Starr had finished. ". . . my man lying here gutted and burnt like he was a hog—T. J.!—and you standing there asking me to come play chil'ren's games with you and your white-trash pussy . . ."

"Wait and hear him," said Dick Rowland softly. "You wouldn't listen to me before you made that deal, now you listen to me telling you to *listen.*"

Bub gave Dick Rowland a look, but waved his hand.

Henry Starr wet his lips to make the talking easier, but spit wasn't enough to grease what he had to say—it pulled through his throat like knotted rope. "I never told anybody else in this life, but I got to tell you . . . What it was I said to Cherokee Bill that made him give up his guns and himself to be hung, and get me a pardon."

That brought Bub up straight and still, his red eyes focused sharply, *Don't you wish you had those words, the words that Henry Starr used to . . .* and Dick Rowland was watching him closely too, standing tense and listening in the same hunched pose he had held that night outside Houston's house while they heard the talk die down, and the lights go out one by one.

"He hated to die that way, Bub. I knew how it was to him. You heard him yourself that time back in Boley, begging you not to let them take and hang him. *It ain't the dying, Henry, it's the nigger of it I hate.* That's what he told me, the night before. That's the death I fooled him into."

Bub stood rigid with strain, but Dick Rowland seemed to wake up and take a sharper look at Henry Starr, who went on now, the words tumbling faster:

"All his life he wanted people to see him as a Hair Twister, as a big man in the Cherokee Nation. I was his friend because I said sure, that's what he was, knowing it was a lie. And there in the prison, at the end: I told him I'd make the lie good forever, I told him I'd write it in lights, like they do in the movies—make people think of him in such a way that his ghost would live forever in the Nation. I told him I'd make his death over for him in a movie, a movie about a Cherokee hero named Cherokee Bill, of the Hair Twister clan, Cherokee Bill and his partner Henry Starr . . .

"I promised him all of that twenty-five years ago, and I ain't kept it to this day, and hell: I ain't even seen how I *could* keep it, and the truth is I didn't *then*, right there when I was telling him, just the two of us there, and the guard pistol-whipped and half dead—that's how much of a lie it was . . ."

Bub brushed it all away like a swarm of flies. "So much damn fuss and it's twenty-five years dead. Man, you should have learned to live with it by now . . ."

"There's things do follow a man, Bub," said Dick Rowland, his eyes locked on Henry Starr's face like he was studying it, his voice tense.

"People die on your account—it don't matter how—but till you've paid what you owe 'em you can't let 'em go, they be in your mind, they be in your bread, you be *breathing* them—running, hiding, anything to just pay 'em off and get shut . . ."

Bub looked grim and glanced at the huddled shape under the tarpaulin. "Yes, you don't have to tell me. But you can't change what was, Dick, you can't bring back the ones they killed or the ones *you* killed, you just got to 'bide what come and take care of the day you living in." He looked at Henry Starr now, his anger tugging against his sympathy. "You make too much of all that old-time stuff, Henry. Nobody would blame what you done: it was your life or his, and he was a dead man any way it come out. All you done was make him feel as good about it as he could feel. It wasn't any fault of yours that the only thing would make Cherokee Bill feel good about himself dying had to be a goddamn lie. Any way at all he died was gonna be *nigger* to him, because that's all he was to himself. You done him all the good a friend could do, lying like that, just like giving a man a drink of whiskey to ease him over when he goin'. And now he don't feel nothing any more at all. Nothing." He pursed up his lips: he was thinking about T. J. Hanks, and what T. J. Hanks had known and felt all that time he was dying.

And just like a sharp trader will see through the other man's bluffs and withdrawals and brags and denials blowing like smoke in the air, see behind his words and behind his eyes just what it is he wants to sell and what's his price, Henry Starr saw suddenly that there were three of them in this trade, or was it six? Yes six, three up and three down, there were three live men here each carrying a dead man around with him, what they wanted was to trade off ghost for ghost, dead man for dead man: Cherokee Bill for Dick Rowland's daddy for T. J. Hanks for Cherokee Bill.

*That's a hard swap to manage, brother, but there's a man I know who's smart enough to swing it.*

He looked at Dick Rowland and saw that Rowland was just waiting on Bub Houston.

Henry Starr leaned forward, he had to press it home now that Bub was softening a little, it was as tight a point of balance as it had been between the narrow stone walls of the prison corridor, staring into the eyes of Cherokee Bill that were like two tiny cells in which a human shadow-shape quivered and raged to get out—he shook that picture away. "But I got a chance now, Bub, to do what I said. To make it all over, and this time get it right."

"Man, but it's still a *lie*, Henry—making that poor blood-simple son of a bitch into some kind of . . ."

"Blood-simple? Maybe he was: but he give up his gun to me, and he must have known I meant to save myself: but he give it up. I thought he was a fool to do that, but maybe he wasn't, maybe he was right to trust that some day I would make his name good in the Nation. Not like it was but like he wished it was, like it should have been if there was any justice. I can't change the facts, but I can change the reasons that go behind the facts, Bub. I can show how inside the thing they hated and was afraid of there was somebody who knew a little bit what justice might taste like."

He had said what he could. Everything that belonged to the trade was on the table now—everything but one: "If you help me, I know how we can take Price down, and maybe the people behind him too."

Bub still shook his head, but now it was with resignation. "All this foolin' around so you can impress that hank of hair." He looked at Dick Rowland like he was disappointed in the boy, but would let him have his way: "If play-actin' around the white folks, helpin' someone else get into the honey pot seem like a man's work to you, Dick, you got my blessing to help Young Henry out."

Rowland smiled, and looked steadily at Henry Starr. "There's worse things a man can do for a friend, Bub. I been play-acting like a half-dead man for white folks and colored both. Hanging around like a picture on the wall. At least Henry Starr's pictures move."

Bub said nothing else. His silence was as good as a handshake; it meant Henry Starr had made his deal. "All right," he said. "I'll lay out how we put Price under; and then Dick and me . . . ."

"Yeah," said Bub slowly, "you do that. But first get you a shovel." He turned away and walked deliberately toward the yellow tarpaulin over which flies buzzed and sparked in the high light of the sun.

## TULSA *May 28–29, 1921*

Henry Starr had not appeared on the set on Tuesday, but Esterhazy had not been concerned. Fog and haze made shooting outside impractical, and everyone needed a break from the continual failure of trying to film the Lady in the Cabin scene. They waited much of Wednesday morning for him to show, Esterhazy was annoyed but used the rest of the day to shoot some extra footage—little bits of detail that he could use to deepen the film's illusion of placement in a real world of cowboys and Indians, farmers and railroad builders. Esterhazy enjoyed himself, it was luxury, having both the chance to do this kind of shooting and an impeccable excuse for using the company's time and resources. But Esterhazy had tried and failed to find Henry Starr in his room or at any of the hangouts in Tulsa that evening, and on Wednesday night he alerted Miss Woodly—they could shoot around Henry Starr tomorrow, but after that . . .

And at first she had refused to be disturbed at all. She saw the fear that made Esterhazy's eyes flicker, but his nervousness only made her feel how much stronger than Esterhazy she was, and always had been. She had Henry Starr's number: he was proud and stubborn and a little childish, of course he would stalk off the set and take a good hard sulk when he struck a hard place like the Lady in the Cabin. But he would be back. She couldn't conceive of any other outcome. No. What else could he do but come back?

Wednesday night and through Thursday she felt strong in stubbornness, she set her chin and wouldn't give him up, but kept recomposing him in her mind, on her yellow sheets of paper, kept taking his ghost apart and putting him together, and maybe if she did that deep and hard and long enough she would bring him there in the flesh.

Friday: the door of his room booming hollow even to *her* fist, his Appaloosa mare missing from the stall in the livery. Esterhazy had looked at her, his face flushed and his eyes racing, "He don't come back this weekend, is *kaput*." She guessed at the mix of feelings in him, he was sorry to lose his movie and glad to get rid of Henry Starr as a rival—for herself, for the right to scheme his way between her legs. The recognition gave her neither anger nor pleasure; she felt like a peeled bone the dogs would fight over, light and dry and empty herself.

She worked in the teller's cage at the Chemical–Cattlemen's Bank all day and lingered there late in the afternoon, nowhere better to go, nothing better for her hands or mind to do. The huge glare of the sun at the windows varnished everything; the air was heavy, the bank like a packing crate full of cottonwool. The slowest time of the day: she could no longer keep her mind on the tasks of taking deposits, paying out, keeping the tally for which she earned her salary. If she was lucky, and if she was an especially good girl, maybe they would let her do this for the rest of her life.

"Would you like that in coin or paper, sir?" The fingers flash one two three four five ten fifteen twenty twenty-five thirty, receipt, record the transaction; keeping correct accounts is the essence of banking.

She had fallen into a deep and narrow hole, and it was just the size and shape of the empty space he made by being so completely gone.

It had been so almost perfect before, even when she had been stuck here behind the brass cage Wilberforce built around her, her eyes full of his money and his account papers and his pale, ring-decked hands. Behind her eyes she was out the door and in her buggy, trotting back to her rooms where Henry Starr sprawled across the yellow sheets of legal paper on which she was composing her movie of him; or out to the movie lot where Poole was waiting, smelling of hair oil and cologne, reminding her that she was due to come for another of those conferences in his office to discuss "the progress of our little project," which was his way of putting a mark upon her, showing her that it was in his power to make her appear in front of him whenever he wanted to look at her. It was his money she was spending, wasn't it? It was his good will that had given her power to make her movie, wasn't it? A man had a right to keep his eye on his investments.

But she didn't have to listen to Poole as long as she could fill her eyes with Henry Starr as he stood under the lights and played the games she made up for him, played himself as old as her father and young as a boy, moved and spoke and acted her dreams so perfectly that he was colored with her colors and the eyes the same as hers, made up out of herself, like herself made strong and compact and self-contained and free.

Who was now absolutely and finally and completely gone. And here she was in her brass cage.

Every move she ever made to give herself freedom had ended up the same way: the same look of the eyes like bars of a prison all around her, saying they had rights, saying if you didn't come across, if you said no, if you didn't *come on honey be a good little girl*—well all right honey if that's what you want, but then you are a bad girl, a welsher, a cheat, a tease, an Indian-giver. Oh and you got punished for it; whether it was Daddy's grim mouth pucker or Poole's knowing smirk, it was all the same judgment.

And she seemed to end up looking at that judgment no matter what she tried, whether she said yes or no, whether she played the whore or the daddy's-girl: because it was the fact of her *playing* it that they hated and made her pay for. Yes: a whore is for me to fuck and a daddy's-girl is for me to buy ice cream, be one or the other and I know what games to play with you, but don't you play any games of your own, because that's man's work, like running a business or robbing a bank.

Looking up through the barred grate in front of her made her feel as if she were finally in jail, paying for all her crimes and presumptions.

She'd never get out of it now, not when Wilberforce and Poole and Foley discovered that Henry Starr had run out on them. *You smug little Cherokee outlaw bastard, you just left me behind as bait for that damned posse. Henry Starr, you treacherous renegade, I thought you stuck by your men?*

And what makes it so hard is I felt like I really was one of yours, when we walked into that bank in Tahlequah I knew you were robbing the bank in your head and I was right there with you. I bet all the cash in this drawer that if you took me back there I'd do it perfectly, drop-rein the horses, check the street, step in the door and cover them with my rifle while you *Thumbs up and stand steady* and clean out the safe, my God I've seen you do it a thousand times between Foley's films and Esterhazy's scenes and all those rehearsals—because you were in my gang too, Henry Starr, how could you forget the Woodly Gang: you played by my rules like I would have played by yours, and the game had almost, almost become something true—

Well, what had broken the spell? Maybe it was the Lady in the Cabin—every time he came back in through that door he changed, and it wasn't just his trying to find some way of acting real with that twit of an Alice: every time he came through the door he was uglier, there was something twisting in his body and his face, twisting tight like a spring, tight and tight so that if he let it go—and he almost did that last time coming through the door like a wolf and Alice nearly crashed herself backwards through the table to get away, and for once I believed her, for once it wasn't fakery, if it had been me I'd have kept backing right on out through the wall . . .

*And Esterhazy said: "You were supposed to keep Cherokee Bill outside, not bring him in with you."*

Cherokee Bill: she had never given much thought to Cherokee Bill, he was always just the side of Henry Starr the outlaw that made for harm and getting punished. And Henry Starr hadn't really told her anything about him, he was vague, just a big nameless shadow hulking beyond the firelight above Tahlequah, all she knew was that they were friends . . . but how good a friend could he have been if Henry Starr gave him up to save himself from hanging? Henry Starr wouldn't do something like that, unless . . .

Unless he wasn't who she imagined him being. And how wide was her imagination if she hadn't thought it was possible for him to throw *her* to the wolves too, to cover his getaway?

There was always too much more of him there than she could dream up. Even when he played her games, rehearsed her dialogue in scenes she made up, he was playing them his way, for his reasons: and then he does something like that damned "rehearsal" he staged in here, walking into the bank like he was the genuine leather-bound gold-embossed edition of Henry Starr the bank robber, six-guns shotguns and bowie knives under the drape of his coat. I asked him *how would you rob my bank* playing games like a little girl, and now he is going to show me and I'm not ready, I'm not.

And then he turns it around again, and doubles the joke—"*B. C. Woodly: what's the B. C. stand for?*"

"*For my name, Henry Starr: which is mine to know and mine to keep. And mine to make, Henry Starr, like you made yours.*" *And he smiled like I had given, like that was all right with him and did we shake hands? It felt like we had, and then he said* "*In the meantime I guess I will just call you Bobcat,*" *and I was afraid first because he had guessed too near, and then because who the hell is Henry Starr to name me my name, even if it's close, even if my brothers my daddy used to call me that name because when I'm hot about something I do look like a goddamn bobcat—because if he knew my name or made it what he wanted I'd have nothing, none of the secrecy a woman needs to make any of the things that were in her to make in a world run by the Pooles and the Wilberforces and even the Henry Starrs . . .*

Except he wasn't Poole: he was Henry Starr, and the difference was instantly as sharp and clear as an image seen by a flash of lightning—the difference being that after all of Henry Starr's teasing in the bank, his pushing at her tender balance, his playing changes back and forth so she went scared and angry and . . . with all of that, he had never afterward called her anything but "Miss Woodly."

If he wanted that badly to get a name to put on her, why when he had nearly done it did he give it all back to her? It was as if—having robbed that bank and come charging back down the street under fire to swoop that dropped saddlebag of money up out of the street—he had just stopped and got off that horse and given the cash back to who it belonged to, and rode off into the blue distance. Well, her "Henry Starr" gave money to the Lady in the Cabin, but this giving back was harder to see, harder to get hold of: a gift so secret and invisible . . . How could you believe a man like Henry Starr would have known how to give it? And how could you be sure it had actually been given?

If he could see secrets that deep, and give them back so carefully that she wasn't even sure they had been taken, then with all her dreaming and inventing she hadn't really seen him at all.

She closed her eyes, blocking out the brass teller's cage and was herself alone, closed in her body, closed in the heavy heat that covered all her skin.

If she ever had "Henry Starr" to invent again she would put the strangeness in too, that ghost or mood in him that was uncontrollable and uncanny, capable of anything, anything absolutely at all: the part that could be friends with Cherokee Bill and then betray him, the part that showed when he killed Floyd Wilson and might have killed any of the hundreds of passengers passersby bankers and yes even female bank tellers who had the luck to get caught up in one of his robberies; the part of him that was outside the smoky power of her dreams, that was real and compact and forty-seven years old and been to prison and been married, that even when he was webbed all over with her knowings and guesses could stand off from her like a stranger and look at her—and ask *her* things, worming her stories out of her as she had done to him, so that in the end he would see her as she had seen him in the firelight, and feel himself the fear of seeing too many of her secrets all at once, afraid, knowing he'd never get to the bottom of her and have it all in his hands, but knowing there was a bottom to her that he wanted more than anything to look and look and look for.

Behind her closed eyes she imagined his eyes on her, stepping through the door of the bank with the sunflares shooting out behind him, and she felt herself divide like the leaves of a book opening to the slide of a finger running up her belly from the socket and groove of her crotch to the eyes of her breasts, into her throat, to the tips of her eyes—

And she was afraid again, afraid: because she realized that even if he hadn't got to the bottom of her yet she had just wished suddenly and sharply and with her whole body that he would come back to the bank and step in through the door with his guns under his jacket and his dangerous eyes, and guess and guess and guess and guess until he had found her all out.

But when she opened her eyes the door was empty. The guard held it open for her, keys dangling from his hand, "Good night, Miss Woodly"; he would close and lock the door after her. On the other side of the door was a night in her empty room, and then a ride to the set in the morning to take whatever kind of defeat they had ready for her.

## TULSA *May 28, 1921*

They had all gotten up early and were out there ahead of her. She saw the three cars parked under the cottonwood—Foley's battered black Model A, Wilberforce's polished touring car, Poole's cream-colored Stutz with a fox's brush streaming from each polished-steel headlamp—so she got herself set before opening the door of the warehouse-studio. They stood in a compact group that centered on Poole, and they raised their eyes in unison to stare her down—all except poor Esterhazy, who ducked his head and moved away from them. He took a cloth from his pocket and began to polish the lens of his camera.

So: Foley had probably been putting the pressure on him, and he had had to talk, couldn't help himself. It was too bad, but it had been bound to happen sooner or later. Esterhazy would be ashamed that it had been sooner.

"I gather you've been having some difficulties with our leading player," said Poole, his mouth composed for gravity but his pale eyebrows lifting in comfortable speculation.

"The safety of our investment . . . ," said Wilberforce. "Insufficient consultations . . ." He clucked his tongue. "Won't happen again I'm . . ."

"Difficulties?" snapped Foley. "He's run off, as I hear it." He addressed Wilberforce loudly, appealingly: "You need to have professional management on something like this, and here's what comes of . . ." But Wilberforce just looked his own appeal to Poole to take things off his hands, he was caught between concern for his money and Foley's importunate demands and . . . and all the *fine hopes* he had invested in Miss Woodly . . .

"Perhaps if you gentlemen will let me talk with Miss Woodly for a moment . . . ?" said Poole, and the others backed off toward Esterhazy though Foley's resentment was a puppet string that had his head continually jerking back toward them.

"Well," said Poole, looking her over, taking inventory before he accepted the goods, a man wants to be sure he gets what he's paid for.

"He's not the first actor around here who ever missed a couple of days of shooting," she said.

Poole brushed that away. "He's gone. It's finished. But it's not the end of the world. If you're patient I'm sure I can put some more chances in your way."

"Is that what you did? Put this chance in my way?"

"Don't be spiteful, Barbara. You aren't a child. There are things that I could do for you. It doesn't have to be complicated: it's going to be necessary for us to have conferences now and again, maybe this evening. As long as you're working for me . . ."

*Henry Starr you Cherokee renegade bastard, you really left me to the wolves.* Then she felt something inside her bristle and rise, words and a grin to go with them that was like a bandanna pulled up to the eyes, eyes loaded cocked and leveled:

"No," she said, "not while I'm working for you."

Behind her she heard the door swing open, and the thud/chink sound of a man in Texas boots and spurs walking slowly across to the set, and she didn't look but trusted who it would be, as if repeating his words for herself had conjured him back. *Thumbs up you weasel prick bastard,* she thought standing eye to eye with Poole, *thumbs up and stand steady.*

Poole's face became studiedly bland. "And if you weren't working for me?"

"Then," she said, "I wouldn't have spent this much time talking about it."

Poole's mouth curled. "I understood from your relations with my partner Mr. Wilberforce that *that* was precisely what you *did* do when you worked for—" And then he saw someone behind Miss Woodly that made him stop.

*Henry Starr,* she thought. "We *can* be mistaken about people," she said quietly.

"Can we?" he snapped, glaring at her again. "No, I think what we all are here is pretty plain."

She turned to find Henry Starr and there he was, like a genie out of a lamp: but there was a strange man standing next to him, a Negro—a tall man, taller than Henry Starr by six or more inches, his features calm and the line of his body relaxed—but where the light from the set touched his eyes it made sharp points.

"Miss Woodly," said Henry Starr, as calmly as if he had been there that whole long time and the last four days a dream, "Miss Woodly, I'd like for you to meet my pardner Dick Rowland. He's come to do Cherokee Bill for us."

Foley, straining to overhear, exploded like a string of Fourth of July backarappers. "What? Impossible! You can't do . . . Nobody would ever stand for it, not one second . . . !"

Wilberforce rose behind him like a baleful moon. "Well well, now, now here . . . I don't think . . ."

Poole nodded his head as if he had expected this, his mouth set in a straight bitter line.

"We signed a contract," Miss Woodly told him, and swung to include Wilberforce and Foley. "Isn't that correct? We signed a contract, and I was to have the right to do the script and cast the performers as I saw fit."

"Subject to my approval!" snapped Foley.

"No," she said, the tilt of her head like an arc in a pressured blade. "No: not till the movie is made the way Esterhazy and I think it should be."

"Ask your associate Mr. Esterhazy what he thinks," said Foley. "You'll find he agrees with me."

"But the final say is still mine," she said, "isn't that right, Mr. Poole?"

"We have the right to edit the film," said Poole, "and it is ours to distribute or not as we see fit."

She just grinned at that, because once the film was made it was *made*; even if Poole was mad enough to want to bury their investment Wilberforce never would, and she could handle Mr. Wilberforce. She turned to smile at Mr. Wilberforce.

Who meanwhile was fleeing the scene, bowing and smiling like a man slapping away the hands of beggars, making his escape. Foley was expostulating at long range to Esterhazy, whose face was turned away from all that had happened, concentrated on his camera, his precious camera, a man's best friend in a troublesome world. Poole walked off and stood near them with his arms folded, ignoring Wilberforce's attempts to say good day.

Miss Woodly smiled at Henry Starr and Dick Rowland. "Pleased to meet you, Cherokee Bill," she said. "I've heard a lot about you." The colored man nodded to the greeting and kept his silence for the rest, but she could tell that Henry Starr was having a real good time. Well, so was she.

"That was some entrance you made, Henry Starr. You've got a talent for this business."

"Yes ma'am," he said. "Just rehearsing my Henry Starr-to-the-rescue scene."

"Like you were rehearsing in my bank a few days ago?"

He looked at her straight. "The truth of it is, I ain't quite sure."

Something in the core of her chest grew hard and tight and began to swell outward to her face and her belly. "I think you were practicing to see how you would rob my bank."

"Maybe so," he said softly.

"You said you would want to have an inside man? Suppose I would be your inside man, Henry Starr: then how would you rob my bank?"

"I'd wait till late in the day," he said softly, "wait for the end of business. Wait till the safes was full. I'd wait for you to be alone behind the cage, like you are at the end of the day's business . . ."

*Yes, she thought, yes he's been watching and keeping track of times and movements and . . .*

"I'd do it quiet. It would just be me and one other man. I come in first and move towards you, take my time so if anyone's in front of me they get ready to clear out. Then the other man comes in, a couple of ticks after, and eases over to where the guard is standing by the door ready to lock when the last customer leaves."

He stopped.

"Yes," she said.

"The other man takes the guard. I draw my gun . . ."

" 'Thumbs up and stand steady,' " she said as if reciting a lesson. "Did I get that right?"

"Yes, Miss Woodly, you've got that right."

"And then I'd have to be ready to show you where everything is, bankers are tricky, they hide things . . ."

"Yes," he said, his eyes narrowing on hers as if something there was suddenly strange to him.

"I'd be ready," she said, grinning her bobcat grin, and all he could say was a soft "Well yes, I guess you would be . . ." but she was ahead of him and meant to stay there:

"But how would I get my share, Henry Starr? Would we have a place to meet?"

"I'd find you," he said.

"Yes," she said with a lift of an eyebrow and an edge in her voice, "after you made your getaway . . ." She stopped. Someone else had come through the door, a lean shape under a broad-brimmed Stetson.

Poole stepped across to greet Bill Tilghman as he came into the light, his badge tipping like a wink from behind the lapel of his jacket. Whatever Poole said made the old man nod once and continue his slow walk toward Henry Starr, Poole now following just behind him, Wilberforce and Foley drifting their way. Esterhazy hid his face in his camera safely out of the picture.

When she looked at Henry Starr he seemed to be gathering himself in, like a wolf might do when in the middle of his rest he gets a scent of something. He looked a little dangerous but he also still looked like he was having a good time.

"I just came by to ask you a couple of questions, Henry," said the marshal.

"Surely."

"I hear you haven't been around this job much the last couple of days."

"Somebody missing something, Bill? Besides me, I mean."

"There was a bank robbed the other day, over in Prue."

"I know the town well. I seem to recollect robbing a bank there once, back in '14 or '15."

"Man who robbed it come in on horseback, wore a fancy shirt, carrying a forty-five. 'Thumbs up and stand steady,' that's what he said to the man."

"Sounds like a feller been reading too many dime books or watching too many of my moving pictures."

"Where you been these last days, Henry?"

"Yes," said Poole, "we'd all like to know . . ."

"He's been with me," she said, *been with me been with* . . . firing the words offhand and snap shot like a kid out hunting and a squirrel flashes by and he knocks it off a limb spinning dead-shot through the air to the earth, *with me been* "with me. He's been staying at my place." *With me.*

"Well!" said Wilberforce turning purple, Foley snorted he might have guessed. Poole lifted the corner of his mouth in a smirk. He turned abruptly and walked with quick strides to the door. Esterhazy, who could have contradicted her, looked up in surprise—safely out of earshot.

She felt loose and soft and empty, the spring of her care and protective self-attention shot and sprung. She had given it all away, given herself away, because even though it wasn't true it *was* true. Now they would all think they knew her right to the bottom, and it didn't matter to her at all, because Henry Starr knew what the truth was now: or he would know if he'd just start guessing, he'd know if he asked her, and she hoped he wouldn't she hoped he already knew so much that he wouldn't have to ask.

"Well . . ." said the old marshal, looking shyly from Henry Starr to Miss Woodly and back again. "Well. I guess you ain't gonna be much help to me then."

Henry Starr kept his eyes on Tilghman's face, and if he felt anything out of what she had said he held it inside himself *because that's what he has to do now, that's the way this part of his game has to work, and if I want to be part of that game I have to keep still myself now.*

"If it was me robbed that bank," said Henry Starr, "I think I'd want to hang out around east of there. Wouldn't have been much of a take, unless Prue got a lot richer since I was there. But there's good cover over between the Caney and the Verdigris, and a couple other banks just as easy to hit. Owasso, for example. They got a real nice bank in Owasso, as I recall."

Tilghman looked Henry Starr in the eyes for a moment, then nodded. "Well, I might do some tracking around there."

"Day after tomorrow," said Henry Starr. "I calculate the likeliest time might be day after tomorrow."

"Yes," said Tilghman, "that's what I was thinking."

"If I get free here, I might come up and show you around that country."

"No need," said Tilghman, "I can find my way." He touched his hat to Miss Woodly, and walked away toward the door, through which Wilberforce and Foley had preceded him.

"*The Lady in the Cabin, take number twelve!*"

"Positions!" said Esterhazy. Miss Woodly stood right next to him, but he was too ashamed to look at her. Shame made his voice seem muffled. *I'm sorry,* he thought, *but Foley . . . you don't know what it is to be a stranger in this country, they can do what they like with you, they* . . . "Henry. I suppose your . . . your friend there knows what this is all about?"

"He's read the script . . ."

Esterhazy had the sense that his camera was now no sanctuary at all, but a window looking out on a morass of quicksand into which he was sinking eyes first. "You know, is impossible now, it really is. We have just two days left to shoot, you bring in new actor—we will have all to start over and . . ."

"You can handle that," said Henry Starr. "Just like you did me in *Buckskin Bill*: just take a few shots of Cherokee Bill here and there and cut 'em up and tie 'em in."

Yes: it was not the technical difficulty he was afraid of, it was Foley and Poole . . . and Henry Starr and his *Neger* and . . . "All right," he said glumly, "places . . ."

"Not yet." Henry Starr stood in the light, a little man talking to a big spider-legged automaton with a twin-bulbed crest on a square black head studded with metal warts. "There's some things have to be changed."

Esterhazy's nerves and conscience were filed to an edge, a hair trigger, and he popped off: "For Christ's sake, Henry, let us just do damned script how it is written. You come in with Cherokee Bill, he scares woman, you give her little protection and . . . We change something now we have to start all over . . ." He looked down at Miss Woodly, he was appealing to her, he was on her side defending her script against Henry Starr.

But she looked only at Henry Starr. "What needs to be changed?" she said.

"She can be scared," said Henry Starr, "she should be scared. But it ain't just him scaring her. It's like he's almost as scared of her as she is of him . . ."

"Big colored man like that?" cried Esterhazy in despair. "He's afraid of woman and little baby?"

"She's scared of him big and tough, and also black," said Henry Starr, "and he's scared of them white and female and so small . . . Do I have to try and explain it? Let me just show you how . . ."

"It won't play," yelped Esterhazy. "I can't see it, and I tell you, won't play."

"Let him show us," said Miss Woodly.

Esterhazy was practically choking. "We got to finish this in two days or Foley . . ."

"You're afraid of Foley," she said turning her eyes on him, "but the contract says this is my movie to make. Maybe you should start being a little afraid of me."

It was as if she had slapped him. His face was numb. "Is your picture. Is your *script*. You tell me now what happens to hero saving guard in prison break? Which we must shoot tomorrow! You wrote him to take gun away from killer, saves guard's life, wins pardon: goes back and marries lady in cabin, no? Is this your story or not? What happens to ending now, if you don't play Cherokee Bill as big bad wolf? Maybe they pardon this hero of yours for taking ribbon off little pussycat . . ."

"That isn't how we'll play it," said Henry Starr. "Story is one thing, but that was just a lie." His look shifted from the camera to the woman standing next to it. "You made me out too much better a man than I was. You see?"

"Tell me," she said.

"We're in the jail, me and my partner, and he busts out, but it's no good, it's just a different way of letting them kill us. But they let me talk to him, and we remember how it used to be, and when I tell him about the woman in the cabin, he's got to remember it just like I would, Miss Woodly. Because it ain't that I fooled him, though it might look like I did mean to . . . But you know he wasn't fooled, no, I don't think he was. I think when he come right down to cases, it was something he decided to do for me. Like a gift he give me, thinking *all right Henry if that is what you want.*" His voice became softer yet: "Because I used to be his pardner, Miss Woodly. Because we rode together from way way back . . . just let me show you," he said.

"Do it the way he wants it done," she said to Esterhazy. "It's his story, isn't it?"

Let them do what they want then, all right, thought Esterhazy, is out of my hands and off my conscience. Even Foley will see that I had no choice. It will not even matter, because scene will not play, and Foley will use most to light cigars, probably saving only robbery scenes, he ought to be able to run those through eight more movies.

They began, and Esterhazy was shamefully glad to see that having Cherokee Bill on hand made no difference, they still could not make anything work. *Take twelve*: the black man standing there like a stick, light-blind and lost and entering too slowly. *Take thirteen* and Alice catches her ass on the end of the table backing away from the outlaw and his tame black bear, well at least she is acting *terror* better than she ever has—twisting face and body away from the Negro's advance, shying *yeee!* when he came close enough for her to need to snatch her skirts away.

"Listen," said Henry Starr, forgetting Esterhazy was supposed to be directing them, so caught up in it that he was almost pleading with Alice. "Listen: this here's your own place. Ain't you got no sand? You think I'd come back here to you when it's over if you didn't have any more backbone than a sack of trash? It's *your* place and these badmen come in, maybe we scare you at first, but you ain't gonna jump out the window. It's your *place.* And if you stand your ground you're gonna find out something: that under the scare we give each other, he . . . he's been some bad places and he's done some killing and they killed on him too, but he's got a man's feelings and he . . . he deserves . . . he deserves justice like anybody else," and all through this unintelligible blither of instructions Alice kept leaning and leaning back away from Henry Starr like he was blowing insects out of his mouth and they were crawling up her front and her face, twisted with disgust—that burst instantly into blind terror when Henry Starr leaned forward suddenly into her face and hissed, "*Listen* you . . . listen: nobody leaves this place till it comes out right."

Miss Woodly stepped into the lights. "Get out of here," she said to Alice, taking the shawl from the woman's shoulders and swinging it around herself. "Can you make me look like her?" she said over her shoulder to Esterhazy.

Crazy. Completely crazy. "Yes." Esterhazy threw up his hands. "Yes. I have enough close pictures of her face. I shoot this from little behind you, nobody sees difference."

"Then do it," she said.

The three of them faced each other in the room: Henry Starr standing in the door, his eyes alert to everything, his muscles tuned like the strings of a guitar; the tall shape of the black man filling the door behind him; Miss Woodly's shape blurred by the shawl, maybe just enough for someone who didn't know it was her small firm shoulders under there and not Alice's soft puffy ones.

"Lady in the Cabin, take fourteen!"

"What should I say?" she called out, and Esterhazy said, "Say anything, we can't see face, just anything so they will react."

They came toward her, and she stepped back once, then leaned like a birch tree in a blow and tilted erect again so that it was the two men who had to stop.

"I am Henry Starr," he said. "This is my pardner, Cherokee Bill. Don't be afraid . . ."

Miss Woodly's mantled head was inclined toward Henry Starr. In Esterhazy's camera the black man's face seemed to shift and change, not stiff with panic as it had been in the first takes but showing now a sudden surprise (maybe it would pass for the kind of fear of small babies and helpless women that Henry Starr wanted), and then his face gathered itself in a kind of intensity as if he saw something in Miss Woodly's face —but her back was to the camera, Esterhazy was as good as blind—

"Henry Starr," he heard her invisible mouth say, "I love you, Henry Starr."

"Yes ma'am," said Henry Starr—and now he swayed back on his boots like a sapling whipping in a blow, and maybe she had just blown the script right out of his head, because he was just standing there looking at her, just repeating his line in an oddly twisted voice, "This here is Cherokee Bill—my pardner—he rides with me."

"Yes," she said, her voice full of breath, "all right. He rides with you, yes."

And Henry Starr had another line in there, he was supposed to say they wouldn't hurt her, but he was in a total funk now, he had seemingly lost his place his cue his words and all. "We got a job to do day after tomorrow, but I'll be back by evening," and Miss Woodly said, "Yes I'll be ready," and God knew what she was talking about or what Henry Starr might have said next.

Of all people it was the Negro who saved the take, remembering at the last instant to say the line Henry Starr had said to give him: "Baby," he said wonderingly, the way you might say *what is* this *all about*—then, as if he had reminded himself of the script, "Baby, that's a fine thing you got here."

*"That's a fine baby you got there," that was the line, but what they had was close enough, the words all out of order but the audience would read "baby" on his lips, and just thank God you can't hear actors talking in a movie*, Esterhazy thought as he kept the film rolling through the camera, *come on, come on, let's get out of this* . . .

Miss Woodly handed the bundle of rags to the black man, and something in her look made him take it as if it were a delicate and precious thing, holding it softly in large black hands that were supposed to be the hands of a congenital lunatic murderer.

"Baby," said the black man again, "little sister, you better take care of yourself."

"I can do that," said Miss Woodly, "if I have to. Or if I want to I can take no damn care at all."

The black man shook his head, and turned as if to show the baby to Henry Starr, and Miss Woodly's head turned to follow him to Henry Starr, but Henry Starr was looking at Miss Woodly, and looking and looking and looking at her hidden face so that Esterhazy wanted to scream. He wished he could see in his camera what was in her face that made the outlaw look like that, but he never wanted to see her face again.

"My real name is Barbara Catherine Woodly," he heard her say, "but I would like it if you called me Bobcat."

## OWASSO *May 30, 1921*

At 9:15 Monday morning Deputy Price—precisely on cue—parked his open-topped Dodge in the alley near the First National Bank of Owasso and walked his usual path to the bank as if stepping off chalk-mark paces laid out in rehearsal: wearing, as before, the terrible yellow suit with the black boxes, and the shoes that gripped his feet in a vise and made him mince awkwardly in the morning sunlight, looking uneasily right and left before he opened the door and stepped inside.

The clerk and the bank president stood behind the counter, staring at him like he was a geek show. "Hey," he groused, "don't you know how to say *howdy* to a customer?"

"Howdy," said a voice behind him, he saw the bank president and clerk shoot their hands straight into the air, and he turned: two of them, one a nigger, bandannas covering everything but their eyes, the dinge had a shotgun and the white man a pistol. The white man jerked his left thumb toward the ceiling and Price raised his hands, his mind struggling to catch up with things. *All right so they would take his money along with the bank's he'd have a hell of a time explaining to MacKinnon, the important thing was to have a reason not to wait for the police to arrive because MacKinnon wouldn't want his name in the paper . . . but whose name would it be in the paper, MacKinnon's? his own?*—all of that lumbering through his head while the white man reached inside the yellow and black jacket and went straight for the envelope as if he'd known it was there.

"Well ain't this a surprise," he said. He riffled the bills with his thumb. "Must be three/four thousand." He tilted his head toward the two men behind the counter and said, "Mr. Banker, this is your lucky day. We won't bother waiting on that time lock you say you got, even if it turns out you ain't got one. I ain't greedy. This here'll do me fine." He dipped the pistol at Price. "You ought to be thankful Mr. Deputy Price here come along."

"That's Mr. MacKinnon . . . !" chirped the clerk; the banker hushed him, but the black bandit said, "No. This here is Mr. Deputy Price, ain't it?"

The black man stepped up to Price and jammed the shotgun up under his chin, lifting it so that the slack skin caught on the barrel end. "Ain't you Mr. Deputy Price?"

"Yes," gasped the deputy, his eyes racing left and right looking for the way out.

"And you Mr. MacKinnon's boy too, ain't you?"

"Yes." It was all deniable anyway, he could say they forced him to—

"And with all that you still got time to go Ku-kluckin' round the countryside," said the black man admiringly. "Catch yo'self some po' black man, you and yo' friends, and tie him up so he can't move, and then you kill on him. Ain't that you, boss?"

"Yes," he croaked, "yes, that's me." *Houston it was Houston's boys—*

"I could kill you," said the black man, "now couldn't I just do that?

You tell me if I *could* kill you. You tell me if I ain't got a *right* to kill you."

"Ahh," said Price. *They were going to blow his head off they were going to shoot him in the guts they were going to—*

"I could kill you, and I got the right," said the black man. He paused, you could hear the clock tick tick tick, and then he said, "But right now it seem I don't got the need." He let Price down off the barrel of the gun and stepped back. The other man had lifted the handcuffs from Price's back pocket, he shoved Price back to the wooden pillar in the middle of the lobby and cuffed him around it with his hands behind him. "If we had some kindling," said the white man, "or even a pile of papers," and the black man stepped up to Price and said, "This is how it feel. Do you feel it?" He waited for Price to answer, but Price's mouth moved like he was gobbling air, his neck stretched out long for breath to scream with, gobbling air like it was pie in a pie-eating contest, snorting like a pig and with your hands behind your back, and the black man said, "Had enough pie?" and punched Price hard in the stomach with the barrels of the shotgun and Price puked up his breakfast and his supper both right down the front of his yellow and black suit, spattering his shoes, the wooden floor. He couldn't think to wish or pray, his head was one blank terrible hum through which he heard the robbers backing out the door, the door closing.

The clerk and bank president came running around the counter. "Get the police!" yelled the bank president, and the clerk slammed out the door as the president helplessly rattled the chained wrists of one of his biggest depositors, the bandits had taken the keys of his . . . handcuffs? Why did a merchant like Mr. MacKinnon carry handcuffs?

There were six pistol shots, and then a *whoof!* of exploding gasoline that rattled the windows, and the boy ducked back in through the door, *the bandits were blowing up the town!* "Get the police! Get the police!" cried the banker, and the clerk picked himself off the floor and ducked outside again.

But there was no need for the clerk to run far, here he was backing into the bank again with a tall gray man in a Stetson hat after him; the tall gray man had a badge.

"I am Marshal Tilghman," said the man, and the banker cried, "Keys! I need keys to get Mr. MacKinnon loose . . ."

Deputy Price raised his face to look at Marshal Tilghman.

"Price," said the marshal, as if that settled *that*. "It looks like somebody blew up Mr. MacKinnon's car too."

"My car," said Price bleakly.

"It must get hard for you to remember which is which," said Tilghman.

"We'll offer a reward for the bandits," said the banker pleadingly to . . . was it Mr. MacKinnon? Mr. Price? His biggest depositor must not think this outrage would go . . . He was frantic, in a fever of anxiety, so that he must either have said the opposite of his meaning or misconstrued the marshal's response:

"I don't think they'll ask for a reward," said the marshal, "beyond the getting away."

## TULSA *May 30, 1921*

But late in the afternoon, after the close of business, Henry Starr came for his reward. He tied his horse in the brush along the creek that twisted behind the rear yard of the house where Miss Woodly boarded, making sure the black-and-white mare could wet her nose in the stream, climbed the cutbank and sidled from tree to bush to woodshed until he reached the sheltered space under the back stairs. There was an empty nail keg there, and he turned it over and sat down on it to wait.

Nearly six o'clock. Miss Woodly would have finished at the bank, had supper at the Palmer Room, her buggy would be licking dust out of the road between here and Tulsa, coming steadily toward him where he sat waiting for her. It had happened, all of it, just as he dreamed and wished and planned, and it would keep happening that way now that he had found his power, now that he could make things come.

It was as sure as if they had signed a treaty. No, surer than that: because trades and treaties were ways people had of tricking each other, and what had come to him from her come as a gift, come before he asked for it, as free as lucky finding, given with that alibi she gave to Tilghman: *he's been in my place, been with me, with me in my place*, and her stepping into Alice's place so that the scene could happen the way it was supposed to.

*How would you rob my bank?*

An inside job.

*I'd be ready.*

I'd find you afterwards.

*Yes you would—after you made your getaway.*

Well she was right about that, he had certainly made his getaway, a getaway to beat them all and maybe to stand even with Jesse James's robbing two banks at the same time—because in one bold stroke he had not only managed to rob the Owasso bank with Bill Tilghman practically watching it done, he had put the finger on Deputy Price and MacKinnon to slam Bub's competition, and paid off T. J.'s lynching by getting Price kicked out from behind his badge so Bub could get him, and finished off his movie and paid his debt to the ghost of Cherokee Bill, and as soon as Esterhazy and Foley were finished editing it he would see his life written on the black in silver fire that would never get sick or old, his life made true and finally perfect going round and round and round and never dying.

It was too bad they had not had cameras in Owasso to film the robbery, because it had been the most perfect bank job of Henry Starr's career, which was absolutely the only way it could have worked: because he had cut this one fine, almost too fine, it had needed perfect timing, and Price keeping his schedule, and Dick Rowland staying cool on his first bank job, and worst of all it hung in the end on whether or not Bill Tilghman had read just what it was Henry Starr meant for him to do in Owasso—read it, and played it the way Henry Starr wanted him to. And it had worked the way such things should but almost never did; for once absolutely everything happened according to his dream and his wish and his plan, as if it had been carefully rehearsed right down to the moment when they blew up Price's Dodge like a big steel firecracker and smoked their horses out of town laughing drunk with victory, the *boom!* of the gas tank as loud in his memory as the yells and shouts and turkey gobbles of the old-time warriors in the big Fourth of July crowd at Tahlequah, the day he had showed the Nation the difference between law and justice—

And then he and Dick Rowland took off down a long straight hard-packed road, at the end of which Dick Rowland would disappear into the cover of his perfect alibi (that janitor friend of his at the Drexel would swear Dick had been hauling bins of waste paper around the basement all morning and into the afternoon)—but for Henry Starr there was something greater than that, waiting for him in the far-away vanishing V of the white road, a small bright living spot that was nobody and nothing but Miss Woodly herself, her hair bright above her blue dress and her blue eyes taking his road in like it was ribbon candy and himself at the other end of it—she looked young and clean and jaunty and fierce, with a magic in her body like the fire that lives in water-white whiskey, pour it down your throat and it makes your blood sing and licks fire round your bones . . .

It was at that moment, sitting at the bottom of the back stairs to Miss Woodly's boardinghouse toward the sunburnt evening of that day, that the blue-white woman/whiskey drunk passed over and he thought: *maybe it was too damn perfect.*

Because it was possible for a man to be too smart and lucky—so smart he fools himself, so lucky that the Powers feel his shadow on them and need to play him a trick.

And if there was a trick in this, then Miss Woodly was it. Just listen to me a minute: sure, she covered my play with Bill Tilghman, an alibi given as free and unasked-for as a bag of gold found in the woods or the deer that suddenly goes sweet on your rifle or the creel springing with fish, *He's been with me at my place, with me, will be with me in my place* —But don't you remember just who it is that gives a man gifts like that?

Now that he ran back over where they had been yesterday, he wasn't so sure he had been able to see behind her eyes and make his words speak inside her head. Their talk had gone so smoothly, just as if they rehearsed it and each knew what was coming next—*How would you rob my bank?*—but in fact he hadn't rehearsed any part of it, words and plans and decisions just jumped out of him when she spoke, like trout jumping at flies, and she was the fisherman.

Now that he thought of it, that sure feeling he had had, of his power to see behind people's eyes and to make things come: it only come to him when Miss Woodly was there, and he never felt it stronger than the minute that she stepped into the lights and took the shawl and the rag baby away from Alice, and made herself the Lady in the Cabin.

But what was it that made her come? It wasn't any power of Henry Starr's because that was something he hadn't even thought to wish, she had jumped him and Esterhazy both, stepping in the middle of things like that, and just for one tick his breath had gone blank in his chest like it did when Paul Curry cut him in half with the hog rifle from behind: stepping across the line into the set she had jumped past anything they had ever played or rehearsed together, out of control entirely, and just who was she where was it she had come from? A place hidden in the light-blind of Esterhazy's lamps, the memory of the light blinded him when he tried to dream her thoughts.

She was coming toward him now, the bank closed and her accounts made up, driving her buggy down the road from Tulsa. But did she know, had she understood, that he would be here waiting for her? Or was it all twisted in his head, and when she sees him on the stairs with his guns and his spurs who she sees is not the Robin Hood of Old Oklahoma nor yet "Henry Starr" who had paid all his debts to all the different kinds of law there were, but the man who robbed the Owasso bank and pistol-whipped Deputy Price, the man who could be brothers to Cherokee Bill, brothers so deep that he could feel the giant's fear and rage humming in his own bones, so mad sometimes that he could have killed out everything between the core of his shadow at noon and the cut of the horizon, just another crazy goddamn half-breed son of a bitch whose blood got dirtied somehow back at the start so even his own kin won't own him, and he can't wash himself clean but by spilling somebody else's.

*"This is my pardner, Cherokee Bill."*

*"Yes," she said. "Yes, he rides with you . . ."*

And then she come into the picture and said, what did she say?—that meant *yes*, that meant *yes* to every and any thing I—

Is that what I heard? Is that what she said she was ready for? Because if I got it wrong when I go up those stairs, and there she is, and if it ain't me she's looking for, then what she sees is a half-breed renegade jailbird felon. And you know how *white* they scream those white ladies, they scream you bone white and stone cold if you're wrong about her.

He was standing on that edge again, like the one he stepped over through the door of the Land Office in Tahlequah in 1892, before Henry Starr was any kind of name at all, and stood there looking at Mr. White Man in the Middle and the man couldn't see him, couldn't know that in one tick of the heart the Injun kid in the doorway would become Henry Starr the Outlaw, with his pistol in his hand—but he hadn't known himself what would happen when he pulled the gun and said *Thumbs up and stand steady*, whether it would work like a charm or blow off like belly wind, whether the banker man would shoot his hands straight up as if "Thumbs up and stand steady" was the cue for which he had been waiting all his life, or laugh and laugh and laugh till little henry starr blew away down the street with the rest of the Fourth of July trash.

You could only rehearse so much, you could only get so ready: but when it come to cases you had to just cross the line and lay yourself open to any and every thing that could ever happen, and if you kept doing it long enough it probably would.

But hell: hadn't *she* stepped over that line, giving herself as my alibi to Tilghman, and then coming into the movie and telling me . . . and what more does she know about me than I do about her? From what I've showed her I might be anything from Robin Hood to Cherokee Bill and if she was wrong about me then she as good as named herself a half-breed renegade's whore and none of them who heard her would lift a goddamn finger if the breed came by that night to make the name good on her.

Well, if she could take her chances, a girl like that, then how about Henry Starr, the smartest and bravest outlaw who ever lived, who had just done the most perfect robbery and made the most perfect getaway in history?

He stood up, his mind running ahead to what she would see when she saw him. He unbuckled his gun belt and rolled it, because he didn't want her to think of . . . and because goddamn it he wasn't some renegade off the reservation, he didn't *need* a gun if she . . . Then he took off his hat, because he didn't want to have to take off his hat when he saw her, *Miss Woodly, ma'am.* So he put the gun into the crown, and hid the hat and gun under the nail keg. His spurs chinked as he moved, the damned silly noise, and he bent to undo them—and there were his boots right under his nose—if they were in her room, if she . . . well he didn't want to stand in front of her hauling his boots off looking like a dog scratching fleas with his hind leg, so he pulled them off, but he'd look like a clodhopper standing there in his dirty socks so he pulled off his socks too and jammed them into the boots, and the boots went under the keg with the hat and the gun.

And he stood at the bottom of the steps for a second thinking *Well if I am wrong about her I better get set for the white scream or the big hee-haw, because so far as keeping my purposes obscure is concerned I might as well go up there buck-naked and dick in the wind as go like this in my bare feet and no gun or . . .*

*Listen:* he said to himself, *hat and gun and boots, or none at all: I am still Henry Starr,* and that sent him lightly up the stairs thinking he would wait for her in the shadow at the end of the upstairs corridor.

But she was there already, standing by the door, the door unlocked and a little open.

He stood there in his bare feet *like a blanket-head Injun in the white folks parlor* until she said, "I knew you, I knew . . ."

. . . Although until that absolute second she hadn't been sure in her mind of *what* she knew. She had driven home in the spring buggy dream-reaching forward over her horse's rhythmically moving back and out up the diminishing V of the road, trying to guess whether he would be there, trying to make his shape there in her room where no one but herself had ever been, no one but herself and the ghostly shape of "Henry Starr" as she had dreamed it out onto her yellow legal-pad pages. Her mind kept devouring the distance with such hungry speed that she would suddenly snap awake shocked to see herself still jogging steadily up the road when, in her mind and body, she had felt herself already there, there with Henry Starr filling the space in the air that her dreaming prepared for him, and how would it how would he be?

But despite her head full of questions there was a stunning sense of assurance in her body like a flow of electricity that made her alive to the tension and slide of muscles beneath the skin in her arms and across her shoulders as she played the reins of the horse—little bursts of energy lifted through her at every tilt and jolt of the buggy, they made her feel the edges and inward curves of herself as clearly as if she had touched them, as if a hand inside her were just forming them, making a place where there hadn't been one. Her heart was banging hard with the effortless labor of it, she was drenched, sweaty and wet inside and out, her dress clung to her breasts barely cooled at all by the breeze of the buggy's riding.

She smelled the strong smell of her own body, a sweet-carroty smell from her skin and the sharp tang of sweat and the sun-warm smell of her clean dress dried on the line, it was odd that she liked all that odor so—and then she recognized it, it was the smell of her mother's skin sweet in itself and washed with its own salt inside the clothes that were full of the smell of her time by the washbasin and the line strung back of the green kitchen garden . . .

As quickly as that she felt panic bubbling in her, she saw her mother's look out of the doorway that had always told her she was no fierce wild Bobcat but just plain little Barbara Catherine, a girl who would grow up to make one of the women. Her mother's scent was breathing out of her own skin, filling her own breathing now, her mother swelling up to fill the shape of her body hidden under the sweaty dress—so she wasn't just Miss Bobcat C. Woodly dashing smartly up the road behind her high-stepping horse to meet the Cherokee half-breed renegade outlaw to whom she had as good as promised to give herself naked and hotly willing, she was also standing inside her mother's body now, watching her own daughter's wild play from her stance in the doorway, clutching her own arms as if she could magically transfer their gripping strength to her wild young daughter who was laughing down her mother's fear as she rode the bucking colt through the kitchen garden—

And between wildness and fear and wish and memory she wondered if this was how it had felt for her mother when she rode to meet her father, "Mr. Woodly"—only he was not her father then, and she had never thought of her mother as riding this way, but now she could see it, could almost see it: and if that was so, then even in her Bobcat Uncas horseback-riding wildness there was no power that could save Barbara Catherine Woodly from her mother's shape and fate, because whether you came to him on a wild mustang or sidesaddle on a grain-fat walking horse, once he really *had* you you were as good as locked in prison, where you couldn't play stories or ride your own horse, where your body was something to carry and labor with and not ride like it was a half-wild mustang, where all you could do was grip your own hands in your own skin in some hopeless horror of impotence that can't keep your little girl from riding or hold her on the horse once she's up—and the worst of it was never that she'd be angry at her daughter's wild badness, the worst of it was in her being who and where and what she was, which was what any girl could become if she let a Mr. Anything get his holts on her long and deep enough.

She saw Curly Joe's blunt clumsiness and the suave easy assumption of Poole and Wilberforce's insistent weight and averted eyes, and she saw Henry Starr, the "Robin Hood of Old Oklahoma," calling her "Miss Woodly, ma'am" as he leaned off his galloping horse to snatch her out of the dust of the street like a bag of stolen money.

Was that how it would be with Henry Starr? "Goddamn it, no!" she yelled, and the horse jumped forward in the traces as if she'd stung it, that wasn't good enough, she wasn't letting this awful pressure in her body race her home through the heat if it was just to play that same old game again. *He smiled at her through the bars of her teller's cage and said well then he guessed he would just call her Bobcat,* and this time she was sure she wanted him to know her, to ask and ask until he'd know absolutely all her secrets and her name—but that was all right with her as long as he knew it was *hers*, as long as he knew he had to ask her things and not just take them for his own like found or stolen money, grinning his luck like Curly Joe or Wilberforce . . .

But he was a robber, wasn't he? He took what he wanted and made his getaway when and as he pleased, with that damned bandanna over his face and you lift it up for a smile that's no closer to the bone or the ghost of him than the bandanna was—only in his eyes maybe there's something else, something like the little shape of a man in a small room trying to wish himself outside and free . . .

She couldn't bear to wait any longer to find out how it would be, only sudden action could override her doubts and speed her past the questioning eyes of her ghosts, and she jerked the buggy to a stop in a grove of trees with the same kind of reckless defiant eagerness that had put her onto the back of that wild two-year-old colt and sent her bucking through the kitchen garden while her mother clutched her own forearms to hold her wild daughter on the horse—because she didn't need didn't want anything to hold her back anymore, not the strength of her mother's hands nor the masks and evasions she had used to ward her mother's weakness off: she was actually fierce with impatience when she reached under her skirts lifting her hips to ease the hasty peeling of her cotton underpants and stockings down her legs and off, as if he were there with her already instead of *maybe* there two miles still farther on—as if that were the last conjure she needed to evoke the power in her own body that would make him be there the way she wished.

And she trusted the conjure's strength so that even when the landing was empty she wouldn't doubt, but waited for the cat's pad of his bare feet on the steps, his shape sudden in the stairwell's frame. "I *knew* you . . . I knew you would be here," she told him.

Her face was suddenly as open to him as a pool of clear water, all her words and looks and even the flashing images of his own reflected face were just the flashes of light on the surface, he could see all the way to the bottom, and he knew he was absolutely right about her, he had been perfectly right from the start, she was a gift as free and lucky as finding . . .

*. . . the woman standing in the orange light of the lantern with the empty counter behind her, he remembered the baby had been sitting there with her the first time he stepped inside the door and saw she was a woman who could have given all she had and never come to the bottom but I ain't a man for gifts I'm a man who . . .*

She backed into the room, which opened behind her—yellow light falling between wooden blinds across a battered sofa, white-shaded lamps, a desk piled with yellow pages and nuggets of yellow paper piled in a wastepaper bin, a washbasin of blue and white china. He closed the door behind him. The room was full of dry hot yellow air, there was a carpet like rough hair under his feet.

"Henry Starr," she said softly, "Henry Henry Henry Henry Starr . . ."

*. . . her female shape black against the pale blue grass of the ranch yard, his ears full of Bob Dalton's hello and Bob Dalton's good-bye, "Thumbs up and stand steady," and she said well Henry Starr it's been quite a day and I guess you got everything else a boy could want but—*

"Call me," she said, "call me my name . . ."

*How do you like it, Henry Starr, or don't you know that yet?*

His mind went around, spinning into blue, *Pearl, Cora,* "Bobcat," he said.

"That's right," she said, "you guessed that right."

She was slim and tall in the yellow light, her face so clear that the edges of her lips and eyes seemed almost sharp, she seemed somehow to be vibrating like a struck blade that made a high singing along his nerves, and he couldn't stand that so he stepped up to her and quelled it by wrapping his arms all around her.

Her hair was in his face, it was sun-hot and smelled like wind. "Ask me," she whispered in his ear, "ask me ask me ask me . . ."

And he wondered *what kind of girl is she, a good girl or a wild girl or a girl who knows how to take care of herself, but if she don't that's her problem* because her odor of hair and skin filled his head and covered his breath, he was like a wolf too close on the scent to raise a howl, he couldn't answer when she said *ask me.* His breath went into his arms and hands and fingers, his fingers like tongues that told the shape and lightness of her small shoulders the groove of her back the deep incurve of her waist, balling and balling the soft cotton of her skirt till it was heaped between his wrists, then he slid his hands down and instead of underpants felt the shocking almost liquid smoothness of her bare skin over the cleft muscle of her buttocks, *is she always naked like this underneath, always ready for it, for me, for this?*

Her fingers were plucking at his belt, dropping it slack—picking the buttons of his pants open to show him to let him loose, his pants sloughing like snakeskin to crumple around his feet.

*Well, how* do *you like it, Henry Starr, hot and ready or cool and reluctant, I don't know but I know* yes *when I hear it.*

There were snakes in his arms and hands, supple and hungry, sliding down over the backs of her thighs and knees and calves like water, his face sliding over the buttons of her pleated blouse, the skirt front drooped under his nose like a swag of bunting, and under the smooth plane of her belly the sudden flare of her bush brushed his face, its smell was dense and strange and without thinking he tasted it with his tongue, and when he felt her hands lightly among his hair his tongue tip touched through to a place that was silk to his tongue with a taste of musk and steel, *that was what her secret tasted like, maybe he was the only man in the world who ever tasted a woman's secrets with his tongue.*

The quick touch of his tongue made her feel that the groove of her sex was a mouth for tasting and drinking, empty mouth, thirsty mouth, her body changed as he touched it. The leaves of the blouse she had managed to unbutton and the skirt lifted and bunched away from her hips felt like dry husks against her naked skin, which felt extraordinarily new and tender—she felt as if a bright seam ran right under her skin upward from the liquid groove of her sex following the line of her opened blouse to the top of her head, and she wanted to open that too, to open herself to his look and touch like a peach split and spread like a mouth against the push of a thirsty tongue.

She cradled his head in her hands and lifted him carefully like a woman bathing lifts two handcups of water to spill down her front, lifted him so that his face divided the leaves of the unbuttoned blouse, giving him one nipple tense as a bud on her small breast and carrying him past it so that she could see his face. He was looking at her, his eyes were dark with intensity and smoky with sex, but she couldn't read his mouth, *his smile like a goddamn bandanna that might mean happy or mad or love or hate and you'd never find out by looking*, and right then she wanted to split him open too, and read him like a book, and get inside his bones and name his name and find him out and—

She grabbed his shirt in two fists and split them, firing buttons like small shot left and right. She was leaning back against the wall and he bent and lifted her from underneath, her heartbeat making her lightly made upper body shake against him, but Henry Starr saw she was smiling like a bobcat and her eyes were open to take him in, her weight rested in his hands and across his shoulders and he felt her legs lift and open around his hips and close across his back as his *ghost his blood his name* gathered itself coiling in his belly and lifted out neck and crest and head and flickering tongue, reached out to touch a small spot like a point of heat, like a small mouth, like an opening mouth. She slid over him like a wedding ring—and she closed her eyes and said Oh-h-h-h-h with a slow shudder that pounded small fists up the front of his chest that was tight as a drum, and the ring dissolved, he was in a flow of warm liquid, he was in a deep closed opening space, her horseback-riding legs were around him her hips twisted and rode him as he rolled and bucked . . .

His hands made a saddle under her rump, she felt her weight come onto her hips as he lifted her and she reached out to hold him with her bare legs, and she remembered her father lifting her to the saddle of her first horse and her legs went around his hips and held him with knees and thighs and her calves and feet curling inward to lock them together, she remembered the taste of the black colt's twisting power that she drank up through legs and hips welded tightly to its bucking body—and she felt herself opening at the groove of her crotch as if she were all thirsty mouth there, and Henry Starr's taste clear and complete as his sweet-salt on her tongue his rough-smooth on her skin in the sliding-opening push of the warm blunt-headed boy-thing man-thing between the lips and in the mouth of her sweet sweet-hole, oh sweet—the black horse was galloping inside her hips, she was locked to him so deep-socketed she didn't know if she was horse or rider, and she opened her eyes to see—and in just that second she saw Henry Starr, Henry without his mask, his face was like her little brother's face sweet and smooth and amazed-looking like the first time she told him *Mohicans* the first time she let him see the new naked points of her breasts—and as his face rushed into her eyes it made a circle with the thrust of his cock-inside her that locked itself right through her center, right through and through as she felt Henry Starr's ghost burst in the throat of her sex like the milk-spurt from a cow's teat . . .

And as he come to the pop he opened his eyes to see her face open-eyed and sharp and clear, and then he blinked as the quick pulse in his balls and hips opened him and squeezed him tight, each blink printing her face inside his head as if each pulse were a camera flash firing shots of light that lit her like a lamp to his eyes: her mouth open to show white teeth pink tongue the pit of the throat going down: her face shuttered and closed to him, delicate lips pinched in strong disapproval: her face masked with a fling of hair: her face rashed with blood raging up against the skin: her face white white white: her face Miss Ma'am, Miss Woodly, Miss B. C. Barbara Catherine Bobcat Woodly . . .

. . . whose deep-grooved hips and horseback-riding thighs gripped and shuddered all around him as he pumped her pulsing belly full of Henry full of Starr full of red-white-and-blue-black Cherokee Indian blood.

She was sleeping, her head pillowed on the couch cushions they had thrown onto the floor, the rumpled cover cloth keeping the bristles of the rug from annoying them. He still didn't know where her bed was, though he guessed it was behind the double doors by the back wall, one of the kind that folds up into a closet.

Blue light fell through the wooden blinds, it made her white skin look blue. Her face was smooth, the bobcat-eyes hidden under closed lids. Her lips made two fine lines in her smooth skin, they were thin like a little girl's lips, they would taste of cold water or cold milk if you . . . Kids have lips like that, boy or girl there's no difference yet, in this light she don't look any older than Jiminy.

Jesus how could she have done what she done, a girl like she looks now, to let me just walk in here and . . . and then how she ran that play yesterday, *he's been with me been at my place* with all those big shots setting at her like hounds at a bitch come in season, it was like her saying "here I am" knowing it could cut them loose for catching and fucking her any way they could she was fair game now . . . Or maybe she don't care, maybe it wasn't nothing at all to her if we had or we hadn't or was or wasn't going to, and half of them there already knew that about her because they, because she . . .

A fist reached down into his throat and knotted itself on his breath. He felt the whole time, everything that they had done, everything since Owasso suddenly drowned in *blue, in the color* . . .

He stood up, and looked down at her. What the hell was she? A young woman who had seen the elephant and knew the score, no damn underpants for Chrissake, like she was always in heat walking around with her crotch open and ready every minute of every day—and now she looks . . .

*Ask me*, she had said, *ask me ask me ask me*. Girl, where do I start asking? And do I have to know right off whether these are gonna be answers I like?

The room seemed closed and safe, but it was hard to trust it. She was smart enough to cover me with Bill Tilghman yesterday, to say just the thing that would stop him asking more questions, and do it without me telling her . . . but if she is *that* smart, then she is smart enough to know that she as good as told Bill Tilghman where to come looking for me if he missed me in Owasso.

No underpants. Maybe she don't never wear no underpants. Like a gunfighter ties his gun down and keeps the scabbard slick: always ready for it.

Her faces flashed behind his closed eyes like faces seen in the flashes of a gun fired four-five-six times in the dark: her face open and eager; closed and shuttered; a girl hurting for the newness; her eyes handling his face as sure and cunning as her hands dropping his belt, his pants like hobbles around his ankles.

*Yeah: Bill Tilghman might figure it out, having caught me two times with my pants down, once with an ass full of buckshot and once with a lady plying her trade.*

It was time to get up and look for his guns. He slipped out of the room, down the stairs in his bare feet—gun and hat were where he had left them, under the keg under the steps. He tiptoed back upstairs holding them in his hands, he'd set them handy, then find that bed and open it up for them and . . .

In the corner where he had leaned her against the wall and lifted her there was a gleam of white. When he picked it up, it was a pair of feminine cotton underpants rumpled by a damp fist. He held it and looked down at her sleeping in the blue light, the delicate line of her lips and eyelids, the round shape of her stubborn chin: his mind made the image of her driving that buggy back from the bank, all the time he's by the back stairs scared silly and trying to think where to hide his gun and how he's gonna get out of his boots, like a randy kid who's never poked the beaver, and while he's doing that she's driving and wondering how and if it is going to be, she don't know any more than I do but suddenly she bets I'm going to be there, and it must happen smooth as water falling over itself down a hill, there's no boots to be a problem her shoes is the slippy kind, but it's these, it's these underpants?—I don't know why, maybe it was just one more thing to be pulled at, pulled up or pulled down, and she wanted to get past the handling to the touching—but when she reached under (where? off the road in a thicket? instantly at her own front door? when she heard a footfall on the stairs that might have been anyone?) and pulled 'em clear she didn't know where to hide 'em, so she balled 'em in her fist and held on till she could drop 'em safe where I wouldn't see and know . . .

Wouldn't know what? That she was as scared as if she never . . .

Well, she wasn't a girl nobody ever touched before.

So I guess it must have been she was just feeling new for me. Like I was for her.

Yes: just like the robbery in Owasso, it come as smooth as if she, as if we had rehearsed it a hundred times before, but underneath it was new to us as mother's milk.

It was like doing anything else that mattered in this world, anything that was big enough to take chances for. You have to get ready in your mind as much as you can for as much as you can figure beforehand, but there's always that thing that comes along and takes you by surprise. You got to be ready for that: got to understand that till it happens, you ain't going to know what it is, and it might be as good as found gold or it might tap you on the back and cut you in half at the waist, no way you can control it, all you can be is ready, look it in the eye and let it come.

Young as she was, she knew all of that, and she could live up to it. She had a lot of sand, and she showed it every time there was a call: that time I come into her bank, and for all she knew of me or could see at the time maybe I *was* getting ready to rob it, and she was scared but she stood her ground, she was ready. And the same when she stood up to Poole and Foley over Cherokee Bill, and when she took a whore's rap on herself to cover my play with Bill Tilghman, and when she come into my movie with me and Cherokee Bill and said—what was it she said?—said quick and blink-fast so that she had the drop on Esterhazy and Alice and Poole and Foley and Henry Starr and Cherokee Bill?

"*I love you, Henry Starr.*" That's what she said.

*And Dick Rowland had looked at her the way he looked at Shaker and Harriet Parker and said, "Baby, little sister, you better take care of yourself."*

He looked at her sleeping. She was young enough to be his child, and here he'd been dicking her like she was Pearl Starr who rode bad men the way horse wranglers rode bad horses. The idea made him uncomfortable, but when he looked at her he knew it made no difference, because he was wishing she would wake up and open herself deep for him again.

*I am a born criminal,* he thought, *it comes with the blood.*

"I'll take care of you," he whispered, hoping that would make a difference, breathing the words on her face that was still closed in sleep.

## TULSA *May 31, 1921*

They were lying in her bed, breakfasttime come and gone and nobody hungry for vittles yet. He was lying on his back and she was grazing up and down the skin of his front like a breeze over clear ground, nibbling bits like a deer in a fern bed. He closed his eyes and felt her mouth here and there all over him, her tongue sliding down from his throat to his chest to his belly to where his dick was filling and lifting as if it came right out of the root of his spine, and he felt himself opening like a book when you slide a finger down between the leaves, the leaves folding back all the way to the spine so she could read she could taste she could drink him word by word till her sweet new mouth and throat were full of him till he was—

"Whoa!" he said.

"Stop?"

"No."

"Whoa or go?" she said. "You don't know your own mind, do you?"

He was on an edge looking over. He opened his eyes and looked up at her face—she was smiling again, a softer smile, a little like Cora, her smile had softened, had aged a little—and very small and clear in the blue mirror of her eye he could see the shape of his old gray ghost.

"You should show more respect for your elders," he said.

"You *ain't* my elders," she said, "not more than half the time. The rest of it you are no older than my baby brother." She brushed his chest with her whole face, then lifted it to look at him again. "Tell me, Henry Starr. Did you ever do anything like this?" Then she answered herself, "Nope: you couldn't have. Because we just made it up."

"Made it up?"

"We made it all up," she said, "we invented everything—'Henry Starr: A Debtor to the Law'!" she crowed, and rolled over faster than he could think and sat on him, pinning his shoulders with hands and arms whose strength reminded him of how firmly and well she could handle a team of horses. She looked down at him, victoriously: " 'Henry Starr,' " she said, " 'Prisoner of Love'!"

*Child*, he thought, *even if you know how to be careful, you just aren't careful with me.* The right thing was to warn her. "Henry Starr the Outlaw," he corrected her. "Henry Starr the Bank Robber."

Behind the vivid look of her face looking down at him and under the memory of what they had been doing all night and morning that filled the air like a scent he remembered that he had come to her in a beeline from Owasso, where they had put it hard to Deputy Price, and if any least little thing of the hundred parts of his plan had gone wrong there would have been Price dead, and himself and Dick, maybe the bank president—and Bill Tilghman too, because if I had been wrong about him that old-time marshal would have come through that door with his pistol drawn cocked and shooting . . .

She shook it all away, the long heavy fingers of her hair swept the memories off the skin of his face. "You can't hide behind those aliases anymore," she said. "Not from me, you can't. I'm the Bobcat, remember? I can smell you out. You are Henry Starr the moviemaker, the actor Henry Starr. Henry Starr the Artist."

"The Bank Artist," he insisted. He lifted his hands and molded her cheekbones with his thumbs; they were a little flattened, her cheekbones, like someone had molded them with thumbs.

It made her whisper, "You don't touch me like a thief, Henry Starr. You touch me like I was . . ." She stopped.

"Was what? Say what you meant."

"I was going to say, 'like I was gold,' but that's not what I . . ."

She stopped again and looked down at him, waiting for him to ask, so he did: "Because you know how it feels when somebody touches you like you were money . . . ?"

"Yes." Her voice snagged on something and tore a little, pulling away. "Yes I know how that feels. I never knew I hated it till I felt it, or I would never have . . ."

"Okay," he said quietly, "it's okay." He heard himself say it, and it was no lie. "You wanted me to ask you things . . ."

"Yes," she said, "I want us to ask and ask each other things till we get right down to the bottom."

"You think we have time for that?" He was beginning to think about breakfast.

"We've got time," she said with her face rubbing him and her lips speaking in his chest, in the eye of his belly. "The movie is done, and we did it. We have all the time we need now for everything."

There was a bathhouse for the use of the boarders, and in the late afternoon she went down to use it. "You have to stay here—Prisoner of Love, remember? Stay here and plan out how we're going to get a place to ourselves so we can take some baths together."

*Prisoner of love*, he thought: just when you think she is a woman grown she jokes like she was a girl playing games out of books. Well: when you come down to it, he wasn't a lot better about that kind of thing, and at his age had a lot less excuse than she did, whether she was the possible twenty-seven she claimed or the probable twenty-two he figured her for. Lying about how old she was—that was another thing like taking off her underpants and being too skittish to find a place to hide them: she kept playing at being strong and sure, hoping that finally the game would take and become real for her.

But she was kin to him in that way too, wasn't she? Because he had joked and fooled his way into more banks than any outlaw including Jesse James, and come away with real money—and a real bullet in the back—to prove that what you play at is what you can become.

The idea that they were somehow a kind of kin to each other—that was a strange thing to think of, and uneasy too, like looking at her in the blue light and seeing his son in her face.

She was out in the bathhouse now, standing in the tub, pouring pitchers of water down the strange shape of her body, that was like a boy's in its fine muscles and a girl's in its delicacy of shoulders and small breasts, a woman's in the depth of her hips and buttocks and a deer's in the long line of her thighs.

He felt suddenly and sharply the emptiness of the room, and blue distances of space and running years opening between her image and himself standing alone in her room. He knew the place, but it was still foreign country. He was like one of those old-time Cherokees come to visit the Great White Father in Washington, stepping out of the same woods you've rode through since Cherokee country into the Capitol or some big city hotel, huge white stone towers walls and windows rising over and looking down at you, closing you inside a world of mirrors and gold carvings, weird perfume in the air.

The air here was full of her odors—something like dried flowers, and underneath a sweetness like fresh carrots or lake water. The room was full of her things, female clothes and boxes of stuff like women keep: all kinds of different little pins and buttons in a lacquered oval box, and another box with medicine things like a small stone bear, a man's watch charm shaped like a locomotive, a black heart locket. On her desk was a fanned-out stack of yellow papers, full of crossed-out bits of talk and action from *Henry Starr: A Debtor to the Law,* some with "?????" next to it, or "!" or commands, "Yes!" "Do this!" "Cut cut cut." On the left side of her desk, neatly typed and stapled, was a thick manuscript:

Henry Starr: A Debtor to the Law.
by B. C. Woodly.

This was where she wrote their movie. It was like finding years later the tracks of a deer you'd hunted and brought home when you were a kid. The movie was over. Everything that went with the movie was done.

What happens when the story is finished? Those old men, Tsigesu and Tom Starr and even Colonel D'Artagnan Arbuthnot, they never let on that things keep rolling after "The End," after, "Now I've told you how it used to be."

What does Henry Starr do now?

*We finished the movie, she said. We have time for everything now, Henry Starr.*

Well, he said to her fragrant ghost, you do, anyway. You got time, and you got things you want to do, and I believe you have the powers to make them happen. But I . . . I feel like I was this story of mine, see? And you helped me make it be, and . . . and now it's done.

I know how keep store . . . He saw Cora standing there in the darkened store, little Jiminy on the counter. No, that's part of what's done, Henry Starr couldn't keep a store, that's why he couldn't stay straight when they pardoned him the first time.

Henry Starr the rancher? That would put bread on the table, but Henry Starr isn't the name for a rancher either, ranchers is named Dodge and Roberts on the face, and Standard Oil in back of their eyes.

Go back to robbing banks? When Henry Starr knows that that road don't have but one ending? And when in any case he had already gone as far in that line as he needed to go—Owasso was perfect, and you can't beat perfect. Let Jesse James keep the record for robbing two banks at once: he wouldn't swap his silver and black lightning-sharp Henry Starr movie against a cheap paper copy of *Jesse James's Double Daring* by Colonel D'Artagnan Arbuthnot any more than he'd have sold New York to the Dutchman for twenty-four bucks worth of beads.

Well then I could just keep on making movies: Henry Starr the Scourge, Henry Starr the Robin Hood, Henry Starr's Revenge, Henry Starr Rides Again, Henry Starr Goes to Chicago, Henry Starr in Gay Paree, Henry Starr and Geronimo and Wild Bill Hickok and Buffalo Bill . . .

What would be the point, when the only story that really matters has already been told? It would just be more ride-rob-and-run for the rest of my life, not even as honest as bank robbing would be. That wasn't ever what I was after with Miss Woodly and Esterhazy: it was just this that I wanted, and now I got it. Now it's just done.

Or keep making love? While we were there, it felt like there could never be a bottom to that, like we'd never even have to stop for food, but just become a pair of mouths and keep on eating each other up. It's like climbing a mountain trying to climb your way up into the sky, climbing and rolling back, climbing and rolling back, and it all feels fine—the climbing and the falling both—but you never get there, do you? You get so close you can touch the sky sometimes, and the mountain falls out under you, but you can't never hang on there, you can't stay. You got to come back down again, or anyway a man does, maybe women got powers for holding on somehow . . .

He thought of the little image of his ghost printed twice in her blue eyes. And maybe a piece of you stays inside her where she has got to, but it ain't you.

But maybe it can be: maybe between you and me we make us a little tribe of breeds, our sign is the Bobcat and the Star, then you can . . . we can tell them the stories, and if we tell them right it will be like they took our ghosts and give them back cleaned up and new—and not take any harm at all, though you have to be careful with stories like that, the stories that say where your blood comes from: tell 'em wrong and those that hear 'em take a twist in their ghosts, like their blood belongs to somebody else, like somebody got in among their bones and left dirty hand marks on their ghost. But maybe Henry Starr could be like old Tsigesu, telling stories about his own old days like they belonged to somebody else—because they *would*, I think, they would belong to somebody else: a young an old a used-to-be outlaw named Henry Starr, who rode the nightland with the wolves and heard the owl hoot, away down in the Cherokee Nation a long time ago. And if that's how it would be . . .

No: because even if you come to a baby with her, and it had your own eyes and mouth and could throw a rope with a Henry Starr loop, it still ain't you yourself coming young again, looking out to see yourself a new road, to find you a horse, and guns, and a word of your own.

So maybe what I do now is live up here in your room, in this neat little book of papers with my name and your name on it, like the papers was the Happy Hunting Ground, where the hunter never misses and the deer you kill ain't dead, and there is nothing more you need to do or even be. And you go out in the world, and you make be whatever it is you aim at. And when you come back here I am, just as I always was, and you open me like I was your book, your redskin-Injun lie in the bed and dream book, and your fingers open me up and you read me word by word by word until I'm done.

The air in the apartment turned blue.

He lifted one slat of the blinds and peered outside. The sun was low, the air was as yellow as old varnish, the cottonwood tree across the road like one of those fern leaves you find in a slice of amber. The bright slash of the white-dirt road ran straight toward Tulsa.

He heard her step on the stairs, the door swung open: she had her hair turbaned in a towel, and her scrubbed face reminded him so forcefully of Jiminy that he could hardly breathe for feeling his fatherhood: because she had trouble in her face too. "The morning newspaper was on the hall table," she said, and put it on the desk.

He didn't see the trouble, what he saw first was the left-hand column whose headline proclaimed his own pure flat-out victory, like pulling the chicken at Tahlequah and this time getting the justice along with the prize:

POLICE CORRUPTION
UNCOVERED

Amazing Turn of Fate

Marshal Summoned in Bank Robbery
Discovers Officer Putting Cash
In Bootlegger's Bank Account

Deputy Sheriff Price Arrested

The trouble was in the right-hand column:

NEGRO ASSAULTS WHITE
WOMAN
IN DREXEL BUILDING ELEVATOR

CITIZENS TO MEET TONIGHT
IN RESPONSE TO THE OUTRAGE

Committee of Safety May Form
To Preserve Public Order
Till the Criminal
Is Brought to Justice

The assault had occurred yesterday afternoon at the close of business.

". . . The Negro suspect has been identified as one 'Dick' Rowland, a veteran discharged from the Army under suspicious circumstances. Rowland is typical of a class of colored soldiers who have not been right in the head since their return from France, where they experienced the brutality of foreign warfare and the moral license of French society; and who have become a danger to public morality and public peace."

Rowland had apparently fled Tulsa, but police were confident of finding the culprit and making an arrest within days. The trial would undoubtedly be a test of the community's pride and self-respect, and would (the *Lamp* trusted) do something to redeem the City from its recent brushes with scandal and show "the color of the blood that runs in our veins."

Henry Starr felt the blood and breath clot in his chest: *those bastards, those murdering peckerwood ku-kluck bastards.* The muscles of his chest and arms and legs went numb, paralyzed like his legs had been when Paul Curry stung him at the base of the spine with his hog-killing gun, *because it's on my head too, mine, just like with Cherokee Bill, because it was me that showed them Dick Rowland and told them his name, it was me made him part of paying off Cherokee Bill, it was alibi-ing my perfect crime that put him in the Drexel Building yesterday afternoon.* Now Mr. Poole was finally going to get his chance to make *Birth of a Nation*, and do it right out in the streets of Tulsa, Oklahoma.

He could imagine what was happening now, Dick on the run, white men waving newspapers rolled into billy-clubs, talking Dick Rowland's name in saloons and barbershops and offices—at first just showing each other just the corner of their fear and rage, just the edge of what they imagined happening between the nigger and the woman, then the tip of what they were beginning to want for themselves, not sure whether what they wanted was exactly the *thing*, a little afraid of finding out whether the rage they felt coming in themselves would be big enough to measure up to what all the other men were feeling, talking each other up, prodding, daring someone to do something about it, to start out the door and make them follow . . . and the marshals and cops out hunting, hoping to get Dick Rowland first despite their believing that it wouldn't make a difference in the long run if the mob got him now or later, and the jailers looking at the strength of the doors and shaking their heads over it like it was already done and past regretting, and unless there was someone around like Bill Tilghman to take a hand for justice, unless there was someone like Bill Tilghman or Henry Starr who knew what to do and how to do it, who could practically see before it started exactly how it would go and so was ready for . . .

And then quick as an eye-blink he felt the blood pulse tingling into his arms and hands, his legs: his head was clear, the blue smoke blown away by a wind as clear as it was cold: because there was no mystery in front of him, he suddenly knew all the answers before anyone could ask the questions, could read it plain and smell all that was left unsaid.

He looked up from the page, his head rising slowly as if he was coming back from a deep distance, and needed to cover wide ground carefully.

Miss Woodly's face kept clenching and unclenching against the black feeling working inside her. "He told me to be careful of myself," she said, "he told me I should be careful."

The Lady in the Cabin: last take, number fifteen. It was a long time ago, that cabin, almost as far off as the days of the Indian Nations. That was a good time, a good place: he had stood there with Miss Bobcat and Dick Rowland being Cherokee Bill, and he had known with perfect assurance that everything from now on would be perfect, running on smooth as bright silver water over black stones to a place where everything come right, like it should have been, it would never get sick or old, it would never change or die.

He had almost got there, almost got into the sky. But it turned out to be just more blue to him, and that made him thinking of roads and running.

He looked away and out the window at the deepening blue twilight, he didn't want to see the grief and fear twisting her, it was what she got for letting him in, he brought black terror with him like a fever, touch him and you catch it.

*The worst of it,* he thought, *is that I don't even feel sorry that it's come this way.* Because the truth was that even in the face of her grieving and his knowing perfectly everything that could still go wrong—every cruel thing that might be done to people that were like kin to him, like blood, like Cherokee water in the Cherokee country—with all of that there was a ghost inside his ghost that felt just that good to know it wasn't over yet, that there was still some call in the world for Henry Starr to get out of blue-smoke prison, and find his guns again, and his horse, and his road, and his word.

# Great Gunfight in Greenwood

TULSA *May 31, 1921*

An Oklahoma National Guard staff car sat in the "Don't Park Here" space in front of the courthouse, glistening in the electric light of the street lamps. Four state troopers in cavalry boots and hussar jackets lounged against the fenders (their motorcycles tilting jauntily on their kickstands nearby), jawing with the Guard corporal behind the wheel, heads bobbing, smiling, they were just agreeing about *everything*, those good old boys in front of the courthouse. The inside corridors were full of state-cop gray, Tulsa blue, Guard khaki and the plainclothes in cheap suits—you could tell the city dicks from the sheriff's and city marshal's deputies by their city shoes instead of Texas boots.

Blaine and Tilghman were looking out the window, and as Henry Starr pushed by the last blue-belly he heard Blaine say, ". . . like Buffalo Bill's Wild West and they haven't even charged him with rape yet."

"It's a good thing they haven't," said Henry Starr, and they turned suddenly. "Even a Tulsa prosecutor can't make just being on an elevator with a white woman into much more than 'simple assault'—unless maybe he also forgot to hold the door for her, then they'd have the cavalry out there, they'd have tanks and aeroplanes, wouldn't they?"

Blaine resented the crack about aeroplanes. "Nothing wrong with being ready for trouble, is there?"

"I knew a man in the Nations used to drink himself crazy every so often. Only way he could tell when the fit was gonna take him was when he'd see his wife hiding the shooting irons and pouring the liniment out the back window." Henry Starr was grinning, but it was an ugly grin. "Sometimes a man don't know what trouble he wants till everybody else starts getting ready for it."

"What can we do for you, Henry?" said Tilghman quietly.

"I come for some legal advice."

"Why?" said Tilghman with an absolute dead pan. "Do you figure we owe you a favor?"

Starr's lips lifted the merest touch. "I forgot to congratulate you on catching that crooked deputy in Owasso."

"You were right," said Tilghman, "the bandits were still working that district. Too bad I missed them. They will likely give up the trade around here, after Owasso."

"They'd be well advised to do so," said Henry Starr.

"Warrants are out for Rowland," said Tilghman, all business now. "State police, marshals, local police are all looking for him. There's talk of a reward for any citizen helps bring him in."

"He took off right after it happened," said Blaine, "like he knew there'd be trouble. If he'd stuck around it would have looked better."

Blaine was either a liar or hopelessly ignorant—he was a Yankee, so he might be both. Henry Starr stuck with Tilghman. "Dick Rowland never run out. Sometimes he just likes to go off by himself, hunting . . . just off in the woods alone. So he finished up work, helping out a friend who does janitoring in the Drexel Building; stopped by Bub's to tell him he was going, and pick up his gear. I've been over at Bub's. You hear what I'm telling you?"

"You mean the girl—the lady he insulted in the elevator is making it all up?" said Blaine, "Is that . . . ?"

"A colored man assaults a white girl in the public elevator of the biggest building in downtown Tulsa in the late afternoon when the halls is jammed with people going home for the day. The lady doesn't scream or call a cop. The colored man doesn't run. Everybody just walks off the elevator and goes off and eats dinner until about seven o'clock when somebody yells rape. How does it smell to you?"

Blaine looked embarrassed; Tilghman looked cold.

"Plus he never said anything about it to Bub," said Henry Starr. "If he even smelled trouble don't you know he would have . . . Dick is no fool, he's an educated man, he don't need to jump women in elevators, and if he needed to jump somebody he wouldn't do it at five o'clock in the goddamn Drexel Building. He's even smart enough to know if something he did or said in the elevator was the kind of thing that afterwards somebody might think it over and decide it was just about as bad as if he *had* jumped a white woman."

"If he's that smart," said Blaine, "maybe he was just playing it close with you."

"Maybe with me," said Henry Starr. "But he wouldn't do that with Bub."

"No," said Tilghman, "not with Bub. So he will be wandering around out there, hunting or whatever it is he does, and he doesn't know he's got the local police, state cops, and National Guard out looking for him."

"If he's not covering his tracks," said Blaine, "why haven't they picked him up yet?"

Starr's look at Blaine was hot: "Because the Tulsa or state cops couldn't either of them track shit across a carpet."

"God damn you to hell," said Blaine, "if you say one more word I swear I'll put you on the next train to McAlester!"

"You know where Dick might have gone to?" asked Tilghman, and Blaine shut up.

Henry Starr was on the edge of telling him. But Bub had been against his even coming here. "*What you gone tell Mr. White-eyes, Young Henry? What you gone ask him to do? There ain't but two things you can do for a nigger in the kind of trouble Dick Rowland's got. One of 'em's to get the charges named on some other poor nigger, because as long as he got the name . . . And the other one is warn him off, so he can get a long start running, and never stop again.*"

"There's people might know how to find him," said Henry Starr. "Bub sent who he could to find and tell Dick to get as far away from here as a man can get."

Tilghman was steady, patient: "That will do him, as long as he don't mind running for the rest of his life. As long as he isn't too attached to his own name or his home or his kinfolks."

"Let him come back and stand trial," said Blaine. "If it's as phony a charge as you think . . ."

"If he's got the name," said Henry Starr, "they'll lynch him as sure as if he had the game."

"It's simple assault on the warrant," said Blaine, "nobody's said rape."

"You just did," said Henry Starr. "You think nobody else has? Look, that simple assault warrant you put out ain't but one small piece of paper. There's ten thousand newspapers on the street calling it rape in six-inch letters and eight columns of type, plus editorials and a letter from the mayor. They're probably striking handbills by now."

"Why would they do all that if it . . . ?" said Blaine.

"There is a deputy sheriff up on charges," said Henry Starr. "Start squeezing Price and all kinds of names start dropping out. The papers would have had to give top billing for his case, but somebody come up with the idea of Dick Rowland jumping some white girl in an elevator, and suddenly Deputy Price ain't nowhere to be seen." He looked at

Tilghman. "Get them to drop the charge," he said, "because you know that nothing else will be worth a damn."

Tilghman was still steady: prepared: patient: "If you're right, Henry, you know it wouldn't do any good to drop the warrant either. Just be like saying to them old boys out there that the law won't take a hand in their play. The name's been laid on him: that's enough to start it."

"Shit," said Henry Starr.

"He's your friend," said Tilghman, "and I know you will side your friends, Henry. But I'm asking you to think if it might not be better if it was me that brought him in. That way you would know there would just be the law, and nothing extra. You got reason to trust that in me, don't you?"

"It seems to me," said Henry Starr, "you asked me that question before."

"And you didn't think much of taking me up on it."

"I thought about it." *Give him the name and be free of Cherokee Bill, Cherokee Bill and whiskey-running, train-robbing, bank-robbing your life away across the Indian Nations, Cherokee Bill and his guns and his killer's eyes and his terror of a cheap-handbill-nigger's death, that I sold him on, that he took for my sake.*

"I have to leave for Oklahoma City tonight," said Tilghman, "to tell the grand jury about Price and MacKinnon and that lot. If you want to talk to me, it's got to be before the train leaves."

"Ten-oh-six for Oklahoma City, stopping at Sapulpa, Bristow, and Stroud," he said. "I remember how it runs."

Tilghman waited silently.

*And he remembered how it had been for him in Stroud. The doctor was sweating, kept wiping his hands again and again with the bloody towel, and the butcher boy's bravado grin had taken a bad set on his face, because they could hear the crowd out in the street, that rising muttering yowl like a pack of wolves so sick for meat they could almost talk and nothing between me and It now but the doctor's glass door—till suddenly the pack hushed down, like they would if a big hunting cat had spooked them, and I knew it had to be Tilghman outside, never mind the trail dodged and the wires cut down he could follow the track of your ghost on a moonless night once he had the scent of it, and once he found you you were caught; and once he had you caught, there was no power on earth could make him stand and deliver you except the law he had swore himself true to.*

"I'll talk to Bub," said Henry Starr. Then he turned and walked out of the office, to do for Dick Rowland what he never did for Cherokee

Bill, which was give him to Bill Tilghman—and maybe for Cherokee Bill it would have made no difference, since either way he was going to end up in Isaac Parker's hands and never get out alive; but it would have made a difference for the half-dozen men he killed in the two years Henry Starr rode with him, and maybe it would have made a difference for Henry Starr, who would still have given his friend to the law but not straight to the Hangman, who never would have had to kill Floyd Wilson by mistake. *I just wonder what kind of difference it will make for Dick Rowland.*

It ain't every man gets a chance to go back and do his life over different, but it seemed like that was Henry Starr's gift—only right now it felt like the kind of gift you get from Jack-the-Devil, the magic pole that makes the fish just keep jumping and jumping and jumping out of that fishing hole, and the last one out is a wart-hided six-eyed turtle-jawed monster that bites your head off at the throat and pops your skull like a grape.

He took the stairs down to the lobby, trying not to feel like an escaping felon, pushed the stairwell door open and walked right into the middle of a movie set.

There was Esterhazy up behind the snouted box of his camera, someone had rigged a portable electric light and Mayor Egan, Police Chief Casey, a National Guard colonel and the commander of the state police were standing in the glare, shaking hands and nodding. Foley was jabbering at them, "*And* blahblahblah, *and* blahblahblah," the four officials turned this way and that way each time he said "and." Then the lights went out, Foley yapped something, and he saw Esterhazy and his crew take hold of the camera by the legs and begin to turn it.

Henry Starr weaseled his way through the crowd, got next to Esterhazy. "What's going on?"

The Hungarian looked up, the sight of Henry Starr seemed to pinch his features into an embarrassed knot. "Ach," he said, "Mr. Poole's instruction. He wants we write some 'history with lightning.' "

"Why ain't you working on my movie?"

Esterhazy set the camera leg down and looked slowly around at Henry Starr. "Is out of my hands, Henry. Foley—you remember, we agree that Foley will do editing. We give him pictures, now he . . ."

There was a long hooting yell from outside, it held on and kept stepping up higher and higher, and then the doors slapped open and a tangle of Tulsa and state police burst through it, a tall black man knotted among them. "Aie!" yelped Esterhazy, leaping to grab his crank. "Go back, wait, I don't get . . ."

They swooped him by so fast that Henry Starr got only a stone look from Dick Rowland, and it hit him then that for all Dick knew he was being nabbed for helping Henry Starr hit that bank in Owasso, there were questions they could ask that might pop that fact right out of him *and you know goddamn well there's things they can do would make you want to give 'em something, somebody, anyone else but you,* but he was already gone up the stairs and Esterhazy was pulling at Henry Starr's sleeve: "Henry! Henry? I know that fellow. Isn't he the one who . . . that was in . . ."

It was Shaker's voice he heard behind the black door challenging, "Who is it?"

"Henry Starr," he answered. The door opened like that was the password, and Shaker said, "You gotta come! Grandpa is fixin' to do somethin' *bad.* And they doin' somethin' bad to Dick . . ."

Faces turned to him lit from above by the hanging lamp over the kitchen table, shadows blanking out the deeps of eyes and masking or distorting the lips into frowns. Bub's heavy mouth was set in a hard line, William Parker looked pale and angry. There was an older gray-haired brown man, and two other black men of about William Parker's age wearing their khaki AEF caps. The older man standing next to Bub held a battered campaign hat in his large hands, marked with sergeant major's chevrons, with the tarnished cords and crossed sabers of the 10th U.S. Cavalry (Colored).

"It's Henry Starr!" said Shaker, *why didn't they all start to feel better?*

By the stove Mrs. Parker stood, her arms wrapped around herself. She had been crying: she was done now.

"You see now," said Bub, glowering at Starr, "what come of playing games around white folks."

"They have him in a cell upstairs at the courthouse," said Henry Starr.

"I was looking for him over on Greenwood," said William Parker, "right across the street when he came out of the alley behind Braxton's . . ."

"He was visitin' that new young woman from Boley, works the tables there," said one of the younger men.

"Yes," said William Parker, as if it hurt to talk, "yes, he was coming around at last, you know?—after all this time." He looked at his wife, she bit her underlip and shook her head hard.

"And they're goin' to take and lynch him," said Bub, glaring at William Parker. "Don't you know? Don't you *know*? Unless his people get up and stop it for him, that's what become of that poor boy."

Parker's strangled voice was down to a hiss. "Don't I know that, damn you, ain't he my, ain't he my, ain't he my friend," and it pinched his eyes till they showed water but he held them open glaring back at Bub.

"Well well well," said Bub twisting away from his son-in-law, "then ain't you got to . . ."

Parker drew himself up: "Where you been living these last months, old man? Maybe you could make a mistake about all those colored barrelhouses and bootleggers getting rousted out, but when you see what they done to T. J.—Bub, they think this is the *day*. They got themselves set to run every colored man woman and child they can find right off the face of the earth. They don't even work at finding reasons no more, any damn lie will do no matter if a backward cracker child could see right through it—Dick Rowland jump some white trash cunt on an elevator in the middle of the Drexel Building! Don't you read the newspapers? That boss of Mr. Starr's, he been laying it out plain. Yeah," he said mockingly, "you know, all them niggers be *crazy*, you got to shoot 'em down 'fo' they be bitin' yo' *laigs* in the street . . ."

"You don't have to tell me about crackers," said Bub, "I been drawing the line on crackers all my . . ."

The wolf was rising in Henry Starr's throat, his spit tasted bitter. *"That boss of Mr. Starr's—" God damn that Parker anyway, drawing that line and me on the other side.* "Where you drawing that line, Bub?" he asked softly.

Bub kept his eyes on Parker, it was still between him and his son-in-law. "I'm drawing it in front of the courthouse. There's a couple dozen men I can name that can handle a gun, or been in the service—killed them some palefaces other side the water, Henry. One kind good as another."

"Daddy," said Harriet Parker, "it don't ever change for you, does it?"

*Well,* thought Henry Starr, *at least I know he don't count me paleface.* It gave him a right to speak. "Your son-in-law Parker is right," said Henry Starr, "they got it all set in their minds." He was thinking about Poole sending Esterhazy to the courthouse, history written with lightning. "They'll kill you, Bub. And they'll take it for license to shoot Greenwood all to hell, and burn it out."

Bub lowered his eyes on Henry Starr. "You got yourself a plan you better let me hear it."

How much of the truth could he say in this crowd? "I've got—Dick and I got a little cash from some business we . . ."

"Movie business?" said William Parker. "Did you send him into the Drexel doing movie business?"

Bub glared at Henry Starr, *you see what come of all that play-foolin', Smart Henry?* but then he blinked—"Movie business is near enough," he muttered. Suddenly it was himself he had to be angry at: if Bub Houston hadn't let them lynch T. J. Hanks there wouldn't have been any debt to pay, no need for Dick Rowland to play in Henry Starr's damned movie or rob the Owasso Bank or make good his alibi by racing back to spend the afternoon in the Drexel Building. Henry watched Bub tasting that idea, bitter, but he ate all of it. When he looked at Henry again his eyes were still grudging, but he had got past hating. "If you got a plan, let's hear it."

"They won't charge him but with simple assault. We can bail him on that," said Henry Starr.

Bub's teeth were showing. "Like somebody bailed T. J."

"No. This time I do the bailing. You come with me. And Bill Tilghman is there to see it through."

"They wait outside," said the old cavalryman, "they take you all three together."

"Four with Bill Tilghman."

"If he with us," said Bub, his eyes drilling Henry Starr's, looking for the bottom.

"I believe I can bring him in," said Henry Starr, thinking *because this time it's law and not just movie business.*

"We pay the money," said Parker eagerly. "Then we get him out a side way . . ."

Bub looked steadily at Henry Starr. "You puttin' a lot of weight on that old white man. You think he can carry it?"

"I've seen him carry it," said Henry Starr, remembering the doctor's office in Stroud, and the pack noise going dead still outside the frosted glass door.

"A long time ago," said Bub Houston, and his eyes lifted off to look out past Henry Starr, out through the walls of his house and past the Dreamland Theater and the city of Tulsa, a place way off out in the country a long time ago. "Yes," said Bub, "used to be Bill Tilghman could carry all the weight there was. Used to be I could too." His eyes came back to Henry Starr. "But times is different, Young Henry. It seem to me the world has got a lot heavier. These city people now: Bill Tilghman just another cop to them, like Price or Casey, who don't carry no more law than what his gun and his badge weighs, and he'll sell that to you for one fistful of green."

"Some of us be waiting," said one of the younger men, "just in case, you know? Tulsa cops be Ku-klucked from the boots up, you never leave without somebody pass the word."

Bub grinned without warmth. "And that bring us back home, don't it? Because unless there is somebody *colored* out there in the street to draw the line, then they gonna kill Dick Rowland." He looked down at Henry Starr, sure of himself again. "Because they mean to have themselves a hanging, don't they, Young Henry? I mean all of them, not just those crackers out in the street, but all them boiled-shirt bastards that sips they whiskey in MacKinnon's speak. Son Parker here got it right: newspapers and police both, they been like a bitch in heat for something like this, and when it don't happen like they want all they got to do is say that it did. Dick Rowland rape a white woman in the Drexel Building elevator and just walk away! Where can they find even a poor dumb cracker dumb enough to believe that's what happened? No, they don't even need to find reasons no more, the reasons is all there already . . . ain't I right, Henry Starr?"

"Yes," said Henry Starr, "yes, you got it right," remembering how Poole had known in advance to put Esterhazy and his camera where they could bushwhack history while it happened.

"So nobody want your damn money, Henry, they want blood. Am I right? Or do you still need to talk to Mr. Tilghman?"

The memory of Bill Tilghman looked smaller now, measured against the dark close presence of Bub Houston—a small shape, very distant and brilliantly white. It was only when you saw Bill Tilghman as the Law, the law not like it was but like it was supposed to be, that the old man took on size and power. But who was there left besides Bub Houston and Henry Starr who could see Bill Tilghman like he used to be? Tilghman would give his word, he'd go down dead before they took any prisoner out of his hands—but Henry Starr believed, suddenly, that that is just what would happen, the mob tearing through all of them to get to Dick Rowland, tearing old Bill Tilghman into shreds of silvery skin.

So there were two men up in the Tulsa jail Henry Starr was responsible for.

Well, Something must have whispered to his ghost that this is the way it would be, because he had come ready: for an answer to Bub's question he lifted and spread open the lapels of his jacket as if baring his breast, and showed them the pair of .45s he had in shoulder holsters, their butts reversed, strapped against the sides of his chest.

Parker was slamming his balled right fist down and down on the counter by the cookstove. Henry Starr felt the small weight of Shaker, hiding behind him, leaning his weight on the back of Henry Starr's legs. Parker didn't see the boy, Parker's eyes were knotted, the pull in opposite directions clenching them tight, "*Then* we *got* to *give* him *up*." He looked back at Harriet Parker, who suddenly balled her apron front and raised it swiftly to her face; if she was crying it was silent, but her whole body seemed to be vibrating though not a sound came out. Parker couldn't look at her; he turned back to Bub. "I don't, I just can't see any way around it. My God, Bub, if they come through here killing people because we . . . and they kill him anyway, once they're done with us, if you got this right—so what's the good of it, Bub?"

Bub's words were those he might have used in cutting argument, but his voice softened them way down. "What you gonna do, son? Take 'em all to Africa? Knowing who you left behind, and what you left him to . . ."

Parker was shaking his head. "The six of us can't just decide we're going to go and shoot it out with every damned cracker in Tulsa to save Dick Rowland, when every colored family in the city is going to pay the cost of what we do." He became fierce again. "This family too, Bub! Your blood and your name. What about Harriet, Bub? What about Shaker?"

Bub wasn't looking at any of them now, he was talking hard to something big and blank that stood against him and was more than all of them put together.

"You can't tell me anything about how mean a cracker can get. They make him eat shit all his life, and smile and say thank you; but he too stupid and cowardly to draw him a line, so he lay it on the nigger. He eat shit, so we got to chew it. Somebody treat him like a dog, so he find somebody and cut on him till he ain't a man. And it don't have to be any particular nigger, first one he see is good enough for . . ."

His look at Parker softened. "You got to see it, son. If we let 'em get Dick, it won't keep 'em satisfied—if you're the kind of people needs to do that thing, one ain't never enough. You got to keep proving you can do it, and do it again, and still be the one who can do it . . . Next they be comin' after me, or you, or Shaker—I seen how they do. They got to teach you the lesson, they got to make you eat shit just like they do."

He looked an appeal at Henry Starr. "But that still ain't what I mean, is it? Give me a hand here, Young Henry? Give me a word I can use here?"

*What do I know,* thought Henry Starr, *what can I tell you? All I can tell you is how it was in the old days, and there never was any good answer then either, no answer that made a difference: whether it was John Ross suffering with his people and dealing soft, or Tom Starr standing off and dealing hard, in the end it was the same, the people shamed and driven and dead and the Old Place gone; whether it was Henry Starr trying so hard to live by justice but not kill anyone, or Cherokee Bill shooting a man off a ladder because he was painting a sign and looked down at Cherokee Bill which was treating him like a nigger, it all come to hanging by the neck in Fort Smith Prison, or betraying your brother to save your own life . . .*

"Sometimes there is no good thing to do," said Henry Starr. "Sometimes you just got to draw the line, and set yourself to take what's coming. Let 'em know if they want to do that thing here they got to be ready to die. Because you are there, and you are ready for it too."

Bub's voice was down to a whisper. "You hear me, son? I ain't sayin' we can stop 'em doing it. I'm just sayin' we got to face it."

"No," said William Parker, "don't tell me, tell your grandson to face it, tell him he's got to face up to his daddy and grandpa shot dead alongside of Dick Rowland lynched, and his house burnt down and his momma . . ."

"I don't know," said Henry Starr, "but it seems to me like there are worse things than dying." He remembered the look of Jiminy, growed up in the yard in front of MUNSON & TODD GENL MDSE throwing somebody else's loop on a horse somebody else taught him to ride. "Dying gets things over with. Living with a thing, remembering something that puts a twist in your soul, that's worse. If it was my son I would want him to remember how I . . . how his father and his grandpa never left Dick Rowland to face that thing alone. He might even hate you for dying like that, but he'll remember, he'll hear people talk about how it was, and when he grows up he'll see for himself how it can be—how sometimes there's no good thing to do, but you got to choose anyway." *It will teach him how to die himself, when it comes to that,* he thought, *and it always comes to that.*

"Everything," said Parker, looking at Shaker who huddled against his mother's hip, "everything we made here, everything and everyone we love, every colored family that worked their way out of cotton and into Tulsa . . ."

Harriet Parker lifted her face from her son to her husband. "Don't let them do him like that, Willy, don't let that happen to Dick. Be like he," she said, "be like it was . . . be like they done it to my own baby, Willy . . ."

Husband and wife looked at each other. "All right," he said. Parker's face took an odd twist, his voice came from far away: "He's like blood to me too, baby: he's like blood to me too." He looked at Shaker, whose face was hidden in his mother's skirt. "I guess whichever thing I do, it's our own blood they are going to spill. It's bad now, but you know, Shaker, later on you wouldn't want to think I just let them do that, and never even tried . . ."

Bub had turned away and unracked a pump shotgun that was hung alongside the rear door. The others turned too, picking up rifles they had leaned against the wall by the kitchen door. "Give Henry Starr one of those Winchesters," said Bub. William Parker gave one agonized look at Bub, at Henry Starr, then opened a closet door and reached out a lever-action Remington.

"You ain't got to go," said Bub. "Be better someone stay here and guard the house, or better yet get these women and kids out to . . ."

Parker answered by levering a shell into the Remington, crack-crack. *My brother Will Parker Dick Rowland called him, Bub said he was a good man, with Bub that means one thing.*

They stood there—five black men and Henry Starr, Mrs. Parker and Shaker standing stiff and straight to one side.

"The rest of the boys is over on Greenwood, supposed to meet at Braxton's," said the old cavalryman. "One of you young folks go tell 'em we's comin'."

Shaker darted over to his father and grabbed him around the hips. "Daddy," he cried, "you ain't supposed to . . . !" and his father put down the Remington and eased his son back with both hands on his shoulders. "You don't want me leaving Dick to get killed, do you?"

"Can't you just let Grandpa and Henry Starr do it, Daddy? Daddy, they could . . ."

"Can't do it without your daddy," said Bub.

"Yes," said Henry Starr, "that's right."

"Then you take care of him!" yelled Shaker as they started filing out of the kitchen. "You take care of him!"

There were about thirty men in Braxton's when the group from Bub's house arrived, most of them showing in one way or another that they had been soldiers—a twin-peaked AEF cap, a badge pinned to a shirt or vest, a Sam Browne belt with a pistol swinging from it. About a dozen had long army Springfields, the rest shotguns, rifles and carbines. Bub's pump shotgun was their heavy artillery: a big-caliber six-shot type they called a trench gun in the army, you could clear a road through a crowded trench with a couple of rounds—Dick Rowland had showed how that could be done.

"Some good boys be comin' up from Muskogee, say they be here by morning," said a big black man in a three-piece suit—Stratford, the owner of the colored hotel.

"That just mean we got to hold them by ourselves tonight," said Bub. He had to raise his voice to be heard over the hubbub, the rattles and clicks and whirrs of breeches being open and closed, cylinders spinning, levers racked open and shut, bullets slotted into their chambers. The place smelled sharp and evil with gun oil and the kind of sweat you put out when it gets so bad it can't get worse, but it does.

"We got a couple dozen people inside the courthouse right now," said Stratford as Bub nodded, his eyes sweeping over the people in the room, laying things out in his mind. "Smitherman, the colored deputy, said they got in okay—side door on Boulder Street while the crowd was up front watching Fifth and Main. That lawyer's heading 'em—Williams. They offered to stay and help Sheriff McCullough protect the prisoner."

Bub showed his teeth. "They gonna help Chief Casey too?"

Stratford broke out in a sudden sweat: "Smitherman says Casey won't call in his off-duty police. Says he don't want to get folks thinking something might go wrong."

"That's what I thought," said Bub. "If the good Lord put that son of a bitch Casey in front of me, I'm gonna shoot his smile out through his asshole." He backed away from Stratford to stand on the steps leading up to the street. "All right!" he bellowed. "All right! We goin' out of here two columns, one each side the street, except for me and two more up the middle. William Parker lead the right side, 'Cavalry' Joe Wright the left." Somebody bugled a slightly flatulent *charge!* and there was a wave of nervous laughter as the older man in the 10th Cavalry hat stepped up next to Bub.

"Stratford and Henry Starr, stick with me," said Bub.

They went down Greenwood on the double, trotting till they crossed Archer. The broad open space of the railroad yards opened in front of them, spotted with white and red lights and slashed by double lines of tracks crosshatching the ground. They went across this more deliberately, but still at a strong pace, Bub and Henry Starr and the big hotel manager walking point and the two files flanked out to left and right.

They followed the Midland Valley track, which paralleled Main, watching the city lights till they came abreast of 5th Street, then Bub led them up a rising slope of poor grass out of the railroad right-of-way and onto the intersection of 5th and Elgin streets, where he halted them—the two files lying down in the grass out of sight, Bub and Henry Starr, Stratford and Parker and Cavalry Joe bellied up to look ahead down the street.

Less than a quarter mile ahead, across Elgin and South Detroit Avenue and up a long city block, just on the other side of Main, stood the courthouse. The darkened warehouses and stores lining the streets made a deep narrow V that exaggerated the distance. The blackness of that narrow canyon was spotlit at intervals by pools of bitter, pale light that fell weirdly from the electric lamps.

The front of the courthouse was illuminated with spotlights, and they could see that there was a crowd there already, milling around filling the space beginning at the double doors and down the stone steps across the sidewalk and into the street, "No Parking Here," and left and right to either side down the street.

"You think they'll let Williams and his people stay inside?" asked Stratford.

"No," said Bub. "If they do"—he shrugged—"then we all right just keeping clear and ready to lend a hand. If they send 'em out the back, we got to figure how to join 'em up."

"I'll put a runner around that way," said Parker.

"We got people in the crowd too," said Stratford. "Couple of boys light enough to pass. They know how we comin' in. I sent 'em from Braxton's after you told me."

"If they sendin' our folks out the front," said Bub, "then they gonna need a diversion, and they gonna need a place to run to, because Casey ain't gonna let 'em back inside. Let's get closer. How you want to play this, Joe?"

"Two lines," said the cavalryman, "deploy as skirmishers. Set the second line back out of the light to cover you, first line forward to start the ball."

"Suppose there's talking first?" asked Stratford.

Bub smiled. "That's why I'm keeping you and Henry Starr close. You a pair of regular Deadeye Dicks with those Winchesters. You find you a couple stands to right and left where you can see the square. If I got to go talk to these crackers, you shoot anybody take a line on me." The smile faded. "And if we got to fall back, you knock *down* any cracker that cross that line, you hear me?" Bub looked around. "We got to fall back, this the way we come."

"Keep swapping lines as we go, one line fires when the other come through," said Cavalry Joe, "till we get here: then lie down under this lip and shoot the legs out from under them."

They looked back across the black expanse of the right-of-way and the jeweled railroad yards, lights enough to run but not to shoot by. Think any crackers will chase you into that big black blank down there? Not likely: they could get back to Greenwood that way, and be ready —for what?

Whatever comes.

They went forward again, in the same two-file formation, crossing Elgin, crossing South Detroit Avenue—Bub kept his eyes rigidly ahead as they crossed it, but Henry Starr swung his eyes north as if in the darkness and down the long distance and past the intervening lights of the depot there was any hope of seeing lights in the house on North Detroit. With his side vision Henry Starr caught William Parker looking that way too.

They marched in the shadows past the light circles of the street lamps, ticking off each one as they passed, *how many between me and the black safety of the yards?* Up ahead they heard the white crowd begin to hoot and yell, saw the white-shirted mass heave back and forth—somebody was pushing open the front doors, a blue-coated policeman leaned out to yell, and Bub raised his right hand to halt them.

Twenty-eight was the number: twenty-eight streetlights behind them when they came to the edge of the courthouse intersection.

The doors of the courthouse were strained open from the inside and were pushed shut again by the press of the mob. The white crowd hooted like a wind rising. A man with a tall white hood stalked through the fringe of the crowd with his arms raised as if in surrender yelling "Hallelujah! Hallelujah!"

The courthouse doors slammed outward and a rush of policemen followed—not many, their dark wedge reached only halfway down the steps—and then the black citizens' delegation started coming down the steps, two policemen in front wading in and shoving the crowd aside. The delegation had come armed to help defend the jail, the huddle of uniformed police and black men in business suits and ties was spiked with rifles held at high port, barrels glistening in the floodlights that beamed down from the courthouse. The black men were in a tight bunch, and when the courthouse door closed behind them they filled only the space from the door to the bottom of the stairs. Not enough to scare a crowd like this, Henry Starr thought; there must be two thousand whites pushing in around them—

And then Bub yelled, "Form as skirmishers!" and pointed sharply ahead to right and left, and as Henry Starr and Stratford ran sidling forward to pick up the cover of a couple of trash barrels down toward the brightly lit courthouse intersection, they heard the rustle of feet on the pavement as William Parker and Cavalry Wright formed their men. Henry Starr crouched behind the trash barrel and looked around its side: the near edge of the crowd was fifty yards off and he had a clear field of fire across two-thirds of its face. If he raised his sights he could pick a man out of a second-floor window in the courthouse if it came to that.

He heard Bub yell "Let's go!" and the first line came stepping forward, twenty men in two staggered lines across the wide street. Henry Starr lifted and looked ahead—there was a bayed storefront on the right and he dashed crouching for that: now the skirmish line was behind him again, and he could see Bub walking steadily forward toward the crowd, the pump shotgun held ready across his chest.

That's when the crowd noticed Bub too: the white-shirted front of the mob split thirty feet ahead of Bub as men began to back away from that point, like earth turning two feet ahead of the part of the plowshare blade that you can see.

There was a lot of confused yelling, hands waving, heaves in the crowd this way and that. He had taken them by surprise, coming up on them while they were getting ready to mob the forty-some Negroes by the courthouse steps—and they hadn't got past yelling nigger yet either, because these niggers had guns—and now here they were flanked and taken from the rear, and they started backing, backing off till here come one white policeman out safely and the crowd of blacks behind him.

The white crowd heaved and buckled in on itself, people behind pushing others forward trying to get a look, the front ones seeing more than they liked and trying to back off, and as they came out of the mob the blacks from the courthouse turned around, holding down on the crowd with rifles and pistols, backing slowly past Bub Houston to get behind Bub's skirmish line.

Someone yelled *they're running* someone yelled *getting away* someone yelled *running, no don't let—get 'em get 'em get 'em you*—and there were only a few blacks left between Bub and the crowd when one of them was grabbed by the shoulder-to-waist strap of his Sam Browne belt. "Nigger, you better give me that gun!" and another white man grabbed the black man's pistol arm. The pistol jerked up and around, and the black man's partner yelled "Drop him!" and cocked his own pistol at the first white man just as the first Negro's pistol went off, and then the second white man fired and hit the second Negro in the belly, and somebody in the front row of the mob fired six wild shots at the black men retreating past Bub Houston. There were at least four bodies on the ground, the gut-shot Negro crawling off while the white man spanged wild shots off the pavement trying to finish him but his hand shaking too much, and it was too mixed up for Bub's people or the mob to shoot because a half-dozen white shirts in the front of the mob jumped ahead to get their hands on the two blacks that were still in reach—nobody had a shot except Henry Starr and maybe Stratford, and Henry Starr leveled and fired on the white shirt still grabbing at the first black man, saw his shoulder blow blood, levered another shell and fired again busting the second man's kneecap, and then another and another, picking them off the wounded blacks by the arm and the leg and the scruff like you'd pick off a louse with your fingertips.

Then suddenly there was clear air between Bub and his men and the mob, a few bodies lying in the street, and Henry Starr heard the shots crackle across the front of the skirmish line and then the hard, bad *whoof! whoof!* of Bub's trench gun. They were shooting high, still aiming to scare the mob off, as if they hoped a little less blood in the street might make some kind of difference. The mob was falling on itself and stepping on itself, there were gunshots coming out of it, people falling or throwing themselves down. You could hear some of the bullets, some of them had the mean tearing sound of rifle shots. Henry Starr looked up to see muzzle flashes up on the courthouse, *fucking Tulsa police.*

Bub was waving them all back down 5th Street—there wasn't but two things to do where they were, one of which was storm the courthouse in the teeth of a mob that had them outnumbered ten or twenty times and the state police and Tulsa cops and militia back of that . . . No, Bub was right, back off and get 'em to come after. He ducked out of the store bay hugging the wall and ran crouching back down the street: William Parker had his skirmishers in a single line across the street, standing and kneeling, and the others poured back through the line, and back at South Detroit Cavalry Wright was drawing another line.

Henry heard the roar of a motor away behind him, and sirens began screeching near the courthouse. He looked back and saw the high bulks of a couple of big cars with searchlights mounted turning out of the alley behind the courthouse and starting to sail slowly through the mob. "That's it!" said Parker. "One of those cars got a Browning machine gun mounted: they used it when the Wobblies tried to shut down the oil field. If they get that thing started, be like putting meat through a grinder." His skirmish line lifted up and backed off down the street, looking back at the dodging white-shirted shapes flowing out of the square and toward them along the sides of the buildings. And now coming up the middle of the street were two big pairs of headlights overlooked by the bright swiveling beams of searchlights—that and the thin smile of metal on the front bumpers were all the glare let them see of the two police cars.

"I'll see you in Greenwood," said Henry Starr, and then he bolted for an alley to his right. There was a side door into the two-story building on his left—and a fire-escape ladder running to the roof. He picked the ladder and went up fast, clutching the Winchester in his right hand. Between the slats of the ladder he saw ricochets sparking off the paving stones, then some white shirts pressing into the alley from the courthouse side.

The roof was tar-tacky under his boots, plucking at them as he ran to the low brick wall that edged it. He crouched behind the wall, put his hat down, and was raising up to look over when the machine gun started up below him with a loud *yatatatatatat* that was as sharp and painful as the impossibly fast repeated going-on-too-long cracking of a bullwhip. He froze, waiting for it to stop. His eyes raced here and there on the roof, the struts of a second ladder were across the way; there was a trapdoor leading down into the building.

The machine gun stopped. He raised up and peeked over the edge hoping there was no police sharpshooter on top of the courthouse drawing a bead on him.

The first car was a plain open-topped police car full of civilians with white armbands carrying rifles and shotguns—and the other a large black car with a thing like Esterhazy's camera tripod mounted over the rear seats: except on top of it was a long-snouted machine gun, with a drooping tongue of bullet belt like unraveled film slopping down into a canister at the shooter's feet. The shooter was a uniformed policeman, so was the driver, but the ammunition feeder and the man with the searchlight wore white shirts and peaked golfing caps.

*And Henry Starr never killed but one man in his life, and that by accident, and he was sorry for it: though it wasn't being sorry that got him out of the noose that Judge Parker named him for, sentencing him to hang dead dead dead for killing a lawman, and the Lord have mercy on his . . .*

But there was only the one way now.

He took the shooter first, one bullet high between the shoulders and before the man could fall Henry Starr was swinging his rifle down and left: the driver next, a head shot blowing his brains out through his face and across the windshield, the car hadn't got speed yet so it just veered slowly, crashing deliberately one after another into a trash can, fire plug, store window as the deadweight of the driver twisted the wheel.

But Henry Starr was already clutched down into himself under the lip of the balustrade as bullets rang off the cheap bricks; it was too bad he never got an angle on the engine of that thing or he could have killed it. Then he was up, crouch-sprinting for the ladder, a quick look—too naked going down the side of the building: the trapdoor. He jerked the handle. It was locked from the inside.

He looked up at the sky, overcast and empty, blue-gray smoke over everything. The roof was an empty box hung out in the middle of the air, they would come pounding up the stairs and ladders and shut the smoky sky down like a lid and his eyes and his memory and his name and his blood would go black . . .

*No!* He jabbed the rifle barrel under the lip of the trapdoor, wedged it, rammed down on it and popped a rotten board loose. His hand fumbled the lock inside, he was on the steps, he closed the door over his head: a black tunnel, stink of mildew. He flared a match: there was a door. He slid his feet toward it through the dark.

In the hallway he listened for people coming into the building. There was yelling, stomping around on the first floor. They were trying to cuss themselves into rushing the roof. Unless they had a hero or a cop or a soldier to lead they'd let somebody else try it.

Time. Time. Time.

The cussing moved away. The first floor was quiet. How do I come down those stairs? If I do it like a rear guard or a skulkin' redskin then they shoot first. No: I come down like the solid citizen of the state of Oklahoma I am, and who says I ain't a white man? Hell, even my own granddad swore I could pass for paleface, I was my poor old mother's pride and . . .

He came down, looking around like a man rousted out of bed by noise, ready to ask what the hell was going on while a man's trying to . . .

But nobody asked, they were all busy rushing up and down the street, on foot and in cars, helping friends limp away toward the hospital, the police station or home, ramping up and down yelling for somebody to try and start something, when are we gonna go finish off those niggers, and nobody thought Henry Starr was any different.

The street was spotted with light where the lamps had not been shot out, and there were people looking at the bodies lying in the street. One man had crawled under a billboard advertising the Majestic Theater, the large pink face of a smiling white lady:

Mary Pickford
AMERICA'S SWEETHEART

in a

Double Bill!!

"The Young American" & "M'liss"

at the Majestic Theater

A white man armed with a pistol stood over the body and a second man knelt and turned it over. The fallen man lifted a hand, palm opened upward and the standing white man fired four shots into his body. The second white man stood up and clapped his hands clean, one-two, and the man who had fired turned to yell something. But whatever he said was drowned in the roar of an engine, they were using one car to haul the other one out of the smashed storefront, but it was hung up on the sill of the display window.

A gang of men, policemen and civilians, were trying to pry the machine-gun car over the sill with muscle and crowbars. A small group stood to one side, with a spare tire ready—the left front tire had blown out when it hit the fireplug. One of the civilians standing by the tire was Price: he had a badge pinned to his jacket, and a white scarf bound as an armband on his left arm.

"I thought you was off the force," said a man near him.

"Suspended," said Price, "but they need every good man they got for the emergency."

"What's the armband?"

"Where are you really from?" Price asked, with grossly exaggerated menace, and the man backed away.

At the far eastern end of the street the lightless square that marked the Midland Railroad right-of-way was quiet—Bub's rear guards were gone. Henry Starr turned and walked toward the courthouse square, just a typical Tulsan out for a night of shooting niggers. There was a crowd pyramided up the steps and Police Chief Casey stood at the peak, framed by the doors, his right hand raised, his walrus mustache bobbing as he deputized the crowd. A man sitting on the curb at Henry Starr's feet muttered "A-men, or whatever you say," his friend was tying a knot in the necktie that bound a lump of cotton waste over a bleeding fleshwound in his upper arm.

Henry Starr turned his back on the courthouse and walked away north up Main Street, pointing toward Archer, and the man called after him, "Hey, ain't you gonna be a deputy?" and his friend said, "Naw, he's one of them likes to hunt by hisself."

As he went up the street the sidewalks filled around him, there was a line by a store selling guns, other people were coming out into the street with guns—though some just sat in front of their doors or in their windows looking grim at any- and everybody, and some were hauling valises out and throwing them into wagons or cars or trucks and getting out of town. There was a slamming sound up ahead like they were shunting fast freights through the yards, and then he recognized it was rifle fire, some of it in volleys, coming pretty steadily from the north where the Frisco tracks split Tulsa parallel with Archer. That was where Bub would be, he guessed, using the cover of cars and raised roadbed, culverts and stray equipment to draw the line in front of Greenwood. If Henry Starr wanted to get through, he'd better swing wide and come around into Greenwood from the west—if he came in from the other end of North Detroit he could see if Mrs. Parker had gotten Shaker and the rest out of town.

North up Main past the junction with Archer. The Oil Field Workers' Hall was dark, though he heard voices. He guessed there might be some Wobblies inside expecting the riot would somehow get turned on them. He had an idea, Henry Starr: walk in and tell 'em what was happening, maybe they'd come out and take a hand with Bub.

Picture of Henry Starr riding to the rescue of Greenwood at the head of a gang of wild Wobblies.

Only how do I get inside without getting shot, when I don't know their passwords. Frank Little, why didn't you ever teach me the damn passwords?

*He probably knew an old-time horseback outlaw never would make any kind of a Wobbly.*

And say I do get in, and I get them to come out—maybe: but ain't they as like to go with their color as the next man? And hell, if any of Bub's boys see a bunch a white men coming up behind them, they won't wait to hear no damn password at all.

He gave the idea another little piece of his time, standing under the darkened windows, waiting for it to get better—but it just got older.

He moved on to where the Katy Railroad tracks cut across Main, arching toward the junction at Greenwood and Archer. The right-of-way was dark all the way to Greenwood, no telltale pinpricks to mark gunfights: Bub must have pulled back again. Henry Starr cut across lots to North Detroit Avenue.

Houston's house was dark. From the distance Starr could hear sirens, the muted rattle of gunfire. A building was burning over toward Greenwood, big black clouds of smoke lit red underneath boiling and turning back on themselves as they lifted up into the overcast.

He saw a candle move across a window: they were still in the house! He stepped out of the bushes into the street, crossing out of the light. Up and down the west side of North Detroit Avenue white men and a few of their women stood by their front doors looking toward downtown.

He went around the back and rattled the door till Harriet Parker opened it.

"Jesus God," she said, "I thought it would be Willy."

"Last I saw, he and Bub were okay. They went back across the yards into Greenwood. I thought you'd be long gone out of here." He stepped inside the kitchen. There was a rifle leaning by the back door, and through the doorways and the hall he could see another by the front window. *And Shaker sitting at the head of the stairs with a shotgun I bet.* "You should have gotten out right after we left."

She stood eye to eye with him and said, "My daddy set himself to do what he's got to, even if he's the only man in Tulsa thinks that way. And he do it even if it mean every other colored family in Tulsa that never got to say *boo* to Bub Houston gone pay the cost of it right along with him. And you think *I'm* gone to take advantage, knowing what that crazy daddy of mine mean to do? Run off and my neighbor friend don't know what's been done till they break her door down . . . ?" She moved in on him, backing him up as she spoke, and Henry Starr said, "All right, all right, I guess you really are Bub Houston's daughter"— "and William Parker's *wife*!" she finished and he was backed against the closed door. Her eyes were swollen with brightness in her dark face, her strong mouth held a tight line.

"The shooting's started," he said quietly, "it's been going for"—his watch said 11:45—"for almost two hours. Anybody doesn't know what's happening by now doesn't want to. Even Bub Houston's daughter and William Parker's wife might think she hadn't no more advantages left to take."

"Nobody been on this street. Maybe I'll wait now, in case William come back."

"Suppose he can't," he said, then saw her eyes squinch so he added, "can't get here in time. They won't leave you alone here for very long. If you're going, north is clear."

"North," she snorted. "North of here there's white folks out as far as you can see. One colored woman out there—just me and a little boy who's like to talk to any white man come up on me just the way his grandpa and his daddy taught him to? If I go I got to try to get back over into Greenwood . . ." She looked out the window, her mouth twisted. "All William ever used to talk about was build us our own home, and get out of Greenwood. Now we be lucky I get us back there in time to die." She looked over at Henry Starr. "That's what's happening over there, isn't it?"

"Take the rifles with you when you go. Or bust 'em. When I see Bub or William I'll tell them what you're planning."

"You're going back to them?" Then she smiled, a better smile even than the one she had given him that first night at dinner "Well, I guess you ain't one to take your advantages either."

"I guess so," he said curtly as he opened the door, "even if I'm no kin to Bub Houston." It wasn't his fault that he had advantages, any one who looked at his life would have to admit he had done his best to throw most of the ones he had away—*most, but not all,* he reminded himself, as he closed the door behind him.

## TULSA *June 1, 1921*

His ruined hip and ham were aching; he'd walked all over Tulsa tonight, but it was too dangerous to sit a horse with all the shooting going on. Henry Starr stuck to the shadows down North Detroit, got his feet on the Katy tracks and started following them toward Greenwood. The shooting, which had been rattling steadily from the Frisco depot and the track line along Archer, was spottier now. There were more fires, and he judged they were inside the colored district that lined the few blocks back from the Frisco tracks. Bub must have pulled his shooters back into Greenwood, if Bub was still alive to do the pulling. Maybe the cops or the Guard had stepped in there. Maybe the whites had busted his line or got around the end somehow.

To his right a two-story loft building was roaring with fire, licking tongues of tiger-colored light across the tracks. Henry Starr eased out beyond the range of the tongues. There were crowds of people silhouetted against the orange blaze. Down at the end of the alleyway next to the building he could see the left rear side of a red fire truck over on Brady Street. People kept trying to climb up onto it. A fireman in a big red helmet and a rubber slicker kept whopping at them with an ax handle. The truck started to back away, the fireman popped a white man off like he was hitting a line drive, and as the truck backed across the frame of the alleyway and disappeared Henry Starr saw that the windshield was blanked out with shatter webs.

Houses and warehouses rose up alongside the tracks. A mob of about twenty-five white men carrying rifles and ax handles came charging around the corner. Henry Starr couldn't duck them so he held up his rifle and waved, and started to run ahead of them. As they came up around him a whiskey-breath whoofed, "Where's it at now? Where's it at?" and Henry Starr said, "Right up here," and they came out into the streets again. The Frisco depot was to their right, and whiskey breath started toward it, but a man with a white armband grabbed him and said, "Don't try it. They got it full of railroad deputies."

"The hell *you*—"

"Don't want nobody messing up their tracks or their stuff. Just keep clear of the depot and . . ."

In the glare of trash burning in big oil drums the Tulsa police were loading black men onto wagons and flatbed trucks. There were about thirty cops, and they kept flinching as stones and junk flew out of the dark at the black men on the trucks—most of the blacks standing, eyes out, backs together. One white man stood outside the police line yelling at the blacks and waving his fist at them. Every once in a while he'd run up and try to break through, and a policeman would bump him back with his hip or shoulder. The blacks looked down, as rigid as cigar store Indians, watching the man yell and run and bump.

There was a small stack of weapons near one of the burning barrels, and whites were walking by in a line and picking up one each, rifle or pistol or shotgun, supervised by another man in a white armband with a police badge pinned to a plaid flannel shirt.

A badge-less white-armband man stepped up next to Henry Starr. "We was just thinkin' about rushing the niggers when the cops came and arrested 'em. Nice work, huh?"

"Tulsa police don't disappoint you," said Henry Starr.

The yelling white man made another run, slipped sideways and broke past the cops. A black man was just climbing up onto the bed of the first truck and the loud white man whipped his gun up and shot him, the *wham!* of the .45 shoving the Negro into the crowd as if he had been kicked and the crowd of black men split, bowed and ducked. The cops swarmed and grabbed the loud white man by the shoulders, slammed him face first into the side of the truck. Two of them picked him up and turned him, and a third one kicked him hard in the ass, shoving him sprawling away from the truck. "Just get the fuck out of here, you simple son of a bitch." The man picked himself up and limped away, the pistol dangling in his right hand.

While everybody was watching the show Henry Starr slipped back into the alley, pointing across back lots and fenced yards into the small back streets of Greenwood.

He went carefully; the shooting was in spots all around him, hard to tell fighting from celebration. There was another fire, westward. If Bub was still alive he'd probably back off the Frisco to the Katy tracks, and if they pushed him off there he'd fire and fall back all the way down Greenwood Avenue. Henry Starr slid into an alley, behind a warehouse, across a yard parked with wagons, smell of rotted hay. He chinned a board fence, there was a small yard on the other side: chinaberry tree, no leaves yet, wrong place for chinaberry, man must be out of Georgia or Mississippi if he—

"Who that?" said a Negro voice.

"A friend," said Henry Starr, then an electric flash from the voice to his nerves made him let go and drop down off the fence as a shotgun slammed and chewed the top of the board fence to splinters spitting all over the place. "Fuck you, friend!" screamed the voice. "I ain't got no friends!"

He snake-walked on his elbows out of line of sight from the yard, found a hole in another fence and went through that. He hugged the shadows along under another house. He heard sounds like sobbing from inside, and somebody hollering at somebody else—man or woman, white or black he couldn't tell.

He came out of the alley onto Greenwood just north of the Dreamland, somebody knocked his hat off and ripped at the swinging tail of his jacket and he dropped down. "Hey! Hey, don't shoot! I'm a friend of Bub Houston!"

In the quiet he could hear the gunfire, steady again, coming from the south end of Greenwood Avenue.

"Henry? Is that you?"

He got up and walked toward the Dreamland as William Parker stepped out from behind the ticket taker's booth. The left sleeves of shirt and jacket were ripped off, his bare arm bound with a bloody wad of cloth. He had a rifle in his right hand, and the pockets of his pants and suit jacket bulged with shells. He held up the rifle. Cavalry Joe Wright and Bub Houston stepped out after him, Bub still holding the pump gun, and now he had a pair of .45s stuck in his belt. From the handle of one dangled a piece of broken lanyard, the kind the police hitched to their gun butts. A silver blink of metal flashed from under the drape of his coat—Bub had pinned his old Boley sheriff's badge to the pocket of his shirt.

"You come down to catch yourself in the picture show?" said Bub.

Henry Starr looked up at the marquee:

DREAMLAND THEATER

NOW SHOWING

A ROMANCE OF HAPPY VALLEY

and

HENRY STARR, THE ROBIN HOOD OF OLD OKLAHOMA

*That was another one of Foley's cut-and-paste jobs. I never even saw it. With all the pictures of me they got in Esterhazy's cans they could keep on making Henry Starr pictures for ten years even if I go down tonight.*

"All the money and time I spent on this place . . ." said William Parker. He looked at Henry Starr. "Here we are standing in front of it, and maybe a couple of hours from now there won't be any of it left. Or me."

"I came by your house . . ."

"She was still there," said Parker, "I knew she . . ."

"Goddamn women," said Bub Houston, "why don't they learn to *mind?*"

"She's your daughter," said Parker, and Bub stepped on the heels of that one with "She's your wife."

"We talked a little," said Henry Starr. "I think she figures she can get out now, without taking unfair advantage of her being related to both of you."

There was a rising rattle of shots at the end of the street, and a whoosh and a glare that said someone had lit off a kerosene barrel in somebody's storefront. People were dodging up Greenwood Avenue, moving quick from storefront to storefront, bundles humped up on their backs, bent over as if walking into a bad wind.

"We could have held them up by the tracks," said Bub, "but somebody let 'em in behind us."

"The Tulsa cops," said Henry Starr. "They arrested a whole crowd by the Frisco depot."

"As soon as the men heard shots from back in Greenwood," said Parker, "they couldn't think of anything but getting back to take care of their own."

"If it was the cav'ry," said Cavalry Joe, "we'd of shot 'em for running."

"Everybody got his own to take care of, Joe," said Bub. "Ain't no Greenwood army except for those got nothing of their own to save."

"You two have your own," said Henry Starr, and Bub snapped, "That's Son Parker's place . . ." and Parker damned his soul for starting that again.

Bub hunched forward, like a tired man leaning on a hoe. "Son, I wish you'd take off home and see to your wife and my daughter, and the child."

"This ain't Boley," said Parker, "it's my town as much as yours. Just like the house is yours as much as mine." They glared at each other, and then Parker looked aside to Henry Starr. "You aren't in the Greenwood army, Mr. Starr. Maybe you could go back and . . ."

There it was again, and he felt the chill of it: "She isn't my wife either."

"You can do a man a favor, can't you?" cried Parker. "You're Dick's friend too, ain't you? If you can't help her for me . . ." and his throat closed as if a fist had grabbed it when he understood what he had almost said out there in the street in front of the Dreamland Theater.

But that didn't change the reasons Parker thought Henry Starr had nothing better to do than get out of Greenwood while there was time. Henry Starr stood there glaring at them, showing Bub and Parker and Cavalry Joe and whoever the hell else was out there watching in the black night that Henry Starr was as at least as good a man as Harriet Houston Parker when it come to not taking his advantages . . .

"God damn the both of you," said Bub, "she can take care of herself. And if she can't now, she's gonna have to start learning."

To prove it there was sudden ripping rattle of gunshots from down the street, and yelling, and the roar of an engine as a big open police car came bellowing up Greenwood from the Frisco tracks.

There was a uniformed policeman at the wheel and about eight men in civilian clothes packed into the car, shotguns and rifles poking out right left and straight up, and as the car came roaring up the street they blasted away, shattering windows, making the people refugeeing up the sidewalk hump and duck and flop on the street. The car swung squealing and fishtailing from side to side, the windows of a parked Ford blew out, a hardware store window. Somebody who had been crouched behind a trash barrel suddenly spooked and sprinted for an alley and the car swung that way and the rifles and shotguns detonated one two three and all together. The car swung toppling as it veered toward the fallen body, the wheels went pop-pop as they ran over it, veered back into the middle of the street again and raced past the four men crouching behind the ticket booth, blasting away at the theater marquee bringing a spray of glass down from the big sign and from the ticket-booth window over their heads as the car roared off up the street.

"Cover me if they come back," yelled William Parker, and he sprinted across the street in a crouch heading for the crumpled body in the gutter. The squeal of tires came from farther up the street, the booming of the shotguns marked in the middle by rifle cracks.

"Get up the street there, in that next alley," Bub snapped at Cavalry Joe. "You stick here, Henry." They were crouched close together behind the ticket booth, broken glass crunching a little as they shifted weight on their boots. "I draw the line here," said Bub. He looked up at the overhanging marquee. "Some goddamn Alamo," he said bitterly.

Henry Starr said nothing.

"You follow my play. I'm gonna kill me that machine. If I do, you pop 'em as they jump out. If I don't, you take 'em out as they go by." He grinned. "Put one in the engine. They might go up like Fourth of July."

"Not a Cherokee holiday," said Henry Starr.

"You show those crackers how we used to do it in the old days."

"I will, Bub."

They heard the engine noise rising up from the far end of the street, the *pow* of the shooting and spray of glass, and Bub Houston levered himself up on the pump gun and then scooted out into the street, an old man bent over on a cane trying to make it over before the white folks and the iron horse come back for him. As soon as the car smelled him it sucked wind and charged, hooting and roaring, and Bub turned white in the glare of the searchlights, which also hinted a ghostly image of Parker crouched across the street leveling his rifle, and here was the car with its eyes burning and its steel lip grinning: here it was: Henry Starr raised his rifle to take a bead on the driver—

—and the tail of his eye caught Bub Houston in the middle of the street with wild shots striking sparks off the paving stones suddenly rising to a bear crouch, the heavy cane lifting to become the barrel of the big trench gun, his left arm pumping the barrel as fire blew out the front of the gun *whoof! whoof! whoof!* like a big bad dog—and the police car windshield blew up like a snowball hitting a brick wall, its two eyes spattered blind, the big thing swerved sideways rocking on two tires and Bub put one in right behind the eyes that blew its radiator like a bomb and another one up its ass that blew a gasoline fart flaring into the street as it spun around on two wheels toppling sideways and smashed over on its side.

Henry Starr's eyes were blue-blind with the fire and searchlight glare, he was cursing and levering the Winchester, maybe if his medicine was good he'd hit somebody firing into that blue-black blank.

"Uh-h-h," said Cavalry Joe—he had shifted forward to get a better shot, and now he knelt down on the sidewalk. Then he threw himself forward on his face.

Then a bullet snagged at Henry Starr's shoulder from behind, and he threw himself down too and crawled over to Cavalry Joe: dead, two bullets in the back. He looked down Greenwood, there were gun flashes, shapes coming forward.

Out across the street: three shapes humped and crawled in the gutter away from the wreck of the overturned car that waved yellow banners of fire over them. No sight of Bub or William Parker, *maybe I can get across before . . .*

There was a cheer up the street, and the roar of another car, and then he heard the *yatatatatatat* and windows crashing in one ceaseless shattering fall, they had got the machine-gun car back on its wheels. He was snaking into his alley before the car got abreast of it, he put his face and belly and his cock and his thighs and his toes as close in to the ground as he could get and squirmed to get closer as the machine gun blasted the front of the Dreamland and flipped some passing rounds up the alley.

They had drawn them a line on Greenwood Avenue, and Bub and Parker were on the other side.

*"You can do a man a favor, can't you?"* But for which man? For William Parker across the street there, who had waited too long to decide whether he'd go home or stay with the Greenwood army? Or for Bub Houston, when like he said, no daughter of his would ever "mind," nor take any advantage that Bub wouldn't take himself? Or for Dick Rowland, who if he was still lucky was sitting in the Tulsa County Jail, if you call that lucky?

"Maybe I should do myself a favor," he said out loud. But he had no idea in the world what that would be. He turned and headed back the way he had come, back lots and alleyways, working across Greenwood toward North Detroit Avenue.

Sometimes he had to get out into the bigger streets, but if he walked like he belonged there they figured he was white as the next man.

There was a long row of small bungalows. Knots of white people, men and women both, were swarming across front yards and into some of the houses, pushing blacks out, men and women, kids. They were "arresting" them, there was the beginning of a coffle in the middle of the street. Some people didn't abuse the blacks, but sweated and balanced hard as they hauled off boxes, chests, sewing machines, a rocker cradle, a couple of lamps with a dirt slash on one of the white satin shades.

Six white women were pushing a black man, his family herded ahead of him, toward the coffle. Four white men with rifles stood by, laughing and calling out suggestions.

One house down the street was burning, but the fire looked pale: it was getting on to sunrise.

In front of some of the bungalows stood white families, arranged like they were mannequins in some kind of store display, or posed to have their pictures taken. They didn't move as the white crowds bustled in and out of the neighboring houses of the Negroes. They didn't help anyone or do anything, they didn't take anything, but just stood there. Nobody bothered their houses or spoke to them. The whites going in and out were careful not to step on the grass strips in front of these houses, one man even laughing as he cut a right-angle turn before running up to throw a rock through a neighboring window.

In front of the burning house there was a row of men like a firing squad. Somebody inside kept trying to open the door, and whenever that happened the line of men would blow off a volley, you could hear the bullets rapping wood even over the harsh whisper of the flames.

*I ain't obliged to stop this*, he thought as he walked on past, *these ain't none of my folks, I ain't in the Greenwood army, I got kin to take care of like everybody else, or no: maybe all it is is I said I'd do a man a favor, and Henry Starr always keeps his word, that word of his—everybody knows that, they saw it in the movie, remember? Yes, and he never broke his word but once, like he never killed but once before today, and both of those times by accident, but it wasn't being sorry that got him out of . . .*

---

He came up out of a brushy ravine and climbed over the board fence that closed Bub Houston's backyard. The kitchen door was locked when he rattled it, there was a sharp reek of kerosene. He ran around to the front of the house.

Someone was crouching on the front porch—it was Harriet Parker; she jumped up and turned on him, snatching a rifle up off the floor. "What are you doing back?" she said while he was saying, "You're supposed to be gone."

"I had things to make sure of," she said. There was a kerosene can on the porch, and a heap of rags and a couple of cane chairs just inside the front door. "And my neighbors needed help"—she gestured toward the street.

Shaker sat on the seat of Bub's delivery wagon and in the box bed behind him a gray-haired colored woman sat, her body twisted around to look toward the house up the street. Henry Starr guessed she was Dr. Jackson's wife. "You waited too long," he said.

Harriet Parker's mouth was set. "The doctor didn't think they would come over this way, so far out of Greenwood. Anyway"—she gestured to the house—"I had to be sure before I . . ."

"Why didn't you just leave it? If they came they'd have burned it for you."

Her face turned furious. "They never live to say they burned me out!"

Shots prickled at the southern end of the street toward Archer. The two of them stood on the porch looking at each other. "I still own my own house," she said. She looked in the front hall. Then she took a box of matches out of the pocket of her skirt, struck one on the box, flipped it into the kerosene-soaked pile of rags, and a stinking orange flame flashed up and ran into the house on the trail of kerosene she had poured for it. They turned and ran for the wagon.

Down the length of the street Henry Starr could see figures darting back and forth across the road. To his right, on the west side of North Detroit Avenue, the white families there had also come out to stand like wooden Indians in front of their houses. By now he knew what that was a sign for.

The wagon dipped, and Henry Starr—riding "shotgun" next to Harriet Parker, who held the reins—turned and saw Dr. Jackson climbing into the back of the wagon, his gray hair and finely textured suit looking queer in the back of Houston's old freighter. He carried a leather instrument bag, the leather stiff and cracked with years of use.

Black smoke was pouring out of Houston's house, flames ate up the curtains and looked out of the windows. Further back a ball of black smoke ballooned up over the trees, there were shots, and Henry Starr figured the way north was closed. Maybe closer in the cops were still taking prisoners.

"Listen to me," he said. "We have to drive through that mob up ahead so I can get us some place safe. The play is that I'm arresting you, taking you downtown . . ."

"*You* arresting *me?*" said Harriet Parker, the orange flames of her house danced crazy shadows across her face. She threw back her head and laughed; it was a real ugly laugh and Shaker stood up and grabbed her and started yelling "No! No! No!" over and over again, and Henry Starr couldn't tell if the *no* was for being arrested or the way his momma was laughing.

"You're my prisoners," he said urgently, watching the darting shapes coming closer up the street, "Shaker, you understand?" He grabbed the boy's shoulder and sat him down hard. "Climb over into the back," he said, his voice grating. "You listen to me now, Shaker," said Henry Starr. "You got to act like you're my prisoner, or we're going to get killed. You understand me? You got to act like you're afraid of me, like I'm a cracker got your momma and you and these neighbor folks here, and I'm taking you to prison. You hear me, Shaker?"

Shaker stood up in the wagon gripping the back of the seat, his face twisted, the smoke of his house blowing into his eyes now, and he seemed suddenly to explode. "No!" he cried. "No! No! Bub Houston and my daddy and Dick never give up to no crackers, they never give up, they never—" and then Mrs. Jackson was hauling him down, aided by the sudden forward jerk of the wagon as Harriet Parker slapped the reins on the horses' rumps and they started up the street. "Don't look back," she said to the doctor's wife.

Henry Starr stood up, bracing his right knee on the seat and his left foot against the front panel of the wagon box, and let himself rock easily and arrogantly as the wagon rolled forward toward the mob, his rifle cocked and ready in his hands; he was wishing he had Bub Houston's pump gun, because it was going to be too close for rifle work.

Henry Starr couldn't look at any of them, Mrs. Parker, Shaker, the doctor and his wife. He was white, he was a white man, why in hell should he *have* to look at a bunch of niggers. In fact, he was mad enough to piss vinegar, got to take these niggers in while everybody else can run around shooting and burning and getting the good pickings. Yeah, he was mad, mad enough so nobody better bother him or . . .

The white families standing in front of their houses watched the wagon pass. Up ahead a different kind of white folks were moving and running around, some in white shirt sleeves and others in business suits, and three or four in old khaki uniforms, running into the east-side houses. There was a bunch of four Negroes, three women and a child, huddled close to one of the street's new-planted trees, tree so small their heads were among the branches. A white woman came out of the house with a sewing machine so heavy she had to keep putting it down. From inside came a sound like somebody banging a piano with a sledgehammer. There was a black woman's body lying face down in the front yard. The morning breeze peeked under her skirt like a mean child.

Then they were all around the wagon, grabbing the horses, pushing up to the wheel, and Henry Starr yelled at them to get their goddamn hands off his wagon, and at the nigger woman to keep driving. The horses were down to an uncertain walk.

"Hey cowboy!" yelled a big man in a khaki shirt. He stood in front of the horses. He had a white armband. "Just you whoa up there." He also had a shotgun. Henry Starr raised his left hand for Mrs. Parker to stop the wagon, and while the man watched that hand Henry Starr eased the rifle around to take a bead in the center of the Ku-kluck's chest.

"Get your ass out of my way," said Henry Starr, "this here is *my* goddamn wagon!"

"Where you taking *them*?"

He felt the wagon rock, the crowd was yelling at the three people in the box behind him, but he had to keep his eyes on the man in front of him, he had to get them moving again. "I arrested these niggers," said Henry Starr, "and I'll take 'em where it suits me."

The wagon pitched and nearly upset; Henry Starr had to whip a look back and see—and see it was nothing he could do anything about, someone had grabbed Dr. Jackson by the jacket and hauled him out of the wagon box into the street. Someone else kicked him so he seemed to make a belly dive into the gutter, and as Henry Starr turned back swiftly to look the way his rifle was still pointing he heard the pistol shots, *slapslap! slap!* and the soft instantaneous thud-home of the bullets. "Listen, you lard-assed son of a bitch," said Henry Starr, "if you don't let go of my niggers I'm gonna put one right in the middle of your ugly face."

The man laughed and shook his head. "You're a tough cowboy all right. But they ain't gonna let you keep any of 'em. You got to turn 'em in at the Convention Center. Courthouse and jail is full up."

"No hard feelings about your swell nigger, Jack," yelled a man in shirt sleeves. "I'll give you three of mine," and everybody laughed at that, laughed as the shirt-sleeve man herded the three women and the child who had been standing by the little tree up into the back of the wagon, laughed as they stood around the wagon, their faces grimed with smoke and sweat, sleeves rolled, men and women together they'd been working hard all night and into the morning, working *hard* and now there was that ease-back feeling, the hard work done, and they stood around laughing and feeling tired and easy as the big Ku-kluck stepped out of the way and Henry Starr clucked and the nigger woman slapped the reins and the loaded wagon moved off.

He threw one glance back. Dr. Jackson's body lay face down in the road, somebody was going through his pockets as he lay there. The leather medical bag had stuck in his hand when they hauled him out, it must have been like part of him after thirty years' practice, and a white man had it open now, turned it over, and shook out a rain of steel surgical tools like a spray of liquid in the early light.

Mrs. Jackson was sobbing in the back of the box, the other women were making comfort sounds, Shaker was screaming something about what Bub Houston and his daddy would do to somebody, but Henry Starr couldn't pay any mind to that. There was a huge hum in the air, a buzz that seemed to fill the sky and the ground from over and under everything, like the mindless buzz of a gigantic insect, the street and the houses quivered like images in a pool. *It's gone too far this time, they busted the wall and let the Nightland in*, if it got any worse they would all melt into smoke and blow away without bodies or names, but it kept getting worse, and worse—

The rush of noise suddenly resolved itself into a roar overhead, Henry Starr looked up and an airplane brushed its shadow over him and climbed higher turning over downtown Tulsa, wings flashing in the new sun. He followed it with his eyes. It seemed to pause at the top of the turn, and then glide down low in the direction of Greenwood. Balloons of fresh fire smoke and broken columns of old burning rose toward it as it disappeared. The rapid pattering of gunshots could be heard from Greenwood.

The wagon bumped over the Katy tracks. The mobs kept rushing by. A Tulsa cop offered Henry Starr some more niggers as long as he was going that way, and he said *sure*.

Shaker was yelling. He was yelling he was nobody's nigger. He was yelling he wouldn't give up. Bub Houston and his daddy were going to . . .

The Convention Hall looked across the Frisco tracks at the Wobblies' union hall—the latter closed up tight, blind eyes turned to the Convention Hall, where guards in uniform and civilian clothes were hustling colored people up the steps and inside, men women and children. "Quick-quickquick, come on, move it there, get along, get in there." There was a spray of brown-red on the white steps as if someone had tossed a bucket of watery slops there. Harriet Parker gave him one look as she climbed down and started in, and he realized he didn't know what would happen now, if the Convention Hall was safe or just a great big barrel for shooting fish.

The world started to buzz and shake again, and the shadow of the plane swept over the face of the Hall. Maybe every place was just a barrel now.

The Parkers, Mrs. Jackson and the rest went in through the doors. Henry Starr got down off the wagon and started walking back toward the courthouse.

There was a National Guardsman in full combat gear in front of the door. "Nobody gets inside unless they're a cop or a deputy."

"You see anybody today who ain't a deputy?" said Henry Starr.

"Brother," said the soldier, "I got my orders."

"I've got some information they want inside," said Henry Starr. "For Captain Blaine of the state police." Tilghman was probably still in Oklahoma City, but maybe something of him had rubbed off on Blaine.

That got him through the door, and as far as the staircase where a state police major in cavalry boots stopped him. Captain Blaine? He grinned, and jerked a thumb upwards. "You want to see Blaine, you need a mighty tall ladder. That's him up in that buzz-bird. You can just give me the information." The policeman misunderstood Henry Starr's hesitation: "Yeah, all right, and I'll tell him you was the one gave it to me."

"It was about that nigger they got in here," said Henry Starr. "Captain wanted me to scout a way out if they wanted to move him."

The state policeman's eyes narrowed, what the hell was Blaine poking his nose in where it didn't belong? "Listen," he said, "that kind of news ain't worth a dime here. You want money, you'll have to see Blaine when he comes down."

He felt a touch of ice. "How come it's old news?"

The state policeman looked smug. "Because they took the nigger out of here a couple of hours ago." He snorted contemptuously. "Brilliant idea, when if they had just opened the goddamn front doors last night they could have saved everybody all this trouble."

"Where'd they take him?"

"How should I know? I don't come from this lousy town. Every town got some place they do that kind of thing . . ."

The people of Tulsa did that kind of thing in a broad-bottomed ravine that cut through the bluffs into the Arkansas west of town, between Tulsa and Sand Springs. It was the Springs Road that Henry Starr rode his horse out along, under the noon sun. He cut off the road before the ravine, busted brush to get to the head of it, and came down through a screen of cottonwood and alder toward the clearing that they would use.

There was a flatbed truck in the clearing, five men loading something on it, and nothing else.

The truck belonged to the Pan American Motion Picture Company of Tulsa. There was a camera set on a riveted stand on the flatbed of the truck, which was the one used to film stagecoach chases, and that was Esterhazy working on it, screwing the machine back into place. A portable tripod lay at his feet among some cans of film, a gas-powered generator and a battery of lights. Henry Starr sidled his horse out of the trees. The men around the truck looked up, saw who it was and waved. Esterhazy turned, saw him and leaned against the camera post.

"Henry," he said.

"You film all of it?" said Henry Starr. He noted that Esterhazy was unarmed but he didn't worry about that, some words a man could say gave you a right to shoot him just as fast and sure as if he had drawed down on you with a cocked and loaded gun.

"Nothing," said Esterhazy. "Henry, nothing happened. We just now hear that colored boy get away safe, Sheriff McCullough and old cowboy marshal you were friends with, they get him away."

*Bill Tilghman*, he thought, *the old man still had the power, maybe if I had* . . . but he would not let anything distract or soften him till he was sure: "Nobody come," he said, "but you was here just in case they did, all nice and set up and ready to go. Camera, lights and everything."

"Henry . . ." said Esterhazy.

"Were you gonna put the makeup on him here? Or were they supposed to do that down at the jail? Or don't you need to put makeup on niggers?"

"It was Poole's idea, Henry. He had information, you know? Something going to happen, we might as well be here and . . ."

*Poole: I guess it's easy to get information like that when you are one of the men that gets to say does it happen, and when and how and where. A man don't get surprised by something he makes up himself, does he, Mr. Editor Poole?*

"Henry!" said Esterhazy. "What I was supposed to do about it? I wouldn't have helped them kill that poor . . ."

"No," said Henry Starr, "you'd only have taken the pictures."

"Pictures is only pictures, Henry. It ain't like I . . . and if I didn't do it, somebody else get my job and I . . ."

"You think pictures is only pictures," said Henry Starr. "I knew a man got himself and his best friend killed about a picture. A cheap lousy handbill picture. It wasn't even no *Birth of a Nation* like you and Poole had going here last night, but it did the job."

"Listen, Henry," said Esterhazy, trying to distract the outlaw's rage, "it ain't me you need to worry about. Is Poole and Foley. They can—I tried to tell her they were too smart, but she's got strong head, she . . ."

"What are you talking about?"

Esterhazy jerked his hand out at the empty clearing. "This wasn't going to be for *Birth of Nation*. He . . . Poole found out that man you put in as Cherokee Bill was same one they have in jail. He said . . . he said, 'Some luck, hey?! Too good to be . . .' " It was going badly, Esterhazy's smile was freezing, this wasn't placating the famous bandit and murderer one bit, but he had to finish. "He figured we get some pictures of hanging and cut them into movie and it . . ."

Henry Starr sat stiff and wooden in his saddle. His eyes were in another place (thank God! thank God! thought Esterhazy), his horse started to move off with his rider's gaze.

Then Henry Starr turned in the saddle. "How could they do that," he said, "when we made those pictures so Cherokee Bill . . ."

Title: **"Drop your guns and clear the way, or this man dies!"**

Cherokee Bill holds the guard tight, pressing the pistol against his head and motions for Starr to pick up a fallen rifle—we see Starr's face in which conflicting emotions war—then his features set:

Starr shakes his head, and holds out his hand.

Title: **"There's been too much killing already, Bill. Give me the gun."**

Cherokee Bill looks fierce, but doubtful.

Henry Starr's face in close-up: and over it the ghostly image of a woman and child in the door of a little cabin . . .

Title: **"Think of your own mother, Bill. She wouldn't want you to kill anymore."**

Cherokee Bill's face in close-up—it softens, his expression is like that of Henry Starr dreaming of the cabin.
He hands Henry Starr his pistol, butt first . . .

"You can write any words you like on cards . . ." said Esterhazy.

"And the pictures?"

Esterhazy shrugged. "Someone like Foley, he can cut them up and put them together how he likes."

*Just like he already did to you how many times and you ain't caught on to the trick yet, you dumb half-breed: Buckskin Bill's Outlaw Trail vs. the Starr Gang, Henry Starr the Bandit the Scourge the Robin Hood the Avenger the Debtor to the Law.*

*Once they got the pictures they can put 'em together to make you anything they want.*

"Maybe now they don't get this here, they won't change so much," said Esterhazy, "if we play careful, Henry, we can maybe get . . ."

Henry Starr was looking right through Esterhazy the camera the truck and all, and Esterhazy suddenly felt naked to the point of transparency standing alone on top of the truck bed. He put his hand on the camera to steady himself, and just then the outlaw reared his spook-gray horse back on its hind legs, and Esterhazy saw the pistol flash in the noon light as it came out of the outlaw's breast, but he had frozen to the camera, he was dead dead dead as the bright fire eye of the pistol winked at him and death made him numb, the jolts were hard but pain-blank.

The outlaw burst away through the screen of brush and vanished, the branches whipping back behind him.

"Holy shit," said one of the crewmen.

Esterhazy looked down and saw that he was alive. Henry Starr had shot out the camera's two lenses and put a third shot between them into the works. It was like seeing a living man mutilated, the eyeballs smashed in his head, the empty sockets full of splinters.

Esterhazy pivoted and puked over the side of the truck.

## TULSA *June 2, 1921*

It wasn't until the following day that Henry Starr got back into Greenwood. A morgue of a kind had been set up on the sidewalks along Greenwood Avenue—bodies laid out, some muffled in blankets or tarpaulins, some lying open to the sky like tramps, dead men and a scattering of women, a child here and there, barefooted where their shoes or boots had been stolen, pockets turned out like white tongues or the clothes lifted cut or torn open to show what the children should not see, lying in the street with just an open newspaper tented over their faces—

GREAT GUNFIGHT IN GREENWOOD

CITIZENS ARMING TO SUPPRESS
THE RIOTERS

A 'War of Races' Commenced
in the Magic City

Under the eyes of National Guardsmen there were black families going up and down the street, peeking under blankets, lifting the newspapers to look into faces.

Bub Houston was laid out in front of the fire-scarred shell of the Dreamland. The marquee had fallen when the beams anchoring its support wires had burned away, breaking the lettered panels:

HAPPY ALLEY

ROBIN HO OKL MA

Harriet Parker stood over the body. Bub's shirt was bloody—three blackened holes in front—the old man's face was rigid and wooden, his dead lips snicked to show his corner teeth. Shaker was sitting next to the old man, his hand stuck into the torn chest pocket of the shirt, *like he was looking for candy*.

"They took his badge," said Harriet Parker. "William said when he went back to the Dreamland, he pinned his badge on again, his old sheriff badge from Boley." She looked up at Henry Starr. "William come through just a little bit shot. He's hiding out with some of his people in Muskogee."

"I think Marshal Tilghman got Dick Rowland clear of town yesterday morning."

"Praise God," she said. She looked down at her son sitting next to the dead body of her father. "The boy wanted the badge to remember his grandpa by. I told him, he don't need no badge to remember a grandpa like he had." She looked down at her father, and said what his praise would be. "When he saw there was nothing a human man could do anymore but die, he come back here. Started out on the roof, and come down to the sign when the plane come after him. He had lots of shells." She looked up fiercely. "And do you think he didn't hit everything he aimed at, sitting up there, and them howling like a pack of dogs under his feet? Do you think he ever missed a shot?"

"No," said Henry Starr, "I don't think he missed a one." *You tell the story just that way, because that's not only how it used to be, that's also how it should have been, and that's how it should be remembered. It was no lie I told Cherokee Bill: how they remember how you die, that's more important even than how you did die: because you yourself only die the once, but in the picture in the memory of the Nation your death keeps being time and time again, praising or shaming you time and time and time . . .*

Shaker still sat with his hand burrowed like a mouse into his grandfather's torn shirt pocket, but his grandfather's face was sealed, blank and dead as the rind of a dry gourd, and Henry Starr thought of himself standing in front of the dead standing stump of Tom Starr on the Fourth of July in Tahlequah, holding out the smoked specs he had bought as a gift—but the gift had no power, the Old Man as dead to him as a cigar store Sitting Bull or a dead tree with black holes in it like eyes, black holes in which your name is black and your memory has stopped being, and you have no clan and no name, you are deader than the dead man himself. "Shaker," said Henry Starr, because he did not want the little boy to hear his grandfather's silence, "Shaker—you know your grandfather, he was the biggest man ever lived in the Nations . . ."

Shaker looked up, and finally he saw who it was. "Get out of here, you cracker," he said.

"Shaker," said his mother softly, "it's Henry Starr."

"My grandpa is dead!" Shaker screamed, his fist gripping and jerking the dead man's bloody shirt. "And you and you ain't you *ain't* Henry Starr! You used to be, but you ain't no more!"

# The Return of Henry Starr

> "While working at the Liberty which had been the Majestic I ran Henry Starr the outlaw's picture and he gave a talk between shows it was good advice for people who thought of a life of crime. He visited a lot in the booth with me. He was dressed nice, was no braggart and could of been taken for a salesman in a men's store."
>
> —EDWARD MILLER, "From Flickers to Todd A-O"

## STROUD *December 10, 1921*

Paul Curry was down at the depot to pick up the load of canned goods Brogan had ordered, coming down on the Tulsa train. There were a half-dozen city people getting off, the oddest one an Irishman in a pocket-y jacket and riding pants with mumps, and with him a little peeping sort of man who looked familiar—Curry remembered him suddenly as the man who had come to town with Henry Starr back in the spring, he woke up and looked sharp: and there, climbing down out of a freight car, was Henry Starr himself, giving orders to some men off-loading boxes of equipment into a pair of wagons.

He kept an eye and an ear on Henry Starr while they heaped Brogan's cases on his wagon, and when Starr stood up and clapped dust off his hands to say *his* work was done, Paul Curry was right there. "Mr. Starr? Remember me?"

The outlaw/movie star let his smile come up slow: "I'm not likely to forget you, Mr. Curry. First impressions are strong impressions, mother used to say."

"I've seen every one of them!" blurted Curry, like a kid thrusting a gift at a teacher, awkward and apologetic at his own generosity. "Every one of them, and this last one was just . . . the greatest ever, I . . ."

Starr's face had an odd look, and Curry thought with excitement that that was how a man like Henry Starr should be, shy with his own fame and greatness, and not any put-on fake modesty either.

"I went up to Tulsa the day they opened it: *Henry Starr: A Debtor to the Law.* Good God, it was . . . and there's talk they'll open up the Opera House here again, some Tulsa people, to show your—but that's why you come to town again, ain't it?" Of course, what a dumb kid he was not to have seen it right off.

"Not exactly," said Henry Starr. "We're just locating around here, looking for places to make some more movies in. We've been up in Sperry and Howitt last week, and . . ."

Curry leaped at it like a trout at a fly. "Maybe this time you'll make one here in Stroud, hey? I mean, not that the way you done it in the picture was wrong . . ."

Starr tipped his head toward the Irishman in the mumps pants and the little peeper man: "Not my say-so. The bossmen there, they didn't think Stroud looked enough like Stroud, so they shot her in a made-up town outside Tulsa."

"It looked great," said Curry, "it was perfect. My God, it was almost like living through it again, the way those pictures just kept rolling along." He laughed, giddily. "You know, watching it roll out like that, it made me scared for *you*, knowing there wasn't no getting out of the way things was coming on. I never . . . I mean, every time I used to remember that day, it was *myself* I was scared for—I'd dream it over and wake up in a sweat, thinking it was all real again only this time I'd never be able to do it, never be able to pull the trigger or the gun wouldn't . . ."

Fear suddenly froze him as he realized what he was saying, and to whom. But Henry Starr was just nodding and looking softly at him like he understood.

"I'm sorry," said Curry, "I didn't mean . . ."

"It's all right," said Henry Starr. "I'm glad the picture did somebody some good."

"It was great," said Paul Curry, "all of it: seeing that kid playing me was real queer, but I loved the rest of it—when they strung up that nigger I was ready to holler."

Henry Starr stiffened up, and his look made Curry blink. "Listen," he said, "I had nothing to do with that. If it was up to me they'd have shot the damned thing in Stroud, and used you to play yourself instead of that little punk. If it had been my doing, you'd have bust out crying when they hung Cherokee Bill."

Paul Curry didn't know what to say, but with everything that had fallen out of his mouth today, "nigger" was the last thing he'd have thought would get Henry Starr down on him.

Henry Starr looked at him straight. "Listen," said the movie star, "you don't need to talk like that. You got something behind you to give you some pride. A man like you don't need to call somebody a nigger, unless he's trying to pass for mean."

"A man like me?" said Paul Curry, rage and grief rising in his throat like bile. "What do you mean, a man like me? The only thing in my life I got to take pride in is shooting you in the back six years ago, and every time I think of that . . . especially since I saw that wonderful . . . every time I think of that it seems like the worst goddamn mistake I ever made!" He glared at Henry Starr bitterly, as if the outlaw had betrayed him. "If I had it to do over again, I'd have shot Charles and that stupid clerk you had with you, and Brogan too, goddamn it, and I'd have gone out of there with *you* instead of . . ." His arm jerked in a broken movement at the wagonload of canned goods.

Starr was looking at him steadily and quietly. "Yes," he said, "I know what you mean. It ain't fair a man should get only one crack at the important things. Mostly they come at you when you ain't experienced enough to know what it is you really want for yourself. It ought to be that you could take another run at something like that: go back and try it again, or find you a second chance somewhere."

"You show me where they let you do like that, and I'll take the next train out of here," said Curry.

"I'm thinking about doing another movie," said Henry Starr. "Like that last one, only better. Maybe you'd like to be in it this time?"

"Oh Lord!" said Paul Curry. "Try me!"

"I got to get some money together," said Henry Starr. "That's why I'm working for these fellers. We're going out to scout up some more what they call 'real old-time western banks'—we done Sperry and Howitt and we'll ride out by Kendrick tomorrow, then likely swing down through Micawber and Okfuskee and Beggs and Tuskegee." He named the places carefully, as if he expected Paul Curry to remember them.

"How long till you start your movie?"

Henry Starr's eyes focused intently on Curry's. "It might take a while for me to get my capital together. This ain't gonna be any one-reel bullshit cowboy movie. This is gonna be like . . . this one is gonna make *Debtor to the Law* and *Birth of a Nation* both look like nickelodeon."

"Are you gonna do all of it again, I mean Stroud too?"

Henry Starr nodded slowly. "So that when you see 'em you'll know they ain't never *really* been done before. But we won't stop with Stroud, either . . ."

"But I thought Stroud was the last . . ."

"*Starr!*" yelled the Irishman in the mumps pants.

"Stroud ain't the last," said Henry Starr. "The last of Henry Starr ain't yet been seen by the general public."

Faster than thought, Paul Curry's hand leapt out to grip Henry Starr's hand and shake it. "This time," he said, "this time I . . ."

"I'll write and tell you when and where," said Henry Starr.

"Yes," said Paul Curry, "yes, I'll be ready."

## BEGGS *December 22, 1921*

On December 22, 1921, Billy Claybo rode his bicycle to work at the Chalmers' General Store in Beggs, Oklahoma, just as he did every morning when school was out. At twelve years old he was just tall enough for his legs to make the stretch to the pedals without straining too hard on his crotch, but he still rode standing at first to pedal up a good burst of speed down the oiled dirt of the County Road, whoofing frosty smoke out of his nostrils on this icy morning, then sitting back in the seat for a glide, one hand on the handlebars and one hanging loose at his side: a cowpoke on a slow lonely lope across the prairie, keen eyes scanning the stubble rows for Injun sign. It was less than a mile to the wooden bridge over the irrigation ditch, but as soon as "Old Blue's" hooves drummed the hollow boards of the bridge he reined the cayuse to a stop, eased down from the saddle and patted the sturdy faithful beast on the withers. "Good boy." A cowhand always takes care of his animal before anything else.

Below him the narrow canal was skinned with ice, frost come too early this year . . . how thick? He chunked a rock in and broke the bland gray mirror skin . . . *less'n an inch.*

But the sound . . . it would wake every skulkin' renegade for miles!

The rear yard of Chalmers' Store backed on the canal, and Chalmers kept a colt and a bull calf back there; they trotted to the fence along the County Road to greet Billy. Luckily he had spotted the varmints before they could see him, and Billy became grim and implacable, his vengeance long delayed but certain as death and judgment, and he shot them down without a tremor from behind Old Blue.

The colt and the bull calf bunched up along the fence, huffing and bumping each other and the heavy boards, eagerly expecting the sugar he always gave them in the morning—their wet noses and their friendliness made Billy suddenly ashamed. He forgave them for the blood they'd shed, didn't know any better, and anyway Injuns get abused by *white* renegades, don't they? So they were just wounded. Billy healed them and they became blood brothers after that, tracked down those white renegades selling guns and whiskey to the Injuns just like Tom Mix in *Apache Rescue* or Henry Starr in *Cherokee Justice* at the Tulsa Lyric.

Billy mounted again on the other side of the bridge, and this time when he stomped forward on the pedal his engine roared suddenly to life and his squealing tires flared dust as he roared across the bridge and into Beggs, Oklahoma: on the town side of the bridge the county road was asphalted, and Billy became Deputy Charlie Bascomb in his cut-down blue Olds touring car with the police stars on the doors, the spotlight mount and the wild-whooping siren.

Chalmers' General Store sat in the notch of a Y intersection, the paved County Road forming its main stem and (from the perspective of the store) its left side. Chalmers' Lane was the other branch of the Y, a dirt road running thirty yards down to the canal where a low, weathered, whitewashed picket fence ended it. Chalmers' Livery Stable was across the lane—wide echoing barns with stalls for horses full of the good sweet smell of rotting hay and horse apples. Chalmers' Store was shaped to fit its triangle corner, its door set at the apex like the prow of a ship looking westward up the County Road to the intersection with the north-south Tulsa Pike, a hundred and fifty yards away.

Sweeping the three steps before the double glass doors, Billy Claybo was the lookout in the forepeak, *'ware shoals!* as they slipped through fog-shrouded seas toward the Windward Passage, *rich pickings, me hearties* among the galleons passing homeward from the Spanish Main. The big gear-grinding produce trucks, high closed vans, oil riggers and fast shiny touring cars were always rolling on the Tulsa Pike, hitting the potholes with a cannon-shot sound fired across Billy's bows. *Missed again, lads! Steady at that, hold her.* They ran out the guns while he laid her in her marks, bearing five points off the big plate-glass front of the Chemical–Cattlemen's Bank halfway down the street. Its signboard swung in the small cold wind as it hung from its cast-iron gallows.

At 2:30 Billy was greasing the chain on Old Blue and tucking the bag with Mrs. Robinson's grocery order into the big wicker basket slung forward of the handlebars, when he looked up and saw three men—three *hombres*—turn up the County Road from the Pike. Two Stetsons and one derby, the Stetsons in pale linen dusters and the derby in a dark brown suit and vest. They rode big strong horses, long in the leg but heavily muscled, their coats rough with winter hair, their hocks brushy. The men didn't tie up, but dropped their reins by the post in front of the Chemical–Cattlemen's Bank and looked up and down the street.

The three men fumbled something at their necks—*what?*—and glided swiftly through the doors of the bank.

*Neckerchers.* Billy's heart jumped and hit him a hard punch in the throat. *Pulled up their neckerchers over their faces. They pulled their neckerchers over their faces and went into the bank.*

There wasn't a sound. The big plate-glass front of the bank was bland and blank with reflected winter light, like the ice on the canal.

Billy waited for the bank to explode in red fire.

Then he waited for the great electric gong inside the door to begin yammering, but he remembered: it only rang in the police station now.

Sweat broke out on him and he chilled, his attention jittering to be in two places at once: at the front of the bank where the three high backed horses switched their broomtails and smelt the ground by the dangling reins; and the far end of the County Road where it crossed the Pike, at the corner around which Deputy Charlie Bascomb and Sheriff Bodine would come barreling any second now in the cut-down Olds, siren raging, shotguns blazing.

Nothing.

Mr. Jessup of the hardware across the street from the bank stepped out with a barrel of waste paper, set it on the curb, went back inside.

A truck rammed its load over a pothole on the Tulsa Pike. Mr. Chalmers called "Billy!" and footsteps thumped toward him out of the deep store.

The two Stetsons burst out of the bank, the linen dusters hiding their bodies so that they almost seemed to glide legless on the air, each with a handful of cut-down twin-barreled big-bore shotgun, and they went up onto the high backs of the horses in a single liquid flow of cloth as the derby hat came backing out the door, a red bandanna covering his face to the eyes looking strange with the brown three-piece suit, and stranger still the pair of heavy hog's-leg Colt's pistols he had in his hands. He spun, took the saddle in a spraddle jump and the bandanna dropped and Billy saw his face—light brown Injun or Mex, a flash of white teeth—and the man rammed the left-hand pistol into a shoulder rig, then the right, swooped up the reins and yelled, "*Eeee*-hah!"

The big horses seemed to gather their legs under them, then suddenly spring out toward the Tulsa Pike seventy yards away, hitting a gallop in two jumps, right toward the gap in the buildings into which Charlie

Bascomb's big blue Olds was going to come barreling any second now, and they raced toward it three abreast, linen dusters flying and the derby gone to blazes rolling behind them in the street, and here was Banker Ford and Mr. Jessup out in the street again, and the bank clerks pushing out of the bank yelling and waving, bumping Banker Ford toward the street, the banker with a long shotgun too heavy for him to lift properly—and down at the end of the street the three galloping horses suddenly seemed to rear and lean back into the wake of their own flying charge, and Billy saw the one with brown suit on him actually skid ten feet on his haunches as the brown man wrung his head around.

And suddenly the three had turned and were charging back down the street right toward the front stoop of Chalmers' Store that pointed back like an accusing finger right in the eye of the street, the horseshoes ringing and clashing sparks, the horses roaring smoke out of their nostrils in the frigid air like the horsemen of the Apocalypse in the Bible picture, and yelling as they come *Yee! Yee! Yipyipyip!* and one shotgun boomed and blew the bank sign to flinders on its iron gallows, and another made the gaslight blow like a bomb, and Mr. Jessup leaped back sprawling into his doorway and the banker ducked and shot his too big shotgun into the air as they raced by, the first cowboy blasting the bank's big plate-glass front into bright flashes of frozen light with the second barrel of the sawed-off, and Billy saw the brown man swing low off the side of his smoking horse hanging on with his legs to reach and swoop that derby hat out of the dust as if all the whooping and shooting and galloping was just because he'd dropped his hat and wanted to come back and get it . . .

At which point the blue Olds materialized at the end of the street fishtailing round the corner and into the County Road on fleering tires, lights on, siren shrieking, motor roaring like an express train as the car spun dust, gathered itself, and shot like a bolt down the street after the horsemen gaining every second as it come.

The thundering riders and the roaring car came straight for Billy Claybo on the stoop of Chalmers' Store, hooves and necks and smoking horseheads reaching for him and the blue fury of the shrieking Olds behind them driving them madly onward, and Billy saw himself wiped out at the next instant in the unappeasable rage of their piled up momentum—horses shotguns riders blue touring car—when the three men leaned their bodies "like they was hauled on one string" and the horses deflected to his right, not down the County Road for the bridge and the open road beyond but down Chalmers' Lane direct for the dead-end fence and the frozen canal.

As the brown man swept by he gave Billy Claybo a smile and a wave of the derby, white teeth flashing in a smooth brown face above the red bandanna he had slipped, and it was like a sudden call or command that sent Billy's heart leaping into hands and feet—so that before he had thought about it he had jumped Old Blue in as near a straddle as he could without doing himself an injury, and then he was furiously pedaling along with them, dropping behind in their dust but still following, the blue Olds now raging up behind him roaring in his left ear, and it was through dust and tears that he saw the three horsemen race up to the picket fence never slacking off or drawing rein but right at it with perfect and unquenchable speed till, at the last of seconds, the men seemed to shrug their shoulders in despair . . . and magically lifted their horses into the air sailing over the fence in a clean jump six feet up and it would have to be fifteen feet straight across—

Which Billy could not see because just as they lifted Deputy Charlie Bascomb and Sheriff Bodine came barreling past him in a wipe-out boil-up of dust, siren wailing, the brims of their Stetsons blown back, shotguns at high port, and Billy (almost at the fence now) saw Charlie Bascomb heave up against the steering wheel with the thrust of his whole upper body like a man trying to lift his horse into the jump as the blue Olds, never slacking speed or drawing rein, blew right through that goddamn picket fence smashing it to kindling, flew eight feet through the air and *whump!* flat ass and withers deep in the irrigation canal. The ice water hit the radiator and it blew its top like a gusher, and Billy could hear Charlie Bascomb and Sheriff Bodine splashing and cursing, Charlie sitting in the water with the steering wheel and a piece of the column in his hands.

Billy was off the bike by then, Old Blue lying on one side with the back wheel still spinning from the wild gallop down the lane, Mrs. Robinson's grocery bag disemboweled beside it, Billy perched on the remaining fence post straining to see three galloping figures, their horses' hooves smoking the dust and powdery snow out of the stubble field as they raced flat out for the dark line of wooded hills in the distance. Even then, sitting on the post with Charlie Bascomb and Sheriff Bodine splashing and cussing below him, he knew he would always be able to see this as sharp and clear and hard as he saw it now—all of it, the tall rough-haired horses trotting up the street, the fumble with the bandannas, the swift glide into the bank, the silence and emptiness of the street, the bland plate glass; the sudden eruption, the men backing out guns leveled, horses turning as they mounted, wheeling and racing for the end of the street with everything flying loose till the brown smiling man slid his horse to a flaring halt at the Tulsa Pike and brought the three of them charging straight back for him, smoke and lightning and thunder shots with the blue Olds screaming round the corner in pursuit—the brown man smiling, swooping down alongside the galloping horse to snatch his derby out of the dust and the grin and wave as he passed (white teeth flashing in a smooth brown Indian face) that was like a command to get up and follow—

The shrug of the shoulders that hauled the three giant horses right up into the sky.

Every tick as sharp and clear as every other for the rest of his life, whether he was daydreaming or nightdreaming, or telling it to his pals at the Beggs School after the Christmas holiday, or to the folks coming into Chalmers' Store for months afterward, or years later to his own small children, or to his grandchildren: *I was standing right there the time they robbed the Chemical–Cattlemen's Bank in '21—three of 'em, big hombres on big horses—with sawed-off shotguns and a couple of Colt's Dragoon pistols, the old-time kind like you see in the pictures, like a haunch off a pig. They looked like* business, *them fellers. And what they did to the law . . . ! Don't let nobody tell you a horse ain't good as a car, for some things anyway—if you know what you're doin'. Yes: There was two of 'em cowboys, and a dude in a derby hat and a brown suit that everybody said was a* Mex: *but I saw him plain, it was like he wanted me to see him: so somebody—me—would know who done it . . .*

That was all the crowd in the bank could say, "Who done it? Who was it? *Two cowboys and a goddamn greaser.*" The door to the bank was jammed with tellers, weeping women customers and secretaries, Mr. Jessup, Mr. Chalmers, and more running up every minute from down the County Road and round the corner on the Pike. Deputy Bascomb and Sheriff Bodine had to bull their way through the door, their khaki uniforms black to the armpits with ditchwater and mud, hanging on them like sheets of cold iron.

Billy wormed his way to the shot-out plate-glass window, and skipped in between the standing blades of glass that made a V in the middle. Charlie Bascomb was cranking the phone and calling in the law from all points north south and west of Beggs, cranking and cussing till he could raise the operator for another one. The sheriff stood in the middle of the bank, dripping water around his high-heeled boots and trying to question Banker Ford while the clerks and tellers fussed and buzzed at him.

"How do you know the son of a bitch was a Mex?" the sheriff was asking, his voice rising to cut through the palaver. "How could you tell he was a Mex if his face was covered?"

" 'Cause he talked Mex!" said one of the tellers, and they all started to agree, yes, talked like a Mex, he was talking Mex to them, and the Sheriff wanted to know did any of them *speak* any Mex themselves?

And they didn't.

"Well then how in the hell did you know he was talking Mex?" He glared around at all of them and they shut up. "How do you know he wasn't an Injun talking Choctaw? Or one of these Eye-talian dagoes from Chicago we got now? Or a Chinaman, for Chrissake?"

It was when he said *Injun* that the face flashed its grin again for Billy, and he was sure who the man in the derby was.

The banker looked embarrassed now, but he answered anyway: "He kept calling his buddies *hombre*, and me *señor*. And he said *ándale* when he meant us to hurry. That's Mex, isn't it? It isn't Italian . . . ?"

"The two is pretty much the same . . ." grumped the sheriff, but he looked away from Banker Ford as if he wasn't on sure ground. "The other two was white enough though, wasn't they?" He started glaring again: "Wasn't they?"

"Well, I guess . . ." said the first teller. "I mean, they *looked* like they was white, their foreheads and eyes I mean . . . but they understood all that Mex, and there's Mexicans is pretty near white . . ."

"Well shee-*it!*" said the sheriff. "If you can't tell . . . didn't anybody in this goddamn place see anything at all?" and Billy piped up: "I did."

The whole room turned to look at him and the palaver shut up. Billy was the center of a circle of eyes and mouths—the tellers, the banker, Mr. Chalmers, the sheriff and Deputy Charlie Bascomb himself on the inside, and the crowd pressing in at the jammed-up door and leaning gingerly against the broken glass front.

"What did you see, son?" asked Charlie Bascomb.

It was the first time Billy would be telling the story, but he knew he would be telling it for the rest of his life, one way or another. And always he would suit the first lines to the occasion, depending on how he had brought the talk round to it, and on who his listeners were and how much they already knew—this time not having to remind people of the robbery, which was all around them, as he would have to remind them later. But the rest of it was set: "I was sweeping off the porch of Mr. Chalmers' Store, like I always do. Just a plain old afternoon. And I was just greasing up Old . . . my bike to go and deliver the stuff to Mrs. Robinson, and that's when I saw 'em—three of 'em coming up the street real slow on them big horses . . ." He couldn't tell it smooth as he would have liked to, as he would later, because they kept interrupting him with questions, and the sheriff had to keep shutting people up to let the boy tell it his own way, and finally he came to the moment when the three riders charging straight for the door of Chalmers' General Store, leaned their horses into the lane and came roaring past him.

"With no masks on?" asked the sheriff and Billy said "No."

"So you saw what they looked like? Who they was?" said Charlie Bascomb. "Did you know 'em?"

Billy looked into Charlie's eyes. *Charlie Bascomb: the biggest, bravest man in the town of Beggs, and once when I was little he picked me up and put me on the saddle of his horse, talking to my dad down by the post box at our road.*

"Two of 'em was cowboys . . . was white, like they said. I never saw 'em before."

"What about the other one, the Mex . . . the one in the suit with the derby?" asked the sheriff.

Billy looked at him. This part of the story was different from the way he would tell it afterwards, because it was going to be a lie. (He was grateful that he didn't have to say it to Charlie Bascomb, but he would have.) As he told it he saw the smiling face sweep by, the wave of the hand holding the swooped-up derby, the smooth brown face he had seen once at the Tulsa Lyric, whose gray ghost he had seen many times since, sweeping in silence across the flickering square of the movie screen at the Tulsa Lyric.

"No sir," said Billy, "I never knowed him. But he looked like a Mex to me, and not no Injun nor a Chinaman." Billy swept his hand across his mouth as if to cover the lower half of his face. "He had a big black mustache, like they do. And"—he remembered the man's smile, clean white teeth in a smooth brown face—"and these teeth like the greasers have, you know, these teeth all black and with lots of gold in 'em, big lumps of it like . . ."

## TULSA *December 22–23, 1921*

". . . and even a man with a skull as thick as Peter Bodine's ought to be able to find a greaser with that kind of face. Teeth big and black and gold enough for a shirttail kid to practically count 'em in the, what is it?—three seconds it takes for the horses to go galloping past down the road, yelling like lunatics and shooting up the street with shotguns and pistols, and if you believe them other witnesses hand grenades and tommyguns to boot . . . I'll take two cards." Fire Chief Adkinson dropped his discards and accepted two more from the thick hands of the dealer, Sheriff McCullough. "Sounds like the same bunch that hit the Chemical–Cattlemen's in Okfuskee four days ago," said the sheriff. "Somebody in the Creek Nation got a bone to pick with our Mr. Wilberforce." There were grunts of agreement from the others around the green-cloth covered table in Judge Meis's large chambers in the Tulsa County Courthouse.

Most of Tulsa's executive power was at the table. There was Adkinson, the fire chief, looking rumpled and sleepy; Sheriff McCullough, his round face framed in luxuriant sidewhiskers; Editor Dexter C. Poole of the Tulsa *Lamp* and Pan American Motion Picture Company, with the sleeves of his dazzling white shirt turned back above his lean hairy wrists so that the green cloth wouldn't soil the French cuffs.

Mayor Egan had the head of the table—"Judge" Egan, who had made his name sending the forty Wobblies to Tulsa Jail four years ago, the jail from which they were taken by the mob, whipped tarred and feathered while Casey's deputies regulated traffic in the streets below. Egan's thin red lips looked oddly prominent against his withered pasty indoor skin.

Judge Meis was Egan's replacement on the bench, and it was Meis who had organized the evening's entertainment, needing (he said) something to break up an extremely taxing and difficult session. Meis had taken sharp criticism for dismissing the charge against Dick Rowland, but around this table there was appreciation for the good judgment he had shown: because he had now to deal with the far more numerous and important cases arising from the riot, for which those trigger-happy Greenwood coons were going to be held responsible—and the Rowland judgment had given him the all-important appearance of impartiality. Poole admired Meis extravagantly and in print; and on the strength of this felt entitled to kid him a little about the case.

There were also Major Bowles and young Captain Blaine of the state police, Blaine the youngest man in the bunch, trim and trig in his short flyer's jacket. And there was Marshal Bill Tilghman, his lean form lounging back in his chair, five cards stacked under his hand, standing pat.

There was a time last year when Casey would have been at the table: but since the riot you would never find Casey and Tilghman in the same room together for longer than it took Old White Eyes to look at the police chief once.

Blaine shut his own hand nervously and spoke up. "The problem is we don't use modern methods in police work. If we had had just one plane for your department or the state police to use, all it would have taken was one call—or the alarm ringing in a central office somewhere—and I'd have been in the air over 'em before they'd gotten up into the timber. And even if they had got in, I'd have hung around up there, circling, gliding to save gas, watching to spot 'em the first time they hit a clearing or made a break. A man in a plane can see anything that moves for fifty miles."

Mayor Egan grinned over at Sheriff McCullough. "Sheriff, this is a sneaky way for you and the chief to pitch for your appropriation. I thought we were here to play poker?" He tossed a stack of chips into the center. "That's me. Anybody want to call?" And the betting went around.

Blaine expected no sympathy, not even from Tilghman, who was the best of them. Tilghman was a professional, but also still an old-time horseback lawman who couldn't (or wouldn't) look beyond the range of his .45 pistol. Tilghman had spent the first part of the night sitting next to the Negro's cell with a shotgun and a pair of .45s, as if one solitary nigger was the point when all hell was breaking loose outside. The only thing he'd got out of his chair for was to bully McCullough into helping him get the prisoner out of town on the sly. But by that time the mob probably wasn't even interested in Dick Rowland, being busy over in Greenwood.

They kidded him for taking to the air in the Guard observation plane, but Blaine felt that at the least he had tried to meet extraordinary crises with extraordinary measures. At least he had been able to see what was happening, study it, and think through the measures they should prepare against the next such outbreak.

When I was up there, thought Blaine, I could see everything: streets and railroad tracks like chains of lights in the gray predawn, the gun flashes, the buildings on fire lighting everything up for blocks. I was up in the sun as soon as it rose, and I came in with it behind me the first time, and the city got clearer as I glided down on it, laid out like a map, like a picture getting clearer and clearer as I came down till I could see the mobs running in the streets, the cars, objects lying in the road (bodies or garbage or barrels?), but by then my speed was up, too fast too fast, the closer I got the faster till things smeared across my eyes in a single blur. I had to pull up, lifting and turning, all of it under and behind me and falling falling away as I climbed and looked for the sun again.

It wasn't like flying in France. When you were across the lines there anything was a target—if it moved you went down on it like a hawk on a hare; but the problem here (it was in his report) was that you couldn't tell who was rioting and who needed protection. Either you were slow enough to study it but too far off to see, or you were close enough but going too fast to work it out. He'd tried different things: buzzing a mob in a residential district, rioters he thought, he'd seen them duck: machine guns and he'd have bagged the lot, but then there were wagons in the streets that looked to be people trying to get away, women and children—it was hard to be sure.

He looked for shooters: buzzed a car, but it was a police car. None-theless, if it had been in use by rioters, and if he had had a machine gun mounted, he could have shot that Ford into a fine spray of metal filings.

Not to mention snipers up on the roofs. Even without guns he had made one duck and run for the street just by buzzing the flat roof of the building on which he had hidden. Couldn't tell, though, if it was colored or white. But perhaps the difference was unimportant. The point was to stop the riot, to knock the shooters down no matter who they were or why they were shooting, and from his aerial distance Blaine could have done that with perfect safety and disinterested precision.

After a while Bill Tilghman—who had been laying back while Egan pushed the betting—took the pot, sweeping the chips toward him with his freckled hand. He looked at Blaine coolly—"Old Peter and Charlie Bascomb, they believed in modern police methods. Traded their hosses for that blue police car. The one they're going to try and haul out of that irrigation ditch, if she ain't rusted away by now?" The laugh went round with the cards that Egan dealt.

Blaine looked at his hand impatiently, then back up at Tilghman. "You can't take a man that thinks it's just some new kind of horse, put him in the seat and expect him to do the job for you. What in hell made Charlie Bascomb think he could put a '19 Olds touring car over the jumps like a goddamn steeplechaser?"

McCullough said, "Those three cowboys done just fine on horseback, though—didn't they, Bill? Nothing modern about them. They just took Mr. Ford's bank the good old-fashioned way: pistols and shotguns, in fast and quiet and come out blazing to keep the citizens ducking for cover. Yup, they hoo-rawed Beggs good and proper, just like Jesse James himself, lost the law and run for the tall timber."

Bill Tilghman glanced at his hand and flipped a chip into the center. "Thought the witnesses said they wasn't running for the timber at first. Said they was heading back up the Tulsa Pike."

"Right," said McCullough. "Not so damn smart after all. Did they think three men on horses, with shotguns pistols masks and three sad-dlebags full of gold certificates was gonna just slip into the courthouse traffic on a Thursday morning in Beggs, Oklahoma? They were just plumb lucky they spotted Peter and Charlie coming while they still had time to turn and run for the open."

"And luckier still that Charlie couldn't tell the difference between a '19 Olds and a jumping horse," added Blaine. "I'll take two cards."

Bill Tilghman stood pat. They all looked over at him, sharply and covertly, then back to their cards.

"If you think about it," said Bill Tilghman, "it don't make any sense. They was smart enough to take that bank. And if they done any checking beforehand, they had to know about the alarm ringing in the police station, and Charlie coming down on them in the car . . . So why run towards the Pike?" The question held them for a minute. Tilghman had to gesture with his hand to remind them to bet. Each man checked his cards again. The bets went around, only Blaine and Tilghman staying to the end: Tilghman raising again and Blaine thinking—then folding his cards in deference to the stand-pat hand, which Tilghman closed and folded blind into the pack that he began to shuffle.

"It was a sucker play," said Blaine and the others looked up sharply. "That's called a bluff, son," said McCullough.

But Tilghman nodded his head: "He don't mean poker. He means those three cowboys . . . two cowboys and a Mex in a derby hat. They run up the street knowing Charlie was coming, fast as he could come and hot for blood. Then they run back *down* the street, with Charlie hard on their heels and not thinking about anything but jamming in the spurs and running those broomtails down. They knew Charlie was an old-time horseback lawman stuck into a '19 Olds, and that he'd come on so hard he'd never think about not being able to take the jump with them."

"So they'd shake him at the start," said Blaine, "and not have to race the car across the flats for the timber."

"Or maybe just for the fun of seeing Charlie fly that car into the canal," said Tilghman.

"That's some smart Mex," said McCullough.

Judge Meis grimaced: "And Horace Ford's bank is out more than $20,000 in gold notes . . . plus a bundle of the paper he was holding on some of the farmers and wildcat drillers around here."

Mayor Egan looked truculent: "Maybe it was one of those farmers did it? Or the drillers, they're tough enough, some of 'em. And there's plenty of those Wobblies left around, mean enough to try it. Aren't the Reds connected up with this Villa fellow down in Mexico?"

Editor Poole looked up keenly. "That's an idea," he said. "It all fits together, doesn't it?"

"Just like in a movie," said Tilghman quietly.

Poole flashed a glare at Tilghman, pursing his lips: then seemed to think better of it. He pushed a short laugh out. "Well, you may be right." He smiled more broadly. "You know, if those badhats had come a week sooner I might have had them in the movies too." He leaned forward, looking at Mayor Egan. "Wouldn't that have been something!"

"Why if they'd come sooner?" asked Egan.

"Because I had Henry Starr out there a week ago with my camera crew, scouting locations and shooting some footage for our next picture—*Henry Starr, the Sagebrush Scout.*"

"It would almost make up to you for missing out on Dick Rowland's lynching," said Tilghman softly.

Poole blushed; this was the first he knew that Tilghman was aware of his plan to use Esterhazy out at the hang-tree. He stole a glance at Judge Meis, but the judge's poker face was impenetrable. Uneasy under Tilghman's eyes, Poole wished Meis would step in and get him off the hook.

But it was Mayor Egan who came to his rescue. "Yes," said the mayor. "You know, Bill, we're all grateful to the sheriff here, and yourself, for preventing anything of the kind. This city's reputation has suffered enough as it is. Especially since the boy turns out to have been innocent, at least according to Judge Meis"—his smile was his appeal across the table to their host—"although if they *had* lynched him that would have been tantamount to a finding of guilt," and he glanced over at Tilghman—and suddenly froze, because the old marshal had the kind of expression that if you let yourself recognize it there was going to be more kinds of trouble than anybody wanted.

It was getting worse with the old man. Now Poole had to get the mayor off the hook. He cleared his throat: "Well, lynching's a dangerous business—stirs up more trouble than it settles sometimes. I sure could have used that robbery though. Damn that Henry Starr anyway. Now that I think of it, this is the second time it's happened—he was about a week too early for that robbery up in Howitt last month. The man has a downright perverse sense of timing."

"Where else has he been?" asked Tilghman softly.

"Well let's see," said Poole, annoyed at being quizzed like a schoolboy. "We had him in Howitt and Sperry the middle of November, and after that down around Stroud, I think, and Micawber . . ."

". . . then Beggs," said Tilghman, finishing the sentence for him, "and after that Okfuskee."

"Well yes," said Poole looking puzzled, and Blaine thought again that just when you thought Tilghman had lost the trail for good, you looked ahead and saw him up there waiting for you.

But Bill Tilghman didn't answer Poole. His pale eyes seemed to concentrate and focus on something not there, something outside the walls of the Tulsa Police Headquarters and miles out in the darkened empty country. Then they tightened to a point—it was the same look they had had in the old days, sighting down the long barrel of his Sharps buffalo gun at the distant formless bulk of the bull he would have to single out and kill.

The poker game broke up as usual at around two in the morning. Tilghman lingered awhile, and as Blaine left he saw him sifting through some files on his desk.

The building was empty except for the prisoners in the cells and the nightwatch when Tilghman came out the back door of the courthouse and got his horse from the stable. As he was coming out of the alley out onto Main a black Ford driving fast and without lights came roaring up from the south, the noise of its engine spooking Tilghman's horse so that the animal reared back just as the marshal's eye caught the stuttering spark and brisk mechanical *yatatatatatat* of the tommy gun and the vile singing of its ricochets and the ripping thump of half a dozen bullets hitting home in the horse's guts, the animal *whee*, wheezing as it thumped down on its hooves—then dropped forward to a kneeling position, and as Tilghman kicked out of the stirrups and stepped off, dropped its rear as sharply as if the string holding it up had been cut. It whee, wheezed again, a foam of bloody snot bursting out of its nostrils as Tilghman shot it swiftly between the ears, the gunshot rapping hard against the brick walls.

There was a distant squeal as the lightless Ford took the turn on Archer and roared northeast toward the ruins of Greenwood.

## TULSA *June 1, 1921*

The night of the riot was not the worst of it for Miss Woodly. When she saw the story about Dick Rowland in the paper a wave of pure terror had almost drowned her, she could hardly breathe under it. Although the reasons were pure mystery to her, she knew absolutely that Henry Starr would never have come back to her and to the movie if he had not somehow discovered or sought out or conjured up Dick Rowland and convinced him to play Cherokee Bill. She could not see him as he had been, playing that Lady in the Cabin scene alone: the black man had to be standing with him. And even more than that—she knew that without Dick Rowland standing in that make-believe cabin, she would never have had the chance or the license to step out from behind the camera and into the white-lit room she had composed for "Henry Starr" and become his dream lady—or was it only *her* dream lady? It might have been either one, but then Dick Rowland called her *little sister* and told her to *take care*—as if the black man were somehow kin to Henry Starr, like a man's shadow is kin, part of him but different, or like an older brother or uncle—as if he had given them a family blessing and named them for love and opened the door through which she had stepped to find Henry Starr.

Everything on the other side of that door had the crazy look and feel of living dreams, as if she had dreamed a horse and it had run away with her and run away, a dream horse whose hard barrel she could still feel ghostly between her thighs, whose vanished hoofbeats still made her bones shake, a wild horse with smoking nostrils, a terrible beautiful great horse whose speed made her body feel alive to its edges and filled her belly with the fear of death, carrying her where in the world? Where? Someplace so different that you could lose your name and body getting there, but it was so much more than *this* place could ever be, a place full of Henry Starr and Henry Starr's names and people . . . one of them was Dick Rowland and maybe he was dead already, and Henry Starr riding after him, searching.

He had ridden off in the early evening. The sun had gone down while she waited. The darkness in her window made a blank black square, she heard distant popping sounds like firecrackers, the far vibration of a fire bell. She sat there alone, trying to imagine Henry Starr riding back into Tulsa, trying to dream her shadow around him like a shield.

She was used to dreaming him that way and after a while her fear began to diminish, or she felt more comfortable in it. Even when blots of fire splashed suddenly across the pattern of sparkling lights that marked the city her fear was in a kind of suspense, there was even a kind of eagerness in her. Although it was night, she still saw him riding in fading daylight, and she remembered how he looked taking the news and getting ready and riding off: calm and compact, ready for anything, as if none of this surprised him at all, as if his plans had been laid long before and now he would carry them out to the letter, carefully and completely. She knew he would save Dick Rowland.

Her belief in that carried her right up to the moment when Henry Starr came back, waking her from half-sleep with the sound of his boots on the floor of her landing. She threw the door opened but she couldn't see him, her eyes were blinded by light as bright and painful as the magnesium flare of a camera flash-pan and she buried her face in his chest. "Dick's safe," she heard him say and she said, "I knew you would . . ."

"No," he said, "I had nothing to do with it."

There was a tone in his voice, bleak and dead, which promised her that worse was going to start happening now. But it still was not real to her, it was all just a terrible story, like his story of Cherokee Bill and his evil old grandfather, like his story of Stroud—Dick was safe but scores, maybe hundreds of people were killed in Greenwood, their homes wrecked and burnt out, Dick's whole family ruined or killed—friends of Henry Starr's they were, friends from his old life, almost like kin to hear the grief in his voice, so that the thought flashed through her that maybe there *was* blood kindred between Dick Rowland and Henry Starr, maybe that was why he had to bring him into her movie—

She thought *nigger between my legs nigger in my* and she looked up with a sudden electric shock of pure blue terror that made her body and soul rigid.

He was looking at her steadily, dark brown eyes half-masked by heavy lids. The claw marks in the corners of his eyes and mouth were sharp and deep, the bulge of his cheekbones told you he was Indian at best, there were flecks of gray in the stubble on his tan cheeks. He was old enough to be her father. He was the reason mothers gave their good little girls why they must never flirt or talk to strange men or walk alone after dark in certain streets and woods.

He was also the Last of the Mohicans and Robin Hood and Jesse James, and she remembered how he smiled at her that day on the movie lot just before he swung his horse around and charged back down the street to swoop the saddlebag out of the dust. She remembered how that first day when she said "Show me" he had done just exactly that, without thought or hesitation or caution, swift as a rattlesnake. She remembered that when she had come to him with her dream of a movie she had not had to wheedle or make a bargain of herself with him—she had just said it, and he answered, "All right. I'll work with you."

The room spun around her and came back: she felt that she had almost lost or thrown him away because of the terrible things that had happened about Dick Rowland. But she was back with him—so the worst still had not happened.

That came the next day, when they had to go out to the studio to preview *Henry Starr: A Debtor to the Law.*

## TULSA *June 2, 1921*

He sat next to her in the Lyric Theater among the crowd of Pan American employees and privileged guests (judges and policemen, aldermen and Chamber of Commerce officers, the Pioneers of Tulsa Cinema) invited to attend the sneak preview. But he might as well have been a ghost or a wooden statue. She was purely alone with that crowd in the darkness as the screen lit up, and for the last time in her life let herself imagine that what she would see on the screen would be her dream as she had dreamed it, as she and Henry Starr had played and worked it out:

The Pan American
Motion Picture Company of Tulsa
Presents

—O—

HENRY STARR: A DEBTOR TO
THE LAW

—O—

Produced by H. F. Foley
Directed by S. Esterhazy
Photoplay by B. C. Woodly

—O—

The Players

HENRY STARR . . . . . . Henry Starr
Laetitia Wilder . . . . . Alice Farnham
Morgan . . . . . . . Vincent C. McClain
Cherokee Bill . . . . . . Richard Rowland

—O—

[ Gasps here and there in the audience, a single district *hiss*, a sputter of questioning murmurs—a rising sense of dangerous exciting expectation . . .]

Here were the pictures now, just as they had imagined them, just as Miss Woodly and Esterhazy and Henry Starr had made them be, flowing out as smoothly and predictably as water running downhill, the pastoral scene, the dreamy boy reading his book in the cornfield, and she thought *how much can they have changed? a few images here and there, a few words in the title cards.*

It wasn't until the rodeo scene that she began to realize what had been done: because there was Dick Rowland skulking around the corral, there was the image of a dark hand with a knife in it cutting Henry Starr's saddle girth so he would lose his chance to win the prize and save his mother's farm inside the law.

Here were titles, and some of them she had written herself long before Dick Rowland had appeared on the set, when Cherokee Bill was nothing to her but a name and a huge dark shadow standing against Henry Starr in the night—written and then taken out of the script when Henry Starr came back bringing a piece of his real old life with him, and they had changed the words together. But now the old words were back, *renegade* and *murderous* and *treacherous mixture of poisonous bloods* and *Cherokee Bill, a man capable of anything but good.*

And to go with the words and give them life there were bits of film cut and spliced in, test shots Esterhazy had made before and after the cabin scene, the Negro framed by the board walls of the warehouse and of the horse stalls where the prison scenes were shot, to see what sorts of lighting worked on Dick Rowland's skin—and these little bits and flashes showed the black man's face sinister in its moments of immobility, threatening when the light changed, shadows covering now this part of his face and now that, making it seem plastic and secretive and unstable.

She couldn't even blink, it was as if her eyelids were pried open and the pictures poured in, pictures that were exactly what she had dreamed and helped Esterhazy make, but now something had changed them, some awful color or smell was in them that made them ugly and terrible without making them any less her own, without allowing her to cut the strings of memory that wove her into them.

They carried her along toward the Cabin, knowing what would happen there but helpless to stop it, helpless even to fool herself any longer into an ignorance that would allow her to be surprised when it happened: so that when it came she expected and anticipated it, so it felt as if she had dreamed up the horror by herself:

Dick Rowland's face in terrifying close-up, glistening with niggersweat licking his niggerlips, and the lady in the cabin leaning back and away as if his eyes were fingers, filthy fingers pulling at her,
the Lady: whose face from one angle was Alice Farnham, but from another was herself, her head covered in a shawl that made her an image of the Madonna and Dick Rowland a helldemon created to defile her: except for
Henry Starr, who stood between her and the nigger, his skin shining with a glossy white pallor in the excessive glare of the artificial light.

And all of the rest of it ran on out of that moment, so clear and logical and predictable that she couldn't say *no* to it, but instead her mind kept predicting it, as if they had found a way to compel her to invent frame by frame the ugly thing they wished for:

As they are marching Henry Starr and Cherokee Bill to the scaffold, Cherokee Bill suddenly breaks free and seizes a gun from one of the guards—the crowd falls back as the outlaw savagely menaces all around with the weapon, thrusting it against the head of the guard who kneels at his feet:
Title: **"Spare me! I have a wife and child . . ."**
Cherokee Bill grimaces savagely and motions for Starr to pick up a fallen rifle.
We see Starr's face in close-up. We see the cloudy image of the woman and child in the cabin . . .
Title: **The instincts of a just man triumph over temptation.**
Cherokee Bill holds the guard tight, pressing the pistol against his head and motions for Starr to pick up a fallen rifle—we see Starr's face in which conflicting emotions war—then his features set:
NIGGERFACE:
NIGGEREYES
NIGGERTEETH
NIGGER-WITH-A-GUN
Title: **"Drop your guns and clear the way, or this man dies!"**
Henry Starr shakes his head, and holds out his hand.
Title: **"You owe the law a debt, Bill. And Henry Starr will see that you pay what you owe!"**

And the rest of it rolled out as smooth and clear and irresistibly as water rushing over a long sleek fall, so swift and sharp and hard that everybody there in the dark seemed to suck breath at once and then blow it out in one big Rebel-yelling war whoop; *Hi! Yay! Hurray! That's done it! That's what we should have . . . ! Got him! String the nigger up!*

Guards and citizens come pouring into the cell block, they seize Cherokee Bill . . .

[Who is not Dick Rowland, she doesn't know who it is, but what is the difference so long as it looks like—]

a nigger carried kicking and screaming and twisting, rolling his eyes till the whites show, twisting his body in snaky curls like a weasel in a leg trap, his legs and arms gripped in bunches of white hands that reached in and pulled him spreadeagled, his head held back by the hair and a white gag rammed through his lips and into his throat . . .

She should have known better; if you let a man do it to you and take money from him it doesn't matter if it's only once and only a little money, it makes you a whore. She had let them do it, let them put their hands all over it, she had said yes, thinking it will only hurt a little bit and then I will have—but it was as if that little *yes* had given them a right to hold her down and open her up, and rape her between her legs—all of them, Wilberforce Poole Foley Esterhazy—between her legs and then rape her again in her open eyes and her mouth, her throat, and she couldn't speak to say *no* while they twisted themselves into knots inside her and carried her to

The Hanging Tree:

(The very gallows-limbed cottonwood any Tulsan would recognize as his from a dozen handbills and news photos)

from which the limber noose dangles, and they put Cherokee Bill's head in a black bag, then rope and clinch it, the soundless straining of his body against the bag and the ropes are screams as dense as the absolute silence in which the picture moves as they throw him into the air—

In shadow silhouette, we see Cherokee Bill hanging against a transfiguring blaze of light:

Title: **The Law takes its Course . . . The human beast is made to pay his debt to civilization.**

*"Just a few changes on the title cards, a picture snipped out here and spliced in there. Oh, and a few unscripted scenes we had to shoot for continuity. A very simple process, really, when you understand the technique."*

We see Starr's face, calm and pale, with a light on it like that which illuminated the sleeping woman in the cabin.

Tilghman appears at the door of Starr's cell. He holds out a paper:

Title: **. . . but Mercy hath its place.**

Starr looks at Tilghman; at the guard whose life he saved.

Title: **Marshal Tilghman: "I have pursued you for ten years, Henry Starr. You have courage, and you always played square. In your heart, you are a good man. Go and sin no more."**

We see Henry Starr riding his horse slowly over a hill. He pauses and looks down—dreamily, as at the beginning. We see that he is looking into a valley, in which sits a poor small lonely cabin, with a curl of smoke at the chimney.

Fade out as Starr rides down the hill toward the cabin which is haloed in yet another sunset glory . . .

—O—

THE END.

The screen blanked, light popped out of the ceiling fixtures exposing Henry Starr's face pale and sickly, his lips pressed thin and looking greenish—they sat there as the audience rose to its feet around them applauding, jabbering praises, as if the two of them were sinking slowly through the floor on a pair of mechanically operated lifts. But his eyes had a tight set on the backs rising between him and the blank square of the screen. "What's done can be fixed," he said, and then shifted his eyes to her. "I'll see to it they do right by us."

She couldn't answer a word, because looking at him in that light she knew suddenly and surely that he was going to fail, that even Henry Starr was not equal to what had been done to them—knew that, because she knew he could not feel in the same way how deep and wide and completely they had been ruined, and she didn't have the words to tell him. It was as if she had had a child inside her, a small free ghost living in the strings of her blood, and she had opened herself meaning to give it to the light—but instead she had let them reach inside and put a twist in it and it had come out wrong, like a dead stick with human eyes, like a baby's face with Henry Starr's smile and her own blue eyes and the tusky snout of a boar hog.

There was no power in Henry Starr to do anything at all about that. In that ugly light she saw him *smaller*, as if the glare of the fixtures had shrunk his long shadow to a black puddle at his feet.

So she would go with him to the banker's office, not to help him win or even to watch him fight, but just so that her body would lend him a little more shadow, as if shadow were a kind of ghostly armor that could stop Poole and Wilberforce and Foley doing inside Henry Starr what they had already done to her.

## TULSA *June 3, 1921*

They met in the bank, just like the last time, except that Esterhazy was not waiting with them. Mr. Armbruster sat talking loans with another farmer. This time the janitor sweeping the marble floor was a white man.

The contracts they had signed were laid out in a line on Wilberforce's desk. It was a line Henry Starr had no power to cross. If the banker had been plain Mr. *Wilberforce* maybe Henry Starr could have made him dance to his tune; but those papers made the banker Party of the First Part, and no Party of the Second Part that ever lived could climb over Mr. Wilberforce if he was First.

They let her say her piece—what was it? The words came out, predictable and so absolutely beside the point that it was like saying yama yama yama, she hardly listened to it herself. When she was through with it Poole said, "I'm sorry you dislike what Mr. Foley has done. But we feel he has fulfilled our expectations and produced a fine bit of historical drama."

It was useless, but Henry Starr couldn't let her stand there and not side her. "They used to print up cheap handbills to advertise their hangings," he said. "I guess this is progress, making a handbill that moves. But it's still ugly, and it's still cheap."

"You are a man of talents, Mr. Starr," said Poole affably. "You were hired as an actor and technical adviser—I had no idea that you were a critic as well."

Foley guffawed. "Actor? You call that . . . ?"

"However," Poole continued, "I'm afraid we already employ a drama critic at the *Lamp*. He and I are eminently satisfied with the results."

"Even if you didn't get to hang your nigger," said Henry Starr.

"I believe we made our point," said Poole softly; it was so obviously true it hardly needed the breath he gave it.

"The contract gives us the right to make any editorial changes which, in *our* judgment, are necessary to the commercial success of the venture," said Wilberforce patiently. "The selection of editor likewise is within our choice, pursuant to the consideration previously stated."

"You made a liar out of me," Henry Starr said, shifting his glare to Foley. But the red-faced director just grinned, he was feeling pretty cocksure. "Me? I didn't make the pictures, boy. I just ran them together."

"I'm going to call you on that," said Henry Starr.

"No," said Poole quietly, "you won't." He got up, looking lean and sharp in a light-striped beige suit. "It also says in your contract that you will do nothing to obstruct or impair the success of the venture. I don't know what you have in mind—perhaps standing out front of the theater and telling the patrons it's all a damn lie? Perhaps a letter to the editor of a rival paper: Miss Woodly could write that for you too. But if you do any of those things we'll charge you with breach of contract and creating a public disorder—the police are being quite stiff about disorders just now . . ."

"And back you go to McAlester!" chortled Foley.

"Mr. Wilberforce," said Henry Starr quietly, "I'm not working for you anymore."

"You can't walk away from us either, Starr," said Poole quickly. "I guess you prefer cheap fiction to more demanding prose, but you really ought to read your contracts. You're signed up for three more movies with us. You can't work for any other company till you finish that. The law of contracts," he mused, "it's too bad you don't know it. The fundamental basis of civilization as we know it is—"

"I don't have to work movies," said Henry Starr, and Foley yapped at him from the side, "What else you gonna do, Starr? You're too old to work cattle, and I can't see you picking cotton. Of course there's always *banks* but . . ."

"And then," said Poole, "there's the further matter of that camera you shot up. Malicious and willful destruction of company property: you're liable for that. I could charge you right now with malicious mischief, and you a man on parole, too. But I'll forbear, as long as you stay on to work out the cost. You'll scout locations for us—I believe Mr. Foley already has an itinerary planned—and you will perform in seven more films, as Mr. Foley directs you. Seven films . . . with the rate we're paying you, yes: a percentage out of your wages plus your royalty on *Debtor to the Law*—that should bring you square."

He looked at Miss Woodly. "You chose a good name for that movie," he said, "*A Debtor to the Law*. Between us we'll see that Henry Starr pays his debts—after all, he has said in our movie that he always pays what he owes, and it would breach our contract if we did anything to discredit our own movie."

They didn't light the lamps in her room. She sat at one end of the sofa and he sat at the other, and it would have hurt if either one had tried to touch the other.

He was closed in on himself, staring at the black square of the window. He thought about Shaker sitting by Bub's corpse jerking at the shirt pocket from which the badge had been torn, *You ain't you ain't you ain't Henry Starr, you used to be but you ain't no more.* He was thinking about Shaker, and when he looked harder he saw he was also thinking about himself: standing in the street of Tahlequah in front of a Grandfather as big and dead to him as a dead standing tree or a cigar store Indian. *The little white man who stole my son's blood: spit on the tobacco and grin, your name is nothing, I have climbed over your spirit, your name is blue!—is blue smoke! Your name is black, your name is no, is no-name.* "That's what my name will be in the Nations from now on down," he said, "and that's what Cherokee Bill's name will be, and Dick Rowland's and Bub's, all of us."

"Oh," she said and she bent over herself as if she were a dry stick and he had just cracked her. "I got you into it," she said. "If I hadn't thought of it . . ."

Her hair fell away from the delicate line of her neck and her small shoulders, and she seemed not just a small-made woman, but a girl, a child; he remembered the look of Jiminy when something took him deep-sad and he thought, *Poor kid, poor little kid, I wish I could . . .*

"Listen," he said, "it isn't on your shoulders. They tricked me too, and I should have known better. After everything I been taught about signing treaties and bank papers . . ."

She lifted herself straight again, a woman grown, whatever it was she had done she wasn't going to ask him to carry it for her—not now that she knew Henry Starr wasn't some giant tireless sure-shooting see-through-the-walls hero out of a storybook, but just . . . just what he had been this afternoon in Wilberforce's office, just what he was right now.

"You trusted me to take care of the business end," she said. "I told you I would handle it, and then got so tied up in writing about you that I . . . and anyway I got you into it, if I hadn't talked you into . . ."

"No," he said, "it was my idea from the start . . ."

"What?" she said. "Your idea . . . ?" It was pure reflex, her jealousy, but for that second she forgot that the thing she was protecting was dead or twisted ugly.

Her look made him smile at her. "Well, Bobcat," he said.

"What's so damn funny?" she said, embarrassed that her blood was shining in her cheeks and sure he could see it even in the twilight.

He kept smiling and smiling. "You look like you looked that day I came into the bank, and you thought . . . you give me that *look* of yours, like saying 'What? You think you're going to rob *my* bank?' "

She remembered. "It never was my bank," she said, "but it *was* my idea to make the movie." She was sitting up straight again, the thin fracture line where she had broken through the middle was weak and tender, but it held.

"Yes," he said, "all I meant was, even before I come out to the set that first time, I was thinking I had to make me a movie. I guess you were thinking the same when I come along: but you were ready to go and had an idea *how*—you were a lot quicker on the draw than I was."

"Yes," she said, her sadness a little theatrical now, "I drew fast and shot myself in the foot. Shot us both in the foot."

"Nice shooting for one bullet," he said. "Same fella teach you that who taught you to drive a team?"

She started to laugh but was afraid it would crack her apart again, but it broke away from her, the laugh came choking out, the tears bled into her eyes instead of running and then the crying just ran away with her and she let it go. "Yes," she said, "they sure taught me . . ."

He came and sat next to her, and let her lean her weight into him, turning her face into the groove of his neck. He smelled of sweat and horses, that was how he smelled after riding up and down in front of the cameras all day. He said quietly, "I just want you to know, this isn't the last of it. One way or another, you and I will run this game back on them."

She could imagine how his face must look, up there looking out over the top of her head, she imagined the skin smoothed and the eyes sharply focused by the strength of his determination. It was a child's look, a look she remembered from her younger brother's face, when you have been mastered by mother or father or larger, stronger children, and there is nothing left but to dream an impossible triumph and wear the dream on your face like a mask. "All right," she said, hoping he would believe she meant it, hoping he would not feel how she did not really believe he had that power—because she knew what that did to you, when people you love won't believe you are what you know you have to be, and she would do anything in her power to keep that knowledge from him. She curled her body smaller against him to lend him the size he would need.

She felt him gather and lift himself a little. "I been down before this and come back up again," he said. He touched her cheek to make her lift and look at him. "You always make mistakes first time out, and I guess we made some. That's nothing to be ashamed of. First bank I robbed I didn't clear enough to make expenses, burnt the wrong kind of papers. But all I lost was money and a little of my time. As long as they ain't bad enough to get you killed, mistakes is just a way of learning how. You pay attention to 'em and then you come back smarter the next time."

*Next time.* She didn't know what that would mean, exactly. But if you believed there was such a thing, it meant that there was going to be life for her outside of *this time*, and that was good news because this time was pretty bad, she wanted it to be over.

In the blue moonlight that came through the slats of her blinds, Henry Starr's face was masked in blue and black horizontal bars. She touched his mouth with her finger and drew its lines, trying to learn their shape by blind touch. She traced the bony ridge of his cheek and drew the circles of his eyes. She found that despite the lessons she'd been taught by Poole and Wilberforce and all the rest she still wasn't ready to stop learning, especially not about her favorite subject. She said, "Why did you ever want to make a movie?"

"Well," he said, "that's a long story."

"Tell me," she said, and he became very still.

"It isn't that easy to tell it."

She pushed him back against the sofa cushions with both hands, pinning him for a second, then sat back herself in a straight-backed hands-on-lap pose that was a satire on the good little girl paying formal attention to the grown-ups. "Just tell it the best way you can," she said, laughing. "Don't be ashamed if you get it wrong the first time, everybody makes mistakes. But you just keep at it, Henry Starr, and maybe next time you will get it right."

He had started to talk to her, his voice quiet and stiff and slow at first, then softening and becoming smooth and limber and rhythmic, as if his speaking breath was like a horse: he had to let her work the kinks out and warm and loosen before he could let her run.

His voice, talking talking talking to her in the blue-and-black-striped darkness, filled her head with so many pictures that her room became strange, it was like going away from Tulsa to a different place, riding with him over the old ground they had covered together when she was making the movie. Only now that *A Debtor to the Law* was done, ruined and done, it seemed to her that her movie dreams had been like a cloud of blue smoke, obscuring or distorting the real shapes of things. The familiar names and places and deeds as Henry Starr told them again seemed small and clear and far away, like images in a photograph: Tom Starr and Belle Starr and the Tahlequah rodeo, how Cherokee Bill was his friend and the promise Henry Starr had made him; and why he couldn't stay with his wife and child, and how he rode out to get some justice and set the balance right; what was wrong about Stroud, and why in the end he needed to make it all into a movie to pay his debt to his friend and his Grandfather and his Nation, and leave a name that would be good to remember.

Did she sleep sometimes while he was telling it? It was hard to be sure, but it was all so familiar—like the secrets of the day that are sometimes revealed when you dream them—all so familiar that it seemed she had heard it before, could recognize every turn. When he stopped, the blue bars had turned gray, and she felt that finally the story was done. He was leaning back against the cushions, eyes closed with the weary boneless ease of an empty sack or a thrown blanket.

She felt a difference in herself—she wasn't tired or empty, as Henry Starr looked. Her insides felt sore and punished, but his talking all night had been like a soothing syrup that took the raw cut feeling away, and made her feel stronger than he looked: a little better rested, not quite so empty. It was morning, the worst was over, maybe now *next time* could start happening.

## SPRINGS ROAD, TULSA *June 3–December 22, 1921*

But the days afterward were still like bad dreams in which nothing felt right or belonged with anything else. She moved out of her boardinghouse, and they rented a cottage on the Springs Road between Tulsa and the movie lot. The air was spring warm and then summer hot, but she felt cold inside every time she stepped into the light. They would get up early and leave for work at the bank and on the movie lot, she in the buggy and Henry Starr on his neat-footed Appaloosa, they'd ride their lane to the main road and turn their backs to each other—he would swing the horse west and she would swing the buggy eastward into Tulsa. He didn't want to think about her working in her cage under Wilberforce's eyes; she didn't want to think about him riding into make-believe towns robbing fake banks and riding out again and again and again, while Esterhazy's camera ate his ghost and shat pictures and Foley yelled "Cut! Cut!" and made him do it over again and again and again.

At first she couldn't bear to remember the Woodly Gang and *Henry Starr: A Debtor to the Law.* She could hardly bear to dream. They were quiet with each other too: as if her movie and Henry Starr's story had exhausted all the words they had brought with them. Instead of talking or dreaming, she lived herself into details: columns of figures at the bank, Yes sir, thank you ma'am, nice to see you Doctor. At home there were other kinds of details. The cottage got dusty and she swept it herself, as she had when she was a child. She made dinner, or Henry Starr did; the house was full of food smells sometimes.

There were all kinds of smells: dry dust, grass from the hay field behind their house, the reek off an oil well when the wind was wrong.

Their sheets smelled of sunlight and fresh air after she had washed and aired them. After a few days the smells of their bodies would get woven into the sheets—he left a dry smell, like leather; she thought her own smell was sharper, like cut grass. When they made love the scent of it lingered, and when she lay quiet afterwards she liked to breathe deep and imagine her breath was full of the mixed-up odor whose center was the furry socket of her hips.

Since she was a little girl she had never lived so long with someone. When she thought back over how things had happened between them —his appearing like a genie on the movie set to give her the chance to do the thing she wished for, the way her dreams of him mixed with the truth of what he was so you couldn't tell which was which, the way he had gone away and come back, the way he had come to her room and . . . It had been like living inside a story in which she herself was the hero, a good story that had turned overnight into a bad fairy tale with a hideous moral. But what struck her now as she remembered that time was not its being good or bad, but its having been like a story: moving from scene to scene, from feeling to feeling, secret to secret, driving toward its one predictable end and never repeating anything, never doing the same thing or feeling the same thing or making the same discovery twice.

Now she found that things kept happening and happening, kept going around and coming around again, varying only a little in manner or detail. It made the bad times more frightening. If she felt despairing, angry, dirty, twisted or lost with Henry Starr, disappointed and then they got past it—still she couldn't be sure the same feeling wouldn't come back again, sneaking up on her maybe from a different quarter, but all of a sudden she'd realize it was the thing that had happened before and she felt surrounded, cornered.

But that happened with the good things too. And when she thought about it, good times were happening more lately. There was a broken place in her that still ached: but the bone had knit. She got up earlier than he did to make breakfast, so they could look at each other for a while before they had to go apart, so they could talk if they wanted to.

More and more she wanted to, again: not storytelling, this time—although she knew that they would do that again, she loved the prospect of years she would spend with him, swapping her "Miss Woodly" stories against more of his "Henry Starr" stories—not storytelling, but talk about daytime things, tasty in the mouth and warm in the belly like breakfast.

When he had to go away for days at a time, scouting locations for Foley and Esterhazy, she missed him—but there was no fear in the feeling. He left behind a space that was still full of his looks and touches and smells, solid guarantees that he had truly been there and that he would come back.

It was getting on toward Christmas and the year's ending. When she was a little girl the December air used to freeze so hard it could be shattered, but inside it was always warm and smelled of ginger, roasting beef, and cut pine boughs. Since she had left home she had treated each year like a chapter in a book that must be read straight through, shut each year behind her like the door to a room she must never go back to, nor even look back, as if the sight would freeze her dead. But she was feeling at home now, here with Henry Starr, and she found she could let herself run her memories freely back and forth like the gleaning birds scooting over the frozen ruts of the stubble fields. Going back didn't freeze her or keep her from flying forward again, and flying forward didn't mean she had no home to come back to. She cut some pine boughs and stacked them in a pail of water to keep fresh until she could weave them into a wreath for their front door.

## TULSA *December 22, 1921*

On a slack day at the bank she took time to add up some figures for herself: how much it cost the two of them to live, how much was still owed to pay off the camera Henry Starr had killed, how long till Foley finished the last two of the seven pictures they owed the company (*Henry Starr's Vengeance Trail, Henry Starr, Sagebrush Scout*) and they could walk away from this world. The facts were not as bad as she had felt them to be. Even with the winter weather and at the rate Foley was shooting, Henry Starr's contract might be fulfilled in two months. But better than that: if she sold her team and buggy and used a saddle horse to get to work, they could pay off their owings after the New Year—and he could quit.

He wouldn't be able to work for another movie company in this state with his contract to Pan American unfulfilled. If it wasn't for his parole they could go out west to Hollywood in California, Esterhazy said if you were serious about getting into movies . . . but they could hire a lawyer to figure a way around his parole, and in the meantime he could do something else, ranching maybe; storekeeping. Foley was wrong, Henry Starr was probably good at lots of things besides movies and robbing banks.

She imagined him being good at lots of things: but when she closed her eyes all she could see was a man swinging down off the side of a galloping horse to snatch a fallen money bag out of a dusty street while the banker and the citizens blazed away with rifles shotguns pistols . . .

It didn't matter. She looked up sharply, looked around the bank. It didn't matter, because whatever he was or wasn't good at, she herself was equal to just about anything. She felt cool and compact in herself: she had good sharp edges. Wilberforce, crossing the lobby to his office, cast a proprietary eye her way—paused—shook his head and moved on, and she smiled. His eyes were just eyes. Not hands: eyes. Let Wilberforce come by her cage and look at her all he liked, think or even—damn him—remember all he liked. Neither he nor Poole had anything to do with her anymore. She didn't even need the bars of the cage, all she needed was to say, "Not while I'm working for you"—better, all she had to say was *no*.

And when she wanted to, she could say *yes*. She knew just what kinds of things she would say yes or no to. Maybe she couldn't really rob a bank or ride a horse like Henry Starr, but even the famous outlaw admitted she could handle a team. Well: she could. Her muscles felt light and tight and well knit to her beautifully articulated bones. There was nothing in the world outside, or in her own mind, or in her own body, that she wasn't equal to.

That included Henry Starr, story ghost body and all.

She had never been at home with someone else's body. No one had ever been at home with hers. But she felt at home now, with herself and with Henry Starr. Her feeling for Henry Starr had been huge and ghostly, shook her like a big blank wind. Now it had—crumbled?—down into the look of him riding or eating, the look of him reading a book, the smell of sweat, horse, and leather on him when he came back from the day's work, the smell of soap on him after he had washed off under the backyard pump, the look of him talking to her, laughing at her and calling her Bobcat or Ma'am or Miss Woodly or Barbara Catherine or whatever name he had for her that day—he had different names for her, changing with his look and his mood, they were a part of his expression like the different tastes and smells and sweats he had depending on what he was doing. But so did she, she could match him look for look and thought for thought story for story and name for name. If there was work she did it, she didn't mind labor and sweat, sometimes she got so slick that he would slide against her like an otter in a mud chute and she'd laugh in the middle of her pleasure and hold him harder so he wouldn't slide right off. And she had names for him too, hundreds of them; inventing or discovering his names was another thing she was good at, she hadn't even begun finding or making them up yet, but she would now that they had time.

But she had names for herself too, that was the surprise, she had been so caught up dreaming and making up "Henry Starr" that she had lost that sense of herself—as if his story were something she could have instead of her own. But his story—it was just a story, and in any case it was *his*. Now her memory ran her body's trace back and back, through *Debtor to the Law* and Miss B. C. Woodly in Wilberforce's bank, to Barbara with Curly Joe and Bobtail-cat with her brothers and Barbara Catherine in her mother's kitchen-call, back to the days when her body was slim as a peeled birch and she was Uncas the Son of Uncas, the last and noblest chief of the ancient race of the Mohicans. If you want a story, children, let me tell you of Miss Barbara Bobtail Catherine Uncas B. C. Bobcat Woodly . . . and if she wanted to she could tack on the name *Starr*—because whether they ever married or not, her name and her story included Henry Starr now. Maybe it didn't have bank robberies and jailbreaks and Indian Nations in it, but it had Henry Starr and a lot more than that already, and here she had barely begun to write it, had only just this moment come to see that what she had been and would be added up to a story equal to the story of Henry Starr.

She could ride and shoot almost as well as he could, and write or drive a team better, and taking one kind of strength with another she'd match her body with his too, running or swimming or jumping or riding, riding or making love, even if he started above her mounted and set for the buck she could roll and ride him, she was as much rider as horse, and sometimes in the quiet afternoon with the brilliant white winter sun through the bare windows heating the whole bedroom, waiting for him to come back the smell of her own body filled her up like a warm liquid and she felt as keen and swift and compact in herself as ever she had dreamed Henry Starr could be, so strong and balanced within herself that she could have leaned down off the side of the fastest wildest colt she'd ever rode and snatched Henry Starr himself out of the flying dust.

---

That night, just like in the "old days," she had a dream of him as a young man, discovered him in fact standing with her brothers in the yard of her father's ranch, dressed like them in Indian feathers and breechclouts. She stepped slowly out of the house into a sunlight that was also the pleasure in their eyes when they saw who she had become.

She woke up, smiling. There was gray false-dawn in the window. In the pale light Henry Starr was lying asleep next to her, breathing a little coarsely. The shadows threw his Cherokee cheekbones into prominence and deepened the tanned-leather heaviness of his skin. He was a redskin Injun all right, the blood showed in his face, if he was or he wasn't part nigger too hardly mattered: white girls who get that redskin thing inside them, that redskin blood or juice, you just throw 'em away like trash, their own blood and kin treat 'em like strangers, you wish 'em dead the way you'd wish a good child Merry Christmas. And what do they say about white girls who get the taste for it, get the taste in both of their mouths, tongue hole and finger hole both . . .

Well I like the way you taste, Henry Starr. If your color was paint I would paint myself all over with you. Or no I wouldn't: because I love how strange you are, and how I will never get to the bottom of you, but you will always surprise me.

The light picked up silver splinters among the bristles of his unshaven chin. The squint lines at the corners of his eyes were like incisions, and below each eye the soft skin crumpled in crepey ridges. Counting his years didn't tell you what his age was, she thought. He's lived the kind of life . . . in some ways he might be a hundred years old. He'll never be a kid again, he'll never be my little brother. He's old enough to be my father.

If he's a *hundred* years old, that makes him my great-great-grandfather not . . .

But no, she wouldn't make that joke, because when she looked at him straight she had to admit to herself that there were times, that he could be like . . . like her little, her young—when she felt she had to big-sister him because he: because sometimes, when he was most quiet, thinking over his long secrets, he looked as blank and pure and open as a baby, and it made you want to do something for him, because the world can put a twist to a child that will turn him cross to everything, even love; and you had to have strong clever hands to reach inside and change that, like she remembered her mother's hands. She looked at her own hands—they could handle a team or write a book, she used to think of them as being like her brothers' hands only thinner. But they weren't thin, they were like her mother's hands, long fingers and palms with solid pads of muscle, soft-skinned flexible mothering hands, with long fingers supple as tongues to reach inside and turn him round back again, so his ghost would lie right along the line of his bones the way it always should have.

She woke his eyes with her fingers, drawing the line of his eyebrows, then his lips. She woke the rest of him with her hair, pouring it forward onto his face like a dry cool kind of water. His eyes were fleckless brown, deep-pupiled, she split into tiny twins and fell into them. She rolled onto him and trailed the nipple of her right breast like a blind thumb till it touched his mouth, and he opened and accepted it. This time when he slid inside her it seemed as if she had grown deeper inside, as if all of Henry Starr became complete and compact inside her, filling her like a cup—but she kept opening deeper still, as much of him as there was or could be she would always be able to contain him, she felt her womb unfold itself inside her and she called him Baby baby, my baby, my little baby.

## SPRINGS ROAD *December 23, 1921*

They were eating breakfast: strong coffee, eggs, bread and bacon. The morning newspapers, delivered by a boy on a motorcycle. The cool smell of the cut pine boughs drifted in. It was Friday and week's end, no shooting after today at the Springs meant the next two days were all for them. She kept smiling and smiling. "It really is going to be all right, I did some figuring and made some plans. They haven't got us where they think they've got us, Henry Starr."

Henry Starr was happy too: "No," he said, "they aren't as smart as they think they are."

"It will cost us something to get clear, one way or another. If you don't want to work out the rest of the contract we can . . ." and she laid it out for him.

He reached across the table and touched the side of her head. "You keep thinking about me," he said. "I can't believe how you keep thinking about me, and . . . You thought till you figured a way I could get clear of this, if I needed to." He squinted, puzzled: "I . . . it's enough for me,

I guess: knowing if I needed to, I could. I don't think I need to, that's all."

Her surprise showed.

"I don't want to quit movies," he said. "I like movies, I like thinking I *could* do 'em, anyway."

"After everything that's come of it?"

"You come of it," he said. "You come of it, along with the rest." His look was serious, direct. "I'm not ready to let it drop, not with me still on the losing end." He smiled. "You don't want to give it up either, do you? Photoplay by Miss B. C. Woodly, Miss Bobcat, Miss Bobcat C. Woodly. Not when you're just getting good at it."

It was one more thing she hadn't been letting herself think about, but he'd spotted it in her. Under the denial and firm resignation was a stubborn hope that Henry Starr would still think of some way to redeem their failure with *A Debtor to the Law.* She told herself it was childish to keep thinking about it, but as she laid out her denial for him she wondered if maybe he could change it: "Poole and Foley will never let us make another movie by ourselves."

"When I get finished with them," said Henry Starr, "maybe we can start up a little company by ourselves."

"Where will we get the money?"

"You like the idea," he said, "if you're thinking that far into it."

"Where?" she insisted.

"America is the land of opportunity," said Henry Starr. "And there's two of us working on it. You at your trade, me at mine."

"I'm looking for different work," she said, reaching for the paper; there might be something advertised she could work at . . . her eye caught a headline low on page one:

DARING BANK ROBBERY IN BEGGS

From the Muskogee Tribune

Beggs, Oklahoma—December 22. Our local branch of the Chemical–Cattlemen's Bank has had some unexpected withdrawals made. It would appear from a casual survey of the case that the Daltons have been outdone altogether. For coolness, smoothness, and daring this adventure has not perhaps its equal since the days of the Daltons and the Jameses.

Three men, armed with revolvers and shotguns, walked coolly into the bank just before the close of business at 2:30 P.M. yesterday.

The bandit leader—a well-dressed Mexican in a derby hat—entered the bank with two companions, armed with shotguns and Colt's revolvers, and immediately took command of the situation, ordering all present—Bank President Ford, Cashier Symons, and Clerks Rayford and Thomason—to line up in front of the safe, admonishing them in heavily accented English to "hold up their hands and stand steady."

She looked across the table at him. His eyes held steadily on hers, but she saw that his face had become smooth and masklike as if a bandanna had been drawn up to his eyes.

*No*, she said inside, and then she said "No," and shook her head, and shook herself *no* from hips to hair. "You can't be doing it," she said, "you can't be."

"Bobcat," he said softly, but she wasn't having any of it. "You *are*," she told him. "Oh God, you are."

"If we can get a little bit of money together . . ."

"No," she said, "we already have a little bit of money together. I just finished telling you how I figured out ways we could get more, get enough to . . ."

"It wouldn't be enough," he said, "your way it wouldn't be enough."

"Not enough? Not enough? For what—oh God, Henry, for what? We're not going to open a bank . . ."

"The movie," he said. "We have to finish . . ."

"No." She said it and she meant it, as deep inside as she could mean anything: *no*. "That's done. We did that. We don't have to do that anymore, we can just get out of this city and be . . ."

"I can't," he said, "it isn't done for me. It isn't done. I can't give it up till it's done. I got to keep trying till I get it right."

"Get what right?" she cried. "Get what? That idiot's dream of a movie? Or is it still Jesse James you're trying to beat, still trying to knock over two banks in one day?"

His brows wrinkled, he looked puzzled. "No," he said, "I swear it isn't any such fool's game as that. It's for the movie, I . . ."

His face was absolutely clear in the white light that poured through the window and she could see all of him clearly now, Henry Starr as he had been and as he was, his face young and old, hidden behind a bandanna or naked and smiling—there was no difference in the faces, none, none at all. "No," she said, "it's always the same thing to you. You don't change. People think you change, but you just go under cover for a while, you change your clothes or think up some new way to act and then out you come again just the way you were before."

The smooth masklike expression seemed to rise like a hood until it covered the expression in his eyes as well, glazing them like a skin of ice on a pond, and she knew that meant she had touched where it hurt him. But she saw in that same instant that knowing she had gotten inside his guard this last time was not going to be any comfort to her at all when she remembered today, because that mask was going to be his final answer to her.

"The movie isn't an idiot's game," he said. "It's the real thing, you know? Bobcat? The real thing. Whatever we have, it was the movie that gave it to us."

She remembered herself as she had been then, flaunting and smart, robber chief of the Woodly Gang, she had been so happy playing that game. The memory: it was like a picture in an album, as gone from her as being a happy child among her brothers, gone. "No," she said, "maybe it was that way at the start, for me too. But it stopped being that when we . . ." She was crying, and she cried more freely knowing that even if she had been trying to use her tears to work him back she would have failed. She gathered her breath back slowly and said, "But that's still how it is for you, Henry Starr. You still think you made us up, like that movie."

She cleared her eyes with her fingers. She said: "No, I guess it was always only yourself that you can't stop making up: Henry Starr. That's why you keep coming back to the same thing. That's why you won't stop any of this."

"Make myself up?" he said. "Like I was in somebody else's story? All I ever did in my life was try to figure out what my name and story was supposed to be. When I tried keeping store, having a family—it went bad on me, because 'Henry Starr the Storekeeper' just wasn't a thing that could happen to my name, see? Not without making me somebody I wasn't." His eyes focused brightly and sharply on her. "You," he said, "you said you . . . who was it you said you loved, Bobcat? Some little mouse of a storekeeper Henry Starr, or was it Henry *Starr* . . ."

. . . *who rode the nightland with the wolves and heard the owl hoot, away down in the Indian Nations, a long time ago.*

"It was Henry Starr," she said, "and maybe it was the Robin Hood of Oklahoma too at the start. But it isn't anymore. I've seen you, Henry: you let me look underneath that damned bandanna, and I know you, oh God I *do*—" The words spinning out of her, she wished they were like ropes that could catch and hold him. "I know you by taste and smell and feel, and hear and speak and listen, I know you and I'm telling you if you were just a human person named Henry Starr you could be anything else too, even Henry Starr the Greengrocer and it wouldn't hurt. You could, you could be with me, and we could and we—

"But we won't," she said as the skein of breath and intense feeling suddenly broke off in her chest. "I'm out of the movie, Henry Starr. It isn't one whole day since I finally figured out how I can live in my own skin and take care of myself and get anything done that I need to. I'm too new at it to take any more chances of getting stuck inside somebody else's movie. Because I think everybody in your movie is all only you, Henry; and soon they are all going to die, just the way you think they should, and I don't want to be a part of that."

He stood up. She wouldn't look at his face. Whether deliberately smoothed or twisted by grief, it was not a face for her to trust anymore, and she didn't want it to be the last of him she saw.

"I'm sorry," he said, "though I know that's not . . ."

She wondered if he even knew just what it was he was saying *no* to now, and she rushed back and forth between wishing he did and hoping for his sake that he didn't, since in neither case was he going to do or be any different.

She let him go out the door, heard him saddling his black and white mare, remembered the black-splattered moon-white glare of the animal's hindquarters, heard her quick clever feet dancing the hard-packed frozen earth in the yard. Then the rhythm of her hoofbeats quickened and spoke distance, diminishing already as Miss Woodly came to the uncurtained window; her last sight of him was man and horse together passing the gate in a smooth boneless lope, man and horse down the lane swinging eastward into Tulsa.

## TULSA

It was a good day for December: bright as steel, the air stiffened with chill and the bite of iron in its taste. There were small birds spinning among the corn stubble and frost rimes between the rows, just like it was supposed to be when the season came around, just like it had always been. The barrel of his spook-gray mare was solid between his legs again, the .45 riding in a hip holster under the drape of his jacket, and the road opening out ahead of him, everything in the world the way it should be, hard and clear and solid, with clean edges and sharp colors.

For a few minutes back there in the breakfast room, she had made him feel like he was buried in blue smoke, everything gone blurred, the insides out of things, no colors—like one of Esterhazy's pictures—talking and talking to him, she had very nearly blown his vision out of him like you blow a candle.

But it was clear and perfect again. This was the only way to deal with the blue smoke people blew around you, all that powwow his Grandfather laid on him, all those dreams she spelled on him, all those blue-smoke dreams his own mind conjured when his body was stopped or prisoned somehow—the only thing was to get up and go, step out the door into the world again and find you a horse and a gun, and a road to ride and place to ride it to. And if a man as old and smart as he was couldn't pick himself a road and figure the best way to ride it . . .

So she didn't like it. But then, she *wouldn't* at first look, would she? Just taking whatever it was you held out in your hand, that wasn't her style. But let her get a taste of it for herself and she was bound to like it, this *was* her kind of play, she would know just how to look and think and act, the kind of thing that come as natural to her as handling horses or shooting a rifle—he had seen that from the beginning, way back in Tahlequah when she walked with him through the front door of the Katy Bank with . . . Yeah, she would like it once she got the taste of it again, and then she'd come back strong, she'd be on it like a bear once she got ahold of it—no, not a bear, he grinned, like a spike-tailed bobcat, quick and fierce and dead-sure, that was Miss Bobcat C. Woodly when she made her move.

So that was one he could count on. Plus three he already had in hand, and the letter in his pocket promising a fifth. That left only two to win this morning, and then he'd have seven—like a hand of stud, four cards open and three aces in the hole—and seven was his number, seven: the sign his powers were working.

Greenwood Avenue was lined with burned-out storefronts, windows still boarded up, facades black-washed with soot, gaps heaped with brick and the broken slants of remnant beams and pillars where buildings had fallen or been torn down. Dick Rowland was working at Braxton's, music in the evenings and tending bar. This morning he was sitting out in back chording his guitar a little. Henry Starr winked at a colored kid of twelve sitting on a barrel at the head of the alley lazy-whittling on a piece of stick, Braxton's lookout in case any crackers came around for Dick Rowland.

Henry Starr leaned off the horse to shake hands. "This isn't the work for you, Dick."

"It is for now," he said. "I'm thinking about later."

"How much *later* do you think they'll let you have around here? They took your name once, Dick—do you think they will forget it?"

"No I don't," said Rowland. "But I can't waste time thinking about what can't be helped. They were always there, Henry. They could have come any time at all. Being ready is all you can do. Then you got to just get on with your work."

"There's work you and I could do. We were good at it."

Rowland shook his head. "I'm not really Cherokee Bill, Henry. I don't rob banks. Not as a regular calling, anyway."

"This would be special, Dick. I just need to put together enough money for the movie I'm thinking about. It would be the real thing this time, Dick. We'd lay it all out right between their eyes, from the Indian Nations right down to Bub Houston and Greenwood, just like it used to be and like it still is."

"Well, that would be good," said Dick, "that would be a good thing to do, Henry. But that ain't my . . ."

"It isn't just for me this time, Dick. But so they'd remember Bub and you, what you did, why. So they wouldn't just look at you like they do now, and they know there's all of this . . . all these things that happened standing in back of Dick Rowland, and can't put the names to them. We could make it as clear as words on a sign, make it so bright it would be like it was in colors . . ."

Dick threw back his head, laughing. "Yeah, old Henry Starr—I'd like to see that movie, I'd like to see somebody do the United States of America in *colors* for a change: black and blue, brother—and red and white, brown and yellow, even with spots like that zebra horse you ride."

"I need you to do it with me," said Henry Starr softly. "If you won't do it it won't work. It's hard enough I got to find a way of making them see the ghosts, if I got to fake the real people too it will never . . ."

"I can't do it," said Dick Rowland softly. "I guess I don't believe in it anymore." He looked searchingly at Henry Starr, trying to see what was behind the intense calm that had taken hold of the outlaw's face, smoothing and blanking his expression. "Even if you made it, it wouldn't do what you say. If people won't learn from their own lives, how you gonna trick 'em into learning from something somebody just made up? If they see me walking around in the street here, like I am, knowing who I am, and then they forget who I am and where I come from and what I did, then there isn't anything will save me—or them, I guess. But if I thought they were that far gone, Henry—I wouldn't stick around.

"Besides," said Dick—his voice roughened as it sank deep into his chest—"besides, I owe these people, I got a debt to pay. Because they did all this dying on my account, to keep the Klan from doing me like they did my daddy." Rowland shook his head. "With all the thinking I did, all the education, that was the one thing I never thought of happening. I used to think they depended on my daddy, to talk for 'em and to die for 'em. And me—I thought they needed me to do their killing for 'em, to get 'em a piece of their own back, a piece of justice. But how it happened was . . . was them killing and dying for me. So I got to stay with 'em and help 'em to . . . well, or maybe just stay with 'em to take what comes, I can't see yet what to do. But I got to stay and look for it."

Dick wouldn't come this time. There was a kind of gray thickening in the air between them, it made Henry Starr feel like Dick was already moving away, so far he would never hear or see him again, his friend, his partner, they had taken the Owasso Bank and Deputy Price together, they had put Cherokee Bill's ghost to sleep and Dick had helped him past the Lady in the Cabin, he said *baby, take care little sister* and then Miss Woodly said *I love you Henry Starr*, maybe it was Dick Rowland opened that door for me at the top of her stairs . . . "I guess it's goodbye then," he said. He was going away, his eyes were already looking to the far place he aimed at, and Dick's image was a little bit hazy, you could almost see trees through it, and two-three miles of empty country—so Henry Starr talked like it was to himself: "I guess we come from different places, Dick. You owe it to your people to stay and try to get them some justice. The problem I got is any people I might have done that for are all pretty much dead. How do you get a piece of justice for a bunch of ghosts? That's my problem. They got some special notions about what they want, you got to hear what they say and answer 'em just the right way—but it's hard because they ain't really there."

He turned his horse away, time was getting shorter. "That makes it harder," he said. Thinking: *It's all getting harder, I won't have seven but only six but that don't mean it can't be done, I didn't have Cherokee Bill with me in Stroud, nor back when I needed him making that movie, but I found Dick to put in his place, and what you've done one time you can do better the second.*

He looked at his watch—it was getting on toward noon and he still had some things to do before 2:45. He turned again and reached down to shake Dick Rowland's hand, smiling, there was no real harm done, he just had to go ahead with the job under certain disadvantages—but there were always disadvantages, they were just the conditions you had to work with, the season and the situation of the bank, the opportunities and the surprises, all you could hope to be was ready, and if Henry Starr wasn't ready by now, with all the times he'd rehearsed this day since Fourth of July in Tahlequah thirty years ago . . .

There was a strike of white sunlight through the east window of the Tulsa County Courthouse, along with the stink of oil from Red Fork. Blaine sat at his desk watching the clouds in the north window disappearing behind the bulk of the Standard Oil Building.

Tilghman was sitting square in the middle of the white light, and it made him look almost ghostlike—the whiteness blanked shadows and perspectives and made him seem depthless, his skin had that translucence you sometimes see in the extremely old, and his pale-gray mustache and hair seemed white. Old: since the attempt on his life Bill Tilghman was an old man.

Blaine kept trying to get him talking. "I'm trying to figure out . . . to get you to help me figure out who was trying to kill you. Negroes gunning for any policeman they could catch out alone—not likely, but possible. Or somebody from the Klan, because you got the colored boy out of town? But I think it has to be someone connected with bootlegging, with the Price case . . . Dammit, Bill: it's not just you, there's something big here, something . . . and we don't have that much time to work on it. Once the papers get ahold of the story there'll be reporters all over the place, and the ones who were behind it running for cover as fast as . . ." Nothing. No reaction. Blaine stiffened, it was a little theatrical but he had to try something: "Or maybe you don't trust me? Maybe you figure I'm part of whatever it is . . ."

Blaine felt he was losing dignity, pleading with the old man like this, but something made him feel again and again the impulse to apologize. But why should *he* apologize to Tilghman? They had worked on the Price case together. Neither of them could help it if Judge Meis had done nothing but fine him and kick him off the force.

The old marshal stirred; it was as uncanny as if a statue had breathed and he spoke with stone lips barely moving. "No, you're not part of it. You been flying right over it, but you're not in it."

Blaine wasn't to be deflected by their old argument over airplanes, he was on the track now. "Then tell me."

Maybe Tilghman was going to speak, but just then Blaine saw the old man's white eyes shift off his face to something behind him, and when the captain turned there was that incubus of an ex-outlaw, the movie actor Henry Starr.

Blaine felt a sense of helpless despair that unstrung his muscles and left him slumped in his chair.

"Hello, Bill," said Henry Starr.

"Somehow I figured you'd turn up," said Tilghman.

"Jesus," said Blaine, "like a bad penny."

"I've come for some more legal advice, Bill," Henry Starr said. The former outlaw sat erect in his chair: the posture of a military cadet at a formal dinner, or of a child perched on the edge of his seat at school. He looked steadily at the marshal.

"Getting or giving?" the old marshal asked Henry Starr.

"Maybe both," said the former outlaw. "They've let Dick Rowland out of jail."

"The judge said they had no case," said Tilghman. "I'd say that was about right."

"It doesn't take the name off him," said Henry Starr. "You figure it's justice if they put a name on you, and they got it wrong, but the name sticks anyway?"

"The law goes as far as it can," said Tilghman. "For me that's far enough."

"Did it go far enough on Deputy Price?"

"Wherever it goes, it's far enough for me," said Tilghman quietly. "I just bring them to the judge."

"You made sure it was the law that got Dick Rowland. Nobody or nothing else."

There was nothing for Tilghman to answer in that, one way or another. That was what you did if you swore yourself to the law: unless you had a twist in you like Price or Casey or . . .

"You can't lose the game if you play it that way, can you, Bill?" said Henry Starr. "If that's how it is for you, then however it comes out, it's got to be right. I guess that was the advice you been trying to give me for thirty years, and me too big a fool to take it."

"What kind of advice you asking now, Henry?"

"Those movie people—Poole, Wilberforce—they got my sign on these papers, contracts . . . Is there law for busting something like that?"

"Ask a lawyer, Henry."

Henry Starr smiled a bad smile. "Yeah, and I know what you think of lawyers. They took that work we done, me and my . . . my partner, and they made liars out of us. I don't suppose you've seen it?"

Tilghman's answer was his silence.

Starr nodded his head *yes* acknowledging Tilghman's right to judge, and said, "Well, I guess what they did was let us tell some lies on ourselves, and put us where we can't get out of having to live behind them. If I could stop them showing those pictures . . ."

Tilghman said, "Stop 'em making more. Get out of it."

Starr's lip lifted sharply. "That's just the thing I can't do. According to the papers I signed. I don't figure that any lawyer I can afford can break a contract like they have written."

"You must be making a pile on that last one," said Blaine bitterly. "Everybody but the two of us has been to see it at least once."

Henry Starr looked like he had a headache. "Yeah, just about every white man in Tulsa. But all I get out of it is my same ten dollars a day, and the fun of seeing my name in lights on that pack of lies, *Henry Starr: A Debtor to the Law*: my little two percent gets kicked in to pay off some debts I kind of accumulated."

Tilghman raised his eyebrows.

"Some equipment I accidentally busted," Starr said blandly.

"Movie business has its risks," said Tilghman.

"Well," said Henry Starr, "all of this has surely been a lesson to me. From here on I'm just trying to do like my momma always told me—making a virtue of necessity. I'll work hard and save my pennies, and maybe someday open a little business of my own."

"Storekeeping?" Tilghman asked.

"Nope," said Starr with a grin: "Movies."

This time, to Blaine's heightened sensibilities, Tilghman's silence had a different quality—less of judgment than of attentive listening.

"Sure you won't join me in it?" said Henry Starr. "If I'd had you riding shotgun for me on that last one, they'd never have skinned me as bad as they did."

"It was never your trade, Henry."

The outlaw smiled. "Well, you wouldn't let me keep practicing the only trade I ever learned. I had to try something new."

The smile lingered on Starr's face, but his eyes became more intent on the old man's white face, and his voice took on an odd, musical, seductive quality that made Blaine deeply uneasy. "And I did learn movies, Bill. There's more to it than a man would ever guess, seeing the kinds of cheap trash they make. But once I got my hand in it was like . . . You know, there are horses you ride one time, and it's like you hand-raised 'em from a colt, she'll move as easy under you as your own legs. Or you can be blood kin to a bunch of people way back to the Cherokee Nation that used to be, and they don't come nearer to you than Tulsa is to Jerusalem, when they talk it's just wind under the door; and then you'll meet somebody one time, a woman maybe, or a man, and it's like you know each other by the inside, you can hear what they're saying when the words is still just breath. There's jobs you can work at all your born days, and never get the good of them because they don't belong to you; and there's things you do one time and it's as easy and natural as remembering your own name—or it's like a kid, like having a son of your own, he's got your looks, you know? and you can teach him the way you ride a horse and throw a rope . . ."

"And rob a bank," said Blaine disgustedly.

"And rob a bank," said Henry Starr, "if that's what he's born and bound to do."

Tilghman answered thoughtfully: "A man can stay with something too long. There's a time to go in, and a time to get out."

Blaine saw with growing anger and despair that Tilghman took the outlaw–movie star's blather more to heart than all of Blaine's own labor and concern. *I guess Starr is kin and I am just wind under the door.* He thought, A *time to go in and a time to get out: listen to yourself, old man, if you won't listen to me.*

Henry Starr seemed to hear the same thought, but he took it the other way. "You don't quit," he said to Tilghman, "you never went back on any track you ever followed till you come to the end. No more than you'd go back on your word. You never even looked back . . ."

"Maybe I should have," said Tilghman, and Blaine heard something in the soft voice that was like the crackle ice makes when you pour warm whiskey on it and the split lines run through it.

"Thanks for the legal advice." Starr was rising to leave, but just then a tremor went through the old man's arms lying before him on the desk, as if he had felt a shock, as if he had felt and instantly suppressed a gesture to keep the former outlaw from leaving just then.

Starr read the sign and he froze—waiting.

"I gave you some advice," said the marshal softly. "Now I want to ask you." The white light whitened the mustache that concealed the expression of his lips. "When I was on your trail, back then. You always knew I was back there, didn't you?"

"I didn't always know just how close," said Henry Starr. "But knowing it was you, I figured you had to be back there somewhere."

"No more than that?"

The square bolt of white light pouring in from the window caught them like still images in the blitz of a camera flash—Starr standing, Tilghman seated: like an image in an old photograph album, frozen, long-dead people standing in a light that died decades ago.

"Well, I don't know," said Henry Starr, "but it did seem to me sometimes I could feel your shadow fall across me. The thing is, I never did know if you were that close: those weren't the times you caught me."

"That time in Stroud?"

Starr's voice was quiet. "I knew you were nearly there."

"But you went on with it, anyway?"

"Closer or further off, Bill, you were always going to be back there. I wasn't disrespecting you, but I couldn't let your being there run me off either, could I? If I wasn't going to just quit, I had to do every job knowing you were behind me and the Judge behind you. Besides," he said, "a man doesn't leave off doing his work, just because it begins to get a little interesting."

"No," said Tilghman, "if he can still get it done, I guess he can't quit."

There was a pause which the old marshal's frozen white study threatened to hold forever. It was Starr who broke it. "If you think you feel something behind you, Bill, then you'd better believe it's there."

"Yes," said Tilghman, gathering his attention to a sudden point and leaning forward, "even if it can't make a difference in what you do. Thanks for the expert advice."

"No trouble." Starr rose to go.

He's an old man, Blaine told himself, and it's finally caught up with him. Tilghman was feeling that shadow on him the way Starr said he had felt Tilghman. Blaine knew the feel of it: even up in a sky burning with sun, he had felt it cold between his own shoulder blades. You don't have to be an old man to feel it, he's a lucky old man that it's taken this long.

Then to Blaine's surprise, Tilghman went back to Henry Starr's proposal, still reluctantly, but now also seriously: "I'm not a play actor, Henry," said Tilghman.

"That's just why I got to have you," said Henry Starr. "I got nearly everybody else that's left lined up for this one. I went down to Stroud and got that kid with the hog-killing gun, Paul Curry—that shot me in the ass that time, and busted up my big double. He ain't a kid no more, but we can fix that . . . and, between us, a couple of old boys that used to ride with me, though they never got named"—he glanced over at Blaine—"and the statute is out on them by now." He fastened on Tilghman again. "No fooling around, taking pictures of lies, Bill. This time we're going to show 'em how it used to be.

"You see, I figured out how it works, how you have to do it. That weasely son of a bitch Poole, setting his cameras up to show Dick Rowland lynched—it stinks, *he* stinks, but there's something there, Bill. If you could get the story part and the real life part so they were kind of working into each other, swapping knives, running 'em in and out like, like . . ."

"Like taking time out of making pictures to point me up to Owasso," said Tilghman softly, and Starr answered: "Yes. That's it."

The outlaw looked steadily at the old marshal and his smile became very easy, almost sweet. "You know," he said, "they kinda made me a little crazy there for a while, play-acting like I was somebody else's idea of a real old-time western badman. But I . . . I climbed over that, I got outside of it. You can play around with that ghost kind of stuff all you want, as long as you keep your hand on what's real: as long as every little while you can find your own horse, and your guns, and your road out of there, as long as you can get back to . . ." He smiled. "Oh hell, you know."

Tilghman said, "Yes, I guess I do know. It's been a lesson watching you these last few months, Henry. Yes, it's been an education."

Blaine snorted and threw up his hands in a good imitation of disgust, but what he was feeling was grief and despair: because if Tilghman could sit there and listen to this crap and keep putting Blaine off, keep putting off looking at who was trying to kill Tilghman and why . . .

"You'll think it over," said Starr as if he was sure the marshal would. He smiled his charming smile, touched his hat to Blaine, backed and turned away.

The doors closed behind Henry Starr, and Tilghman looked across the bustling office after him. Then he got up slowly, reached his worn gun belt down from the hat rack and put it around his waist.

"I don't believe I'm seeing this," said Blaine. "You won't talk to me, when I'm not only trying to do some real police work but trying to find out who's trying to kill *you*. And then this cheap ex-con walks in here, sings some kind of old sweet song, and you're out the door to go act in his goddamn minstrel show!"

Tilghman stopped, his eyes staring after Henry Starr with a white intensity. "It's not a movie, exactly . . . that isn't exactly what he means."

"Since that first day he has never *said* exactly what he means . . ."

Tilghman looked over at Blaine, he looked surprised at what the young man had said. "Well I don't know," said Tilghman, "I guess I understood him right along. It's just his way of talking . . . I guess I know what he's saying because we come from the same place, away back there."

Blaine's frustration made him reach for eloquence: "So you're going to let him lead you around by the nose instead of putting your shoulder to the wheel here with me. I thought you had devoted your life to police work. If you won't hold up our side of it . . ."

"Our side," said Tilghman, turning the words over slowly. "I never thought of it that way. It was always just the law to me. When I gave my word to it, that's what I called it. I never thought of it as a side, but maybe I was wrong—or maybe it changed on me—but"—he blinked as if the white light was finally blinding him—"I guess it does come down to different sides, and who was on them. You see, I had Judge Parker behind me starting out, and he . . . he was hard, but he was square. The law was always one thing to him, and nothing turned him aside, neither mercy on the one hand or the influence of powerful men on the other, but he went straight at it. It wasn't always kind or right. It wasn't even always justice. But there was never any foolery about what the law was and what a judge had to do with it.

"It made the Judge a little bit narrow in his views, I reckon. For him a man was either inside the law or outside, and if it was outside then God have mercy on your soul, for he would have none. He had a contempt and a hate for Henry Starr that made me sorry to see. Because for me it wasn't that easy, not being a judge but . . . To me it was like, you believed in the law so you brought it out there with you to make it work out on the land; but there was other things out there, they was there first, they had a kind of justice that belonged to them, and belonged out there, just like all those buffalo we used to . . ." *two thousand head, I remember, we killed everything from the edge of our shadows out to the skyline in three days.*

Tilghman seemed to lose the thread, but Blaine couldn't help him, he had no idea where the old man was or thought he was going.

But the old man picked it up again. "You know, law and justice can't always be the same thing," said Tilghman. "You got to make a choice which one you're going to live by. I made mine a long time ago. But that don't make Henry Starr mean for choosing different. You got to give a man grace according to his lights and his circumstances, that's only fair and just. Sometimes if you've got a pure set on justice the law becomes something you can't live with. So you choose justice and you live by that, and I got no bad name for a man who does that even if I swore myself to take him in for judgment. The thing about Henry Starr . . . the thing about Henry Starr was when you talked with him you could see that he knew all that, and that he give you grace too, to follow the law if you chose it, and still he give you your due as a man. He even give the law its due." Tilghman's eyes focused on Blaine again. "Yes, he even give the law its due. When I come to take him" *ass-naked in that fancy house in Colorado or ass-shot and lying there paralyzed waiting for the white mob and the ropes and the razors* "he knew it was what come of his own choosing: that me and him was doing what we done for the same kind of . . ." Tilghman's eyes were off again. "So that sometimes when I'd be tracking that smart little Cherokee son of a bitch I'd lie awake figuring and figuring, trying to get inside his head, trying to guess his next move and then I'd have it, clear as if I could hear the words moving behind his eyes, and I'd know how and when and where I was going to take him—and then I'd dream about it: instead of me running him down and shooting it out with him, it was like he was waiting for me, or I was waiting for him, and we would meet like it'd all been arranged long ago—and we'd shake hands on something, like we would talk something out to the bottom and then shake on it, and when we come back to Fort Smith I'd put him, I'd walk him in and sit him down with Judge Parker, and the two of them would go at it talking and talking it through like I never could talk it, but Henry Starr and the old Judge they sure could have, and just as they was standing up to shake on it I'd . . ."

Tilghman's face flinched as if he had been pinched awake. Blaine stared at him, too appalled to hide what he was thinking, *the old man had gone over the border this time, old Bill Tilghman . . .*

"But I guess I just had all of that wrong," said Tilghman, "or like I said, maybe the times just changed. Judge Parker is long gone, and they got men wear the robe and spit on the law every time they speak it. How can you go and bring that kind of law out to where it's got to look somebody like Henry Starr eye for eye, and make the name of what I'm living by as good as the name of what he is living by? So that when I take him in, it ain't just that I got the drop on him, but it's . . . but it's the right thing, it's a thing that's got some right to it and both of us know it." He looked at Blaine and his eyes had become impossibly white as if he might cry bright dry tears. "If the kind of judge I got behind me is the kind that that Meis is, then who do I bring Henry Starr *to*? You see why I'm asking?"

"Meis!" said Blaine, and the pattern flashed before him like the gridwork of fields and towns from five thousand feet up. "Who else knew when and where that poker game was going to be, and you in it? Meis!" *But actually* . . . "Or I suppose Egan might have told Casey," he conceded, "or even Poole, if he . . ." Suddenly Blaine felt afraid, he tore his eyes away from Tilghman and found the bulk of the Standard Oil skyscraper filling the north window. "Any one of them, or they all might have, maybe . . ." It was big, bigger than the courthouse, it filled the window and stretched up out of the frame into the unseeable sky.

"You think I can't track a man anymore," said the marshal. "Whatever a man does, if he does it long and hard enough, he writes his name on it as clear as daylight. There's a pattern, like there always was. The robbery in Owasso. The robberies in Okfuskee and Beggs and Howitt."

What did Howitt and Beggs and Okfuskee have to do with it? The old man was wandering off again. "Price and MacKinnon," said Blaine, "Egan and Meis and Casey and Poole—the nigger they lynched, bootleggers getting busted by the Klan—that's the pattern, Bill! Damnit! We can run that trail too, if we . . ."

The old man was fading again, the white light flattening him to the thinness and shine of an overexposed photograph. "You got a call to run it, son, I wish you well. But it don't belong to me. I don't want any part of it."

"It's you they tried to kill," said Blaine, pleading.

The old man looked at the blazing window, then back at Blaine. "They can try, if they're bound to. I can't stop that. But they ain't my business. I'm done with them."

"They're poisoning this whole stinking city, and everything and everyone in it. Isn't it any part of your duty to keep the crooks from taking over? Don't you care what they do to these people . . . ?"

"I gave my word I'd bring the law to them, that's all. If they take and sell it to a whiskey peddler or throw it away like it was trash, that's their business. I got nothing . . . nothing to say to them, one way or the other." He took the Peacemaker out of its soft worn scabbard and spun the cylinder with a sound like a well-oiled steel rattlesnake, then holstered it again. "Henry Starr was always outside the law, but he give it its due."

The marshal moved swiftly toward the door, lean and direct as a greyhound, never looking back.

Blaine turned away in anger and grief. The Standard Oil skyscraper clogged the north window, there were clouds behind it. *I'd rather be up there,* he thought, *I'd rather be so high above the streets they look like a road map.*

Sign by sign, like a dealer turning cards one at a time, the world kept showing Henry Starr his power and his luck. He'd planned for seven plus himself, and Dick Rowland wouldn't come—but he still had seven, counting himself as one. Three were waiting for him in an alley off Main Street: all he could find of his old Stroud bunch, the black man Shields and Bergman and Romero, a little grayer than they were ten years ago when he'd run his circle around Tulsa and had the sheriffs the police the federal marshals and the goddamn militia chasing their tails looking for the ghost of Henry Starr, never knowing who it was until he told them.

Except for Bill Tilghman. Bill Tilghman knew it was Henry Starr. So he had been waiting up the road from Stroud, and when the time come, cut wires or not, there he was.

"You got it all in your heads?" he asked them.

Yes, yes sure, sure they did. They let the street fill with the truck and wagon traffic to and from the 2:10 and 2:30 freights on the Katy and the Frisco. They take the left-side bank on the tick of 2:50 while Henry Starr took the right, shots and alarm bells from both sides of the street and with the noise and the traffic freezing Main Street solid so nothing on wheels could move, those old-time horseback outlaws would jump a back fence to where their mounts were waiting and adjourn to "the jungles of the Osage Nation" like they used to in the old days. But this wasn't the time to be talking it, it was time to do it. They rackracked the levers of the Winchesters, broke and looked down the shotgun barrels, spun the oiled cylinders of their revolvers with a sound like iron crickets.

Henry Starr stepped out first into the street: sign by sign, everything spoke to him, everything was the sign of his luck. The hard bright December air showed things sharp and clear—the crowds in the street shopping for the holiday, the wind slatting the banner that swept overhead

WELCOME TO TULSA, ALL-AMERICAN MAGIC CITY
OF THE SOUTHWEST

and under it in smaller letters a streamer saying

"Merry Christmas Tulsa Boosters"

—the gas flares waving like banners off the tops of the oil wells, the looping swags of electric Christmas lights swung from lightpost to lightpost, evergreen boughs tied to the uprights.

There was only three things he didn't have or couldn't see:

Miss Bobcat was one, it felt like he had left her a long time ago and way off, but really it was just this morning, and not more than eight miles of white road and cold air—no more than she put between them every day she went to work at the bank. But he knew she'd be in the bank now, just as she was supposed to be, just like she always was this time of day. And if she was there she would know, she would be ready like she always was, and when he come through that door . . .

All those words this morning, they were wind under the door when you put them next to the fact of her, with her blue eyes and her bobcat grin—she had grit and she had bottom, and she knew him like he knew her, which was by the ghost. What did it matter if she said *no* to him, when the breath in her chest meant *yes*?

And the second was Dick Rowland—who should have been his second inside the bank, that's how he had told her it would be when she asked him "How would you rob my bank?" But in a way Dick was inside the picture too, because he was right where he was supposed to be, and so his not being here in the street was no worse a thing than not being able to talk to Tom Starr or Bub or Aunt Belle or Cherokee Bill when he needed to. Not seeing them didn't mean they wasn't in the picture.

It was real strange, but suddenly the one he missed was Esterhazy—the man ran scared so you couldn't trust him to stick by you, but he wished he had Esterhazy working for him today, because the cameraman would have appreciated what it was to do a job in one perfect seamless take, and because Esterhazy filming this would have made and kept it perfect, he could have arranged it so you wouldn't notice the cars and trucks, the gasoline stink, the paved street and the paved sidewalk, the electric lights up and down the street on cast-iron gallows, SEQUOYAH HOTEL in electric letters, and then MAGIC CITY HARDWARE / CRYSTAL SETS REPAIRED, then the marquee of the Lyric Theater:

NOW SHOWING
THE BIRTH OF A NATION
BY POPULAR DEMAND!!!!

then the Chemical–Cattlemen's Bank, and off in the distance the skeleton of an oil gantry like a naked church steeple waving a long banner of blue and yellow flame—Esterhazy, he could look you right past all of it to what was still there underneath, black and white and gray, the ghosts that were underneath . . .

"Let's go," he said, and they stepped out of the alley and into the street, Henry Starr crossing just under the nose of a big rusty Reo truck that came on grating its gears and heaving forward on its springs, a flare of blue smoke at its asshole.

His men stayed behind and began to loiter their way up the east side of the street toward the First National Bank, just as he had laid it out in his mind, just as he had showed them, telling them first then walking it through with his men, just as he always used to do: and they would go into their bank on the tick of the watch three minutes after he stepped inside the Chemical–Cattlemen's Bank. And then this: and then that: everything as it used to be, as it always was, time after time after time, *Thumbs up and stand steady*, bust the safe burn the mortgage papers and then—

He walked slowly up the street, thinking how he had gauged the crowds and the traffic and the fall of sunlight against the windows just right, he was okay so far for this world, it was the other one was worrying him. *Give me a sign I got it working there too*, he said, *that's what I need. Hey, Grandfather: give me a sign.*

He stopped in front of the Sequoyah Hotel and looked ahead to the Lyric Theater. Paul Curry stood in the shade of the marquee, in an ill-fitting go-to-town suit that showed his wrist knobs. He carried a rifle in a scabbard and shoulder sling: a short rifle, a hog-killing gun. He kept peering out into the bright sunlight, looking for someone. Then he would stand and fidget. Then he would look at his watch.

December 19, 1921

Dear Mr. Starr,

I will gladly meet you at the time you say, waiting for you at the Lyric Theater, and bring the rifle one way or another. If Mr. Brogan will not lend it, I will have it anyway, and as you say who has a better right?

Thank you Mr. Starr, I am in your debt for giving me a chance. But I am ready for it, and believe I will not disappoint you.

Thank you Mr. Starr,
Yours sincerely,
*Paul Curry*

*No need to thank me, Henry Starr thought, it's only fair that a man should get a second chance at the things that make a difference to him.*

Curry made six, he was almost there.

The wind blew a cloud across the sun, darkening the street, brightening the lights in the shop windows. Henry Starr stepped into the bay of the hardware storefront—took a deep breath, stepped out onto the sidewalk again as the sunlight nailed him like a spotlight—and the tail of his eye caught a lean gray shape under a gray Stetson vanishing back into the storefronts like smoke fading in a breeze.

Henry Starr smiled. *Old Bill must be getting a little slower or . . .*

Or what?

He didn't finish the thought. *Sometimes my conjures work so good, I even scare myself.*

He had his seven. He looked around at the world. Everything was in its place, everything as it should be, everyone moving and standing and speaking and keeping still just as he had imagined it, just as it was supposed to be. The long street ran out ahead of him past the hotel and the movie house and the bank out to a vanishing V point, a small white place where the sky was tacked to the edge of the earth. When he was done here he would ride that road to the end, and sweep that white point up in his hand as easy as snapping a chicken head, leaning off the side of your smoking horse as he blows you through the judges and the barriers and into the blue distance of your perfect getaway.

Yes, perfect: because this time they couldn't bushwhack him by pure dumb luck, some jerk of a kid with a hog gun shooting him in the ass like they had done in Stroud. Live or die now, Henry Starr could not lose this game. He had his seven, Henry Starr and his three men, and Miss Bobcat waiting in the bank, and Curry and Tilghman, so this time even if they got him it wouldn't be any damn surprise, it would be the kind of death a man would choose for himself, like in a book or a picture, everything in its place, everything as it should be, hundreds of people watching, the whole city of Tulsa, every newspaper in the Nations in the state of Oklahoma in the United States of America *I came here to die, not to make a speech, that's what Cherokee Bill said, but I got more than that to say . . .:*

*Now I walk towards the Chemical–Cattlemen's Bank, moving quickly, giving Paul Curry his chance to see me go in and to see that I will not notice him waiting there, and it is just as if we had rehearsed it before, and I guess in a way we have. The windowed door of the bank glazed by the white sunlight is like a screen, and I can see my ghost coming towards me out of the bright screen, my hand on the door will shake the hand of my own ghost and then we'll take the bank together, the last bank, the second bank of two banks robbed by the Henry Starr Gang at the same and single time, the twenty-ninth and thirtieth banks Henry Starr robbed, for his clan and his Nation and for Bub Houston's Nation and for the Nation that was lost or sold away and Frank Little's and Preacher Brown's Nation of Nations that never was yet but maybe will be, and it will go all of it just as I wish it, so that as I come up close enough to my ghost to feel its breath I will see the flash of her golden head behind the shadow of my face like a signal in the dark of the bank, a signal saying yes . . .*

She'd watch him come in, and she'd know—even without Dick Rowland with him, she would know and it would be just the way he told her when she asked him *How would you rob my bank?* knowing like she must have even then that someday it would come true like it was her prayer or her dream. So she'd be ready, she was always ready for things like this, her body worked slick as a cat's and her head was faster than electricity, *Thumbs up and stand steady*, and she'd start playing the lady in distress so perfectly that no man in the place would think of his gun for wanting to reach her a handkerchief; and one way or another between tears and fainting and throwing up her hands she'd show him whatever they had that he couldn't find for himself. And when he was gone, when he had made his getaway, when he was gone in the blue distance of the most perfect getaway ever known in the Nations, she'd come away and wait for him, and he'd find her again—

And this time he'd take the stairs two at a time, the way Jesse James took banks, two at a time till he come to her landing and opened her door and found her waiting for him, leaning against the wall, her blue eyes open to the bottom saying henry henry henry henry Henry Starr . . .

*And now I'm standing at the door but in another second my hand will reach out and open it and I will be—*

He pushed the door open. A tiny bell above his head tinkled! There never was a bell before, and it froze him for one tick of the heart.

His eyes opened to the darker light of the bank, the dark walnut of the counters, the tarnished brass bars of the cage—

There was no flash of light hair behind the bars of the teller's cage.

There was no sight or sound or smell of her anywhere.

The bank was quiet as a church, except for the sound of small cash falling on itself like a little steel rain.

He heard a bellow from the street behind him, a yell! Breaking glass, the wrong sound from the wrong place, maybe the boys were spotted, maybe they missed their timing maybe it is all falling in pieces . . .

He stood in the door. He looked at the empty cage. She just wasn't there.

*But in just another second I will be Henry Starr, who robbed the Katy the Caney the Prue the Beggs the Owasso the Tulsa Chemical–Cattlemen's Bank with his pistol in his—*

People were scurrying past the door behind him, a man was bellowing loudly, harassingly, people were running to find out what the ruckus was all about, there wasn't supposed to be any ruckus.

He tilted back out of the doorframe and glanced back up the street.

Past the marquee of the Lyric Theater a circle of passersby was closing in on and then backing away from two men who seemed to be arguing violently: Deputy Price in a dented derby and Bill Tilghman in his gray Stetson.

Henry Starr looked back into the bank. It had a look that was uncanny, repellent, the air smelt bad, it was dark where there should be light and nothing was right about it, the wood had eyes and the marble floor looked like a sheet of ice full of frozen snakes. There were strangers in the teller's cages, their faces were like dead blocks of wood with eyes in them, and Miss Woodly had disappeared in the blue, the black . . .

*No,* he thought. *No I guess she, I guess this is not . . .*

He stepped back out the door, stepping in his own footprints to cover his trace, reversing himself like the film of his movie scenes running backwards through Esterhazy's projector, and she had grinned like a bobcat and they had laughed their fool heads off.

Everything in the bank was exactly as it had been when he stepped through the door, everyone going about his or her business, they hadn't noticed him nobody said his name.

Out in the street the marshal and the ex-deputy were the center of an uneasy knot of onlookers. Price's hooting bull voice kept insisting on something, and he kept pushing himself in on Tilghman, who glided back, then tried to shift past Price toward the bank. The two men sketched a broken circle on the sidewalk, they seemed to be dancing an odd two-step toward the Lyric marquee—

BY POPULAR DEMAND!!!!!

"You'd better sober up, Price," he heard Bill Tilghman say.

The big ex-deputy had on his terrible yellow suit, grease-stained as if he'd slept under a car, he kept trying to grab Tilghman by the lapels of his jacket and pull him close. "You had no right to do that to me, I got a family to think of!"

Tilghman kept fending him off with his arms and stepping back out of the range of Price's ugly breath; his gray suit gleamed almost white in the intolerable afternoon sun, and it was disgusting to see that lard-assed slob of a deputy putting his hands all over Bill Tilghman, making him have to back off just to keep clean, anybody with any more soul than a rooting hog would know better than to get that close to Bill Tilghman let alone put a hand on him.

Henry Starr started that way.

Deputy Price lunged forward, grabbed Tilghman and swung the old man right toward the gutter just as the black Ford that had been idling its motor up the street gunned forward with a squeal of tires, the snout of a tommy gun jutted out the window, stuttering stuttering shattering the windows of the SEQUOYAH HOTEL, MAGIC CITY HARDWARE/CRYSTAL SETS REPAIRED, the Lyric Theater's ticket booth, the windows of the Chemical–Cattlemen's Bank, spraying a rain of watery sparks into the street, into the screaming of people, men and women ducking, falling down and screaming.

The street scene froze like a photograph in silver and black: men and women scattered half-curled on the street or crouched behind trash bins and light posts and parked cars, the shattered ice of the windows as sharp as bits of mirror all around them.

Paul Curry, standing faithfully in the shadow of the Lyric Theater's marquee, had had a gash torn in the left side of his go-to-town jacket. He stood there, fingering the wound. He looked up and met Henry Starr's eyes.

Henry Starr said, "I'm sorry," and walked past him, but the boy still stood there thinking *it isn't even three o'clock yet.*

People were picking themselves up off the pavement, there was pink color in their faces, there was red, a woman was having hysterics and a man was yelling for the police, for an ambulance.

Tilghman had been thrown into Price's arms and the fat ex-deputy had reflexively embraced him. Now Price screamed, and threw the marshal away from him backward into the street. There were big red-flower sunbursts across the front of Tilghman's gray jacket and blood blots printed up and down Price's terrible yellow suit. Price was still standing there, unhurt although he was crying and bellowing, holding up the bullet-torn facing and sleeve of his yellow and black jacket so that everybody could see and bear witness to what had almost happened to him.

The crowd drew in, hiding the two men in a circle of bodies, the circle thickening till the outer edge of it was backed up against the picture of Lillian Gish on the movie-house door—Miss Gish had a slanting row of three machine-gun bullet holes stitched across her from her left shoulder to her right-most bottle curl, and there was one ragged black hole where her nose should have been.

The crowd had not gotten past the first burst of crying and feeling of its body parts when there were three loud shots from across the street and the hysterical yammer of an alarm bell, someone came out yelling, "They robbed the bank! They robbed the bank!" and it was all to be gone through again, the yelling and the hiding and the terror.

But this time no cars or bullets menaced them across the barrier of stalled traffic. So the crowd in front of the Lyric stopped ducking and started looking around and asking each other questions, as if they were veterans now and knew how to judge the danger. By the time the police arrived it was all old news to them. They were even amused that the police seemed so shocked by the dead man on the sidewalk and the screaming drunk in the loud suit—they were used to them already, had begun taking them for granted.

"That's Marshal Tilghman and Deputy Price," said the reporter of the Tulsa *Lamp*, the first newshawk on the scene. He looked out across the street and squinted his eyes like he was taking a sight. "They must have been trying to stop those yeggmen making their getaway," he said.

The man on the street wasn't so sure. It seemed to him the car come first, then the bank alarm. But that didn't faze the reporter: eyewitnesses were usually rattled and confused, his own version made better sense, as even the eyewitness would have to admit when he saw it in print the next day.

## HARRISON, ARKANSAS *February 23, 1922*

*Let me tell you how it used to be in the old days.*
*Just as I heard it.*
*Just as it was told to me:*

From the Harrison *Democrat*:

. . . at the close of an ordinary business day. Officers and employees of the bank had been instructed to be particularly watchful, because of the continuing epidemic of bank robberies that has afflicted this and neighboring states. Nevertheless, the robbers took them completely by surprise.

The three men had not entered in a group and were an oddly assorted lot —such that no similarity of age or dress or color would have caught the eye of either the uniformed guards or the watchful cashier, G. C. Hoffman. The leader was a well-dressed man, apparently a wealthy Indian from the western part of the county.

*And Henry Starr was the smartest outlaw that ever lived, so smart: he could charm the bark off a hickory, Henry Starr.*

*Two times they locked him in stone prison, and two times he come out again to find his horse and his guns and his road, and his word . . .*

He approached Mr. Hoffman's desk, smiling in a friendly manner, and in response to the cashier's wishing him good afternoon pulled from inside his jacket a large Colt's revolver and said in a clear and penetrating voice: . . .

*—that word of his with which he had robbed twenty-eight banks, one for every farm the Starr family had taken from them in Georgia and Carolina, in the United States and the Southern Confederacy and the Indian Nations: . . .*

. . .: "Thumbs up and stand steady!"

At this signal his companions suddenly revealed their presence in the bank. According to witnesses these were a large colored man carrying his "savings" in a rolled neckerchief, and an elderly gray-haired gentleman who, according to witnesses, "looked like a lawyer or a preacher." They had placed themselves so as to take control of the bank upon their leader's signal, and now uncovered their weapons, the Negro unwrapping the pistol concealed in the rolled neckerchief and the elderly "lawyer" pulling a sawed-off shotgun from under the skirt of his Prince Albert coat.

*. . . the outlaw Henry Starr and his partner Cherokee Bill, who rode the nightland with the wolves and heard the owl hoot.*

*Away down in the Indian Nations, a long time ago.*

*Just as I heard it, just as . . .*

These events were observed by W. J. Meyers, a stockholder and former president of the People's Bank, who was standing near the open vault, and on hearing the bandit's command instantly stepped behind the security of its iron door. His action, as will be seen, was not motivated by a desire to avoid danger, but rather to take advantage of certain security measures which the bank's officers, in their anxiety over the recent crime wave, had provided. He was, he said later, somewhat dismayed when he heard the bandit order Mr. Hoffman to open the safe, since it was the bank's policy to store cash only in the safe, reserving the vault space for its records and papers. He feared that robbers so well acquainted with the bank's procedures might also be aware of the danger to their enterprise that might be posed by someone concealed in the vault.

Happily, this proved not to be the case. After emptying the cash drawers and safe of perhaps $20,000 . . .

*. . . they give like they took, with a free hand. They was brave men and they kept their road, and they kept their word. They knew the taste*

*of justice,* hyenh! *I'm telling you: so the law could never hold them . . .*

*Twenty-eight farms, twenty-eight banks: and the twenty-ninth bank for the Nation that was lost so long ago, among the waters and the trees of that Old Place in the mountains, the bank that was too many for Henry Starr.*

*Listen! This is how it used to be.*

Then the outlaw chief ordered Mr. Hoffman to "show him where the mortgage papers were kept." It was now Mr. Hoffman's turn to be torn between emotions of hopeful elation and profound anxiety, since he had no idea whether or not anyone had taken control of the vault and its protective resources; or if they had, whether they would use them with sufficient skill and care to spare his own life. In this condition, Mr. Hoffman stepped inside the vault, and being temporarily blinded by the transition from the sunlit bank lobby to the dark chamber neither he nor the robber noticed Mr. Meyers standing just inside the door, until . . .

The vault was full up to the steel rim of the door with light-blind darkness, the cashier stepped into it and as Henry Starr followed him the center of the light-blind winked! *Exploplodloded* bright-blast-printing the steel doorframe through eyes and eyelids and into the back wall of his skull, so that as Henry Starr was thrown hurtling backwards out of eye-light into closed-eye-dark into inside-the-skull blue-blackness the image of the open door stayed with him, its colors changing from steel gray to phosphorous green to a glowing blue like a gas flame: and when the door turned that blue he felt his heart and lungs explode in the center of his chest like a bomb going off—

First a blast of pure-white pain that filled him to his tips and then:

. . . it became a black hole, blue, black, black empty hole that bulged and swole and rode outward after the white flame, he was the rider on that emptiness, it was a horse and he was a rider, *If I ride, Mr. Dodge, you can bet on me* and they did they bet on their blood *your Injun blood damn you or your son's blood which?* blood, bloodloodloodlood he tasted it in his mouth *he smeared it on his face for warpaint, he was on the horse like a bear and wouldn't let go, two times they locked him in stone prison and two times he come out again, to find his horse and his guns and his road, and his word . . .*

His eyes popped open. Faces peered down the hole in which he lay. The hole ran from their faces into the center of his chest, the hole was the center of his chest and he could make no air in it, bring no air in it, his throat clicked and glocked but there was a hole in his center that wouldn't suck air.

. . . and it was at this point that one of the tellers, Miss Gloria Montag, identified the bandit, whose face she had seen on the screen in a local movie house: "Why, it is Henry Starr!"

It was indeed the notorious Oklahoma badman, whose aunt—the infamous Belle Starr—was the chief or paramour of several of those figures whose crimes disfigure the early history of our section, over whose misdeeds the light of sentimentality and romance has too often been cast. Indeed, this last fatal foray of Henry Starr might serve some minister as text for a sermon denouncing the tendency of our pulp magazines and cinemas to romanticize criminal behavior, to find in every common thief a Robin Hood who robs from the rich to aid the poor—a myth pernicious at any time to inflict upon the rising generation, never more so than in these hard times. Indeed, there was a measure of poetic justice in this bloody affray, in that Starr was for a time himself an actor in movies of this description; and we might call it Providential that he should himself fall into the pit which his own works had digged for impressionable and adventurous youth.

. . . a hole where his chest was and all he could say was a sound like "lk. lk. lk. lk."

*Let me Let me tell you tell how it was how in the old*

"He's trying to talk," said a man.

"My God," said a voice, "it *is* Henry Starr."

Yh Yh Yh, said the dead man:

*Used to be.*

# The Ballad of Henry Starr

Tune: Buffalo Skinners (Traditional)

Words by Richard Slotkin

If you want a story, children, then listen here to me,
About Henry Starr the outlaw, and the days that used to be.
He robbed a-many banks and railroad trains also
Way down in the Indian Nations, a long time ago.

'Twas in the town of Tahlequah, that's where it all began,
When Henry Starr robbed the Katy Bank with his pistol in his hand.
"Thumbs up and stand steady!" were the words that he did say,
And he burned the mortgage papers when he made his getaway.

Now Henry Starr was running with the posse on his track,
When Deputy Floyd Wilson approached him from the back.
A rifle shot he fired, the bullet it went wide:
Henry Starr he turned and shot Wilson in the side.

"I know that I am dying," the Deputy did say,
"And for my bloody murder the law will make you pay.
For robbing banks and property is laid unto your score:
You owe a life for my life, a debtor to the law."

"Oh yes I robbed the Katy Bank with my pistol in my hand,
And for the laws and property I do not give a damn.
The white man robbed the Indian, the banker robs the white,
And so I rob the banker to set the balance right."

They called out twenty posses, and the Fed'ral Marshals
come
With rifles, ropes and pistols and a great big Gatling gun.
They called out the militia, they called the Ku Klux Klan,
They chased him for a thousand miles and never caught their
man.

Now I do not hold with robbery, and murder is a sin,
But between the banks and the weevils a farmer cannot win,
And if we don't get justice soon then things may go too far,
Like they did in the Indian Nations, in the days of Henry
Starr.

# Acknowledgments

I am grateful to Christina L. Zwarg for her careful and incisive reading of my first draft; and to Willie Holtzman, for his helpful suggestions and advice. I also want to thank Robert N. Powers, Curator of the Tulsa County Historical Society for his answers to my inquiries; and Linda Hindman, Miriam Horn and Marsha Morgan of the Stroud, Oklahoma Public Library for taking the time to answer my questions and provide me with maps and newspapers descriptive of Stroud at the time of Starr's attempted double robbery.

I would also like to acknowledge my debt to the careful research of Glenn Shirley, *The Last of the Real Badmen*, the definitive biography of Henry Starr; and Scott Ellison, *Death in a Promised Land*, a history of the Tulsa Race Riot of 1921. It should go without saying that they are not accountable for the novelistic license I have taken in telling this story.

**Richard Slotkin** was born in Brooklyn, New York, and educated in New York City public schools. He received his B.A. from Brooklyn College (1963) and his Ph.D. in American Civilization from Brown University (1967). His first book, *Regeneration Through Violence: The Mythology of the American Frontier, 1600–1860*, was awarded the American Historical Association's Albert J. Beveridge Award as the best book on American History in 1973, and was nominated for a National Book Award. His most recent book, *The Fatal Environment: The Myth of the Frontier in the Age of Industrialization, 1800–1890*, is its sequel, and was awarded the Little Big Horn Associates Literary Award for 1985. Professor Slotkin is also the author of *The Crater* (1980), a highly praised first novel set during the American Civil War.

Since 1966 he has taught at Wesleyan University in Middletown, Connecticut, where he is Olin Professor of English and Director of American Studies. He lives in Middletown with his wife and their son.